# HARLEM RENAISSANCE

## FOUR NOVELS OF THE 1930S

# Harlem Renaissance

## FOUR NOVELS OF THE 1930s

*Not Without Laughter* • Langston Hughes
*Black No More* • George Schuyler
*The Conjure-Man Dies* • Rudolph Fisher
*Black Thunder* • Arna Bontemps

Rafia Zafar, *editor*

THE LIBRARY OF AMERICA

Manufactured in the United States of America

*Harlem Renaissance: Four Novels of the 1930s*
is published with support from

**THE SHELLEY & DONALD RUBIN FOUNDATION**

# Contents

# NOT WITHOUT LAUGHTER

*Langston Hughes*

*To*
*J. E. and Amy Spingarn*

# Contents

# ONE

## *Storm*

A UNT HAGER WILLIAMS stood in her doorway and looked out at the sun. The western sky was a sulphurous yellow and the sun a red ball dropping slowly behind the trees and house-tops. Its setting left the rest of the heavens grey with clouds.

"Huh! A storm's comin'," said Aunt Hager aloud.

A pullet ran across the back yard and into a square-cut hole in an unpainted piano-box which served as the roosting-house. An old hen clucked her brood together and, with the tiny chicks, went into a small box beside the large one. The air was very still. Not a leaf stirred on the green apple-tree. Not a single closed flower of the morning-glories trembled on the back fence. The air was very still and yellow. Something sultry and oppressive made a small boy in the doorway stand closer to his grandmother, clutching her apron with his brown hands.

"Sho is a storm comin'," said Aunt Hager.

"I hope mama gets home 'fore it rains," remarked the brown child holding to the old woman's apron. "Hope she gets home."

"I does, too," said Aunt Hager. "But I's skeared she won't."

Just then great drops of water began to fall heavily into the back yard, pounding up little clouds of dust where each drop struck the earth. For a few moments they pattered violently on the roof like a series of hammer-strokes; then suddenly they ceased.

"Come in, chile," said Aunt Hager.

She closed the door as the green apple-tree began to sway in the wind and a small hard apple fell, rolling rapidly down the top of the piano-box that sheltered the chickens. Inside the kitchen it was almost dark. While Aunt Hager lighted an oil-lamp, the child climbed to a chair and peered through the square window into the yard. The leaves and flowers of the morning-glory vines on the back fence were bending with the rising wind. And across the alley at the big house, Mrs.

Kennedy's rear screen-door banged to and fro, and Sandy saw her garbage-pail suddenly tip over and roll down into the yard, scattering potato-peelings on the white steps.

"Sho gwine be a terrible storm," said Hager as she turned up the wick of the light and put the chimney on. Then, glancing through the window, she saw a black cloud twisting like a ribbon in the western sky, and the old woman screamed aloud in sudden terror: "It's a cyclone! It's gwine be a cyclone! Sandy, let's get over to Mis' Carter's quick, 'cause we ain't got no cellar here. Come on, chile, let's get! Come on, chile! . . . Come on, chile!"

Hurriedly she blew out the light, grabbed the boy's hand; and together they rushed through the little house towards the front. It was quite dark in the inner rooms, but through the parlor windows came a sort of sooty grey-green light that was rapidly turning to blackness.

"Lawd help us, Jesus!"

Aunt Hager opened the front door, but before she or the child could move, a great roaring sound suddenly shook the world, and, with a deafening division of wood from wood, they saw their front porch rise into the air and go hurtling off into space. Sailing high in the gathering darkness, the porch was soon lost to sight. And the black wind blew with terrific force, numbing the ear-drums.

For a moment the little house trembled and swayed and creaked as though it were about to fall.

"Help me to shut this do'," Aunt Hager screamed; "help me to shut it, Lawd!" as with all her might she struggled against the open door, which the wind held back, but finally it closed and the lock caught. Then she sank to the floor with her back against the wall, while her small grandson trembled like a leaf as she took him in her lap, mumbling: "What a storm! . . . O, Lawdy! . . . O, ma chile, what a storm!"

They could hear the crackling of timbers and the rolling limbs of trees that the wind swept across the roof. Her arms tightened about the boy.

"Dear Jesus!" she said. "I wonder where is yo' mama? S'pose she started out fo' home 'fore this storm come up!" Then in a scream: "Have mercy on ma Annjee! O, Lawd, have mercy on this chile's mamma! Have mercy on all ma chillens! Ma

Harriett, an' ma Tempy, an' ma Annjee, what's maybe all of 'em out in de storm! O, Lawd!"

A dry crack of lightning split the darkness, and the boy began to wail. Then the rain broke. The old woman could not see the crying child she held, nor could the boy hear the broken voice of his grandmother, who had begun to pray as the rain crashed through the inky blackness. For a long while it roared on the roof of the house and pounded at the windows, until finally the two within became silent, hushing their cries. Then only the lashing noise of the water, coupled with the feeling that something terrible was happening, or had already happened, filled the evening air.

After the rain the moon rose clear and bright and the clouds disappeared from the lately troubled sky. The stars sparkled calmly above the havoc of the storm, and it was still early evening as people emerged from their houses and began to investigate the damage brought by the twisting cyclone that had come with the sunset. Through the rubbish-filled streets men drove slowly with horse and buggy or automobile. The fire-engine was out, banging away, and the soft tang-tang-tang of the motor ambulance could be heard in the distance carrying off the injured.

Black Aunt Hager and her brown grandson put their rubbers on and stood in the water-soaked front yard looking at the porchless house where they lived. Platform, steps, pillars, roof, and all had been blown away. Not a semblance of a porch was left and the front door opened bare into the yard. It was grotesque and funny. Hager laughed.

"Cyclone sho did a good job," she said. "Looks like I ain't never had no porch."

Madam de Carter, from next door, came across the grass, her large mouth full of chattering sympathy for her neighbor.

"But praise God for sparing our lives! It might've been worse, Sister Williams! It might've been much more calamitouser! As it is, I lost nothin' more'n a chimney and two washtubs which was settin' in the back yard. A few trees broke down don't 'mount to nothin'. We's livin', ain't we? And we's more importanter than trees is any day!" Her gold teeth sparkled in the moonlight.

" 'Deed so," agreed Hager emphatically. "Let's move on down de block, Sister, an' see what mo' de Lawd has 'stroyed or spared this evenin'. He's gin us plenty moonlight after de storm so we po' humans can see this lesson o' His'n to a sinful world."

The two elderly colored women picked their way about on the wet walk, littered with twigs and branches of broken foliage. The little brown boy followed, with his eyes wide at the sight of baby-carriages, window-sashes, shingles, and tree-limbs scattered about in the roadway. Large numbers of people were out, some standing on porches, some carrying lanterns, picking up useful articles from the streets, some wringing their hands in a daze.

Near the corner a small crowd had gathered quietly.

"Mis' Gavitt's killed," somebody said.

"Lawd help!" burst from Aunt Hager and Madam de Carter simultaneously.

"Mister and Mis' Gavitt's both dead," added a nervous young white man, bursting with the news. "We live next door to 'em, and their house turned clean over! Came near hitting us and breaking our side-wall in."

"Have mercy!" said the two women, but Sandy slipped away from his grandmother and pushed through the crowd. He ran round the corner to where he could see the overturned house of the unfortunate Gavitts.

Good white folks, the Gavitts, Aunt Hager had often said, and now their large frame dwelling lay on its side like a doll's mansion, with broken furniture strewn carelessly on the wet lawn—and they were dead. Sandy saw a piano flat on its back in the grass. Its ivory keys gleamed in the moonlight like grinning teeth, and the strange sight made his little body shiver, so he hurried back through the crowd looking for his grandmother. As he passed the corner, he heard a woman sobbing hysterically within the wide house there.

His grandmother was no longer standing where he had left her, but he found Madam de Carter and took hold of her hand. She was in the midst of a group of excited white and colored women. One frail old lady was saying in a high determined voice that she had never seen a cyclone like this in her whole life, and she lived here in Kansas, if you please, going on seventy-three years. Madam de Carter, chattering nervously, began to tell them how she had recognized its coming and had rushed to the cellar the minute she saw the sky turn green. She had not come up until the rain stopped, so frightened had she been. She was extravagantly enjoying the telling of her fears as Sandy kept tugging at her hand.

"Where's my grandma?" he demanded. Madam de Carter, however, did not cease talking to answer his question.

"What do you want, sonny?" finally one of the white women asked, bending down when he looked as if he were about to cry. "Aunt Hager? . . . Why, she's inside helping them calm poor Mrs. Gavitt's niece. Your grandmother's good to have around when folks are sick or grieving, you know. Run and set on the steps like a nice boy and wait until she comes out." So Sandy left the women and went to sit in the dark on the steps of the big corner house where the niece of the dead Mrs. Gavitt lived. There were some people on the porch, but they soon passed through the screen-door into the house or went away down the street. The moonlight cast weird shadows across the damp steps where Sandy sat, and it was dark there under the trees in spite of the moon, for the old house was built far back from the street in a yard full of oaks and maples, and Sandy could see the light from an upstairs window reflecting on the wet leaves of their nearest boughs. He heard a girl screaming, too, up there where the light was burning, and he knew that Aunt Hager was putting cold cloths on her head, or rubbing her hands, or driving folks out of the room, and talking kind to her so that she would soon be better.

All the neighborhood, white or colored, called his grandmother when something happened. She was a good nurse, they said, and sick folks liked her around. Aunt Hager always came when they called, too, bringing maybe a little soup that she had made or a jelly. Sometimes they paid her and sometimes they didn't. But Sandy had never had to sit outdoors in the darkness waiting for her before. He leaned his small back against the top step and rested his elbows on the porch behind him. It was growing late and the people in the streets had all disappeared.

There, in the dark, the little fellow began to think about his mother, who worked on the other side of town for a rich white lady named Mrs. J. J. Rice. And suddenly frightful thoughts came into his mind. Suppose she had left for home just as the storm came up! Almost always his mother was home before dark—but she wasn't there tonight when the storm came—and she should have been home! This thought appalled him. She should have been there! But maybe she had been caught by the storm and blown away as she walked down Main Street! Maybe Annjee had been carried off by the great black wind that had overturned the Gavitt's house and taken his grandma's porch flying through the air! Maybe the cyclone had gotten his mother, Sandy thought. He wanted her! Where was she? Had something terrible happened to her? Where was she now?

The big tears began to roll down his cheeks—but the little fellow held back the sobs that wanted to come. He decided he wasn't going to cry and make a racket there by himself on the strange steps of these white folks' house. He wasn't going to cry like a big baby in the dark. So he wiped his eyes, kicked his heels against the cement walk, lay down on the top step, and, by and by, sniffled himself to sleep.

"Wake up, son!" Someone was shaking him. "You'll catch your death o' cold sleeping on the wet steps like this. We're going home now. Don't want me to have to carry a big man like you, do you, boy? . . . Wake up, Sandy!" His mother stooped to lift his long little body from the wide steps. She held him against her soft heavy breasts and let his head rest on one of her shoulders while his feet, in their muddy rubbers, hung down against her dress.

"Where you been, mama?" the boy asked drowsily, tightening his arms about her neck. "I been waiting for you."

"Oh, I been home a long time, worried to death about you and ma till I heard from Madam Carter that you-all was down here nursing the sick. I stopped at your Aunt Tempy's house when I seen the storm coming."

"I was afraid you got blowed away, mama," murmured Sandy sleepily. "Let's go home, mama. I'm glad you ain't got blowed away."

On the porch Aunt Hager was talking to a pale white man and two thin white women standing at the door of the lighted hallway. "Just let Mis' Agnes sleep," she was saying. "She'll be all right now, an' I'll come back in de mawnin' to see 'bout her. . . . Good-night, you-all."

The old colored woman joined her daughter and they started home, walking through the streets filled with debris and puddles of muddy water reflecting the moon.

"You're certainly heavy, boy," remarked Sandy's mother to the child she held, but he didn't answer.

"I'm right glad you come for me, Annjee," Hager said. "I wonder is yo' sister all right out yonder at de country club. . . . An' I was so worried 'bout you I didn't know what to do—skeared you might a got caught in this twister, 'cause it were cert'ly awful!"

"I was at Tempy's!" Annjee replied. "And I was nearly crazy, but I just left everything in the hands o' God. That's all." In silence they walked on, a piece; then hesitantly, to her mother: "There wasn't any mail for me today, was there, ma?"

"Not a speck!" the old woman replied shortly. "Mail-man passed on by."

For a few minutes there was silence again as they walked. Then, "It's goin' on three weeks he's been gone, and he ain't written a line," the younger woman complained, shifting the child to her right arm. "Seems like Jimboy would let a body know where he is, ma, wouldn't it?"

"Huh! That ain't nothin'! He's been gone before this an' he ain't wrote, ain't he? Here you is worryin' 'bout a letter from that good-for-nothing husband o' your'n—an' there's ma house settin' up without a porch to its name! . . . Ain't you seed what de devil's done done on earth this evenin', chile? . . . An' yet de first thing you ask me 'bout is de mail-man! . . . Lawd! Lawd! . . . You an' that Jimboy!"

Aunt Hager lifted her heavy body over fallen tree-trunks and across puddles, but between puffs she managed to voice her indignation, so Annjee said no more concerning letters from her husband. Instead they went back to the subject of the cyclone. "I'm just thankful, ma, it didn't blow the whole house down and you with it, that's all! I was certainly worried! . . . And

then you-all was gone when I got home! Gone on out—
nursing that white woman. . . . It's too bad 'bout poor Mis'
Gavitt, though, and old man Gavitt, ain't it?"

"Yes, indeedy!" said Aunt Hager. "It's sho too bad. They
was certainly good old white folks! An' her married niece is
takin' it mighty hard, po' little soul. I was nigh two hours,
her husband an' me, tryin' to bring her out o' de hysterics.
Tremblin' like a lamb all over, she was." They were turning
into the yard. "Be careful with that chile, Annjee, you don't
trip on none o' them boards nor branches an' fall with him."

"Put me down, 'cause I'm awake," said Sandy.

The old house looked queer without a porch. In the moonlight he could see the long nails that had held the porch roof
to the weather-boarding. His grandmother climbed slowly
over the door-sill, and his mother lifted him to the floor level
as Aunt Hager lit the large oil-lamp on the parlor table. Then
they went back to the bedroom, where the youngster took off
his clothes, said his prayers, and climbed into the high feather
bed where he slept with Annjee. Aunt Hager went to the next
room, but for a long time she talked back and forth through
the doorway to her daughter about the storm.

"We was just startin' out fo' Mis' Carter's cellar, me an' Sandy,"
she said several times. "But de Lawd was with us! He held us
back! Praise His name! We ain't harmed, none of us—'ceptin' I
don't know 'bout ma Harriett at de club. But you's all right.
An' you say Tempy's all right, too. An' I prays that Harriett
ain't been touched out there in de country where she's workin'.
Maybe de storm ain't passed that way."

Then they spoke about the white people where Annjee
worked . . . and about the elder sister Tempy's prosperity.
Then Sandy heard his grandmother climb into bed, and a few
minutes after the springs screaked under her, she had begun to
snore. Annjee closed the door between their rooms and slowly
began to unlace her wet shoes.

"Sandy," she whispered, "we ain't had no word yet from
your father since he left. I know he goes away and stays away
like this and don't write, but I'm sure worried. Hope the cyclone ain't passed nowhere near wherever he is, and I hope
ain't nothin' hurt him. . . . I'm gonna pray for him, Sandy.
I'm gonna ask God right now to take care o' Jimboy. . . . The

Lawd knows, I wants him to come back! . . . I loves him. . . . We both loves him, don't we, child? And we want him to come on back!"

She knelt down beside the bed in her night-dress and kept her head bowed for a long time. Before she got up, Sandy had gone to sleep.

# TWO

## *Conversation*

---

IT WAS broad daylight in the town of Stanton and had been for a long time.

"Get out o' that bed, boy!" Aunt Hager yelled. "Here's Buster waitin' out in de yard to play with you, an' you still sleepin'!"

"Aw, tell him to cut off his curls," retorted Sandy, but his grandmother was in no mood for fooling.

"Stop talkin' 'bout that chile's haid and put yo' clothes on. Nine o'clock an' you ain't up yet! Shame on you!" She shouted from the kitchen, where Sandy could hear the fire crackling and smell coffee boiling.

He kicked the sheet off with his bare feet and rolled over and over on the soft feather tick. There was plenty of room to roll now, because his mother had long since got up and gone to Mrs. J. J. Rice's to work.

"Tell Bus I'm coming," Sandy yelled, jumping into his trousers and running with bare feet towards the door. "Is he got his marbles?"

"Come back here, sir, an' put them shoes on," cried Hager, stopping him on his way out. "Yo' feet'll get long as yard-sticks and flat as pancakes runnin' round barefooted all de time. An' wash yo' face, sir. Buster ain't got a thing to do but wait. An' eat yo' breakfast."

The air was warm with sunlight, and hundreds of purple and white morning-glories laughed on the back fence. Earth and sky were fresh and clean after the heavy night-rain, and the young corn-shoots stood straight in the garden, and green pea-vines wound themselves around their crooked sticks. There was the mingled scent of wet soil and golden pollen on the breeze that blew carelessly through the clear air.

Buster sat under the green apple-tree with a pile of black mud from the alley in front of him.

"Hey, Sandy, gonna make marbles and put 'em in the sun to dry," he said.

"All right," agreed Sandy, and they began to roll mud balls in the palms of their hands. But instead of putting them in the sun to dry they threw them against the back of the house, where they flattened and stuck beautifully. Then they began to throw them at each other.

Sandy's playmate was a small ivory-white Negro child with straight golden hair, which his mother made him wear in curls. His eyes were blue and doll-like and he in no way resembled a colored youngster; but he was colored. Sandy himself was the shade of a nicely browned piece of toast, with dark, brown-black eyes and a head of rather kinky, sandy hair that would lie smooth only after a rigorous application of vaseline and water. That was why folks called him Annjee's sandy-headed child, and then just—Sandy.

"He takes after his father," Sister Lowry said, "'cept he's not so light. But he's gonna be a mighty good-lookin' boy when he grows up, that's sho!"

"Well, I hopes he does," Aunt Hager said. "But I'd rather he'd be ugly 'fore he turns out anything like that good-for-nothing Jimboy what comes here an' stays a month, goes away an' stays six, an' don't hit a tap o' work 'cept when he feels like it. If it wasn't for Annjee, don't know how we'd eat, 'cause Sandy's father sho don't do nothin' to support him."

All the colored people in Stanton knew that Hager bore no love for Jimboy Rodgers, the tall good-looking yellow fellow whom her second daughter had married.

"First place, I don't like his name," she would say in private. "Who ever heard of a nigger named Jimboy, anyhow? Next place, I ain't never seen a yaller dude yet that meant a dark woman no good—an' Annjee is dark!" Aunt Hager had other objections, too, although she didn't like to talk evil about folks. But what she probably referred to in her mind was the question of his ancestry, for nobody knew who Jimboy's parents were.

"Sandy, look out for the house while I run down an' see how is Mis' Gavitt's niece. An' you-all play outdoors. Don't bring no chillen in, litterin' up de place." About eleven o'clock Aunt Hager pulled a dustcap over her head and put on a clean white apron. "Here, tie it for me, chile," she said, turning her broad back. "An' mind you don't hurt yo'self on no rusty nails and rotten boards left from de storm. I'll be back atter while." And she disappeared around the house, walking proudly, her black face shining in the sunlight.

Presently the two boys under the apple-tree were joined by a coal-colored little girl who lived next door, one Willie-Mae Johnson, and the mud balls under her hands became mud pies carefully rounded and patted and placed in the sun on the small box where the little chickens lived. Willie-Mae was the mama, Sandy the papa, and Buster the baby as the old game of "playing house" began anew.

By and by the mail-man's whistle blew and the three children scampered towards the sidewalk to meet him. The carrier handed Sandy a letter. "Take it in the house," he said. But instead the youngsters sat on the front-door-sill, their feet dangling where the porch had been, and began to examine the envelope.

"I bet that's Lincoln's picture," said Buster.

"No, 'taint," declared Willie-Mae. "It's Rossiefelt!"

"Aw, it's Washington," said Sandy. "And don't you-all touch my mama's letter with your hands all muddy. It might be from my papa, you can't tell, and she wants it kept clean."

"'Tis from Jimboy," Aunt Hager declared when she returned, accompanied by her old friend, Sister Whiteside, who peddled on foot fresh garden-truck she raised herself. Aunt Hager had met her at the corner.

"I knows his writin'," went on Hager. "An' it's got a postmark, K-A-N-, Kansas City! That's what 'tis! Niggers sho do love Kansas City! . . . Huh! . . . So that's where he's at. Well, yo' mama'll be glad to get it. If she knowed it was here, she'd quit work an' come home now. . . . Sit down, Whiteside. We gwine eat in a few minutes. You better have a bite with us an' stay an' rest yo'self awhile, 'cause I knows you been walkin' this mawnin'!"

"'Deed I is," the old sister declared, dropping her basket of lettuce and peas on the floor and taking a chair next to the table in the kitchen. "An' I ain't sold much neither. Seems like folks ain't got no buyin' appetite after all that storm an' wind last night—but de Lawd will provide! I ain't worried."

"That's right," agreed Hager. "Might o' been me blowed away maself, 'stead o' just ma porch, if Jesus hadn't been with us. . . . You Sandy! Make haste and wash yo' hands, sir. Rest o' you chillens go on home, 'cause I know yo' ma's lookin' for you. . . . Huh! This wood fire's mighty low!"

Hager uncovered a pot that had been simmering on the stove all morning and dished up a great bowlful of black-eyed peas and salt pork. There was biscuit bread left from breakfast. A plate of young onions and a pitcher of lemonade stood on the white oilcloth-covered table. Heads were automatically bowed.

"Lawd, make us thankful for this food. For Christ's sake, amen," said Hager; then the two old women and the child began to eat.

"That's Elvira's boy, ain't it—that yaller-headed young-one was here playin' with Sandy?" Sister Whiteside had her mouth full of onions and beans as she asked the question.

"Shsss! . . . That's her child!" said Hager. "But it ain't Eddie's!" She gave her guest a meaning glance across the table, then lowered her voice, pretending all the while that Sandy's ears were too young to hear. "They say she had that chile 'fore she married Eddie. An' black as Eddie is, you knows an' I knows ain't due to be no golden hair in de family!"

"I knowed there must be something funny," whispered the old sister, screwing up her face. "That's some white man's chile!"

"Sho it is!" agreed Hager. . . . "I knowed it all de time. . . . Have some mo' meat, Whiteside. Help yo'self! We ain't got much, but such as 'tis, you're welcome. . . . Yes, sir, Buster's some white man's chile. . . . Stop reachin' cross de table for bread, Sandy. Where's yo' manners, sir? I declare, chillens do try you sometimes. . . . Pass me de onions."

"Truth, they tries you, yit I gits right lonesome since all ma young-ones is gone." Sister Whiteside worked her few good teeth vigorously, took a long swallow of lemonade, and smacked her lips. "Chillen an' grandchillen all in Chicago an' St. Louis an' Wichita, an' nary chick nor child left with me in de house. . . . Pass me de bread, thank yuh. . . . I feels kinder sad an' sorry at times, po' widder-woman that I is. I has ma garden an' ma hens, but all ma chillens done grown and married. . . . Where's yo' daughter Harriett at now, Hager? Is she married, too? I ain't seen her lately."

Hager pulled a meat skin through her teeth; then she answered: "No, chile, she too young to marry yet! Ain't but sixteen, but she's been workin out this summer, waitin' table at de Stanton County Country Club. Been in de country three weeks now, since school closed, but she comes in town on Thursdays, though. It's nigh six miles from here, so de women-help sleeps there at night. I's glad she's out there, Sister. Course Harriett's a good girl, but she likes to be frisky—wants to run de streets 'tendin' parties an' dances, an' I can't do much with her no mo', though I hates to say it."

"But she's a songster, Hager! An' I hears she's sho one smart chile, besides. They say she's up with them white folks when it comes to books. An' de high school where she's goin' ain't easy. . . . All ma young ones quit 'fore they got through with it—wouldn't go—ruther have a good time runnin' to Kansas City an' galavantin' round."

"De Lawd knows it's a hard job, keepin' colored chillens in school, Sister Whiteside, a mighty hard job. De niggers don't help 'em, an' de white folks don't care if they stay or not. An' when they gets along sixteen an' seventeen, they wants this, an' they wants that, an' t'other—an' when you ain't got it to give to 'em, they quits school an' goes to work. . . . Harriett say she ain't goin' back next fall. I feels right hurt over it, but she 'clares she ain't goin' back to school. Says there ain't no use in learnin' books fo' nothin' but to work in white folks' kitchens when she's graduated."

"Do she, Hager? I's sho sorry! I's gwine to talk to that gal. Get Reverend Berry to talk to her, too. . . . You's struggled to bring up yo' chillens, an' all we Christians in de church ought to help you! I gwine see Reverend Berry, see can't he 'suade her to stay in school." The old woman reached for the onions. "But you ain't never raised no boys, though, has you, Hagar?"

"No, I ain't. My two boy-chillens both died 'fore they was ten. Just these three girls—Tempy, an' Annjee, an' Harriett— that's all I got. An' this here grandchile, Sandy. . . . Take yo' hands off that meat, sir! You had 'nough!"

"Lawd, you's been lucky! I done raised seven grandchillen 'sides eight o' ma own. An' they don't thank me. No, sir! Go off and kick up they heels an' git married an' don't thank me a bit! Don't even write, some of 'em. . . . Waitin' fo' me to die, I reckon, so's they can squabble over de little house I owns an' ma garden." The old visitor pushed back her chair. "Huh! Yo' dinner was sho good! . . . Waitin' fo' me to die."

"Unhuh! . . . That's de way with 'em, Sister Whiteside. Chillens don't care—but I reckon we old ones can't kick much. They's got to get off fo' themselves. It's natural, that's what 'tis. Now, my Tempy, she's married and doin' well. Got a fine house, an' her husband's a mail-clerk in de civil service makin' good money. They don't 'sociate no mo' with none but de high-toned colored folks, like Dr. Mitchell, an' Mis' Ada Walls, an' Madam C. Frances Smith. Course Tempy don't come to see me much 'cause I still earns ma livin' with ma arms in de tub. But Annjee run in their house out o' the storm last night an' she say Tempy's just bought a new pianer, an' de house looks fine. . . . I's glad fo' de chile."

"Sho, sho you is, Sister Williams, you's a good mother an' I knows you's glad. But I hears from Reverend Berry that Tempy's done withdrawed from our church an' joined de Episcopals!"

"That's right! She is. Last time I seed Tempy, she told me she couldn't stand de Baptist no mo'—too many low niggers belonging, she say, so she's gonna join Father Hill's church, where de best people go. . . . I told her I didn't think much o' joinin' a church so far away from God that they didn't want nothin' but yaller niggers for members, an' so full o' forms an' fashions that a good Christian couldn't shout—but she went on an' joined. It's de stylish temple, that's why, so I ain't said no mo'. Tempy's goin' on thirty-five now, she's ma oldest chile, an' I reckon she knows how she wants to act."

"Yes, I reckon she do. . . . But there ain't no church like de Baptist, praise God! Is there, Sister? If you ain't been dipped in that water an' half drowned, you ain't saved. Tempy don't know like we do. No, sir, she don't know!"

There was no fruit or dessert, and the soiled plates were not removed from the table for a long time, for the two old women, talking about their children, had forgotten the dishes. Young flies crawled over the biscuit bread and hummed above the bowl of peas, while the wood fire died in the stove, and Sandy went out into the sunshine to play.

"Now, ma girl, Maggie," said Sister Whiteside; "de man she married done got to be a big lawyer in St. Louis. He's in de politics there, an' Maggie's got a fine job herself—social servin', they calls it. But I don't hear from her once a year. An' she don't send me a dime. Ma boys looks out for me, though, sometimes, round Christmas. There's Lucius, what runs on de railroad, an' then Andrew, what rides de horses, an' John, in Omaha, sends me a little change now an' then—all but Charlie, an' he never was thoughtful 'bout his mother. He ain't never sent me nothin'."

"Well, you sho is lucky," said Hager; "'cause they ain't no money comes in this house, Christmas nor no other time, less'n me an' Annjee brings it here. Jimboy ain't no good, an' what Harriett makes goes for clothes and parties an' powderin'-rags. Course, I takes some from her every week, but I gives it right back for her school things. An' I ain't taken nothin' from her these three weeks she's been workin' at de club. She say she's savin' her money herself. She's past sixteen now, so I lets her have it. . . . Po' little thing! . . . She does need to look purty." Hager's voice softened and her dark old face was half abashed, kind and smiling. "You know, last month I bought her a gold watch—surprise fo' her birthday, de kind you hangs on a little pin on yo' waist. Lawd knows, I couldn't 'ford it— took all de money from three week's o' washin', but I knowed she'd been wantin' a watch. An' this front room—I moved ma bed out last year an' bought that new rug at de second-hand store an' them lace curtains so's she could have a nice place to entertain her comp'ny. . . . But de chile goes with such a kinder wild crowd o' young folks, Sister Whiteside! It worries me! The boys, they cusses, an' the girls, they paints, an' some of 'em live in de Bottoms. I been tried to get her out of it right along, but seems like I can't. That's why I's glad she's in de country fo' de summer an' comes in but only once a week, an' then she's home with me. It's too far to come in town at night, she say, so she gets her rest now, goin' to bed early an' all, with de country air round her. I hopes she calms down from runnin' round when she comes back here to stay in de fall. . . . She's a good chile. She don't lie to me 'bout where she goes, nor nothin' like that, but she's just wild, that's all, just wild."

"Is she a Christian, Sister Williams?"

"No, she ain't. I's sorry to say it of a chile o' mine, but she ain't. She's been on de moaner's bench time after time, Sunday mawnins' an' prayer-meetin' evenin's, but she never would rise. I prays for her."

"Well, when she takes Jesus, she'll see de light! That's what de matter with her, Sister Williams, she ain't felt Him yit. Make her go to church when she comes back here. . . . I reckon you heard 'bout when de big revival's due to come off this year, ain't you?"

"No, I ain't, not yet."

"Great colored tent-meetin' with de Battle-Ax of de Lawd, Reverend Braswell preachin'! Yes, sir! Gwine start August eighteenth in de Hickory Woods yonder by de edge o' town."

"Good news," cried Hager. "Mo' sinners than enough's in need o' savin'. I's gwine to take Sandy an' get him started right with de Lawd. An' if that onery Jimboy's back here, I gwine make him go, too, an' look Jesus in de face. Annjee an' me's saved, chile! . . . You Sandy, bring us some drinkin'-water from de pump." Aunt Hager rapped on the window with her knuckles to the boy playing outside. "An' stop wrastlin' with that gal."

Sandy rose triumphant from the prone body of black little Willie-Mae, lying squalling on the cinder-path near the back gate. "She started it," he yelled, running towards the pump. The girl began a reply, but at that moment a rickety wagon drawn by a white mule and driven by a grey-haired, leather-colored old man came rattling down the alley.

"Hy, there, Hager!" called the old Negro, tightening his reins on the mule, which immediately began to eat corn-tops over the back fence. "How you been treatin' yo'self?"

"Right tolable," cried Hager, for she and Sister Whiteside had both emerged from the kitchen and were approaching the driver. "How you doin', Brother Logan?"

"Why, if here ain't Sis' Whiteside, too!" said the old beau, sitting up straight on his wagon-seat and showing a row of ivory teeth in a wide grin. "I's doin' purty well for a po' widower what ain't got nobody to bake his bread. Doin' purty well. Hee! Hee! None o' you all ain't sorry for me, is you? How de storm treat you, Hager? . . . Says it carried off yo' porch? . . . That's certainly too bad! Well, it did some o' these white folks worse'n that. I got 'nough work to do to last me de next fo' weeks, cleanin' up yards an' haulin' off trash, me an' dis mule here. . . . How's yo' chillen, Sis' Williams?"

"Oh, they all right, thank yuh. Annjee's still at Mis' Rice's, an' Harriet's in de country at de club."

"Is she?" said Brother Logan. "I seed her in town night 'fore last down on Pearl Street 'bout ten o'clock."

"You ain't seed Harriett no night 'fore last," disputed Hager vigorously. "She don't come in town 'ceptin' Thursday afternoons, an' that's tomorrow."

"Sister, I ain't blind," said the old man, hurt that his truth should be doubted. "I—seen—Harriett Williams on Pearl Street . . . with Maudel Smothers an' two boys 'bout ten o'clock day before yestidy night! An' they was gwine to de Waiters' Ball, 'cause I asked Maudel where they was gwine, an' she say so. Then I says to Harriett: 'Does yo' mammy know you's out this late?' an' she laughed an' say: 'Oh, that's all right!' . . . Don't tell me I ain't seen Harriett, Hager."

"Well, Lawd help!" Aunt Hager cried, her mouth open. "You done seed my chile in town an' she ain't come anear home! Stayed all night at Maudel's, I reckon. . . . I tells her 'bout runnin' with that gal from de Bottoms. That's what makes her lie to me—tellin' me she don't come in town o' nights. Maudel's folks don't keep no kind o' house, and mens goes there, an' they sells licker, an' they gambles an' fights. . . . Is you sho that's right, Brother Logan, ma chile done been in town an' ain't come home?"

"It ain't wrong!" said old man Logan, cracking his long whip on the white mule's haunches. "Gittiyap! You ole jinny!" and he drove off.

"Um-uh!" said Sister Whiteside to Hager as the two toil-worn old women walked toward the house. "That's de way they does you!" The peddler gathered up her things. "I better be movin', 'cause I got these greens to sell yit, an' it's gittin' 'long towards evenin'. . . . That's de way chillens does you, Sister Williams! I knows! That's de way they does!"

# THREE

## *Jimboy's Letter*

KANSAS CITY, MO.
13 June 1912

D EAR ANNJELICA,
I been laying off to written you ever since I left
home but you know how it is. Work has not been so good
here. Am with a section gang of coloreds and greeks and
somehow strained my back on the Union Pacific laying
ties so I will be home on Saturday. Will do my best to try
and finish out weak here. Love my darling wife also kiss
my son Sandy for me. Am dying to see you,
affectionately as ever and allways
till the judgment day,
Jimboy Rogers

"Strained his back, has he? Unhuh! An' then comes writin'
'bout till de judgment day!" Hager muttered when she heard it.
"Always something wrong with that nigger! He'll be back here
now, layin' 'round, doin' nothin' fo' de rest o' de summer, turnin'
ma house into a theatre with him an' Harriett singin' their rag-
time, an' that guitar o' his'n wangin' ever' evenin'! 'Tween him
an' Harriett both it's a wonder I ain't plumb crazy. But Harriett
do work fo' her livin'. She ain't no loafer. . . . Huh! . . .
Annjee, you was sho a fool when you married that boy, an'
you still is! . . . I's gwine next do' to Sister Johnson's!" Aunt
Hager went out the back and across the yard, where, next door,
Tom and Sarah Johnson, Willie-Mae's grandparents, sat on a
bench against the side-wall of an unpainted shanty. They were
both quietly smoking their corn-cob pipes in the evening
dusk.

Sandy, looking at the back of the letter that his mother held,
stood at the kitchen-table rapidly devouring a large piece of
fresh lemon pie, which she had brought from Mrs. J. J. Rice's.
Annjee had said to save the two cold fried lamb chops until tomorrow, or Sandy would have eaten those, too.

23

"Wish you'd brought home some more pie," the boy declared, his lips white with meringue, but Annjee, who had just got in from work, paid no attention to her son's appreciative remarks on her cookery.

Instead she said: "Ma certainly ain't got no time for Jimboy, has she?" and then sat down with the open letter still in her hand—a single sheet of white paper pencilled in large awkward letters. She put it on the table, rested her dark face in her hands, and began to read it again. . . . She knew how it was, of course, that her husband hadn't written before. That was all right now. Working all day in the hot sun with a gang of Greeks, a man was tired at night, besides living in a box-car, where there was no place to write a letter anyway. He was a great big kid, that's what Jimboy was, cut out for playing. But when he did work, he tried to outdo everybody else. Annjee could see him in her mind, tall and well-built, his legs apart, muscles bulging as he swung the big hammer above his head, driving steel. No wonder he hurt his back, trying to lay more ties a day than anybody else on the railroad. That was just like Jimboy. But she was kind of pleased he had hurt it, since it would bring him home.

"Ain't you glad he's comin', Sandy?"

"Sure," answered the child, swallowing his last mouthful of pie. "I hope he brings me that gun he promised to buy last Easter." The boy wiped his sticky hands on the dish-cloth and ran out into the back yard, calling: "Willie-Mae! Willie-Mae!"

"Stay right over yonder!" answered his grandmother through the dusk. "Willie-Mae's in de bed, sir, an' we old folks settin' out here tryin' to have a little peace." From the tone of Hager's voice he knew he wasn't wanted in the Johnson's yard, so he went back into the house, looked at his mother reading her letter again, and then lay down on the kitchen-floor.

"Affectionately as ever and allways till the judgment day," she read, "Jimboy Rogers."

He loved her, Annjee was sure of that, and it wasn't another woman that made him go away so often. Eight years they'd been married. No, nine—because Sandy was nine, and he was ready to be born when they had had the wedding. And Jimboy left the week after they were married, to go to Omaha, where he worked all winter. When he came back, Sandy was in the world, sitting up sucking meat skins. It was springtime and they bought a piano for the house—but later the instalment man came and took it back to the store. All that summer her husband stayed home and worked a little, but mostly he fished, played pool, taught Harriett to buck-dance, and quarrelled with Aunt Hager. Then in the winter he went to Jefferson City and got a job at the Capitol.

Jimboy was always going, but Aunt Hager was wrong about his never working. It was just that he couldn't stay in one place all the time. He'd been born running, he said, and had run ever since. Besides, what was there in Stanton anyhow for a young colored fellow to do except dig sewer ditches for a few cents an hour or maybe porter around a store for seven dollars a week. Colored men couldn't get many jobs in Stanton, and foreigners were coming in, taking away what little work they did have. No wonder he didn't stay home. Hadn't Annjee's father been in Stanton forty years and hadn't he died with Aunt Hager still taking in washings to help keep up the house?

There was no well-paid work for Negro men, so Annjee didn't blame Jimboy for going away looking for something better. She'd go with him if it wasn't for her mother. If she went, though, Aunt Hager wouldn't have anybody for company but Harriett, and Harriett was the youngest and wildest of the three children. With Pa Williams dead going on ten years, Hager washing every day, Tempy married, and Annjee herself out working, there had been nobody to take much care of the little sister as she grew up. Harriett had had no raising, even though she was smart and in high school. A female child needed care. But she could sing! Lawdy! And dance, too! That was another reason why Aunt Hager didn't like Jimboy. The devil's musicianer, she called him, straight from hell, teaching Harriett buck-and-winging! But when he took his soft-playing guitar and picked out spirituals and old-time Christian hymns on its sweet strings, Hager forgot she was his enemy, and sang and rocked with the rest of them. When Jimboy was home, you couldn't get lonesome or blue.

"Gee, I'll be glad when he comes!" Annjee said to herself. "But if he goes off again, I'll feel like dying in this dead old town. I ain't never been away from here nohow." She spoke aloud to the dim oil-lamp smoking on the table and the sleeping boy on the floor. "I believe I'll go with him next time. I declare I do!" And then, realizing that Jimboy had never once told her when he was leaving or for what destination, she amended her utterance. "I'll follow him, though, as soon as he writes." Because, almost always after he had been away two or three weeks, he would write. "I'll follow him, sure, if he goes off again. I'll leave Sandy here and send money back to mama. Then Harriett could settle down and take care of ma and stop runnin' the streets so much. . . . Yes, that's what I'll do next time!"

This going away was a new thought, and the dark, strong-bodied young woman at the table suddenly began to dream of the cities she had never seen to which Jimboy would lead her. Why, he had been as far north as Canada and as far south as New Orleans, and it wasn't anything for him to go to Chicago or Denver any time! He was a travelling man—and she, Annjee, was too meek and quiet, that's what she was—too stay-at-homish. Never going nowhere, never saying nothing back to those who scolded her or talked about her, not even sassing white folks when they got beside themselves. And every colored girl in town said that Mrs. J. J. Rice was no easy white woman to work for, yet she had been there now five years, accepting everything without a murmur! Most young folks, girls and boys, left Stanton as soon as they could for the outside world, but here she was, Annjelica Williams, going on twenty-eight, and had never been as far as Kansas City!

"I want to travel," she said to herself. "I want to go places, too."

But that was why Jimboy married her, because she wasn't a runabout. He'd had enough of those kind of women before he struck Stanton, he said. St. Louis was full of them, and Chicago running over. She was the first nice girl he'd ever met who lived at home, so he took her. . . . There were mighty few dark women had a light, strong, good-looking young husband, really a married husband, like Jimboy, and a little brown kid like Sandy.

"I'm mighty lucky," Annjee thought, "even if he ain't here." And two tears of foolish pride fell from the bright eyes in her round black face. They trickled down on the letter, with its blue lines and pencil-scrawled message, and some of the words on the paper began to blur into purple blots because the pencil had been an indelible one. Quickly she fumbled for a handkerchief to wipe the tears away, when a voice made her start.

"You Annjee!" cried Aunt Hager in the open door. "Go to bed, chile! Go on! Settin' up here this late, burnin' de light an' lurin' all sorts o' night-bugs an' creepers into de house!" The old woman came in out of the dark. "Lawd! I might anigh stumbled over this boy in de middle o' de flo'! An' you ain't even took off yo' hat since you got home from work! Is you crazy? Settin' up here at night with yo' hat on, an' lettin' this chile catch his death o' cold sleepin' down on de flo' long after his bedtime!"

Sheepishly Annjee folded her letter and got up. It was true that she still had on her hat and the sweater she had worn to Mrs. Rice's. True, too, the whole room was alive with soft-winged moths fluttering against the hot glass of the light—and on the kitchen floor a small, brown-skin, infinitely lovable edition of Jimboy lay sprawled contentedly in his grandmother's path, asleep!

"He's my baby!" Annjee said gently, stooping to pick him up. "He's my baby—me and Jimboy's baby!"

# FOUR

## *Thursday Afternoon*

H AGER had risen at sunrise. On Thursdays she did the Reinharts' washing, on Fridays she ironed it, and on Saturdays she sent it home, clean and beautifully white, and received
as pay the sum of seventy-five cents. During the winter Hager
usually did half a dozen washings a week, but during the hot
season her customers had gone away, and only the Reinharts,
on account of an invalid grandmother with whom they could
not travel, remained in Stanton.

Wednesday afternoon Sandy, with a boy named Jimmy Lane,
called at the back door for their soiled clothes. Each child took
a handle and between them carried the large wicker basket
seven blocks to Aunt Hager's kitchen. For this service Jimmy
Lane received five cents a trip, although Sister Lane had repeatedly said to Hager that he needn't be given anything. She
wanted him to learn his Christian duties by being useful to old
folks. But Jimmy was not inclined to be Christian. On the contrary, he was a very bad little boy of thirteen, who often led
Sandy astray. Sometimes they would run with the basket for no
reason at all, then stumble and spill the clothes out on the
sidewalk—Mrs. Reinhart's summer dresses, and drawers, and
Mr. Reinhart's extra-large B.V.D.'s lying generously exposed to
the public. Sometimes, if occasion offered, the youngsters
would stop to exchange uncouth epithets with strange little
white boys who called them "niggers." Or, again, they might
neglect their job for a game of marbles, or a quarter-hour of
scrub baseball on a vacant lot; or to tease any little colored girl
who might tip timidly by with her hair in tight, well-oiled
braids—while the basket of garments would be left forlornly in
the street without guardian. But when the clothes were safe in
Aunt Hager's kitchen, Jimmy would usually buy candy with
his nickel and share it with Sandy before he went home.

After soaking all night, the garments were rubbed through
the suds in the morning; and in the afternoon the colored arti-

cles were on the line while the white pieces were boiling seriously in a large tin boiler on the kitchen-stove.

"They sho had plenty this week," Hager said to her grandson, who sat on the stoop eating a slice of bread and apple butter. "I's mighty late gettin' 'em hung out to dry, too. Had no business stoppin' this mawnin' to go see sick folks, and me here got all I can do maself! Looks like this warm weather old Mis' Reinhart must change ever' piece from her dress to her shimmy three times a day—sendin' me a washin' like this here!" They heard the screen-door at the front of the house open and slam. "It's a good thing they got me to do it fo' 'em! . . . Sandy, see who's that at de do'."

It was Harriett, home from the country club for the afternoon, cool and slender and pretty in her black uniform with its white collar, her smooth black face and neck powdered pearly, and her crinkly hair shining with pomade. She smelled nice and perfumy as Sandy jumped on her like a dog greeting a favorite friend. Harriett kissed him and let him hang to her arm as they went through the bedroom to the kitchen. She carried a brown cardboard suit-case and a wide straw hat in one hand.

"Hello, mama," she said.

Hager poked the boiling clothes with a vigorous splash of her round stick. The steam rose in clouds of soapy vapor.

"I been waitin' for you, madam!" her mother replied in tones that were not calculated to welcome pleasantly an erring daughter. "I wants to know de truth—was you in town last Monday night or not?"

Harriett dropped her suit-case against the wall. "You seem to have the truth," she said carelessly. How'd you get it? . . . Here, Sandy, take this out in the yard and eat it, seed and all." She gave her nephew a plum she had brought in her pocket. "I *was* in town, but I didn't have time to come home. I had to go to Maudel's because she's making me a dress."

"To Maudel's! . . . Unhuh! An' to de Waiters' Ball, besides galavantin' up an' down Pearl Street after ten o'clock! I wouldn't cared so much if you'd told me beforehand, but you said you didn't come in town 'ceptin' Thursday afternoon, an' here I was believing yo' lies."

"It's no lies! I haven't been in town before."

"Who brung you here at night anyhow—an' there ain't no trains runnin'?"

"O, I came in with the cook and some of the boys, mama, that's who! They hired an auto for the dance. What would be the use coming home, when you and Annjee go to bed before dark like chickens?"

"That's all right, madam! Annjee's got sense—savin' her health an' strength!"

Harriett was not impressed. "For what? To spend her life in Mrs. Rice's kitchen?" She shrugged her shoulders.

"What you bring yo' suit-case home fo'?"

"I'm quitting the job Saturday," she said. "I've told them already."

"Quitting!" her mother exclaimed. "What fo'? Lawd, if it ain't one thing, it's another!"

"What for?" Harriett retorted angrily. "There's plenty what for! All that work for five dollars a week with what little tips those pikers give you. And white men insulting you besides, asking you to sleep with 'em. Look at my finger-nails, all broke from scrubbing that dining-room floor." She thrust out her dark slim hands. "Waiting table and cleaning silver, washing and ironing table-linen, and then scrubbing the floor besides —that's too much of a good thing! And only three waitresses on the job. That old steward out there's a regular white folks' nigger. He don't care how hard he works us girls. Well, I'm through with the swell new Stanton County Country Club this coming Saturday—I'm telling everybody!" She shrugged her shoulders again.

"What you gonna do then?"

"Maudel says I can get a job with her."

"Maudel? . . . Where?" The old woman had begun to wring the clothes dry and pile them in a large dish-pan.

"At the Banks Hotel, chambermaid, for pretty good pay."

Hager stopped again and turned decisively towards her daughter. "You ain't gonna work in no hotel. You hear me! They's dives o' sin, that's what they is, an' a child o' mine ain't goin' in one. If you was a boy, I wouldn't let you go, much less a girl! They ain't nothin' but strumpets works in hotels."

"Maudel's no strumpet." Harriett's eyes narrowed.

"I don't know if she is or ain't, but I knows I wants you to stop runnin' with her—I done tole you befo'. . . . Her mammy ain't none too straight neither, raisin' them chillen in sin. Look at Sammy in de reform school 'fore he were fifteen for gamblin'. An' de oldest chile, Essie, done gone to Kansas City with that yaller devil she ain't married. An' Maudel runnin' de streets night an' day, with you tryin' to keep up with her! . . . Lawd a mercy! . . . Here, hang up these clothes!"

Her mother pointed to the tin pan on the table filled with damp, twisted, white underwear. Harriett took the pan in both hands. It was heavy and she trembled with anger as she lifted it to her shoulders.

"You can bark at me if you want to, mama, but don't talk about my friends. I don't care what they are! Maudel'd do anything for me. And her brother's a good kid, whether he's been in reform school or not. They oughtn't to put him there just for shooting dice. What's that? I like him, and I like Mrs. Smothers, too. She's not always scolding people for wanting a good time and for being lively and trying to be happy."

Hot tears raced down each cheek, leaving moist lines in the pink powder. Sandy, playing marbles with Buster under the apple-tree, heard her sniffling as she shook out the clothes and hung them on the line in the yard.

"You Sandy," Aunt Hager called loudly from the kitchen-door. "Come in here an' get me some water an' cut mo' firewood." Her black face was wet with perspiration and drawn from fatigue and worry. "I got to get the rest o' these clothes out yet this evenin'. . . . That chile Harriett's aggravatin' me to death! Help me, Sandy, honey."

They ate supper in silence, for Hager's attempts at conversation with her young daughter were futile. Once the old woman said: "That onery Jimboy's comin' home Saturday," and Harriett's face brightened a moment.

"Gee, I'm glad," she replied, and then her mouth went sullen again. Sandy began uncomfortably to kick the table-leg.

"For Christ's sake!" the girl frowned, and the child stopped, hurt that his favorite aunt should yell at him peevishly for so slight an offense.

"Lawd knows, I wish you'd try an' be mo' like yo' sisters, Annjee an' Tempy," Hager began as she washed the dishes, while Harriett stood near the stove, cloth in hand, waiting to dry them. "Here I is, an old woman, an' you tries ma soul! After all I did to raise you, you don't even hear me when I speak." It was the old theme again, without variation. "Now, there's Annjee, ain't a better chile livin'—if she warn't crazy 'bout Jimboy. An' Tempy married an' doin' well, an' respected ever'where. . . . An' you runnin' wild!"

"Tempy?" Harriett sneered suddenly, pricked by this comparison. "So respectable you can't touch her with a ten-foot pole, that's Tempy! . . . Annjee's all right, working herself to death at Mrs. Rice's, but don't tell me about Tempy. Just because she's married a mail-clerk with a little property, she won't even see her own family any more. When niggers get up in the world, they act just like white folks—don't pay you no mind. And Tempy's that kind of a nigger—she's up in the world now!"

"Close yo' mouth, talking that way 'bout yo' own sister! I ain't asked her to be always comin' home, is I, if she's satisfied in her own house?"

"No, you aren't asking her, mama, but you're always talking about her being so respectable. . . . Well, I don't want to be respectable if I have to be stuck up and dicty like Tempy is. . . . She's colored and I'm colored and I haven't seen her since before Easter. . . . It's not being black that matters with her, though, it's being poor, and that's what we are, you and me and Annjee, working for white folks and washing clothes and going in back doors, and taking tips and insults. I'm tired of it, mama! I want to have a good time once in a while."

"That's 'bout all you does have is a good time," Hager said. "An' it ain't right, an' it ain't Christian, that's what it ain't! An' de Lawd is takin' notes on you!" The old woman picked up the heavy iron skillet and began to wash it inside and out.

"Aw, the church has made a lot of you old Negroes act like Salvation Army people," the girl returned, throwing the dried knives and forks on the table. "Afraid to even laugh on Sundays, afraid for a girl and boy to look at one another, or for people to go to dances. Your old Jesus is white, I guess, that's why! He's white and stiff and don't like niggers!"

Hager gasped while Harriett went on excitedly, disregarding her mother's pain: "Look at Tempy, the highest-class Christian in the family—Episcopal, and so holy she can't even visit her own mother. Seems like all the good-time people are bad, and all the old Uncle Toms and mean, dried-up, long-faced niggers fill the churches. I don't never intend to join a church if I can help it."

"Have mercy on this chile! Help her an' save her from hell-fire! Change her heart, Jesus!" the old woman begged, standing in the middle of the kitchen with uplifted arms. "God have mercy on ma daughter."

Harriett, her brow wrinkled in a steady frown, put the dishes away, wiped the table, and emptied the water with a splash through the kitchen-door. Then she went into the bedroom that she shared with her mother, and began to undress. Sandy saw, beneath her thin white underclothes, the soft black skin of her shapely young body.

"Where you goin'?" Hager asked sharply.

"Out," said the girl.

"Out where?"

"O, to a barbecue at Willow Grove, mama! The boys are coming by in an auto at seven o'clock."

"What boys?"

"Maudel's brother and some fellows."

"You ain't goin' a step!"

A pair of curling-irons swung in the chimney of the lighted lamp on the dresser. Harriett continued to get ready. She was making bangs over her forehead, and the scent of scorching hair-oil drifted by Sandy's nose.

"Up half de night in town Monday, an' de Lawd knows how late ever' night in de country, an' then you comes home to run out agin! . . . You ain't goin'!" continued her mother.

Harriett was pulling on a pair of red silk stockings, bright and shimmering to her hips.

"You quit singin' in de church choir. You say you ain't goin' back to school. You won't keep no job! Now what *is* you gonna do? Yo' pappy said years ago, 'fore he died, you was too purty to 'mount to anything, but I ain't believed him. His last dyin' words was: 'Look out fo' ma baby Harriett.' You was his favourite chile. . . . Now look at you! Runnin' de streets an' wearin' red silk stockings!" Hager trembled. " 'Spose yo' pappy was to come back an' see you?"

Harriett powdered her face and neck, pink on ebony, dashed

white talcum at each arm-pit, and rubbed her ears with perfume from a thin bottle. Then she slid a light blue dress of
many ruffles over her head. The skirt ended midway between
the ankle and the knee, and she looked very cute, delicate, and
straight, like a black porcelain doll in a Vienna toy shop.

"Some o' Maudel's makin's, that dress—anybody can tell,"
her mother went on quarrelling. "Short an' shameless as it can
be! Regular bad gal's dress, that's what 'tis. . . . What you
puttin' it on fo' anyhow, an' I done told you you ain't goin'
out? You must think I don't mean ma words. Ain't more'n sixteen last April an' runnin' to barbecues at Willer Grove! De
idee! When I was yo' age, wasn't up after eight o'clock, 'ceptin'
Sundays in de church house, that's all. . . . Lawd knows
where you young ones is headin'. An' me prayin' an' washin'
ma fingers to de bone to keep a roof over yo' head."

The sharp honk of an automobile horn sounded from the
street. A big red car, full of laughing brown girls gaily dressed,
and coatless, slick-headed black boys in green and yellow silk
shirts, drew up at the curb. Somebody squeezed the bulb of
the horn a second time and another loud and saucy honk!
struck the ears.

"You Sandy," Hager commanded. "Run out there an' tell
them niggers to leave here, 'cause Harriett ain't goin' no place."

But Sandy did not move, because his young and slender
aunt had gripped him firmly by the collar while she searched
feverishly in the dresser-drawer for a scarf. She pulled it out,
long and flame-colored, with fiery, silky fringe, before she released the little boy.

"You ain't gwine a step this evenin'!" Hager shouted. "Don't
you hear me?"

"O, no?" said Harriett coolly in a tone that cut like knives.
"You're the one that says I'm not going—*but I am!*"

Then suddenly something happened in the room—the anger
fell like a veil from Hager's face, disclosing aged, helpless eyes
full of fear and pain.

"Harriett, honey, I wants you to be good," the old woman
stammered. The words came pitiful and low—not a command
any longer—as she faced her terribly alive young daughter in
the ruffled blue dress and the red silk stockings. "I just wants you
to grow up decent, chile. I don't want you runnin' to Willer

Grove with them boys. It ain't no place fo' you in the night-time—an' you knows it. You's mammy's baby girl. She wants you to be good, honey, and follow Jesus, that's all."

The baritone giggling of the boys in the auto came across the yard as Hager started to put a timid, restraining hand on her daughter's shoulder—but Harriett backed away.

"You old fool!" she cried. "Lemme go! You old Christian fool!"

She ran through the door and across the sidewalk to the waiting car, where the arms of the young men welcomed her eagerly. The big machine sped swiftly down the street and the rapid sput! sput! sput! of its engine grew fainter and fainter. Finally, the auto was only a red tail-light in the summer dusk. Sandy, standing beside his grandmother in the doorway, watched it until it disappeared.

# FIVE

## *Guitar*

Throw yo' arms around me, baby,
Like de circle round de sun!
Baby, throw yo' arms around me
Like de circle round de sun,
An' tell yo' pretty papa
How you want yo' lovin' done!

JIMBOY was home. All the neighborhood could hear his rich low baritone voice giving birth to the blues. On Saturday night he and Annjee went to bed early. On Sunday night Aunt Hager said: "Put that guitar right up, less'n it's hymns you plans on playin'. An' I don't want too much o' them, 'larmin' de white neighbors."

But this was Monday, and the sun had scarcely fallen below the horizon before the music had begun to float down the alley, over back fences and into kitchen-windows where nice white ladies sedately washed their supper dishes.

Did you ever see peaches
Growin' on a watermelon vine?
Says did you ever see peaches
On a watermelon vine?
Did you ever see a woman
That I couldn't get for mine?

Long, lazy length resting on the kitchen-door-sill, back against the jamb, feet in the yard, fingers picking his sweet guitar, left hand holding against its finger-board the back of an old pocket-knife, sliding the knife upward, downward, getting thus weird croons and sighs from the vibrating strings:

O, I left ma mother
An' I cert'ly can leave you.
Indeed I left ma mother
An' I cert'ly can leave you,

36

> For I'd leave any woman
> That mistreats me like you do.

Jimboy, remembering brown-skin mamas in Natchez, Shreveport, Dallas; remembering Creole women in Baton Rouge, Louisiana:

> O, yo' windin' an' yo' grindin'
> Don't have no effect on me,
> Babe, yo' windin' an' yo' grindin'
> Don't have no 'fect on me,
> 'Cause I can wind an' grind
> Like a monkey round a coconut-tree!

Then Harriett, standing under the ripening apple-tree, in the back yard, chiming in:

> Now I see that you don't want me,
> So it's fare thee, fare thee well!
> Lawd, I see that you don't want me,
> So it's fare—thee—well!
> I can still get plenty lovin',
> An' you can go to—Kansas City!

"O, play it, sweet daddy Jimboy!" She began to dance.

Then Hager, from her seat on the edge of the platform covering the well, broke out: "Here, madam! Stop that prancin'! Bad enough to have all this singin' without turnin' de yard into a show-house." But Harriett kept on, her hands picking imaginary cherries out of the stars, her hips speaking an earthly language quite their own.

"You got it, kid," said Jimboy, stopping suddenly, then fingering his instrument for another tune. "You do it like the stage women does. You'll be takin' Ada Walker's place if you keep on."

"Wha! Wha! . . . You chillen sho can sing!" Tom Johnson shouted his compliments from across the yard. And Sarah, beside him on the bench behind their shack, added: "Minds me o' de ole plantation times, honey! It sho do!"

"Unhuh! Bound straight fo' de devil, that's what they is," Hager returned calmly from her place beside the pump. "You an' Harriett both—singin' an' dancin' this stuff befo' these

chillens here." She pointed to Sandy and Willie-Mae, who sat
on the ground with their backs against the chicken-box. "It's a
shame!"

"I likes it," said Willie-Mae.

"Me too," the little boy agreed.

"Naturally you would—none o' you-all's converted yet,"
countered the old woman to the children as she settled back
against the pump to listen to some more.

The music rose hoarse and wild:

> I wonder where ma easy rider's gone?
> He done left me, put ma new gold watch in pawn.

It was Harriett's voice in plaintive moan to the night sky.
Jimboy had taught her that song, but a slight, clay-colored
brown boy who had hopped bells at the Clinton Hotel for a
couple of months, on his way from Houston to Omaha, discovered its meaning to her. Puppy-love, maybe, but it had hurt
when he went away, saying nothing. And the guitar in Jimboy's
hands echoed that old pain with an even greater throb than
the original ache itself possessed.

Approaching footsteps came from the front yard.

"Lord, I can hear you-all two blocks away!" said Annjee,
coming around the house, home from work, with a bundle of
food under her left arm. "Hello! How are you, daddy? Hello,
ma! Gimme a kiss Sandy. . . . Lord, I'm hot and tired and
most played out. This late just getting from work! . . . Here,
Jimboy, come on in and eat some of these nice things the white
folks had for supper." She stepped across her husband's outstretched legs into the kitchen. "I brought a mighty good
piece of cold ham for you, hon', from Mis' Rice's."

"All right, sure, I'll be there in a minute," the man said, but
he went on playing *Easy Rider*, and Harriett went on singing,
while the food was forgotten on the table until long after
Annjee had come outdoors again and sat down in the cool,
tired of waiting for Jimboy to come in to her.

Off and on for nine years, ever since he had married Annjee,
Jimboy and Harriett had been singing together in the evenings.
When they started, Harriett was a little girl with braided hair,
and each time that her roving brother-in-law stopped in
Stanton, he would amuse himself by teaching her the old

Southern songs, the popular rag-time ditties, and the hundreds
of varying verses of the blues that he would pick up in the big
dirty cities of the South. The child, with her strong sweet voice
(colored folks called it alto) and her racial sense of rhythm,
soon learned to sing the songs as well as Jimboy. He taught
her the *parse me la*, too, and a few other movements peculiar
to Southern Negro dancing, and sometimes together they
went through the buck and wing and a few taps. It was all
great fun, and innocent fun except when one stopped to think,
as white folks did, that some of the blues lines had, not only
double, but triple meanings, and some of the dance steps required very definite movements of the hips. But neither
Harriett nor Jimboy soiled their minds by thinking. It was music, good exercise—and they loved it.

"Do you know this one, Annjee?" asked Jimboy, calling his
wife's name out of sudden politeness because he had forgotten
to eat her food, had hardly looked at her, in fact, since she
came home. Now he glanced towards her in the darkness
where she sat plump on a kitchen-chair in the yard, apart from
the others, with her back to the growing corn in the garden.
Softly he ran his fingers, light as a breeze, over his guitar
strings, imitating the wind rustling through the long leaves of
the corn. A rectangle of light from the kitchen-door fell into
the yard striking sidewise across the healthy orange-yellow of
his skin above the unbuttoned neck of his blue laborer's shirt.

"Come on, sing it with us, Annjee," he said.

"I don't know it," Annjee replied, with a lump in her throat,
and her eyes on the silhouette of his long, muscular, animal-
hard body. She loved Jimboy too much, that's what was the
matter with her! She knew there was nothing between him and
her young sister except the love of music, yet he might have
dropped the guitar and left Harriett in the yard for a little while
to come eat the nice cold slice of ham she had brought him.
She hadn't seen him all day long. When she went to work this
morning, he was still in bed—and now the blues claimed him.

In the starry blackness the singing notes of the guitar became a plaintive hum, like a breeze in a grove of palmettos;
became a low moan, like the wind in a forest of live-oaks strung
with long strands of hanging moss. The voice of Annjee's
golden, handsome husband on the door-step rang high and far

away, lonely-like, crying with only the guitar, not his wife, to understand; crying grotesquely, crying absurdly in the summer night:

> I got a mule to ride.
> I got a mule to ride.
> Down in the South somewhere
> I got a mule to ride.

Then asking the question as an anxious, left-lonesome girl-sweetheart would ask it:

> You say you goin' North.
> You say you goin' North.
> How 'bout yo' . . . lovin' gal?
> You say you goin' North.

Then sighing in rhythmical despair:

> O, don't you leave me here.
> Babe, don't you leave me here.
> Dog-gone yo' comin' back!
> Said don't you leave me here.

On and on the song complained, man-verses and woman-verses, to the evening air in stanzas that Jimboy had heard in the pine-woods of Arkansas from the lumber-camp workers; in other stanzas that were desperate and dirty like the weary roads where they were sung; and in still others that the singer created spontaneously in his own mouth then and there:

> O, I done made ma bed,
> Says I done made ma bed.
> Down in some lonesome grave
> I done made ma bed.

It closed with a sad eerie twang.

"That's right decent," said Hager. "Now I wish you-all'd play some o' ma pieces like *When de Saints Come Marchin' In* or *This World Is Not Ma Home*—something Christian from de church."

"Aw, mama, it's not Sunday yet," said Harriett.

"Sing *Casey Jones*," called old man Tom Johnson. "That's ma song."

So the ballad of the immortal engineer with another mama in the Promised Land rang out promptly in the starry darkness, while everybody joined in the choruses.

"Aw, pick it, boy," yelled the old man. "Can't nobody play like you."

And Jimboy remembered when he was a lad in Memphis that W. C. Handy had said: "You ought to make your living out of that, son." But he hadn't followed it up—too many things to see, too many places to go, too many other jobs.

"What song do you like, Annjee?" he asked, remembering her presence again.

"O, I don't care. Any ones you like. All of 'em are pretty." She was pleased and petulant and a little startled that he had asked her.

"All right, then," he said. "Listen to me:"

> Here I is in de mean ole jail.
> Ain't got nobody to go ma bail.
> Lonesome an' sad an' chain gang bound—
> Ever' friend I had's done turned me down.

"That's sho it!" shouted Tom Johnson in great sympathy. "Now, when I was in de Turner County Jail . . ."

"Shut up yo' mouth!" squelched Sarah, jabbing her husband in the ribs.

The songs went on, blues, shouts, jingles, old hits: *Bon Bon Buddy, the Chocolate Drop; Wrap Me in Your Big Red Shawl; Under the Old Apple Tree; Turkey in the Straw*—Jimboy and Harriett breaking the silence of the small-town summer night until Aunt Hager interrupted:

"You-all better wind up, chillens, 'cause I wants to go to bed. I ain't used to stayin' 'wake so late, nohow. Play something kinder decent there, son, fo' you stops."

Jimboy, to tease the old woman, began to rock and moan like an elder in the Sanctified Church, patting both feet at the same time as he played a hymn-like, lugubrious tune with a dancing overtone:

> Tell me, sister,
> Tell me, brother,
> Have you heard de latest news?

Then seriously as if he were about to announce the coming of the Judgment:

> A woman down in Georgia
> Got her two sweet-men confused.

How terrible! How sad! moaned the guitar.

> One knocked on de front do',
> One knocked on de back—

Sad, sad . . . sad, sad! said the music.

> Now that woman down in Georgia's
> Door-knob is hung with black.

O, play that funeral march, boy! while the guitar laughed a dirge.

> An' de hearse is comin' easy
> With two rubber-tired hacks!

Followed by a long-drawn-out, churchlike:

> Amen . . . !

Then with rapid glides, groans, and shouts the instrument screamed of a sudden in profane frenzy, and Harriett began to ball-the-jack, her arms flopping like the wings of a headless pigeon, the guitar strings whining in ecstasy, the player rocking gaily to the urgent music, his happy mouth crying: "Tack 'em on down, gal! Tack 'em on down, Harrie!"

But Annjee had risen.

"I wish you'd come in and eat the ham I brought you," she said as she picked up her chair and started towards the house. "And you, Sandy! Get up from under that tree and go to bed." She spoke roughly to the little fellow, whom the songs had set a-dreaming. Then to her husband: "Jimboy, I wish you'd come in."

The man stopped playing, with a deep vibration of the strings that seemed to echo through the whole world. Then he leaned his guitar against the side of the house and lifted straight up in his hairy arms Annjee's plump, brown-black little body while he kissed her as she wriggled like a stubborn child, her soft breasts rubbing his hard body through the coarse blue shirt.

"You don't like my old songs, do you, baby? You don't want to hear me sing 'em," he said, laughing. "Well, that's all right. I like you, anyhow, and I like your ham, and I like your kisses, and I like everything you bring me. Let's go in and chow down." And he carried her into the kitchen, where he sat with her on his knees as he ate the food she so faithfully had brought him from Mrs. J. J. Rice's dinner-table.

Outside, Willie-Mae went running home through the dark. And Harriett pumped a cool drink of water for her mother, then helped her to rise from her low seat, Sandy aiding from behind, with both hands pushing firmly in Aunt Hager's fleshy back. Then the three of them came into the house and glanced, as they passed through the kitchen, at Annjee sitting on Jim-boy's lap with both dark arms tight around his neck.

"Looks like you're clinging to the Rock of Ages," said Harriett to her sister. "Be sure you don't slip, old evil gal!"

But at midnight, when the owl that nested in a tree near the corner began to hoot, they were all asleep—Annjee and Jimboy in one room, Harriett and Hager in another, with Sandy on the floor at the foot of his grandmother's bed. Far away on the railroad line a whistle blew, lonesome and long.

# SIX

## *Work*

THE sunflowers in Willie-Mac's back yard were taller than Tom Johnson's head, and the hollyhocks in the fence corners were almost as high. The nasturtiums, blood-orange and gold, tumbled over themselves all around Madam de Carter's house. Aunt Hager's sweet-william, her pinks, and her tiger-lilies were abloom and the apples on her single tree would soon be ripe. The adjoining yards of the three neighbors were gay with flowers. "Watch out for them dogs!" his grandmother told Sandy hourly, for the days had come when the bright heat made gentle animals go mad. Bees were heavy with honey, great green flies hummed through the air, yellow-black butterflies suckled at the rambling roses . . . and watermelons were on the market.

The Royal African Knights and Ladies of King Solomon's Scepter were preparing a drill for the September Emancipation celebration, a "Drill of All Nations," in which Annjee was to represent Sweden. It was not to be given for a month or more, but the first rehearsal would take place tonight.

"Sandy," his mother said, shaking him early in the morning as he lay on his pallet at the foot of Aunt Hager's bed, "listen here! I want you to come out to Mis' Rice's this evening and help me get through the dishes so's I can start home early, in time to wash and dress myself to go to the lodge hall. You hears me?"

"Yes'm," said Sandy, keeping his eyes closed to the bright stream of morning sunlight entering the window. But half an hour later, when Jimboy kicked him and said: "Hey, bo! You wanta go fishin'?" he got up at once, slid into his pants; and together they went out in the garden to dig worms. It was seldom that his father took him anywhere, and, of course, he wanted to go. Sandy adored Jimboy, but Jimboy, amiable and indulgent though he was, did not often care to be bothered with his ten-year-old son on his fishing expeditions.

Harriett had gone to her job, and Hager had long been at the tubs under the apple-tree when the two males emerged from the kitchen-door. "Huh! You ain't workin' this mawnin', is you?" the old woman grunted, bending steadily down, then up, over the wash-board.

"Nope," her tall son-in-law answered. "Donahoe laid me off yesterday on account o' the white bricklayers said they couldn't lay bricks with a nigger."

"Always something to keep you from workin'," panted Hager.

"Sure is," agreed Jimboy pleasantly. "But don't worry, me and Sandy's gonna catch you a mess o' fish for supper today. How's that, ma?"

"Don't need no fish," the old woman answered. "An' don't come ma-in' me! Layin' round here fishin' when you ought to be out makin' money to take care o' this house an' that chile o' your'n." The suds rose foamy white about her black arms as the clothes plushed up and down on the zinc wash-board. "Lawd deliver me from a lazy darky!"

But Jimboy and Sandy were already behind the tall corn, digging for bait near the back fence.

"Don't never let no one woman worry you," said the boy's father softly, picking the moist wriggling worms from the up-turned loam. "Treat 'em like chickens, son. Throw 'em a little corn and they'll run after you, but don't give 'em too much. If you do, they'll stop layin' and expect you to wait on 'em."

"Will they?" asked Sandy.

The warm afternoon sun made the river a languid sheet of muddy gold, glittering away towards the bridge and the flour-mills a mile and a half off. Here in the quiet, on the end of a rotting jetty among the reeds, Jimboy and his son sat silently. A long string of small silver fish hung down into the water, keeping fresh, and the fishing-lines were flung far out in the stream, waiting for more bites. Not a breeze on the flat brown-gold river, not a ripple, not a sound. But once the train came by behind them, pouring out a great cloud of smoke and cinders and shaking the jetty.

"That's Number Five," said Jimboy. "Sure is flyin'," as the

train disappeared between rows of empty box-cars far down the track, sending back a hollow clatter as it shot past the flour-mills, whose stacks could be dimly seen through the heat haze. Once the engine's whistle moaned shrilly.

"She's gone now," said Jimboy as the last click of the wheels died away. And, except for the drone of a green fly about the can of bait, there was again no sound to disturb the two fishermen.

Jimboy gazed at his lines. Across the river Sandy could make out, in the brilliant sunlight, the gold of wheat-fields and the green of trees on the hills. He wondered if it would be nice to live over there in the country.

"Man alive!" his father cried suddenly, hauling vigorously at one of the lines. "Sure got a real bite now. . . . Look at this catfish." From the water he pulled a large flopping lead-colored creature, with a fierce white mouth bleeding and gaping over the hook.

"He's on my line!" yelled Sandy. "I caught him!"

"Pshaw!" laughed Jimboy. "You was setting there dreaming."

"No, I wasn't!"

But just then, at the mills, the five-o'clock whistles blew. "Oh, gee, dad!" cried the boy, frightened. "I was s'posed to go to Mis' Rice's to help mama, and I come near forgetting it. She wants to get through early this evenin' to go to lodge meeting. I gotta hurry and go help her."

"Well, you better beat it then, and I'll look out for your line like I been doing and bring the fishes home."

So the little fellow balanced himself across the jetty, scrambled up the bank, and ran down the railroad track towards town. He was quite out of breath when he reached the foot of Penrose Street, with Mrs. Rice's house still ten blocks away, so he walked awhile, then ran again, down the long residential street, with its large houses sitting in green shady lawns far back from the sidewalk. Sometimes a sprinkler attached to a long rubber hose, sprayed fountain-like jets of cold water on the thirsty grass. In one yard three golden-haired little girls were playing under an elm-tree, and in another a man and some children were having a leisurely game of croquet.

Finally Sandy turned into a big yard. The delicious scent of frying beefsteak greeted the sweating youngster as he reached the screen of the white lady's kitchen-door. Inside, Annjee was standing over the hot stove seasoning something in a saucepan, beads of perspiration on her dark face, and large damp spots under the arms of her dress.

"You better get here!" she said. "And me waiting for you for the last hour. Here, take this pick and break some ice for the tea." Sandy climbed up on a stool and raised the ice-box lid while his mother opened the oven and pulled out a pan of golden-brown biscuits. "Made these for your father," she remarked. "The white folks ain't asked for 'em, but they like 'em, too, so they can serve for both. . . . Jimboy's crazy about biscuits. . . . Did he work today?"

"No'm," said Sandy, jabbing at the ice. "We went fishing."

At that moment Mrs. Rice came into the kitchen, tall and blond, in a thin flowered gown. She was a middle-aged white woman with a sharp nasal voice.

"Annjee, I'd like the potatoes served just as they are in the casserole. And make several slices of very thin toast for my father. Now, be sure they *are* thin!"

"Yes, m'am," said Annjee stirring a spoonful of flour into the frying-pan, making a thick brown gravy.

"Old thin toast," muttered Annjee when Mrs. Rice had gone back to the front. "Always bothering round the kitchen! Here 'tis lodge-meeting night—dinner late anyhow—and she coming telling me to stop and make toast for the old man! He ain't too indigestible to eat biscuits like the rest of 'em. . . . White folks sure is a case!" She laid three slices of bread on top of the stove. "So spoiled with colored folks waiting on 'em all their days! Don't know what they'll do in heaven, 'cause I'm gonna sit down up there myself."

Annjee took the biscuits, light and brown, and placed some on a pink plate she had warmed. She carried them, with the butter and jelly, into the dining-room. Then she took the steak from the warmer, dished up the vegetables into gold-rimmed serving-dishes, and poured the gravy, which smelled deliciously onion-flavored.

"Gee, I'm hungry," said the child, with his eyes on the big steak ready to go in to the white people.

"Well, just wait," replied his mother. "You come to work, not to eat. . . . Whee! but it's hot today!" She wiped her wet face and put on a large white bungalow apron that had been hanging behind the door. Then she went with the iced tea and a pitcher of water into the dining-room, struck a Chinese gong, and came back to the kitchen to get the dishes of steaming food, which she carried in to the table.

It was some time before she returned from waiting on the table; so Sandy, to help her, began to scrape out the empty pans and put them to soak in the sink. He ate the stewed corn that had stuck in the bottom of one, and rubbed a piece of bread in the frying-pan where the gravy had been. His mother came out with the water-pitcher, broke some ice for it, and returned to the dining-room where Sandy could hear laughter, and the clinking of spoons in tea-glasses, and women talking. When Annjee came back into the kitchen, she took four custards from the ice-box and placed them on gold-rimmed plates.

"They're about through," she said to her son. "Sit down and I'll fix you up."

Sandy was very hungry and he hoped Mrs. Rice's family hadn't eaten all the steak, which had looked so good with its brown gravy and onions.

Shortly, his mother returned carrying the dishes that had been filled with hot food. She placed them on the kitchen-table in front of Sandy, but they were no longer full and no longer hot. The corn had thickened to a paste, and the potatoes were about gone; but there was still a ragged piece of steak left on the platter.

"Don't eat it all," said Annjee warningly. "I want to take some home to your father."

The bell rang in the dining-room. Annjee went through the swinging door and returned bearing a custard that had been but little touched.

"Here, sonny—the old man says it's too sweet for his stomach, so you can have this." She set the yellow cornstarch before Sandy. "He's seen these ripe peaches out here today and he wants some, that's all. More trouble than he's worth, po' old soul, and me in a hurry!" She began to peel the fruit. "Just like a chile, 'deed he is!" she added, carrying the sliced peaches into the dining-room and leaving Sandy with a plate of food before him, eating slowly. "When you rushing to get out, seems like white folks tries theirselves."

In a moment she returned, ill-tempered, and began to scold Sandy for taking so long with his meal.

"I asked you to help me so's I can get to the lodge on time, and you just set and chew and eat! . . . Here, wipe these dishes, boy!" Annjee began hurriedly to lay plates in a steaming row on the shelf of the sink; so Sandy got up and, between mouthfuls of pudding, wiped them with a large dish-towel.

Soon Mrs. Rice came into the kitchen again, briskly, through the swinging door and glanced about her. Sandy felt ashamed for the white woman to see him eating a left-over pudding from her table, so he put the spoon down.

"Annjee," the mistress said sharply. "I wish you wouldn't put quite so much onion in your sauce for the steak. I've mentioned it to you several times before, and you know very well we don't like it."

"Yes, m'am," said Annjee.

"And do *please* be careful that our drinking water is cold before meals are served. . . . You were certainly careless tonight. You must think more about what you are doing, Annjee."

Mrs. Rice went out again through the swinging door, but Sandy stood near the sink with a burning face and eyes that had suddenly filled with angry tears. He couldn't help it—hearing his sweating mother reprimanded by this tall white woman in the flowered dress. Black, hard-working Annjee answered: "Yes, m'am," and that was all—but Sandy cried.

"Dry up," his mother said crossly when she saw him, thinking he was crying because she had asked him to work. "What's come over you, anyway?—can't even wipe a few plates for me and act nice about it!"

He didn't answer. When the dining-room had been cleared and the kitchen put in order, Annjee told him to empty the garbage while she wrapped in newspapers several little bundles of food to carry to Jimboy. Then they went out the back door, around the big house to the street, and trudged the fourteen blocks to Aunt Hager's, taking short cuts through alleys, passing under arc-lights that sputtered whitely in the deepening twilight, and greeting with an occasional "Howdy" other poor colored folks also coming home from work.

"How are you, Sister Jones?"

"Right smart, I thank yuh!" as they passed.

Once Annjee spoke to her son. "Evening's the only time we niggers have to ourselves!" she said. "Thank God for night . . . 'cause all day you gives to white folks."

# SEVEN
## *White Folks*

WHEN they got home, Aunt Hager was sitting in the cool of the evening on her new porch, which had been rebuilt for thirty-five dollars added to the mortgage. The old woman was in her rocking-chair, with Jimboy, one foot on the ground and his back against a pillar, lounging at her feet. The two were quarrelling amicably over nothing as Annjee and Sandy approached.

"Good-evenin', you-all," said Annjee. "I brought you a nice piece o' steak, Jimboy-sugar, and some biscuits to go with it. Come on in and eat while I get dressed to go to the drill practice. I got to hurry."

"We don't want no steak now," Jimboy answered without moving. "Aunt Hager and me had fresh fish for supper and egg-corn-bread and we're full. We don't need nothin' more."

"Oh! . . ." said Annjee disappointedly. "Well, come on in anyhow, honey, and talk while I get dressed." So he rose lazily and followed his wife into the house.

Shortly, Sister Johnson, pursued by the ever-present Willie-Mae, came through the blue-grey darkness from next door. "Good-evenin', Sister Williams; how you been today?"

"Tolable," answered Hager, "'ceptin' I's tired out from washin' an' rinsin'. Have a seat. . . . You Sandy, go in de house an' get Sister Johnson a settin'-chair. . . . Where's Tom?"

"Lawd, chile, he done gone to bed long ago. That there sewer-diggin' job ain't so good fer a man old as Tom. He 'bout played out. . . . I done washed fer Mis' Cohn maself today. . . . Umh! dis cheer feels good! . . . Looked like to me she had near 'bout fifty babies' diddies in de wash. You know she done got twins, 'sides dat young-'un born last year."

The conversation of the two old women rambled on as their grandchildren ran across the front yard laughing, shrieking, wrestling; catching fire-flies and watching them glow in closed fists, then releasing them to twinkle in the sultry night-air.

Harriett came singing out of the house and sat down on the

51

edge of the porch. "Lord, it's hot! . . . How are you, Mis' Johnson? I didn't see you in the dark."

"Jest tolable, chile," said the old woman, "but I can't kick. Honey, when you gits old as I is, you'll be doin' well if you's livin' a-tall, de way you chillens runs round now 'days! How come you ain't out to some party dis evenin'?"

"O, there's no party tonight," said Harriett laughing. "Besides, this new job of mine's a heart-breaker, Mis' Johnson. I got to stay home and rest now. I'm kitchen-girl at that New Albert Restaurant, and time you get through wrestling with pots and arguing with white waitresses and colored cooks, you don't feel much like running out at night. But the shifts aren't bad, though, food's good, and—well, you can't expect everything." She shrugged her shoulders against the two-by-four pillar on which her back rested.

"Long's it keeps you off de streets, I's glad," said Hager, rocking contentedly. "Maybe I can git you goin' to church agin now."

"Aw, I don't like church," the girl replied.

"An', chile, I can't blame you much," said Sister Johnson, fumbling in the pocket of her apron. "De way dese churches done got now'days. . . . Sandy, run in de house an' ask yo' pappy fo' a match to light ma pipe. . . . It ain't 'Come to Jesus' no mo' a-tall. Ministers dese days an' times don't care nothin' 'bout po' Jesus. 'Stead o' dat it's rally dis an' collection dat, an' de aisle wants a new carpet, an' de pastor needs a 'lectric fan fer his red-hot self." The old sister spat into the yard. "Money! That's all 'tis! An' white folkses' religion—Lawd help! 'Taint no use in mentionin' them."

"True," agreed Hager.

"Cause if de gates o' heaven shuts in white folkses' faces like de do's o' dey church in us niggers' faces, it'll be too bad! Yes, sir! One thing sho, de Lawd ain't prejudiced!"

"No," said Hager; "but He don't love ugly, neither in niggers nor in white folks."

"Now, talking about white folks' religion," said Annjee, emerging from the house with a fresh white dress on, "why, Mis' Rice where I work don't think no more about playing bridge on Sunday than she does about praying—and I ain't never seen her pray yet."

"You're nuts," said Jimboy behind her. "People's due to have a little fun on Sundays. That's what's the matter with colored folks now—work all week and then set up in church all day Sunday, and don't even know what's goin' on in the rest of the world."

"Huh!" grunted Hager.

"Well, we won't argue, daddy," Annjee smiled. "Come on and walk a piece with me, sweetness. Here 'tis nearly nine and I should a been at the hall at eight, but colored folks are always behind the clock. Come on, Jimboy."

"Good-bye, mama," yelled Sandy from the lawn as his parents strolled up the street together.

"Jimboy's right," said Harriett. "Darkies do like the church too much, but white folks don't care nothing about it at all. They're too busy getting theirs out of this world, not from God. And I don't blame 'em, except that they're so mean to niggers. They're right, though, looking out for themselves . . . and yet I hate 'em for it. They don't have to mistreat us besides, do they?"

"Honey, don't talk that way," broke in Hager. "It ain't Christian, chile. If you don't like 'em, pray for 'em, but don't feel evil against 'em. I was in slavery, Harrie, an' I been knowin' white folks all ma life, an' they's good as far as they can see—but when it comes to po' niggers, they just can't see far, that's all."

Harriett opened her mouth to reply, but Jimboy, who left Annjee at the corner and had returned to the porch, beat her to it. "We too dark for 'em, ma," he laughed. "How they gonna see in the dark? You colored folks oughta get lighter, that's what!"

"Shut up yo' mouth, you yaller rooster!" said Sister Johnson. "White folks is white folks, an' dey's mean! I can't help what Hager say," the old woman disagreed emphatically with her crony. "Ain't I been knowin' crackers sixty-five years, an' ain't dey de cause o' me bein' here in Stanton 'stead o' in ma home right today? De dirty buzzards! Ain't I nussed t'ree of 'em up from babies like ma own chillens, and ain't dem same t'ree boys done turned round an' helped run me an' Tom out o' town?"

The old sister took a long draw on her corn-cob pipe, and a fiery red spot glowed in its bowl, while Willie-Mae and Sandy stopped playing and sat down on the porch as she began a tale they had all heard at least a dozen times.

"I's tole you 'bout it befo', ain't I?" asked Sister Johnson.

"Not me," lied Jimboy, who was anxious to keep her going.

"No, you haven't," Harriett assured her.

"Well, it were like dis," and the story unwound itself, the preliminary details telling how, as a young freed-girl after the Civil War, Sister Johnson had gone into service for a white planter's family in a Mississippi town near Vicksburg. While attached to this family, she married Tom Johnson, then a field-hand, and raised five children of her own during the years that followed, besides caring for three boys belonging to her white mistress, nursing them at her black breasts and sometimes leaving her own young ones in the cabin to come and stay with her white charges when they were ill. These called her mammy, too, and when they were men and married, she still went to see them and occasionally worked for their families.

"Now, we niggers all lived at de edge o' town in what de whites called Crowville, an' most of us owned little houses an' farms, an' we did right well raisin' cotton an' sweet 'taters an' all. Now, dat's where de trouble started! We was doin' too well, an' de white folks said so! But we ain't paid 'em no 'tention, jest thought dey was talkin' fer de pastime of it. . . . Well, we all started fixin' up our houses an' paintin' our fences, an' Crowville looked kinder decent-like when de white folks 'gin to 'mark, so's we servants could hear 'em, 'bout niggers livin' in painted houses an' dressin' fine like we was somebody! . . . Well, dat went on fer some time wid de whites talkin' an' de coloreds doin' better'n better year by year, sellin' mo' cotton ever' day an' gittin' nice furniture an' buyin' pianers, till by an' by a prosp'rous nigger named John Lowdins up an' bought one o' dese here new autimobiles—an' dat settled it! . . . A white man in town one Sat'day night tole John to git out o' dat damn car 'cause a nigger ain't got no business wid a autimobile nohow! An' John say: 'I ain't gonna git out!' Den de white man, what's been drinkin', jump up on de runnin'-bo'ad an' bust John in de mouth fer talkin' back to him—he a white man, an' Lowdins nothin' but a nigger. 'De very idee!' he say, and hit John in de face six or seven times. Den John drawed his gun! One! two! t'ree! he fiah, hit dis old red-neck cracker in

de shoulder, but he ain't dead! Aint nothin' meant to kill a
cracker what's drunk. But John think he done kilt this white
man, an' so he left him kickin' in de street while he runs that
car o' his'n lickety-split out o' town, goes to Vicksburg, an'
catches de river boat. . . . Well, sir! Dat night Crowville's
plumb full o' white folks wid dogs an' guns an' lanterns,
shoutin' an' yellin' an' scarin' de wits out o' us coloreds an'
wakin' us up way late in de night-time lookin' fer John, an' dey
don't find him. . . . Den dey say dey gwine teach dem
Crowville niggers a lesson, all of 'em, paintin' dey houses an'
buyin' cars an' livin' like white folks, so dey comes to our do's
an' tells us to leave our houses—git de hell out in de fields,
'cause dey don't want to kill nobody there dis evenin'! . . . Well,
sir! Niggers in night-gowns an' underwear an' shimmies, half-
naked an' barefooted, was runnin' ever' which way in de
dark, scratchin' up dey legs in de briah patches, fallin' on dey
faces, scared to death! Po' ole Pheeny, what ain't moved from
her bed wid de paralytics fo' six years, dey made her daughters
carry her out, screamin' an' wall-eyed, an' set her in de middle
o' de cotton-patch. An' Brian, what was sleepin' naked, jumps
up an' grabs his wife's apron and runs like a rabbit with not another blessed thing on! Chillens squallin' ever'where, an' mens
a-pleadin' an' a-cussin', an' womens cryin' 'Lawd 'a' Mercy' wid
de whites of dey eyes showin'! . . . Den looked like to me
'bout five hundred white mens took torches an' started burnin'
wid fiah ever' last house, an' hen-house, an' shack, an' barn, an'
privy, an' shed, an' cow-slant in de place! An' all de niggers,
when de fiah blaze up, was moanin' in de fields, callin' on de
Lawd fer help! An' de fiah light up de whole country clean
back to de woods! You could smell fiah, an' you could see it
red, an' taste de smoke, an' feel it stingin' yo' eyes. An' you
could hear de bo'ads a-fallin' an' de glass a-poppin', an' po' animals roastin' an' fryin' an' a-tearin' at dey halters. An' one cow
run out, fiah all ovah, wid her milk streamin' down. An' de
smoke roll up, de cotton-fields were red . . . an' dey ain't
been no mo' Crowville after dat night. No, sir! De white folks
ain't left nothin' fer de niggers, not nary bo'ad standin' one
'bove another, not even a dog-house. . . . When it were done
—nothin' but ashes! . . . De white mens was ever'where wid
guns, scarin' de po' blacks an' keepin' 'em off, an' one of 'em

say: 'I got good mind to try yo'-all's hide, see is it bullet proof—gittin' so prosp'rous, paintin' yo' houses an' runnin ovah white folks wid yo' damn gasoline buggies! Well, after dis you'll damn sight have to bend yo' backs an' work a little!' . . . Dat's what de white man say. . . . But we didn't—not yit! 'Cause ever' last nigger moved from there dat Sunday mawnin'. It were right funny to see ole folks what ain't never been out o' de backwoods pickin' up dey feet an' goin'. Ma Bailey say: 'De Lawd done let me live eighty years in one place, but ma next eighty'll be spent in St. Louis.' An' she started out walkin' wid neither bag nor baggage. . . . An' me an' Tom took Willie-Mae an' went to Cairo, an' Tom started railroad-workin' wid a gang; then we come on up here, been five summers ago dis August. We ain't had not even a rag o' clothes when we left Crowville—so don't tell me 'bout white folks bein' good, Hager, 'cause I knows 'em. . . . Yes, indeedy, I really knows 'em. . . . Dey done made us leave our home."

The old woman knocked her pipe against the edge of the porch, emptying its dead ashes into the yard, and for a moment no one spoke. Sandy, trembling, watched a falling star drop behind the trees. Then Jimboy's deep voice, like a bitter rumble in the dark, broke the silence.

"I know white folks, too," he said. "I lived in the South."

"And I ain't never been South," added Harriett hoarsely, "but I know 'em right here . . . and I hate 'em!"

"De Lawd hears you," said Hager.

"I don't care if He does hear me, mama! You and Annjee are too easy. You just take whatever white folks give you—*coon* to your face, and *nigger* behind your backs—and don't say nothing. You run to some white person's back door for every job you get, and then they pay you one dollar for five dollars' worth of work, and fire you whenever they get ready."

"They do that all right," said Jimboy. "They don't mind firin' you. Wasn't I layin' brick on the *Daily Leader* building and the white union men started sayin' they couldn't work with me because I wasn't in the union? So the boss come up and paid me off. 'Good man, too,' he says to me, 'but I can't buck the union.' So I said I'd join, but I knew they wouldn't let me before I went to the office. Anyhow, I tried. I told the guys there I was a bricklayer and asked 'em how I was gonna work if I couldn't be in the union. And the fellow who had the cards, secretary I guess he was, says kinder sharp, like he didn't want to be bothered: 'That's your look-out, big boy, not mine.' So you see how much the union cares if a black man works or not."

"Ain't Tom had de same trouble?" affirmed Sister Johnson. "Got put off de job mo'n once on 'count o' de white unions."

"O, they've got us cornered, all right," said Jimboy. "The white folks are like farmers that own all the cows and let the niggers take care of 'em. Then they make you pay a sweet price for skimmed milk and keep the cream for themselves—but I reckon cream's too rich for rusty-kneed niggers anyhow!"

They laughed.

"That's a good one!" said Harriett. "You know old man Wright, what owns the flour-mill and the new hotel—how he made his start off colored women working in his canning factory? Well, when he built that orphan home for colored and gave it to the city last year, he had the whole place made just about the size of the dining-room at his own house. They got the little niggers in that asylum cooped up like chickens. And the reason he built it was to get the colored babies out of the city home, with its nice playgrounds, because he thinks the two races oughtn't to mix! But he don't care how hard he works his colored help in that canning factory of his, does he? Wasn't I there thirteen hours a day in tomato season? Nine cents an hour and five cents overtime after ten hours—and you better work overtime if you want to keep the job! . . . As for the races mixing—ask some of those high yellow women who work there. They know a mighty lot about the races mixing!"

"Most of 'em lives in de Bottoms, where de sportin' houses are," said Hager. "It's a shame de way de white mens keeps them sinful places goin'."

"It ain't Christian, is it?" mocked Harriett. . . . "White folks!" . . . And she shrugged her shoulders scornfully. Many disagreeable things had happened to her through white folks. Her first surprising and unpleasantly lasting impression of the pale world had come when, at the age of five, she had gone alone one day to play in a friendly white family's yard. Some mischievous small boys there, for the fun of it, had taken hold of her short kinky braids and pulled them, dancing round and round her and yelling: "Blackie! Blackie! Blackie!" while she screamed and tried to run away. But they held her and pulled her hair terribly, and her friends laughed because she *was* black and she *did* look funny. So from that time on, Harriett had been uncomfortable in the presence of whiteness, and that early hurt had grown with each new incident into a rancor that she could not hide and a dislike that had become pain.

Now, because she could sing and dance and was always amusing, many of the white girls in high school were her friends. But when the three-thirty bell rang and it was time to go home, Harriett knew their polite "Good-bye" was really a kind way of saying: "We can't be seen on the streets with a colored girl." To loiter with these same young ladies had been all right during their grade-school years, when they were all younger, but now they had begun to feel the eyes of young white boys staring from the windows of pool halls, or from the tennis-courts near the park—so it was not proper to be seen with Harriett.

But a very unexpected stab at the girl's pride had come only a few weeks ago when she had gone with her class-mates, on tickets issued by the school, to see an educational film of the under-sea world at the Palace Theatre, on Main Street. It was a special performance given for the students, and each class had had seats allotted to them beforehand; so Harriett sat with her class and had begun to enjoy immensely the strange wonders of the ocean depths when an usher touched her on the shoulder.

"The last three rows on the left are for colored," the girl in the uniform said.

"I— But— But I'm with my class," Harriett stammered. "We're all supposed to sit here."

"I can't help it," insisted the usher, pointing towards the rear of the theatre, while her voice carried everywhere. "Them's the house rules. No argument now—you'll have to move."

So Harriett rose and stumbled up the dark aisle and out into the sunlight, her slender body hot with embarrassment and rage. The teacher saw her leave the theatre without a word of protest, and none of her white classmates defended her for being black. They didn't care.

"All white people are alike, in school and out," Harriett concluded bitterly, as she told of her experiences to the folks sitting with her on the porch in the dark.

Once, when she had worked for a Mrs. Leonard Baker on Martin Avenue, she accidentally broke a precious cut-glass pitcher used to serve some out-of-town guests. And when she tried to apologize for the accident, Mrs. Baker screamed in a rage: "Shut up, you impudent little black wench! Talking back to me after breaking up my dishes. All you darkies are alike—careless sluts—and I wouldn't have a one of you in my house if I could get anybody else to work for me without paying a fortune. You're all impossible."

"So that's the way white people feel," Harriett said to Aunt Hager and Sister Johnson and Jimboy, while the two children listened. "They wouldn't have a single one of us around if they could help it. It don't matter to them if we're shut out of a job. It don't matter to them if niggers have only the back row at the movies. It don't matter to them when they hurt our feelings without caring and treat us like slaves down South and like beggars up North. No, it don't matter to them. . . . White folks run the world, and the only thing colored folks are expected to do is work and grin and take off their hats as though it don't matter. . . . O, I hate 'em!" Harriett cried, so fiercely that Sandy was afraid. "I hate white folks!" she said to everybody on the porch in the darkness. "You can pray for 'em if you want to, mama, but I hate 'em! . . . I hate white folks! . . . I hate 'em all!"

# EIGHT

## *Dance*

M RS. J. J. RICE and family usually spent ten days during
the August heat at Lake Dale, and thither they had gone
now, giving Annjee a forced vacation with no pay. Jimboy was
not working, and so his wife found ten days of rest without
income not especially agreeable. Nevertheless, she decided that
she might as well enjoy the time; so she and Jimboy went to
the country for a week with Cousin Jessie, who had married
one of the colored farmers of the district. Besides, Annjee
thought that Jimboy might help on the farm and so make a
little money. Anyway, they would get plenty to eat, because
Jessie kept a good table. And since Jessie had eight children of
her own, they did not take Sandy with them—eight were
enough for a woman to be worried with at one time!

Aunt Hager had been ironing all day on the Reinharts'
clothes—it was Friday. At seven o'clock Harriett came home,
but she had already eaten her supper at the restaurant where
she worked.

"Hello, mama! Hy, Sandy!" she said, but that was all, because she and her mother were not on the best of terms. Aunt
Hager was attempting to punish her youngest daughter by not
allowing her to leave the house after dark, since Harriett, on
Tuesday night, had been out until one o'clock in the morning
with no better excuse than a party at Maudel's. Aunt Hager
had threatened to whip her then and there that night.

"You ain't had a switch on yo' hide fo' three years, but don't
think you's gettin' too big fo' me not to fan yo' behind,
madam. 'Spare de rod an' spoil de chile,' that's what de Bible
say, an' Lawd knows you sho is spoiled! De idee of a young gal
yo' age stayin' out till one o'clock in de mawnin', an' me not
knowed where you's at. . . . Don't you talk back to me! . . .
You rests in this house ever' night this week an' don't put yo'
foot out o' this yard after you comes from work, that's what
you do. Lawd knows I don't know what I's gonna do with

60

you. I works fo' you an' I prays fo' you, an' if you don't mind, I's sho gonna whip you, even if you is goin' on seventeen years old!"

Tonight as soon as she came from work Harriett went into her mother's room and lay across the bed. It was very warm in the little four-room house, and all the windows and doors were open.

"We's got some watermelon here, daughter," Hager called from the kitchen. "Don't you want a nice cool slice?"

"No," the girl replied. She was fanning herself with a palm-leaf fan, her legs in their cheap silk stockings hanging over the side of the bed, and her heels kicking the floor. Benbow's Band played tonight for the dance at Chaver's Hall, and everybody was going—but her. Gee, it was hard to have a Christian mother! Harriett kicked her slippers off with a bang and rolled over on her stomach, burying her powdery face in the pillows. . . . Somebody knocked at the back door.

A boy's voice was speaking excitedly to Hager: "Hemorrhages . . . and papa can't stop 'em . . . she's coughin' something terrible . . . says can't you please come over and help him"— frightened and out of breath.

"Do, Jesus!" cried Hager. "I'll be with you right away, chile. Don't worry." She rushed into the bedroom to change her apron. "You Harriett, listen; Sister Lane's taken awful sick an' Jimmy says she's bleedin' from de mouth. If I ain't back by nine o'clock, see that that chile Sandy's in de bed. An' you know you ain't to leave this yard under no circumstances. . . . Po' Mis' Lane! She sho do have it hard." In a whisper: "I 'spects she's got de T. B., that what I 'spects!" And the old woman hustled out to join the waiting youngster. Jimmy was leaning against the door, looking at Sandy, and neither of the boys knew what to say. Jimmy Lane wore his mother's cast-off shoes to school, and Sandy used to tease him, but tonight he didn't tease his friend about his shoes.

"You go to bed 'fore it gets late," said his grandmother, starting down the alley with Jimmy.

"Yes'm," Sandy called after her. "So long, Jim!" He stood under the apple-tree and watched them disappear.

Aunt Hager had scarcely gotten out of sight when there was

a loud knock at the front door, and Sandy ran around the house to see Harriett's boy friend, Mingo, standing in the dusk outside the screen-door, waiting to be let in.

Mingo was a patent-leather black boy with wide, alive nostrils and a mouth that split into a lighthouse smile on the least provocation. His body was heavy and muscular, resting on bowed legs that curved backward as though the better to brace his chunky torso; and his hands were hard from mixing concrete and digging ditches for the city's new water-mains.

"I know it's tonight, but I can't go," Sandy heard his aunt say at the door. They were speaking of Benbow's dance. "And his band don't come here often, neither. I'm heart-sick having to stay home, dog-gone it all, especially this evening!"

"Aw, come on and go anyway," pleaded Mingo. "After I been savin' up my dough for two weeks to take you, and got my suit cleaned and pressed and all. Heck! If you couldn't go and knew it yesterday, why didn't you tell me? That's a swell way to treat a fellow!"

"Because I wanted to go," said Harriett; "and still want to go. . . . Don't make so much difference about mama, because she's mad anyhow . . . but what could we do with this kid? We can't leave him by himself." She looked at Sandy, who was standing behind Mingo listening to everything.

"You can take me," the child offered anxiously, his eyes dancing at the delightful prospect. "I'll behave, Harrie, if you take me, and I won't tell on you either. . . . Please lemme go, Mingo. I ain't never seen a big dance in my life. I wanta go."

"Should we?" asked Harriett doubtfully, looking at her boy friend standing firmly on his curved legs.

"Sure, if we got to have him . . . damn 'im!" Mingo replied. "Better the kid than no dance. Go git dressed." So Harriett made a dash for the clothes-closet, while Sandy ran to get a clean waist from one of his mother's dresser-drawers, and Mingo helped him put it on, cussing softly to himself all the while. "But it ain't your fault, pal, is it?" he said to the little boy.

"Sure not," Sandy replied. "I didn't tell Aunt Hager to make Harrie stay home. I tried to 'suade grandma to let her go," the child lied, because he liked Mingo. "I guess she won't care about her goin' to just one dance." He wanted to make everything all right so the young man wouldn't be worried. Besides, Sandy very much wanted to go himself.

"Let's beat it," Harriett shrilled excitedly before her dress was fastened, anxious to be gone lest her mother come home. She was powdering her face and neck in the next room, nervous, happy, and afraid all at once. The perfume, the voice, and the pat, pat, pat of the powder-puff came out to the waiting gentleman.

"Yo' car's here, madam," mocked Mingo. "Step right this way and let's be going!"

Wonder where ma easy rider's gone—
He done left me, put ma new gold watch in pawn!

Like a blare from hell the second encore of *Easy Rider* filled every cubic inch of the little hall with hip-rocking notes. Benbow himself was leading and the crowd moved like jellyfish dancing on individual sea-shells, with Mingo and Harriett somewhere among the shakers. But they were not of them, since each couple shook in a world of its own, as, with a weary wail, the music abruptly ceased.

Then, after scarcely a breath of intermission, the band struck up again with a lazy one-step. A tall brown boy in a light tan suit walked his partner straight down the whole length of the floor and, when he reached the corner, turned leisurely in one spot, body riding his hips, eyes on the ceiling, and his girl shaking her full breasts against his pink silk shirt. Then they recrossed the width of the room, turned slowly, repeating themselves, and began again to walk rhythmically down the hall, while the music was like a lazy river flowing between mountains, carving a canyon coolly, calmly, and without insistence. The *Lazy River One-Step* they might have called what the band was playing as the large crowd moved with the greatest ease about the hall. To drum-beats barely audible, the tall boy in the tan suit walked his partner round and round time after time, revolving at each corner with eyes uplifted, while the piano was the water flowing, and the high, thin chords of the banjo were the mountains floating in the clouds. But in sultry tones, alone and always, the brass cornet spoke harshly about the earth.

Sandy sat against the wall in a hard wooden folding chair. There were other children scattered lonesomely about on chairs, too, watching the dancers, but he didn't seem to know any of them. When the music stopped, all the chairs quickly filled with loud-talking women and girls in brightly colored dresses who fanned themselves with handkerchiefs and wiped their sweating brows. Sandy thought maybe he should give his seat to one of the women when he saw Maudel approaching.

"Here, honey," she said. "Take this dime and buy yourself a bottle of something cold to drink. I know Harriett ain't got you on her mind out there dancin'. This music is certainly righteous, chile!" She laughed as she handed Sandy a coin and closed her pocketbook. He liked Maudel, although he knew his grandmother didn't. She was a large good-natured brown-skinned girl who walked hippishly and used too much rouge on her lips. But she always gave Sandy a dime, and she was always laughing.

He went through the crowd towards the soft-drink stand at the end of the hall. "Gimme a bottle o' cream soda," he said to the fat orange-colored man there, who had his sleeves rolled up and a white butcher's-apron covering his barrel-like belly. The man put his hairy arms down into a zinc tub full of ice and water and began pulling out bottles, looking at their caps, and then dropping them back into the cold liquid.

"Don't seem like we got no cream, sonny. How'd a lemon do you?" he asked above the bedlam of talking voices.

"Naw," said Sandy. "It's too sour."

On the improvised counter of boards the wares displayed consisted of cracker-jacks, salted peanuts, a box of gum, and Sen Sens, while behind the counter was a lighted oil-stove holding a tin pan full of spare-ribs, sausage, and fish; and near it an ice-cream freezer covered with a brown sack. Some cases of soda were on the floor beside the zinc tub filled with bottles, in which the man was still searching.

"Nope, no cream," said the fat man.

"Well, gimme a fish sandwich then," Sandy replied, feeling very proud because some kids were standing near, looking at him as he made his purchase like a grown man.

"Buy me one, too," suggested a biscuit-colored little girl in a frilly dirty-white dress.

"I only got a dime," Sandy said. "But you can have half of mine." And he gallantly broke in two parts the double square of thick bread, with its hunk of greasy fish between, and gravely handed a portion to the grinning little girl.

"Thanks," she said, running away with the bread and fish in her hands.

"Shame on you!" teased a small boy, rubbing his forefingers at Sandy. "You got a girl! You got a girl!"

"Go chase yourself!" Sandy replied casually, as he picked out the bones and smacked his lips on the sweet fried fish. The orchestra was playing another one-step, with the dancers going like shuttles across the floor. Sandy saw his Aunt Harriett and a slender yellow boy named Billy Sanderlee doing a series of lazy, intricate steps as they wound through the crowd from one end of the hall to the other. Certain less accomplished couples were watching them with admiration.

Sandy, when he had finished eating, decided to look for the wash-room, where he could rinse his hands, because they were greasy and smelled fishy. It was at the far corner of the hall. As he pushed open the door marked GENTS, a thick grey cloud of cigarette-smoke drifted out. The stench of urine and gin and a crowd of men talking, swearing, and drinking licker surrounded the little boy as he elbowed his way towards the wash-bowls. All the fellows were shouting loudly to one another and making fleshy remarks about the women they had danced with.

"Boy, you ought to try Velma," a mahogany-brown boy yelled. "She sure can go."

"Hell," answered a whisky voice somewhere in the smoke. "That nappy-headed black woman? Gimme a high yaller for mine all de time. I can't use no coal!"

"Well, de blacker de berry, de sweeter de juice," protested a slick-haired ebony youth in the center of the place. . . . "Ain't that right, sport?" he demanded of Sandy, grabbing him jokingly by the neck and picking him up.

"I guess it is," said the child, scared, and the men laughed.

"Here, kid, buy yourself a drink," the slick-headed boy said, slipping Sandy a nickel as he set him down gently at the door. "And be sure it's pop—not gin."

Outside, the youngster dried his wet hands on a handkerchief, blinked his smoky eyes, and immediately bought the soda, a red strawberry liquid in a long, thick bottle.

Suddenly and without warning the cornet blared at the other end of the hall in an ear-splitting wail: "Whaw! . . . Whaw! . . . Whaw! . . . Whaw!" and the snare-drum rolled in answer. A pause . . . then the loud brassy notes were repeated and the banjo came in, "Plinka, plink, plink," like timid drops of rain after a terrific crash of thunder. Then quite casually, as though nothing had happened, the piano lazied into a slow drag, with all the other instruments following. And with the utmost nonchalance the drummer struck into time.

"Ever'body shake!" cried Benbow, as a ribbon of laughter swirled round the hall.

Couples began to sway languidly, melting together like candy in the sun as hips rotated effortlessly to the music. Girls snuggled pomaded heads on men's chests, or rested powdered chins on men's shoulders, while wild young boys put both arms tightly around their partners' waists and let their hands hang down carelessly over female haunches. Bodies moved ever so easily together—ever so easily, as Benbow turned towards his musicians and cried through cupped hands: "Aw, screech it, boys!"

A long, tall, gangling gal stepped back from her partner, adjusted her hips, and did a few easy, gliding steps all her own before her man grabbed her again.

"Eu-o-oo-oooo-oooo!" moaned the cornet titillating with pain, as the banjo cried in stop-time, and the piano sobbed aloud with a rhythmical, secret passion. But the drums kept up their hard steady laughter—like somebody who don't care.

"I see you plowin', Uncle Walt," called a little autumn-leaf brown with switching skirts to a dark-purple man grinding down the center of the floor with a yellow woman. Two short prancing blacks stopped in their tracks to quiver violently. A bushy-headed girl threw out her arms, snapped her fingers, and began to holler: "Hey! . . . Hey!" while her perspiring partner held doggedly to each hip in an effort to keep up with her. All over the hall, people danced their own individual movements to the scream and moan of the music.

"Get low . . . low down . . . down!" cried the drummer, bouncing like a rubber ball in his chair. The banjo scolded in diabolic glee, and the cornet panted as though it were out of breath, and Benbow himself left the band and came out on the floor to dance slowly and ecstatically with a large Indian-brown woman covered with diamonds.

"Aw, do it, Mister Benbow!" one of his admirers shouted frenziedly as the hall itself seemed to tremble.

"High yallers, draw nigh! Brown-skins, come near!" somebody squalled. "But black gals, stay where you are!"

"Whaw! Whaw! Whaw!" mocked the cornet—but the steady tomtom of the drums was no longer laughter now, no longer even pleasant: the drum-beats had become sharp with surly sound, like heavy waves that beat angrily on a granite rock. And under the dissolute spell of its own rhythm the music had got quite beyond itself. The four black men in Benbow's wandering band were exploring depths to which mere sound had no business to go. Cruel, desolate, unadorned was their music now, like the body of a ravished woman on the sun-baked earth; violent and hard, like a giant standing over his bleeding mate in the blazing sun. The odors of bodies, the stings of flesh, and the utter emptiness of soul when all is done—these things the piano and the drums, the cornet and the twanging banjo insisted on hoarsely to a beat that made the dancers move, in that little hall, like pawns on a frenetic checker-board.

"Aw, play it, Mister Benbow!" somebody cried.

The earth rolls relentlessly, and the sun blazes for ever on the earth, breeding, breeding. But why do you insist like the earth, music? Rolling and breeding, earth and sun for ever relentlessly. But why do you insist like the sun? Like the lips of women? Like the bodies of men, relentlessly?

"Aw, play it, Mister Benbow!"

But why do you insist, music?

Who understands the earth? Do you, Mingo? Who understands the sun? Do you, Harriett? Does anybody know—among you high yallers, you jelly-beans, you pinks and pretty daddies, among you sealskin browns, smooth blacks, and chocolates to-the-bone—does anybody know the answer?

"Aw, play it, Benbow!"

"It's midnight. De clock is strikin' twelve, an' . . ."

"Aw, play it, Mister Benbow!"

*

During intermission, when the members of the band stopped making music to drink gin and talk to women, Harriett and Mingo bought Sandy a box of cracker-jacks and another bottle of soda and left him standing in the middle of the floor holding both. His young aunt had forgotten time, so Sandy decided to go upstairs to the narrow unused balcony that ran the length of one side of the place. It was dusty up there, but a few broken chairs stood near the railing and he sat on one of them. He leaned his arms on the banister, rested his chin in his hands, and when the music started, he looked down on the mass of moving couples crowding the floor. He had a clear view of the energetic little black drummer eagle-rocking with staccato regularity in his chair as his long, thin sticks descended upon the tightly drawn skin of his small drum, while his foot patted the pedal of his big bass-drum, on which was painted in large red letters: "BENBOW'S FAMOUS KANSAS CITY BAND."

As the slow shuffle gained in intensity (and his cracker-jacks gave out), Sandy looked down drowsily on the men and women, the boys and girls, circling and turning beneath him. Dresses and suits of all shades and colors, and a vast confusion of bushy heads on swaying bodies. Faces gleaming like circus balloons—lemon-yellow, coal-black, powder-grey, ebony-black, blue-black faces; chocolate, brown, orange, tan, creamy-gold faces—the room full of floating balloon faces—Sandy's eyes were beginning to blur with sleep—colored balloons with strings, and the music pulling the strings. No! Girls pulling the strings—each boy a balloon by a string. Each face a balloon.

Sandy put his head down on the dusty railing of the gallery. An odor of hair-oil and fish, of women and sweat came up to him as he sat there alone, tired and a little sick. It was very warm and close, and the room was full of chatter during the intervals. Sandy struggled against sleep, but his eyes were just about to close when, with a burst of hopeless sadness, the *St. Louis Blues* spread itself like a bitter syrup over the hall. For a moment the boy opened his eyes to the drowsy flow of sound, long enough to pull two chairs together; then he lay down on them and closed his eyes again. Somebody was singing:

St. Louis woman with her diamond rings . . . .

as the band said very weary things in a loud and brassy manner and the dancers moved in a dream that seemed to have forgotten itself:

Got ma man tied to her apron-strings . . .

Wah! Wah! Wah! . . . The cornet laughed with terrible rudeness. Then the drums began to giggle and the banjo whined an insulting leer. The piano said, over and over again: "St. Louis! That big old dirty town where the Mississippi's deep and wide, deep and wide . . ." and the hips of the dancers rolled.

Man's got a heart like a rock cast in de sea . . .

while the cynical banjo covered unplumbable depths with a plinking surface of staccato gaiety, like the sparkling bubbles that rise on deep water over a man who has just drowned himself:

Or else he never would a gone so far from me . . .

then the band stopped with a long-drawn-out wail from the cornet and a flippant little laugh from the drums.

A great burst of applause swept over the room, and the musicians immediately began to play again. This time just blues, not the *St. Louis*, nor the *Memphis*, nor the *Yellow Dog*—but just the plain old familiar blues, heart-breaking and extravagant, ma-baby's-gone-from-me blues.

Nobody thought about anyone else then. Bodies sweatily close, arms locked, cheek to cheek, breast to breast, couples rocked to the pulse-like beat of the rhythm, yet quite oblivious each person of the other. It was true that men and women were dancing together, but their feet had gone down through the floor into the earth, each dancer's alone—down into the center of things—and their minds had gone off to the heart of loneliness, where they didn't even hear the words, the sometimes lying, sometimes laughing words that Benbow, leaning on the piano, was singing against this background of utterly despondent music:

> When de blues is got you,
> Ain't no use to run away.

> When de blue-blues got you,
> Ain't no use to run away,
> 'Cause de blues is like a woman
> That can turn yo' good hair grey.

Umn-ump! . . . Umn! . . . Umn-ump!

> Well, I tole ma baby,
> Says baby, baby, babe, be mine,
> But ma baby was deceitful.
> She must a thought that I was blind.

De-da! De-da! . . . De da! De da! Dee!

> O, Lawdy, Lawdy, Lawdy,
> Lawdy, Lawdy, Lawd . . . Lawd . . . Lawd!
> She quit me fo' a Texas gambler,
> So I had to git another broad.

Whaw-whaw! . . . Whaw-whaw-whaw! As though the laughter of a cornet could reach the heart of loneliness.

These mean old weary blues coming from a little orchestra of four men who needed no written music because they couldn't have read it. Four men and a leader—Rattle Benbow from Galveston; Benbow's buddy, the drummer, from Houston; his banjoist from Birmingham; his cornetist from Atlanta; and the pianist, long-fingered, sissyfied, a coal-black lad from New Orleans who had brought with him an exaggerated rag-time which he called jazz.

"I'm jazzin' it, creepers!" he sometimes yelled as he rolled his eyes towards the dancers and let his fingers beat the keys to a frenzy. . . . But now the piano was cryin' the blues!

Four homeless, plug-ugly niggers, that's all they were, playing mean old loveless blues in a hot, crowded little dance-hall in a Kansas town on Friday night. Playing the heart out of loneliness with a wide-mouthed leader, who sang everybody's troubles until they became his own. The improvising piano, the whanging banjo, the throbbing bass-drum, the hard-hearted little snare-drum, the brassy cornet that laughed, "Whaw-whaw-whaw. . . . Whaw!" were the waves in this lonesome sea of harmony from which Benbow's melancholy voice rose:

> You gonna wake up some mawnin'
> An' turn yo' smilin' face.
> Wake up some early mawnin',
> Says turn yo' smilin' face,
> Look at yo' sweetie's pillow—
> An' find an' empty place!

Then the music whipped itself into a slow fury, an awkward, elemental, foot-stamping fury, with the banjo running terrifiedly
away in a windy moan and then coming back again, with the
cornet wailing like a woman who don't know what it's all
about:

> Then you gonna call yo' baby,
> Call yo' lovin' baby dear—
> But you can keep on callin',
> 'Cause I won't be here!

And for a moment nothing was heard save the shuf-shuf-shuffle
of feet and the immense booming of the bass-drum like a living vein pulsing at the heart of loneliness.

"Sandy! . . . Sandy! . . . My stars! Where is that child? . . .
Has anybody seen my little nephew?" All over the hall. . . .
"Sandy! . . . Oh-o-o, Lord!" Finally, with a sigh of relief:
"You little brat, darn you, hiding up here in the balcony where
nobody could find you! . . . Sandy, wake up! It's past four
o'clock and I'll get killed."

Harriett vigorously shook the sleeping child, who lay
stretched on the dusty chairs; then she began to drag him
down the narrow steps before he was scarcely awake. The hall
was almost empty and the chubby little black drummer was
waddling across the floor carrying his drums in canvas cases.
Someone was switching off the lights one by one. A mustard-
colored man stood near the door quarrelling with a black
woman. She began to cry and he slapped her full in the mouth,
then turned his back and left with another girl of maple-sugar
brown. Harriett jerked Sandy past this linked couple and pulled
the boy down the long flight of stairs into the street, where
Mingo stood waiting, with a lighted cigarette making a white
line against his black skin.

"You better git a move on," he said. "Daylight ain't holdin' itself back for you!" And he told the truth, for the night had already begun to pale.

Sandy felt sick at the stomach. To be awakened precipitately made him cross and ill-humored, but the fresh, cool air soon caused him to feel less sleepy and not quite so ill. He took a deep breath as he trotted rapidly along on the sidewalk beside his striding aunt and her boy friend. He watched the blue-grey dawn blot out the night in the sky; and then pearl-grey blot out the blue, while the stars faded to points of dying fire. And he listened to the birds chirping and trilling in the trees as though they were calling the sun. Then, as he became fully awake, the child began to feel very proud of himself, for this was the first time he had ever been away from home all night.

Harriett was fussing with Mingo. "You shouldn't 've kept me out like that," she said. "Why didn't you tell me what time it was? . . . I didn't know."

And Mingo came back: "Hey, didn't I try to drag you away at midnight and you wouldn't come? And ain't I called you at one o'clock and you said: 'Wait a minute'—dancin' with some yaller P. I. from St. Joe, with your arms round his neck like a life-preserver? . . . Don't tell me I didn't want to leave, and me got to go to work at eight o'clock this mornin' with a pick and shovel when the whistle blows! What de hell?"

But Harriett did not care to quarrel now when there would be no time to finish it properly. She was out of breath from hurrying and almost in tears. She was afraid to go home.

"Mingo, I'm scared."

"Well, you know what you can do if your ma puts you out," her escort said quickly, forgetting his anger. "I can take care of you. We could get married."

"Could we, Mingo?"

"Sure!"

She slipped her hand in his. "Aw, daddy!" and the pace became much less hurried.

When they reached the corner near which Harriett lived, she lifted her dark little purple-powdered face for a not very lingering kiss and sent Mingo on his way. Then she frowned anxiously and ran on. The sky was a pale pearly color, waiting for the warm gold of the rising sun.

"I'm scared to death!" said Harriett. "Lord, Sandy, I hope ma ain't up! I hope she didn't come home last night from Mis' Lane's. We shouldn't 've gone, Sandy . . . I guess we shouldn't 've gone." She was breathing hard and Sandy had to run fast to keep up with her. "Gee, I'm scared!"

The grass was diamond-like with dew, and the red bricks of the sidewalk were damp, as the small boy and his young aunt hurried under the leafy elms along the walk. They passed Madam de Carter's house and cut through the wet grass into their own yard as the first rays of the morning sun sifted through the trees. Quietly they tiptoed towards the porch; quickly and quietly they crossed it; and softly, ever so softly, they opened the parlor door.

In the early dusk the oil-lamp still burned on the front-room table, and in an old arm-chair, with the open Bible on her lap, sat Aunt Hager Williams, a bundle of switches on the floor at her feet.

# NINE

## *Carnival*

B ETWEEN the tent of Christ and the tents of sin there
stretched scarcely a half-mile. Rivalry reigned: the revival
and the carnival held sway in Stanton at the same time. Both
were at the south edge of town, and both were loud and musical in their activities. In a dirty white tent in the Hickory
Woods the Reverend Duke Braswell conducted the services of
the Lord for the annual summer tent-meeting of the First
Ethiopian Baptist Church. And in Jed Galoway's meadow lots
Swank's Combined Shows, the World's Greatest Midway
Carnival, had spread canvas for seven days of bunko games and
cheap attractions. The old Negroes went to the revival, and
the young Negroes went to the carnival, and after sundown
these August evenings the mourning songs of the Christians
could be heard rising from the Hickory Woods while the profound syncopation of the minstrel band blared from Galoway's
Lots, strangely intermingling their notes of praise and joy.

Aunt Hager with Annjee and Sandy went to the revival every
night (Sandy unwillingly), while Jimboy, Harriett, and Maudel
went to the carnival. Aunt Hager prayed for her youngest
daughter at the meetings, but Harriett had not spoken to her
mother, if she could avoid it, since the morning after the dance,
when she had been whipped. Since their return from the country Annjee and Jimboy were not so loving towards each other,
either, as they had been before. Jimboy tired of Jessie's farm, so
he came back to town three days before his wife returned. And
now the revival and the carnival widened the breach between
the Christians and the sinners in Aunt Hager's little household.
And Sandy would rather have been with the sinners—Jimboy
and Harriett—but he wasn't old enough; so he had to go to
meetings until, on Thursday morning, when he and Buster
were climbing over the coal-shed in the back yard, Sandy accidentally jumped down on a rusty nail, which penetrated the
heel of his bare foot. He set up a wail, cried until noon over
the pain, and refused to eat any dinner; so finally Jimboy said

74

that if he would only hush hollering he'd take him to the carnival that evening.

"Yes, take de rascal," said Aunt Hager. "He ain't doin' no good at de services, wiggling and squirming so's we can't hardly hear de sermon. He ain't got religion in his heart, that chile!"

"I hope he ain't," said his father, yawning.

"All you wants him to be is a good-fo'-nothin' rounder like you is," retorted Hager. And she and Jimboy began their daily quarrel, which lasted for hours, each of them enjoying it immensely. But Sandy kept pulling at his father and saying: "Hurry up and let's go," although he knew well that nothing really started at the carnival until sundown. Nevertheless, about four o'clock, Jimboy said: "All right, come on," and they started out in the hot sun towards Galoway's Lots, the man walking tall and easy while the boy hobbled along on his sore foot, a rag tied about his heel.

At the old cross-bar gate on the edge of town, through which Jed Galoway drove his cows to pasture, there had been erected a portable arch strung with electric lights spelling out "SWANK'S SHOWS" in red and yellow letters, but it was not very impressive in the day-time, with the sun blazing on it, and no people about. And from this gate, extending the whole length of the meadow on either side, like a roadway, were the tents and booths of the carnival: the Galatea illusion, the seal and sea-lion circus, the Broadway musical-comedy show, the freaks, the games of chance, the pop-corn- and lemonade-stands, the colored minstrels, the merry-go-round, the fun house, the hoochie-coochie, the Ferris wheel, and, at the far end, a canvas tank under a tiny platform high in the air from which the World's Most Dangerous and Spectacular High Dive took place nightly at ten-thirty.

"We gonna stay to see that, ain't we, papa?" Sandy asked.

"Sure," said Jimboy. "But didn't I tell you there wouldn't be nothin' runnin' this early in the afternoon? See! Not even the band playin', and ain't a thing open but the freak-show and I'll bet all the freaks asleep." But he bought Sandy a bag of peanuts and planked down twenty cents for two tickets into the sultry tent where a perspiring fat woman and a tame-looking wild-man were the only attractions to be found on the platforms.

The sword-swallower was not yet at work, nor the electric marvel, nor the human glass-eater. The terrific sun beat fiercely through the canvas on this exhibit of two lone human abnormalities, and the few spectators in the tent kept wiping their faces with their handkerchiefs.

Jimboy struck up a conversation with the Fat Woman, a pink and white creature who said she lived in Columbus, Ohio; and when Jimboy said he'd been there, she was interested. She said she had always lived right next door to colored people at home, and she gave Sandy a postcard picture of herself for nothing, although it had "10¢" marked on the back. She kept saying she didn't see how anybody could stay in Kansas and it a dry state where a soul couldn't even get beer except from a bootlegger.

When Sandy and his father came out, they left the row of tents and went across the meadow to a clump of big shade-trees beneath which several colored men who worked with the show were sitting. A blanket had been spread on the grass, and a crap game was going on to the accompaniment of much arguing and good-natured cussing. But most of the men were just sitting around not playing, and one or two were stretched flat on their faces, asleep. Jimboy seemed to know several of the fellows, so he joined in their talk while Sandy watched the dice roll for a while, but since the boy didn't understand the game, he decided to go back to the tents.

"All right, go ahead," said his father. "I'll pick you up later when the lights are lit and things get started; then we can go in the shows."

Sandy limped off, walking on the toe of his injured foot. In front of the sea-lion circus he found Earl James, a little white boy in his grade at school; the two of them went around together for a while, looking at the large painted canvas pictures in front of the shows or else lying on their stomachs on the ground to peep under the tents. When they reached the minstrel-show tent near the end of the midway, they heard a piano tinkling within and the sound of hands clapping as though someone was dancing.

"Jeezus! Let's see this," Earl cried, so the two boys got down on their bellies, wriggled under the flap of the tent on one side, and looked in.

A battered upright piano stood on the ground in front of the stage, and a fat, bald-headed Negro was beating out a rag. A big white man in a checkered vest was leaning against the piano, derby on head, and a long cigar stuck in his mouth. He was watching a slim black girl, with skirts held high and head thrown back, prancing in a mad circle of crazy steps. Two big colored boys in red uniforms were patting time, while another girl sat on a box, her back towards the peeping youngsters staring up from under the edge of the tent. As the girl who was dancing whirled about, Sandy saw that it was Harriett.

"Pretty good, ain't she, boss?" yelled the wrinkle-necked Negro at the piano as he pounded away.

The white man nodded and kept his eyes on Harriett's legs. The two black boys patting time were grinning from ear to ear.

"Do it, Miss Mama!" one of them shouted as Harriett began to sashay gracefully.

Finally she stopped, panting and perspiring, with her lips smiling and her eyes sparkling gaily. Then she went with the white man and the colored piano-player behind the canvas curtains to the stage. One of the show-boys put his arms around the girl sitting on the box and began tentatively to feel her breasts.

"Don't be so fresh, hot papa," she said. And Sandy recognized Maudel's voice, and saw her brown face as she leaned back to look at the showman. The boy in the red suit bent over and kissed her several times, while the other fellow kept imitating the steps he had just seen Harriett performing.

"Let's go," Earl said to Sandy, rolling over on the ground. The two small boys went on to the next tent, where one of the carnival men caught them, kicked their behinds soundly, and sent them away.

The sun was setting in a pink haze, and the show-grounds began to take on an air of activity. The steam calliope gave a few trial hoots, and the merry-go-round circled slowly without passengers. The paddle-wheels and the get-'em-hot men, the lemonade-sellers and the souvenir-venders were opening their booths to the evening trade. A barker began to ballyhoo in front of the freak-show. By and by there would be a crowd. The lights came on along the Midway, the Ferris wheel swept languidly up into the air, and when Sandy found his father, the colored band had begun to play in front of the minstrel show.

"I want to ride on the merry-go-round," Sandy insisted. "And go in the Crazy House." So they did both; then they bought hamburger sandwiches with thick slices of white onion and drank strawberry soda and ate pop-corn with butter on it. They went to the sea-lion circus, tried to win a Kewpie doll at the paddle-wheel booth, and watched men losing money on the hidden pea, then trying to win it back at four-card monte behind the Galatea attraction. And all the while Sandy said nothing to his father about having seen Harriett dancing in the minstrel tent that afternoon.

Sandy had lived too long with three women not to have learned to hold his tongue about the private doings of each of them. When Annjee paid two dollars a week on a blue silk shirt for his father at Cohn's cut-rate credit store, and Sandy saw her make the payments, he knew without being told that the matter was never to be mentioned to Aunt Hager. And if his grandmother sometimes threw Harriett's rouge out in the alley, Sandy saw it with his eyes, but not with his mouth. Because he loved all three of them—Harriett and Annjee and Hager—he didn't carry tales on any one of them to the others. Nobody would know he had watched his Aunt Harrie dancing on the carnival lot today in front of a big fat white man in a checkered vest while a Negro in a red suit played the piano.

"We got a half-dollar left for the minstrel show," said Jimboy. "Come on, let's go." And he pulled his son through the crowd that jammed the long Midway between the booths.

All the bright lights of the carnival were on now, and everything was running full blast. The merry-go-round whirled to the ear-splitting hoots of the calliope; bands blared; the canvas paintings of snakes and dancing-girls, human skeletons, fire-eaters, billowed in the evening breeze; pennants flapped, barkers shouted, acrobats twirled in front of a tent; a huge paddle-wheel clicked out numbers. Folks pushed and shoved and women called to their children not to get lost. In the air one smelled the scent of trampled grass, peanuts, and hot dogs, animals and human bodies.

The large white man in the checkered vest was making the

ballyhoo in front of the minstrel show, his expansive belly turned towards the crowd that had been attracted by the band. One hand pointed towards a tawdry group of hard-looking Negro performers standing on the platform.

"Here we have, ladies and gents, Madam Caledonia Watson, the Dixie song-bird; Dancing Jenkins, the dark strutter from Jacksonville; little Lizzie Roach, champeen coon-shouter of Georgia; and last, but not least, Sambo and Rastus, the world's funniest comedians. Last performance this evening! . . . Strike her up, perfesser! . . . Come along, now, folks!"

The band burst into sound, Madam Watson and Lizzie Roach opened their brass-lined throats, the men dropped into a momentary clog-dance, and then the whole crowd of performers disappeared into the tent. The ticket-purchasing townspeople followed through the public opening beneath a gaudily painted sign picturing a Mississippi steamboat in the moonlight, and two black bucks shooting gigantic dice on a street-corner.

Jimboy and Sandy followed the band inside and took seats, and soon the frayed curtain rose, showing a plantation scene in the South, where three men, blackened up, and two women in bandannas sang longingly about Dixie. Then Sambo and Rastus came out with long wooden razors and began to argue and shoot dice, but presently the lights went out and a ghost appeared and frightened the two men away, causing them to leave all the money on the stage. (The audience thought it screamingly funny—and just like niggers.) After that one of the women sang a ragtime song and did the eagle-rock. Then a man with a banjo in his hands began to play, but until then the show had been lifeless.

"Listen to him," Jimboy said, punching Sandy. "He's good!"

The piece he was picking was full of intricate runs and trills long drawn out, then suddenly slipping into tantalizing rhythms. It ended with a vibrant whang!—and the audience yelled for more. As an encore he played a blues and sang innumerable verses, always ending:

> An' Ah can't be satisfied,
> 'Cause all Ah love has
> Done laid down an' died.

And to Sandy it seemed like the saddest music in the world—but the white people around him laughed.

Then the stage lights went on, the band blared, and all the black actors came trooping back, clapping their hands before the cotton-field curtain as each one in turn danced like fury, vigorously distorting agile limbs into the most amazing positions, while the scene ended with the fattest mammy and the oldest uncle shaking jazzily together.

The booths were all putting out their lights as the people poured through the gate towards town. Sandy hobbled down the road beside his father, his sore heel, which had been forgotten all evening, paining him terribly until Jimboy picked him up and carried him on his shoulder. Automobiles and buggies whirled past them in clouds of gritty dust, and young boys calling vulgar words hurried after tittering girls. When Sandy and his father reached home, Aunt Hager and Annjee had not yet returned from the revival. Jimboy said he thought maybe they had stopped at Mrs. Lane's to sit up all night with the sick woman, so Sandy spread his pallet on the floor at the foot of his grandmother's bed and went to sleep. He did not hear his Aunt Harriett when she came home, but late in the night he woke up with his heel throbbing painfully, his throat dry, and his skin burning, and when he tried to bend his leg, it hurt him so that he began to cry.

Harriett, awakened by his moans, called drowsily: "What's the matter, honey?"

"My foot," said Sandy tearfully.

So his young aunt got out of bed, lit the lamp, and helped him to the kitchen, where she heated a kettle of water, bathed his heel, and covered the nail-wound with vaseline. Then she bound it with a fresh white rag.

"Now that ought to feel better," she said as she led him back to his pallet, and soon they were both asleep again.

The next morning when Hager came from the sickbed of her friend, she sent to the butcher-shop for a bacon rind, cut from it a piece of fat meat, and bound it to Sandy's heel as a cure.

"Don't want you havin' de blood-pisen here," she said. "An' don't you run round an' play on that heel. Set out on de porch

an' study yo' reader, 'cause school'll be startin' next month."
Then she began Mrs. Reinhart's ironing.

The next day, Saturday, the last day of the carnival, Jimboy
carried the Reinharts' clothes home for Hager, since Sandy
was crippled and Jimmy Lane's mother was down in bed. But
after delivering the clothes Jimboy did not come home for
supper. When Annjee and Hager wanted to leave for the revival
in the early evening, they asked Harriett if she would stay home
with the little boy, for Sandy's heel had swollen purple where
the rusty nail had penetrated and he could hardly walk at all.

"You been gone ever' night this week," Hager said to the
girl. "An' you ain't been anear de holy tents where de Lawd's
word is preached; so you ought to be willin' to stay home one
night with a po' little sick boy."

"Yes'm," Harriett muttered in a noncommittal tone. But
shortly after her mother and Annjee had gone, she said to her
nephew: "You aren't afraid to stay home by yourself, are you?"

And Sandy answered: "Course not, Aunt Harrie."

She gave him a hot bath and put a new piece of fat meat on
his festering heel. Then she told him to climb into Annjee's
bed and go to sleep, but instead he lay for a long time looking
out the window that was beside the bed. He thought about
the carnival—the Ferris wheel sweeping up into the air, and the
minstrel show. Then he remembered Benbow's dance a few
weeks ago and how his Aunt Harriett had stood sullenly the
next morning while Hager whipped her—and hadn't cried at
all, until the welts came under her silk stockings. . . . Then
he wondered what Jimmy Lane would do if his sick mother
died from the T. B. and he were left with nobody to take care
of him, because Jimmy's step-father was no good. . . . Eu-
uuu! His heel hurt! . . . When school began again, he would
be in the fifth grade, but he wished he'd hurry up and get to
high school, like Harriett was. . . . When he got to be a man,
he was going to be a railroad engineer. . . . Gee, he wasn't
sleepy—and his heel throbbed painfully.

In the next room Harriett had lighted the oil-lamp and was
moving swiftly about taking clothes from the dresser-drawers
and spreading them on the bed. She thought Sandy was asleep,
he knew—but he couldn't go to sleep the way his foot hurt
him. He could see her through the doorway folding her dresses

in little piles and he wondered why she was doing that. Then she took an old suit-case from the closet and began to pack it, and when it was full, she pulled a new bag from under the bed, and into it she dumped her toilet-articles, powder, vaseline, nail-polish, straightening comb, and several pairs of old stockings rolled in balls. Then she sat down on the bed between the two closed suit-cases for a long time with her hands in her lap and her eyes staring ahead of her.

Finally she rose and closed the bureau-drawers, tidied up the confusion she had created, and gathered together the discarded things she had thrown on the floor. Then Sandy heard her go out into the back yard towards the trash-pile. When she returned, she put on a tight little hat and went into the kitchen to wash her hands, throwing the water through the back door. Then she tip-toed into the room where Sandy was lying and kissed him gently on the head. Sandy knew that she thought he was asleep, but in spite of himself he suddenly threw his arms tightly around her neck. He couldn't help it.

"Where you going, Aunt Harriett?" he said, sitting up in bed, clutching the girl.

"Honey, you won't tell on me, will you?" Harriett asked.

"No," he answered, and she knew he wouldn't. "But where are you going, Aunt Harrie?"

"You won't be afraid to stay here until grandma comes?"

"No," burying his face on her breast. "I won't be afraid."

"And you won't forget Aunt Harrie?"

"Course not."

"I'm leaving with the carnival," she told him.

For a moment they sat close together on the bed. Then she kissed him, went into the other room and picked up her suit-cases—and the door closed.

# TEN

## *Punishment*

O LD white Dr. McDillors, beloved of all the Negroes in
Stanton, came on Sunday morning, swabbed Sandy's festering foot with iodine, bound it up, and gave him a bottle of
green medicine to take, and by the middle of the week the boy
was able to hobble about again without pain; but Hager continued to apply fat meat instead of following the doctor's
directions.

When Harriett didn't come back, Sandy no longer slept on a
pallet on the floor. He slept in the big bed with his grandma
Hager, and the evenings that followed weren't so jolly, with his
young aunt off with the carnival, and Jimboy spending most of
his time at the pool hall or else loafing on the station platform
watching the trains come through—and nobody playing music
in the back yard.

They went to bed early these days, and after that eventful
week of carnival and revival, a sore heel, and a missing Aunt
Harriett, the muscles of Sandy's little body often twitched and
jerked in his sleep and he would awaken suddenly from dreaming that he heard sad raggy music playing while a woman
shouted for Jesus in the Gospel tent, and a girl in red silk stockings cried because the switches were cutting her legs. Sometimes
he would lie staring into the darkness a long time, while Aunt
Hager lay snoring at his side. And sometimes in the next room,
where Annjee and Jimboy were, he could hear the slow rhythmical creaking of the bedsprings and the low moans of his
mother, which he already knew accompanied the grown-up
embraces of bodily love. And sometimes through the window
he could see the moonlight glinting on the tall, tassel-crowned
stalks of corn in the garden. Perhaps he would toss and turn
until he had awakened Aunt Hager and she would say drowsily: "What's de matter with you, chile? I'll put you back on de
flo' if you can't be still!" Then he would go to sleep again, and
before he knew it, the sun would be flooding the room with

warm light, and the coffee would be boiling on the stove in the kitchen, and Annjee would have gone to work.

Summer days were long and drowsy for grown-ups, but for Sandy they were full of interest. In the mornings he helped Aunt Hager by feeding the chickens, bringing in the water for her wash-tubs and filling the buckets from which they drank. He chopped wood, too, and piled it behind the kitchen-stove; then he would take the broom and sweep dust-clean the space around the pump and under the apple-tree where he played. Perhaps by that time Willie-Mae would come over or Buster would be there to shoot marbles. Or maybe his grandmother would send him to the store to get a pound of sugar or ten cents' worth of meal for dinner, and on the way there was certain to be an adventure. Yesterday he had seen two bad little boys from the Bottoms, collecting scrap-iron and junk in the alleys, get angry at each other and pretend to start a fight.

The big one said to the smaller one: "I'm a fast-black and you know I sho won't run! Jest you pick up that piece o' iron that belongs to me. Go ahead, jest you try!"

And the short boy replied: "I'm your match, long skinny! Strike me an' see if you don't get burnt up!" And then they started to play the dozens, and Sandy, standing by, learned several new and very vulgar words to use when talking about other peoples' mothers.

The tall kid said finally: "Aw, go on, you little clay-colored nigger, you looks too much like mustard to me anyhow!" Picking up the disputed piece of scrap-iron, he proceeded on his quest for junk, looking into all the trash-piles and garbage-cans along the alley, but the smaller of the two boys took his gunnysack and went in the opposite direction alone.

"Be careful, sissy, and don't break your dishes," his late companion called after his retreating buddy, and Sandy carefully memorized the expression to try on Jimmy Lane some time—that is, if Jimmy's mother got well, for Mrs. Lane now was in the last stages of consumption. But if she got better, Sandy was going to tell her son to be careful and not break his dishes—always wearing his mother's shoes, like a girl.

By that time he had forgotten what Hager sent him to the store to buy, and instead of getting meal he bought washing-powder. When he came home, after nearly an hour's absence, his grandmother threatened to cut an elm switch, but she satisfied herself instead by scolding him for staying so long, and then sending him back to exchange the washing-powder for meal—and she waiting all that time to make corn dumplings to put in the greens!

In the afternoon Sandy played in his back yard or next door at the Johnson's, but Hager never allowed him outside their block. The white children across the street were frequently inclined to say "Nigger," so he was forbidden to play there. Usually Buster, who looked like a white kid, and Willie-Mae, who couldn't have been blacker, were his companions. The three children would run at hide-and-seek, in the tall corn; or they would tag one another in the big yard, or play house under the apple-tree.

Once when they were rummaging in the trash-pile to see what they could find, Sandy came across a pawn ticket which he took into the kitchen to Hager. It was for a watch his Aunt Harriett had pawned the Saturday she ran away.

Sometimes in the late afternoon the children would go next door to Madam de Carter's and she would give them ginger cookies and read to them from the *Bible Story Reader*. Madam de Carter looked very pompous and important in her silk waist as she would put on her *pince-nez* and say: "Now, children, seat yourselves and preserve silence while I read you-all this moralizing history of Samson's treacherous hair. Now, Buster, who were Samson? Willie-Mae, has you ever heard of Delilah?"

Sometimes, if Jimboy was home, he would take down his old guitar and start the children to dancing in the sunlight—but then Hager would always call Sandy to pump water or go to the store as soon as she heard the music.

"Out there dancin' like you ain't got no raisin'!" she would say. "I tells Jimboy 'bout playin' that ole ragtime here! That's what ruint Harriett!"

And on Sundays Sandy went to Sabbath school at the Shiloh Baptist Church, where he was given a colored picture card with a printed text on it. The long, dull lessons were taught by Sister Flora Garden, who had been to Wilberforce College, in Ohio. There were ten little boys in Sandy's class, ranging from nine to fourteen, and they behaved very badly, for Miss Flora Garden, who wore thick-lensed glasses on her roach-colored face, didn't understand little boys.

"Where was Moses when the lights went out?" Gritty Smith asked her every Sunday, and she didn't even know the answer.

Sandy didn't think much of Sunday-school, and frequently instead of putting his nickel in the collection basket he spent it for candy, which he divided with Buster—until one very hot Sunday Hager found it out. He had put a piece of the sticky candy in his shirt-pocket and it melted, stuck, and stained the whole front of his clean clothes. When he came home, with Buster behind him the first thing Hager said was: "What's all this here stuck up in yo' pocket?" and Buster commenced to giggle and said Sandy had bought candy.

"Where'd you get the money, sir?" demanded Aunt Hager searchingly of her grandson.

"I—we—er—Madam Carter gimme a nickel," Sandy replied haltingly, choosing the first name he could think of, which would have been all right had not Madam de Carter herself stopped by the house, almost immediately afterwards, on her way home from church.

"Is you give Sandy a nickel to buy candy this mawnin'?" Hager asked her as soon as she entered the parlor.

"Why, no, Sister Williams, I isn't. I had no coins about me a-tall at services this morning."

"Umn-huh! I thought so!" said Hager. "You Sandy!"

The little boy, guilt written all over his face, came in from the front porch, where he had been sitting with his father after Buster went home.

"Where'd you tell me you got that nickel this mawnin'?" And before he could answer, she spat out: "I'm gonna whip you!"

"Jehovah help us! Children sure is bad these days," said Madam de Carter, shaking her head as she left to go next door to her own house. "They sure *are* bad," she added, self-consciously correcting her English.

"I'm gonna whip you," Hager continued, sitting down amazed in her plush chair. "De idee o' withholdin' yo' Sunday-school money from de Lawd an' buyin' candy."

"I only spent a penny," Sandy lied, wriggling.

"How you gwine get so much candy fo' a penny that you has some left to gum up in yo' pocket? Tell me that, how you gonna do it?"

Sandy, at a loss for an answer, was standing with lowered eyelids, when the screen door opened and Jimboy came in. Sandy looked up at him for aid, but his father's usually amiable face was stern this time.

"Come here!" he said. The man towered very tall above the little fellow who looked up at him helplessly.

"I's gwine whip him!" interposed Hager.

"Is that right, you spent your Sunday-school nickel for candy?" Jimboy demanded gravely.

Sandy nodded his head. He couldn't lie to his father, and had he spoken now, the sobs would have come.

"Then you told a lie to your grandma—and I'm ashamed of you," his father said.

Sandy wanted to turn his head away and escape the slow gaze of Jimboy's eyes, but he couldn't. If Aunt Hager would only whip him, it would be better; then maybe his father wouldn't say any more. But it was awful to stand still and listen to Jimboy talk to him this way—yet there he stood, stiffly holding back the sobs.

"To take money and use it for what it ain't s'posed to be used is the same as stealing," Jimboy went on gravely to his son. "That's what you done today, and then come home and lie about it. Nobody's ugly as a liar, you know that! . . . I'm not much, maybe. Don't mean to say I am. I won't work a lot, but what I do I do honest. White folks gets rich lyin' and stealin'—and some niggers gets rich that way, too—but I don't need money if I got to get it dishonest, with a lot o' lies trailing behind me, and can't look folks in the face. It makes you feel dirty! It's no good! . . . Don't I give you nickels for candy whenever you want 'em?"

The boy nodded silently, with the tears trickling down his chin.

"And don't I go with you to the store and buy you ice-cream and soda-pop any time you ask me?"

The child nodded again.

"And then you go and take the Sunday-school nickel that your grandma's worked hard for all the week, spend it on candy, and come back home and lie about it. So that's what you do! And then lie!"

Jimboy turned his back and went out on the porch, slamming the screen door behind him. Aunt Hager did not whip her grandson, but returned to the kitchen and left him standing disgraced in the parlor. Then Sandy began to cry, with one hand in his mouth so no one could hear him, and when Annjee came home from work in the late afternoon, she found him lying across her bed, head under the pillows, still sobbing because Jimboy had called him a liar.

# ELEVEN

# *School*

---

SOME weeks later the neighbors were treated to an early morning concert:

> I got a high yaller
> An' a little short black,
> But a brown-skin gal
> Can bring me right on back!
> I'm singin' brown-skin!
> Lawdy! . . . Lawd!
> Brown-skin! . . . O, ma Lawd!

"It must be Jimboy," said Hager from the kitchen. "A lazy coon, settin' out there in the cool singin', an' me in here sweatin' and washin' maself to dust!"

> Kansas City Southern!
> I mean de W. & A.!
> I'm gonna ride de first train
> I catch goin' out ma way.
> I'm got de railroad blues—

"I wish to God you'd go on, then!" mumbled Hager over the wash-boilers.

> But I ain't got no railroad fare!
> I'm gwine to pack ma grip an'
> Beat ma way away from here!

"Learn me how to pick a cord, papa," Sandy begged as he sat beside his father under the apple-tree, loaded with ripe fruit.

"All right, look a-here! . . . You put your thumb like this. . . ." Jimboy began to explain. "But, doggone, your fingers ain't long enough yet!"

Still they managed to spend a half-day twanging at the old instrument, with Sandy trying to learn a simple tune.

The sunny August mornings had become September mornings, and most of Aunt Hager's "white folks" had returned from their vacations; her kitchen was once more a daily laundry. Great boilers of clothes steamed on the stove and, beside the clothes, pans of apple juice boiled to jelly, and the peelings of peaches simmered to jam.

There was no news from the runaway Harriett. . . . Mrs. Lane died one sultry night, with Hager at the bedside, and was buried by the lodge with three hacks and a fifty-dollar coffin. . . . The following week the Drill of All Nations, after much practising by the women, was given with great success and Annjee, dressed in white and wrapped in a Scandinavian flag, marched proudly as Sweden. . . . Madam de Carter's house was now locked and barred, as she had departed for Oklahoma to organize branches of the lodge there. . . . Tempy had stopped to see Hager one afternoon, but she didn't stay long. She told her mother she was out collecting rents and that she and her husband were buying another house. . . . Willie-Mae had a new calico dress. . . . Buster had learned to swear better than Sandy. . . . And next Monday was to be the opening of the new school term.

Sandy hated even to think about going back to school. He was having much fun playing, and Jimboy had been teaching him to box. Then the time to go to classes came.

"Wash yo' face good, sir, put on yo' clean waist, an' polish yo' shoes," Aunt Hager said bright and early, " 'cause I don't want none o' them white teachers sayin' I sends you to school dirty as a 'cuse to put you back in de fourth grade. You hear me, sir!"

"Yes'm," Sandy replied.

This morning he was to enter the "white" fifth grade, having passed last June from the "colored" fourth, for in Stanton the Negro children were kept in separate rooms under colored teachers until they had passed the fourth grade. Then, from the fifth grade on, they went with the other children, and the teachers were white.

When Sandy arrived on the school grounds with his face shining, he found the yard already full of shouting kids. On the girls' side he saw Willie-Mae jumping rope. Sandy found Earl and Buster and some boys whom he knew playing mumble-peg on the boys' side, and he joined them. When the bell rang, they all crowded into the building, as the marching-lines had not yet been formed. Miss Abigail Minter, the principal, stood at the entrance, and there were big signs on all the room doors marking the classes. Sandy found the fifth-grade room upstairs and went in shyly. It was full of whispering youngsters huddled in little groups. He saw two colored children among them, both girls whom he didn't know, but there were no colored boys. Soon the teacher rapped briskly on her desk, and silence ensued.

"Take seats, all of you, please," she rasped out. "Anywhere now until we get order." She rapped again impatiently with the ruler. "Take seats at once." So the children each selected a desk and sat down, most of the girls at the front of the room and most of the boys together at the back, where they could play and look out the windows.

Then the teacher, middle-aged and wearing glasses, passed out tiny slips of paper to each child in the front row, with the command that they be handed backwards, so that every student received one slip.

"Now, write your names on the paper, turning it longways," she said. "Nothing but your names, that's all I want today. You will receive forms to fill out later, but I want to get your seats assigned this morning, however."

Amid much confusion and borrowing of pencils, the slips were finally signed in big awkward letters, and collected by the teacher, who passed up and down the aisles. Then she went to her desk, and there was a delightful period of whispering and wriggling as she sorted the slips and placed them in alphabetical order. Finally she finished.

"Now," she said, "each child rise as I call out your names, so I can see who you are."

The teacher stood up with the papers in her hand.

"Mary Atkins . . . Carl Dietrich . . . Josephine Evans," she called slowly glancing up after each name. "Franklin Rhodes . . . James Rodgers." Sandy stood up quickly. "Ethel Shortlidge . . . Roland Thomas." The roll-call continued, each child standing until he had been identified, then sitting down again.

"Now," the teacher said, "everybody rise and make a line around the walls. Quietly! No talking! As I call your names this time, take seats in order, starting with number one in the first row near the window. . . . Mary Atkins . . . Carl Dietrich. . . ." The roll was repeated, each child taking a seat as she had commanded. When all but four of the children were seated, the two colored girls and Sandy still were standing.

"Albert Zwick," she said, and the last white child sat down in his place. "Now," said the teacher, "you three colored children take the seats behind Albert. You girls take the first two, and you," pointing to Sandy, "take the last one. . . . Now I'm going to put on the board the list of books to buy and I want all of you to copy them correctly." And she went on with her details of schoolroom routine.

One of the colored girls turned round to Sandy and whispered: "She just put us in the back cause we're niggers." And Sandy nodded gravely. "My name's Sadie Butler and she's put me behind the Z cause I'm a nigger."

"An old heifer!" said the first little colored girl, whispering loudly. "I'm gonna tell my mama." But Sandy felt like crying. And he was beginning to be ashamed of crying because he was no longer a small boy. But the teacher's putting the colored children in the back of the room made him feel like crying.

At lunch-time he came home with his list of books, and Aunt Hager pulled her wet arms out of the tub, wiped her hands, and held them up in horror.

"Lawdy! Just look! Something else to spend money for. Ever' year more an' more books, an' chillens learn less an' less! Used to didn't have nothin' but a blue-backed speller, and now look ahere—a list as long as ma arm! Go out there in de yard an' see is yo' pappy got any money to give you for 'em, 'cause I ain't."

Sandy found Jimboy sitting dejectedly on the well-stoop in the sunshine, with his head in his hands. "You got any money, papa?" he asked.

Jimboy looked at the list of books written in Sandy's childish scrawl and slowly handed him a dollar and a half.

"You see what I got left, don't you?" said his father as he turned his pants-pockets inside out, showing the little boy a jack-knife, a half-empty sack of Bull Durham, a key, and a dime. But he smiled, and took Sandy awkwardly in his arms and kissed him. "It's all right, kid."

That afternoon at school they had a long drill on the multiplication table, and then they had a spelling-match, because the teacher said that would be a good way to find out what the children knew. For the spelling-bee they were divided into two sides—the boys and the girls, each side lining up against an opposite wall. Then the teacher gave out words that they should have learned in the lower grades. On the boys' side everyone was spelled down except Sandy, but on the girls' side there were three proud little white girls left standing and Sandy came near spelling them down, too, until he put the *e* before *i* in "chief," and the girls' side won, to the disgust of the boys, and the two colored girls, who wanted Sandy to win.

After school Sandy went uptown with Buster to buy books, but there was so large a crowd of children in the bookstore that it was five o'clock before he was waited on and his list filled. When he reached home, Aunt Hager was at the kitchen-stove frying an egg-plant for supper.

"You stayin' out mighty long," she said without taking her attention from the stove.

"Where's papa?" Sandy asked eagerly. He wanted to show Jimboy his new books—a big geography, with pictures of animals in it, and a *Nature Story Reader* that he knew his father would like to see.

"Look in yonder," said Hager, pointing towards Annjee's bedroom.

Sandy rushed in, then stopped, because there was no one there. Suddenly a queer feeling came over him and he put his books down on the bed. Jimboy's clothes were no longer hanging against the wall where his working-shirts and overalls were kept. Then Sandy looked under the bed. His father's old suit-case was not there either, nor his work-shoes, nor his Sunday patent-leathers. And the guitar was missing.

"Where's papa?" he asked again, running back to the kitchen.

"Can't you see he ain't here?" replied his grandmother,

busily turning slices of egg-plant with great care in the skillet. "Gone—that's where he is—a lazy nigger. Told me to tell Annjee he say goodbye, 'cause his travellin' blues done come on . . . ! Huh! Jimboy's yo' pappy, chile, but he sho ain't worth his salt! . . . an' I's right glad he's took his clothes an' left here, maself."

# TWELVE
## *Hard Winter*

---

SEPTEMBER passed and the corn-stalks in the garden were cut. There were no more apples left on the trees, and chilly rains came to beat down the falling leaves from the maples and the elms. Cold and drearily wet October passed, too, with no hint of Indian summer or golden forests. And as yet there was no word from the departed Jimboy. Annjee worried herself sick as usual, hoping every day that a letter would come from this wandering husband whom she loved. And each night she hurried home from Mrs. Rice's, looked on the parlor table for the mail, and found none. Harriett had not written, either, since she went away with the carnival, and Hager never mentioned her youngest daughter's name. Nor did Hager mention Jimboy except when Annjee asked her, after she could hold it no longer: "Are you sure the mail-man ain't left me a letter today?" And then Aunt Hager would reply impatiently: "You think I'd a et it if he did? You know that good-for-nothin', upsettin' scoundrel ain't wrote!"

But in spite of daily disappointments from the postal service Annjee continued to rush from Mrs. Rice's hot kitchen as soon after dinner as she could and to trudge through the chill October rains, anxious to feel in the mail-box outside her door, then hope against hope for a letter inside on the little front-room table—which would always be empty. She caught a terrible cold tramping through the damp streets, forgetting to button her cloak, then sitting down with her wet shoes on when she got home, a look of dumb disappointment in her eyes, too tired and unhappy to remove her clothes.

"You's a fool," said her mother, whose tongue was often much sharper than the meaning behind it. "Mooning after a worthless nigger like Jimboy. I tole you years ago he were no good, when he first come, lookin' like he ought to be wearin' short pants, an' out here courtin' you. Ain't none o' them bell-hoppin', racehoss-followin' kind o' darkies worth havin', an' that's all Jimboy was when you married him an' he ain't much mo'n that now. An' you older'n he is, too!"

"But you know why I married, don't you?"

"You Sandy, go outdoors an' get me some wood fo' this stove. . . . Yes, I knows why, because he were de father o' that chile you was 'bout to bring here, but I don't see why it couldn't just well been some o' these steady, hard-workin' Stanton young men's what was courtin' you at de same time. . . . But, chile or no chile, I couldn't hear nothin' but Jimboy, Jimboy, Jimboy! I told you you better stay in de high school an' get your edication, but no, you had to marry this Jimboy. Now you see what you got, don't you?"

"Well, he ain't been so bad, ma! And I don't care, I love him!"

"Umn-huh! Try an' live on love, daughter! Just try an' live on love. . . . You's made a mistake, that's all, honey. . . . But I guess there ain't no use talkin' 'bout it now. Take off yo' wet shoes 'fore you catch yo' death o' cold!"

On Thanksgiving at Mrs. Rice's, so Annjee reported, they had turkey with chestnut dressing; but at Aunt Hager's she and Sandy had a nice juicy possum, a present from old man Logan, parboiled and baked sweet and brown with yams in the pan. Aunt Hager opened a jar of peach preserves. And she told Sandy to ask Jimmy Lane in to dinner because, since his mother died, he wasn't faring so well and the people he was staying with didn't care much about him. But since Jimmy had quit school, Sandy didn't see him often; and the day before Thanksgiving he couldn't find him at all, so they had no company to help them eat the possum.

The week after Thanksgiving Annjee fell ill and had to go to bed. She had the grippe, Aunt Hager said, and she began to dose her with quinine and to put hot mustard-plasters on her back and gave her onion syrup to drink, but it didn't seem to do much good, and finally she had to send Sandy for Dr. McDillors.

"System's all run down," said the doctor. "Heavy cold on the chest—better be careful. And stay in the bed!" But the warning was unnecessary. Annjee felt too tired and weak ever to rise, and only the mail-man's whistle blowing at somebody else's house would cause her to try to lift her head. Then she would demand weakly: "Did he stop here?"

Hager's home now was like a steam laundry. The kitchen was always hung with lines of clothes to dry, and in the late afternoon and evenings the ironing-board was spread from the table to a chair-back in the middle of the floor. All of the old customers were sending their clothes to Hager again during the winter. And since Annjee was sick, bringing no money into the house on Saturdays, the old woman had even taken an extra washing to do. Being the only wage-earner, Hager kept the suds flying—but with the wet weather she had to dry the clothes in the kitchen most of the time, and when Sandy came home from school for lunch, he would eat under dripping lines of white folks' garments while he listened to his mother coughing in the next room.

In the other rooms of the house there were no stoves, so the doors were kept open in order that the heat might pass through from the kitchen. They couldn't afford to keep more than one fire going; therefore the kitchen was living-room, dining-room, and work-room combined. In the mornings Sandy would jump out of bed and run with his clothes in his hands to the kitchen-stove, where his grandmother would have the fire blazing, the coffee-pot on, and a great tub of water heating for the washings. And in the evenings after supper he would open his geography and read about the strange countries far away, the book spread out on the oilcloth-covered kitchen-table. And Aunt Hager, if her ironing was done, would sit beside the stove and doze, while Annjee tossed and groaned in her chilly bedroom. Only in the kitchen was it really bright and warm.

In the afternoons when Sandy came home from school he would usually find Sister Johnson helping Hager with her ironing, and keeping up a steady conversation.

"Dis gonna be a hard winter. De papers say folks is out o' work ever' where, an', wid all dis sleet an' rain, it's a terror fo' de po' peoples, I tells you! Now, ma Tom, he got a good job tendin' de furnace at de Fair Buildin', so I ain't doin' much washin' long as he's workin'—but so many colored men's out o' work here, wid Christmas comin', it sho is too bad! An' you, Sis Williams, wid yo' daughter sick in bed! Any time yo' clothes git kinder heavy fo' you, I ain't mind helpin' you out. Jest send dis chile atter me or holler 'cross de yard if you kin make me hear! . . . How you press dis dress, wid de collar turn up or down? Which way do Mis' Dunset like it?"

"I always presses it down," returned Hager, who was ironing handkerchiefs and towels on the table. "Better let me iron that, an' you take these here towels."

"All right," agreed Sister Johnson, "'cause you knows how yo' white folks likes dey things, an' I don't. Folks have so many different ways!"

"Sho do," said Hager. "I washed for a woman once what even had her sheets starched."

"But you's sure got a fine repertation as a washer, Sis Williams. One o' de white ladies what I washes fo' say you washes beautiful."

"I reckon white folks does think right smart of me," said Hager proudly. "They always likes you when you tries to do right."

"When you tries to do yo' work right, you means. Dey ain't carin' nothin' 'bout you 'yond workin' fo' 'em. Ain't dey got all de little niggers settin' off in one row at dat school whar Sandy an' Willie-Mae go at? I's like Harriett—ain't got no time fo' white folks maself, 'ceptin' what little money dey pays me. You ain't been run out o' yo' home like I is, Hager. . . . Sandy, make haste go fetch my pipe from over to de house, an' don't stay all day playin' wid Willie-Mae! Tote it here quick! . . . An' you oughter hear de way white folks talks 'bout niggers. Says dey's lazy, an' says dey stinks, an' all. Huh! Dey ought to smell deyselves! You's smelled white peoples when dey gets to sweatin' ain't you? Smells jest like sour cream, only worser, kinder sickenin' like. And some o' dese foriners what's been eating garlic—phew! Lawdy!"

When Sandy returned with the pipe, the conversation had shifted to the deaths in the colored community. "Hager, folks dyin' right an' left already dis winter. We's had such a bad fall, dat's de reason why. You know dat no-'count Jack Smears passed away last Sunday. Dey had his funeral yesterday an' I went. Good thing he belonged to de lodge, too, else he'd been buried in de po'-field, 'cause he ain't left even de copper cents to put on his eyes. Lodge beared his funeral bill, but I heard more'n one member talkin' 'bout how dey was puttin' a ten-dollar nigger in a hundred-dollar coffin! . . . An' his wife were at de funeral. Yes, sir! A hussy! After she done left him last year wid de little chillens to take care of, an' she runnin' round de streets showin' off. Dere she sot, big as life, in front wid de moaners, long black veil on her face and done dyed her coat black, an' all de time Reverend Butler been preachin' 'bout how holy Jack were, she turn an' twist an' she coughed an' she whiffled an' blowed an' she wiped—tryin' her best to cry an' couldn't, deceitful as she is! Then she jest broke out to screamin', but warn't a tear in her eye; makin' folks look at her, dat's all, 'cause she ain't cared nothin' 'bout Jack. She been livin' in de Bottoms since last Feb'ary wid a young bell-hop ain't much older'n her own son, Bert!"

"Do Jesus!" said Hager. "Some womens is awful."

"Worse'n dat," said Sister Johnson. . . . "Lawdy! Listen at dat sleet beatin' on dese winders! Sho gwine be a real winter! An' how time do pass. Ain't but t'ree mo' weeks till Christmas!"

"Truth!" said Sandy's grandmother. "An' we ain't gwine have no money a-tall. Ain't no mo'n got through payin' ma taxes good, an' de interest on ma mortgage, when Annjee get sick here! Lawd, I tells you, po' colored womens have it hard!"

"Sho do!" said Sister Johnson, sucking at her pipe as she ironed. "How long you been had this house, Sis Williams?"

"Fo' nigh on forty years, even sence Cudge an' me come here from Montgomery. An' I been washin' fo' white folks ever' week de Lawd sent sence I been here, too. Bought this house washin', and made as many payments myself as Cudge come near; an' raised ma chillens washin'; an' when Cudge taken sick an' laid on his back for mo'n a year, I taken care o' him washin'; an' when he died, paid de funeral bill washin', cause he ain't belonged to no lodge. Sent Tempy through de high school and edicated Annjee till she marry that onery pup of a Jimboy, an' Harriett till she left home. Yes, sir. Washin', an' here I is with me arms still in de tub! . . . But they's one mo' got to go through school yet, an' that's ma little Sandy. If de Lawd lets me live, I's gwine make a edicated man out o' him. He's gwine be another Booker T. Washington." Hager turned a voluminous white petticoat on the ironing-board as she carefully pressed its emroidered hem. "I ain't never raised no boy o' ma own yet, so I wants this one o' Annjee's to 'mount to something. I wants him to know all they is to know, so's he can help this black race o' our'n to come up and see de light and take they places in de world. I wants him to be a Fred Douglass leadin' de people, that's what, an' not followin' in de tracks o' his good-for-nothin' pappy, worthless an' wanderin' like Jimboy is."

"O, don't say that, ma," Annjee cried weakly from her bed in the other room. "Jimboy's all right, but he's just too smart to do this heavy ditch-digging labor, and that's all white folks gives the colored a chance at here in Stanton; so he had to leave."

"There you go excitin' yo'self agin, an' you sick. I thought you was asleep. I ain't meant nothin', honey. Course he's all right," Hager said to quiet her daughter, but she couldn't resist mumbling: "But I ain't seen him doin' you no good."

"Well, he ain't beat her, has he?" asked Sister Johnson, who, for the sake of conversation, often took a contrary view-point. "I's knowed many a man to beat his wife. Tom used to tap me a few times 'fo' I found out a way to stop him, but dat ain't nedder here nor dere!" She folded a towel decisively and gave it a vigorous rub with the hot iron. "Did I ever tell you 'bout de man lived next do' to us in Cairo what cut his wife in de stomach wid a razor an' den stood ovah her when de doctor was sewin' her up moanin': 'I don't see why I cut her in de stomach! O, Lawd! She always told me she ain't want to be cut in de stomach!' . . . An' it warn't two months atter dat dat he done sliced her in de stomach agin when she was tryin' to git away from him! He were a mean nigger, that man were!"

"Annjee, is you taken yo' medicine yet? It's past fo' o'clock," Hager called. "Sandy, here, take this fifteen cents, chile, and run to do store an' get me a soup bone. I gwine try an' make a little broth for yo' mother. An' don't be gone all day neither, 'cause I got to send these clothes back to Mis' Dunset." Hager was pressing out the stockings as she turned her attention to the conversation again. "They tells me, Sister Johnson, that Seth Jones done beat up his wife something terrible."

"He did, an' he oughter! She was always stayin' way from

home an' settin' up in de church, not even cookin' his meals, an' de chillens runnin' ragged in de street."

"She's a religious frantic, ain't she?" asked Hager. . . . "You Sandy, hurry up, sir! an' go get that soup bone!"

"No, chile, 'tain't that," said Sister Johnson. "She ain't carin' so much 'bout religion. It's Reverend Butler she's runnin' atter. Ever' time de church do' opens, there she sets in de preacher's mouth, tryin' to 'tract de shepherd from his sheep. She de one what taken her husband's money an' bought Reverend Butler dat gold-headed walkin'-cane he's got. I ain't blame Seth fer hittin' her bap on de head, an' she takin' his money an' buyin' canes fer ministers!"

"Sadie Butler's in my school," said Sandy, putting on his stocking cap. "Reverend Butler's her step-father."

"Shut up! You hears too much," said Hager. "Ain't I told you to go on an' get that soup bone?"

"Yes'm. I'm going."

"An' I reckon I'll be movin' too," said Sister Johnson, placing the iron on the stove. "It's near 'bout time to be startin' Tom's supper. I done told Willie-Mae to peel de taters 'fo' I come ovah here, but I spects she ain't done it. Dat's de worse black gal to get to work! Soon as she eat, she run outdo's to de privy to keep from washin' de dishes!"

Sandy started to the store, and Sister Johnson, with on old coat over her head, scooted across the back yard to her door. It was a chill December afternoon and the steady sleet stung Sandy in the face as he ran along, but the air smelled good after the muggy kitchen and the stale scent of Annjee's sick-room. Near the corner Sandy met the mail-man, his face red with cold.

"Got anything for us?" asked the little boy.

"No," said the man as he went on without stopping.

Sandy wished his mother would get well soon. She looked so sad lying there in bed. And Aunt Hager was always busy washing and ironing. His grandmother didn't even have time to mend his stockings any more and there were great holes in the heels when he went to school. His shoes were worn out under the bottoms, too. Yesterday his mother had said: "Honey, you better take them high brown shoes of mine from underneath the bed and put 'em on to keep your feet dry this wet weather. I can't afford to buy you none now, and you ain't got no rubbers."

"You want me to wear old women's shoes like Jimmy Lane?" Sandy objected. "I won't catch cold with my feet wet."

But Hager from the kitchen overruled his objections. "Put on them shoes, sir, an' don't argue with yo' mother, an' she sick in de bed! Put 'em on an' hush yo' mouth, till you get something better."

So this morning at recess Sandy had to fight a boy for calling him "sissy" on account of his mother's shoes he was wearing.

But only a week and a half more and the Christmas vacation would come! Uptown the windows were already full of toys, dolls, skates, and sleds. Sandy wanted a Golden Flyer sled for Christmas. That's all he wanted—a Golden Flyer with flexible rudders, so you could guide it easy. Boy! Wouldn't he come shooting down that hill by the Hickory Woods where the fellows coasted every year! They cost only four dollars and ninety-five cents and surely his grandma could afford that for him, even if his mother was sick and she had just paid her taxes. Four ninety-five—but he wouldn't want anything else if Aunt Hager would buy that sled for Santa Claus to bring him! Every day, after school, he passed by the store, where many sleds were displayed, and stood for a long time looking at this Golden Flyer of narrow hard-wood timbers varnished a shiny yellow. It had bright red runners and a beautiful bar with which to steer.

When he told Aunt Hager about it, all she said was: "Boy, is you crazy?" But Annjee smiled from her bed and answered: "Wait and see." Maybe they would get it for him—but Santa Claus was mean to poor kids sometimes, Sandy knew, when their parents had no money.

"Fifteen cents' worth of hamburger," he said absentmindedly to the butcher when he reached the market. . . . And when Sandy came home, his grandmother whipped him for bringing ground meat instead of the soup bone for which she had sent him.

So the cold days passed, heavy and cloudy, with Annjee still in bed, and the kitchen full of garments hanging on lines to dry because, out of doors, the frozen rain kept falling. Always in Hager's room a great pile of rough-dried clothes eternally waited to be ironed. Sandy helped his grandmother as much as he could, running errands, bringing in coal and wood, pumping water in the mornings before school, and sitting by his mother in the evenings, reading to her from his *Nature Story Reader* when it wasn't too cold in her bedroom.

Annjee was able to sit up now and she said she felt better, but she looked ashen and tired. She wanted to get back to work, so she would have a little money for Christmas and be able to help Hager with the doctor's bill, but she guessed she couldn't. And she was still worrying about Jimboy. Three months had passed since he went away—a longer time than usual that he hadn't written. Maybe something *had* happened to him. Maybe he was out of work and hungry, because this was a hard winter. *Maybe he was dead!*

"O, my God, no!" Annjee cried as the thought struck her.

But one Sunday morning, ten days before Christmas, the door-bell rang violently and a special-delivery boy stood on the front porch. Annjee's heart jumped as she sat up in bed. She had seen the youngster approaching from the window. Word from Jimboy surely—or word about him!

"Ma! Sandy! Go quick and see what it is!"

"Letter for Mrs. Annjelica Rodgers," said the boy, stamping the snow from his feet. "Sign here."

While Sandy held the door open, letting the cold wind blow through the house, Hager haltingly scrawled something on the boy's pink pad. Then, with the child behind her, the old woman hurried to her daughter's bed with the white envelope.

"It's from him!" Annjee cried; "I know it's from Jimboy," as she tore open the letter with trembling fingers.

A scrap of dirty tablet-paper fell on the quilt, and Annjee quickly picked it up. It was written in pencil in a feminine hand.

>   Dear Sister,
>       I am stranded in Memphis, Tenn. and the show has gone on to New Orleans. I can't buy anything to eat because I am broke and don't know anybody in this town.

Annjee, please send me my fare to come home and mail it to the Beale Street Colored Hotel. I'm sending my love to you and mama.

Your baby sister,
Harriett

# THIRTEEN

# *Christmas*

---

"Po' little thing," said Hager. "Po' little thing. An' here we ain't got no money."

The night before, on Saturday, Hager had bought a sack of flour, a chunk of salt pork, and some groceries. Old Dr. McDillors had called in the afternoon, and she had paid him, too.

"I reckon it would take mo'n thirty dollars to send fo' Harriett, an' Lawd knows we ain't got three dollars in de house."

Annjee lay limply back on her pillows staring out of the window at the falling snow. She had been crying.

"But never mind," her mother went on, "I's gwine see Mr. John Frank tomorrow an' see can't I borry a little mo' money on this mortgage we's got with him."

So on Monday morning the old lady left her washing and went uptown to the office of the money-lender, but the clerk there said Mr. Frank had gone to Chicago and would not be back for two weeks. There was nothing the clerk could do about it, since he himself could not lend money.

That afternoon Annjee sat up in bed and wrote a long letter to Harriett, telling her of their troubles, and before she sealed it, Sandy saw his mother slip into the envelope the three one-dollar bills that she had been guarding under her pillow.

"There goes your Santa Claus," she said to her son, "but maybe Harriett's hungry. And you don't want Aunt Harrie to be hungry, do you?"

"No'm," Sandy said.

The grey days passed and Annjee was able to get up and sit beside the kitchen-stove while her mother ironed. Every afternoon Sandy went downtown to look at the shop windows, gay with Christmas things. And he would stand and stare at the Golden Flyer sleds in Edmondson's hardware-shop. He could feel himself coasting down a long hill on one of those light, swift, red and yellow coasters, the envy of all the other boys, white and colored, who looked on.

When he went home, he described the sled minutely to Annjee and Aunt Hager and wondered aloud if that might be what he would get for Christmas. But Hager would say: "Santa Claus are just like other folks. He don't work for nothin'!" And his mother would add weakly from her chair: "This is gonna be a slim Christmas, honey, but mama'll see what she can do." She knew his heart was set on a sled, and he could tell that she knew; so maybe he would get it.

One day Annjee gathered her strength together, put a woollen dress over her kimono, wrapped a heavy cloak about herself, and went out into the back yard. Sandy, from the window, watched her picking her way slowly across the frozen ground towards the outhouse. At the trash-pile near the alley fence she stopped and, stooping down, began to pull short pieces of boards and wood from the little pile of lumber that had been left there since last summer by the carpenters who had built the porch. Several times in her labor she rose and leaned weakly against the back fence for support, and once Sandy ran out to see if he could help her, but she told him irritably to get back in the house out of the weather or she would put him to bed without any supper. Then, after placing the boards that she had succeeded in unearthing in a pile by the path, she came wearily back to the kitchen, trembling with cold.

"I'm mighty weak yet," she said to Hager, "but I'm sure much better than I was. I don't want to have the grippe no more. . . . Sandy, look in the mail-box and see has the mailman come by yet."

As the little boy returned empty-handed, he heard his mother talking about old man Logan, who used to be a carpenter.

"Maybe he can make it," she was saying, but stopped when she heard Sandy behind her. "I guess I'll lay back down now."

Aunt Hager wrung out the last piece of clothes that she had been rinsing. "Yes, chile," she said, "you go on and lay down. I's gwine make you some tea after while." And the old woman went outdoors to take from the line the frozen garments blowing in the sharp north wind.

After supper that night Aunt Hager said casually: "Well, I reckon I'll run down an' see Brother Logan a minute whilst I got nothin' else to do. Sandy, don't you let de fire go out, and take care o' yo' mama."

"Yes'm," said the little boy, drawing pictures on the oilcloth-covered table with a pin. His grandmother went out the back door and he looked through the frosty window to see which way she was going. The old woman picked up the boards that his mother had piled near the alley fence, and with them in her arms she disappeared down the alley in the dark.

After a little, Aunt Hager returned puffing and blowing.

"Can he do it?" Annjee demanded anxiously from the bed-room when she heard her mother enter.

"Yes, chile," Hager answered. "Lawd, it sho is cold out yon-der! Whee! Lemme git here to this stove!"

That night it began to snow again. The great heavy flakes fell with languid gentility over the town and silently the white-ness covered everything. The next morning the snow froze to a hard sparkling crust on roofs and ground, and in the late afternoon when Sandy went to return the Reinharts' clothes, you could walk on top of the snow without sinking.

At the back door of the Reinharts' house a warm smell of plum-pudding and mince pies drifted out as he waited for the cook to bring the money. When she returned with seventy-five cents, she had a nickel for Sandy, too. As he slid along the street, he saw in many windows gay holly wreaths with red berries and big bows of ribbon tied to them. Sandy wished he could buy a holly wreath for their house. It might make his mother's room look cheerful. At home it didn't seem like Christmas with the kitchen full of drying clothes, and no Christmas-tree.

Sandy wondered if, after all, Santa Claus might, by some good fortune, bring him that Golden Flyer sled on Christmas morning. How fine this hard snow would be to coast on, down the long hill past the Hickory Woods! How light and swift he would fly with his new sled! Certainly he had been a good boy, carrying Aunt Hager's clothes for her, waiting on his mother when she was in bed, emptying the slops and cutting wood every day. And at night when he said his prayers:

Now I lay me down to sleep.
Pray the Lord my soul to keep.
If I should die before I wake,
Pray the Lord my soul to take. . . .

he had added with great earnestness: "And let Santa bring me a Golden Flyer sled, please, Lord. Amen."

But Sandy knew very well that there wasn't really any Santa Claus! He knew in his heart that Hager and his mother were Santa Claus—and that they didn't have any money. They were poor people. He was wearing his mama's shoes, as Jimmy Lane had once done. And his father and Harriett, who used to make the house gay, laughing and singing, were far away somewhere. . . . There wasn't any Santa Claus.

"I don't care," he said, tramping over the snow in the twilight on his way from the Reinharts'.

Christmas Eve. Candles and poinsettia flowers. Wreaths of evergreen. Baby trees hung with long strands of tinsel and fragile ornaments of colored glass. Sandy passed the windows of many white folks' houses where the curtains were up and warm floods of electric light made bright the cozy rooms. In Negro shacks, too, there was the dim warmth of oil-lamps and Christmas candles glowing. But at home there wasn't even a holly wreath. And the snow was whiter and harder than ever on the ground.

Tonight, though, there were no clothes drying in the kitchen when he went in. The ironing-board had been put away behind the door, and the whole place was made tidy and clean. The fire blazed and crackled in the little range; but nothing else said Christmas—no laughter, no tinsel, no tree.

Annjee had been about all day, still weak, but this afternoon she had made a trip to the store for a quarter's worth of mixed candies and nuts and a single orange, which she had hidden away until morning. Hager had baked a little cake, but there was no frosting on it such as there had been in other years, and there were no strange tissue-wrapped packages stuck away in the corners of trunks and drawers days ahead of time.

Although the little kitchen was warm enough, the two bedrooms were chilly, and the front room was freezing-cold because they kept the door there closed all the time. It was hard to afford a fire in one stove, let alone two, Aunt Hager kept saying, with nobody working but herself.

"I's thinking about Harriett," she remarked after their Christmas Eve supper as she rocked before the fire, "and how I's always tried to raise her right."

"And I'm thinking about—well, there ain't no use mentionin' him," Annjee said.

A sleigh slid by with jingling bells and shouts of laughter from the occupants, and a band of young people passed on their way to church singing carols. After a while another sleigh came along with a jolly sound.

"Santa Claus!" said Annjee, smiling at her serious little son. "You better hurry and go to bed, because he'll be coming soon. And be sure to hang up your stocking."

But Sandy was afraid that she was fooling, and, as he pulled off his clothes, he left his stockings on the floor, stuck into the women's shoes he had been wearing. Then, leaving the bedroom door half open so that the heat and a little light from the kitchen would come in, he climbed into his mother's bed. But he wasn't going to close his eyes yet. Sandy had discovered long ago that you could hear and see many things by not going to sleep when the family expected you to; therefore he remained awake tonight.

His mother was talking to Aunt Hager now: "I don't think he'll charge us anything, do you, ma?" And the old woman answered: "No, chile, Brother Logan's been tryin' to be ma beau for twenty years, an' he ain't gonna charge us nothin'."

Annjee came into the half-dark bedroom and looked at Sandy, lying still on the side of the bed towards the window. Then she took down her heavy coat from the wall and, sitting on the edge of a chair, began to pull on her rubbers. In a few moments he heard the front door close softly. His mother had gone out.

Where could she be going, he wondered, this time of night? He heard her footsteps crunching the hard snow and, rolling over close to the window, he pulled aside the shade a little and looked out. In the moonlight he saw Annjee moving slowly down the street past Sister Johnson's house, walking carefully over the snow like a very weak woman.

"Mama's still sick," the child thought, with his nose pressed against the cold window-pane. "I wish I could a bought her a present today."

Soon an occasional snore from the kitchen told Sandy that Hager dozed peacefully in her rocker beside the stove. He sat up in bed, wrapped a quilt about his shoulders, and remained looking out the window, with the shade hanging behind his back.

The white snow sparkled in the moonlight, and the trees made striking black shadows across the yard. Next door at the Johnson's all was dark and quiet, but across the street, where white folks lived, the lights were burning brightly and a big Christmas-tree with all its candles aglow stood in the large bay window while a woman loaded it with toys. Sandy knew that four children lived there, three boys and a girl, whom he had often watched playing on the lawn. Sometimes he wished he had a brother or sister to play with him, too, because it was very quiet in a house with only grown-ups about. And right now it was dismal and lonely to be by himself looking out the window of a cold bedroom on Christmas Eve.

Then a woman's cloaked figure came slowly back past Sister Johnson's house in the moonlight, and Sandy saw that it was his mother returning, her head down and her shadow moving blackly on the snow. You could hear the dry grate of her heels on the frozen whiteness as she walked, leaning forward, dragging something heavy behind her. Sandy prepared to lie down quickly in bed again, but he kept his eyes against the window-pane to see what Annjee was pulling, and, as she came closer to the house, he could distinguish quite clearly behind her a solid, home-made sled bumping rudely over the snow.

Before Anjee's feet touched the porch, he was lying still as though he had been asleep a long time.

The morning sunlight was tumbling brightly into the windows when Sandy opened his eyes and blinked at the white world outside.

"Aren't you ever going to get up?" asked Annjee, smiling timidly above him. "It's Christmas morning, honey. Come see what Santa Claus brought you. Get up quick."

But he didn't want to get up. He knew what Santa Claus had brought him and he wanted to stay in bed with his face to the wall. It wasn't a Golden Flyer sled—and now he couldn't even hope for one any longer. He wanted to pull the covers over his head and cry, but, "Boy! You ain't up yet?" called Aunt Hager cheerily from the kitchen. "De little Lawd Jesus is in His manger fillin' all de world with light. An' old Santa done been here an' gone! Get out from there, chile, an' see!"

"I'm coming, grandma," said Sandy slowly, wiping his tear-filled eyes and rolling out of bed as he forced his mouth to smile wide and steady at the few little presents he saw on the floor—for the child knew he was expected to smile.

"O! A sled!" he cried in a voice of mock surprise that wasn't his own at all; for there it stood, heavy and awkward, against the wall and beside it on the floor lay two picture-books from the ten-cent store and a pair of white cotton gloves. Above the sled his stocking, tacked to the wall, was partly filled with candy, and the single orange peeped out from the top.

But the sled! Home-made by some rough carpenter, with strips of rusty tin nailed along the wooden runners, and a piece of clothes-line to pull it with!

"It's fine," Sandy lied, as he tried to lift it and place it on the floor as you would in coasting; but it was very heavy, and too wide for a boy to run with in his hands. You could never get a swift start. And a board was warped in the middle.

"It's a nice sled, grandma," he lied. "I like it, mama."

"Mr. Logan made it for you," his mother answered proudly, happy that he was pleased. "I knew you wanted a sled all the time."

"It's a nice sled," Sandy repeated, grinning steadily as he held the heavy object in his hands. "It's an awful nice sled."

"Well, make haste and look at de gloves, and de candy, and them pretty books, too," called Hager from the kitchen, where she was frying strips of salt pork. "My, you sho is a slow chile on Christmas mawnin'! Come 'ere and lemme kiss you." She came to the bedroom and picked him up in her arms. "Christmas gift to Hager's baby chile! Come on, Annjee, bring his clothes out here behind de stove an' bring his books, too. . . . This here's Little Red Riding Hood and the Wolf, and this here's Hansee and Gretsle on de cover—but I reckon you can read 'em better'n I can. . . . Daughter, set de table. Breakfast's 'bout ready now. Look in de oven an' see 'bout that corn-bread. . . . Lawd, this here Sandy's just like a baby lettin' ole Hager hold him and dress him. . . . Put yo' foot in that stocking, boy!" And Sandy began to feel happier, sitting on his grandmother's lap behind the stove.

Before noon Buster had come and gone, showing off his new shoes and telling his friend about the train he had gotten that ran on a real track when you wound it up. After dinner Willie-Mae appeared bringing a naked rag doll and a set of china dishes in a blue box. And Sister Johnson sent them a mince pie as a Christmas gift.

Almost all Aunt Hager's callers knocked at the back door, but in the late afternoon the front bell rang and Annjee sent Sandy through the cold parlor to answer it. There on the porch stood his Aunt Tempy, with several gaily wrapped packages in her arms. She was almost a stranger to Sandy, yet she kissed him peremptorily on the forehead as he stood in the doorway. Then she came through the house into the kitchen, with much the air of a mistress of the manor descending to the servants' quarters.

"Land sakes alive!" said Hager, rising to kiss her.

Tempy hugged Annjee, too, before she sat down, stiffly, as though the house she was in had never been her home. To little black Willie-Mae she said nothing.

"I'm sorry I couldn't invite you for Christmas dinner today, but you know how Mr. Siles is," Tempy began to explain to her mother and sister. "My husband is home so infrequently, and he doesn't like a house full of company, but of course Dr. and Mrs. Glenn Mitchell will be in later in the evening. They drop around any time. . . . But I had to run down and bring you a few presents. . . . You haven't seen my new piano yet, have you, mother? I must come and take you home with me some nice afternoon." She smiled appropriately, but her voice was hard.

"How is you an' yo' new church makin' it?" asked Hager, slightly embarrassed in the presence of her finely dressed society daughter.

"Wonderful!" Tempy replied. "Wonderful! Father Hill is so dignified, and the services are absolutely refined! There's never anything niggerish about them—so you know, mother, they suit me."

"I's glad you likes it," said Hager.

There was an awkward silence; then Tempy distributed her gifts, kissed them all as though it were her Christian duty, and went her way, saying that she had calls to make at Lawyer and Mrs. Moore's, and Professor Booth's, and Madam Temple's before she returned home. When she had gone, everybody felt relieved—as though a white person had left the house. Willie-Mae began to play again, and Hager pushed her feet out of her shoes once more, while Annjee went into the bedroom and lay down.

Sandy sat on the floor and untied his present, wrapped in several thicknesses of pink tissue paper, and found, in a bright Christmas box, a big illustrated volume of *Andersen's Fairy Tales* decorated in letters of gold. With its heavy pages and fine pictures, it made the ten-cent-store books that Hager had bought him appear cheap and thin. It made his mother's sled look cheap, too, and shamed all the other gifts the ones he loved had given him.

"I don't want it," he said suddenly, as loud as he could. "I don't want Tempy's old book!" And from where he was sitting, he threw it with all his might underneath the stove.

Hager gasped in astonishment. "Pick that up, sir," she cried amazed. "Yo' Aunt Tempy done bought you a fine purty book an' here you throwin' it un'neath de stove in de ashes! Lawd have mercy! Pick it up, I say, this minute!"

"I won't!" cried Sandy stubbornly. "I won't! I like my sled what you-all gave me, but I don't want no old book from Tempy! I won't pick it up!"

Then the astonished Hager grabbed him by the scruff of the neck and jerked him to his feet.

"Do I have to whip you yet this holy day? . . . Pick up that book, sir!"

"No!" he yelled.

She gave him a startled rap on the head with the back of her hand. "Talkin' sassy to yo' old grandma an' tellin' her no!"

"What is it?" Annjee called from the bedroom, as Sandy began to wail.

"Nothin'," Hager replied, " 'ceptin' this chile's done got beside hisself an' I has to hit him—that's all!"

But Sandy was not hurt by his grandmother's easy rap. He

was used to being struck on the back of the head for misde-
meanors, and this time he welcomed the blow because it gave
him, at last, what he had been looking for all day—a sufficient
excuse to cry. Now his pent-up tears flowed without ceasing
while Willie-Mae sat in a corner clutching her rag doll to her
breast, and Tempy's expensive gift lay in the ashes beneath the
stove.

# FOURTEEN
## *Return*

A FTER Christmas there followed a period of cold weather, made bright by the winter sun shining on the hard crusty snow, where children slid and rolled, and over which hay-wagons made into sleighs on great heavy runners drove jingling into town from the country. There was skating on the frozen river and fine sledding on the hills beyond the woods, but Sandy never went out where the crowds were with his sled, because he was ashamed of it.

After New Year's Annjee went back to work at Mrs. Rice's, still coughing a little and still weak. But with bills to pay and Sandy in need of shoes and stockings and clothes to wear to school, she couldn't remain idle any longer. Even with her mother washing and ironing every day except the Sabbath, expenses were difficult to meet, and Aunt Hager was getting pretty old to work so hard. Annjee thought that Tempy ought to help them a little, but she was too proud to ask her. Besides, Tempy had never been very affectionate towards her sisters even when they were all girls together—but she ought to help look out for their mother. Hager, however, when Annjee brought up the subject of Tempy's help, said that she was still able to wash, thank God, and wasn't depending on any of her children for anything—not so long as white folks wore clothes.

At school Sandy passed all of his mid-year tests and, along with Sadie Butler, was advanced to the fifth A, but the other colored child in the class, a little fat girl named Mary Jones, failed and had to stay behind. Mary's mother, a large sulphur-yellow woman who cooked at the Drummer's Hotel, came to the school and told the teacher, before all the children, just what she thought of her for letting Mary fail—and her thoughts were not very complimentary to the stiff, middle-aged white lady who taught the class. The question of color came up, too, during the discussion.

"Look at ma chile settin' back there behind all de white

ones," screamed the sulphur-yellow woman. "An' me payin' as much taxes as anybody! You treats us colored folks like we ain't citizerzens—that's what you does!" The argument had to be settled in the principal's office, where the teacher went with the enraged mother, while the white children giggled that a fat, yellow colored lady should come to school to quarrel about her daughter's not being promoted. But the colored children in the class couldn't laugh.

St. Valentine's day came and Sadie Butler sent Sandy a big red heart. But for Annjee, "the mail-man passed and didn't leave no news," because Jimboy hadn't written yet, nor had Harriett thanked her for the three dollars she had mailed to Memphis before Christmas. There were no letters from anybody.

The work at Mrs. Rice's was very heavy, because Mrs. Rice's sister, with two children, had come from Indiana to spend the winter, and Annjee had to cook for them and clean their rooms, too. But she was managing to save a little money every week. She bought Sandy a new blue serge suit with a Norfolk coat and knickerbocker pants. And then he sat up very stiffly in Sterner's studio and had his picture taken.

The freckled-faced white boy, Paul Biggers, who sat across from Sandy in school, delivered the *Daily Leader* to several streets in Sandy's neighborhood, and Sandy sometimes went with him, helping to fold and throw the papers in the various doorways. One night it was almost seven o'clock when he got home.

"I had a great mind not to wait for you," said Aunt Hager, who had long had the table set for supper. "Wash yo' face an' hands, sir! An' brush that snow off yo' coat 'fo' you hang it up."

His grandmother took a pan of hot spoon-bread from the oven and put it on the table, where the little oil-lamp glowed warmly and the plain white dishes looked clean and inviting. On the stove there was a skillet full of fried apples and bacon, and Hager was making a pot of tea.

"Umn-nn! Smells good!" said Sandy, speaking of everything at once as he slid into his chair. "Gimme a lot o' apples, grandma."

"Is that de way you ask fo' 'em, sir? Can't you say please no mo'?"

"Please, ma'am," said the boy, grinning, for Hager's sharpness wasn't serious, and her old eyes were twinkling.

While they were eating, Annjee came in from work with a small bucket of oyster soup in her hands. They heated this and added it to their supper, and Sandy's mother sat down in front of the stove, with her feet propped up on the grate to dry quickly. It was very comfortable in the little kitchen.

"Seems like the snow's melting," said Annjee. "It's kinder sloppy and nasty underfoot. . . . Ain't been no mail today, has they?"

"No, honey," said Hager. "Leastwise, I been washin' so hard ain't had no time to look in de box. Sandy, run there to de front do' an' see. But I knows there ain't nothin', nohow."

"Might be," said Annjee as Sandy took a match and went through the dark bedroom and parlor to the front porch. There was no mail. But Sandy saw, coming across the slushy dirty-white snow towards the house, a slender figure approaching in the gloom. He waited, shivering in the doorway a moment to see who it was; then all at once he yelled at the top of his lungs: "Aunt Harrie's here!"

Pulling her by the hand, after having kissed and hugged and almost choked her, he ran back to the kitchen. "Look, here's Aunt Harrie!" he cried. "Aunt Harrie's home!" And Hager turned from the table, upsetting her tea, and opened wide her arms to take her to her bosom.

"Ma chile!" she shouted. "Done come home again! Ma baby chile come home!"

Annjee hugged and kissed Harriett, too, as her sister sat on Hager's knees—and the kitchen was filled with sound, warm and free and loving, for the prodigal returned.

"Ma chile's come back!" her mother repeated over and over. "Thank de Lawd! Ma chile's back!"

"You want some fried apples, Harrie?" asked Sandy, offering her his plate. "You want some tea?"

"No, thank you, honey," she replied when the excitement had subsided and Aunt Hager had released her, with her little black hat askew and the powder kissed off one side of her face.

She got up, shook herself, and removed her hat to brush down her hair, but she kept her faded coat on as she laid her little purse of metal mesh on the table. Then she sat down on the chair that Annjee offered her near the fire. She was thinner and her hair had been bobbed, giving her a boyish appearance, like the black pages in old Venetian paintings. But her lips were red and there were two little spots of rouge burning on each cheek, although her eyes were dark with heavy shadows as though she had been ill.

Hager was worried. "Has you been sick, chile?" she asked.

"No, mama," Harriett said. "I've been all right—just had a hard time, that's all. I got mad, and quit the show in Memphis, and they wouldn't pay me—so that was that! The minstrels left the carnival for the winter and started playing the theatres, and the new manager was a cheap skate. I couldn't get along with him."

"Did you get my letter and the money?" Annjee asked. "We didn't have no more to send you, and afterwards, when you didn't write, I didn't know if you got it."

"I got it and meant to thank you, sis, but I don't know—just didn't get round to it. But, anyway, I'm out of the South now. It's a hell—I mean it's an awful place if you don't know anybody! And more hungry niggers down there! I wonder who made up that song about *Dear Old Southland*. There's nothing dear about it that I can see. Good God! It's awful! . . . But I'm back." She smiled. "Where's Jimboy? . . . O, that's right, Annjee—you told me in the letter. But I sort-a miss him around here. Lord, I hope he didn't go to Memphis!"

"Did you find a job down there?" Annjee asked, looking at her sister's delicate hands.

"Sure, I found a *job* all right," Harriett replied in a tone that made Annjee ask no more questions. "Jobs are like hen's teeth —try and find 'em." And she shrugged her shoulders as Sandy had so often seen her do, but she no longer seemed to him like a little girl. She was grown-up and hard and strange now, but he still loved her.

"Aunt Harrie, I passed to the fifth A," he announced proudly.

"That's wonderful," she answered. "My, but you're smart! You'll be a great man some day, sure, Sandy."

"Where's yo' suit-case, honey?" Hager interrupted, too happy to touch her food on the table or to take her eyes away from the face of her returned child. "Didn't you bring it back with you? Where is it?"

"Sure, I got it. . . . But I'm gonna live at Maudel's this time, mama. . . . I left it at the station. I didn't think you-all'd want me here." She tried to make the words careless-like, but they were pitifully forced.

"Aw, honey!" Annjee cried, the tears coming.

The shadow of inner pain passed over Hager's black face, but the only reply she made was: "You's growed up now, chile. I reckon you knows what you's doin'. You's been ten thousand miles away from yo' mammy, an' I reckon you knows. . . . Come on, Sandy, let's we eat." Slowly the old woman returned to the cold food on her plate. "Won't you eat something with us, daughter?"

Harriett's eyes lowered and her shoulders drooped. "No, mama, thank you. I'm—not hungry."

Then a long, embarrassing silence followed while Hager gulped at her tea, Sandy tried to swallow a mouthful of bread that seemed to choke him, and Annjee stared stupidly at the stove.

Finally Harriett said: "I got to go now." She stood up to button her coat and put on her hat. Then she took her metal purse from the table.

"Maudel'll be waiting for me, but I'll be seeing you-all again soon, I guess. Good-bye, Sandy honey! I got to go. . . . Annjee, I got to go now. . . . Good-bye, mama!" She was trembling. As she bent down to kiss Hager, her purse slipped out of her hands and fell in a little metal heap on the floor. She stooped to pick it up.

"I got to go now."

A tiny perfume-bottle in the bag had broken from the fall, and as she went through the cold front room towards the door, the odor of cheap and poignant drugstore violets dripped across the house.

# FIFTEEN

## *One by One*

---

YOU could smell the spring.

"'Tain't gwine be warm fo' weeks yet!" Hager said.

Nevertheless, you could smell the spring. Little boys were already running in the streets without their overcoats, and the ground-hog had seen its shadow. Snow remained in the fence corners, but it had melted on the roofs. The yards were wet and muddy, but no longer white.

It was a sunny afternoon in late March that a letter came. On his last delivery the mail-man stopped, dropped it in the box—and Sandy saw him. It was addressed to his mother and he knew it must be from Jimboy.

"Go on an' take it to her," his grandma said, as soon as she saw the boy coming with it in his hand. "I knows that's what you want to do. Go on an' take it." And she bent over her ironing again.

Sandy ran almost all the way to Mrs. Rice's, dropping the letter more than once on the muddy sidewalk, so excited he did not think to put it in his pocket. Into the big yard and around to the white lady's back door he sped—and it was locked! He knocked loudly for a long time, and finally an upper window opened and Annjee, a dust-rag around her head, looked down, squinting in the sunlight.

"Who's there?" she called stridently, thinking of some peddler or belated tradesman for whom she did not wish to stop her cleaning.

Sandy pantingly held up the letter and was about to say something when the window closed with a bang. He could hear his mother almost falling down the back stairs, she was coming so fast. Then the key turned swiftly in the lock, the door opened, and, without closing it, Annjee took the letter from him and tore it open where she stood.

"It's from Jimboy!"

Sandy stood on the steps looking at his mother, her bosom

heaving, her sleeves rolled up, and the white cloth tied about her head, doubly white against her dark-brown face.

"He's in Detroit, it says. . . . Umn! I ain't never seen him write such a long letter. 'I had a hard time this winter till I landed here,' it says, 'but things look pretty good now, and there is lots of building going on and plenty of work opening up in the automobile plants . . . a mighty lot of colored folks here . . . hope you and Sandy been well. Sorry couldn't send you nothing Xmas, but I was in St. Paul broke. . . . Kiss my son for me. . . . Tell ma hello even if she don't want to hear it. Your loving husband, Jimboy Rogers.'"

Annjee did her best to hold the letter with one hand and pick up Sandy with the other, but he had grown considerably during the winter and she was still a little weak from her illness; so she bent down to his level and kissed him several times before she re-read the letter.

"From your daddy!" she said. "Umn-mn. . . . Come on in here and warm yourself. Lemme see what he says again!" . . . She lighted the gas oven in the white kitchen and sat down in front of it with her letter, forgetting the clock and the approaching time for Mrs. Rice's dinner, forgetting everything. "A letter from my daddy! From my far-off sugar-daddy!"

"From *my* daddy," corrected Sandy. . . . "Say, gimme a nickel to buy some marbles, mama. I wanta go play."

Without taking her eyes from the precious note Annjee fumbled in her apron and found a coin. "Take it and go on!" she said.

It was a dime. Sandy skipped around the house and down the street in the chilly sunshine. He decided to stop at Buster's for a while before going home, since he had to pass there anyway, and he found his friend in the house trying to carve boats from clothes-pins with a rusty jack-knife.

Buster's mother was a seamstress, and, after opening the front door and greeting Sandy with a cheery "Hello," she returned to her machine and a friend who was calling on her. She was a tall young light-mulatto woman, with skin like old ivory. Maybe that was why Buster was so white. But her husband was a black man who worked on the city's garbage-trucks and was active politically when election time came, getting colored men to vote Republican. Everybody said he made lots of money, but that he wasn't really Buster's father.

The golden-haired child gave Sandy a butcher-knife and together they whacked at the clothes-pins. You could hear the two women talking plainly in the little sewing-room, where the machine ran between snatches of conversation.

"Yes," Buster's mother was saying, "I have the hardest time keeping that boy colored! He goes on just like he was white. Do you know what he did last week? Cut all the blossoms off my geranium plants here in the house, took them to school, and gave them to Dorothy Marlow, in his grade. And you know who Dorothy is, don't you? Senator Marlow's daughter! . . . I said: 'Buster, if you ever cut my flowers to carry to any little girl again, I'll punish you severely, but if you cut them to carry to little white girls, I don't know what I'll do with you. . . . Don't you know they hang colored boys for things like that?' I wanted to scare him—because you know there might be trouble even among kids in school over such things. . . . But I had to laugh."

Her friend laughed too. "He's a hot one, taking flowers to the women already, and a white girl at that! You've got a fast-working son, Elvira, I must say. . . . But, do you know, when you first moved here and I saw you and the boy going in and out, I thought sure you were both white folks. I didn't know you was colored till my husband said: 'That's Eddie's wife!' You-all sure looked white to me."

The machine started to whir, making the conversation inaudible for a few minutes, and when Sandy caught their words again, they were talking about the Elks' club-house that the colored people were planning to build.

"Can you go out?" Sandy demanded of Buster, since they were making no headway with the tough clothes-pins and dull knives.

"Maybe," said Buster. "I'll go see." And he went into the other room and asked his mother.

"Put on your overcoat," she commanded. "It's not summer yet. And be back in here before dark."

"All right, Vira," the child said.

The two children went to Mrs. Rumford's shop on the corner and bought three cents' worth of candy and seven cents' worth of peewees with which to play marbles when it got warm. Then Sandy walked back past Buster's house with him and they played for a while in the street before Sandy turned to run home.

Aunt Hager was making mush for supper. She sent him to the store for a pint bottle of milk as soon as he arrived, but he forgot to take the bottle and had to come back for it.

"You'd forget yo' head if it wasn't tied to you!" the old woman reminded him.

They were just finishing supper when Annjee got home with two chocolate éclairs in her coat-pocket, mashed together against Jimboy's letter.

"Huh! I'm crazy!" she said, running her hand down into the sticky mess. "But listen, ma! He's got a job and is doing well in Detroit, Jimboy says. . . . And I'm going to him!"

"You what?" Hager gasped, dropping her spoon in her mush-bowl. "What you sayin'?"

"I said I'm going to him, ma! I got to!" Annjee stood with her coat and hat still on, holding the sticky letter. "I'm going where my heart is, ma! . . . Oh, not today." She put her arms around her mother's neck. "I don't mean today, mama, nor next week. I got to save some money first. I only got a little now. But I mean I'm going to him soon's I can. I can't help it, ma—I love him!"

"Lawd, is you foolish?" cried Hager. "What's you gwine do with this chile, trapesin' round after Jimboy? What you gwine do if he leaves you in Detroiter or wherever he are? What you gwine do then? You loves him! Huh!"

"But he ain't gonna leave me in Detroit, 'cause I'm going with him everywhere he goes," she said, her eyes shining. "He ain't gonna leave me no more!"

"An' Sandy?"

"Couldn't he stay with you, mama? And then maybe we'd come back here and live, Jimboy and me, some time, when we get a little money ahead, and could pay off the mortgage on the house. . . . But there ain't no use arguing, mama, I got to go!"

Hager had never seen Annjee so positive before; she sat speechless, looking at the bowl of mush.

"I got to go where it ain't lonesome and where I ain't

unhappy—and that's where Jimboy is! I got to go soon as I can."

Hager rose to put some water on the stove to heat for the dishes.

"One by one you leaves me—Tempy, then Harriett, then you," she said. "But Sandy's gonna stick by me, ain't you, son? He ain't gwine leave his grandma."

The youngster looked at Hager, moving slowly about the kitchen putting away the supper things.

"And I's gwine to make a fine man out o' you, Sandy. I's gwine raise one chile right yet, if de Lawd lets me live—just one chile right!" she murmured.

That night the March wind began to blow and the window-panes rattled. Sandy woke up in the dark, lying close and warm beside his mother. When he went back to sleep again, he dreamed that his Aunt Tempy's Christmas book had been turned into a chariot, and that he was riding through the sky with Tempy standing very dignifiedly beside him as he drove. And he couldn't see anybody down on earth, not even Hager.

When his mother rolled out at six o'clock to go to work, he woke up again, and while she dressed, he lay watching his breath curl mistily upwards in the cold room. Outside the window it was bleak and grey and the March wind, humming through the leafless branches of the trees, blew terrifically. He heard Aunt Hager in the kitchen poking at the stove, making up a blaze to start the coffee boiling. Then the front door closed when his mother went out and, as the door slammed, the wind howled fiercely. It was nice and warm in bed, so he lay under the heavy quilts half dreaming, half thinking, until his grandmother shook him to get up. And many were the queer, dream-drowsy thoughts that floated through his mind —not only that morning, but almost every morning while he lay beneath the warm quilts until Hager had called him three or four times to get ready for school.

He wondered sometimes whether if he washed and washed his face and hands, he would ever be white. Someone had told him once that blackness was only skin-deep. . . . And would he ever have a big house with electric lights in it, like his Aunt Tempy—but it was mostly white people who had such fine things, and they were mean to colored. . . . Some white folks were nice, though. Earl was nice at school, but not the little boys across the street, who called him "nigger" every day . . . and not Mrs. Rice, who scolded his mother. . . . Aunt Harrie didn't like any white folks at all. . . . But Jesus was white and wore a long, white robe, like a woman's, on the Sunday-school cards. . . . Once Jimmie Lane said: "God damn Jesus" when the teacher scolded him for not knowing his Bible lesson. He said it out loud in church, too, and the church didn't fall down on him, as Sandy thought it might. . . . Grandma said it was a sin to cuss and swear, but all the fellows at school swore—and Jimboy did, too. But every time Sandy said "God damn," he felt bad, because Aunt Hager said God was mighty good and it was wrong to take His name in vain. But he would like to learn to say "God damn" without feeling anything like most boys said it—just "God damn! . . . God damn! . . . God damn!" without being ashamed of himself. . . . The Lord never seemed to notice, anyhow. . . . And when he got big, he wanted to travel like Jimboy. He wanted to be a railroad engineer, but Harriett had said there weren't any colored engineers on trains. . . . What would he be, then? Maybe a doctor; but it was more fun being an engineer and travelling far away.

Sandy wished Annjee would take him with her when she went to join Jimboy—but then Aunt Hager would be all by herself, and grandma was so nice to him he would hate to leave her alone. Who would cut wood for her then? . . . But when he got big, he would go to Detroit. And maybe New York, too, where his geography said they had the tallest buildings in the world, and trains that ran under the river. . . . He wondered if there were any colored people in New York. . . . How ugly African colored folks looked in the geography—with bushy heads and wild eyes! Aunt Hager said her mother was an African, but she wasn't ugly and wild; neither was Aunt Hager; neither was little dark Willie-Mae, and they were all black like Africans. . . . And Reverend Braswell was as black as ink, but he knew God. . . . God didn't care if people were black, did He? . . . What was God? Was He a man or a lamb or what? Buster's mother said God was a light, but Aunt Hager said He was a King and had a throne and wore a crown—she intended to sit down by His side by and by. . . . Was Buster's father white? Buster was white and colored both. But he didn't look like he was colored. What made Buster not colored? . . . And what made girls different from boys? . . . Once when they were playing house, Willie-Mae told him how girls were different from boys, but they didn't know why. Now Willie-Mae was in the seventh grade and had hard little breasts that stuck out sharp-like, and Jimmy Lane said dirty things about Willie-Mae. . . . Once he asked his mother what his navel was for and she said, "Layovers to catch meddlers." What did that mean? . . . And how come ladies got sick and stayed in bed when they had babies? Where did babies come from, anyhow? Not from storks—a fairy-story like Santa Claus. . . . Did God love people who told fairy-stories and lied to kids about storks and Santa Claus? . . . Santa Claus was no good, anyhow! God damn Santa Claus for not bringing him the sled he wanted Christmas! It was all a lie about Santa Claus!

The sound of Hager pouring coal on the fire and dragging her wash-tubs across the kitchen-floor to get ready for work broke in on Sandy's drowsy half-dreams, and as he rolled over in bed, his grandmother, hearing the springs creak, called loudly: "You Sandy! Get up from there! It's seven and past! You want to be late gettin' to yo' school?"

"Yes'm, I'm coming, grandma!" he said under the quilts. "But it's cold in here."

"You knows you don't dress in yonder! Bring them clothes on out behind this stove, sir."

"Yes'm." So with a kick of the feet his covers went flying back and Sandy ran to the warmth of the little kitchen, where he dressed, washed, and ate. Then he yelled for Willie-Mae—when he felt like it—or else went on to school without her, joining some of the boys on the way.

So spring was coming and Annjee worked diligently at Mrs. Rice's day after day. Often she did something extra for Mrs. Rice's sister and her children—pressed a shirtwaist or ironed some stockings—and so added a few quarters or maybe even a dollar to her weekly wages, all of which she saved to help carry her to Jimboy in Detroit.

For ten years she had been cooking, washing, ironing, scrubbing—and for what? For only the few weeks in a year, or a half-year, when Jimboy would come home from some strange place and take her in his strong arms and kiss her and murmur: "Annjee, baby!" That's what she had been working for—then the dreary months were as nothing, and the hard years faded away. But now he had been gone all winter, and, from his letter, he might not come back soon, because he said Detroit was a fine place for colored folks. . . . But Stanton—well, Annjee thought there must surely be better towns, where a woman wouldn't have to work so hard to live. . . . And where Jimboy was.

So before the first buds opened on the apple-tree in the back yard, Annjee had gone to Detroit, leaving Sandy behind with his grandmother. And when the apple blossoms came in full bloom, there was no one living in the little house but a grey-headed old woman and her grandchild.

"One by one they leaves you," Hager said slowly. "One by one yo' chillen goes."

# SIXTEEN

## *Nothing but Love*

"A YEAR ago tonight was de storm what blowed ma porch away! You 'members, honey? . . . Done seem like this year took more'n ma porch, too. My baby chile's left home an' gone to stay down yonder in de Bottoms with them triflin' Smothers family, where de piano's goin' night an' day. An' yo' mammy's done gone a-trapesin' after Jimboy. . . . Well, I thanks de Lawd you ain't gone too. You's mighty little an' knee-high to a duck, but you's ma stand-by. You's all I got, an' you ain't gwine leave yo' old grandma, is you?"

Hager had turned to Sandy in these lonely days for comfort and companionship. Through the long summer evenings they sat together on the front porch and she told her grandchild stories. Sometimes Sister Johnson came over and sat with them for a while smoking. Sometimes Madam de Carter, full of chatter and big words about the lodge and the race, would be there. But more often the two were alone—the black wash-woman with the grey hair and the little brown boy. Slavery-time stories, myths, folk-tales like the Rabbit and the Tar Baby; the war, Abe Lincoln, freedom; visions of the Lord; years of faith and labor, love and struggle filled Aunt Hager's talk of a summer night, while the lightning-bugs glowed and glimmered and the katydids chirruped, and the stars sparkled in the far-off heavens.

Sandy was getting to be too big a boy to sit in his grandmother's lap and be rocked to sleep as in summers gone by; now he sat on a little stool beside her, leaning his head on her legs when he was tired. Or else he lay flat on the floor of the porch listening, and looking up at the stars. Tonight Hager talked about love.

"These young ones what's comin' up now, they calls us ole fogies, an' handkerchief heads, an' white folks' niggers 'cause we don't get mad an' rar' up in arms like they does 'cause things is kinder hard, but, honey, when you gets old, you knows they

128

ain't no sense in gettin' mad an' sourin' yo' soul with hatin' peoples. White folks is white folks, an' colored folks is colored, an' neither one of 'em is bad as t'other make out. For mighty nigh seventy years I been knowin' both of 'em, an' I ain't never had no room in ma heart to hate neither white nor colored. When you starts hatin' people, you gets uglier than they is—an' I ain't never had no time for ugliness, 'cause that's where de devil comes in—in ugliness!

"They talks 'bout slavery time an' they makes out now like it were de most awfullest time what ever was, but don't you believe it, chile, 'cause it weren't all that bad. Some o' de white folks was just as nice to their niggers as they could be, nicer than many of 'em is now, what makes 'em work for less than they needs to eat. An' in those days they had to feed 'em. An' they ain't every white man beat his slaves neither! Course I ain't sayin' 'twas no paradise, but I ain't going to say it were no hell either. An' maybe I's kinder seein' it on de bestest side 'cause I worked in de big house an' ain't never went to de fields like most o' de niggers did. Ma mammy were de big-house cook an' I grewed up right with her in de kitchen an' played with little Miss Jeanne. An' Miss Jeanne taught me to read what little I knowed. An' when she growed up an' I growed up, she kept me with her like her friend all de time. I loved her an' she loved me. Miss Jeanne were de mistress' daughter, but warn't no difference 'tween us 'ceptin' she called me Hager an' I called her Miss Jeanne. But what difference do one word like 'Miss' make in yo' heart? None, chile, none. De words don't make no difference if de love's there.

"I disremembers what year it were de war broke out, but white folks was scared, an' niggers, too. Didn't know what might happen. An' we heard talk o' Abraham Lincoln 'way down yonder in de South. An' de ole marster, ole man Winfield, took his gun an' went to war, an' de young son, too, an' de superintender and de overseer—all of 'em gone to follow Lee. Ain't left nothin' but womens an' niggers on de plantation. De womens was a-cryin' an' de niggers was, too, 'cause they was sorry for de po' grievin' white folks.

"Is I ever told you how Miss Jeanne an' Marster Robert was married in de springtime o' de war, with de magnolias all a-bloomin' like candles for they weddin'? Is I ever told you,

Sandy? . . . Well, I must some time. An' then Marster Robert had to go right off with his mens, 'cause he's a high officer in de army an' they heard Sherman were comin'. An' he left her a-standin' with her weddin'-clothes on, leanin' 'gainst a pillar o' de big white porch, with nobody but me to dry her eyes—ole Missis done dead an' de men-folks all gone to war. An' nobody in that big whole mansion but black ole deaf Aunt Granny Jones, what kept de house straight, an' me, what was stayin' with ma mistress.

"O, de white folks needed niggers then mo'n they ever did befo', an' they ain't a colored person what didn't stick by 'em when all they men-folks were gone an' de white womens was a-cryin' an' a-faintin' like they did in them days.

"But lemme tell you 'bout Miss Jeanne. She just set in her room an' cry. A-holdin' Marster Bob's pitcher, she set an' cry, an' she ain't come out o' her room to see 'bout nothin'—house, horses, cotton—nothin'. But de niggers, they ain't cheat her nor steal from her. An' come de news dat her brother done got wounded an' died in Virginia, an' her cousins got de yaller fever. Then come de news that Marster Robert, Miss Jeanne's husband, ain't no mo'! Killed in de battle! An' I thought Miss Jeanne would like to go crazy. De news say he died like a soldier, brave an' fightin'. But when she heard it, she went to de drawer an' got out her weddin'-veil an' took her flowers in her hands like she were goin' to de altar to meet de groom. Then she just sink in de flo' an' cry till I pick her up an' hold her like a chile.

"Well, de freedom come, an' all de niggers scatter like buckshot, goin' to live in town. An' de yard niggers say I's a ole fool! I's free now—why don't I come with them? But I say no, I's gwine stay with Miss Jeanne—an' I stayed. I 'lowed ain't nary one o' them colored folks needed me like Miss Jeanne did, so I ain't went with 'em.

"An' de time pass; it pass an' it pass, an' de ole house get rusty for lack o' paint, an' de things, they 'gin to fall to pieces. An' Miss Jeanne say: 'Hager, I ain't got nobody in de world but you.' An' I say: 'Miss Jeanne, I ain't got nobody in de world but you neither.'

"And then she'd start talkin' 'bout her young husband what died so handsome an' brave, what ain't even had time that last

day fo' to 'scort her to de church for de weddin', nor to hold
her in his arms 'fore de orders come to leave. An' we would set
on de big high ole porch, with its tall stone pillars, in de evenin's
twilight till de bats start flyin' overhead an' de sunset glow
done gone, she in her wide white skirts a-billowin' round her
slender waist, an' me in ma apron an' cap an' this here chain
she gimme you see on ma neck all de time an' what's done
wore so thin.

"They was a ole stump of a blasted tree in de yard front o'
de porch 'bout tall as a man, with two black pieces o' branches
raised up like arms in de air. We used to set an' look at it, an'
Miss Jeanne could see it from her bedroom winder upstairs,
an' sometimes this stump, it look like it were movin' right up
de path like a man.

"After she done gone to bed, late one springtime night when
de moon were shinin', I hear Miss Jeanne a-cryin': 'He's come!
. . . Hager, ma Robert's come back to me!' An' I jumped out
o' ma bed in de next room where I were sleepin' an' run in to
her, an' there she was in her long, white night-clothes standin'
out in de moonlight on de little balcony, high up in de middle
o' that big stone porch. She was lookin' down into de yard at
this stump of a tree a-holdin' up its arms. An' she thinks it's
Marster Robert a-callin' her. She thinks he's standin' there in
his uniform, come back from de war, a-callin' her. An' she say:
'I'm comin', Bob, dear'; . . . I can hear her now. . . . She
say: 'I'm comin'!' . . . An' 'fore I think what she's doin', Miss
Jeanne done stepped over de little rail o' de balcony like she
were walkin' on moonlight. An' she say: 'I'm comin', Bob!'

"She ain't left no will, so de house an' all went to de State,
an' I been left with nothin'. But I ain't care 'bout that. I followed her to de grave, an' I been with her all de time, 'cause
she's ma friend. An' I were sorry for her, 'cause I knowed that
love were painin' her soul, an' warn't nobody left to help her
but me.

"An' since then I's met many a white lady an' many a white
gentleman, an' some of 'em's been kind to me an' some of 'em
ain't; some of 'em's cussed me an' wouldn't pay me fo' ma
work; an' some of 'em's hurted me awful. But I's been sorry fo'
white folks, fo' I knows something inside must be aggravatin'
de po' souls. An' I's kept a room in ma heart fo' 'em, 'cause

white folks needs us, honey, even if they don't know it. They's like spoilt chillens what's got too much o' ever'thing—an' they needs us niggers, what ain't got nothin'.

"I's been livin' a long time in yesterday, Sandy chile, an' I knows there ain't no room in de world fo' nothin' mo'n love. I knows, chile! Ever'thing there is but lovin' leaves a rust on yo' soul. An' to love sho 'nough, you got to have a spot in yo' heart fo' ever'body—great an' small, white an' black, an' them what's good an' them what's evil—'cause love ain't got no crowded-out places where de good ones stays an' de bad ones can't come in. When it gets that way, then it ain't love.

"White peoples maybe mistreats you an' hates you, but when you hates 'em back, you's de one what's hurted, 'cause hate makes yo' heart ugly—that's all it does. It closes up de sweet door to life an' makes ever'thing small an' mean an' dirty. Honey, there ain't no room in de world fo' hate, white folks hatin' niggers, an' niggers hatin' white folks. There ain't no room in this world fo' nothin' but love, Sandy chile. That's all they's room fo'—nothin' but love."

# SEVENTEEN

# Barber–Shop

M R. LOGAN, hearing that Aunt Hager had an empty room
since all her daughters were gone, sent her one evening
a new-comer in town looking for a place to stay. His name was
Wim Dogberry and he was a brickmason and hod-carrier, a
tall, quiet, stoop-shouldered black man, neither old nor young.
He took, for two dollars and a half a week, the room that had
been Annjee's, and Hager gave him a key to the front door.

Wim Dogberry was carrying hod then on a new moving-
picture theatre that was being built. He rose early and came in
late, face, hands, and overalls covered with mortar dust. He
washed in a tin basin by the pump and went to bed, and about
all he ever said to Aunt Hager and Sandy was "Good-mornin' "
and "Good-evenin'," and maybe a stumbling "How is you?"
But on Sunday mornings Hager usually asked him to breakfast
if he got up on time—for on Saturday nights Wim drank licker
and came home mumbling to himself a little later than on a
week-day evenings, so sometimes he would sleep until noon
Sundays.

One Saturday night he wet the bed, and when Hager went
to make it up on the Sabbath morning, she found a damp yellow spot in the middle. Of this act Dogberry was so ashamed
that he did not even say "Good-mornin'" for several days, and
if, from the corner, he saw Aunt Hager and her grandson sitting on the porch in the twilight when he came towards home,
he would pass his street and walk until he thought they had
gone inside to bed. But he was a quiet roomer, he didn't give
anyone any trouble, and he paid regularly. And since Hager
was in no position to despise two dollars and a half every week,
she rather liked Dogberry.

Now Hager kept the growing Sandy close by her all the time
to help her while she washed and ironed and to talk to her
while she sat on the porch in the evenings. Of course, he played
sometimes in his own yard whenever Willie-Mae or Buster or,

on Sundays, Jimmie Lane came to the house. But Jimmie Lane was running wild since his mother died, and Hager didn't like him to visit her grandson any more. He was bad.

When Sandy wanted to go to the vacant lot to play baseball with the neighbor boys, his grandmother would usually not allow him to leave her. "Stay here, sir, with Hager. I needs you to pump ma water fo' me an' fill up these tubs," she would say. Or else she would yell: "Ain't I told you you might get hurt down there with them old rough white boys? Stay here in yo' own yard, where you can keep out o' mischief."

So he grew accustomed to remaining near his grandmother, and at night, when the other children would be playing duck-on-the-rock under the arc-light at the corner, he would be sitting on the front porch listening to Aunt Hager telling her tales of slavery and talking of her own far-off youth. When school opened in the fall, the old woman said: "I don't know what I's gwine do all day without you, Sandy. You sho been company to me, with all my own chillens gone." But Sandy was glad to get back to a roomful of boys and girls again.

One Indian-summer afternoon when Aunt Hager was hanging up clothes in the back yard while the boy held the basket of clothes-pins, old man Logan drove past on his rickety trash-wagon and bowed elaborately to Hager. She went to the back fence to joke and gossip with him as usual, while his white mule switched off persistent flies with her tail.

Before the old beau drove away, he said: "Say, Hager, does you want that there young one o' your'n to work? I knows a little job he can have if you does," pointing to Sandy.

"What'll he got to do?" demanded Hager.

"Well, Pete Scott say he need a boy down yonder at de barber-shop on Saturdays to kinder clean up where de kinks fall, an' shine shoes fo' de customers. Ain't nothin' hard 'bout it, an' I was thinkin' it would just 'bout be Sandy's size. He could make a few pennies ever' week to kinder help things 'long."

"True, he sho could," said Hager. "I'll have him go see Pete."

So Sandy went to see Mr. Peter Scott at the colored barber-shop on Pearl Street that evening and was given his first regular job. Every Saturday, which was the barber-shop's only busy day, when the working-men got paid off, Sandy went on the job at noon and worked until eight or nine in the evening. His duties were to keep the place swept clean of the hair that the three barbers sheared and to shine the shoes of any customer who might ask for a shine. Only a few customers permitted themselves that last luxury, for many of them came to the shop in their working-shoes, covered with mud or lime, and most of them shined their own boots at home on Sunday mornings before church. But occasionally Cudge Windsor, who owned a pool hall, or some of the dressed-up bootleggers, might climb on the stand and permit their shoes to be cleaned by the brown youngster, who asked shyly: "Shine, mister?"

The barber-shop was a new world to Sandy, who had lived thus far tied to Aunt Hager's apron-strings. He was a dreamy-eyed boy who had grown to his present age largely under the dominant influence of women—Annjee, Harriett, his grand-mother—because Jimboy had been so seldom home. But the barber-shop then was a man's world, and, on Saturdays, while a dozen or more big laborers awaited their turns, the place was filled with loud man-talk and smoke and laughter. Baseball, Jack Johnson, racehorses, white folks, Teddy Roosevelt, local gossip, Booker Washington, women, labor prospects in Topeka, Kansas City, Omaha, religion, politics, women, God—discussions and arguments all afternoon and far up into the night, while crisp kinks rolled to the floor, cigarette and cigar-butts were thrown on the hearth of the monkey-stove, and Sandy called out: "Shine, mister?"

Sometimes the boy earned one or two dollars from shines, but on damp or snowy days he might not make anything except the fifty cents Pete Scott paid him for sweeping up. Or perhaps one of the barbers, too busy to go out for supper, would send Sandy for a sandwich and a bottle of milk, and thus he would make an extra nickel or dime.

The patrons liked him and often kidded him about his sandy hair. "Boy, you's too dark to have hair like that. Ain't nobody but white folks s'posed to have sandy-colored hair. An' your'n's nappy at that!" Then Sandy would blush with embarrassment —if the change from a dry chocolate to a damp chocolate can be called a blush, as he grew warm and perspired—because he didn't like to be kidded about his hair. And he hadn't been around uncouth fellows long enough to learn the protective art of turning back a joke. He had discovered already, though, that so-called jokes are often not really jokes at all, but rather unpleasant realities that hurt unless you can think of something equally funny and unpleasant to say in return. But the men who patronized Pete Scott's barber-shop seldom grew angry at the hard pleasantries that passed for humor, and they could play the dozens for hours without anger, unless the parties concerned became serious, when they were invited to take it on the outside. And even at that a fight was fun, too.

After a winter of Saturday nights at Pete's shop Sandy himself became pretty adept at "kidding"; but at first he was timid about it and afraid to joke with grown-up people, or to give smart answers to strangers when they teased him about his crinkly, sand-colored head. One day, however, one of the barbers gave him a tin of Madam Walker's and told him: "Lay that hair down an' stop these niggers from laughin' at you." Sandy took his advice.

Madam Walker's—a thick yellow pomade—and a good wetting with water proved most efficacious to the boy's hair, when aided with a stocking cap—the top of a woman's stocking cut off and tied in a knot at one end so as to fit tightly over one's head, pressing the hair smooth. Thereafter Sandy appeared with his hair slick and shiny. And the salve and water together made it seem a dark brown, just the color of his skin, instead of the peculiar sandy tint it possessed in its natural state. Besides he soon advanced far enough in the art of "kidding" to say: "So's your pa's," to people who informed him that his head was nappy.

During the autumn Harriett had been home once to see her mother and had said that she was working as chambermaid with Maudel at the hotel. But in the barber-shop that winter Sandy often heard his aunt's name mentioned in less proper connections. Sometimes the boy pretended not to hear, and if Pete Scott was there, he always stopped the men from talking.

"Tired o' all this nasty talk 'bout women in ma shop," he said one Saturday night. "Some o' you men better look after your own womenfolks if you got any."

"Aw, all de womens in de world ain't worth two cents to me," said a waiter sitting in the middle chair, his face covered with lather. "I don't respect no woman but my mother."

"An' neither do I," answered Greensbury Jones. "All of em's evil, specially if they's black an' got blue gums."

"I's done told you to hush," said Pete Scott behind the first chair, where he was clipping Jap Logan's hair. "Ma wife's black herself, so don't start talkin' 'bout no blue gums! I's tired o' this here female talk anyhow. This is ma shop, an' ma razors sho can cut somethin' else 'sides hair—so now just keep on talkin' 'bout blue gums!"

"I see where Bryant's runnin' for president agin," said Greensbury Jones.

But one Saturday, while the proprietor was out to snatch a bite to eat, a discussion came up as to who was the prettiest colored girl in town. Was she yellow, high-brown, chocolate, or black? Of course, there was no agreement, but names were mentioned and qualities were described. One girl had eyes like Eve herself; another had hips like Miss Cleopatra; one smooth brown-skin had legs like—like—like—

"Aw, man! De Statue of Liberty!" somebody suggested when the name of a famous beauty failed the speaker's memory.

"But, feller, there ain't nothin' in all them rainbow shades," a young teamster argued against Uncle Dan Givens, who preferred high yellows. "Gimme a cool black gal ever' time! They's too dark to fade—and when they are good-looking, I mean they *are* good-looking! I'm talkin' 'bout Harrietta Williams, too! That's who I mean! Now, find a better-looking gal than she is!"

"I admits Harrietta's all right," said the old man; "all right to look at but—sput-t-tsss!" He spat contemptuously at the stove.

"O, I know that!" said the teamster; "but I ain't talkin' 'bout what she is! I'm talkin' 'bout how she looks. An' a songster out o' this world don't care if she is a—!"

"S-s-s-sh! Soft-pedal it brother." One of the men nudged the speaker. "There's one o' the Williamses right here—that kid over yonder shinin' shoes's Harriett's nephew or somethin' 'nother."

"You niggers talks too free, anyhow," one of the barbers added. "Somebody gwine cut your lips off some o' these days. De idee o' ole Uncle Dan Givens' arguin' 'bout women and he done got whiskers all round his head like a wore-out cheese."

"That's all right, you young whip-snapper," squeaked Uncle

Dan heatedly. "Might have whiskers round ma head, but I ain't
wore out!"

Laughter and smoke filled the little shop, while the winter
wind blew sleet against the big plate-glass window and whistled
through the cracks in the doorway, making the gas lights flicker
overhead. Sandy smacked his polishing cloth on the toes of a
gleaming pair of brown button shoes belonging to a stranger
in town, then looked up with a grin and said: "Yes, sir!" as the
man handed him a quarter.

"Keep the change," said the new-comer grandly.

"That guy's an actor," one of the barbers said when the man
went out. "He's playin' with the *Smart Set* at the Opery House
tonight. I bet the top gallery'll be full o' niggers sence it's a jig
show, but I ain't goin' anear there myself to be Jim-Crowed,
cause I don't believe in goin' nowhere I ain't allowed to set
with the rest of the folks. If I can't be the table-cloth, I won't
be the dish-rag—that's my motto. And if I can't buy the seats I
want at a show, I sure God can keep my change!"

"Yes, and miss all the good shows," countered a little red-
eyed porter. "Just as well say if you can't eat in a restaurant
where white folks eat, you ain't gonna eat."

"Anybody want a shine?" yelled Sandy above the racket.
"And if you don't want a shine, stay out of my chair and do
your arguing on the floor!"

A brown-skin chorus girl, on her way to the theatre, stepped
into the shop and asked if she could buy a *Chicago Defender*
there. The barber directed her to the colored restaurant, while
all the men immediately stopped talking to stare at her until
she went out.

"Whew! . . . Some legs!" the teamster cried as the door
closed on a vision of silk stockings. "How'd you like to shine
that long, sweet brown-skin mama's shoes, boy?"

"She wouldn't have to pay me!" said Sandy.

"Whoopee! Gallery or no gallery," shouted Jap Logan, "I'm
gonna see that show! Don't care if they do Jim-Crow niggers
in the white folks' Opery House!"

"Yes," muttered one of the barbers, "that's just what's the
matter now—you ain't got no race-pride! You niggers ain't got
no shame!"

# EIGHTEEN

# *Children's Day*

WHEN Easter came that spring, Sandy had saved enough money to buy himself a suit and a new cap from his earnings at the barber-shop. He was very proud of this accomplishment and so was Aunt Hager.

"You's a 'dustrious chile, sho is! Gwine make a smart man even if yo' daddy warn't nothin'. Gwine get ahead an' do good fo' yo'self an' de race, yes, sir!"

The spring came early and the clear balmy days found Hager's back yard billowing with clean white clothes on lines in the sun. Her roomer had left her when the theatre was built and had gone to work on a dam somewhere up the river, so Annjee's room was empty again. Sandy had slept with his grandmother during the cold weather, but in summer he slept on a pallet.

The boy did not miss his mother. When she had been home, Annjee had worked out all day, and she was quiet at night because she was always tired. Harriett had been the one to keep the fun and laughter going—Harriett and Jimboy, whenever he was in town. Sandy wished Harrie would live at home instead of staying at Maudel's house, but he never said anything about it to his grandmother. He went to school regularly, went to work at the barber-shop on Saturdays and to Sunday-School on Sundays, and remained with Aunt Hager the rest of his time. She was always worried if she didn't know where he was.

"Colored boys, when they gets round twelve an' thirteen, they gets so bad, Sandy," she would say. "I wants you to stay nice an' make something out o' yo'self If Hager lives, she ain't gonna see you go down. She's gonna make a fine man out o' you fo' de glory o' God an' de black race. You gwine to 'mount to something in this world. You hear me?"

Sandy did hear her, and he knew what she meant. She meant a man like Booker T. Washington, or Frederick Douglass, or like Paul Lawrence Dunbar, who did poetry-writing. Or maybe

Jack Johnson. But Hager said Jack Johnson was the devil's kind of greatness, not God's.

"That's what you get from workin' round that old barber-shop where all they talks 'bout is prize-fightin' an' hossracin'. Jack Johnson done married a white woman, anyhow! What he care 'bout de race?"

The little boy wondered if Jack Johnson's kids looked like Buster. But maybe he didn't have any kids. He must ask Pete Scott about that when he went back to work on Saturday.

In the summer a new amusement park opened in Stanton, the first of its kind in the city, with a merry-go-round, a shoot-the-shoots, a Ferris wheel, a dance-hall, and a bandstand for week-end concerts. In order to help popularize the park, which was far on the north edge of town, the *Daily Leader* announced, under its auspices, what was called a Free Children's Day Party open to all the readers of that paper who clipped the coupons published in each issue. On July 26 these coupons, presented at the gate, would entitle every child in Stanton to free admittance to the park, free popcorn, free lemonade, and one ride on each of the amusement attractions—the merry-go-round, the shoot-the-shoots, and the Ferris wheel. All you had to do was to be a reader of the *Daily Leader* and present the coupons cut from that paper.

Aunt Hager and Sister Johnson both took the *Leader* regularly, as did almost everybody else in Stanton, so Sandy and Willie-Mae started to clip coupons. All the children in the neighborhood were doing the same thing. The Children's Day would be a big event for all the little people in town. None of them had ever seen a shoot-the-shoots before, a contrivance that pulled little cars full of folks high into the air and then let them come whizzing down an incline into an artificial pond, where the cars would float like boats. Sandy and Willie-Mae looked forward to thrill after thrill.

When the afternoon of the great day came at last, Willie-Mae stopped for Sandy, dressed in her whitest white dress and her new patent-leather shoes, which hurt her feet awfully. Sandy's grandmother was making him wash his ears when she came in.

"You gwine out yonder 'mongst all them white chillens, I wants you to at least look clean!" said Hager.

They started out.

"Here!" called Aunt Hager. "Ain't you gwine to take yo' coupons?" In his rush to get away, Sandy had forgotten them.

It was a long walk to the park, and Willie-Mae stopped and took off her shoes and stockings and carried them in her hands until she got near the gate; then she put them on again and limped bravely along, clutching her precious bits of newspaper. They could hear the band playing and children shouting and squealing as the cars on the shoot-the-shoots shot downward with a splash into the pond. They could see the giant Ferris wheel, larger than the one the carnival had had, circling high in the air.

"I'm gonna ride on that first," said Sandy.

There were crowds of children under the bright red and white wooden shelter at the park entrance. They were lining up at the gate—laughing, merry, clean little white children, pushing and yelling and giggling amiably. Sandy let Willie-Mae go first and he got in line behind her. The band was playing gaily inside. . . . They were almost to the entrance now. . . . There were just two boys in front of them. . . . Willie-Mae held out her black little hand clutching the coupons. They moved forward. The man looked down.

"Sorry," he said. "This party's for white kids."

Willie-Mae did not understand. She stood holding out the coupons, waiting for the tall white man to take them.

"Stand back, you two," he said, looking at Sandy as well. "I told you little darkies this wasn't your party. . . . Come on—next little girl." And the line of white children pushed past Willie-Mae and Sandy, going into the park. Stunned, the two dark ones drew aside. Then they noticed a group of a dozen or more other colored youngsters standing apart in the sun, just without the bright entrance pavilion, and among them was Sadie Butler, Sandy's class-mate. Three or four of the colored children were crying, but most of them looked sullen and angry, and some of them had turned to go home.

"My papa takes the *Leader*," Sadie Butler was saying. "And you see what it says here on the coupons, too—'Free Admittance to Every Child in Stanton.' Can't you read it, Sandy?"

"Sure, I can read it, but I guess they didn't mean colored," he answered, as the boy watched the white children going in the gate. "They wouldn't let us in."

Willie-Mae, between the painful shoes and the hurt of her disappointment, was on the verge of tears. One of the small boys in the crowd, a hard-looking little fellow from Pearl Street, was cursing childishly.

"God damn old sons of biscuit-eaters, that what they are! I wish I was a big man, dog-gone, I'd shoot 'em all, that's what I'd do!"

"I suppose they didn't mean colored kids," said Sandy again.

"Buster went in all right," said Sadie. "I seen him. But they didn't know he was colored, I guess. When I went up to the gate, the man said: 'Whoa! Where you goin'?' just like I was a horse. . . . I'm going home now and tell my papa."

She walked away, followed by five or six other little girls in their Sunday dresses. Willie-Mae was sitting on the ground taking off her shoes again, sweat and tears running down her black cheeks. Sandy saw his white schoolmate, Earl, approaching.

"What's matter, Sandy? Ain't you goin' in?" Earl demanded, looking at his friend's worried face. "Did the little girl hurt her foot?"

"No," said Sandy. "We just ain't going in. . . . Here, Earl, you can have my coupons. If you have extra ones, the papers says you get more lemonade . . . so you take 'em."

The white boy, puzzled, accepted the proffered coupons, stood dumbly for a moment wondering what to say to his brown friend, then went on into the park.

"It's yo' party, white chile!" a little tan-skin girl called after him, mimicking the way the man at the gate had talked. "Whoa! Stay out! You's a nigger!" she said to Sandy.

The other children, in spite of themselves, laughed at the accuracy of her burlesque imitation. Then, with the music of the merry-go-round from beyond the high fence and the laughter of happy children following them, the group of dark-skinned ones started down the dusty road together—and to all the colored boys and girls they met on the way they called out, "Ain't no use, jigaboos! That party's for white folks!"

When Willie-Mae and Sandy got home and told their story, Sister Johnson was angry as a wet hen.

"Crackers is devils," she cried. "I 'spected as much! Dey ain't nary hell hot 'nough to burn ole white folks, 'cause dey's devils deyselves! De dirty hounds!"

But all Hager said was: "They's po' trash owns that park what don't know no better, hurtin' chillens' feelin's, but we'll forgive 'em! Don't fret yo'self, Sister Johnson. What good can frettin' do? Come on here, let's we have a party of our own." She went out in the yard and took a watermelon from a tub of well-water where it had been cooling and cut it into four juicy slices; then they sat down on the grass at the shady side of the house and ate, trying to forget about white folks.

"Don't you mind, Willie-Mae," Hager said to the little black girl, who was still crying. "You's colored, honey, an' you's liable to have a hard time in this life—but don't cry. . . . You Sandy, run round de house an' see didn't I heard de mail-man blowin'."

"Yes'm," said Sandy when he came back. "Was the mail-man, and I got a letter from mama." The boy sat on the grass to read it, anxious to see what Annjee said. And later, when the company had gone, he read it aloud to Hager.

Dear little Son:

How have you all been? how is grandma? I get worried about you when I do not hear. You know Aunt Hager is old and can't write much so you must do it for her because she is not used to adress letters and the last one was two weeks getting here and had went all around everywhere. Your father says tell you hello. I got a job in a boarding house for old white folks what are cranky about how they beds is made. There are white and colored here in the auto business and women to. Tell Madam de Carter I will send my Lodge dues back because I do not want to be transfer as I might come home sometime. I ain't seen you all now for more'n a year. Jimboy he keeps changing jobs from one thing to another but he likes this town pretty well. You know he broke his guitar carrying it in a crowded street car. Ma says you are growing and have bought yourself a new suit last Easter. Mama certainly does right well to keep on washing and ironing at her age and worrying with you besides. Tempy ought to help ma but seem like she don't think so. Do you ever see your Aunt Harrie? I hope she is settling down in her ways. If ma wasn't all by herself maybe I could send for you to come live with us in Detroit but maybe I will be home to see you if I ever get any money ahead. Rent is so high here I never wittnessed so many folks in one house, rooming five and six together, and nobody can save a dime. Are you still working at the barber shop. I heard Sister Johnson was under the weather but I couldn't make out from ma's scribbling what was the matter with her. Did she have a physicianer? You behave yourself with Willie-Mae because you are getting to be a big boy now and she is a girl older then you are. I am going to send you some pants next time I go down town but I get off from work so late I don't have a chance to do nothing and your father eats in the restaurant count of me not home to fix for him and I don't care where you go colored folks has a hard time. I want you to mind your grandma and help her work. She is too old to be straining at the pump drawing water to wash clothes with. Now write to me. Love to you all both and seven kisses XXXXXXX right here on the paper,

Your loving mother,<br>Annjelica Rogers

Sandy laughed at the clumsy cross-mark kisses. He was glad to get a letter from his mother, and word in it about Jimboy. And he was sorry his father had broken his guitar. But not even watermelon and the long letter could drive away his sick feeling about the park.

"I guess Kansas is getting like the South, isn't it, ma?" Sandy said to his grandmother as they came out on the porch that evening after supper. "They don't like us here either, do they?"

But Aunt Hager gave him no answer. In silence they watched the sunset fade from the sky. Slowly the evening star grew bright, and, looking at the stars, Hager began to sing, very softly at first:

> From this world o' trouble free,
>      Stars beyond!
>      Stars beyond!

And Sandy, as he stood beside his grandmother on the porch, heard a great chorus out of the black past—singing generations of toil-worn Negroes, echoing Hager's voice as it deepened and grew in volume:

> There's a star fo' you an' me,
>      Stars beyond!

# NINETEEN

## Ten Dollars and Costs

I N THE fall Sandy found a job that occupied him after school
hours, as well as on Saturday and Sunday. One afternoon at
the barber-shop, Charlie Nutter, a bell-hop who had come to
have his hair cut, asked Sandy to step outside a minute. Once
out of earshot of the barbers and loafers within, Charlie went
on: "Say, kid, I got some dope to buzz to yuh 'bout a job. Joe
Willis, the white guy what keeps the hotel where I work, is
lookin' for a boy to kinder sweep up around the lobby every
day, dust off, and sort o' help the bell-boys out sometimes.
Ain't nothin' hard attached to it, and yuh can bring 'long your
shine-box and rub up shoes in the lobby, too, if yuh wants to.
I though maybe yuh might like to have the job. Yuh'd make
more'n yuh do here. And more'n that, too, when yuh got on
to the ropes. Course yuh'd have to fix me up with a couple o'
bucks o' so for gettin' yuh the job, but if yuh want it, just
lemme know and I'll fix it with the boss. He tole me to start
lookin' for somebody and that's what I'm doin'." Charlie Nutter went on talking, without stopping to wait for an answer.
"Course a boy like you don't know nothin' 'bout hotel work,
but yuh ain't never too young to learn, and that's a nice easy
way to start. Yuh might work up to me some time, yuh never
can tell—head bell-hop! 'Cause I ain't gonna stay in this burg
all my life; I figger if I can hop bells here, I can hop bells in
Chicago or some place worth livin' at. But the tips ain't bad
down there at the Drummer's though—lots o' sportin' women
and folks like that what don't mind givin' yuh a quarter any
time. . . . And yuh can get well yourself once in a while.
What yuh say? Do yuh want it?"

Sandy thought quick. With Christmas not far off, his shoes
about worn out, and the desire to help Aunt Hager, too—"I
guess I better take it," he said. "But do I have to pay you
now?"

"Hell, naw, not now! I'll keep my eye on yuh, and yuh can
just slip me a little change now and then down to the hotel

when you start workin.' Other boy ain't quittin' nohow till next week. S'pose yuh come round there Sunday morning and I'll kinder show yuh what to do. And don't pay no mind to Willis when he hollers at yuh. He's all right—just got a hard way about him with the help, that's all—but he ain't a bad boss. I'll see yuh, then! Drop by Sunday and lemme know for sure. So long!"

But Aunt Hager was not much pleased when Sandy came home that night and she heard the news. "I ain't never wanted none o' my chillens to work in no ole hotels," she said. "They's evil, full o' nastiness, an' you don't learn nothin' good in 'em. I don't want you to go there, chile."

"But grandma," Sandy argued, "I want to send mama a Christmas present. And just look at my shoes, all worn out! I don't make much money any more since that new colored barber-shop opened up. It's all white inside and folks don't have to wait so long 'cause there's five barbers. Jimmy Lane's got the porter's job down there . . . and I have to start working regular some time, don't I?"

"I reckons you does, but I hates to see you workin' in hotels, chile, with all them low-down Bottoms niggers, and bad womens comin' an' goin'. But I reckon you does need de job. Yo' mammy ain't sent no money here fo' de Lawd knows when, an' I ain't able to buy you nice clothes an' all like you needs to go to school in. . . . But don't forget, honey, no matter where you works—you be good an' do right. . . . I reckon you'll get along."

So Sandy found Charlie Nutter on Sunday and told him for sure he would take the job. Then he told Pete Scott he was no longer coming to work at his barber-shop, and Pete got mad and told him to go to hell, quitting when business was bad after all he had done for Sandy, besides letting him shine shoes and keep all his earnings. At other shops he couldn't have done that; besides he had intended to teach Sandy to be a barber when he got big enough.

"But go on!" said Pete Scott. "Go on! I don't need you. Plenty other boys I can find to work for me. But I bet you won't stay at that Drummer's Hotel no time, though—I can tell you that!"

The long Indian summer lingered until almost Thanksgiving, and the weather was sunny and warm. The day before Sandy went to work on his new job, he came home from school, brought in the wood for the stove, and delivered a basket of newly ironed clothes to the white folks. When he returned, he found his grandmother standing on the front porch in the sun-set, reading the evening paper, which the boy had recently delivered. Sandy stopped in the twilight beside Hager, breathing in the crisp cool air and wondering what they were going to have for supper.

Suddenly his grandmother gave a deep cry and leaned heavily against the door-jamb, letting the paper fall from her hands. "O, ma Lawd!" she moaned. "O, ma Lawd!" and an expression of the uttermost pain made the old woman's eyes widen in horror. "Is I read de name right?"

Sandy, frightened, picked up the paper from the porch and found on the front page the little four-line item that his grandmother had just read:

### NEGRESSES ARRESTED

Harrietta Williams and Maudel Smothers, two young negresses, were arrested last night on Pearl Street for street-walking. They were brought before Judge Brinton and fined ten dollars and costs.

"What does that mean, ma—street-walking?" the child asked, but his grandmother raised her apron to her eyes and stumbled into the house. Sandy stopped, perplexed at the meaning of the article, at his aunt's arrest, at his grandmother's horror. Then he followed Hager, the open newspaper still in his hands, and found her standing at the window in the kitchen, crying. Racking sobs were shaking her body and the boy, who had never seen an old person weep like that before, was terribly afraid. He didn't know that grown-up people cried, except at funerals, where it was the proper thing to do. He didn't know they ever cried alone, by themselves in their own houses.

"I'm gonna get Sister Johnson," he said, dropping the paper on the floor. "I'm gonna get Sister Johnson quick!"

"No, honey, don't get her," stammered the old woman. "She can't help us none, chile. Can't nobody help us . . . but de Lawd."

In the dusk Sandy saw that his grandmother was trying hard to make her lips speak plainly and to control her sobs.

"Let's we pray, son, fo' yo' po' lost Aunt Harriett—fo' ma own baby chile, what's done turned from de light an' is walkin' in darkness."

She dropped on her knees near the kitchen-stove with her arms on the seat of a chair and her head bowed. Sandy got on his knees, too, and while his grandmother prayed aloud for the body and soul of her daughter, the boy repeated over and over in his mind: "I wish you'd come home, Aunt Harrie. It's lonesome around here! Gee, I wish you'd come home."

# TWENTY

## *Hey, Boy!*

---

IN THE lobby of the Drummer's Hotel there were six large brass spittoons—one in the center of the place, one in each corner, and one near the clerk's desk. It was Sandy's duty to clean these spittoons. Every evening that winter after school he came in the back door of the hotel, put his books in the closet where he kept his brooms and cleaning rags, swept the two short upper halls and the two flights of stairs, swept the lobby and dusted, then took the spittoons, emptied their slimy contents into the alley, rinsed them out, and polished them until they shone as brightly as if they were made of gold. Except for the stench of emptying them, Sandy rather liked this job. He always felt very proud of himself when, about six o'clock, he could look around the dingy old lobby and see the six gleaming brass bowls catching the glow of the electric lamps on their shining surfaces before they were again covered with spit. The thought that he himself had created this brightness with his own hands, aided by a can of brass-polish, never failed to make Sandy happy.

He liked to clean things, to make them beautiful, to make them shine. Aunt Hager did, too. When she wasn't washing clothes, she was always cleaning something about the house, dusting, polishing the range, or scrubbing the kitchen-floor until it was white enough to eat from. To Hager a clean thing was beautiful—also to Sandy, proud every evening of his six unblemished brass spittoons. Yet each day when he came to work, they were covered anew with tobacco juice, cigarette-butts, wads of chewing-gum, and phlegm. But to make them clean was Sandy's job—and they were beautiful when they were clean.

Charlie Nutter was right—there was nothing very hard about the work and he liked it for a while. The new kinds of life which he saw in the hotel interested and puzzled him, but, being naturally a silent child, he asked no questions, and, beyond the directions for his work, nobody told him anything.

Sandy did his cleaning well and the boss had not yet had occasion to bellow at him, as he often bellowed at the two bell-boys.

The Drummer's Hotel was not a large hotel, nor a nice one. A three-story frame structure, dilapidated and run down, it had not been painted for years. In the lobby two large panes of plate glass looked on the street, and in front of these were rows of hard wooden chairs. At the rear of the lobby was the clerk's desk, a case of cigars and cigarettes, a cooler for water, and the door to the men's room. It was Sandy's duty to clean this toilet, too.

Upstairs on the second and third floors were the bedrooms. Only the poorest of travelling salesmen, transient railroad workers, occasionally a few show-people, and the ladies of the streets with their clients rented them. The night trade was always the most brisk at the Drummer's Hotel, but it was only on Saturdays that Sandy worked after six o'clock. That night he would not get home until ten or eleven, but Aunt Hager would always be waiting for him, keeping the fire warm, with the wash-tub full of water for his weekly bath.

There was no dining-room attached to the hotel, and, aside from Sandy, there were only five employees. The boss himself, Joe Willis, was usually at the desk. There were two chamber-maids who worked in the mornings, an old man who did the heavy cleaning and scrubbing once or twice a week, and two bell-boys—one night boy and one day boy supposedly, but both bellmen had been there so long that they arranged the hours to suit themselves. Charlie Nutter had started small, like Sandy, and had grown up there. The other bell-boy, really no boy at all, but an old man, had been in the hotel ever since it opened, and Sandy was as much afraid of him as he was of the boss.

This bellman's name was Mr. George Clark. His uniform was frayed and greasy, but he wore it with the air of a major, and he acted as though all the burdens of running the hotel were on his shoulders. He knew how everything was to be done, where everything was kept, what every old guest liked. And he could divine the tastes of each new guest before he had been there a day. Subservient and grinning to white folks, evil and tyrannical to the colored help, George was the chief authority, next to Joe Willis, in the Drummer's Hotel. He it was who found some fault with Sandy's work every day until he learned to like the child because Sandy never answered back or tried to be fly, as George said most young niggers were. After a time the old fellow seldom bothered to inspect Sandy's spittoons or to look in the corners for dust, but, nevertheless, he remained a person to be humored and obeyed if one wished to work at the Drummer's Hotel.

Besides being the boss's right-hand man, George Clark was the official bootlegger for the house, too. In fact, he kept his liquor-supply in the hotel cellar. When he was off duty, Charlie, the other bell-hop, sold it for him if there were any calls from the rooms above. They made no sales other than to guests of the house, but such sales were frequent. Some of the white women who used the rooms collected a commission from George for the sales they helped make to their men visitors.

Sandy was a long time learning the tricks of hotel work. "Yuh sure a dumb little joker," Charlie was constantly informing him. "But just stay around awhile and yuh'll get on to it."

Christmas came and Sandy sent his mother in Detroit a big box of drugstore candy. For Aunt Hager he started to buy a long pair of green ear-rings for fifty cents, but he was afraid she might not like them, so he bought her white handkerchiefs instead. And he sent a pretty card to Harriett, for one snowy December day his aunt had seen him through the windows sweeping out the lobby of the hotel and she had called him to the door to talk to her. She thrust a little piece of paper into his hand with her new address on it.

"Maudel's moved to Kansas City," she said, "so I don't live there any more. You better keep this address yourself and if mama ever needs me, you can know where I am."

Then she went on through the snow, looking very pretty in a cheap fur coat and black, high-heeled slippers, with grey silk stockings. Sandy saw her pass the hotel often with different men. Sometimes she went by with Cudge Windsor, the owner of the pool hall, or Billy Sanderlee. Almost always she was with sporty-looking fellows who wore derbies and had gold teeth. Sandy noticed that she didn't urge him to come to see her at this new house-number she had given him, so he put the paper in his pocket and went back to his sweeping, glad, anyway, to have seen his Aunt Harriett.

One Saturday afternoon several white men were sitting in the lobby smoking and reading the papers. Sandy swept around their chairs, dusted, and then took the spittoons out to clean. This work did not require his attention; while he applied the polish with a handful of soft rags, he could let his mind wander to other things. He thought about Harriett. Then he thought about school and what he would do when he was a man; about Willie-Mae, who had a job washing dinner dishes for a white family; about Jimmy Lane, who had no mama; and Sandy wondered what his own mother and father were doing in another town, and if they wanted him with them. He thought how old and tired and grey-headed Aunt Hager had become; how she puffed and blowed over the wash-tubs now, but never complained; how she waited for him on Saturday nights with the kitchen-stove blazing, so he would be warm after walking so far in the cold; and how she prayed he would be a great man some day. . . . Sitting there in the back room of the hotel, Sandy wondered how people got to be great, as, one by one, he made the spittoons bright and beautiful. He wondered how people made themselves great.

That night he would have to work late picking up papers in the lobby, running errands for the boss, and shining shoes. After he had put the spittoons around, he would go out and get a hamburger sandwich and a cup of coffee for supper; then he would come back and help Charlie if he could. . . . Charlie was a good old boy. He had taken only a dollar for getting Sandy his job and he often helped him make tips by allowing Sandy to run to the telegraph office or do some other little odd job for a guest upstairs. . . . Sure, Charlie was a nice guy.

Things were pretty busy tonight. Several men had their shoes shined as they sat tipped back in the lobby chairs while Sandy with his boot-black box let them put up a foot at a time to be polished. One tall farmer gave him a quarter tip and a pat on the head.

"Bright little feller, that," he remarked to the boss.

About ten o'clock the blond Miss Marcia McKay's bell rang, and, Charlie being engaged, Joe Willis sent Sandy up to see what she wanted. Miss McKay had just come in out of the snow a short time before with a heavy-set ugly man. Both of them were drunk. Sandy knocked timidly outside her room.

"Come in," growled the man's voice.

Sandy opened the door and saw Miss McKay standing naked in the middle of the floor combing her hair. He stopped on the threshold.

"Aw, come in," said the man. "She won't bite you! Where's that other bell-boy? We want some licker! . . . Damn it! Say, send Charlie up here! He knows what I want!"

Sandy scampered away, and when he found Charlie, he told him about Miss McKay. The child was scared because he had often heard of colored boys' being lynched for looking at white women, even with their clothes on—but the bell-boy only laughed.

"Yuh're a dumb little joker!" he said. "Just stay around here awhile and yuh'll see lots more'n that!" He winked and gave Sandy a nudge in the ribs. "Boy, I done sold ten quarts o' licker tonight," he whispered jubilantly. "And some a it was mine, too!"

Sandy went back to the lobby and the shining of shoes. A big, red-necked stranger smoking and drinking with a crowd of drummers in one corner of the room called to him "Hey, boy! Shine me up here!" So he edged into the center of the group of men with his blacking-box, got down on his knees before the big fellow, took out his cans and his cloths, and went to work.

The white men were telling dirty stories, uglier than any Sandy had heard at the colored barber-shop and not very funny—and some of them made him sick at the stomach.

The big man whose shoes he was shining said: "Now I'm gonna tell one." He talked with a Southern drawl and a soft slurring of word-endings like some old colored folks. He had been drinking, too. "This is 'bout a nigger went to see Aunt Hanner one night. . . ."

A roar of laughter greeted his first effort and he was encouraged to tell another.

"Old darky caught a gal on the levee . . ." he commenced.

Sandy finished polishing the shoes and put the cloths inside his wooden box and stood up waiting for his pay, but the speaker did not notice the colored boy until he had finished his tale and laughed heartily with the other men. Then he looked at Sandy. Suddenly he grinned.

"Say, little coon, let's see you hit a step for the boys! . . . Down where I live, folks, all our niggers can dance! . . . Come on, boy, snap it up!"

"I can't," Sandy said, frowning instead of smiling, and growing warm as he stood there in the smoky circle of grinning white men. "I don't know how to dance."

"O, you're one of them stubborn Kansas coons, heh?" said the red-necked fellow disgustedly, the thickness of whisky on his tongue. "You Northern darkies are dumb as hell, anyhow!" Then, turning to the crowd of amused lobby loungers, he announced: "Now down in Mississippi, whar I come from, if you offer a nigger a dime, he'll dance his can off . . . an' they better dance, what I mean!"

He turned to the men around him for approbation, while Sandy still waited uncomfortably to be paid for the shine. But the man kept him standing there, looking at him drunkenly, then at the amused crowd of Saturday-night loungers.

"Now, a nigger his size down South would no more think o' not dancin' if a white man asked him than he would think o' flyin'. This boy's jest tryin' to be smart, that's all. Up here you-all've got darkies spoilt, believin' they're somebody. Now, in my home we keep 'em in their places." He again turned his attention to Sandy. "Boy! I want to see you dance!" he commanded.

But Sandy picked up his blacking-box and had begun to push through the circle of chairs, not caring any longer about his pay, when the southerner rose and grabbed him roughly by the arm, exhaling alcoholic breath in the boy's face as he jokingly pulled him back.

"Com'ere, you little—" but he got no further, for Sandy, strengthened by the anger that suddenly possessed him at the touch of this white man's hand, uttered a yell that could be heard for blocks.

Everyone in the lobby turned to see what had happened, but before Joe Willis got out from behind the clerk's desk, the boy, wriggling free, had reached the street-door. There Sandy turned, raised his boot-black box furiously above his head, and flung it with all his strength at the group of laughing white men in which the drunken southerner was standing. From one end of the whizzing box a stream of polish-bottles, brushes, and cans fell clattering across the lobby while Sandy disappeared through the door, running as fast as his legs could carry him in the falling snow.

"Hey! You black bastard!" Joe Willis yelled from the hotel entrance, but his voice was blown away in the darkness. As Sandy ran, he felt the snow-flakes falling in his face.

TWENTY-ONE

## *Note to Harriett*

---

SEVERAL days later, when Sandy took out of his pocket the piece of paper that his Aunt Harriett had given him that day in front of the hotel, he noticed that the address written on it was somewhere in the Bottoms. He felt vaguely worried, so he did not show it to his grandmother, because he had often heard her say that the Bottoms was a bad place. And when he was working at the barber-shop, he had heard the men talking about what went on there—and in a sense he knew what they meant.

It was a gay place—people did what they wanted to, or what they had to do, and didn't care—for in the Bottoms folks ceased to struggle against the boundaries between good and bad, or white and black, and surrendered amiably to immorality. Beyond Pearl Street, across the tracks, people of all colors came together for the sake of joy, the curtains being drawn only between themselves and the opposite side of the railroad, where the churches were and the big white Y.M.C.A.

At night in the Bottoms victrolas moaned and banjos cried ecstatically in the darkness. Summer evenings little yellow and brown and black girls in pink or blue bungalow aprons laughed invitingly in doorways, and dice rattled with the staccato gaiety of jazz music on long tables in rear rooms. Pimps played pool; bootleggers lounged in big red cars; children ran in the streets until midnight, with no voice of parental authority forcing them to an early sleep; young blacks fought like cocks and enjoyed it; white boys walked through the streets winking at colored girls; men came in autos; old women ate pigs' feet and watermelon and drank beer; whisky flowed; gin was like water; soft indolent laughter didn't care about anything; and deep nigger-throated voices that had long ago stopped rebelling against the ways of this world rose in song.

To those who lived on the other side of the railroad and never realized the utter stupidity of the word "sin," the Bottoms was vile and wicked. But to the girls who lived there, and the boys who pimped and fought and sold licker there, "sin" was a silly word that did not enter their heads. They had never looked at life through the spectacles of the Sunday-School. The glasses good people wore wouldn't have fitted their eyes, for they hung no curtain of words between themselves and reality. To them, things were—what they were.

"Ma bed is hard, but I'm layin' in it jest de same!"

sang the raucous-throated blues-singer in her song;

"Hey! . . . Hey! Who wants to lay with me?"

It was to one of these streets in the Bottoms that Sandy came breathlessly one bright morning with a note in his hand. He knocked at the door of a big grey house.

"Is this where Harriett Williams lives?" he panted.

"You means Harrietta?" said a large, sleek yellow woman in a blue silk kimono who opened the door. "Come in, baby, and sit down. I'll see if she's up yet." Then the woman left Sandy in the parlor while she went up the stairs calling his aunt in a clear, lazy voice.

There were heavy velvet draperies at the windows and doors in this front room where Sandy sat, and a thick, well-worn rug on the floor. There was a divan, a davenport covered with pillows, a centre table, and several chairs. Through the curtains at the double door leading into the next room, Sandy saw a piano, more sofas and chairs, and a cleared oiled floor that might be used for dancing. Both rooms were in great disorder, and the air in the house smelled stale and beerish. Licker-bottles and ginger-ale bottles were underneath the center table, underneath the sofas, and on top of the piano. Ash-trays were everywhere, overflowing with cigar-butts and cigarette-ends—on the floor, under chairs, overturned among the sofa-pillows. A small brass tray under one of the sofas held a half-dozen small glasses, some of them still partly full of whisky or gin.

Sandy sat down to wait for his aunt. It was very quiet in the house, although it was almost ten o'clock. A man came down the stairs with his coat on his arm, blinking sleepily. He passed through the hall and out into the street. Bedroom-slippered feet shuffled to the head of the steps on the second floor, and the lazy woman's voice called: "She'll be down in a minute, darling. Just wait there."

Sandy waited. He heard the splash of water above and the hoarse gurgling of a bath-tub being emptied. Presently Harriett appeared in a little pink wash dress such as a child wears, the skirt striking her just above the knees. She smelled like cashmere-bouquet soap, and her face was not yet powdered, nor her hair done up, but she was smiling broadly, happy to see her nephew, as her arms went round his neck.

"My! I'm glad to see you, honey! How'd you happen to come? How'd you find me?"

"Grandma's sick," said Sandy. "She's awful sick and Aunt Tempy sent you this note."

The girl opened the letter. It read:

> Your mother is not expected to live. You better come to see her since she has asked for you. Tempy.

"O! . . . Wait a minute," said Harriett softly. "I'll hurry."

Sandy sat down again in the room full of ash-trays and licker-bottles. Many feet pattered upstairs, and, as doors opened and closed, women's voices were heard: "Can I help you, girlie? Can I lend you anything? Does you need a veil?"

When Harriett came down, she was wearing a tan coat-suit and a white turban, pulled tight on her head. Her face was powdered and her lips rouged ever so slightly. The bag she carried was beaded, blue and gold.

"Come on, Sandy," she said. "I guess I'm ready."

As they went out, they heard a man's voice in a shabby house across the street singing softly to a two-finger piano accompaniment:

> Sugar babe, I'm leavin'
> An' it won't be long. . . .

While outside, on his front door-step, two nappy-headed little yellow kids were solemnly balling-the-jack.

Two days before, Sandy had come home from school and found his grandmother lying across the bed, the full tubs still standing in the kitchen, her clothes not yet hung out to dry.

"What's the matter?" he asked.

"I's washed down, chile," said the old woman, panting. "I feels kinder tired-like, that's all."

But Sandy knew that there must be something else wrong with Aunt Hager, because he had never seen her lying on the bed in broad daylight, with her clothes still in the tubs.

"Does your back ache?" asked the child.

"I does feel a little misery," sighed Aunt Hager. "But seems to be mo' ma side an' not ma back this time. But 'tain't nothin'. I's just tired."

But Sandy was scared. "You want some soda and water, grandma?"

"No, honey." Then, in her usual tones of assumed anger: "Go on away from here an' let a body rest. Ain't I told you they ain't nothin' the matter 'ceptin' I's all washed out an' just got to lay down a minute? Go on an' fetch in yo' wood . . . an' spin yo' top out yonder with Buster and them. Go on!"

It was nearly five o'clock when the boy came in again. Aunt Hager was sitting in the rocker near the stove then, her face drawn and ashy. She had been trying to finish her washing.

"Chile, go get Sister Johnson an' ask her if she can't wring out ma clothes fo' me—Mis' Dunset ain't sent much washin' this week, an' you can help her hang 'em up. I reckon it ain't gonna rain tonight, so's they can dry befo' mawnin'."

Sandy ran towards the door.

"Now, don't butt your brains out!" said the old lady. "Ain't no need o' runnin'."

Not only did Sister Johnson come at once and hang out the washing, but she made Hager get in bed, with a hot-water bottle on her paining side. And she gave her a big dose of peppermint and water.

"I 'spects it's from yo' stomick," she said. "I knows you et cabbage fo' dinner!"

"Maybe 'tis," said Hager.

Sister Johnson took Sandy to her house for supper that evening and he and Willie-Mae ate five sweet potatoes each.

"You-all gwine bust!" said Tom Johnson.

About nine o'clock the boy went to bed with his grandmother, and all that night Hager tossed and groaned, in spite of her efforts to lie quiet and not keep Sandy awake. In the morning she said: "Son, I reckon you better stay home from school, 'cause I's feelin' mighty po'ly. Seems like that cabbage ain't digested yet. Feels like I done et a stone. . . . Go see if you can't make de fire up an' heat me a cup o' hot water."

About eleven o'clock Madam de Carter came over. "I thought I didn't perceive you nowhere in the yard this morning and the sun 'luminating so bright and cheerful. You ain't indispensed, are you? Sandy said you was kinder ill." She chattered away. "You know it don't look natural not to see you hanging out clothes long before the noon comes."

"I ain't well a-tall this mawnin'," said Hager when she got a chance to speak. "I's feelin' right bad. I suffers with a pain in ma side; seems like it ain't gettin' no better. Sister Johnson just left here from rubbin' it, but I still suffers terrible an' can't eat nothin'. . . . You can use de phone, can't you, Sister Carter?"

"Why, yes! Yes indeedy! I oftens phones from over to Mis' Petit's. You think you needs a physicianer?"

In spite of herself a groan came from the old woman's lips as she tried to turn towards her friend. Aunt Hager, who had never moaned for lesser hurts, did not intend to complain over this one—but the pain!

"It's cuttin' me in two." She gasped. "Send fo' old Doc McDillors an' he'll come."

Madam de Carter, proud and important at the prospect of using her white neighbor's phone, rushed away.

"I didn't know you were so sick, grandma!" Sandy's eyes were wide with fright and sympathy. "I'm gonna get Mis' Johnson to come rub you again."

"O! . . . O, ma Lawd, help!" Alone for a moment with no one to hear her, she couldn't hold back the moans any longer. A cold sweat stood on her forehead.

The doctor came—the kind old white man who had known Hager for years and in whom she had faith.

"Well," he said, "It's quite a surprise to see you in bed, Aunty." Then, looking very serious and professional, he took her pulse.

"Go out and close the door," he said gently to Madam de Carter and Sister Johnson, Willie-Mae and Sandy, all of whom had gathered around the bed in the little room. "Somebody heat some water." He turned back the quilts from the woman's body and unbuttoned her gown.

Ten minutes later he said frankly, but with great kindness in his tones: "You're a sick woman, Hager, a very sick woman."

That afternoon Tempy came, like a stranger to the house, and took charge of things. Sandy felt uncomfortable and shy in her presence. This aunt of his had a hard, cold, correct way of talking that resembled Mrs. Rice's manner of speaking to his mother when Annjee used to work there. But Tempy quickly put the house in order, bathed her mother, and spread the bed with clean sheets and a white counterpane. Before evening, members of Hager's Lodge began to drop in bringing soups and custards. White people of the neighborhood stopped, too, to inquire if there was anything they could do for the old woman who had so often waited on them in their illnesses. About six o'clock old man Logan drove up the alley and tied his white mule to the back fence.

The sun was setting when Tempy called Sandy in from the back yard, where he was chopping wood for the stove. She said: "James"—how queerly his correct name struck his ears as it fell from the lips of this cold aunt!—"James, you had better send this telegram to your mother. Now, here is a dollar bill and you can bring back the change. Look on her last letter and get the correct address."

Sandy took the written sheet of paper and the money that his aunt gave him. Then he looked through the various drawers in the house for his mother's last letter. It had been nearly a month since they had heard from her, but finally the boy found the letter in the cupboard, under a jelly-glass full of small coins that his grandmother kept there. He carried the envelope with him to the telegraph office, and there he paid for a message to Annjee in Detroit:

Mother very sick, come at once. Tempy.

As the boy walked home in the gathering dusk, he felt strangely alone in the world, as though Aunt Hager had already gone away, and when he reached the house, it was full of lodge members who had come to keep watch. Tempy went home, but Sister Johnson remained in the sick-room, changing the hot-water bottles and administering, every three hours, the medicine the doctor had left.

There were so many people in the house that Sandy came

out into the back yard and sat down on the edge of the well. It was cool and clear, and a slit of moon rode in a light-blue sky spangled with stars. Soon the apple-trees would bud and the grass would be growing. Sandy was a big boy. When his next birthday came, he would be fourteen, and he had begun to grow tall and heavy. Aunt Hager said she was going to buy him a pair of long pants this coming summer. And his mother would hardly know him when she saw him again, if she ever came home.

Tonight, inside, there were so many old sisters from the lodge that Sandy couldn't even talk to his grandmother while she lay in bed. They were constantly going in and out of the sick-room, drinking coffee in the kitchen, or gossiping in the parlor. He wished they would all go away. He could take care of his grandmother himself until she got well—he and Sister Johnson. They didn't even need Tempy, who, he felt, shouldn't be there, because he didn't like her.

"They callin' you inside," Willie-Mae came out to tell him as he sat by himself in the cold on the edge of the well. She was taller than Sandy now and had a regular job taking care of a white lady's baby. She no longer wore her hair in braids. She did it up, and she had a big leather pocket-book that she carried on her arm like a woman. Boys came to take her to the movies on Saturday nights. "They want you inside."

Sandy got up, his legs stiff and numb, and went into the kitchen. An elderly brown woman, dressed in black silk that swished as she moved, opened the door to Hager's bedroom and whispered to him loudly: "Be quiet, chile."

Sandy entered between a lane of old women. Hager looked up at him and smiled—so grave and solemn he appeared.

"Is they takin' care o' you?" she asked weakly. "Ain't it bed-time, honey? Is you had something to eat? Come on an' kiss yo' old grandma befo' you go to sleep. She'll be better in de mawnin'."

She couldn't seem to lift her head, so Sandy sat down on the bed and kissed her. All he said was: "I'm all right, grandma," because there were so many old women in there that he couldn't talk. Then he went out into the other room.

The air in the house was close and stuffy and the boy soon became groggy with sleep. He fell across the bed that had been

Annjee's, and later Dogberry's, with all his clothes on. One of the lodge women in the room said: "You better take off yo' things, chile, an' go to sleep right." Then she said to the other sisters: "Come on in de kitchen, you-all, an' let this chile go to bed."

In the morning Tempy woke him. "Are you sure you had Annjee's address correct last night?" she demanded. "The telegraph office says she couldn't be found, so the message was not delivered. Let me see the letter."

Sandy found the letter again, and the address was verified.

"Well, that's strange," said Tempy. "I suppose, as careless and irresponsible as Jimboy is, they've got it wrong, or else moved. . . . Do you know where Harriett can be? I don't suppose you do, but mother has been calling for her all night. I suppose we'll have to try to get her, wherever she is."

"I got her address," said Sandy. "She wrote it down for me when I was working at the hotel this winter. I can find her."

"Then I'll give you a note," said Tempy. "Take it to her."

So Sandy went to the big grey house in the Bottoms that morning to deliver Tempy's message, before the girls there had risen from their beds.

# TWENTY-TWO

# *Beyond the Jordan*

D URING the day the lodge members went to their work in the various kitchens and restaurants and laundries of the town. And Madam de Carter was ordered to Tulsa, Oklahoma, where a split in her organization was threatened because of the elections of the grand officers. Hager was resting easy, no pain now, but very weak.

"It's only a matter of time," said the doctor. "Give her the medicine so she won't worry, but it does no good. There's nothing we can do."

"She's going to die!" Sandy thought.

Harriett sat by the bedside holding her mother's hand as the afternoon sunlight fell on the white spread. Hager had been glad to see the girl again, and the old woman held nothing against her daughter for no longer living at home.

"Is you happy, chile?" Hager asked. "You looks so nice. Yo' clothes is right purty. I hopes you's findin' what you wants in life. You's young, honey, an' you needs to be happy. . . . Sandy!" She called so weakly that he could hardly hear her, though he was standing at the head of the bed. "Sandy, look in that drawer, chile, under ma night-gowns an' things, an' hand me that there little box you sees down in de corner."

The child found it and gave it to her, a small, white box from a cheap jeweller's. It was wrapped carefully in a soft handkerchief. The old woman took it eagerly and tried to hold it out towards her daughter. Harriett unwound the handkerchief and opened the lid of the box. Then she saw that it contained the tiny gold watch that her mother had given her on her sixteenth birthday, which she had pawned months ago in order to run away with the carnival. Quick tears came to the girl's eyes.

"I got it out o' pawn fo' you," Hager said, "'cause I wanted you to have it fo' yo'self, chile. You know yo' mammy bought it fo' you."

It was such a little watch! Old-timey, with a breast-pin on it.

Harriett quickly put her handkerchief over her wrist to hide the flashy new timepiece she was wearing on a gold bracelet.

That night Hager died. The undertakers came at dawn with their wagon and carried the body away to embalm it. Sandy stood on the front porch looking at the morning star as the clatter of the horses' hoofs echoed in the street. A sleepy young white boy was driving the undertaker's wagon, and the horse that pulled it was white.

The women who had been sitting up all night began to go home now to get their husbands' breakfasts and to prepare to go to work themselves.

"It's Wednesday," Sandy thought. "Today I'm supposed to go get Mrs. Reinhart's clothes, but grandma's dead. I guess I won't get them now. There's nobody to wash them."

Sister Johnson called him to the kitchen to drink a cup of coffee. Harriett was there weeping softly. Tempy was inside busily cleaning the room from which they had removed the body. She had opened all the windows and was airing the house.

Out in the yard a rooster flapped his wings and crowed shrilly at the rising sun. The fire crackled, and the coffee boiling sent up a fragrant aroma. Sister Johnson opened a can of condensed milk by punching it with the butcher-knife. She put some cups and saucers on the table.

"Tempy, won't you have some?"

"No, thank you, Mrs. Johnson," she called from the dead woman's bedroom.

When Aunt Hager was brought back to her house, she was in a long box covered with black plush. They placed it on a folding stand by the window in the front room. There was a crape on the door, and the shades were kept lowered, and people whispered in the house as though someone were asleep. Flowers began to be delivered by boys on bicycles, and the lodge members came to sit up again that night. The time was set for burial, and the *Daily Leader* carried this paragraph in small type on its back page:

Hager Williams, aged colored laundress of 419 Cypress Street, passed away at her home last night. She was known and respected by many white families in the community. Three daughters and a grandson survive.

They tried again to reach Annjee in Detroit by telegram, but without success. On the afternoon of the funeral it was cold and rainy. The little Baptist Church was packed with people. The sisters of the lodge came in full regalia, with banners and insignia, and the brothers turned out with them. Hager's coffin was banked with flowers. There were many fine pieces from the families for whom she had washed and from the white neighbors she had nursed in sickness. There were offerings, too, from Tempy's high-toned friends and from Harriett's girl companions in the house in the Bottoms. Many of the bellboys, porters, and bootleggers sent wreaths and crosses with golden letters on them: "At Rest in Jesus," "Beyond the Jordan," or simply: "Gone Home." There was a bouquet of violets from Buster's mother and a blanket of roses from Tempy herself. They were all pretty, but, to Sandy, the perfume was sickening in the close little church.

The Baptist minister preached, but Tempy had Father Hill from her church to say a few words, too. The choir sang *Shall We Meet Beyond the River?* People wept and fainted. The services seemed interminable. Then came the long drive to the cemetery in horse-drawn hacks, with a few automobiles in line behind. In at the wide gates and through a vast expanse of tombstones the procession passed, across the graveyard, towards the far, lonesome corner where most of the Negroes rested. There Sandy saw the open grave. Then he saw the casket going down . . . down . . . down, into the earth.

The boy stood quietly between his Aunt Tempy and his Aunt Harriett at the edge of the grave while Tempy stared straight ahead into the drizzling rain, and Harriett cried, streaking the powder on her cheeks.

"That's all right, mama," Harriett sobbed to the body in the long, black box. "You won't get lonesome out here. Harrie'll come back tomorrow. Harrie'll come back every day and bring you flowers. You won't get lonesome, mama."

They were throwing wet dirt on the coffin as the mourners walked away through the sticky clay towards their carriages. Some old sister at the grave began to sing:

> Dark was the night,
> Cold was the ground . . .

in a high weird monotone. Others took it up, and, as the mourners drove away, the air was filled with the minor wailing of the old women. Harriett was wearing Hager's gift, the little gold watch, pinned beneath her coat.

When they got back to the house where Aunt Hager had lived for so long, Sister Johnson said the mail-man had left a letter under the door that afternoon addressed to the dead woman. Harriett was about to open it when Tempy took it from her. It was from Annjee.

"Dear mama," it began.

> We have moved to Toledo because Jimboy thought he would do better here and the reason I haven't written, we have been so long getting settled. I have been out of work but we both got jobs now and maybe I will be able to send you some money soon. I hope you are well, ma, and all right. Kiss Sandy for me and take care of yourself. With love and God's blessings from your daughter,
>
> Annjee

Tempy immediately turned the letter over and wrote on the back:

> We buried your mother today. I tried to reach you in Detroit, but could not get you, since you were no longer there and neglected to send us your new address. It is too bad you weren't here for the funeral. Your child is going to stay with me until I hear from you.
>
> Tempy

Then she turned to the boy, who stood dazed beside Sister Johnson in the silent, familiar old house. "You will come home with me, James," she said. "We'll see that this place is locked first. You try all the windows and I'll fasten the doors; then we'll go out the front. . . . Mrs. Johnson, it's been good of you to help us in our troubles. Thank you."

Sister Johnson went home, leaving Harriett in the parlor. When Sandy and Tempy returned from locking the back windows and doors, they found the girl still standing there, and for a moment the two sisters looked at one another in silence. Then Tempy said coldly: "We're going."

Harriett went out alone into the drizzling rain. Tempy tried the parlor windows to be sure they were well fastened; then, stepping outside on the porch, she locked the door and put the key in her bag.

"Come on," she said.

Sandy looked up and down the street, but in the thick twilight of fog and rain Harriet had disappeared, so he followed his aunt into the waiting cab. As the hack clattered off, the boy gave an involuntary shiver.

"Do you want to hold my hand," Tempy asked, unbending a little.

"No," Sandy said. So they rode in silence.

# TWENTY-THREE

## *Tempy's House*

"JAMES, you must get up on time in this house. Breakfast has been ready twenty minutes. I can't come upstairs every morning to call you. You are old enough now to wake yourself and you must learn to do so—you've too far to walk to school to lie abed."

Sandy tumbled out. Tempy left the room so that he would be free to dress, and soon he came downstairs to breakfast.

He had never had a room of his own before. He had never even slept in a room alone, but here his aunt had given him a small chamber on the second floor which had a window that looked out into a tidy back yard where there was a brick walk running to the back gate. The room, which was very clean, contained only the bed, one chair, and a dresser. There was, too, a little closet in which to hang clothes, but Sandy did not have many to put in it.

The thing that impressed him most about the second floor was the bathroom. He had never lived where there was running water indoors. And in this room, too, everything was so spotlessly clean that Sandy was afraid to move lest he disturb something or splash water on the wall.

When he came downstairs for breakfast, he found the table set for two. Mr. Siles, being in the railway postal service, was out on a trip. The grapefruit was waiting as Sandy slid shyly into his place opposite the ash-brown woman who had become his guardian since his grandma's death. She bowed her head to say a short grace; then they ate.

"Have you been accustomed to drinking milk in the mornings?" Tempy asked as they were finishing the meal. "If you have, the milkman can leave another bottle. Young people should have plenty of milk."

"Yes'm, I'd like it, but we only had coffee at home."

"You needn't say 'yes'm' in this house. We are not used to slavery talk here. If you like milk, I'll get it for you. . . . Now, how are your clothes? I see your stocking has a hole in it, and one pants-leg is hanging."

"It don't stay fastened."

"It *doesn't*, James! I'll buy you some more pants tomorrow. What else do you need?"

Sandy told her, and in a few days she took him to Wertheimer's, the city's largest store, and outfitted him completely. And, as they shopped, she informed him that she was the only colored woman in town who ran a bill there.

"I want white people to know that Negroes have a little taste; that's why I always trade at good shops. . . . And if you're going to live with me, you'll have to learn to do things right, too."

The tearful letter that came from Annjee when she heard of her mother's death said that Toledo was a very difficult place to get work in, and that she had no money to send railroad fare for Sandy, but that she would try to send for him as soon as she could. Jimboy was working on a lake steamer and was seldom home, and she couldn't have Sandy with her anyway until they got a nicer place to stay; so would Tempy please keep him a little while?

By return post Tempy replied that if Annjee had any sense, she would let Sandy remain in Stanton, where he could get a good education, and not be following after his worthless father all over the country. Mr. Siles and she had no children, and Sandy seemed like a quiet, decent child, smart in his classes. Colored people needed to encourage talent so that the white race would realize Negroes weren't all mere guitar-players and housemaids. And Sandy could be a credit if he were raised right. Of course, Tempy knew he hadn't had the correct environment to begin with—living with Jimboy and Harriett and going to a Baptist church, but undoubtedly he could be trained. He was young. "And I think it would be only fair to the boy that you let him stay with us, because, Annjee, you are certainly not the person to bring him up as he should be reared." The letter was signed: "Your sister, Tempy," and written properly with pen and ink.

So it happened that Sandy came to live with Mr. and Mrs.

Arkins Siles, for that was the name by which his aunt and uncle
were known in the Negro society of the town. Mr. Siles was a
mail-clerk on the railroad—a position that colored people considered a high one because you were working for "Uncle Sam."
He was a paste-colored man of forty-eight who had inherited
three houses from his father.

Tempy, when she married, had owned houses too, one of
which had been willed her by Mrs. Barr-Grant, for whom she
had worked for years as personal maid. She had acquired her
job while yet in high school, and Mrs. Barr-Grant, who travelled a great deal in the interest of woman suffrage and prohibition, had taken Tempy east with her. On their return to
Stanton she allowed the colored maid to take charge of her
home, where she also employed a cook and a parlor girl. Thus
was the mistress left free to write pamphlets and prepare lec-
tures on the various evils of the world standing in need of
correction.

Tempy pleased Mrs. Barr-Grant by being prompt and exact
in obeying orders and by appearing to worship her Puritan
intelligence. In truth Tempy did worship her mistress, for the
colored girl found that by following Mrs. Barr-Grant's early
directions she had become an expert housekeeper; by imitating
her manner of speech she had acquired a precise flow of language; and by reading her books she had become interested in
things that most Negro girls never thought about. Several
times the mistress had remarked to her maid: "You're so smart
and such a good, clean, quick little worker, Tempy, that it's too
bad you aren't white." And Tempy had taken this to heart, not
as an insult, but as a compliment.

When the white lady died, she left one of her small houses to
her maid as a token of appreciation for faithful services. By dint
of saving, and of having resided with her mistress where there
had been no living expenses, Tempy had managed to buy another house, too. When Mr. Siles asked her to be his wife, everybody said it was a fine match, for both owned property, both
were old enough to know what they wanted, and both were emi-
nently respectable. . . . Now they prospered together.

Tempy no longer worked out, but stayed home, keeping
house, except that she went each month to collect her rents
and those of her husband. She had a woman to do the laundry

and help with the cleaning, but Tempy herself did the cooking, and all her meals were models of economical preparation. Just enough food was prepared each time for three people. Sandy never had a third helping of dessert in her house. No big pots of black-eyed peas and pigtails scented her front hall, either. She got her recipes from *The Ladies' Home Journal*—and she never bought a watermelon.

White people were for ever picturing colored folks with huge slices of watermelon in their hands. Well, she was one colored woman who did not like them! Her favorite fruits were tangerines and grapefruit, for Mrs. Barr-Grant had always eaten those, and Tempy had admired Mrs. Barr-Grant more than anybody else—more, of course, than she had admired Aunt Hager, who spent her days at the wash-tub, and had loved watermelon.

Colored people certainly needed to come up in the world, Tempy thought, up to the level of white people—dress like white people, talk like white people, think like white people— and then they would no longer be called "niggers."

In Tempy this feeling was an emotional reaction, born of white admiration, but in Mr. Siles, who shared his wife's views, the same attitude was born of practical thought. The whites had the money, and if Negroes wanted any, the quicker they learned to be like the whites, the better. Stop being lazy, stop singing all the time, stop attending revivals, and learn to get the dollar—because money buys everything, even the respect of white people.

Blues and spirituals Tempy and her husband hated because they were too Negro. In their house Sandy dared not sing a word of *Swing Low, Sweet Chariot*, for what had darky slave songs to do with respectable people? And rag-time belonged in the Bottoms with the sinners. (It was ironically strange that the Bottoms should be the only section of Stanton where Negroes and whites mingled freely on equal terms.) That part of town, according to Tempy, was lost to God, and the fact that she had a sister living there burned like a hidden cancer in her breast. She never mentioned Harriett to anyone.

Tempy's friends were all people of standing in the darker world—doctors, school-teachers, a dentist, a lawyer, a hair-dresser. And she moved among these friends as importantly as

Mrs. Barr-Grant had moved among a similar group in the white race. Many of them had had washwomen for mothers and day-laborers for fathers; but none ever spoke of that. And while Aunt Hager lived, Tempy, after getting her position with Mrs. Barr-Grant, was seldom seen with the old woman. After her marriage she was even more ashamed of her family connections—a little sister running wild, and another sister married for the sake of love—Tempy could never abide Jimboy, or understand why Annjee had taken up with a rounder from the South. One's family as a topic of conversation, however, was not popular in high circles, for too many of Stanton's dark society folks had sprung from humble family trees and low black bottoms.

"But back in Washington, where I was born," said Mrs. Doctor Mitchell once, "we really have blood! All the best people at the capital come from noted ancestry—Senator Bruce, John M. Langston, Governor Pinchback, Frederick Douglass. Why, one of our colored families on their white side can even trace its lineage back to George Washington! . . . O, yes, we have a background! But, of course, we are too refined to boast about it."

Tempy thought of her mother then and wished that black Aunt Hager had not always worn her apron in the streets, uptown and everywhere! Of course, it was clean and white and seemed to suit the old lady, but aprons weren't worn by the best people. When Tempy was in the hospital for an operation shortly after her marriage, they wouldn't let Hager enter by the front door—and Tempy never knew whether it was on account of her color or the apron! The Presbyterian Hospital was prejudiced against Negroes and didn't like them to use the elevator, but certainly her mother should not have come there in an apron!

Well, Aunt Hager had meant well, Tempy thought, even if she didn't dress right. And now this child, Sandy—James was his correct name! At that first breakfast they ate together, she asked him if he had a comb and brush of his own.

"No'm, I ain't," said Sandy.

"I haven't," she corrected him. "I certainly don't want my white neighbors to hear you saying 'ain't' . . . You've come to live with me now and you must talk like a gentleman."

# TWENTY-FOUR

# A Shelf of Books

THAT spring, shortly after Sandy went to stay with Tempy, there was an epidemic of mumps among the schoolchildren in Stanton, and, old as he was, he was among its early victims. With jaws swollen to twice their normal size and a red sign, MUMPS, on the house, he was forced to remain at home for three weeks. It was then that the boy began to read books other than the ones he had had to study for his lessons. At Aunt Hager's house there had been no books, anyway, except the Bible and the few fairytales that he had been given at Christmas; but Tempy had a case full of dusty volumes that were used to give dignity to her sitting-room: a row of English classics bound in red, an *Encyclopedia of World Knowledge* in twelve volumes, a book on household medicine full of queer drawings, and some modern novels—*The Rosary, The Little Shepherd of Kingdom Come*, the newest Harold Bell Wright, and all that had ever been written by Gene Stratton Porter, Tempy's favorite author. The Negro was represented by Chestnut's *House Behind the Cedars*, and the *Complete Poems* of Paul Lawrence Dunbar, whom Tempy tolerated on account of his fame, but condemned because he had written so much in dialect and so often of the lower classes of colored people. Tempy subscribed to *Harper's Magazine*, too, because Mrs. Barr-Grant had taken it. And in her sewing-room closet there was also a pile of *The Crisis*, the thin Negro monthly that she had been taking from the beginning of its publication.

Sandy had heard of that magazine, but he had never seen a copy; so he went through them all, looking at the pictures of prominent Negroes and reading about racial activities all over the country, and about racial wrongs in the South. In every issue he found, too, stirring and beautifully written editorials about the frustrated longings of the black race, and the hidden beauties in the Negro soul. A man named Du Bois wrote them.

"Dr. William Edward Burghardt Du Bois," said Tempy, "and he is a great man."

"Great like Booker T. Washington?" asked Sandy.

"Teaching Negroes to be servants, that's all Washington did!" Tempy snorted in so acid a tone that Sandy was silent. "Du Bois wants our rights. He wants us to be real men and women. He believes in social equality. But Washington—huh!" The fact that he had established an industrial school damned Washington in Tempy's eyes, for there were enough colored workers already. But Du Bois was a doctor of philosophy and had studied in Europe! . . . That's what Negroes needed to do, get smart, study books, go to Europe! "Don't talk to me about Washington," Tempy fumed. "Take Du Bois for your model, not some white folks' nigger."

"Well, Aunt Hager said—" then Sandy stopped. His grand-mother had thought that Booker T. was the greatest of men, but maybe she had been wrong. Anyway, this Du Bois could write! Gee, it made you burn all over to read what he said about a lynching. But Sandy did not mention Booker Washington again to Tempy, although, months later, at the library he read his book called *Up from Slavery*, and he was sure that Aunt Hager hadn't been wrong. "I guess they are both great men," he thought.

Sandy's range of reading increased, too, when his aunt found a job for him that winter in Mr. Prentiss's gift-card- and print-ing-shop, where he kept the place clean and acted as delivery boy. This shop kept a shelf of current novels and some volumes of the new poetry—Sandburg, Lindsay, Masters—which the Young Women's Club of Stanton was then studying, to the shocked horror of the older white ladies of the town. Sandy knew of this because Mr. Prentiss's daughter, a student at Goucher College, used to keep shop and she pointed out vol-umes for the boy to read and told him who their authors were and what the books meant. She said that none of the colored boys they had employed before had ever been interested in reading; so she often lent him, by way of encouragement, shop-worn copies to be taken home at night and returned the next day. Thus Sandy spent much of his first year with Tempy deep in novels too mature for a fourteen-year-old boy. But Tempy was very proud of her studious young nephew. She began to decide that she had made no mistake in keeping him with her, and when he entered the high school, she bought him his first long-trouser suit as a spur towards further application.

Sandy became taller week by week, and it seemed to Tempy as if his shirt-sleeves became too short for him overnight. His voice was changing, too, and he had acquired a liking for football, but his after-school job at Prentiss's kept him from playing much. At night he read, or sometimes went to the movies with Buster—but Tempy kept him home as much as she could. Occasionally he saw Willie-Mae, who was keeping company with the second cook at Wright's Hotel. And sometimes he saw Jimmy Lane, who was a bell-hop now and hung out with a sporty crowd in the rear room of Cudge Windsor's pool hall. But whenever Sandy went into his old neighborhood, he felt sad, remembering Aunt Hager and his mother, and Jimboy, and Harriett—for his young aunt had gone away from Stanton, too, and the last he heard about her rumored that she was on the stage in Kansas City. Now the little house where Sandy had lived with his grandmother belonged to Tempy, who kept it rented to a family of strangers.

In high school Sandy was taking, at his aunt's request, the classical course, which included Latin, ancient history, and English, and which required a great deal of reading. His teacher of English was a large, masculine woman named Martha Fry, who had once been to Europe and who loved to talk about the splendors of old England and to read aloud in a deep, mannish kind of voice, dramatizing the printed words. It was from her that Sandy received an introduction to Shakespeare, for in the spring term they studied *The Merchant of Venice*. In the spring also, under Miss Fry's direction, the first-year students were required to write an essay for the freshman essay prizes of both money and medals. And in this contest Sandy won the second prize. It was the first time in the history of the school that a colored pupil had ever done anything of the sort, and Tempy was greatly elated. There was a note in the papers about it, and Sandy brought his five dollars home for his aunt to put away. But he gave his bronze medal to a girl named Pansetta Young, who was his class-mate and a new-found friend.

From the first moment in school that he saw Pansetta, he knew that he liked her, and he would sit looking at her for hours in every class that they had together—for she was a little baby-doll kind of girl, with big black eyes and a smooth pinkish-brown skin, and her hair was curly on top of her head. Her widowed mother was a cook at the Goucher College dining-hall; and she was an all-alone little girl, for Pansetta had no brothers or sisters. After Thanksgiving Sandy began to walk part of the way home with her every day. He could not accompany her all the way because he had to go to work at Mr. Prentiss's shop. But on Christmas he bought her a box of candy—and sent it to her by mail. And at Easter-time she gave him a chocolate egg.

"Unh-huh! You got a girl now, ain't you?" teased Buster one April afternoon when he caught Sandy standing in front of the high school waiting for Pansetta to come out.

"Aw, go chase yourself!" said Sandy, for Buster had a way of talking dirty about girls, and Sandy was afraid he would begin that with Pansetta; but today his friend changed the subject instead.

"Say come on round to the pool hall tonight and I'll teach you to play billiards."

"Don't think I'd better, Bus. Aunt Tempy might get sore," Sandy replied, shaking his head. "Besides, I have to study."

"Are you gonna read yourself to death?" Buster demanded indignantly. "You've got to come out some time, man! Tell her you're going to the movies and we'll go down to Cudge's instead."

Sandy thought for a moment.

"All the boys come round there at night."

"Well, I might."

"Little apron-string boy!" teased Buster.

"If I hit you a couple of times, you'll find out I'm not!" Sandy doubled up his fists in pretended anger. "I'll black your blue eyes for you!"

"Ya-a-a-a?" yelled his friend, running up the street. "See you tonight at Cudge's—apron-string boy!"

And that evening Sandy didn't finish reading, as he had planned, *Moby Dick*, which Mr. Prentiss's daughter had lent him. Instead he practised handling a cue-stick under the tute-lage of Buster.

# TWENTY-FIVE

## *Pool Hall*

---

THERE were no community houses in Stanton and no recreation centres for young men except the Y.M.C.A., which was closed to you if you were not a white boy; so, for the Negro youths of the town, Cudge Windsor's pool hall was the evening meeting-place. There one could play billiards, shoot dice in a back room, or sit in summer on the two long benches outside, talking and looking at the girls as they passed. In good weather these benches were crowded all the time.

Next door to the pool hall was Cudge Windsor's lunchroom. Of course, the best colored people did not patronize Cudge's, even though his business was not in the Bottoms. It was located on Pearl Street, some three or four blocks before that thoroughfare plunged across the tracks into the low terrain of tinkling pianos and ladies who loved for cash. But since Cudge catered to what Mr. Siles called "the common element," the best people stayed away.

After months of bookishness and subjection to Tempy's prim plans for his improvement, Sandy found the pool hall an easy and amusing place in which to pass time. It was better than the movies, where people on the screen were only shadows. And it was much better than the Episcopal Church, with its stoop-shouldered rector, for here at Cudge's everybody was alive, and the girls who passed in front swinging their arms and grinning at the men were warm-bodied and gay, while the boys rolling dice in the rear room or playing pool at the tables were loud-mouthed and careless. Life sat easily on their muscular shoulders.

Adventurers and vagabonds who passed through Stanton on the main line would often drop in at Cudge's to play a game or get a bite to eat, and many times on summer nights reckless black boys, a long way from home, kept the natives entertained with tales of the road, or trips on side-door Pullmans, and of far-off cities where things were easy and women generous. They had a song that went:

O, the gals in Texas,
They never be's unkind.
They feeds their men an'
Buys 'em gin an' wine.
But these women in Stanton,
Their hearts is hard an' cold.
When you's out of a job, they
Denies you jelly roll.

Then, often, arguments would begin—boastings, proving
and fending; or telling of exploits with guns, knives, and razors,
with cops and detectives, with evil women and wicked men;
out-bragging and out-lying one another, all talking at once.
Sometimes they would create a racket that could be heard for
blocks. To the uninitiated it would seem that a fight was imminent. But underneath, all was good-natured and friendly—and
through and above everything went laughter. No matter how
belligerent or lewd their talk was, or how sordid the tales they
told—of dangerous pleasures and strange perversities—these
black men laughed. That must be the reason, thought Sandy,
why poverty-stricken old Negroes like Uncle Dan Givens lived
so long—because to them, no matter how hard life might be,
it was not without laughter.

Uncle Dan was the world's champion liar, Cudge Windsor
said, and the jolly old man's unending flow of fabulous remi-
niscences were entertaining enough to earn him a frequent
meal in Cudge's lunch-room or a drink of licker from the
patrons of the pool hall, who liked to start the old fellow
talking.

One August evening when Tempy was away attending a
convention of the Midwest Colored Women's Clubs, Sandy
and Buster, Uncle Dan, Jimmy Lane, and Jap Logan sat until
late with a big group of youngsters in front of the pool hall
watching the girls go by. A particularly pretty high yellow
damsel passed in a thin cool dress of flowered voile, trailing the
sweetness of powder and perfume behind her.

"Dog-gone my soul!" yelled Jimmy Lane. "Just gimme a
bone and lemme be your dog—I mean your salty dog!" But
the girl, pretending not to hear, strolled leisurely on, followed
by a train of compliments from the pool-hall benches.

"Sweet mama Venus!" cried a tall raw-bony boy, gazing after her longingly.

"If angels come like that, lemme go to heaven—and if they don't, lemme be lost to glory!" Jap exclaimed.

"Shut up, Jap! What you know 'bout women?" asked Uncle Dan, leaning forward on his cane to interrupt the comments. "Here you-all is, ain't knee-high to ducks yit, an' talkin' 'bout womens! Shut up, all o' you! Nary one o' you's past sebenteen, but when I were yo' age—Hee! Hee! You-all want to know what dey called me when I were yo' age?" The old man warmed to his tale. "Dey called me de 'stud nigger'! Yes, dey did! On 'count o' de kind o' slavery-time work I was doin'—I were breedin' babies fo' to sell!"

"Another lie!" said Jap.

"No, 'tain't, boy! You listen here to what I's gwine tell you. I were de onliest real healthy nigger buck ma white folks had on de plantation, an' dese was ole po' white folks what can't 'ford to buy many slaves, so dey figures to raise a heap o' darky babies an' sell 'em later on—dat's why dey made me de breeder. . . . Hee! Hee! . . . An' I sho breeded a gang o' pickaninnies, too! But I were young then, jest like you-all is, an' I ain't had a pint o' sense—laying wid de womens all night, ever' night."

"Yes, we believe you," drawled Jimmy.

"An' it warn't no time befo' little yaller chillens an' black chillens an' red chillens an' all kinds o' chillens was runnin' round de yard eatin' out o' de hog-pen an' a-callin' me pappy. . . . An' here I is today gwine on ninety-three year ole an' I done outlived 'em all. Dat is, I done outlived all I ever were able to keep track on after de war, 'cause we darkies sho scattered once we was free! Yes, sah! But befo' de fightin' ended I done been pappy to forty-nine chillens—an' thirty-three of 'em were boys!"

"Aw, I know you're lying now, Uncle Dan," Jimmy laughed.

"No, I ain't, sah! . . . Hee! Hee! . . . I were a great one when I were young! Yes, sah!" The old man went on undaunted. "I went an' snuck off to a dance one night, me an' nudder boy, went 'way ovah in Macon County at ole man Laird's plantation, who been a bitter enemy to our white folks. Did I ever tell you 'bout it? We took one o' ole massa's best hosses out

de barn to ride, after he done gone to his bed. . . . Well,
sah! It were late when we got started, an' we rid dat hoss lickety-
split uphill an' down holler, ovah de crick an' past de mill, me an'
ma buddy both on his back, through de cane-brake an' up
anudder hill, till he wobble an' foam at de mouth like he's 'bout
to drap. When we git to de dance, long 'bout midnight, we
jump off dis hoss an' ties him to a post an' goes in de cabin whar
de music were—an' de function were gwine on big. Man! We
grabs ourselves a gal an' dance till de moon riz, kickin' up our
heels an' callin' figgers, an' jest havin' a scrumptious time. Ay,
Lawd! We sho did dance! . . . Well, come 'long 'bout two
o'clock in de mawnin', niggers all leavin', an' we goes out in de
yard to git on dis hoss what we had left standin' at de post. . . .
An' Lawd have mercy—de hoss were dead! Yes, sah! He done
fell down right whar he were tied, eyeballs rolled back, mouth a-
foamin', an' were stone-dead! . . . Well, we ain't knowed how
we gwine git home ner what we gwine do 'bout massa's hoss—an'
we was skeered, Lawdy! 'Cause we know he beat us to death if
he find out we done rid his best hoss anyhow—let lone ridin' de
crittur to death. . . . An' all de low-down Macon niggers what
was at de party was whaw-whawin' fit to kill, laughin' cause it
were so funny to see us gittin' ready to git on our hoss an' de
hoss were dead! . . . Well, sah, me an' ma buddy ain't wasted
no time. We took dat animule up by de hind legs an' we drug
him all de way home to massa's plantation befo' day! We sho
did! Uphill an' down holler, sixteen miles! Yes, sah! An' put dat
damn hoss back in massa's barn like he war befo' we left. An'
when de sun riz, me an' ma buddy were in de slavery quarters
sleepin' sweet an' lowly-like as if we ain't been nowhar. . . . De
next day old massa 'maze how dat hoss die all tied up in his stall
wid his halter on! An' we niggers 'maze, too, when we heard dat
massa's hoss been dead, 'cause we ain't knowed a thing 'bout it.
No, sah! Ain't none o' us niggers knowed a thing! Hee! Hee!
Not a thing!"

"Weren't you scared?" asked Sandy.

"Sho, we was scared," said Uncle Dan, "but we ain't act like
it. Niggers was smart in them days."

"They're still smart," said Jap Logan, "if they can lie like
you."

"I mean!" said Buster.

"Uncle Dan's the world's champeen liar," drawled a tall lanky boy. "Come on, let's chip in and buy him a sandwich, 'cause he's lied enough fo' one evening."

They soon crowded into the lunch-room and sat on stools at the counter ordering soda or ice-cream from the fat good-natured waitress. While they were eating, a gambler bolted in from the back room of the pool hall with a handful of coins he had just won.

"Gonna feed ma belly while I got it in ma hand," he shouted. "Can't tell when I might lose, 'cause de dice is runnin' they own way tonight. Say, Mattie," he yelled, "tell chef to gimme a beefsteak all beat up like Jim Jeffries, cup o' coffee strong as Jack Johnson, an' come flyin' like a airship so I can get back in the game. Tell that kitchen buggar sweet-papa Stingaree's out here!"

"All right, keep yo' collar on," said Mattie. "De steak's got to be cooked."

"What you want, Uncle Dan?" yelled the gambler to the old man. "While I's winnin', might as well feed you, too. Take some ham and cabbage or something. That sandwich ain't 'nough to fill you up."

Uncle Dan accepted a plate of spareribs, and Stingaree threw down a pile of nickels on the counter.

"Injuns an' buffaloes," he said loudly. "Two things de white folks done killed, so they puts 'em on de backs o' nickels. . . . Rush up that steak there, gal, I's hongry!"

Sandy finished his drink and bought a copy of the *Chicago Defender*, the World's Greatest Negro Weekly, which was sold at the counter. Across the front in big red letters there was a headline: *Negro Boy Lynched*. There was also an account of a race riot in a Northern industrial city. On the theatrical page a picture of pretty Baby Alice Whitman, the tap-dancer, attracted his attention, and he read a few of the items there concerning colored shows; but as he was about to turn the page, a little article in the bottom corner made him pause and put the paper down on the counter.

ACTRESS MAKES HIT

St. Louis, Mo., Aug. 3: Harrietta Williams, sensational young blues-singer, has been packing the Booker

Washington Theatre to the doors here this week. Jones and Jones are the headliners for the all-colored vaudeville bill, but the singing of Miss Williams has been the outstanding drawing card. She is being held over for a continued engagement, with Billy Sanderlee at the piano.

"Billy Sanderlee," said Buster, who was looking over Sandy's shoulder. "That's that freckled-faced yellow guy who used to play for dances around here, isn't it? He could really beat a piano to death, all right!"

"Sure could," replied Sandy. "Gee, they must make a great team together, 'cause my Aunt Harrie can certainly sing and dance!"

"Ain't the only thing she can do!" bellowed the gambler, swallowing a huge chunk of steak. "Yo' Aunt Harrie's a whang, son!"

"Shut yo' mouth!" said Uncle Dan.

# TWENTY-SIX

# *The Doors of Life*

DURING Sandy's second year at high school Tempy was busy sewing for the local Red Cross and organizing Liberty Bond clubs among the colored population of Stanton. She earnestly believed that the world would really become safe for democracy, even in America, when the war ended, and that colored folks would no longer be snubbed in private and discriminated against in public.

"Colored boys are over there fighting," she said. "Our men are buying hundreds of dollars' worth of bonds, colored women are aiding the Red Cross, our clubs are sending boxes to the camps and to the front. White folks will see that the Negro can be trusted in war as well as peace. Times will be better after this for all of us."

One day a letter came from Annjee, who had moved to Chicago. She said that Sandy's father had not long remained in camp, but had been sent to France almost immediately after he enlisted, and she didn't know what she was going to do, she was so worried and alone! There had been but one letter from Jimboy since he left. And now she needed Sandy with her, but she wasn't able to send for him yet. She said she hoped and prayed that nothing would happen to his father at the front, but every day there were colored soldiers' names on the casualty list.

"Good thing he's gone," grunted Tempy when she read the letter as they were seated at the supper-table. Then, suddenly changing the subject, she asked Sandy: "Did you see Dr. Frank Crane's beautiful article this morning?"

"No, I didn't," said the boy.

"You certainly don't read as much as you did last winter," complained his aunt. "And you're staying out entirely too late to suit me. I'm quite sure you're not at the movies all that time, either. I want these late hours stopped, young man. Every night in the week out somewhere until ten and eleven o'clock!"

"Well, boys do have to get around a little, Tempy," Mr. Siles objected. "It's not like when you and I were coming up."

"I'm raising this boy, Mr. Siles," Tempy snapped. "When do you study, James? That's what I want to know."

"When I come in," said Sandy, which was true. His light was on until after twelve almost every night. And when he did not study late, his old habit of lying awake clung to him and he could not go to sleep early.

"You think too much," Buster once said. "Stop being so smart; then you'll sleep better."

"Yep," added Jimmy Lane. "Better be healthy and dumb than smart and sick like some o' these college darkies I see with goggles on their eyes and breath smellin' bad."

"O, I'm not sick," objected Sandy, "but I just get to thinking about things at night—the war, and white folks, and God, and girls, and—O, I don't know—everything in general."

"Sure, keep on thinking," jeered Buster, "and turn right ashy after while and be all stoop-shouldered like Father Hill." (The Episcopalian rector was said to be the smartest colored man in town.) "But I'm not gonna worry about being smart myself. A few more years, boy, and I'll be in some big town passing for white, making money, and getting along swell. And I won't need to be smart, either—I'll be ofay! So if you see me some time in St. Louis or Chi with a little blond on my arm— don't recognize me, hear! I want my kids to be so yellow-headed they won't have to think about a color line."

And Sandy knew that Buster meant what he said, for his light-skinned friend was one of those people who always go directly towards the things they want, as though the road is straight before them and they can see clearly all the way. But to Sandy himself nothing ever seemed quite that clear. Why was his country going stupidly to war? . . . Why were white people and colored people so far apart? Why was it wrong to desire the bodies of women? . . . With his mind a maelstrom of thoughts as he lay in bed night after night unable to go to sleep quickly, Sandy wondered many things and asked himself many questions.

Sometimes he would think about Pansetta Young, his classmate with the soft brown skin, and the pointed and delicate breasts of her doll-like body. He had never been alone with

Pansetta, never even kissed her, yet she was "his girl" and he liked her a great deal. Maybe he loved her! . . . But what did it mean to love a girl? Were you supposed to marry her then and live with her for ever? . . . His father had married his mother—good-natured, guitar-playing Jimboy—but they weren't always together, and Sandy knew that Jimboy was enjoying the war now, just as he had always enjoyed everything else.

"Gee, he must of married early to be my father and still look so young!" he thought. "Suppose I marry Pansetta now!" But what did he really know about marriage other than the dirty fragments he had picked up from Jimmy and Buster and the fellows at the pool hall?

On his fifteenth birthday Tempy had given him a book written for young men on the subject of love and living, called *The Doors of Life*, addressed to all Christian youths in their teens— but it had been written by a white New England minister of the Presbyterian faith who stood aghast before the flesh; so its advice consisted almost entirely in how to pray in the orthodox manner, and in how *not* to love.

"Avoid evil companions lest they be your undoing (see Psalms cxix, 115–20); and beware of lewd women, for their footsteps lead down to hell (see Proverbs vii, 25–7)," said the book, and that was the extent of its instructions on sex, except that it urged everyone to marry early and settle down to a healthy, moral, Christian life. . . . But how could you marry early when you had no money and no home to which to take a wife, Sandy wondered. And who were evil companions. Neither Aunt Hager nor Annjee had ever said anything to Sandy about love in its bodily sense; Jimboy had gone away too soon to talk with him; and Tempy and her husband were too proper to discuss such subjects; so the boy's sex knowledge consisted only in the distorted ideas that youngsters whisper; the dirty stories heard in the hotel lobby where he had worked; and the fact that they sold in drugstores articles that weren't mentioned in the company of nice people.

But who were nice people anyway? Sandy hated the word "nice." His Aunt Tempy was always using it. All of her friends were nice, she said, respectable and refined. They went around with their noses in the air and they didn't speak to porters and washwomen—though they weren't nearly so much fun as the folks they tried to scorn. Sandy liked Cudge Windsor or Jap Logan better than he did Dr. Mitchell, who had been to college—and never forgotten it.

Sandy wondered if Booker T. Washington had been like Tempy's friends? Or if Dr. Du Bois was a snob just because he was a college man? He wondered if those two men had a good time being great. Booker T. was dead, but he had left a living school in the South. Maybe he could teach in the South, too, Sandy thought, if he ever learned enough. Did colored folks need to know the things he was studying in books now? Did French and Latin and Shakespeare make people wise and happy? Jap Logan never went beyond the seventh grade and he was happy. And Jimboy never attended school much either. Maybe school didn't matter. Yet to get a good job you had to be smart—and white, too. That was the trouble, you had to be white!

"But I want to learn!" thought Sandy as he lay awake in the dark after he had gone to bed at night. "I want to go to college. I want to go to Europe and study. 'Work and make ready and maybe your chance will come,' it said under the picture of Lincoln on the calendar given away by the First National Bank, where Earl, his white friend, already had a job promised him when he came out of school. . . . It was not nearly so difficult for white boys. They could work at anything—in stores, on newspapers, in offices. They could become president of the United States if they were clever enough. But a colored boy. . . . No wonder Buster was going to pass for white when he left Stanton.

"I don't blame him," thought Sandy. "Sometimes I hate white people, too, like Aunt Harrie used to say she did. Still, some of them are pretty decent—my English-teacher, and Mr. Prentiss where I work. Yet even Mr. Prentiss wouldn't give me a job clerking in his shop. All I can do there is run errands and scrub the floor when everybody else is gone. There's no advancement for colored fellows. If they start as porters, they stay porters for ever and they can't come up. Being colored is like being born in the basement of life, with the door to the light locked and barred—and the white folks live upstairs. They don't want us up there with them, even when we're respectable like Dr. Mitchell, or smart like Dr. Du Bois. . . . And guys like Jap Logan—well, Jap don't care anyway! Maybe it's best not to care, and stay poor and meek waiting for heaven like Aunt Hager did. . . . But I don't want heaven! I want to live first!" Sandy thought. "I want to live!"

He understood then why many old Negroes said: "Take all this world and give me Jesus!" It was because they couldn't get this world anyway—it belonged to the white folks. They alone had the power to give or withhold at their back doors. Always back doors—even for Tempy and Dr. Mitchell if they chose to go into Wright's Hotel or the New Albert Restaurant. And no door at all for Negroes if they wanted to attend the Rialto Theatre, or join the Stanton Y.M.C.A., or work behind the grilling at the National Bank.

*The Doors of Life.* . . . God damn that simple-minded book that Tempy had given him! What did an old white minister know about the doors of life for him and Pansetta and Jimmy Lane, for Willie-Mae and Buster and Jap Logan and all the black and brown and yellow youngsters standing on the threshold of the great beginning in a Western town called Stanton? What did an old white minister know about the doors of life anywhere? And, least of all, the doors to a Negro's life? . . . Black youth. . . . Dark hands knocking, knocking! Pansetta's little brown hands knocking on the doors of life! Baby-doll hands, tiny autumn-leaf girl-hands! . . . Gee, Pansetta! . . . The Doors of Life . . . the great big doors. . . . Sandy was asleep . . . of life.

# TWENTY-SEVEN

# Beware of Women

"I WON'T permit it," said Tempy. "I won't stand for it. You'll have to mend your ways, young man! Spending your evenings in Windsor's pool parlor and running the streets with a gang of common boys that have had no raising, that Jimmy Lane among them. I won't stand for it while you stay in my house. . . . But that's not the worst of it. Mr. Prentiss tells me you've been getting to work late after school three times this week. And what have you been doing? O, don't think I don't know! I saw you with my own eyes yesterday walking home with that girl Pansetta Young! . . . Well, I want you to understand that I won't have it!"

"I didn't walk home with her," said Sandy. "I only go part way with her every day. She's in my class in high school and we have to talk over our lessons. She's the only colored kid in my class I have to talk to."

"Lessons! Yes, I know it's lessons," said Tempy sarcastically. "If she were a girl of our own kind, it would be all right. I don't see why you don't associate more with the young people of the church. Marie Steward or Grace Mitchell are both nice girls and you don't notice them. No, you have to take up with this Pansetta, whose mother works out all day, leaving her daughter to do as she chooses. Well, she's not going to ruin you, after all I've done to try to make something out of you."

"Beware of women, son," said Mr. Siles pontifically from his deep morris-chair. It was one of his few evenings home and Tempy had asked him to talk to her nephew, who had gotten beyond her control, for Sandy no longer remained in at night even when she expressly commanded it; and he no longer attended church regularly, but slept on Sunday mornings instead. He kept up his school-work, it was true, but he seemed to have lost all interest in acquiring the respectable bearing and attitude towards life that Tempy thought he should have. She bought him fine clothes and he went about with ruffians.

"In other words, he has been acting just like a nigger, Mr. Siles!" she told her husband. "And he's taken up with a girl who's not of the best, to say the least, even if she does go to the high school. Mrs. Francis Cannon, who lives near her, tells me that this Pansetta has boys at her house all the time, and her mother is never at home until after dark. She's a cook or something somewhere. . . . A fine person for a nephew of ours to associate with, this Pansy daughter of hers!"

"Pansetta's a nice girl," said Sandy. "And she's smart in school, too. She helps me get my Latin every day, and I might fail if she didn't."

"Huh! It's little help you need with your Latin, young man! Bring it here and I'll help you. I had Latin when I was in school. And certainly you don't need to walk on the streets with her in order to study Latin, do you? First thing you know you'll be getting in trouble with her and she'll be having a baby—I see I have to be plain—and whether it's yours or not, she'll say it is. Common girls like that always want to marry a boy they think is going to amount to something— going to college and be somebody in the world. Besides, you're from the Williams family and you're good-looking! But I'm going to stop this affair right now. . . . From now on you are to leave that girl alone, do you understand me? She's dangerous!"

"Yes," grunted Mr. Siles. "She's dangerous."

Angry and confused, Sandy left the room and went upstairs to bed, but he could not sleep. What right had they to talk that way about his friends? Besides, what did they mean about her being dangerous? About his getting in trouble with her? About her wanting to marry him because her mother was a cook and he was going to college?

A white boy in Sandy's high-school class had "got in trouble" with an Italian girl and they had had to go to the juvenile court to fix it up, but it had been kept quiet. Even now Sandy couldn't quite give an exact explanation of what getting in trouble with a girl meant. Did a girl have to have a baby just because a fellow walked home with her when he didn't even go in? Pansetta had asked him into her house often, but he always had to go back uptown to work. He was due at work at four o'clock—besides he knew it wasn't quite correct to call on a young lady if her mother was not at home. But it wasn't necessarily bad, was it? And how could a girl have a baby and say it was his if it wasn't his? Why couldn't he talk to his Aunt Tempy about such things and get a clear and simple answer instead of being given an old book like *The Doors of Life* that didn't explain anything at all?

Pansetta hadn't said a word to him about babies, or anything like that, but she let him kiss her once and hold her on his lap at Sadie Butler's Christmas party. Gee, but she could kiss—and such a long time! He wouldn't care if she did make him marry her, only he wanted to travel first. If his mother would send for him now, he would like to go to Chicago. His Aunt Tempy was too cranky, and too proper. She didn't like any of his friends, and she hated the pool hall. But where else was there for a fellow to play? Who wanted to go to those high-toned people's houses, like the Mitchells', and look bored all the time while they put Caruso's Italian records on their new victrola? Even if it was the finest victrola owned by a Negro in Stanton, as they always informed you, Sandy got tired of listening to records in a language that none of them understood.

"But this is opera!" they said. Well, maybe it was, but he thought that his father and Harriett used to sing better. And they sang nicer songs. One of them was:

> Love, O love, O careless love—
> Goes to your head like wine!

"And maybe I really am in love with Pansetta. . . . But if she thinks she can fool me into marrying her before I've travelled all around the world, like my father, she's wrong," Sandy thought. "She can't trick me, not this kid!" Then he was immediately sorry that he had allowed Tempy's insinuations to influence his thoughts.

"Pretty, baby-faced Pansetta! Why, she wouldn't try to trick anybody into anything. If she wanted me to love her, she'd let me, but she wouldn't try to trick a fellow. She wouldn't let me love her that way anyhow—like Tempy meant. Gee, that was ugly of Aunt Tempy to say that! . . . But Buster said she would. . . . Aw, he always talked that way about girls! He said no women were any good—as if he knew! And Jimmy

Lane said white women were worse than colored—but all the boys who worked at hotels said that."

Let 'em talk! Sandy liked Pansetta anyhow. . . . But maybe his Aunt Tempy was right! Maybe he had better stop walking home with her. He didn't want to "get in trouble" and not be able to travel to Chicago some time, where his mother was. Maybe he could go to Chicago next summer if he began to save his money now. He wanted to see the big city, where the buildings were like towers, the trains ran overhead, and the lake was like a sea. He didn't want to "get in trouble" with Pansetta even if he did like her. Besides, he had to live with Tempy for awhile yet and he hated to be quarrelling with his aunt all the time. He'd stop going to the pool hall so much and stay home at night and study. . . . But, heck! it was too beautiful out of doors to stay in the house—especially since spring had come!

Through his open window, as he lay in bed after Tempy's tirade about the girl, he could see the stars and the tops of the budding maple-trees. A cool earth-smelling breeze lifted the white curtains, scattering the geometry papers that he had left lying on his study table. He got out of bed to pick up the papers and put them away, and stood for a moment in his pyjamas looking out of the window at the roofs of the houses and the tops of the trees under the night sky.

"I wish I had a brother," Sandy thought as he stood there. "Maybe I could talk to him about things and I wouldn't have to think so much. It's no fun being the only kid in the family, and your father never home either. . . . When I get married, I'm gonna have a lot of children; then they won't have to grow up by themselves."

The next day after school he walked nearly home with Pansetta as usual, although he was still thinking of what Tempy had said, but he hadn't decided to obey his aunt yet. At the corner of the block in which the girl lived, he gave her her books.

"I got to beat it back to the shop now. Old man Prentiss'll have a dozen deliveries waiting for me just because I'm late."

"All right," said Pansetta in her sweet little voice. "I'm sorry you can't come on down to my house awhile. Say, why don't you work at the hotel, anyway? Wouldn't you make more money there?"

"Guess I would," replied the boy. "But my aunt thinks it's better where I am."

"Oh," said Pansetta. "Well, I saw Jimmy Lane last night and he's making lots of money at the hotel. He wanted to meet me around to school this afternoon, but I told him no. I said you took me home."

"I do," said Sandy.

"Yes," laughed Pansetta; "but I didn't tell him you wouldn't ever come in."

During the sunny spring weeks that followed, Sandy did not walk home with her any more after school. Having to go to work earlier was the excuse he gave, but at first Pansetta seemed worried and puzzled. She asked him if he was mad at her, or something, but he said he wasn't. Then in a short time other boys were meeting her on the corner near the school, buying her cones when the ice-cream wagon passed and taking her home in the afternoons. To see other fellows buying her ice-cream and walking home with her made Sandy angry, but it was his own fault, he thought. And he felt lonesome having no one to walk with after classes.

Pansetta, in school, was just as pleasant as before, but in a kind of impersonal way, as though she hadn't been his girl once. And now Sandy was worried, because it had been easy to drop her, but would it be easy to get her back again if he should want her? The hotel boys had money, and once or twice he saw her talking with Jimmy Lane. Gee, but she looked pretty in her thin spring dresses and her wide straw hat.

Why had he listened to Tempy at all? She didn't know Pansetta, and just because her mother worked out in service she wanted him to snub the girl. What was that to be afraid of—her mother not being home after school? Even if Pansetta would let him go in the house with her and put his arms around her and love her, why shouldn't he? Didn't he have a right to have a girl like that, as well as the other fellows? Didn't he have a right to be free with women, too, like all the rest of the young men? . . . But Pansetta wasn't that kind of girl!

. . . What made his mind run away with him? Because of what Tempy had said? . . . To hell with Tempy!

"She's just an old-fashioned darky Episcopalian, that's what Tempy is! And she wanted me to drop Pansetta because her mother doesn't belong to the Dunbar Whist Club. Gee, but I'm ashamed of myself. I'm a cad and a snob, that's all I am, and I'm going to apologize." Subconsciously he was living over a scene from an English novel he had read at the printing-shop, in which the Lord dropped the Squire's daughter for a great Lady, but later returned to his first love. Sandy retained the words "cad" and "snob" in his vocabulary, but he wasn't thinking of the novel now. He really believed, after three weeks of seeing Pansetta walking with other boys, that he had done wrong, and that Tempy was the villainess in the situation. It was worrying him a great deal; he decided to make up with Pansetta if he could.

One Friday afternoon she left school with a great armful of books. They had to write an English composition for Monday and she had taken some volumes from the school library for reference. He might have offered to carry them for her, but he hadn't. Instead he went to work—and there had been no other colored boys on the corner waiting for her as she went out. Now he could have kicked himself for his neglect, he thought, as he cleaned the rear room of Mr. Prentiss's gift-card shop. Suddenly he dropped the broom with which he was sweeping, grabbed his cap, and left the place, for the desire to make friends with Pansetta possessed him more fiercely than ever, and he no longer cared about his work.

"I'm going to see her right now," he thought, "before I go home to supper. Gee, but I'm ashamed of the way I've treated her."

On the way to Pansetta's house the lawns looked fresh and green and on some of them tulips were blooming. The late afternoon sky was aglow with sunset. Little boys were out in the streets with marbles and tops, and little girls were jumping rope on the sidewalks. Workmen were coming home, empty dinner-pails in their hands, and a band of Negro laborers passed Sandy, singing softly together.

"I must hurry," the boy thought. "It will soon be our

supper-time." He ran until he was at Pansetta's house—then came the indecision: Should he go in? Or not go in? He was ashamed of his treatment of her and embarrassed. Should he go on by as if he had not meant to call? Suppose she shut the door in his face! Or, worse, suppose she asked him to stay awhile! Should he stay? What Tempy had said didn't matter any more. He wanted to be friends with Pansetta again. He wanted her to know he still liked her and wanted to walk home with her. But how could he say it? Had she seen him from the window? Maybe he could turn around and go back, and see her Monday at school.

"No! I'm not a coward," he declared. "Afraid of a girl! I'll walk right up on the front porch and knock!" But the small house looked very quiet and the lace curtains were tightly drawn together at the windows. . . . He knocked again. Maybe there was no one home. . . . Yes, he heard somebody.

Finally Pansetta peeped through the curtains of the glass in the front door. Then she opened the door and smiled surprisingly, her hair mussed and her creamy-brown skin pink from the warm blood pulsing just under the surface. Her eyes were dark and luminous, and her lips were moist and red.

"It's Sandy!" she said, turning to address someone inside the front room.

"O, come in, old man," a boy's voice called in a tone of forced welcome, and Sandy saw Jimmy Lane sitting on the couch adjusting his collar self-consciously. "How's everything, old scout?"

"All right," Sandy stammered. "Say, Pansy, I—I— Do you know— I mean, what is the subject we're supposed to write on for English Monday? I must of forgotten to take it down."

"Why, 'A Trip to Shakespeare's England.' That's easy to remember, silly. You must have been asleep. . . . Won't you sit down?"

"No, thanks, I've— I guess I got to get back to supper."

"Jesus!" cried Jimmy jumping up from the sofa. "Is it that late? I'm due on bells at six o'clock. Wait a minute, Sandy, and I'll walk up with you as far as the hotel. Boy, I'm behind time!" He picked up his coat from the floor, and Pansetta held it for him while he thrust his arms into the sleeves, glancing around meanwhile for his cap, which lay among the sofa-pillows. Then he kissed the girl carelessly on the lips as he slid one arm familiarly around her waist.

"So long, baby," he said, and the two boys went out. On the porch Jimmy lit a cigarette and passed the pack to Sandy.

Jimmy Lane looked and acted as if he were much older than his companion, but Jimmy had been out of school several years, and hopping bells taught a fellow a great deal more about life than books did—and also about women. Besides, he was supporting himself now, which gave him an air of independence that boys who still lived at home didn't have.

When they had walked about a block, the bell-boy said carelessly: "Pansetta can go! Can't she, man?"

"I don't know," said Sandy.

"Aw, boy, you're lying," Jimmy Lane returned. "Don't try to hand me that kid stuff! You had her for a year, didn't you?"

"Yes," replied Sandy slowly, "but not like you mean."

"Stop kidding," Jimmy insisted.

"No, honest, I never touched her that way," the boy said. "I never was at her house before."

Jimmy opened his mouth astonished. "What!" he exclaimed. "And her old lady out working till eight and nine every night! Say, Sandy, we're friends, but you're either just a big liar—or else a God-damn fool!" He threw his cigarette away and put both hands in his pockets. "Pansetta's easy as hell, man!"

# TWENTY-EIGHT

# *Chicago*

CHICAGO, ILL.
May 16, 1918

D EAR SANDY:
Have just come home from work and am very tired but thought I would write you this letter right now while I had time and wasn't sleepy. You are a big boy and I think you can be of some help to me. I don't want you to stay in Stanton any longer as a burden on your Aunt Tempy. She says in her letters you have begun to stay out late nights and not pay her any mind. You ought to be with your mother now because you are all she has since I do not know what has happened to your father in France. The war is awful and so many mens are getting killed. Have not had no word from Jimboy for 7 months from Over There and am worried till I'm sick. Will try and send you how much money you need for your fare before the end of the month so when school is out in june you can come. Let me know how much you saved and I will send you the rest to come to Chicago because Mr. Harris where I stay is head elevator man at a big hotel in the Loop and he says he can put you on there in July. That will be a good job for you and maybe by saving your money you can go back to school in Sept. I will help you if I can but you will have to help me too because I have not been do-ing so well. Am working for a colored lady in her hair dressing parlor and am learning hairdressing myself, sham-poo and straighten and give massauges on the face and all. But colored folks are hard people to work for. Madam King is from down south somewhere and these southern Negroes are not like us in their ways, but she seems to like me. Mr. Harris is from the south too in a place called Baton Rouge. They eat rice all the time. Well I must close hoping to see you soon once more because it has been five

years since I have looked at my child. With love to you
and Tempy, be a good boy,

Your mother,
Annjelica Rogers.

A week later another letter came to Sandy from his mother.
This time it was a registered special-delivery, which said: "If
you'll come right away you can get your job at once. Mr. Harris
says he will have a vacancy Saturday because one of the elevator boys are quitting." And sufficient bills to cover Sandy's fare
tumbled out.

With a tremendous creaking and grinding and steady clack-
ing of wheels the long train went roaring through the night
towards Chicago as Sandy, in a day coach, took from his pocket
Annjee's two letters and re-read them for the tenth time since
leaving Stanton. He could hardly believe himself actually at
that moment on the way to Chicago!

In the stuffy coach papers littered the floor and the scent of
bananas and human feet filled the car. The lights were dim and
most of the passengers slumbered in the straight-backed greenplush seats, but Sandy was still awake. The thrill of his first all-
night rail journey and his dream-expectations of the great city
were too much to allow a sixteen-year-old boy to go calmly to
sleep, although the man next to him had long been snoring.

Annjee's special-delivery letter had come that morning.
Sandy had discovered it when he came home for lunch, and
upon his return to the high school for the afternoon classes he
went at once to the principal to inquire if he might be excused
from the remaining days of the spring term.

"Let me see! Your record's pretty good, isn't it, Rogers?"
said Professor Perkins looking over his glasses at the young
colored fellow standing before him. "Going to Chicago, heh?
Well, I guess we can let you transfer and give you full credit for
this year's work without your waiting here for the examinations
—there are only ten days or so of the term remaining. You are
an honor student and would get through your exams all right.
Now, if you'll just send us your address when you get to
Chicago, we'll see that you get your report. . . . Intending
to go to school there, are you? . . . That's right! I like to see

your people get ahead. . . . Well, good luck to you, James."
The old gentleman rose and held out his hand.

"Good old scout," thought Sandy. "Miss Fry was a good
teacher, too! Some white folks *are* nice all right! Not all of
them are mean. . . . Gee, old man Prentiss hated to see me
quit his place. Said I was the best boy he ever had working
there, even if I was late once in awhile. But I don't mind leaving Stanton. Gee, Chicago ought to be great! And I'm sure
glad to get away from Tempy's house. She's too tight!"

But Tempy had not been glad to see her nephew leave. She
had grown fond of the boy in spite of her almost nightly lec-
tures to him recently on his behavior and in spite of his never
having become her model youth. Not that he was bad, but he
might have been so much better! She wanted to show her
white neighbors a perfect colored boy—and such a boy certainly wouldn't be a user of slang, a lover of pool halls and non-
Episcopalian ways. Tempy had given Sandy every opportunity
to move in the best colored society and he had not taken advantage of it. Nevertheless, she cried a little as she packed a
lunch for him to eat on the train. She had done all she could.
He was a good-looking boy, and quite smart. Now, if he
wanted to go to his mother, well—"I can only hope Chicago
won't ruin you," she said. "It's a wicked city! Goodbye, James.
Remember what I've tried to teach you. Stand up straight and
look like you're somebody!"

Stanton, Sandy's Kansas home, was back in the darkness,
and the train sped towards the great center where all the small-
town boys in the whole Middle West wanted to go.

"I'm going now!" thought Sandy. "Chicago now!"

A few weeks past he had gone to see Sister Johnson, who
was quite feeble with the rheumatism. As she sat in the corner
of her kitchen smoking a corn-cob pipe, no longer able to wash
clothes, but still able to keep up a rapid flow of conversation,
she told him all the news.

"Tom, he's still at de bank keepin' de furnace goin' an' sort
o' handy man. . . . Willie-Mae, I 'spects you knows, is figurin'
on gettin' married next month to Mose Jenkins, an' I tells her
she better stay single, young as she is, but she ain't payin' me
no mind. Umn-unh! Jest let her go on! . . . Did you heerd
Sister Whiteside's daughter done brought her third husband

home to stay wid her ma—an' five o' her first husband's chillens there too? Gals ain't got no regard for de old folks. Sister Whiteside say if she warn't a Christian in her heart, she don't believe she could stand it! . . . I tells Willie-Mae she better not bring no husbands here to stay wid me—do an' I'll run him out! These mens ought be shame o' demselves comin' livin' on de womenfolks."

As the old woman talked, Sandy, thinking of his grandmother, gazed out of the window towards the house next door, where he had lived with Aunt Hager. Some small children were playing in the back yard, running and yelling. They belonged to the Southern family to whom Tempy had rented the place. . . . Madam de Carter, who still owned the second house, had been made a national grand officer in the women's division of the lodge and many of the members of the order now had on the walls of their homes a large picture of her dressed in full regalia, inscribed: "Yours in His Grace," and signed: "Madam Fannie Rosalie de Carter."

"Used to be just plain old Rose Carter befo' she got so important," said Sister Johnson, explaining her neighbor's lengthy name. "All these womens dey mammy named Jane an' Mary an' Cora, soon's dey gets a little somethin', dey changes dey names to Janette or Mariana or Corina or somethin' mo' flowcry then what dey had. Willie-Mae say she gwine change her'n to Willetta-Mayola, an' I tole her if she do, I'll beat her—don't care how old she is!"

Sandy liked to listen to the rambling talk of old colored folks. "I guess there won't be many like that in Chicago," he thought, as he doubled back his long legs under the greenplush seat of the day coach. "I better try to get to sleep—there's a long ways to go until morning."

Although it was not yet June, the heat was terrific when, with the old bags that Tempy had given him, Sandy got out of the dusty train in Chicago and walked the length of the sheds into the station. He caught sight of his mother waiting in the crowd, a fatter and much older woman than he had remembered her to be; and at first she didn't know him among the stream of people coming from the train. Perhaps, unconsciously, she was looking for the little boy she left in Stanton;

but Sandy was taller than Annjee now and he looked quite a young man in his blue serge suit with long trousers. His mother threw both plump arms around him and hugged and kissed him for a long time.

They went uptown in the street-cars, Annjee a trifle out of breath from helping with the bags, and both of them perspiring freely from the heat. And they were not very talkative either. A strange and unexpected silence seemed to come between them. Annjee had been away from her son for five growing years and he was no longer her baby boy, small and eager for a kiss. She could see from the little cuts on his face that he had even begun to shave on the chin. And his voice was like a man's, deep and musical as Jimboy's, but not so sure of itself.

But Sandy was not thinking of his mother as they rode uptown on the street-car. He was looking out of the windows at the blocks of dirty grey warehouses lining the streets through which they were passing. He hadn't expected the great city to be monotonous and ugly like this and he was vaguely disappointed. No towers, no dreams come true! Where were the thrilling visions of grandeur he had held? Hidden in the dusty streets? Hidden in the long, hot alleys through which he could see at a distance the tracks of the elevated trains?

"Street-cars are slower, but I ain't got used to them air lines yet," said Annjee, searching her mind for something to say. "I always think maybe them elevated cars'll fall off o' there sometimes. They go so fast!"

"I believe I'd rather ride on them, though," said Sandy, as he looked at the monotonous box-like tenements and dismal alleys on the ground level. No trees, no yards, no grass such as he had known at home, and yet, on the other hand, no bigness or beauty about the bleak warehouses and sorry shops that hugged the sidewalk. Soon, however, the street began to take on a racial aspect and to become more darkly alive. Negroes leaned from windows with heads uncombed, or sat fanning in doorways with legs apart, talking in kimonos and lounging in overalls, and more and more they became a part of the passing panorama.

"This is State Street," said Annjee. "They call it the Black Belt. We have to get off in a minute. You got your suit-case?"

She rang the bell and at Thirty-seventh Street they walked over to Wabash Avenue. The cool shade of the tiny porch that Annjee mounted was more than welcome, and as she took out her key to unlock the front door, Sandy sat on the steps and mopped his forehead with a grimy handkerchief. Inside, there was a dusky gloom in the hallway, that smelled of hair-oil and cabbage steaming.

"Guess Mis' Harris is in the kitchen," said Annjee. "Come on—we'll go upstairs and I'll show you our room. I guess we can both stay together till we can do better. You're still little enough to sleep with your mother, ain't you?"

They went down the completely dark hall on the second floor, and his mother opened a door that led into a rear room with two windows looking out into the alley, giving an extremely near view of the elevated structure on which a downtown train suddenly rushed past with an ear-splitting roar that made the entire house tremble and the window-sashes rattle. There was a wash-stand with a white bowl and pitcher in the room, Annjee's trunk, a chair, and a brass bed, covered with a fresh spread and starched pillow-covers in honor of Sandy's arrival.

"See," said Annjee. "There's room enough for us both, and we'll be saving rent. There's no closet, but we can drive a few extra nails behind the door. And with the two windows we can get plenty of air these hot nights."

"It's nice, mama," Sandy said, but he had to repeat his statement twice, because another L train thundered past so that he couldn't hear his own words as he uttered them. "It's awful nice, mama!"

He took off his coat and sat down on the trunk between the two windows. Annjee came over and kissed him, rubbing her hand across his crinkly brown hair.

"Well, you're a great big boy now. . . . Mama's baby—in long pants. And you're handsome, just like your father!" She had Jimboy's picture stuck in a corner of the wash-stand—a postcard photo in his army uniform, in which he looked very boyish and proud, sent from the training-camp before his company went to France. "But I got no time to be setting here petting you, Sandy, even if you have just come. I got to get on back to the hairdressing-parlor to make some money."

So Annjee went to work again—as she had been off only long enough to meet the train—and Sandy lay down on the bed and slept the hot afternoon away. That evening as a treat they had supper at a restaurant, where Annjee picked carefully from the cheap menu so that their bill wouldn't be high.

"But don't think this is regular. We can't afford it," she said. "I bring things home and fix them on an oil-stove in the room and spread papers on the trunk for a table. A restaurant supper's just in honor of you."

When they came back to the house that evening, Sandy was introduced to Mrs. Harris, their landlady, and to her husband, the elevator-starter, who was to give him the job at the hotel.

"That's a fine-looking boy you got there, Mis' Rogers," he said, appraising Sandy. "He'll do pretty well for one of them main lobby cars, since we don't use nothing but first-class intelligent help down where I am, like I told you. And we has only the best class o' white folks stoppin' there, too. . . . Be up at six in the mornin', buddy, and I'll take you downtown with me."

Annjee was tired, so they went upstairs to the back room and lit the gas over the bed, but the frequent roar of the L trains prevented steady conversation and made Sandy jump each time that the long chain of cars thundered by. He hadn't yet become accustomed to them, or to the vast humming of the city, which was strange to his small-town ears. And he wanted to go out and look around a bit, to walk up and down the streets at night and see what they were like.

"Well, go on if you want to," said his mother, "but don't forget this house number. I'm gonna lie down, but I guess I'll be awake when you come back. Or somebody'll be setting on the porch and the door'll be open."

At the corner Sandy stopped and looked around to be sure of his bearings when he returned. He marked in his mind the sign-board advertising CHESTERFIELDS and the frame-house with the tumbledown stairs on the outside. In the street some kids were playing hopscotch under the arc-light. Somebody stopped beside him.

"Nice evening?" said a small yellow man with a womanish kind of voice, smiling at Sandy.

"Yes," said the boy, starting across the street, but the stranger followed him, offering Pall Malls. He smelled of perfume, and his face looked as though it had been powdered with white talcum as he lit a tiny pocket-lighter.

"Stranger?" murmured the soft voice, lighting Sandy's cigarette.

"I'm from Stanton," he replied, wishing the man had not chosen to walk with him.

"Ah, Kentucky," exclaimed the perfumed fellow. "I been down there. Nice women in that town, heh?"

"But it's not Kentucky," Sandy objected. "It's Kansas."

"Oh, out west where the girls are raring to go! I know! Just like wild horses out there—so passionate, aren't they?"

"I guess so," Sandy ventured. The powdered voice was softly persistent.

"Say, kid," it whispered smoothly, touching the boy's arm, "listen, I got some swell French pictures up in my room—naked women and everything! Want to come up and see them?"

"No," said Sandy quickening his pace. "I got to go somewhere."

"But I room right around the corner," the voice insisted. "Come on by. You're a nice kid, you know it? Listen, don't walk so fast. Stop, let me talk to you."

But Sandy was beginning to understand. A warm sweat broke out on his neck and forehead. Sometimes, at the pool hall in Stanton, he had heard the men talk about queer fellows who stopped boys in the streets and tried to coax them to their rooms.

"He thinks I'm dumb," thought Sandy, "but I'm wise to him!" Yet he wondered what such men did with the boys who accompanied them. Curious, he'd like to find out—but he was afraid; so at the next corner he turned and started rapidly towards State Street, but the queer fellow kept close beside him, begging.

". . . and we'll have a nice time. . . . I got wine in the room, if you want some, and a vic, too."

"Get away, will you!"

They had reached State Street where the lights were bright and people were passing all the time. Sandy could see the fellow's anxious face quite clearly now.

"Listen, kid . . . you . . ."

But suddenly the man was no longer beside him—for Sandy commenced to run. On the brightly lighted avenue panic seized him. He had to escape this powdered face at his shoulder. The whining voice made him sick inside—and, almost without knowing it, his legs began swerving swiftly between the crowds along the curb. When he stopped in front of the Monogram Theatre, two blocks away, he was freed of his companion.

"Gee, that's nice," panted Sandy, grinning as he stood looking at the pictures in front of the vaudeville house, while hundreds of dark people passed up and down on the sidewalk behind him. Lots of folks were going into the theatre, laughing and pushing, for one of the great blues-singing Smiths was appearing there. Sandy walked towards the ticket-booth to see what the prices were.

"Buy me a ticket, will you?" said a feminine voice beside him. This time it was a girl—a very ugly, skinny girl, whose smile revealed a row of dirty teeth. She sidled up to the startled boy whom she had accosted and took his hand.

"I'm not going in," Sandy said shortly, as he backed away, wiping the palm of his hand on his coat-sleeve.

"All right then, stingy!" hissed the girl, flouncing her hips and digging into her own purse for the coins to buy a ticket. "I got money."

Some men standing on the edge of the sidewalk laughed as Sandy went up the street. A little black child in front of him toddled along in the crowd, seemingly by itself, licking a big chocolate ice-cream cone that dripped down the front of its dress.

So this was Chicago where the buildings were like towers and the lake was like a sea . . . State Street, the greatest Negro street in the world, where people were always happy, lights for ever bright; and where the prettiest brown-skin women on earth could be found—so the men in Stanton said.

"I guess I didn't walk the right way. But maybe tomorrow I'll see other things," Sandy thought, "the Loop and the lake and the museum and the library. Maybe they'll be better."

He turned into a side street going back towards Wabash Avenue. It was darker there, and near the alley a painted woman called him, stepping out from among the shadows.

"Say, baby, com'ere!" But the boy went on.

Crossing overhead an L train thundered by, flashing its flow of yellow light on the pavement beneath.

Sandy turned into Wabash Avenue and cut across the street. As he approached the colored Y.M.C.A., three boys came out with swimming suits on their arms, and one of them said: "Damn, but it's hot!" They went up the street laughing and talking with friendly voices, and at the corner they turned off.

"I must be nearly home," Sandy thought, as he made out a group of kids still playing under the streetlight. Then he distinguished, among the other shabby buildings, the brick house where he lived. The front porch was still crowded with roomers trying to keep cool, and as the boy came up to the foot of the steps, some of the fellows seated there moved to let him pass.

"Good-evenin', Mr. Rogers," Mrs. Harris called, and as Sandy had never been called Mr. Rogers before, it made him feel very manly and a little embarrassed as he threaded his way through the group on the porch.

Upstairs he found his mother sleeping deeply on one side of the bed. He undressed, keeping on his underwear, and crawled in on the other side, but he lay awake a long while because it was suffocatingly hot, and very close in their room. The bedbugs bit him on the legs. Every time he got half asleep, an L train roared by, shrieking outside their open windows, lighting up the room, and shaking the whole house. Each time the train came, he started and trembled as though a sudden dragon were rushing at the bed. But then, after midnight, when the elevated cars passed less frequently, and he became more used to their passing, he went to sleep.

# TWENTY-NINE
## *Elevator*

---

T HE following day Sandy went to work as elevator-boy at the hotel in the Loop where Mr. Harris was head bellman, and during the hot summer months that followed, his life in Chicago gradually settled into a groove of work and home—work, and home to Annjee's stuffy little room against the elevated tracks, where at night his mother read the war news and cried because there had been no letter from Jimboy. Whether Sandy's father was in Brest or Saint-Lazare with the labor battalions, or at the front, she did not know. The *Chicago Defender* said that colored troops were fighting in the Champagne sector with great distinction, but Annjee cried anew when she read that.

"No news is good news," Sandy repeated every night to comfort his mother, for he couldn't imagine Jimboy dead. "Papa's all right!" But Annjee worried and wept, half sick all the time, for ever reading the death lists fearfully for her husband's name.

That summer the heat was unbearable. Uptown in the Black Belt the air was like a steaming blanket around your head. In the Loop the sky was white-hot metal. Even on the lake front there was no relief unless you hurried into the crowded water. And there were long stretches of beach where the whites did not want Negroes to swim; so it was often dangerous to bathe if you were colored.

Sandy sweltered as he stood at the door of his box-like, mirrored car in the big hotel lobby. He wore a red uniform with brass buttons and a tight coat that had to be kept fastened no matter how warm it was. But he felt very proud of himself holding his first full-time job, helping his mother with the room rent, and trying to save a little money out of each pay in order to return to high school in the fall.

The prospects of returning to school, however, were not bright. Some weeks it was impossible for Sandy to save even a half-dollar. And Annjee said now that she believed he should stay out of school and work to take care of himself, since he was as large as a man and had more education already than she'd had at his age. Aunt Hager would not have felt that way, though, Sandy thought, remembering his grandmother's great ambition for him. But Annjee was different, less far-seeing than her mother had been, less full of hopes for her son, not ambitious about him—caring only for the war and Jimboy.

At the hotel Sandy's hours on duty were long, and his legs and back ached with weariness from standing straight in one spot all the time, opening and closing the bronze door of the elevator. He had been assigned the last car in a row of six, each manned by a colored youth standing inside his metal box in a red uniform, operating the lever that sent the car up from the basement grill to the roof-garden restaurant on the fifteenth floor and then back down again all day. Repeating up-down—up-down—up-down interminably, carrying white guests.

After two months of this there were times when Sandy felt as though he could stand it no longer. The same flow of people week after week—fashionable women, officers, business men; the fetid air of the elevator-shaft, heavy with breath and the perfume of bodies; the same doors opening at the same unchanging levels hundreds of times each innumerable, monotonous day. The L in the morning; the L again at night. The street or the porch for a few minutes of air. Then bed. And the same thing tomorrow.

"I've got to get out of this," Sandy thought. "It's an awful job." Yet some of the fellows had been there for years. Three of the elevator-men on Sandy's shift were more than forty years old—and had never gotten ahead in life. Mr. Harris had been a bell-hop since his boyhood, doing the same thing day after day—and now he was very proud of being head bell-boy in Chicago.

"I've got to get out of this," Sandy kept repeating. "Or maybe I'll get stuck here, too, like they are, and never get away. I've got to go back to school."

Yet he knew that his mother was making very little money—serving more or less as an apprentice in the hairdressing-shop, trying to learn the trade. And if he quit work, how would he live? Annjee did not favor his returning to school. And could he study if he were hungry? Could he study if he were worried about having no money? Worried about Annjee's displeasure?

"Yes! I can!" he said. "I'm going to study!" He thought about Booker Washington sleeping under the wooden pavements at Richmond—because he had had no place to stay on his way to Hampton in search of an education. He thought about Frederick Douglass—a fugitive slave, owning not even himself, and yet a student. "If they could study, I can, too! When school opens, I'm going to quit this job. Maybe I can get another one at night or in the late afternoon—but it doesn't matter—I'm going back to my classes in September. . . . I'm through with elevators."

Jimboy! Jimboy! Like Jimboy! something inside him warned, quitting work with no money, uncaring.

"Not like Jimboy," Sandy countered against himself. "Not like my father, always wanting to go somewhere. I'd get as tired of travelling all the time, as I do of running this elevator up and down day after day. . . . I'm more like Harriett—not wanting to be a servant at the mercies of white people for ever. . . . I want to do something for myself, by myself. . . . Free. . . . I want a house to live in, too, when I'm older—like Tempy's and Mr. Siles's. . . . But I wouldn't want to be like Tempy's friends—or her husband, dull and colorless, putting all his money away in a white bank, ashamed of colored people."

"A lot of minstrels—that's all niggers are!" Mr. Siles had said once. "Clowns, jazzers, just a band of dancers—that's why they never have anything. Never be anything but servants to the white people."

Clowns! Jazzers! Band of dancers! . . . Harriett! Jimboy! Aunt Hager! . . . A band of dancers! . . . Sandy remembered his grandmother whirling around in front of the altar at revival meetings in the midst of the other sisters, her face shining with light, arms outstretched as though all the cares of the world had been cast away; Harriett in the back yard under the apple-tree, eagle-rocking in the summer evenings to the tunes of the guitar; Jimboy singing. . . . But was that why Negroes were poor, because they were dancers, jazzers, clowns? . . . The other way round would be better: dancers because of their poverty; singers because they suffered; laughing all the time because they must forget. . . . It's more like that, thought Sandy.

A band of dancers. . . . Black dancers—captured in a white world. . . . Dancers of the spirit, too. Each black dreamer a captured dancer of the spirit. . . . Aunt Hager's dreams for Sandy dancing far beyond the limitations of their poverty, of their humble station in life, of their dark skins.

"I wants you to be a great man, son," she often told him, sitting on the porch in the darkness, singing, dreaming, calling up the deep past, creating dreams within the child. "I wants you to be a great man."

"And I won't disappoint you!" Sandy said that hot Chicago summer, just as though Hager were still there, planning for him. "I won't disappoint you!" he said, standing straight in his sweltering red suit in the cage of the hotel elevator. "I won't disappoint you, Aunt Hager," dreaming at night in the stuffy little room in the great Black Belt of Chicago. "I won't disappoint you now," opening his eyes at dawn when Annjee shook him to get up and go to work again.

# THIRTY

# *Princess of the Blues*

ONE hot Monday in August Harrietta Williams, billed as "The Princess of the Blues," opened at the Monogram Theatre on State Street. The screen had carried a slide of her act the week previous, so Sandy knew she would be there, and he and his mother were waiting anxiously for her appearance. They were unable to find out before the performance where she would be living, or if she had arrived in town, but early that Monday evening Sandy hurried home from work, and he and Annjee managed to get seats in the theatre, although it was soon crowded to capacity and people stood in the aisles.

It was a typical Black Belt audience, laughing uproariously, stamping its feet to the music, kidding the actors, and joining in the performance, too. Rows of shiny black faces, gay white teeth, bobbing heads. Everybody having a grand time with the vaudeville, swift and amusing. A young tap-dancer rhymed his feet across the stage, grinning from ear to ear, stepping to the tantalizing music, ending with a series of intricate and amazing contortions that brought down the house. Then a sister act came on, with a stock of sentimental ballads offered in a wholly jazzy manner. They sang even a very melancholy mammy song with their hips moving gaily at every beat.

> O, what would I do
> Without dear you,
> Sweet mammy?

they moaned reverently, with their thighs shaking.

"Aw, step it, sweet gals!" the men and boys in the audience called approvingly. "We'll be yo' mammy and yo' pappy, too! Do it, pretty mamas!"

A pair of black-faced comedians tumbled on the stage as the girls went off, and began the usual line of old jokes and razor comedy.

"Gee, I wish Aunt Harriett's act would come on," Sandy said as he and Annjee laughed nervously at the comedians.

Finally the two blacked-up fellows broke into a song called *Walking the Dog*, flopping their long-toed shoes, twirling their middles like egg-beaters, and made their exit to a roar of laughter and applause. Then the canvas street-scene rose, disclosing a gorgeous background of blue velvet, with a piano and a floor-lamp in the centre of the stage.

"This is Harriett's part now," Sandy whispered excitedly as a tall, yellow, slick-headed young man came in and immediately began playing the piano. "And, mama, that's Billy Sanderlee!"

"Sure is!" said Annjee.

Suddenly the footlights were lowered and the spotlight flared, steadied itself at the right of the stage, and waited. Then, stepping out from among the blue curtains, Harriett entered in a dress of glowing orange, flame-like against the ebony of her skin, barbaric, yet beautiful as a jungle princess. She swayed towards the footlights, while Billy teased the keys of the piano into a hesitating delicate jazz. Then she began to croon a new song—a popular version of an old Negro melody, refashioned with words from Broadway.

"Gee, Aunt Harrie's prettier than ever!" Sandy exclaimed to his mother.

"Same old Harriett," said Annjee. "But kinder hoarse."

"Sings good, though," Sandy cried when Harriett began to snap her fingers, putting a slow, rocking pep into the chorus, rolling her bright eyes to the tune of the melody as the piano rippled and cried under Billy Sanderlee's swift fingers.

"She's the same Harrie," murmured Annjee.

When she appeared again, in an apron of blue calico, with a bandanna handkerchief knotted about her head, she walked very slowly. The man at the piano had begun to play blues—the old familiar folk-blues—and the audience settled into a receptive silence broken only by a "Lawdy! . . . Good Lawdy! Lawd!" from some southern lips at the back of the house, as Harriett sang:

> Red sun, red sun, why don't you rise today?
> Red sun, O sun! Why don't you rise today?
> Ma heart is breakin'—ma baby's gone away.

A few rows ahead of Annjee a woman cried out: "True, Lawd!" and swayed her body.

> Little birds, little birds, ain't you gonna sing this morn?
> Says, little chirpin' birds, ain't you gonna sing this morn?
> I cannot sleep—ma lovin' man is gone.

"Whee-ee-e! . . . Hab mercy! . . . Moan it, gal!" exclamations and shouts broke loose in the understanding audience.

"Just like when papa used to play for her," said Sandy. But Annjee was crying, remembering Jimboy, and fumbling in her bag for a handkerchief. On the stage the singer went on—as though singing to herself—her voice sinking to a bitter moan as the listeners rocked and swayed.

> It's a mighty blue mornin' when yo' daddy leaves yo'
>     bed.
> I says a blue, blue mornin' when yo' daddy leaves yo'
>     bed—
> 'Cause if you lose yo' man, you'd just as well be dead!

Her final number was a dance-song which she sang in a sparkling dress of white sequins, ending the act with a mad collection of steps and a swift sudden whirl across the whole stage as the orchestra joined Billy's piano in a triumphant arch of jazz.

The audience yelled and clapped and whistled for more, stamping their feet and turning to one another with shouted comments of enjoyment.

"Gee! She's great," said Sandy. When another act finally had the stage after Harriett's encores, he was anxious to get back to the dressing-room to see her.

"Maybe they won't let us in," Annjee objected timidly.

"Let's try," Sandy insisted, pulling his mother up. "We don't want to hear this fat woman with the flag singing *Over There*. You'll start crying, anyhow. Come on, mama."

When they got backstage, they found Harriett standing in the dressing-room door laughing with one of the black-face comedians, a summer fur over her shoulders, ready for the street. Billy Sanderlee and the tap-dancing boy were drinking gin from a bottle that Billy held, and Harriett was holding her glass, when she saw Sandy coming.

Her furs slipped to the floor. "My Lord!" she cried, enveloping them in kisses. "What are you doing in Chicago, Annjee?

My, I'm mighty glad to see you, Sandy! . . . I'm certainly surprised—and so happy I could cry. . . . Did you catch our act tonight? Can't Billy play the piano, though? . . . Great heavens! Sandy, you're twice as tall as me! When did you leave home? How's that long-faced sister o' mine, Tempy?"

After repeated huggings the new-comers were introduced to everybody around. Sandy noticed a certain harshness in his aunt's voice. "Smoking so much," she explained later. "Drinking, too, I guess. But a blues-singer's supposed to sing deep and hoarse, so it's all right."

Beyond the drop curtain Sandy could hear the audience laughing in the theatre, and occasionally somebody shouting at the performers.

"Come on! Let's go and get a bite to eat," Harriett suggested when they had finally calmed down enough to decide to move on. "Billy and me are always hungry. . . . Where's Jimboy, Annjee? In the war, I suppose! It'd be just like that big jigaboo to go and enlist first thing, whether he had to or not. Billy here was due to go, too, but licker kept him out. This white folk's war for democracy ain't so hot, nohow! . . . Say, how'd you like to have some chop suey instead of going to a regular restaurant?"

In a Chinese café they found a quiet booth, where the two sisters talked until past midnight—with Sandy and Billy silent for the most part. Harriett told Annjee about Aunt Hager's death and the funeral that chill rainy day, and how Tempy had behaved so coldly when it was all over.

"I left Stanton the week after," Harriett said, "and haven't been back since. Had hard times, too, but we're kinder lucky now, Billy and me—got some dates booked over the Orpheum circuit soon. Liable to get wind of us at the Palace on Broadway one o' these days. Can't tell! Things are breakin' pretty good for spade acts—since Jews are not like the rest of the white folks. They will give you a break if you've got some hot numbers to show 'em, whether you're colored or not. And Jews control the theatres."

But the conversation went back to Stanton, when Hager and Jimboy and all of them had lived together, laughing and quarrelling and playing the guitar—while the tea got cold and the chop suey hardened to a sticky mess as the sisters wept.

Billy marked busily on the table-cloth meanwhile with a stubby pencil, explaining to Sandy a new and intricate system he had found for betting on the numbers.

"Harrie and me plays every day. Won a hundred forty dollars last week in Cleveland," he said.

"Gee! I ought to start playing," Sandy exclaimed. "How much do you put on each number?"

"Well, for a nickel you can win . . ."

"No, you oughtn't," checked Harriett, suddenly conscious of Billy's conversation, turning towards Sandy with a handkerchief to her eyes. "Don't you fool with those numbers, honey! . . . What are you trying to do, Billy, start the boy off on your track? . . . You've got to get your education, Sandy, and amount to something. . . . Guess you're in high school now, aren't you, kid?"

"Third year," said Sandy slowly, dreading a new argument with his mother.

"And determined to keep on going here this fall, in spite o' my telling him I don't see how," put in Annjee. "Jimboy's over yonder, Lord knows where, and I certainly can't take care of Sandy and send him to school, too. No need of my trying— since he's big enough and old enough to hold a job and make his own living. He ought to be wanting to help me, anyway. Instead of that, he's determined to go back to school."

"Make his own living!" Harriett exclaimed, looking at Annjee in astonishment. "You mean you want Sandy to stay out of school to help you? What good is his little money to you?"

"Well, he helps with the room rent," his mother said. "And gets his meals where he works. That's better'n we'd be doing with him studying and depending on me to keep things up."

"What do you mean better?" Harriett cried, glaring at her sister excitedly, forgetting they had been weeping together five minutes before. "For crying out loud—better? Why, Aunt Hager'd turn over in her grave if she heard you talking so calmly about Sandy leaving school—the way she wanted to make something out of this kid. . . . How much do you earn a week?" Harriett asked suddenly, looking at her nephew across the table.

"Fourteen dollars."

"Pshaw! Is that all? I can give you that much myself," Harriett said. "We've got straight bookings until Christmas—then cabaret work's good around here. Bill and I can always make the dough—and you go to school."

"I want to, Aunt Harrie," Sandy said, suddenly content.

"Yea, old man," put in Billy. "And I'll shoot you a little change myself—to play the numbers," he added, winking.

"Well," Annjee began, "what about . . ."

But Harriett ignored Billy's interjection as well as her sister's open mouth. "Running an elevator for fourteen dollars a week and losing your education!" she cried. "Good Lord! Annjee, you ought to be ashamed, wanting him to keep that up. This boy's gotta get ahead—all of us niggers are too far back in this white man's country to let any brains go to waste! Don't you realize that? . . . You and me was foolish all right, breaking mama's heart, leaving school, but Sandy can't do like us. He's gotta be what his grandma Hager wanted him to be—able to help the black race, Annjee! You hear me? Help the whole race!"

"I want to," Sandy said.

"Then you'll stay in school!" Harriett affirmed, still looking at Annjee. "You surely wouldn't want him stuck in an elevator for ever—just to help you, would you, sister?"

"I reckon I wouldn't," Annjee murmured, shaking her head.

"You know damn well you wouldn't," Harriett concluded. And, before they parted, she slipped a ten-dollar bill into her nephew's hand.

"For your books," she said.

When Sandy and his mother started home, it was very late, but in a little Southern church in a side street, some old black worshippers were still holding their nightly meeting. High and fervently they were singing:

> By an' by when de mawnin' comes,
> Saints an' sinners all are gathered home. . . .

As the deep volume of sound rolled through the open door, Annjee and her son stopped to listen.

"It's like Stanton," Sandy said, "and the tent in the Hickory Woods."

"Sure is!" his mother exclaimed. "Them old folks are still singing—even in Chicago! . . . Funny how old folks like to sing that way, ain't it?"

"It's beautiful!" Sandy cried—for, vibrant and steady like a stream of living faith, their song filled the whole night:

An' we'll understand it better by an' by!

# BLACK NO MORE

Being an Account of the Strange
and Wonderful Workings of
Science in the Land of the
Free, a.d. 1933–1940

*George S. Schuyler*

THIS BOOK IS DEDICATED TO ALL CAUCASIANS IN THE GREAT REPUBLIC WHO CAN TRACE THEIR ANCESTRY BACK TEN GENERATIONS AND CONFIDENTLY ASSERT THAT THERE ARE NO BLACK LEAVES, TWIGS, LIMBS OR BRANCHES ON THEIR FAMILY TREES.

# PREFACE

OVER twenty years ago a gentleman in Asbury Park, N. J. began manufacturing and advertising a preparation for the immediate and unfailing straightening of the most stubborn Negro hair. This preparation was called Kink-No-More, a name not wholly accurate since users of it were forced to renew the treatment every fortnight.

During the intervening years many chemists, professional and amateur, have been seeking the means of making the downtrodden Aframerican resemble as closely as possible his white fellow citizen. The temporarily effective preparations placed on the market have so far proved exceedingly profitable to manufacturers, advertising agencies, Negro newspapers and beauty culturists, while millions of users have registered great satisfaction at the opportunity to rid themselves of kinky hair and grow several shades lighter in color, if only for a brief time. With America's constant reiteration of the superiority of whiteness, the avid search on the part of the black masses for some key to chromatic perfection is easily understood. Now it would seem that science is on the verge of satisfying them.

Dr. Yusaburo Noguchi, head of the Noguchi Hospital at Beppu, Japan, told American newspaper reporters in October 1929, that as a result of fifteen years of painstaking research and experiment he was able to change a Negro into a white man. While he admitted that this racial metamorphosis could not be effected overnight, he maintained that "Given time, I could change the Japanese into a race of tall blue-eyed blonds." The racial transformation, he asserted, could be brought about by glandular control and electrical nutrition.

Even more positive is the statement of Mr. Bela Gati, an electrical engineer residing in New York City, who, in a letter dated August 18, 1930 and addressed to the National Association for the Advancement of Colored People said, in part:

> "Once I myself was very strongly tanned by the sun and a European rural population thought that I was a Negro, too. I did not suffer much but the situation was disagreeable. Since that time I have studied the problem and I am convinced that the

surplus of the pigment could be removed. In case you are interested and believe that with the aid of your physicians we could carry out the necessary experiments, I am willing to send you the patent specification . . . and my general terms relating to this invention. . . . The expenses are so to say negligible."

I wish to express my sincere thanks and appreciation to Mr. V. F. Calverton for his keen interest and friendly encouragement and to my wife, Josephine Schuyler, whose coöperation and criticism were of great help in completing *Black No More*.

GEORGE S. SCHUYLER

NEW YORK CITY,
*September 1, 1930*

# Chapter One

MAX DISHER stood outside the Honky Tonk Club puffing a panatela and watching the crowds of white and black folk entering the cabaret. Max was tall, dapper and smooth coffee-brown. His negroid features had a slightly satanic cast and there was an insolent nonchalance about his carriage. He wore his hat rakishly and faultless evening clothes underneath his raccoon coat. He was young, he wasn't broke, but he was damnably blue. It was New Year's Eve, 1933, but there was no spirit of gaiety and gladness in his heart. How could he share the hilarity of the crowd when he had no girl? He and Minnie, his high "yallah" flapper, had quarreled that day and everything was over between them.

"Women are mighty funny," he mused to himself, "especially yallah women. You could give them the moon and they wouldn't appreciate it." That was probably the trouble; he'd given Minnie too much. It didn't pay to spend too much on them. As soon as he'd bought her a new outfit and paid the rent on a three-room apartment, she'd grown uppity. Stuck on her color, that's what was the matter with her! He took the cigar out of his mouth and spat disgustedly.

A short, plump, cherubic black fellow, resplendent in a narrow-brimmed brown fedora, camel's hair coat and spats, strolled up and clapped him on the shoulder: "Hello, Max!" greeted the newcomer, extending a hand in a fawn-colored glove, "What's on your mind?"

"Everything, Bunny," answered the debonair Max. "That damn yallah gal o' mine's got all upstage and quit."

"Say not so!" exclaimed the short black fellow. "Why I thought you and her were all forty."

"Were, is right, kid. And after spending my dough, too! It sure makes me hot. Here I go and buy two covers at the Honky Tonk for tonight, thinkin' surely she'd come and she starts a row and quits!"

"Shucks!" exploded Bunny, "I wouldn't let that worry me none. I'd take another skirt. I wouldn't let no dame queer my New Year's."

"So would I, Wise Guy, but all the dames I know are dated up. So here I am all dressed up and no place to go."

"You got two reservations, aint you? Well, let's you and me go in," Bunny suggested. "We may be able to break in on some party."

Max visibly brightened. "That's a good idea," he said. "You never can tell, we might run in on something good."

Swinging their canes, the two joined the throng at the entrance of the Honky Tonk Club and descended to its smoky depths. They wended their way through the maze of tables in the wake of a dancing waiter and sat down close to the dance floor. After ordering ginger ale and plenty of ice, they reared back and looked over the crowd.

Max Disher and Bunny Brown had been pals ever since the war when they soldiered together in the old 15th regiment in France. Max was one of the Aframerican Fire Insurance Company's crack agents, Bunny was a teller in the Douglass Bank and both bore the reputation of gay blades in black Harlem. The two had in common a weakness rather prevalent among Aframerican bucks: they preferred yellow women. Both swore there were three things essential to the happiness of a colored gentleman: yellow money, yellow women and yellow taxis. They had little difficulty in getting the first and none at all in getting the third but the yellow women they found flighty and fickle. It was so hard to hold them. They were so sought after that one almost required a million dollars to keep them out of the clutches of one's rivals.

"No more yallah gals for me!" Max announced with finality, sipping his drink. "I'll grab a black gal first."

"Say not so!" exclaimed Bunny, strengthening his drink from his huge silver flask. "You aint thinkin' o' dealin' in coal, are you?"

"Well," argued his partner, "it might change my luck. You can trust a black gal; she'll stick to you."

"How do you know? You ain't never had one. Ever' gal I ever seen you with looked like an ofay."

"Humph!" grunted Max. "My next one may be an ofay, too! They're less trouble and don't ask you to give 'em the moon."

"I'm right with you, pardner," Bunny agreed, "but I gotta

have one with class. None o' these Woolworth dames for me! Get you in a peck o' trouble. . . Fact is, Big Boy, ain't none o' these women no good. They all get old on the job."

They drank in silence and eyed the motley crowd around them. There were blacks, browns, yellows, and whites chatting, flirting, drinking; rubbing shoulders in the democracy of night life. A fog of tobacco smoke wreathed their heads and the din from the industrious jazz band made all but the loudest shrieks inaudible. In and out among the tables danced the waiters, trays balanced aloft, while the patrons, arrayed in colored paper caps, beat time with the orchestra, threw streamers or grew maudlin on each other's shoulders.

"Looky here! Lawdy Lawd!" exclaimed Bunny, pointing to the doorway. A party of white people had entered. They were all in evening dress and in their midst was a tall, slim, titian-haired girl who had seemingly stepped from heaven or the front cover of a magazine.

"My, my, my!" said Max, sitting up alertly.

The party consisted of two men and four women. They were escorted to a table next to the one occupied by the two colored dandies. Max and Bunny eyed them covertly. The tall girl was certainly a dream.

"Now that's my speed," whispered Bunny.

"Be yourself," said Max. "You couldn't touch her with a forty-foot pole."

"Oh, I don't know, Big Boy," Bunny beamed self-confidently, "You never can tell! You never can tell!"

"Well, I can tell," remarked Disher, "'cause she's a cracker."

"How you know that?"

"Man, I can tell a cracker a block away. I wasn't born and raised in Atlanta, Georgia, for nothin', you know. Just listen to her voice."

Bunny listened. "I believe she is," he agreed.

They kept eyeing the party to the exclusion of everything else. Max was especially fascinated. The girl was the prettiest creature he'd ever seen and he felt irresistibly drawn to her. Unconsciously he adjusted his necktie and passed his well-manicured hand over his rigidly straightened hair.

Suddenly one of the white men rose and came over to their

table. They watched him suspiciously. Was he going to start something? Had he noticed that they were staring at the girl? They both stiffened at his approach.

"Say," he greeted them, leaning over the table, "do you boys know where we can get some decent liquor around here? We've run out of stuff and the waiter says he can't get any for us."

"You can get some pretty good stuff right down the street," Max informed him, somewhat relieved.

"They won't sell none to him," said Bunny. "They might think he was a Prohibition officer."

"Could one of you fellows get me some?" asked the man.

"Sure," said Max, heartily. What luck! Here was the very chance he'd been waiting for. These people might invite them over to their table. The man handed him a ten dollar bill and Max went out bareheaded to get the liquor. In ten minutes he was back. He handed the man the quart and the change. The man gave back the change and thanked him. There was no invitation to join the party. Max returned to his table and eyed the group wistfully.

"Did he invite you in?" asked Bunny.

"I'm back here, aint I?" answered Max, somewhat resentfully.

The floor show came on. A black-faced comedian, a corpulent shouter of mammy songs with a gin-roughened voice, three chocolate soft-shoe dancers and an octette of wriggling, practically nude, mulatto chorines.

Then midnight and pandemonium as the New Year swept in. When the din had subsided, the lights went low and the orchestra moaned the weary blues. The floor filled with couples. The two men and two of the women at the next table rose to dance. The beautiful girl and another were left behind.

"I'm going over and ask her to dance," Max suddenly announced to the surprised Bunny.

"Say not so!" exclaimed that worthy. "You're fixin' to get in dutch, Big Boy."

"Well, I'm gonna take a chance, anyhow," Max persisted, rising.

This fair beauty had hypnotized him. He felt that he would give anything for just one dance with her. Once around the floor with her slim waist in his arm would be like an eternity in heaven. Yes, one could afford to risk repulse for that.

"Don't do it, Max!" pleaded Bunny. "Them fellows are liable to start somethin'."

But Max was not to be restrained. There was no holding him back when he wanted to do a thing, especially where a comely damsel was concerned.

He sauntered over to the table in his most sheikish manner and stood looking down at the shimmering strawberry blond. She was indeed ravishing and her exotic perfume titilated his nostrils despite the clouds of cigarette smoke.

"Would you care to dance?" he asked, after a moment's hesitation.

She looked up at him haughtily with cool green eyes, somewhat astonished at his insolence and yet perhaps secretly intrigued, but her reply lacked nothing in definiteness.

"No," she said icily, "I never dance with niggers!" Then turning to her friend, she remarked: "Can you beat the nerve of these darkies?" She made a little disdainful grimace with her mouth, shrugged daintily and dismissed the unpleasant incident.

Crushed and angry, Max returned to his place without a word. Bunny laughed aloud in high glee.

"You said she was a cracker," he gurgled, "an' now I guess you know it."

"Aw, go to hell," Max grumbled.

Just then Billy Fletcher, the headwaiter passed by. Max stopped him. "Ever see that dame in here before?" he asked.

"Been in here most every night since before Christmas," Billy replied.

"Do you know who she is?"

"Well, I heard she was some rich broad from Atlanta up here for the holidays. Why?"

"Oh, nothin'; I was just wondering."

From Atlanta! His home town. No wonder she had turned him down. Up here trying to get a thrill in the Black Belt but a thrill from observation instead of contact. Gee, but white folks were funny. They didn't want black folks' game and yet they were always frequenting Negro resorts.

\*

At three o'clock Max and Bunny paid their check and ascended to the street. Bunny wanted to go to the breakfast dance at the Dahomey Casino but Max was in no mood for it.

"I'm going home," he announced laconically, hailing a taxi. "Good night!"

As the cab whirled up Seventh Avenue, he settled back and thought of the girl from Atlanta. He couldn't get her out of his mind and didn't want to. At his rooming house, he paid the driver, unlocked the door, ascended to his room and undressed, mechanically. His mind was a kaleidoscope: Atlanta, sea-green eyes, slender figure, titian hair, frigid manner. "I never dance with niggers." Then he fell asleep about five o'clock and promptly dreamed of her. Dreamed of dancing with her, dining with her, motoring with her, sitting beside her on a golden throne while millions of manacled white slaves prostrated themselves before him. Then there was a nightmare of grim, gray men with shotguns, baying hounds, a heap of gasoline-soaked faggots and a screeching, fanatical mob.

He awoke covered with perspiration. His telephone was ringing and the late morning sunshine was streaming into his room. He leaped from bed and lifted the receiver.

"Say," shouted Bunny, "did you see this morning's *Times?*"

"Hell no," growled Max, "I just woke up. Why, what's in it?"

"Well, do you remember Dr. Junius Crookman, that colored fellow that went to Germany to study about three years ago? He's just come back and the *Times* claims he's announced a sure way to turn darkies white. Thought you might be interested after the way you fell for that ofay broad last night. They say Crookman's going to open a sanitarium in Harlem right away. There's your chance, Big Boy, and it's your only chance." Bunny chuckled.

"Oh, ring off," growled Max. "That's a lot of hooey."

But he was impressed and a little excited. Suppose there was something to it? He dressed hurriedly, after a cold shower, and went out to the newsstand. He bought a *Times* and scanned its columns. Yes, there it was:

NEGRO ANNOUNCES REMARKABLE
DISCOVERY
Can Change Black to White in Three Days.

Max went into Jimmy Johnson's restaurant and greedily read the account while awaiting his breakfast. Yes, it must be true. To think of old Crookman being able to do that! Only a few years ago he'd been just a hungry medical student around Harlem. Max put down the paper and stared vacantly out of the window. Gee, Crookman would be a millionaire in no time. He'd even be a multi-millionaire. It looked as though science was to succeed where the Civil War had failed. But how could it be possible? He looked at his hands and felt at the back of his head where the straightening lotion had failed to conquer some of the knots. He toyed with his ham and eggs as he envisioned the possibilities of the discovery.

Then a sudden resolution seized him. He looked at the newspaper account again. Yes, Crookman was staying at the Phyllis Wheatley Hotel. Why not go and see what there was to this? Why not be the first Negro to try it out? Sure, it was taking a chance, but think of getting white in three days! No more jim crow. No more insults. As a white man he could go anywhere, be anything he wanted to be, do most anything he wanted to do, be a free man at last . . . and probably be able to meet the girl from Atlanta. What a vision!

He rose hurriedly, paid for his breakfast, rushed out of the door, almost ran into an aged white man carrying a sign advertising a Negro fraternity dance, and strode, almost ran, to the Phyllis Wheatley Hotel.

He tore up the steps two at a time and into the sitting room. It was crowded with white reporters from the daily newspapers and back reporters from the Negro weeklies. In their midst he recognized Dr. Junius Crookman, tall, wiry, ebony black, with a studious and polished manner. Flanking him on either side were Henry ("Hank") Johnson, the "Numbers" banker and Charlie ("Chuck") Foster, the realtor, looking very grave, important and possessive in the midst of all the hullabaloo.

"Yes," Dr. Crookman was telling the reporters while they eagerly took down his statements, "during my first year at college I noticed a black girl on the street one day who had several irregular white patches on her face and hands. That intrigued me. I began to study up on skin diseases and found out that the girl was evidently suffering from a nervous disease known as vitiligo. It is a very rare disease. Both Negroes and

Caucasians occasionally have it, but it is naturally more conspicuous on blacks than whites. It absolutely removes skin pigment and sometimes it turns a Negro completely white but only after a period of thirty or forty years. It occurred to me that if one could discover some means of artificially inducing and stimulating this nervous disease at will, one might possibly solve the American race problem. My sociology teacher had once said that there were but three ways for the Negro to solve his problem in America," he gestured with his long slender fingers, "'To either get out, get white or get along.' Since he wouldn't and couldn't get out and was getting along only indifferently, it seemed to me that the only thing for him was to get white." For a moment his teeth gleamed beneath his smartly waxed mustache, then he sobered and went on:

"I began to give a great deal of study to the problem during my spare time. Unfortunately there was very little information on the subject in this country. I decided to go to Germany but I didn't have the money. Just when I despaired of getting the funds to carry out my experiments and studies abroad, Mr. Johnson and Mr. Foster," he indicated the two men with a graceful wave of his hand, "came to my rescue. I naturally attribute a great deal of my success to them."

"But how is it done?" asked a reporter.

"Well," smiled Crookman, "I naturally cannot divulge the secret any more than to say that it is accomplished by electrical nutrition and glandular control. Certain gland secretions are greatly stimulated while others are considerably diminished. It is a powerful and dangerous treatment but harmless when properly done."

"How about the hair and features?" asked a Negro reporter.

"They are also changed in the process," answered the biologist. "In three days the Negro becomes to all appearances a Caucasian."

"But is the transformation transferred to the offspring?" persisted the Negro newspaperman.

"As yet," replied Crookman, "I have discovered no way to accomplish anything so revolutionary but I am able to transform a black infant to a white one in twenty-four hours."

"Have you tried it on any Negroes yet?" queried a sceptical white journalist.

"Why of course I have," said the Doctor, slightly nettled. "I would not have made my announcement if I had not done so. Come here, Sandol," he called, turning to a pale white youth standing on the outskirts of the crowd, who was the most Nordic looking person in the room. "This man is a Senegalese, a former aviator in the French Army. He is living proof that what I claim is true."

Dr. Crookman then displayed a photograph of a very black man, somewhat resembling Sandol but with bushy Negro hair, flat nose and full lips. "This," he announced proudly, "is Sandol as he looked before taking my treatment. What I have done to him I can do to any Negro. He is in good physical and mental condition as you all can see."

The assemblage was properly awed. After taking a few more notes and a number of photographs of Dr. Crookman, his associates and of Sandol, the newspapermen retired. Only the dapper Max Disher remained.

"Hello, Doc!" he said, coming forward and extending his hand. "Don't you remember me? I'm Max Disher."

"Why certainly I remember you, Max," replied the biologist rising cordially. "Been a long time since we've seen each other but you're looking as sharp as ever. How's things?"

The two men shook hands.

"Oh, pretty good. Say, Doc, how's chances to get you to try that thing on me? You must be looking for volunteers."

"Yes, I am, but not just yet. I've got to get my equipment set up first. I think now I'll be ready for business in a couple of weeks."

Henry Johnson, the beefy, sleek-jowled, mulatto "Numbers" banker, chuckled and nudged Dr. Crookman. "Old Max ain't losin' no time, Doc. When that niggah gits white Ah bet he'll make up fo' los' time with these ofay girls."

Charlie Foster, small, slender, grave, amber colored, and laconic, finally spoke up: "Seems all right, Junius, but there'll be hell to pay when you whiten up a lot o' these darkies and them mulatto babies start appearing here and there. Watcha gonna do then?"

"Oh, quit singin' th' blues, Chuck," boomed Johnson. "Don't cross bridges 'til yuh come tuh 'em. Doc'll fix that okeh. Besides, we'll have mo' money'n Henry Ford by that time."

"There'll be no difficulties whatever," assured Crookman rather impatiently.

"Let's hope not."

Next day the newspapers carried a long account of the interview with Dr. Junius Crookman interspersed with photographs of him, his backers and of the Senegalese who had been turned white. It was the talk of the town and was soon the talk of the country. Long editorials were written about the discovery, learned societies besieged the Negro biologist with offers of lecture engagements, magazines begged him for articles, but he turned down all offers and refused to explain his treatment. This attitude was decried as unbecoming a scientist and it was insinuated and even openly stated that nothing more could be expected from a Negro.

But Crookman ignored the clamor of the public, and with the financial help of his associates planned the great and lucrative experiment of turning Negroes into Caucasians.

The impatient Max Disher saw him as often as possible and kept track of developments. He yearned to be the first treated and didn't want to be caught napping. Two objects were uppermost in his mind: To get white and to Atlanta. The statuesque and haughty blonde was ever in his thoughts. He was head over heels in love with her and realized there was no hope for him to ever win her as long as he was brown. Each day he would walk past the tall building that was to be the Crookman Sanitarium, watching the workmen and delivery trucks; wondering how much longer he would have to wait before entering upon the great adventure.

At last the sanitarium was ready for business. Huge advertisements appeared in the local Negro weeklies. Black Harlem was on its toes. Curious throngs of Negroes and whites stood in front of the austere six-story building gazing up at its windows.

Inside, Crookman, Johnson and Foster stood nervously about while hustling attendants got everything in readiness. Outside they could hear the murmur of the crowd.

"That means money, Chuck," boomed Johnson, rubbing his beefsteak hands together.

"Yeh," replied the realtor, "but there's one more thing I wanna get straight: How about that darky dialect? You can't change that."

"It isn't necessary, my dear Foster," explained the physician, patiently. "There is no such thing as Negro dialect, except in literature and drama. It is a well-known fact among informed persons that a Negro from a given section speaks the same dialect as his white neighbors. In the South you can't tell over the telephone whether you are talking to a white man or a Negro. The same is true in New York when a Northern Negro speaks into the receiver. I have noticed the same thing in the hills of West Virginia and Tennessee. The educated Haitian speaks the purest French and the Jamaican Negro sounds exactly like an Englishman. There are no racial or color dialects; only sectional dialects."

"Guess you're right," agreed Foster, grudgingly.

"I know I'm right. Moreover, even if my treatment did not change the so-called Negro lips, even that would prove to be no obstacle."

"How come, Doc," asked Johnson.

"Well, there are plenty of Caucasians who have lips quite as thick and noses quite as broad as any of us. As a matter of fact there has been considerable exaggeration about the contrast between Caucasian and Negro features. The cartoonists and minstrel men have been responsible for it very largely. Some Negroes like the Somalis, Filanis, Egyptians, Hausas and Abyssinians have very thin lips and nostrils. So also have the Malagasys of Madagascar. Only in certain small sections of Africa do the Negroes possess extremely pendulous lips and very broad nostrils. On the other hand, many so-called Caucasians, particularly the Latins, Jews and South Irish, and frequently the most Nordic of peoples like the Swedes, show almost Negroid lips and noses. Black up some white folks and they could deceive a resident of Benin. Then when you consider that less than twenty per cent of our Negroes are without Caucasian ancestry and that close to thirty per cent have American Indian ancestry, it is readily seen that there cannot be the wide difference in Caucasian and Afro-American facial characteristics that most people imagine."

"Doc, you sho' knows yo' onions," said Johnson, admiringly. "Doan pay no 'tenshun to that ole Doubtin' Thomas. He'd holler starvation in a pie shop."

There was a commotion outside and an angry voice was heard above the hum of low conversation. Then Max Disher burst in the door with a guard hanging onto his coat tail.

"Let loose o' me, Boy," he quarreled. "I got an engagement here. Doc, tell this man something, will you."

Crookman nodded to the guard to release the insurance man. "Well, I see you're right on time, Max."

"I told you I'd be Johnny-on-the-spot, didn't I?" said Disher, inspecting his clothes to see if they had been wrinkled.

"Well, if you're all ready, go into the receiving room there, sign the register and get into one of those bathrobes. You're first on the list."

The three partners looked at each other and grinned as Max disappeared into a small room at the end of the corridor. Dr. Crookman went into his office to don his white trousers, shoes and smock; Johnson and Foster entered the business office to supervise the clerical staff, while white-coated figures darted back and forth through the corridors. Outside, the murmuring of the vast throng grew more audible.

Johnson showed all of his many gold teeth in a wide grin as he glanced out the window and saw the queue of Negroes already extending around the corner. "Man, man, man!" he chuckled to Foster, "at fifty dollars a th'ow this thing's gonna have th' numbah business beat all hollow."

"Hope so," said Foster, gravely.

Max Disher, arrayed only in a hospital bathrobe and a pair of slippers, was escorted to the elevator by two white-coated attendants. They got off on the sixth floor and walked to the end of the corridor. Max was trembling with excitement and anxiety. Suppose something should go wrong? Suppose Doc should make a mistake? He thought of the Elks' excursion every summer to Bear Mountain, the high yellow Minnie and her colorful apartment, the pleasant evenings at the Dahomey Casino doing the latest dances with the brown belles of Harlem, the prancing choruses at the Lafayette Theater, the hours he had whiled away at Boogie's and the Honky Tonk Club, and he hesitated. Then he envisioned his future as a white man, probably as the husband of the tall blonde from Atlanta, and with firm resolve, he entered the door of the mysterious chamber.

He quailed as he saw the formidable apparatus of sparkling nickel. It resembled a cross between a dentist's chair and an electric chair. Wires and straps, bars and levers protruded from it and a great nickel headpiece, like the helmet of a knight, hung over it. The room had only a skylight and no sound entered it from the outside. Around the walls were cases of instruments and shelves of bottles filled with strangely colored fluids. He gasped with fright and would have made for the door but the two husky attendants held him firmly, stripped off his robe and bound him in the chair. There was no retreat. It was either the beginning or the end.

# Chapter Two

Slowly, haltingly, Max Disher dragged his way down the hall to the elevator, supported on either side by an attendant. He felt terribly weak, emptied and nauseated; his skin twitched and was dry and feverish; his insides felt very hot and sore. As the trio walked slowly along the corridor, a blue-green light would ever and anon blaze through one of the doorways as a patient was taken in. There was a low hum and throb of machinery and an acrid odor filled the air. Uniformed nurses and attendants hurried back and forth at their tasks. Everything was quiet, swift, efficient, sinister.

He felt so thankful that he had survived the ordeal of that horrible machine so akin to the electric chair. A shudder passed over him at the memory of the hours he had passed in its grip, fed at intervals with revolting concoctions. But when they reached the elevator and he saw himself in the mirror, he was startled, overjoyed. White at last! Gone was the smooth brown complexion. Gone were the slightly full lips and Ethiopian nose. Gone was the nappy hair that he had straightened so meticulously ever since the kink-no-more lotions first wrenched Aframericans from the tyranny and torture of the comb. There would be no more expenditures for skin whiteners; no more discrimination; no more obstacles in his path. He was free! The world was his oyster and he had the open sesame of a pork-colored skin!

The reflection in the mirror gave him new life and strength. He now stood erect, without support and grinned at the two tall, black attendants. "Well, Boys," he crowed, "I'm all set now. That machine of Doc's worked like a charm. Soon's I get a feed under my belt I'll be okeh."

Six hours later, bathed, fed, clean-shaven, spry, blonde and jubilant, he emerged from the out-patient ward and tripped gaily down the corridor to the main entrance. He was through with coons, he resolved, from now on. He glanced in a superior manner at the long line of black and brown folk on one side of the corridor, patiently awaiting treatment. He saw many persons whom he knew but none of them recognized him. It thrilled him to feel that he was now indistinguishable from nine-tenths of the people of the United States; one of the great majority. Ah, it was good not to be a Negro any longer!

As he sought to open the front door, the strong arm of a guard restrained him. "Wait a minute," the man said, "and we'll help you get through the mob."

A moment or two later Max found himself the center of a flying wedge of five or six husky special policemen, cleaving through a milling crowd of colored folk. From the top step of the Sanitarium he had noticed the crowd spread over the sidewalk, into the street and around the corners. Fifty traffic policemen strained and sweated to keep prospective patients in line and out from under the wheels of taxicabs and trucks.

Finally he reached the curb, exhausted from the jostling and squeezing, only to be set upon by a mob of newspaper photographers and reporters. As the first person to take the treatment, he was naturally the center of attraction for about fifteen of these journalistic gnats. They asked a thousand questions seemingly all at once. What was his name? How did he feel? What was he going to do? Would he marry a white woman? Did he intend to continue living in Harlem?

Max would say nothing. In the first place, he thought to himself, if they're so anxious to know all this stuff, they ought to be willing to pay for it. He needed money if he was going to be able to thoroughly enjoy being white; why not get some by selling his story? The reporters, male and female, begged him almost with tears in their eyes for a statement but he was adamant.

While they were wrangling, an empty taxicab drove up. Pushing the inquisitive reporters to one side, Max leaped into it and yelled "Central Park!" It was the only place he could think of at the moment. He wanted to have time to compose his mind, to plan the future in this great world of whiteness. As the cab lurched forward, he turned and was astonished to find another occupant, a pretty girl.

"Don't be scared," she smiled. "I knew you would want to get away from that mob so I went around the corner and got a cab for you. Come along with me and I'll get everything fixed up for you. I'm a reporter from *The Scimitar*. We'll give you a lot of money for your story." She talked rapidly. Max's first impulse had been to jump out of the cab, even at the risk of having to face again the mob of reporters and photographers he had sought to escape, but he changed his mind when he heard mention of money.

"How much?" he asked, eyeing her. She was very comely and he noted that her ankles were well turned.

"Oh, probably a thousand dollars," she replied.

"Well, that sounds good." A thousand dollars! What a time he could have with that! Broadway for him as soon as he got paid off.

As they sped down Seventh Avenue, the newsboys were yelling the latest editions. "Ex—try! Ex—try! Blacks turning white! Blacks turning white! . . . Read all about the gr-r-reat dis—covery! Paper, Mister! Paper! . . . Read all about Dr. Crookman."

He settled back while they drove through the park and glanced frequently at the girl by his side. She looked mighty good; wonder could he talk business with her? Might go to dinner and a cabaret. That would be the best way to start.

"What did you say your name was?" he began.

"I didn't say," she stalled.

"Well, you have a name, haven't you?" he persisted.

"Suppose I have?"

"You're not scared to tell it, are you?"

"Why do you want to know my name?"

"Well, there's nothing wrong about wanting to know a pretty girl's name, is there?"

"Well, my name's Smith, Sybil Smith. Now are you satisfied?"

"Not yet. I want to know something more. How would you like to go to dinner with me tonight?"

"I don't know and I won't know until I've had the experience." She smiled coquettishly. Going out with him, she figured, would make the basis of a rattling good story for tomorrow's paper. "Negro's first night as a Caucasian!" Fine!

"Say, you're a regular fellow," he said, beaming upon her. "I'll get a great kick out of going to dinner with you because you'll be the only one in the place that'll know I'm a Negro."

Down at the office of *The Scimitar*, it didn't take Max long to come to an agreement, tell his story to a stenographer and get a sheaf of crisp, new bills. As he left the building a couple of hours later with Miss Smith on his arm, the newsboys were already crying the extra edition carrying the first installment of his strange tale. A huge photograph of him occupied the entire front page of the tabloid. Lucky for him that he'd given his name as William Small, he thought.

He was annoyed and a little angered. What did they want to put his picture all over the front of the paper for? Now everybody would know who he was. He had undergone the tortures of Doc Crookman's devilish machine in order to escape the conspicuousness of a dark skin and now he was being made conspicuous because he had once had a dark skin! Could one never escape the plagued race problem?

"Don't worry about that," comforted Miss Smith. "Nobody'll recognize you. There are thousands of white people, yes millions, that look like you do." She took his arm and snuggled up closer. She wanted to make him feel at home. It wasn't often a poor, struggling newspaper woman got a chap with a big bankroll to take her out for the evening. Moreover, the description she would write of the experience might win her a promotion.

They walked down Broadway in the blaze of white lights to a dinner-dance place. To Max it was like being in heaven. He had strolled through the Times Square district before but never with such a feeling of absolute freedom and sureness. No one now looked at him curiously because he was with a white girl, as they had when he came down there with Minnie, his former octoroon lady friend. Gee, it was great!

They dined and they danced. Then they went to a cabaret, where, amid smoke, noise and body smells, they drank what was purported to be whiskey and watched a semi-nude chorus do its stuff. Despite his happiness Max found it pretty dull. There was something lacking in these ofay places of amusement or else there was something present that one didn't find in the black-and-tan resorts in Harlem. The joy and abandon here was obviously forced. Patrons went to extremes to show each other they were having a wonderful time. It was all so strained and quite unlike anything to which he had been accustomed. The Negroes, it seemed to him, were much gayer, enjoyed themselves more deeply and yet they were more restrained, actually more refined. Even their dancing was different.

They followed the rhythm accurately, effortlessly and with easy grace; these lumbering couples, out of step half the time and working as strenuously as stevedores emptying the bowels of a freighter, were noisy, awkward, inelegant. At their best they were gymnastic where the Negroes were sensuous. He felt a momentary pang of mingled disgust, disillusionment and nostalgia. But it was only momentary. He looked across at the comely Sybil and then around at the other white women, many of whom were very pretty and expensively gowned, and the sight temporarily drove from his mind the thoughts that had been occupying him.

They parted at three o'clock, after she had given him her telephone number. She pecked him lightly on the cheek in payment, doubtless, for a pleasant evening's entertainment. Somewhat disappointed because she had failed to show any interest in his expressed curiosity about the interior of her apartment, he directed the chauffeur to drive him to Harlem. After all, he argued to himself in defense of his action, he had to get his things.

As the cab turned out of Central Park at 110th Street he felt, curiously enough, a feeling of peace. There were all the old familiar sights: the all-night speakeasies, the frankfurter stands, the loiterers, the late pedestrians, the chop suey joints, the careening taxicabs, the bawdy laughter.

He couldn't resist the temptation to get out at 133rd Street and go down to Boogie's place, the hangout of his gang. He tapped, an eye peered through a hole, appraised him critically, then disappeared and the hole was closed. There was silence.

Max frowned. What was the matter with old Bob? Why didn't he open that door? The cold January breeze swept down into the little court where he stood and made him shiver. He knocked a little louder, more insistently. The eye appeared again.

"Who's 'at?" growled the doorkeeper.

"It's me, Max Disher," replied the ex-Negro.

"Go 'way f'm here, white man. Dis heah place is closed."

"Is Bunny Brown in there?" asked Max in desperation.

"Yeh, he's heah. Does yuh know him? Well, Ah'll call 'im out heah and see if he knows you."

Max waited in the cold for about two or three minutes and

then the door suddenly opened and Bunny Brown, a little unsteady, came out. He peered at Max in the light from the electric bulb over the door.

"Hello Bunny," Max greeted him. "Don't know me do you? It's me, Max Disher. You recognize my voice, don't you?"

Bunny looked again, rubbed his eyes and shook his head. Yes, the voice was Max Disher's, but this man was white. Still, when he smiled his eyes revealed the same sardonic twinkle—so characteristic of his friend.

"Max," he blurted out, "is that you, sure enough? Well, for cryin' out loud! Damned 'f you ain't been up there to Crookman's and got fixed up. Well, hush my mouth! Bob, open that door. This is old Max Disher. Done gone up there to Crookman's and got all white on my hands. He's just too tight, with his blond hair, 'n everything."

Bob opened the door, the two friends entered, sat down at one of the small round tables in the narrow, smoke-filled cellar and were soon surrounded with cronies. They gazed raptly at his colorless skin, commented on the veins showing blue through the epidermis, stroked his ash-blond hair and listened with mouths open to his remarkable story.

"Whatcha gonna do now, Max?" asked Boogie, the rangy, black, bullet-headed proprietor.

"I know just what that joker's gonna do," said Bunny. "He's goin' back to Atlanta. Am I right, Big Boy?"

"You ain't wrong," Max agreed. "I'm goin' right on down there, brother, and make up for lost time."

"Whadayah mean?" asked Boogie.

"Boy, it would take me until tomorrow night to tell you and then you wouldn't understand."

The two friends strolled up the avenue. Both were rather mum. They had been inseparable pals since the stirring days in France. Now they were about to be parted. It wasn't as if Max was going across the ocean to some foreign country; there would be a wider gulf separating them: the great sea of color. They both thought about it.

"I'll be pretty lonesome without you, Bunny."

"It ain't you, Big Boy."

"Well, why don't you go ahead and get white and then we could stay together. I'll give you the money."

"Say not so! Where'd you get so much jack all of a sudden?" asked Bunny.

"Sold my story to *The Scimitar* for a grand."

"Paid in full?"

"Wasn't paid in part!"

"All right, then, I'll take you up, Heavy Sugar." Bunny held out his plump hand and Max handed him a hundred-dollar bill.

They were near the Crookman Sanitarium. Although it was five o'clock on a Sunday morning, the building was brightly lighted from cellar to roof and the hum of electric motors could be heard, low and powerful. A large electric sign hung from the roof to the second floor. It represented a huge arrow outlined in green with the words BLACK-NO-MORE running its full length vertically. A black face was depicted at the lower end of the arrow while at the top shone a white face to which the arrow was pointed. First would appear the outline of the arrow; then, BLACK-NO-MORE would flash on and off. Following that the black face would appear at the bottom and beginning at the lower end the long arrow with its lettering would appear progressively until its tip was reached, when the white face at the top would blazon forth. After that the sign would flash off and on and the process would be repeated.

In front of the sanitarium milled a half-frozen crowd of close to four thousand Negroes. A riot squad armed with rifles, machine guns and tear gas bombs maintained some semblance of order. A steel cable stretched from lamp post to lamp post the entire length of the block kept the struggling mass of humanity on the sidewalk and out of the path of the traffic. It seemed as if all Harlem were there. As the two friends reached the outskirts of the mob, an ambulance from the Harlem Hospital drove up and carried away two women who had been trampled upon.

Lined up from the door to the curb was a gang of tough special guards dredged out of the slums. Grim Irish from Hell's Kitchen, rough Negroes from around 133rd Street and 5th Avenue (New York's "Beale Street") and tough Italians from the lower West Side. They managed with difficulty to keep an aisle cleared for incoming and outgoing patients. Near the curb were stationed the reporters and photographers.

The noise rose and fell. First there would be a low hum of voices. Steadily it would rise and rise in increasing volume as the speakers became more animated and reach its climax in a great animal-like roar as the big front door would open and a whitened Negro would emerge. Then the mass would surge forward to peer at and question the ersatz Nordic. Sometimes the ex-Ethiopian would quail before the mob and jump back into the building. Then the hardboiled guards would form a flying squad and hustle him to a waiting taxicab. Other erstwhile Aframericans issuing from the building would grin broadly, shake hands with friends and relatives and start to graphically describe their experience while the Negroes around them enviously admired their clear white skins.

In between these appearances the hot dog and peanut vendors did a brisk trade, along with the numerous pickpockets of the district. One slender, anemic, ratty-looking mulatto Negro was almost beaten to death by a gigantic black laundress whose purse he had snatched. A Negro selling hot roasted sweet potatoes did a land-office business while the neighboring saloons, that had increased so rapidly in number since the enactment of the Volstead Law that many of their Italian proprietors paid substantial income taxes, sold scores of gallons of incredibly atrocious hootch.

"Well, bye, bye, Max," said Bunny, extending his hand. "I'm goin' in an' try my luck."

"So long, Bunny. See you in Atlanta. Write me general delivery."

"Why, ain't you gonna wait for me, Max?"

"Naw! I'm fed up on this town."

"Oh, you ain't kiddin' me, Big Boy. I know you want to look up that broad you saw in the Honky Tonk New Year's Eve," Bunny beamed.

Max grinned and blushed slightly. They shook hands and parted. Bunny ran up the aisle from the curb, opened the sanitarium door and without turning around, disappeared within.

For a minute or so, Max stood irresolutely in the midst of the gibbering crowd of people. Unaccountably he felt at home here among these black folk. Their jests, scraps of conversation and lusty laughter all seemed like heavenly music. Momentarily he felt a disposition to stay among them, to share again their troubles which they seemed always to bear with a lightness that was yet not indifference. But then, he suddenly realized with just a tiny trace of remorse that the past was forever gone. He must seek other pastures, other pursuits, other playmates, other loves. He was white now. Even if he wished to stay among his folk, they would be either jealous or suspicious of him, as they were of most octoroons and nearly all whites. There was no other alternative than to seek his future among the Caucasians with whom he now rightfully belonged.

And after all, he thought, it was a glorious new adventure. His eyes twinkled and his pulse quickened as he thought of it. Now he could go anywhere, associate with anybody, be anything he wanted to be. He suddenly thought of the comely miss he had seen in the Honky Tonk on New Year's Eve and the greatly enlarged field from which he could select his loves. Yes, indeed there were advantages in being white. He brightened and viewed the tightly-packed black folk around him with a superior air. Then, thinking again of his clothes at Mrs. Blandish's, the money in his pocket and the prospect for the first time of riding into Atlanta in a Pullman car and not as a Pullman porter, he turned and pushed his way through the throng.

He strolled up West 139th Street to his rooming place, stepping lightly and sniffing the early morning air. How good it was to be free, white and to possess a bankroll! He fumbled in his pocket for his little mirror looked at himself again and again from several angles. He stroked his pale blond hair and secretly congratulated himself that he would no longer need to straighten it nor be afraid to wet it. He gazed raptly at his smooth, white hands with the blue veins showing through. What a miracle Dr. Crookman had wrought!

As he entered the hallway, the mountainous form of his landlady loomed up. She jumped back as she saw his face.

"What you doing in here?" she almost shouted. "Where'd you get a key to this house?"

"It's me, Max Disher," he assured her with a grin at her astonishment. "Don't know me, do you?"

She gazed incredulously into his face. "Is that you sure enough, Max? How in the devil did you get so white?"

He explained and showed her a copy of *The Scimitar*

containing his story. She switched on the hall light and read it. Contrasting emotions played over her face, for Mrs. Blandish was known in the business world as Mme. Sisseretta Blandish, the beauty specialist, who owned the swellest hair-straightening parlor in Harlem. Business, she thought to herself, was bad enough, what with all of the competition, without this Dr. Crookman coming along and killing it altogether.

"Well," she sighed, "I suppose you're going down town to live, now. I always said niggers didn't really have any race pride."

Uneasy, Max made no reply. The fat, brown woman turned with a disdainful sniff and disappeared into a room at the end of the hall. He ran lightly upstairs to pack his things.

An hour later, as the taxicab bearing him and his luggage bowled through Central Park, he was in high spirits. He would go down to the Pennsylvania Station and get a Pullman straight into Atlanta. He would stop there at the best hotel. He wouldn't hunt up any of his folks. No, that would be too dangerous. He would just play around, enjoy life and laugh at the white folks up his sleeve. God! What an adventure! What a treat it would be to mingle with white people in places where as a youth he had never dared to enter. At last he felt like an American citizen. He flecked the ash of his panatela out of the open window of the cab and sank back in the seat feeling at peace with the world.

# Chapter Three

D R. JUNIUS CROOKMAN, looking tired and worn, poured himself another cup of coffee from the percolator near by and turning to Hank Johnson, asked "What about that new electrical apparatus?"

"On th' way, Doc. On th' way," replied the former Numbers baron. "Just talkin' to th' man this mornin'. He says we'll get it tomorrow, maybe."

"Well, we certainly need it," said Chuck Foster, who sat beside him on the large leather divan. "We can't handle all of the business as it is."

"How about those new places you're buying?" asked the physician.

"Well, I've bought the big private house on Edgecombe Avenue for fifteen thousand and the workmen are getting it in shape now. It ought to be ready in about a week if nothing happens," Foster informed him.

"If nuthin' happens?" echoed Johnson. "Whut's gonna happen? We're settin' on th' world, ain't we? Our racket's within th' law, ain't it? We're makin' money faster'n we can take it in, ain't we? Whut could happen? This here is the best and safest graft I've ever been in."

"Oh, you never can tell," cautioned the quondom realtor. "These white newspapers, especially in the South, are beginning to write some pretty strong editorials against us and we've only been running two weeks. You know how easy it is to stir up the fanatical element. Before we know it they're liable to get a law passed against us."

"Not if I c'n git to th' legislature first," interrupted Johnson. "Yuh know, Ah knows how tuh handle these white folks. If yuh 'Say it with Bucks' you c'n git anything yuh want."

"There is something in what Foster says, though," Dr. Crookman said. "Just look at this bunch of clippings we got in this morning. Listen to these: 'The Viper in Our Midst,' from the Richmond *Blade;* 'The Menace of Science' from the Memphis *Bugle;* 'A Challenge to Every White Man' from the Dallas

*Sun;* 'Police Battle Black Mob Seeking White Skins,' from the Atlanta *Topic;* 'Negro Doctor Admits Being Taught by Germans,' from the St. Louis *North American.* Here's a line or two from an editorial in the Oklahoma City *Hatchet:* 'There are times when the welfare of our race must take precedence over law. Opposed as we always have been to mob violence as the worst enemy of democratic government, we cannot help but feel that the intelligent white men and women of New York City who are interested in the purity and preservation of their race should not permit the challenge of Crookmanism to go unanswered, even though these black scoundrels may be within the law. There are too many criminals in this country already hiding behind the skirts of the law.'

"And lastly, one from the Tallahassee *Announcer* says: 'While it is the right of every citizen to do what he wants to do with his money, the white people of the United States cannot remain indifferent to this discovery and its horrible potentialities. Hundreds of Negroes with newly-acquired white skins have already entered white society and thousands will follow them. The black race from one end of the country to the other has in two short weeks gone completely crazy over the prospect of getting white. Day by day we see the color line which we have so laboriously established being rapidly destroyed. There would not be so much cause for alarm in this, were it not for the fact that this vitiligo is not hereditary. In other words, THE OFFSPRING OF THESE WHITENED NEGROES WILL BE NEGROES! This means that your daughter, having married a supposed white man, may find herself with a black baby! Will the proud white men of the Southland so far forget their traditions as to remain idle while this devilish work is going on?"

"No use singin' th' blues," counseled Johnson. "We ain' gonna be both'ed heah, even if them crackahs down South do raise a little hell. Jus' lissen to th' sweet music of that mob out theah! Eve'y scream means fifty bucks. On'y reason we ain't makin' mo' money is 'cause we ain't got no mo' room."

"That's right," Dr. Crookman agreed. "We've turned out one hundred a day for fourteen days." He leaned back and lit a cigarette.

"At fifty bucks a th'ow," interrupted Johnson, "that means we've took in seventy thousand dollahs. Great Day in th' mornin'! Didn't know tha was so much jack in Harlem."

"Yes," continued Crookman, "we're taking in thirty-five thousand dollars a week. As soon as you and Foster get that other place fixed up we'll be making twice that much."

From the hallway came the voice of the switchboard operator monotonously droning out her instructions: "No, Dr. Crookman cannot see anyone. . . . Dr. Crookman has nothing to say. . . . Dr. Crookman will issue a statement shortly. . . . Fifty Dollars. . . . No, Dr. Crookman isn't a mulatto. . . . I'm very sorry but I cannot answer that question."

The three friends sat in silence amid the hum of activity around them. Hank Johnson smiled down at the end of his cigar as he thought back over his rather colorful and hectic career. To think that today he was one of the leading Negroes of the world, one who was taking an active and important part in solving the most vexatious problem in American life, and yet only ten years before he had been working on a Carolina chain gang. Two years he had toiled on the roads under the hard eye and ready rifle of a cruel white guard; two years of being beaten, kicked and cursed, of poor food and vermin-infested habitations; two years for participating in a little crap game. Then he had drifted to Charleston, got a job in a pool room, had a stroke of luck with the dice, come to New York and landed right in the midst of the Numbers racket. Becoming a collector or "runner," he had managed his affairs well enough to be able to start out soon as a "banker." Money had poured in from Negroes eager to chance one cent in the hope of winning six dollars. Some won but most lost and he had prospered. He had purchased an apartment house, paid off the police, dabbled in the bail bond game, given a couple of thousand dollars to advance Negro Art and been elected Grand Permanent Shogun of the Ancient and Honorable Order of Crocodiles, Harlem's largest and most prosperous secret society. Then young Crookman had come to him with his proposition. At first he had hesitated about helping him but later was persuaded to do so when the young man bitterly complained that the dicty Negroes would not help to pay for the studies abroad. What a stroke of luck, getting in on the ground floor like this! They'd all be richer than Rockefeller inside of a year. Twelve million Negroes at fifty dollars apiece! Great Day in the morning! Hank spat regally into the brass cuspidor across the office and reared back contentedly on the soft cushion of the divan.

Chuck Foster was also seeing his career in retrospect. His life had not been as colorful as that of Hank Johnson. The son of a Birmingham barber, he had enjoyed such educational advantages as that community afforded the darker brethren; had become a schoolteacher, an insurance agent and a social worker in turn. Then, along with the tide of migration, he had drifted first to Cincinnati, then to Pittsburgh and finally to New York. There the real estate field, unusually lucrative because of the paucity of apartments for the increasing Negro population, had claimed him. Cautious, careful, thrifty and devoid of sentimentality, he had prospered, but not without some ugly rumors being broadcast about his sharp business methods. As he slowly worked his way up to the top of Harlem society, he had sought to live down this reputation for double-dealing and shifty practices, all too true of the bulk of his fellow realtors in the district, by giving large sums to the Young Men's and Young Women's Christian Associations, by offering scholarships to young Negroes, by staging elaborate parties to which dicty Negroes of the community were invited. He had been glad of the opportunity to help subsidize young Crookman's studies abroad when Hank Johnson pointed out the possibilities of the venture. Now, although the results so far exceeded his wildest dreams, his natural conservatism and timidity made him somewhat pessimistic about the future. He supposed a hundred dire results of their activities and only the day before he had increased the amount of his life insurance. His mind was filled with doubts. He didn't like so much publicity. He wanted a sort of genteel popularity but no notoriety.

Despite the coffee and cigarettes, Dr. Junius Crookman was sleepy. The responsibility, the necessity of overseeing the work of his physicians and nurses, the insistence of the newspapers and the medical profession that he reveal the secrets of his treatment and a thousand other vexatious details had kept him from getting proper rest. He had, indeed, spent most of his time in the sanitarium.

This hectic activity was new to him. Up until a month ago his thirty-five years had been peaceful and, in the main, studious ones. The son of an Episcopal clergyman, he had been born and raised in a city in central New York, his associates carefully selected in order to protect him as much as possible from the defeatist psychology so prevalent among American Negroes and given every opportunity and inducement to learn his profession and become a thoroughly cultivated and civilized man. His parents, though poor, were proud and boasted that they belonged to the Negro aristocracy. He had had to work his way through college because of the failure of his father's health but he had come very little in contact with the crudity, coarseness and cruelty of life. He had been monotonously successful but he was sensible enough to believe that a large part of it was due, like most success, to chance. He saw in his great discovery the solution to the most annoying problem in American life. Obviously, he reasoned, if there were no Negroes, there could be no Negro problem. Without a Negro problem, Americans could concentrate their attention on something constructive. Through his efforts and the activities of Black-No-More, Incorporated, it would be possible to do what agitation, education and legislation had failed to do. He was naïvely surprised that there should be opposition to his work. Like most men with a vision, a plan, a program or a remedy, he fondly imagined people to be intelligent enough to accept a good thing when it was offered to them, which was conclusive evidence that he knew little about the human race.

Dr. Crookman prided himself above all on being a great lover of his race. He had studied its history, read of its struggles and kept up with its achievements. He subscribed to six or seven Negro weekly newspapers and two of the magazines. He was so interested in the continued progress of the American Negroes that he wanted to remove all obstacles in their path by depriving them of their racial characteristics. His home and office were filled with African masks and paintings of Negroes by Negroes. He was what was known in Negro society as a Race Man. He was wedded to everything black except the

black woman—his wife was a white girl with remote Negro ancestry, of the type that Negroes were wont to describe as being
"able to pass for white." While abroad he had spent his spare
time ransacking the libraries for facts about the achievements
of Negroes and having liaisons with comely and available fraus
and fräuleins.

"Well, Doc," said Hank Johnson, suddenly, "you'd bettah
go on home 'n git some sleep. Ain' no use killin' you'sef.
Eve'thing's gonna be all right heah. You ain' gotta thing tuh
worry 'bout."

"How's he gonna get out of here with that mob in front?"
Chuck inquired. "A man almost needs a tank to get through
that crowd of darkies."

"Oh, Ah've got all that fixed, Calamity Jane," Johnson remarked casually. "All he's gotta do is tuh go on down staihs
tuh the basem'nt, go out th' back way an' step into th' alley.
My car'll be theah waitin' fo' 'im."

"That's awfully nice of you, Johnson," said the physician. "I
am dead tired. I think I'll be a new man if I can get a few hours
of sleep."

A black man in white uniform opened the door and announced: "Mrs. Crookman!" He held the door open for the
Doctor's petite, stylishly-dressed wife to enter. The three men
sprang to their feet. Johnson and Foster eyed the beautiful little
octoroon appreciatively as they bowed, thinking how easily she
could "pass for white," which would have been something akin
to a piece of anthracite coal passing for black.

"Darling!" she exclaimed, turning to her husband. "Why
don't you come home and get some rest? You'll be ill if you
keep on in this way."

"Jus' whut Ah bin tellin' him, Mrs. Crookman," Johnson
hastened to say. "He got eve'ything fixed tuh send 'im off."

"Well, then, Junius, we'd better be going," she said decisively.

Putting on a long overcoat over his white uniform, Dr.
Crookman, wearily and meekly followed his spouse out of the
door.

"Mighty nice looking girl, Mrs. Crookman," Foster observed.

"Nice lookin'!" echoed Johnson, with mock amazement.

"Why, nigguh, that ooman would make uh rabbit hug uh houn'. Doc sez she's cullud, an' she sez so, but she looks mighty white tuh me."

"Everything that looks white ain't white in this man's country," Foster replied.

Meantime there was feverish activity in Harlem's financial institutions. At the Douglass Bank the tellers were busier than bootleggers on Christmas Eve. Moreover, they were short-handed because of the mysterious absence of Bunny Brown. A long queue of Negroes extended down one side of the bank, out of the front door and around the corner, while bank attendants struggled to keep them in line. Everybody was drawing out money; no one was depositing. In vain the bank officials pleaded with them not to withdraw their funds. The Negroes were adamant: they wanted their money and wanted it quick. Day after day this had gone on ever since Black-No-More, Incorporated, had started turning Negroes white. At first, efforts were made to bulldoze and intimidate the depositors but that didn't succeed. These people were in no mood to be trifled with. A lifetime of being Negroes in the United States had convinced them that there was great advantage in being white.

"Mon, whutcha tahlk ab't?" scoffed a big, black British West Indian woman with whom an official was remonstrating not to draw out her money. "Dis heah's mah mahney, ain't it? Yuh use mah mahney alla time, aintcha? Whutcha mean, Ah shouldn't draw't out? . . . You gimme mah mahney or Ah broke up dis place!"

"Are you closing your account, Mr. Robinson?" a soft-voiced mulatto teller inquired of a big, rusty stevedore.

"Ah ain't openin' it," was the rejoinder. "Ah wants th' whole thing, an' Ah don't mean maybe."

Similar scenes were being enacted at the Wheatley Trust Company and at the local Post Office station.

An observer passing up and down the streets would have noted a general exodus from the locality. Moving vans were backed up to apartment houses on nearly every block.

The "For Rent" signs were appearing in larger number in Harlem than at any time in twenty-five years. Landlords looked on helplessly as apartment after apartment emptied and was not filled. Even the refusal to return deposits did not prevent the tenants from moving out. What, indeed, was fifty, sixty or seventy dollars when one was leaving behind insult, ostracism, segregation and discrimination? Moreover, the whitened Negroes were saving a great deal of money by being able to change localities. The mechanics of race prejudice had forced them into the congested Harlem area where, at the mercy of white and black real estate sharks, they had been compelled to pay exorbitant rentals because the demand for housing far exceeded the supply. As a general rule the Negroes were paying one hundred per cent more than white tenants in other parts of the city for a smaller number of rooms and worse service.

The installment furniture and clothing houses in the area were also beginning to feel the results of the activities of Black-No-More, Incorporated. Collectors were reporting their inability to locate certain families or the articles they had purchased on time. Many of the colored folk, it was said, had sold their furniture to second-hand stores and vanished with the proceeds into the great mass of white citizenry.

At the same time there seemed to be more white people on the streets of Harlem than at any time in the past twenty years. Many of them appeared to be on the most intimate terms with the Negroes, laughing, talking, dining and dancing in a most un-Caucasian way. This sort of association had always gone on at night but seldom in the daylight.

Strange Negroes from the West and South who had heard the good news were to be seen on the streets and in public places, patiently awaiting their turn at the Crookman Institute.

Madame Sisseretta Blandish sat disconsolately in an armchair near the front door of her ornate hair-straightening shop, looking blankly at the pedestrians and traffic passing to and fro. These two weeks had been hard ones for her. Everything was going out and nothing coming in. She had been doing very well at her vocation for years and was acclaimed in the community as one of its business leaders. Because of her prominence as the proprietor of a successful enterprise engaged in making Negroes appear as much like white folks as possible, she had recently been elected for the fourth time a Vice-President of the American Race Pride League. She was also head of the Woman's Committee of the New York Branch of the Social Equality League and held an important place in local Republican politics. But all of these honors brought little or no money with them. They didn't help to pay her rent or purchase the voluminous dresses she required to drape her Amazonian form. Only that day her landlord had brought her the sad news that he either wanted his money or the premises.

Where, she wondered, would she get the money. Like most New Yorkers she put up a big front with very little cash behind it, always looking hopefully forward to the morrow for a lucky break. She had two-thirds of the rent money already, by dint of much borrowing, and if she could "do" a few nappy heads she would be in the clear; but hardly a customer had crossed her threshold in a fortnight, except two or three Jewish girls from downtown who came up regularly to have their hair straightened because it wouldn't stand inspection in the Nordic world. The Negro women had seemingly deserted her. Day after day she saw her old customers pass by hurriedly without even looking in her direction. Verily a revolution was taking place in Negro society.

"Oh, Miss Simpson!" cried the hair-straightener after a passing young lady. "Ain't you going to say hello?"

The young woman halted reluctantly and approached the doorway. Her brown face looked strained. Two weeks before she would have been a rare sight in the Black Belt because her kinky hair was not straightened; it was merely combed, brushed and neatly pinned up. Miss Simpson had vowed that she wasn't going to spend any dollar a week having her hair "done" when she only lacked fifteen dollars of having money enough to quit the Negro race forever.

"Sorry, Mrs. Blandish," she apologized, "but I swear I didn't see you. I've been just that busy that I haven't had eyes for anything or anybody except my job and back home again. You know I'm all alone now. Yes, Charlie went over two weeks ago and I haven't heard a word from him. Just think of that! After all I've done for that nigger. Oh well! I'll soon be over there myself. Another week's work will fix me all right."

"Humph!" snorted Mme. Blandish. "That's all you niggers

are thinking about nowadays. Why don't you come down here and give me some business? If I don't hurry up and make some more money I'll have to close up this place and go to work myself."

"Well, I'm sorry, Mrs. Blandish," the girl mumbled indifferently, moving off toward the corner to catch the approaching street car, "but I guess I can hold out with this here bad hair until Saturday night. You know I've taken too much punishment being dark these twenty-two years to miss this opportunity. . . . Well," she flung over her shoulder, "Goodbye! See you later."

Madame Blandish settled her 250 pounds back into her armchair and sighed heavily. Like all American Negroes she had desired to be white when she was young and before she entered business for herself and became a person of consequence in the community. Now she had lived long enough to have no illusions about the magic of a white skin. She liked her business and she liked her social position in Harlem. As a white woman she would have to start all over again, and she wasn't so sure of herself. Here at least she was somebody. In the great Caucasian world she would be just another white woman, and they were becoming a drug on the market, what with the simultaneous decline of chivalry, the marriage rate and professional prostitution. She had seen too many elderly, white-haired Caucasian females scrubbing floors and toiling in sculleries not to know what being just another white woman meant. Yet she admitted to herself that it would be nice to get over being the butt for jokes and petty prejudice.

The Madame was in a quandary and so also were hundreds of others in the upper stratum of Harlem life. With the Negro masses moving out from under them, what other alternative did they have except to follow. True, only a few hundred Negroes had so far vanished from their wonted haunts, but it was known that thousands, tens of thousands, yes, millions would follow them.

# Chapter Four

MATTHEW FISHER, alias Max Disher, joined the Easter Sunday crowds, twirling his malacca stick and ogling the pretty flappers who passed giggling in their Spring finery. For nearly three months he had idled around the Georgia capital hoping to catch a glimpse of the beautiful girl who on New Year's Eve had told him "I never dance with niggers." He had searched diligently in almost every stratum of Atlanta society, but he had failed to find her. There were hundreds of tall, beautiful, blonde maidens in the city; to seek a particular one whose name one did not know was somewhat akin to hunting for a Russian Jew in the Bronx or a particular Italian gunman in Chicago.

For three months he had dreamed of this girl, carefully perused the society columns of the local newspapers on the chance that her picture might appear in them. He was like most men who have been repulsed by a pretty girl, his desire for her grew stronger and stronger.

He was not finding life as a white man the rosy existence he had anticipated. He was forced to conclude that it was pretty dull and that he was bored. As a boy he had been taught to look up to white folks as just a little less than gods; now he found them little different from the Negroes, except that they were uniformly less courteous and less interesting.

Often when the desire for the happy-go-lucky, jovial good-fellowship of the Negroes came upon him strongly, he would go down to Auburn Avenue and stroll around the vicinity, looking at the dark folk and listening to their conversation and banter. But no one down there wanted him around. He was a white man and thus suspect. Only the black women who ran the "Call Houses" on the hill wanted his company. There was nothing left for him except the hard, materialistic, grasping, ill-bred society of the whites. Sometimes a slight feeling of regret that he had left his people forever would cross his mind, but it fled before the painful memories of past experiences in this, his home town.

The unreasoning and illogical color prejudice of most of the people with whom he was forced to associate, infuriated him. He often laughed cynically when some coarse, ignorant white man voiced his opinion concerning the inferior mentality and morality of the Negroes. He was moving in white society now and he could compare it with the society he had known as a Negro in Atlanta and Harlem. What a let-down it was from the good breeding, sophistication, refinement and gentle cynicism to which he had become accustomed as a popular young man about town in New York's Black Belt. He was not able to articulate this feeling but he was conscious of the reaction nevertheless.

For a week, now, he had been thinking seriously of going to work. His thousand dollars had dwindled to less than a hundred. He would have to find some source of income and yet the young white men with whom he talked about work all complained that it was very scarce. Being white, he finally concluded, was no Open Sesame to employment for he sought work in banks and insurance offices without success.

During his period of idleness and soft living, he had followed the news and opinion in the local daily press and confessed himself surprised at the antagonistic attitude of the newspapers toward Black-No-More, Incorporated. From the vantage point of having formerly been a Negro, he was able to see how the newspapers were fanning the color prejudice of the white people. Business men, he found were also bitterly opposed to Dr. Crookman and his efforts to bring about chromatic democracy in the nation.

The attitude of these people puzzled him. Was not Black-No-More getting rid of the Negroes upon whom all of the blame was placed for the backwardness of the South? Then he recalled what a Negro street speaker had said one night on the corner of 138th Street and Seventh Avenue in New York: that unorganized labor meant cheap labor; that the guarantee of cheap labor was an effective means of luring new industries into the South; that so long as the ignorant white masses could be kept thinking of the menace of the Negro to Caucasian race purity and political control, they would give little thought to labor organization. It suddenly dawned upon Matthew Fisher that this Black-No-More treatment was more of a menace to white business than to white labor. And not long afterward he became aware of the money-making possibilities involved in the present situation.

How could he work it? He was not known and he belonged to no organization. Here was a veritable gold mine but how could he reach the ore? He scratched his head over the problem but could think of no solution. Who would be interested in it that he could trust?

He was pondering this question the Monday after Easter while breakfasting in an armchair restaurant when he noticed an advertisement in a newspaper lying in the next chair. He read it and then re-read it

## THE KNIGHTS OF NORDICA

Want 10,000 Atlanta White Men and Women to
Join in the Fight for White Race Integrity.

Imperial Klonklave Tonight

The racial integrity of the Caucasian Race is being
threatened by the activities of a scientific
black Beelzebub in New York

Let us Unite Now Before It Is

## TOO LATE!

Come to Nordica Hall Tonight
Admission Free.
Rev. Henry Givens,
Imperial Grand Wizard

Here, Matthew figured, was just what he had been looking for. Probably he could get in with this fellow Givens. He finished his cup of coffee, lit a cigar and paying his check, strolled out into the sunshine of Peachtree Street.

He took the trolley out to Nordica Hall. It was a big, unpainted barn-like edifice, with a suite of offices in front and a huge auditorium in the rear. A new oil cloth sign reading "THE KNIGHTS OF NORDICA" was stretched across the front of the building.

Matthew paused for a moment and sized up the edifice.

Givens must have some money, he thought, to keep up such a large place. Might not be a bad idea to get a little dope on him before going inside.

"This fellow Givens is a pretty big guy around here, ain't he?" he asked the young man at the soda fountain across the street.

"Yessah, he's one o' th' bigges' men in this heah town. Used to be a big somethin' or other in th' old Ku Klux Klan 'fore it died. Now he's stahtin' this heah Knights o' Nordica."

"He must have pretty good jack," suggested Matthew.

"He oughtta have," answered the soda jerker. "My paw tells me he was close to th' money when he was in th' Klan."

Here, thought Matthew, was just the place for him. He paid for his soda and walked across the street to the door marked "Office." He felt a slight tremor of uneasiness as he turned the knob and entered. Despite his white skin he still possessed the fear of the Klan and kindred organizations possessed by most Negroes.

A rather pretty young stenographer asked him his business as he walked into the ante room. Better be bold, he thought. This was probably the best chance he would have to keep from working, and his funds were getting lower and lower.

"Please tell Rev. Givens, the Imperial Grand Wizard, that Mr. Matthew Fisher of the New York Anthropological Society is very anxious to have about a half-hour's conversation with him relative to his new venture." Matthew spoke in an impressive, businesslike manner, rocked back on his heels and looked profound.

"Yassah," almost whispered the awed young lady, "I'll tell him." She withdrew into an inner office and Matthew chuckled softly to himself. He wondered if he could impress this old fakir as easily as he had the girl.

Rev. Henry Givens, Imperial Grand Wizard of the Knights of Nordica, was a short, wizened, almost-bald, bull-voiced, ignorant ex-evangelist, who had come originally from the hilly country north of Atlanta. He had helped in the organization of the Ku Klux Klan following the Great War and had worked with a zeal only equalled by his thankfulness to God for escaping from the precarious existence of an itinerant saver of souls.

Not only had the Rev. Givens toiled diligently to increase the prestige, power and membership of the defunct Ku Klux Klan, but he had also been a very hard worker in withdrawing as much money from its treasury as possible. He convinced himself, as did the other officers, that this stealing was not stealing at all but merely appropriation of rightful reward for his valuable services. When the morons finally tired of supporting the show and the stream of ten-dollar memberships declined to a trickle, Givens had been able to retire gracefully and live on the interest of his money.

Then, when the newspapers began to recount the activities of Black-No-More, Incorporated, he saw a vision of work to be done, and founded the Knights of Nordica. So far there were only a hundred members but he had high hopes for the future. Tonight, he felt would tell the story. The prospect of a full treasury to dip into again made his little gray eyes twinkle and the palms of his skinny hands itch.

The stenographer interrupted him to announce the newcomer.

"Hum-n!" said Givens, half to himself. "New York Anthropological Society, eh? This feller must know somethin'. Might be able to use him in this business. . . . All right, show him in!"

The two men shook hands and swiftly appraised each other. Givens waved Matthew to a chair.

"How can I serve you, Mr. Fisher?" he began in sepulchral tone dripping with unction.

"It is rather," countered Matthew in his best salesman's croon, "how I can serve you and your valuable organization. As an anthropologist, I have, of course, been long interested in the work with which you have been identified. It has always seemed to me that there was no question in American life more important than that of preserving the integrity of the white race. We all know what has been the fate of those nations that have permitted their blood to be polluted with that of inferior breeds." (He had read some argument like that in a Sunday supplement not long before, which was the extent of his knowledge of anthropology.) "This latest menace of Black-No-More is the most formidable the white people of America have had to face since the founding of the Republic. As a resident of New York City, I am aware, of course, of the extent of the activities of this Negro Crookman and his two associates. Already thousands of blacks have passed over into the white race. Not satisfied with operating in New York City, they have opened their sanitariums in twenty other cities from Coast to Coast. They open a new one almost every day. In their literature and advertisements in the darky newspapers they boast that they are now turning four thousand Negroes white every day." He knitted his blond eyebrows. "You see how great the menace is? At this rate there will not be a Negro in the country in ten years, for you must remember that the rate is increasing every day as new sanitariums are opened. Don't you see that something must be done about this immediately? Don't you see that Congress must be aroused; that these places must be closed?" The young man glared with belligerent indignation.

Rev. Givens saw. He nodded his head as Matthew, now glorying in his newly-discovered eloquence made point after point, and concluded that this pale, dapper young fellow, with his ready tongue, his sincerity, his scientific training and knowledge of the situation ought to prove a valuable asset to the Knights of Nordica.

"I tried to interest some agencies in New York," Matthew continued, "but they are all blind to this menace and to their duty. Then someone told me of you and your valuable work, and I decided to come down here and have a talk with you. I had intended to suggest the organization of some such militant secret order as you have started, but since you've already seen the necessity for it, I want to hasten to offer my services as a scientific man and one familiar with the facts and able to present them to your members."

"I should be very glad," boomed Givens, "very happy, indeed, Brother Fisher, to have you join us. We need you. I believe you can help us a great deal. Would you, er—ah, be interested in coming out to the mass meeting this evening? It would help us tremendously to get members if you would be willing to get up and tell the audience what you have just related about the progress of this iniquitous nigger corporation in New York."

Matthew pretended to think over the matter for a moment or two and then agreed. If he made a hit at the initial meeting, he

would be sure to get on the staff. Once there he could go after
the larger game. Unlike Givens, he had no belief in the racial
integrity nonsense nor any confidence in the white masses
whom he thought were destined to flock to the Knights of
Nordica. On the contrary he despised and hated them. He had
the average Negro's justifiable fear of the poor whites and only
planned to use them as a stepladder to the real money.

When Matthew left, Givens congratulated himself upon the
fact that he had been able to attract such talent to the organization in its very infancy. His ideas must be sound, he concluded, if scientists from New York were impressed by them.
He reached over, pulled the dictionary stand toward him and
opened the big book at A.

"Lemme see, now," he muttered aloud. "Anthropology.
Better git that word straight 'fore I go talkin' too much about
it. . . . Humn! Humn! . . . That boy must know a hull
lot." He read over the definition of the word twice without
understanding it, closed the dictionary, pushed it away from
him, and then cutting off a large chew of tobacco from his
plug, he leaned back in his swivel chair to rest after the unaccustomed mental exertion.

Matthew went gaily back to his hotel. "Man alive!" he chortled to himself. "What a lucky break! Can't keep old Max down
long. . . . Will I speak to 'em? Well, I won't stay quiet!" He
felt so delighted over the prospect of getting close to some real
money that he treated himself to an expensive dinner and a
twenty-five-cent cigar. Afterward he inquired further about
old man Givens from the house detective, a native Atlantan.

"Oh, he's well heeled—the old crook!" remarked the detective. "Damnify could ever understand how such ignorant people get a-hold of th' money; but there y'are. Owns as pretty a
home as you can find around these parts an' damn 'f he ain't
stahtin' a new racket."

"Do you think he'll make anything out of it?" inquired
Matthew, innocently.

"Say, Brother, you mus' be a stranger in these parts. These
damn, ignorant crackers will fall fer anything fer a while. They
ain't had no Klan here fer goin' on three years. Leastwise it
ain't been functionin'." The old fellow chuckled and spat a

stream of tobacco juice into a nearby cuspidor. Matthew sauntered away. Yes, the pickings ought to be good.

Equally enthusiastic was the Imperial Grand Wizard when
he came home to dinner that night. He entered the house humming one of his favorite hymns and his wife looked up from
the evening paper with surprise on her face. The Rev. Givens
was usually something of a grouch but tonight he was as happy
as a pickpocket at a country fair.

"What's th' mattah with you?" she inquired, sniffing suspiciously.

"Oh, Honey," he gurgled, "I think this here Knights of
Nordica is going over big; going over big! My fame is spreading. Only today I had a long talk with a famous anthropologist
from New York and he's going to address our mass meeting
tonight."

"Whut's an anthropologist?" asked Mrs. Givens, wrinkling
her seamy brow.

"Oh-er, well; he's one of these here scientists what knows all
about this here business what's going on up there in New York
where them niggers is turning each other white," explained
Rev. Givens hastily but firmly. "He's a mighty smaht feller and
I want you and Helen to come out and hear him."

"B'lieve Ah will," declared Mrs. Givens, "if this heah rheumatism'll le' me foh a while. Doan know 'bout Helen, though.
Evah since that gal went away tuh school she ain't bin int'rested
in nuthin' up-liftin'!"

Mrs. Givens spoke in a grieved tone and heaved her narrow
chest in a deep sigh. She didn't like all this newfangled foolishness of these young folks. They were getting away from God,
that's what they were, and she didn't like it. Mrs. Givens was a
Christian. There was no doubt about it because she freely admitted it to everybody, with or without provocation. Of course
she often took the name of the Creator in vain when she got to
quarreling with Henry; she had the reputation among her
friends of not always stating the exact truth; she hated Negroes;
her spouse had made bitter and profane comment concerning
her virginity on their wedding night; and as head of the ladies'
auxiliary of the defunct Klan she had copied her husband's financial methods; but that she was a devout Christion no one

doubted. She believed the Bible from cover to cover, except what it said about people with money, and she read it every evening aloud, greatly to the annoyance of the Imperial Grand Wizard and his modern and comely daughter.

Mrs. Givens had probably once been beautiful but the wear and tear of a long life as the better half of an itinerant evangelist was apparent. Her once flaming red hair was turning gray and roan-like, her hatchet face was a criss-cross of wrinkles and lines, she was round-shouldered, hollow-chested, walked with a stoop and her long, bony, white hands looked like claws. She alternately dipped snuff and smoked an evil-smelling clay pipe, except when there was company at the house. At such times Helen would insist her mother "act like civilized people."

Helen was twenty and quite confident that she herself was civilized. Whether she was or not, she was certainly beautiful. Indeed, she was such a beauty that many of the friends of the family insisted that she must have been adopted. Taller than either of her parents, she was stately, erect, well proportioned, slender, vivid and knew how to wear her clothes. In only one way did she resemble her parents and that was in things intellectual. Any form of mental effort, she complained, made her head ache, and so her parents had always let her have her way about studying.

At the age of eleven she had been taken from the third grade in public school and sent to an exclusive seminary for the double purpose of gaining social prestige and concealing her mental incapacity. At sixteen when her instructors had about despaired of her, they were overjoyed by the decision of her father to send the girl to a "finishing school" in the North. The "finishing school" about finished what intelligence Helen possessed; but she came forth, four years later, more beautiful, with a better knowledge of how to dress and how to act in exclusive society, enough superficialities to enable her to get by in the "best" circles and a great deal of that shallow facetiousness that passes for sophistication in American upper-class life. A winter in Manhattan had rounded out her education. Now she was back home, thoroughly ashamed of her grotesque parents, and, like the other girls of her set, anxious to get a husband who at the same time was handsome, intelligent, educated, refined and rolling in wealth. As she was ignorant of the fact that no such man existed, she looked confidently forward into the future.

"I don't care to go down there among all those gross people," she informed her father at the dinner table when he broached the subject of the meeting. "They're so crude and elemental, don't you know," she explained, arching her narrow eyebrows.

"The common people are the salt of the earth," boomed Rev. Givens. "If it hadn't been for the common people we wouldn't have been able to get this home and send you off to school. You make me sick with all your modern ideas. You'd do a lot better if you'd try to be more like your Ma."

Both Mrs. Givens and Helen looked quickly at him to see if he was smiling. He wasn't.

"Why don'tcha go, Helen?" pleaded Mrs. Givens. "Yo fathah sez this heah man f'm N'Yawk is uh—uh scientist or somethin' an' knows a whole lot about things. Yuh might l'arn somethin'. Ah'd go mys'f if 'twasn't fo mah rheumatism." She sighed in self-pity and finished gnawing a drumstick.

Helen's curiosity was aroused and although she didn't like the idea of sitting among a lot of mill hands, she was anxious to see and hear this reputedly brilliant young man from the great metropolis where not long before she had lost both her provincialism and chastity.

"Oh, all right," she assented with mock reluctance. "I'll go."

The Knights of Nordica's flag-draped auditorium slowly filled. It was a bare, cavernous structure, with sawdust on the floor, a big platform at one end, row after row of folding wooden chairs and illuminated by large, white lights hanging from the rafters. On the platform was a row of five chairs, the center one being high-backed and gilded. On the lectern downstage was a bulky bible. A huge American flag was stretched across the rear wall.

The audience was composed of the lower stratum of white working people: hard-faced, lantern-jawed, dull-eyed adult children, seeking like all humanity for something permanent in the eternal flux of life. The young girls in their cheap finery with circus makeup on their faces; the young men, aged before their time by child labor and a violent environment; the middle-aged folk with their shiny, shabby garb and beaten countenances; all ready and eager to be organized for any purpose except improvement of their intellects and standard of living.

Rev. Givens opened the meeting with a prayer "for the success, O God, of this thy work, to protect the sisters and wives and daughters of these, thy people, from the filthy pollution of an alien race."

A choir of assorted types of individuals sang "Onward Christian Soldiers" earnestly, vociferously and badly.

They were about to file off the platform when the song leader, a big, beefy, jovial mountain of a man, leaped upon the stage and restrained them.

"Wait a minute, folks, wait a minute," he commanded. Then turning to the assemblage: "Now people let's put some pep into this. We wanna all be happy and get in th' right spirit for this heah meetin'. Ah'm gonna ask the choir to sing th' first and last verses ovah ag'in, and when they come to th' chorus, Ah wantcha to all join in. Doan be 'fraid. Jesus wouldn't be 'fraid to sing 'Onward Christian Soldiers,' now would he? Come on, then. All right, choir, you staht; an' when Ah wave mah han' you'all join in on that theah chorus."

They obediently followed his directions while he marched up and down the platform, red-faced and roaring and waving his arms in time. When the last note had died away, he dismissed the choir and stepping to the edge of the stage he leaned far out over the audience and barked at them again.

"Come on, now, folks! Yuh caint slow up on Jesus now. He won't be satisfied with jus' one ole measly song. Yuh gotta let 'im know that yuh love 'im; that y're happy an' contented; that yuh ain't got no troubles an' ain't gonna have any. Come on, now. Le's sing that ole favorite what yo'all like so well: 'Pack Up Your Troubles in Your Old Kit Bag and Smile, Smile, Smile.'" He bellowed and they followed him. Again the vast hall shook with sound. He made them rise and grasp each other by the hand until the song ended.

Matthew, who sat on the platform alongside old man Givens, viewed the spectacle with amusement mingled with amazement. He was amused because of the similarity of this meeting to the religious orgies of the more ignorant Negroes and amazed that earlier in the evening he should have felt any qualms about lecturing to these folks on anthropology, a subject with which neither he nor his hearers were acquainted. He quickly saw that these people would believe anything that was shouted at them loudly and convincingly enough. He knew what would fetch their applause and bring in their memberships and he intended to repeat it over and over.

The Imperial Grand Wizard spent a half-hour introducing the speaker of the evening, dwelt upon his supposed scholastic attainments, but took pains to inform them that, despite Matthew's vast knowledge, he still believed in the Word of God, the sanctity of womanhood and the purity of the white race.

For an hour Matthew told them at the top of his voice what they believed: i.e., that a white skin was a sure indication of the possession of superior intellectual and moral qualities; that all Negroes were inferior to them; that God had intended for the United States to be a white man's country and that with His help they could keep it so; that their sons and brothers might inadvertently marry Negresses or, worse, their sisters and daughters might marry Negroes, if Black-No-More, Incorporated, was permitted to continue its dangerous activities.

For an hour he spoke, interrupted at intervals by enthusiastic gales of applause, and as he spoke his eye wandered over the females in the audience, noting the comeliest ones. As he wound up with a spirited appeal for eager soldiers to join the Knights of Nordica at five dollars per head and the half-dozen "planted" emissaries led the march of suckers to the platform, he noted for the first time a girl who sat in the front row and gazed up at him raptly.

She was a titian blonde, well-dressed, beautiful and strangely familiar. As he retired amid thunderous applause to make way for Rev. Givens and the money collectors, he wondered where he had seen her before. He studied her from his seat.

Suddenly he knew. It was she! The girl who had spurned him; the girl he had sought so long; the girl he wanted more than anything in the world! Strange that she should be here. He had always thought of her as a refined, educated and wealthy lady, far above associating with such people as these.

He was in a fever to meet her, some way, before she got out of his sight again, and yet he felt just a little disappointed to find her here.

He could hardly wait until Givens seated himself again before questioning him as to the girl's identity. As the beefy song leader led the roaring of the popular closing hymn, he leaned toward the Imperial Grand Wizard and shouted: "Who is that tall golden-haired girl sitting in the front row? Do you know her?"

Rev. Givens looked out over the audience, craning his skinny neck and blinking his eyes. Then he saw the girl, sitting within twenty feet of him.

"You mean that girl sitting right in front, there?" he asked, pointing.

"Yes, that one," said Matthew, impatiently.

"Heh! Heh! Heh!" chuckled the Wizard, rubbing his stubbly chin. "Why that there's my daughter, Helen. Like to meet her?"

Matthew could hardly believe his ears. Givens's daughter! Incredible! What a coincidence! What luck! Would he like to meet her? He leaned over and shouted "Yes."

# Chapter Five

A HUGE silver monoplane glided gracefully to the surface of Mines Field in Los Angeles and came to a pretty stop after a short run. A liveried footman stepped out of the forward compartment armed with a stool which he placed under the rear door. Simultaneously a high-powered foreign car swept up close to the airplane and waited. The rear door of the airplane opened, and to the apparent surprise of the nearby mechanics a tall, black, distinguished-looking Negro stepped out and down to the ground, assisted by the hand of the footman. Behind him came a pale young man and woman, evidently secretaries. The three entered the limousine which rapidly drove off.

"Who's that coon?" asked one of the mechanics, round-eyed and respectful, like all Americans, in the presence of great wealth.

"Don't you know who that is?" inquired another, pityingly. "Why that's that Dr. Crookman. You know, the fellow what's turnin' niggers white. See that B N M on the side of his plane? That stands for Black-No-More. Gee, but I wish I had just half the jack he's made in the last six months!"

"Why I thought from readin' th' papers," protested the first speaker, "that th' law had closed up his places and put 'im outta business."

"Oh, that's a lotta hockey," said the other fellow. "Why just yesterday th' newspapers said that Black-No-More was openin' a place on Central Avenue. They already got one in Oakland, so a coon told me yesterday."

"'Sfunny," ventured a third mechanic, as they wheeled the big plane into a nearby hangar, "how he don't have nuthin' but white folks around him. He must not like nigger help. His chauffeur's white, his footman's white an' that young gal and feller what was with him are white."

"How do you know?" challenged the first speaker. "They may be darkies that he's turned into white folks."

"That's right," the other replied. "It's gittin' so yuh can't tell who's who. I think that there Knights of Nordica ought to do something about it. I joined up with 'em two months ago but they ain't done nuthin' but sell me an ole uniform an' hold a coupla meetin's."

They lapsed into silence. Sandol, the erstwhile Senegalese, stepped from the cockpit grinning. "Ah, zese Americains," he muttered to himself as he went over the engine, examining everything minutely.

"Where'd yuh come from, buddy?" asked one of the mechanics.

"Den-vair," Sandol replied.

"Whatcha doin', makin' a trip around th' country?" queried another.

"Yes, we air, what you callem, on ze tour inspectione," the aviator continued. They could think of no more to say and soon strolled off.

Around an oval table on the seventh floor of a building on Central Avenue, sat Dr. Junius Crookman, Hank Johnson, Chuck Foster, Ranford the Doctor's secretary and four other men. At the lower end of the table Miss Bennett, Ranford's stenographer, was taking notes. A soft-treading waiter whose Negro nature was only revealed by his mocking obsequiousness, served each with champagne.

"To our continued success!" cried the physician, lifting his glass high.

"To our continued success!" echoed the others.

They drained their glasses, and returned them to the polished surface of the table.

"Dog bite it, Doc!" blurted Johnson. "Us sho is doin' fine. Ain't had a bad break since we stahted, an' heah 'tis th' fust o' September."

"Don't holler too soon," cautioned Foster. "The opposition is growing keener every day. I had to pay seventy-five thousand dollars more for this building than it's worth."

"Well, yuh got it, didn't yuh?" asked Johnson. "Just like Ah allus say: when yuh got money yuh kin git anything in this man's country. Whenever things look tight jes pull out th' ole check book an' eve'ything's all right."

"Optimist!" grunted Foster.

"I ain't no pess'mist," Johnson accused.

"Now gentlemen," Dr. Crookman interrupted, clearing his throat, "let's get down to business. We have met here, as you know, not only for the purpose of celebrating the opening of this, our fiftieth sanitarium, but also to take stock of our situation. I have before me here a detailed report of our business affairs for the entire period of seven months and a half that we've been in operation.

"During that time we have put into service fifty sanitariums from Coast to Coast, or an average of one every four and one-half days, the average capacity of each sanitarium being one hundred and five patients. Each place has a staff of six physicians and twenty-four nurses, a janitor, four orderlies, two electricians, bookkeeper, cashier, stenographer and record clerk, not counting four guards.

"For the past four months we have had an equipment factory in Pittsburgh in full operation and a chemical plant in Philadelphia. In addition to this we have purchased four airplanes and a radio broadcasting station. Our expenditures for real estate, salaries and chemicals have totaled six million, two hundred and fifty-five thousand, eighty-five dollars and ten cents." . . .

"He! He!" chuckled Johnson. "Dat ten cents mus' be fo' one o' them bad ceegars that Fostah smokes."

"Our total income," continued Dr. Crookman, frowning slightly at the interruption, "has been eighteen million, five hundred thousand, three hundred dollars, or three hundred and seventy thousand and six patients at fifty dollars apiece. I think that vindicates my contention at the beginning that the fee should be but fifty dollars—within the reach of the rank and file of Negroes." He laid aside his report and added:

"In the next four months we'll double our output and by the end of the year we should cut the fee to twenty-five dollars," he lightly twirled his waxed mustache between his long sensitive fingers and smiled with satisfaction.

"Yes," said Foster, "the sooner we get this business over with the better. We're going to run into a whole lot more opposition from now on than we have so far encountered."

"Why man!" growled Johnson, "we ain't even stahted on

dese darkies yet. And when we git thu wi' dese heah, we kin work on them in th' West Indies. Believe me, Ah doan *nevah* want dis graft tuh end."

"Now," continued Dr. Crookman, "I want to say that Mr. Foster deserves great praise for the industry and ingenuity he has shown in purchasing our real estate and Mr. Johnson deserves equally great praise for the efficient manner in which he has kept down the opposition of the various city officials. As you know, he has spent nearly a million dollars in such endeavors and almost as much again in molding legislative sentiment in Washington and the various state capitals. That accounts for the fact that every bill introduced in a legislature or municipal council to put us out of business has died in committee. Moreover, through his corps of secret operatives, who are mostly young women, he has placed numbers of officials and legislators in a position where they cannot openly oppose our efforts."

A smile of appreciation went around the circle.

"We'll have a whole lot to do from now on," commented Foster.

"Yeh, Big Boy," replied the ex-gambler, "an' whut it takes tuh do it Ah ain't got nuthin' else but!"

"Certainly," said the physician, "our friend Hank has not been overburdened with scruples."

"Ah doan know whut dat is, Chief," grinned Johnson, "but Ah knows whut a check book'll do. Even these crackers tone down when Ah talks bucks."

"This afternoon," continued Crookman, "we also have with us our three regional directors, Doctors Henry Dogan, Charles Hinckle and Fred Selden, as well as our chief chemist, Wallace Butts. I thought it would be a good idea to bring you all together for this occasion so we could get better acquainted. We'll just have a word from each of them. They're all good Race men, you know, even if they have, like the rest of our staff, taken the treatment."

For the next three-quarters of an hour the three directors and the chief chemist reported on the progress of their work. At intervals the waiter brought in cold drinks, cigars and cigarettes. Overhead whirred the electric fans. Out of the wide open windows could be seen the panorama of bungalows, pavements, palm trees, trundling street cars and scooting automobiles.

"Lawd! Lawd! Lawd!" Johnson exclaimed at the conclusion of the meeting, going to the window and gazing out over the city. "Jes gimme a coupla yeahs o' dis graft an' Ah'll make Henry Foahd look like a tramp."

Meanwhile, Negro society was in turmoil and chaos. The colored folk in straining every nerve to get the Black-No-More treatment, had forgotten all loyalties, affiliations and responsibilities. No longer did they flock to the churches on Sundays or pay dues in their numerous fraternal organizations. They had stopped giving anything to the Anti-Lynching campaign. Santop Licorice, head of the once-flourishing Back-To-Africa Society, was daily raising his stentorian voice in denunciation of the race for deserting his organization.

Negro business was being no less hard hit. Few people were bothering about getting their hair straightened or skin whitened temporarily when for a couple of weeks' pay they could get both jobs done permanently. The immediate result of this change of mind on the part of the Negro public was to almost bankrupt the firms that made the whitening and straightening chemicals. They were largely controlled by canny Hebrews, but at least a half-dozen were owned by Negroes. The rapid decline in this business greatly decreased the revenue of the Negro weekly newspapers who depended upon such advertising for their sustenance. The actual business of hair straightening that had furnished employment to thousands of colored women who would otherwise have had to go back to washing and ironing, declined to such an extent that "To Rent" signs hung in front of nine-tenths of the shops.

The Negro politicians in the various Black Belts, grown fat and sleek "protecting" vice with the aid of Negro votes which they were able to control by virtue of housing segregation, lectured in vain about black solidarity, race pride and political emancipation; but nothing stopped the exodus to the white race. Gloomily the politicians sat in their offices, wondering whether to throw up the sponge and hunt the nearest Black-No-More sanitarium or hold on a little longer in the hope that

the whites might put a stop to the activities of Dr. Crookman
and his associates. The latter, indeed, was their only hope because the bulk of Negroes, saving their dimes and dollars for
chromatic emancipation, had stopped gambling, patronizing
houses of prostitution or staging Saturday-night brawls. Thus
the usual sources of graft vanished. The black politicians appealed to their white masters for succor, of course, but they
found to their dismay that most of the latter had been safely
bribed by the astute Hank Johnson.

Gone was the almost European atmosphere of every Negro
ghetto: the music, laughter, gaiety, jesting and abandon.
Instead, one noted the same excited bustle, wild looks and
strained faces to be seen in a war time soldier camp, around a
new oil district or before a gold rush. The happy-go-lucky
Negro of song and story was gone forever and in his stead was
a nervous, money-grubbing black, stuffing away coin in socks,
impatiently awaiting a sufficient sum to pay Dr. Crookman's fee.

Up from the South they came in increasing droves, besieg-
ing the Black-No-More sanitariums for treatment. There were
none of these havens in the South because of the hostility of
the bulk of white people but there were many all along the
border between the two sections, at such places as Washington,
D. C., Baltimore, Cincinnati, Louisville, Evansville, Cairo, St.
Louis and Denver. The various Southern communities attempted to stem this, the greatest migration of Negroes in the
history of the country, but without avail. By train, boat, wagon,
bicycle, automobile and foot they trekked to the promised
land; a hopeful procession, filtering through the outposts of
police and Knights of Nordica volunteer bands. Where there
was great opposition to the Negroes' going, there would suddenly appear large quantities of free bootleg liquor and crisp
new currency which would make the most vigilant white
opponent of Black-No-More turn his head the other way.
Hank Johnson seemed to be able to cope with almost every
situation.

The national office of the militant Negro organization, the
National Social Equality League, was agog. Telephone bells
were ringing, mulatto clerks were hustling excitedly back and
forth, messenger boys rushed in and out. Located in the Times

Square district of Manhattan, it had for forty years carried on the fight for full social equality for the Negro citizens and the immediate abolition of lynching as a national sport. While this organization had to depend to a large extent upon the charity of white folk for its existence, since the blacks had always been more or less skeptical about the program for liberty and freedom, the efforts of the society were not entirely unprofitable. Vistas of immaculate offices spread in every direction from the elevator and footfalls were muffled in thick imitation-Persian rugs. While the large staff of officials was eager to end all oppression and persecution of the Negro, they were never so happy and excited as when a Negro was barred from a theater or fried to a crisp. Then they would leap for telephones, grab telegraph pads and yell for stenographers; smiling through their simulated indignation at the spectacle of another reason for their continued existence and appeals for funds.

Ever since the first sanitarium of Black-No-More, Incorporated, started turning Negroes into Caucasians, the National Social Equality League's income had been decreasing. No dues had been collected in months and subscriptions to the national mouthpiece, *The Dilemma*, had dwindled to almost nothing. Officials, long since ensconced in palatial apartments, began to grow panic-stricken as pay days got farther apart. They began to envision the time when they would no longer be able for the sake of the Negro race to suffer the hardships of lunching on canvasback duck at the Urban Club surrounded by the white dilettante, endure the perils of first-class Transatlantic passage to stage Save-Dear-Africa Conferences or undergo the excruciating torture of rolling back and forth across the United States in drawing-rooms to hear each other lecture on the Negro problem. On meager salaries of five thousand dollars a year they had fought strenuously and tirelessly to obtain for the Negroes the constitutional rights which only a few thousand rich white folk possessed. And now they saw the work of a lifetime being rapidly destroyed.

Single-handed they felt incapable of organizing an effective opposition to Black-No-More, Incorporated, so they had called a conference of all of the outstanding Negro leaders of the country to assemble at the League's headquarters on December 1, 1933. Getting the Negro leaders together for any purpose except boasting of each other's accomplishments had previously been impossible. As a usual thing they fought each other with a vigor only surpassed by that of their pleas for racial solidarity and unity of action. This situation, however, was unprecedented, so almost all of the representative gentlemen of color to whom invitations had been sent agreed with alacrity to come. To a man they felt that it was time to bury the hatchet before they became too hungry to do any digging.

In a very private inner office of the N. S. E. L. suite, Dr. Shakespeare Agamemnon Beard, founder of the League and a graduate of Harvard, Yale and Copenhagen (whose haughty bearing never failed to impress both Caucasians and Negroes) sat before a glass-topped desk, rubbing now his curly gray head, and now his full spade beard. For a mere six thousand dollars a year, the learned doctor wrote scholarly and biting editorials in *The Dilemma* denouncing the Caucasians whom he secretly admired and lauding the greatness of the Negroes whom he alternately pitied and despised. In limpid prose he told of the sufferings and privations of the downtrodden black workers with whose lives he was totally and thankfully unfamiliar. Like most Negro leaders, he deified the black woman but abstained from employing aught save octoroons. He talked at white banquets about "we of the black race" and admitted in books that he was part-French, part-Russian, part-Indian and part-Negro. He bitterly denounced the Nordics for debauching Negro women while taking care to hire comely yellow stenographers with weak resistance. In a real way, he loved his people. In time of peace he was a Pink Socialist but when the clouds of war gathered he bivouacked at the feet of Mars.

Before the champion of the darker races lay a neatly typed resolution drawn up by him and his staff the day before and addressed to the Attorney General of the United States. The staff had taken this precaution because no member of it believed that the other Negro leaders possessed sufficient education to word the document effectively and grammatically. Dr. Beard re-read the resolution and then placing it in the drawer of the desk, pressed one of a row of buttons. "Tell them to come in," he directed. The mulattress turned and switched out of the room, followed by the appraising and approving eye of the aged scholar. He heaved a regretful sigh as the door closed and his thoughts dwelt on the vigor of his youth.

In three or four minutes the door opened again and several well-dressed blacks, mulattoes and white men entered the large office and took seats around the wall. They greeted each other and the President of the League with usual cordiality but for the first time in their lives they were sincere about it. If anyone could save the day it was Beard. They all admitted that, as did the Doctor himself. They pulled out fat cigars, long slender cigarettes and London briar pipes, lit them and awaited the opening of the conference.

The venerable lover of his race tapped with his knuckle for order, laid aside his six-inch cigarette and rising, said:

"It were quite unseemly for me who lives such a cloistered life and am spared the bane or benefit of many intimate contacts with those of our struggling race who by sheer courage, tenacity and merit have lifted their heads above the mired mass, to deign to take from a more capable individual the unpleasant task of reviewing the combination of unfortunate circumstances that has brought us together, man to man, within the four walls of the office." He shot a foxy glance around the assembly and then went on suavely. "And so, my friends, I beg your august permission to confer upon my able and cultured secretary and confidant, Dr. Napoleon Wellington Jackson, the office of chairman of this temporary body. I need not introduce Dr. Jackson to you. You know of his scholarship, his high sense of duty and his deep love of the suffering black race. You have doubtless had the pleasure of singing some of the many sorrow songs he has written and popularized in the past twenty years, and you must know of his fame as a translator of Latin poets and his authoritative work on the Greek language.

"Before I gratefully yield the floor to Dr. Jackson, however, I want to tell you that our destiny lies in the stars. Ethiopia's fate is in the balance. The Goddess of the Nile weeps bitter tears at the feet of the Great Sphinx. The lowering clouds gather over the Congo and the lightning flashes o'er Togoland. To your tents, O Israel! The hour is at hand."

The president of the N. S. E. L. sat down and the erudite Dr. Jackson, his tall, lanky secretary got up. There was no fear of Dr. Jackson ever winning a beauty contest. He was a sooty black, very broad shouldered, with long, ape-like arms, a diminutive egg-shaped head that sat on his collar like a hen's egg on a demitasse cup and eyes that protruded so far from his head that they seemed about to fall out. He wore pince-nez that were continually slipping from his very flat and oily nose. His chief business in the organization was to write long and indignant letters to public officials and legislators whenever a Negro was mistreated, demanding justice, fair play and other legal guarantees vouchsafed no whites except bloated plutocrats fallen miraculously afoul of the law, and to speak to audiences of sex-starved matrons who yearned to help the Negro stand erect. During his leisure time, which was naturally considerable, he wrote long and learned articles, bristling with references, for the more intellectual magazines, in which he sought to prove conclusively that the plantation shouts of Southern Negro peons were superior to any of Beethoven's symphonies and that the city of Benin was the original site of the Garden of Eden.

"Hhmm! Hu-umn! Now er—ah, gentlemen," began Dr. Jackson, rocking back on his heels, taking off his eye glasses and beginning to polish them with a silk kerchief, "as you know, the Negro race is face to face with a grave crisis. I-ah-presume it is er-ah unnecessary for me to go into any details concerning the-ah activities of Black-No-More, Incorporated. Suffice er-ah umph! ummmmh! to say-ah that it has thrown our society into rather a-ah bally turmoil. Our people are forgetting shamelessly their-ah duty to the-ah organizations that have fought valiantly for them these-ah many years and are now busily engaged chasing a bally-ah will-o-the wisp. Ahem!

"You-ah probably all fully realize that-ah a continuation of the aforementioned activities will prove disastrous to our-ah organizations. You-ah, like us, must feel-uh that something drastic must be done to preserve the integrity of Negro society. Think, gentlemen, what the future will mean to-uh all those who-uh have toiled so hard for Negro society. What-ah, may I ask, will we do when there are no longer any-ah groups to support us? Of course, Dr. Crookman and-ah his associates have a-uh perfect right to-ah engage in any legitimate business, but-ah their present activities cannot-ah be classed under that head, considering the effect on our endeavors. Before we go any further, however, I-ah would like to introduce our research expert Mr. Walter Williams, who will-ah describe the situation in the South."

Mr. Walter Williams, a tall, heavy-set white man with pale blue eyes, wavy auburn hair and a militant, lantern jaw, rose and bowed to the assemblage and proceeded to paint a heartrending picture of the loss of pride and race solidarity among Negroes North and South. There was, he said, not a single local of the N. S. E. L. functioning, dues had dwindled to nothing, he had not been able to hold a meeting anywhere, while many of the stanchest supporters had gone over into the white race.

"Personally," he concluded, "I am very proud to be a Negro and always have been (his great-grandfather, it seemed, had been a mulatto), and I'm willing to sacrifice for the uplift of my race. I cannot understand what has come over our people that they have so quickly forgotten the ancient glories of Ethiopia, Songhay and Dahomey, and their marvelous record of achievement since emancipation." Mr. Williams was known to be a Negro among his friends and acquaintances, but no one else would have suspected it.

Another white man of remote Negro ancestry, Rev. Herbert Gronne of Dunbar University, followed the research expert with a long discourse in which he expressed fear for the future of his institution whose student body had been reduced to sixty-five persons and deplored the catastrophe "that has befallen us black people."

They all listened with respect to Dr. Gronne. He had been in turn a college professor, a social worker and a minister, had received the approval of the white folks and was thus doubly acceptable to the Negroes. Much of his popularity was due to the fact that he very cleverly knew how to make statements that sounded radical to Negroes but sufficiently conservative to satisfy the white trustees of his school. In addition he possessed the asset of looking perpetually earnest and sincere.

Following him came Colonel Mortimer Roberts, principal of the Dusky River Agricultural Institute, Supreme General of the Knights and Daughters of Kingdom Come and president of the Uncle Tom Memorial Association. Colonel Roberts was the acknowledged leader of the conservative Negroes (most of whom had nothing to conserve) who felt at all times that the white folks were in the lead and that Negroes should be careful to guide themselves accordingly.

He was a great mountain of blackness with a head shaped like an upturned bucket, pierced by two pig-like eyes and a cavernous mouth equipped with large tombstone teeth which he almost continually displayed. His speech was a cross between the woofing of a bloodhound and the explosion of an inner tube. It conveyed to most white people an impression of rugged simplicity and sincerity, which was very fortunate since Colonel Roberts maintained his school through their contributions. He spoke as usual about the cordial relations existing between the two races in his native Georgia, the effrontery of Negroes who dared whiten themselves and thus disturb the minds of white people and insinuated alliance with certain militant organizations in the South to stop this whitening business before it went too far. Having spoken his mind and received scant applause, Colonel (some white man had once called him Colonel and the title stuck) puffing and bowing, sat down.

Mr. Claude Spelling, a scared-looking little brown man with big ears, who held the exalted office of president of the Society of Negro Merchants, added his volume of blues to the discussion. The refrain was that Negro business—always anemic—was about to pass out entirely through lack of patronage. Mr. Spelling had for many years been the leading advocate of the strange doctrine that an underpaid Negro worker should go out of his way to patronize a little dingy Negro store instead of going to a cheaper and cleaner chain store, all for the dubious satisfaction of helping Negro merchants grow wealthy.

The next speaker, Dr. Joseph Bonds, a little rat-faced Negro with protruding teeth stained by countless plugs of chewing tobacco and wearing horn-rimmed spectacles, who headed the Negro Data League, almost cried (which would have been terrible to observe) when he told of the difficulty his workers had encountered in their efforts to persuade retired white capitalists, whose guilty consciences persuaded them to indulge in philanthropy, to give their customary donations to the work. The philanthropists seemed to think, said Dr. Bonds, that since the Negroes were busily solving their difficulties, there was no need for social work among them or any collection of data. He almost sobbed aloud when he described how his collections had fallen from $50,000 a month to less than $1000.

His feeling in the matter could easily be appreciated. He was engaged in a most vital and necessary work: i.e., collecting bales of data to prove satisfactorily to all that more money was needed to collect more data. Most of the data were highly informative, revealing the amazing fact that poor people went to jail oftener than rich ones; that most of the people were not getting enough money for their work; that strangely enough there was some connection between poverty, disease and crime. By establishing these facts with mathematical certitude and illustrating them with elaborate graphs, Dr. Bonds garnered many fat checks. For his people, he said, he wanted work, not charity; but for himself he was always glad to get the charity with as little work as possible. For many years he had succeeded in doing so without any ascertainable benefit accruing to the Negro group.

Dr. Bonds' show of emotion almost brought the others to tears and many of them muttered "Yes, Brother" while he was talking. The conferees were getting stirred up but it took the next speaker to really get them excited.

When he rose an expectant hush fell over the assemblage. They all knew and respected the Right Reverend Bishop Ezekiel Whooper of the Ethiopian True Faith Wash Foot Methodist Church for three reasons: viz., his church was rich (though the parishioners were poor), he had a very loud voice and the white people praised him. He was sixty, corpulent and an expert at the art of making cuckolds.

"Our loyal and devoted clergy," he boomed, "are being forced into manual labor and the Negro church is rapidly dying" and then he launched into a violent tirade against Black-No-More and favored any means to put the corporation out of business. In his excitement he blew saliva, waved his long arms, stamped his feet, pummeled the desk, rolled his eyes, knocked down his chair, almost sat on the rug and generally reverted to the antics of Negro bush preachers.

This exhibition proved contagious. Rev. Herbert Gronne, face flushed and shouting amens, marched from one end of the room to the other; Colonel Roberts, looking like an inebriated black-faced comedian, rocked back and forth clapping his hands; the others began to groan and moan. Dr. Napoleon

Wellington Jackson, sensing his opportunity, began to sing a spiritual in his rich soprano voice. The others immediately joined him. The very air seemed charged with emotion.

Bishop Whooper was about to start up again, when Dr. Beard, who had sat cold and disdainful through this outbreak of revivalism, toying with his gold-rimmed fountain pen and gazing at the exhibition through half-closed eyelids, interrupted in sharp metallic tones.

"Let's get down to earth now," he commanded. "We've had enough of this nonsense. We have a resolution here addressed to the Attorney General of the United States demanding that Dr. Crookman and his associates be arrested and their activities stopped at once for the good of both races. All those in favor of this resolution say aye. Contrary? . . . Very well, the ayes have it. . . Miss Hilton please send off this telegram at once!"

They looked at Dr. Beard and each other in amazement. Several started to meekly protest.

"You gentlemen are all twenty-one, aren't you?" sneered Beard. "Well, then be men enough to stand by your decision."

"But Doctor Beard," objected Rev. Gronne, "isn't this a rather unusual procedure?"

"Rev. Gronne," the great man replied, "it's not near as unusual as Black-No-More. I have probably ruffled your dignity but that's nothing to what Dr. Crookman will do."

"I guess you're right, Beard," the college president agreed.

"I know it," snapped the other.

The Honorable Walter Brybe, who had won his exalted position as Attorney General of the United States because of his long and faithful service helping large corporations to circumvent the federal laws, sat at his desk in Washington, D. C. Before him lay the wired resolution from the conference of Negro leaders. He pursed his lips and reached for his private telephone.

"Gorman?" he inquired softly into the receiver. "Is that you?"

"Nossuh," came the reply, "this heah is Mistah Gay's valet."

"Well, call Mister Gay to the telephone at once."

"Yassuh."

"That you, Gorman," asked the chief legal officer of the nation addressing the National Chairman of his party.

"Yeh, what's up?"

"You heard 'bout this resolution from them niggers in New York, aint you? It's been in all of the papers."

"Yes I read it."

"Well, whaddya think we oughtta do about it?"

"Take it easy, Walter. Give 'em the old run around. You know. They ain't got a thin dime; it's this other crowd that's holding the heavy jack. And 'course you know we gotta clean up our deficit. Just lemme work with that Black-No-More crowd. I can talk business with that Johnson fellow."

"All right, Gorman, I think you're right, but you don't want to forget that there's a whole lot of white sentiment against them coons."

"Needn't worry 'bout that," scoffed Gorman. "There's no money behind it much and besides it's in states we can't carry anyhow. Go ahead; stall them New York niggers off. You're a lawyer, you can always find a reason."

"Thanks for the compliment, Gorman," said the Attorney General, hanging up the receiver.

He pressed a button on his desk and a young girl, armed with pencil and pad, came in.

"Take this letter," he ordered: "To Doctor Shakespeare Agamemnon Beard (what a hell of a name!), Chairman of the Committee for the Preservation of Negro Racial Integrity, 1400 Broadway, New York City.

"My dear Dr. Beard:

The Attorney General has received the resolution signed by yourself and others and given it careful consideration.

Regardless of personal views in the matter (I don't give a damn whether they turn white or not, myself) it is not possible for the Department of Justice to interfere with a legitimate business enterprise so long as its methods are within the law. The corporation in question has violated no federal statute and hence there is not the slightest ground for interfering with its activities.

Very truly yours,

WALTER BRYBE.

"Get that off at once. Give out copies to the press. That's all."

Santop Licorice, founder and leader of the Back-to-Africa Society, read the reply of the Attorney General to the Negro leaders with much malicious satisfaction. He laid aside his morning paper, pulled a fat cigar from a box near by, lit it and blew clouds of smoke above his woolly head. He was always delighted when Dr. Beard met with any sort of rebuff or embarrassment. He was doubly pleased in this instance because he had been overlooked in the sending out of invitations to Negro leaders to join the Committee for the Preservation of Negro Racial Integrity. It was outrageous, after all the talking he had done in favor of Negro racial integrity.

Mr. Licorice for some fifteen years had been very profitably advocating the emigration of all the American Negroes to Africa. He had not, of course, gone there himself and had not the slightest intention of going so far from the fleshpots, but he told the other Negroes to go. Naturally the first step in their going was to join his society by paying five dollars a year for membership, ten dollars for a gold, green and purple robe and silver-colored helmet that together cost two dollars and a half, contributing five dollars to the Santop Licorice Defense Fund (there was a perpetual defense fund because Licorice was perpetually in the courts for fraud of some kind), and buying shares at five dollars each in the Royal Black Steamship Company, for obviously one could not get to Africa without a ship and Negroes ought to travel on Negro-owned and operated ships. The ships were Santop's especial pride. True, they had never been to Africa, had never had but one cargo and that, being gin, was half consumed by the unpaid and thirsty crew before the vessel was saved by the Coast Guard, but they had cost more than anything else the Back-To-Africa Society had purchased even though they were worthless except as scrap iron. Mr. Licorice, who was known by his followers as Provisional President of Africa, Admiral of the African Navy, Field Marshal of the African Army and Knight Commander of the Nile, had a genius for being stuck with junk by crafty salesmen. White men only needed to tell him that he was shrewder than white men and he would immediately reach for a check book.

But there was little reaching for check books in his office nowadays. He had been as hard hit as the other Negroes. Why should anybody in the Negro race want to go back to Africa at a cost of five hundred dollars for passage when they could stay in America and get white for fifty dollars? Mr. Licorice saw the point but instead of scuttling back to Demerara from whence he had come to save his race from oppression, he had hung on in the hope that the activities of Black-No-More, Incorporated, would be stopped. In the meantime, he had continued to attempt to save the Negroes by vigorously attacking all of the other Negro organizations and at the same time preaching racial solidarity and coöperation in his weekly newspaper, *"The African Abroad,"* which was printed by white folks and had until a year ago been full of skin-whitening and hair-straightening advertisements.

"How is our treasury?" he yelled back through the dingy suite of offices to his bookkeeper, a pretty mulatto.

"What treasury?" she asked in mock surprise.

"Why, I thought we had seventy-five dollars," he blurted.

"We did, but the Sheriff got most of it yesterday or we wouldn't be in here today."

"Huumn! Well, that's bad. And tomorrow's pay day, isn't it?"

"Why bring that up?" she sneered. "I'd forgotten all about it."

"Haven't we got enough for me to get to Atlanta?" Licorice inquired, anxiously.

"There is if you're gonna hitch-hike."

"Well, of course, I couldn't do that," he smiled deprecatingly.

"I should say not," she retorted surveying his 250-pound, five-feet-six-inches of black blubber.

"Call Western Union," he commanded.

"What with?"

"Over the telephone, of course, Miss Hall," he explained.

"If you can get anything over that telephone you're a better man than I am, Gunga Din."

"Has the service been discontinued, young lady?"

"Try and get a number," she chirped. He gazed ruefully at the telephone.

"Is there anything we can sell?" asked the bewildered Licorice.

"Yeah, if you can get the Sheriff to take off his attachments."

"That's right, I had forgotten."

"You would."

"Please be more respectful, Miss Hall," he snapped. "Somebody might overhear you and tell my wife."

"Which one?" she mocked.

"Shut up," he blurted, touched in a tender spot, "and try to figure out some way for us to get hold of some money."

"You must think I'm Einstein," she said, coming up and perching herself on the edge of his desk.

"Well, if we don't get some operating expenses I won't be able to obtain money to pay your salary," he warned.

"The old songs are the best songs," she wise-cracked.

"Oh, come now, Violet," he remonstrated, pawing her buttock, "let's be serious."

"After all these years!" she declared, switching away.

In desperation, he eased his bulk out of the creaking swivel chair, reached for his hat and overcoat and shuffled out of the office. He walked to the curb to hail a taxicab but reconsidered when he recalled that a worn half-dollar was the extent of his funds. Sighing heavily, he trudged the two blocks to the telegraph office and sent a long day letter to Henry Givens, Imperial Grand Wizard of the Knights of Nordica—collect.

"Well, have you figured it out?" asked Violet when he barged into his office again.

"Yes, I just sent a wire to Givens," he replied.

"But he's a nigger-hater, isn't he?" was her surprised comment.

"You want your salary, don't you?" he inquired archly.

"I have for the past month."

"Well, then, don't ask foolish questions," he snapped.

# Chapter Six

TWO important events took place on Easter Sunday, 1934. The first was a huge mass meeting in the brand new reinforced concrete auditorium of the Knights of Nordica for the double purpose of celebrating the first anniversary of the militant secret society and the winning of the millionth member. The second event was the wedding of Helen Givens and Matthew Fisher, Grand Exalted Giraw of the Knights of Nordica.

Rev. Givens, the Imperial Grand Wizard of the order, had never regretted that he had taken Fisher into the order and made him his right-hand man. The membership had grown by leaps and bounds, the treasury was bursting with money in spite of the Wizard's constant misappropriation of funds, the regalia factory was running night and day and the influence of the order was becoming so great that Rev. Givens was beginning to dream of a berth in the White House or near by.

For over six months the order had been publishing *The Warning*, an eight-page newspaper carrying lurid red headlines and poorly-drawn quarter-page cartoons, and edited by Matthew. The noble Southern working people purchased it eagerly, devouring and believing every word in it. Matthew, in 14-point, one-syllable word editorials painted terrifying pictures of the menace confronting white supremacy and the utter necessity of crushing it. Very cleverly he linked up the Pope, the Yellow Peril, the Alien Invasion and Foreign Entanglements with Black-No-More as devices of the Devil. He wrote with such blunt sincerity that sometimes he almost persuaded himself that it was all true.

As the money flowed in, Matthew's fame as a great organizer spread throughout the Southland, and he suddenly became the most desirable catch in the section. Beautiful women literally threw themselves at his feet, and, as a former Negro and thus well versed in the technique of amour, he availed himself of all offerings that caught his fancy.

At the same time he was a frequent visitor to the Givens home, especially when Mrs. Givens, whom he heartily detested, was away. From the very first Helen had been impressed by

Matthew. She had always longed for the companionship of an educated man, a scientist, a man of literary ability. Matthew to her mind embodied all of these. She only hesitated to accept his first offer of marriage two days after they met because she saw no indication that he had much, if any, money. She softened toward him as the Knights of Nordica treasury grew; and when he was able to boast of a million-dollar bank account, she agreed to marriage and accepted his ardent embraces in the meantime.

And so, before the yelling multitude of nightgowned Knights, they were united in holy wedlock on the stage of the new auditorium. Both, being newlyweds, were happy. Helen had secured the kind of husband she wanted, except that she regretted his association with what she called lowbrows; while Matthew had won the girl of his dreams and was thoroughly satisfied, except for a slight regret that her grotesque mother wasn't dead and some disappointment that his spouse was so much more ignorant than she was beautiful.

As soon as Matthew had helped to get the Knights of Nordica well under way with enough money flowing in to satisfy the avaricious Rev. Givens, he had begun to study ways and means of making some money on the side. He had power, influence and prestige and he intended to make good use of them. So he had obtained audiences individually with several of the leading business men of the Georgia capital.

He always prefaced his proposition by pointing out that the working people were never so contented, profits never so high and the erection of new factories in the city never so intensive; that the continued prosperity of Atlanta and of the entire South depended upon keeping labor free from Bolshevism, Socialism, Communism, Anarchism, trade unionism and other subversive movements. Such un-American philosophies, he insisted had ruined European countries and from their outposts in New York and other Northern cities were sending emissaries to seek a foothold in the South and plant the germ of discontent. When this happened, he warned gloomily, then farewell to high profits and contented labor. He showed copies of books and pamphlets which he had ordered from radical book stores in New York but which he asserted were being distributed to the prospect's employees.

He then explained the difference between the defunct Ku Klux Klan and the Knights of Nordica. While both were interested in public morals, racial integrity and the threatened invasion of America by the Pope, his organization glimpsed its larger duty, the perpetuation of Southern prosperity by the stabilization of industrial relations. The Knights of Nordica, favored by increasing membership, was in a position to keep down all radicalism, he said, and then boldly asserted that Black-No-More was subsidized by the Russian Bolsheviks. Would the gentlemen help the work of the Nordicists along with a small contribution? They would and did. Whenever there was a slump in the flow of cash from this source, Matthew merely had his print shop run off a bale of Communistic tracts which his secret operatives distributed around in the mills and factories. Contributions would immediately increase.

Matthew had started this lucrative side enterprise none too soon. There was much unemployment in the city, wages were being cut and work speeded up. There was dissatisfaction and grumbling among the workers and a small percentage of them was in a mood to give ear to the half-dozen timid organizers of the conservative unions who were being paid to unionize the city but had as yet made no headway. A union might not be so bad after all.

The great mass of white workers, however, was afraid to organize and fight for more pay because of a deepset fear that the Negroes would take their jobs. They had heard of black labor taking the work of white labor under the guns of white militia, and they were afraid to risk it. They had first read of the activities of Black-No-More, Incorporated, with a secret feeling akin to relief but after the orators of the Knights of Nordica and the editorials of *The Warning* began to portray the menace confronting them, they forgot about their economic ills and began to yell for the blood of Dr. Crookman and his associates. Why, they began to argue, one couldn't tell who was who! Herein lay the fundamental cause of all their ills. Times were hard, they reasoned, because there were so many white Negroes in their midst taking their jobs and undermining their American standard of living. None of them had ever attained an American standard of living to be sure, but that fact never occurred to any of them. So they flocked to the meetings of the Knights of Nordica and night after night sat spellbound while Rev. Givens, who had finished the eighth grade in a one-room country school, explained the laws of heredity and spoke eloquently of the growing danger of black babies.

Despite his increasing wealth (the money came in so fast he could scarcely keep track of it), Matthew maintained close contact with the merchants and manufacturers. He sent out private letters periodically to prominent men in the Southern business world in which he told of the marked psychological change that had come over the working classes of the South since the birth of the K. of N. He told how they had been discontented and on the brink of revolution when his organization rushed in and saved the South. Unionism and such destructive nostrums had been forgotten, he averred, when *The Warning* had revealed the latest danger to the white race. Of course, he always added, such work required large sums of money and contributions from conservative, substantial and public-spirited citizens were ever acceptable. At the end of each letter there appeared a suggestive paragraph pointing out the extent to which the prosperity of the New South was due to its "peculiar institutions" that made the worker race conscious instead of class conscious, and that with the passing of these "peculiar institutions" would also pass prosperity. This reasoning proved very effective, financially speaking.

Matthew's great success as an organizer and his increasing popularity was not viewed by Rev. Givens with equanimity. The former evangelist knew that everybody of intelligence in the upper circles of the order realized that the growth and prosperity of the Knights of Nordica was largely due to the industry, efficiency and intelligence of Matthew. He had been told that many people were saying that Fisher ought to be Imperial Grand Wizard instead of Grand Exalted Giraw.

Givens had the ignorant man's fear and suspicion of anybody who was supposedly more learned than he. His position, he felt, was threatened, and he was decidedly uneasy. He neither said nor did anything about it, but he fretted a great deal to his wife, much to her annoyance. He was consequently overjoyed when Matthew asked him for Helen's hand, and gave his consent with alacrity. When the marriage was consummated, he saw his cup filled to overflowing and no clouds on the horizon. The Knights of Nordica was safe in the family.

One morning a week or two after his wedding, Matthew was sitting in his private office, when his secretary announced a caller, one B. Brown. After the usual delay staged for the purpose of impressing all visitors, Matthew ordered him in. A short, plump, well-dressed, soft-spoken man entered and greeted him respectfully. The Grand Exalted Giraw waved to a chair and the stranger sat down. Suddenly, leaning over close to Matthew, he whispered, "Don't recognize me, do you Max?"

The Grand Giraw paled and started. "Who are you?" he whispered hoarsely. How in the devil did this man know him? He peered at him sharply.

The newcomer grinned. "Why it's me, Bunny Brown, you big sap!"

"Well, cut my throat!" Matthew exclaimed in amazement. "Boy, is it really you?" Bunny's black face had miraculously bleached. He seemed now more chubby and cherubic than ever.

"It aint my brother," said Bunny with his familiar beam.

"Bunny, where've you been all this time? Why didn't you come on down here when I wrote you? You must've been in jail."

"Mind reader! That's just where I've been," declared the former bank clerk.

"What for? Gambling?"

"No: Rambling."

"What do you mean: Rambling?" asked the puzzled Matthew.

"Just what I said, Big Boy. Got to rambling around with a married woman. Old story: husband came in unexpectedly and I had to crown him. The fire escape was slippery and I slipped. Couldn't run after I hit the ground and the flatfoot nabbed me. Got a lucky break in court or I wouldn't be here."

"Was it a white woman?" asked the Grand Exalted Giraw.

"She wasn't black," said Bunny.

"It's a good thing you weren't black, too!"

"Our minds always ran in the same channels," Bunny commented.

"Got any jack?" asked Matthew.

"Is it likely?"

"Do you want a job?"

"No, I prefer a position."

"Well, I think I can fix you up here for about five grand to begin with," said Matthew.

"Santa Claus! What do I have to do: assassinate the President?"

"No, kidder; just be my right-hand man. You know, follow me through thick and thin."

"All right, Max; but when things get too thick, I'm gonna thin out."

"For Christ's sake don't call me Max," cautioned Matthew.

"That's your name, aint it?"

"No, simp. Them days has gone forever. It's Matthew Fisher now. You go pulling that Max stuff and I'll have to answer more questions than a traffic officer."

"Just think," mused Bunny. "I been reading about you right along in the papers but until I recognized your picture in last Sunday's paper I didn't know who you were. Just how long have you been in on this graft?"

"Ever since it started."

"Say not so! You must have a wad of cash salted away by this time."

"Well, I'm not appealing for charity," Matthew smiled sardonically.

"How many squaws you got now?"

"Only one, Bunny—regular."

"What's matter, did you get too old?" chided his friend.

"No, I got married."

"Well, that's the same thing. Who's the unfortunate woman?"

"Old man Givens' girl."

"Judas Priest! You got in on the ground floor didn't you?"

"I didn't miss. Bunny, old scout, she's the same girl that turned me down that night in the Honky Tonk," Matthew told him with satisfaction.

"Well, hush my mouth! This sounds like a novel," Bunny chuckled.

"Believe it or not, papa, it's what God loves," Matthew grinned.

"Well, you lucky hound! Getting white didn't hurt you none."

"Now listen, Bunny," said Matthew, dropping to a more serious tone, "from now on you're private secretary to the Grand Exalted Giraw; that's me."

"What's a Giraw?"

"I can't tell you; I don't know myself. Ask Givens sometime. He invented it but if he can explain it I'll give you a grand."

"When do I start to work? Or rather, when do I start drawing money?"

"Right now, Old Timer. Here's a century to get you fixed up. You eat dinner with me tonight and report to me in the morning."

"Fathers above!" said Bunny. "Dixie must be heaven."

"It'll be hell for you if these babies find you out; so keep your nose clean."

"Watch me, Mr. Giraw."

"Now listen, Bunny. You know Santop Licorice, don't you?"

"Who doesn't know that hippo?"

"Well, we've had him on our payroll since December. He's fighting Beard, Whooper, Spelling and that crowd. He was on the bricks and we helped him out. Got his paper to appearing regularly, and all that sort of thing."

"So the old crook sold out the race, did he?" cried the amazed Bunny.

"Hold that race stuff, you're not a shine anymore. Are you surprised that he sold out? You're actually becoming innocent," said Matthew.

"Well, what about the African admiral?" Bunny asked.

"This: In a couple of days I want you to run up to New York and look around and see if his retention on the payroll is justified. I got a hunch that nobody is bothering about his paper or what he says, and if that's true we might as well can him; I can use the jack to better advantage."

"Listen here, Boy, this thing is running me nuts. Here you are fighting this Black-No-More, and so is Beard, Whooper, Gronne, Spelling and the rest of the Negro leaders, yet you have Licorice on the payroll to fight the same people that are fighting your enemy. This thing is more complicated than a flapper's past."

"Simple, Bunny, simple. Reason why you can't understand it is because you don't know anything about high strategy."

"High what?" asked Bunny.

"Never mind, look it up at your leisure. Now you can savvy the fact that the sooner these spades are whitened the sooner this graft will fall through, can't you?"

"Righto," said his friend.

"Well, the longer we can make the process, the longer we continue to drag down the jack. Is that clear?"

"As a Spring day."

"You're getting brighter by the minute, old man," jeered Matthew.

"Coming from you, that's no compliment."

"As I was saying, the longer it takes, the longer we last. It's my business to see that it lasts a long time but neither do I want it to stop because that also would be disastrous."

Bunny nodded: "You're a wise egg!"

"Thanks, that makes it unanimous. Well, I don't want my side to get such an upper hand that it will put the other side out of business, or vice versa. What we want is a status quo."

"Gee, you've got educated since you've been down here with these crackers."

"You flatter them, Bunny; run along now. I'll have my car come by your hotel to bring you to dinner."

"Thanks for the compliment, old man, but I'm staying at the Y.M.C.A. It's cheaper," laughed Bunny.

"But is it safer?" kidded Matthew, as his friend withdrew.

Two days later Bunny Brown left for New York on a secret mission. Not only was he to spy on Santop Licorice and see how effective his work was, but he was also to approach Dr. Shakespeare Agamemnon Beard, Dr. Napoleon Wellington Jackson, Rev. Herbert Gronne, Col. Mortimer Roberts, Prof. Charles Spelling, and the other Negro leaders with a view to getting them to speak to white audiences for the benefit of the Knights of Nordica. Matthew already knew that they were in a precarious economic situation since they now had no means of income, both the black masses and the philanthropic whites having deserted them. Their white friends, mostly Northern plutocrats, felt that the race problem was being satisfactorily solved by Black-No-More, Incorporated, and so did the Negroes. Bunny's job was to convince them that it was better to lecture for the K. of N. and grow fat than to fail to get chances to lecture to Negroes who weren't interested in what they said anyhow. The Grand Exalted Giraw had a personal interest in these Negro leaders. He realized that they were too old or too incompetent to make a living except by preaching and writing about the race problem, and since they had lost their influence with the black masses, they might be a novelty to introduce to the K. of N. audiences. He felt that their racial integrity talks would click with the crackers. They knew more about it too than any of regular speakers, he realized.

As the train bearing Bunny pulled into the station in Charlotte, he bought an evening paper. The headline almost knocked him down:

WEALTHY WHITE GIRL HAS NEGRO BABY

He whistled softly and muttered to himself, "Business picks up from now on." He thought of Matthew's marriage and whistled again.

From that time on there were frequent reports in the daily press of white women giving birth to black babies. In some cases, of course, the white women had recently become white but the blame for the tar-brushed offspring in the public mind always rested on the shoulders of the father, or rather, of the husband. The number of cases continued to increase. All walks of life were represented. For the first time the prevalence of sexual promiscuity was brought home to the thinking people of America. Hospital authorities and physicians had known about it in a general way but it had been unknown to the public.

The entire nation became alarmed. Hundreds of thousands of people, North and South, flocked into the Knights of Nordica. The real white people were panicstricken, especially in Dixie. There was no way, apparently, of telling a real Caucasian from an imitation one. Every stranger was viewed with suspicion, which had a very salutory effect on the standard of sex morality in the United States. For the first time since 1905, chastity became a virtue. The number of petting parties, greatly augmented by the development of aviation, fell off amazingly. One must play safe, the girls argued.

The holidays of traveling salesmen, business men and fraternal delegates were made less pleasant than of yore. The old orgiastic days in the big cities seemed past for all time. It also suddenly began to dawn upon some men that the pretty young thing they had met at the seashore and wanted to rush to the altar might possibly be a whitened Negress; and young women were almost as suspicious. Rapid-fire courtships and gin marriages declined. Matrimony at last began to be approached with caution. Nothing like this situation had been known since the administration of Grover Cleveland.

Black-No-More, Incorporated, was not slow to seize upon this opportunity to drum up more business. With 100 sanitariums going full blast from Coast to Coast, it now announced in full page advertisements in the daily press that it was establishing lying-in hospitals in the principal cities where all prospective mothers could come to have their babies, and that whenever a baby was born black or mulatto, it would immediately be given the 24-hour treatment that permanently turned black infants white. The country breathed easier, particularly the four million Negroes who had become free because white.

In a fortnight Bunny Brown returned. Over a quart of passable rye, the two friends discussed his mission.

"What about Licorice?" asked Matthew.

"Useless. You ought to give him the gate. He's taking your jack but he isn't doing a thing but getting your checks and eating regularly. His followers are scarcer than Jews in the Vatican."

"Well, were you able to talk business with any of the Negro leaders?"

"Couldn't find any of them. Their offices are all closed and they've moved away from the places where they used to live. Broke, I suppose."

"Did you inquire for them around Harlem?"

"What was the use? All of the Negroes around Harlem nowadays are folks that have just come there to get white; the rest of them left the race a long time ago. Why, Boy, darkies are as hard to find on Lenox Avenue now as they used to be in Tudor City."

"What about the Negro newspapers? Are any of them running still?"

"Nope, they're a thing of the past. Shines are too busy get-

ting white to bother reading about lynching, crime and peon-
age," said Bunny.

"Well," said Matthew, "it looks as if old Santop Licorice is
the only one of the old gang left."

"Yeah, and he won't be black long, now that you're cutting
him off the payroll."

"I think he could make more money staying black."

"How do you figure that out?" asked Bunny.

"Well, the dime museums haven't closed down, you know,"
said Matthew.

# Chapter Seven

ONE June morning in 1934, Grand Exalted Giraw Fisher received a report from one of his secret operatives in the town of Paradise, South Carolina, saying:

> "The working people here are talking about going on strike next week unless Blickdoff and Hortzenboff, the owners of the Paradise Mill increase pay and shorten hours. The average wage is around fifteen dollars a week, the work day eleven hours. In the past week the company has speeded up the work so much that the help say they cannot stand the pace.
>
> "The owners are two Germans who came to this country after the war. They employ 1000 hands, own all of the houses in Paradise and operate all of the stores. Most of the hands belong to the Knights of Nordica and they want the organization to help them unionize. Am awaiting instructions."

Matthew turned to Bunny and grinned. "Here's more money," he boasted, shaking the letter in his assistant's face.

"What can you do about it?" that worthy inquired.

"What can I do? Well, Brother, you just watch my smoke. Tell Ruggles to get the plane ready," he ordered. "We'll fly over there at once."

Two hours later Matthew's plane sat down on the broad, close-clipped lawn in front of the Blickdoff-Hortzenboff cotton mill. Bunny and the Grand Giraw entered the building and walked to the office.

"Whom do you wish to see?" asked a clerk.

"Mr. Blickdoff, Mr. Hortzenboff or both; preferably both," Matthew replied.

"And who's calling?"

"The Grand Exalted Giraw of the Ancient and Honorable Order of the Knights of Nordica and his secretary," boomed that gentleman. The awed young lady retired into an inner sanctum.

"That sure is some title," commented Bunny in an undertone.

"Yes, Givens knows his stuff when it comes to that. The longer and sillier a title, the better the yaps like it."

The young lady returned and announced that the two owners would be glad to receive the eminent Atlantan. Bunny and Matthew entered the office marked "Private."

Hands were shaken, greetings exchanged and then Matthew got right down to business. He had received contributions from these two mill owners so to a certain extent they understood one another.

"Gentlemen," he queried, "is it true that your employees are planning to strike next week?"

"So ve haff heardt," puffed the corpulent, under-sized Blickdoff.

"Well, what are you going to do about it?"

"De uszual t'ing, uff coarse," replied Hortzenboff, who resembled a beer barrel on stilts.

"You can't do the usual thing," warned Matthew. "Most of these people are members of the Knights of Nordica. They are looking to us for protection and we mean to give it to them."

"Vy ve t'ought you vas favorable," exclaimed Blickdoff.

"Und villing to be reasonable," added Hortzenboff.

"That's true," Matthew agreed, "but you're squeezing these people too hard."

"But ve can't pay dem any more," protested the squat partner. "Vot ve gonna do?"

"Oh, you fellows can't kid me, I know you're coining the jack; but if you think its worth ten grand to you, I think I can adjust matters," the Grand Giraw stated.

"Ten t'ousand dollars?" the two mill men gasped.

"You've got good ears," Matthew assured them. "And if you don't come across I'll put the whole power of my organization behind your hands. Then it'll cost you a hundred grand to get back to normal."

The Germans looked at each other incredulously.

"Are you t'reatening us, Meester Fisher?" whined Blickdoff.

"You've got a good head at figuring out things, Blickdoff," Matthew retorted, sarcastically.

"Suppose ve refuse?" queried the heavier Teuton.

"Yeah, suppose you do. Can't you imagine what'll happen when I pull these people off the job?"

"Ve'll call oudt de militia," warned Blickdoff.

"Don't make me laugh," Matthew commented. "Half the militiamen are members of my outfit."

The Germans shrugged their shoulders hopelessly while Matthew and Bunny enjoyed their confusion.

"How mutch you say you wandt?" asked Hortzenboff.

"Fifteen grand," replied the Grand Giraw, winking at Bunny.

"Budt you joost said ten t'ousand a minute ago," screamed Blickdoff, gesticulating.

"Well, it's fifteen now," said Matthew, "and it'll be twenty grand if you babies don't hurry up and make up your mind."

Hortzenboff reached hastily for the big check book and commenced writing. In a moment he handed Matthew the check.

"Take this back to Atlanta in the plane," ordered Matthew, handing the check to Bunny, "and deposit it. Safety first." Bunny went out.

"You don't act like you trust us," Blickdoff accused.

"Why should I?" the ex-Negro retorted. "I'll just stick around for a while and keep you two company. You fellows might change your mind and stop payment on that check."

"Ve are honest men, Meester Fisher," cried Hortzenboff.

"Now I'll tell one," sneered the Grand Giraw, seating himself and taking a handful of cigars out of a box on the desk.

The following evening the drab, skinny, hollow-eyed mill folk trudged to the mass meeting called by Matthew in the only building in Paradise not owned by the company—the Knights of Nordica Hall. They poured into the ramshackle building, seated themselves on the wooden benches and waited for the speaking to begin.

They were a sorry lot, under-nourished, bony, vacant-looking, and yet they had seen a dim light. Without suggestion or agitation from the outside world, from which they were almost as completely cut off as if they had been in Siberia, they had talked among themselves and concluded that there was no hope for them except in organization. What they all felt they needed was wise leadership, and they looked to the Knights of

Nordica for it, since they were all members of it and there was
no other agency at hand. They waited now expectantly for the
words of wisdom and encouragement which they expected to
hear fall from the lips of their beloved Matthew Fisher, who
now looked down upon them from the platform with cynical
humor mingled with disgust.

They had not long to wait. A tall, gaunt mountaineer, who
acted as chairman, after beseeching the mill hands to stand together like men and women, introduced the Grand Exalted
Giraw.

Matthew spoke forcefully and to the point. He reminded
them that they were men and women; that they were free,
white and twenty-one; that they were citizens of the United
States; that America was their country as well as Rockefeller's;
that they must stand firm in the defense of their rights as working people; that the worker was worthy of his hire; that nothing
should be dearer to them than the maintenance of white supremacy. He insinuated that even in their midst there probably
were some Negroes who had been turned white by Black-No-
More. Such individuals, he insisted made poor union material
because they always showed their Negro characteristics and
ran away in a crisis. Ending with a fervent plea for liberty, justice and a square deal, he sat down amid tumultuous applause.
Eager to take advantage of their enthusiasm, the chairman began to call for members. Happily the people crowded around
the little table in front of the platform to give their names and
pay dues.

Swanson, the chairman and acknowledged leader of the militant element, was tickled with the results of the meeting. He
slapped his thighs mountaineer fashion, shifted his chew of tobacco from the right cheek to the left, his pale blue eyes twinkling, and "allowed" to Matthew that the union would soon
bring the Paradise Mill owners to terms. The Grand Exalted
Giraw agreed.

Two days later, back in Atlanta, Matthew held a conference
with a half-dozen of his secret operatives in his office. "Go to
Paradise and do your stuff," he commanded, "and do it right."

The next day the six men stepped from the train in the little
South Carolina town, engaged rooms at the local hotel and
got busy. They let it be known that they were officials of the

Knights of Nordica sent from Atlanta by the Grand Exalted
Giraw to see that the mill workers got a square deal. They busied themselves visiting the three-room cottages of the workers,
all of which looked alike, and talking very confidentially.

In a day or so it began to be noised about that Swanson,
leader of the radical element, was really a former Negro from
Columbia. It happened that a couple of years previously he
had lived in that city. Consequently he readily admitted that
he had lived there when asked innocently by one of the strangers in the presence of a group of workers. When Swanson
wasn't looking, the questioner glanced significantly at those in
the group.

That was enough. To the simple-minded workers Swanson's
admission was conclusive evidence that the charge of being a
Negro was true. When he called another strike meeting, no
one came except a few of Fisher's men. The big fellow was almost ready to cry because of the unexplained falling away of
his followers. When one of the secret operatives told him the
trouble he was furious.

"Ah haint no damn nigger a-tall," he shouted. "Ah'm a white
man an' kin prove hit!"

Unfortunately he could not prove to the satisfaction of his
fellow workers that he was not a Negro. They were adamant.
On the streets they passed him without speaking and they
complained to the foremen at the mill that they didn't want to
work with a nigger. Broken and disheartened after a week of
vain effort, Swanson was glad to accept carfare out of the
vicinity from one of Matthew's men who pretended to be
sympathetic.

With the departure of Swanson, the cause of the mill workers was dealt a heavy blow, but the three remaining ringleaders
sought to carry on. The secret operatives of the Grand Exalted
Giraw got busy again. One of the agitators was asked if it was
true that his grandfather was a nigger. He strenuously denied
the charge but being ignorant of the identity of his father he
could not very well be certain about his grandfather. He was
doomed. Within a week the other two were similarly discred-
ited. Rumor was wafted abroad that the whole idea of a strike
was a trick of smart niggers in the North who were in the pay
of the Pope.

The erstwhile class conscious workers became terror-stricken by the specter of black blood. You couldn't, they said, be sure of anybody any more, and it was better to leave things as they were than to take a chance of being led by some nigger. If the colored gentry couldn't sit in the movies and ride in the trains with white folks, it wasn't right for them to be organizing and leading white folks.

The radicals and laborites in New York City had been closely watching developments in Paradise ever since the news of the big mass meeting addressed by Matthew was broadcast by the Knights of Nordica news service. When it seemed that the mill workers were, for some mysterious reason, going to abandon the idea of striking, liberal and radical labor organizers were sent down to the town to see what could be done toward whipping up the spirit of revolt.

The representative of the liberal labor organization arrived first and immediately announced a meeting in the Knights of Nordica Hall, the only obtainable place. Nobody came. The man couldn't understand it. He walked out into the town square, approached a little knot of men and asked what was the trouble.

"Y're from that there Harlem in N'Yawk, haint ye?" asked one of the villagers.

"Why yes, I live in Harlem. What about it?"

"Well, we haint a gonna have no damn nigger leadin' us, an' if ye know whut's healthy fer yuh yo'll git on away f'um here," stated the speaker.

"Where do you get that nigger stuff?" inquired the amazed and insulted organizer. "I'm a white man."

"Yo ain't th' first white nigger whut's bin aroun' these parts," was the reply.

The organizer, puzzled but helpless, stayed around town for a week and then departed. Somebody had told the simple folk that Harlem was the Negro district in New York, after ascertaining that the organizer lived in that district. To them Harlem and Negro became synonymous and the laborite was doomed.

The radical labor organizer, refused permission to use the Knights of Nordica Hall because he was a Jew, was prevented from holding a street meeting when someone started a rumor that he believed in dividing up property, nationalizing women, and was in addition an atheist. He freely admitted the first, laughed at the second and proudly proclaimed the third. That was sufficient to inflame the mill hands, although God had been strangely deaf to their prayers, they owned no property to divide and most of their women were so ugly that they need have had no fears that any outsiders would want to nationalize them. The disciple of Lenin and Trotsky vanished down the road with a crowd of emaciated workers at his heels.

Soon all was quiet and orderly again in Paradise, S. C. On the advice of a conciliator from the United States Labor Department, Blickdoff and Hortzenboff, took immediate steps to make their workers more satisfied with their pay, their jobs and their little home town. They built a swimming pool, a tennis court, shower baths and a playground for their employees but neglected to shorten their work time so these improvements could be enjoyed. They announced that they would give each worker a bonus of a whole day's pay at Christmas time, hereafter, and a week's vacation each year to every employee who had been with them more than ten years. There were no such employees, of course, but the mill hands were overjoyed with their victory.

The local Baptist preacher, who was very thoughtfully paid by the company with the understanding that he would take a practical view of conditions in the community, told his flock their employers were to be commended for adopting a real Christian and American way of settling the difficulties between them and their workers. He suggested it was quite likely that Jesus, placed in the same position, would have done likewise.

"Be thankful for the little things," he mooed. "God works in mysterious ways his wonders to perform. Ye shall know the truth and the truth shall set ye free. The basis of all things is truth. Let us not be led astray by the poison from vipers' tongues. This is America and not Russia. Patrick Henry said 'Give me liberty or give me death' and the true, red-blooded, 100 per cent American citizen says the same thing today. But there are right ways and wrong ways to get liberty. Your employers have gone about it the right way. For what, after all is liberty except the enjoyment of life; and have they not placed within your reach those things that bring happiness and recreation?

"Your employers are interested, just as all true Americans are interested, in the welfare of their fellow citizens, their fellow townsmen. Their hearts beat for you. They are always thinking of you. They are always planning ways to make conditions better for you. They are sincerely doing all in their power. They have very heavy responsibilities.

"So you must be patient. Rome wasn't built in a day. All things turn out well in time. Christ knows what he is doing and he will not permit his children to suffer.

"O, ye of little faith! Let not your hearts store up jealousy, hatred and animosity. Let not your minds be wooed by misunderstanding. Let us try to act and think as God would wish us to, and above all, let us, like those two kindly men yonder, practice Christian tolerance."

Despite this inspiring message, it was apparent to everyone that Paradise would never be the same again. Rumors continued to fill the air. People were always asking each other embarrassing questions about birth and blood. Fights became more frequent. Large numbers of the workers, being of Southern birth, were unable to disprove charges of possessing Negro ancestry, and so were forced to leave the vicinity. The mill hands kept so busy talking about Negro blood that no one thought of discussing wages and hours of labor.

In August, Messrs. Blickdoff and Hortzenboff, being in Atlanta on business, stopped by Matthew's office.

"Well, how's the strike?" asked the Grand Giraw.

"Dot strike!" echoed Blickdoff. "Ach Gott! Dot strike neffer come off. Vat you do, you razscal?"

"That's my secret," replied Matthew, a little proudly. "Every man to his trade, you know."

It had indeed become Matthew's trade and he was quite adept at it. What had happened at Paradise had also happened elsewhere. There were no more rumors of strikes. The working people were far more interested in what they considered, or were told was, the larger issue of race. It did not matter that they had to send their children into the mills to augment the family wage; that they were always sickly and that their death rate was high. What mattered such little things when the very foundation of civilization, white supremacy, was threatened?

# Chapter Eight

For over two years now had Black-No-More, Incorporated, been carrying on its self-appointed task of turning Negroes into Caucasians. The job was almost complete, except for the black folk in prisons, orphan asylums, insane asylums, homes for the aged, houses of correction and similar institutions. Those who had always maintained that it was impossible to get Negroes together for anything but a revival, a funeral or a frolic, now had to admit that they had coöperated well in getting white. The poor had been helped by the well-to-do, brothers had helped sisters, children had assisted parents. There had been revived some of the same spirit of adventure prevalent in the days of the Underground Railroad. As a result, even in Mississippi, Negroes were quite rare. In the North the only Negroes to be seen were mulatto babies whose mothers, charmed by the beautiful color of their offspring, had defied convention and not turned them white. As there had never been more than two million Negroes in the North, the whitening process had been viewed indifferently by the masses because those who controlled the channels of opinion felt that the country was getting rid of a very vexatious problem at absolutely no cost; but not so in the South.

When one-third of the population of the erstwhile Confederacy had consisted of the much-maligned Sons of Ham, the blacks had really been of economic, social and psychological value to the section. Not only had they done the dirty work and laid the foundation of its wealth, but they had served as a convenient red herring for the upper classes when the white proletariat grew restive under exploitation. The presence of the Negro as an under class had also made of Dixie a unique part of the United States. There, despite the trend to industrialization, life was a little different, a little pleasanter, a little softer. There was contrast and variety, which was rare in a nation where standardization had progressed to such an extent that a traveler didn't know what town he was in until someone informed him. The South had always been identified with the

Negro, and vice versa, and its most pleasant memories trea-
sured in song and story, were built around this pariah class.

The deep concern of the Southern Caucasians with chivalry,
the protection of white womanhood, the exaggerated development of race pride and the studied arrogance of even the poorest half-starved white peon, were all due to the presence of the
black man. Booted and starved by their industrial and agricultural feudal lords, the white masses derived their only consola-
tion and happiness from the fact that they were the same color
as their oppressors and consequently better than the mudsill
blacks.

The economic loss to the South by the ethnic migration was
considerable. Hundreds of wooden railroad coaches, long since
condemned as death traps in all other parts of the country, had
to be scrapped by the railroads when there were no longer any
Negroes to jim crow. Thousands of railroad waiting rooms remained unused because, having been set aside for the use of
Negroes, they were generally too dingy and unattractive for
white folk or were no longer necessary. Thousands of miles of
streets located in the former Black Belts, and thus without
sewers or pavement, were having to be improved at the insistent behest of the rapidly increased white population, real and
imitation. Real estate owners who had never dreamed of making
repairs on their tumble-down property when it was occupied
by the docile Negroes, were having to tear down, rebuild and
alter to suit white tenants. Shacks and drygoods boxes that had
once sufficed as schools for Negro children, had now to be
condemned and abandoned as unsuitable for occupation by
white youth. Whereas thousands of school teachers had received
thirty and forty dollars a month because of their Negro ancestry,
the various cities and counties of the Southland were now
forced to pay the standard salaries prevailing elsewhere.

Naturally taxes increased. Chambers of Commerce were
now unable to send out attractive advertising to Northern
business firms offering no or very low taxation as an inducement to them to move South nor were they able to offer as
many cheap building sites. Only through the efforts of the
Grand Exalted Giraw of the Knights of Nordica were they still
able to point to their large reserves of docile, contented,

Anglo-Saxon labor, and who knew how long that condition would last?

Consequently, the upper classes faced the future with some misgivings. As if being deprived of the pleasure of black mistresses were not enough, there was a feeling that there would shortly be widespread revolt against the existing medieval industrial conditions and resultant reduction of profits and dividends. The mill barons viewed with distaste the prospect of having to do away with child labor. Rearing back in their padded swivel chairs, they leaned fat jowls on well-manicured hands and mourned the passing of the halcyon days of yore.

If the South had lost its Negroes, however, it had certainly not lost its vote, and the political oligarchy that ruled the section was losing its old assurance and complacency. The Republicans had made inroads here and there in the 1934 Congressional elections. The situation politically was changing and if drastic steps were not immediately taken, the Republicans might carry the erstwhile Solid South, thus practically destroying the Democratic Party. Another Presidential election was less than two years off. There would have to be fast work to ward off disaster. Far-sighted people, North and South, even foresaw the laboring people soon forsaking both of the old parties and going Socialist. Politicians and business men shuddered at the thought of such a tragedy and saw horrible visions of old-age pensions, eight-hour laws, unemployment insurance, workingmen's compensation, minimum-wage legislation, abolition of child labor, dissemination of birth-control information, monthly vacations for female workers, two-month vacations for prospective mothers, both with pay, and the probable killing of individual initiative and incentive by taking the ownership of national capital out of the hands of two million people and putting it into the hands of one hundred and twenty million.

Which explains why Senator Rufus Kretin of Georgia, one of the old Democratic war horses, an incomparable Negro-baiter, a faithful servitor of the dominant economic interests of his state and the lusty father of several black famillies since whitened, walked into the office of Imperial Grand Wizard Givens one day in March, 1935.

"Boys," he began, as closeted with Rev. Givens, Matthew and Bunny in the new modernistic Knights of Nordica palace, they quaffed cool and illegal beverages, "we gotta do sumpin and do it quick. These heah damn Yankees ah makin' inroads on ouah preserves, suh. Th' Republican vote is a-growin'. No tellin' what's li'ble tuh happen in this heah nex' 'lection."

"What can we do, Senator?" asked the Imperial Grand Wizard. "How can we serve the cause?"

"That's just it. That's just it, suh; jus' what Ah came heah fo'," replied the Senator. "Naow sum o' us was thinkin' that maybe yo'all might be able to he'p us keep these damn hicks in line. Yo'all are intelligent gent'men; you know what Ah'm get-tin' at?"

"Well, that's a pretty big order, Colonel," said Givens.

"Yes," Matthew added. "It'll be a hard proposition. Conditions are no longer what they used to be."

"An'," said Givens, "we can't do much with that nigger business, like we used to do when th' old Klan was runnin'."

"What about one o' them theah Red scares," asked the Senator, hopefully.

"Humph!" the clergyman snorted. "Better leave that there Red business alone. Times ain't like they was, you know. Anyhow, them damn Reds'll be down here soon enough 'thout us encouragin' 'em none."

"Guess that's right, Gen'ral," mused the statesman. Then brightening: "Lookaheah, Givens. This fellah Fisher's gotta good head. Why not let him work out sumpin?"

"Yeah, he sure has," agreed the Wizard, glad to escape any work except minding the treasury of his order. "If he can't do it, ain't nobody can. Him and Bunny here is as shrewd as some o' them old time darkies. He! He! He!" He beamed patronizingly upon his brilliant son-in-law and his plump secretary.

"Well, theah's money in it. We got plenty o' cash; what we want now is votes," the Senator explained. "C'ose yuh caint preach that white supremacy stuff ve'y effectively when they haint no niggahs."

"Leave it to me. I'll work out something," said Matthew. Here was a chance to get more power, more money. Busy as he was, it would not do to let the opportunity slip by.

"Yuh caint lose no time," warned the Senator.

"We won't," crowed Givens.

A few minutes later they took a final drink together, shook

hands and the Senator, bobbing his white head to the young ladies in the outer office, departed.

Matthew and Bunny retired to the private office of the Grand Exalted Giraw.

"What you thinkin' about pullin'?" asked Bunny.

"Plenty. We'll try the old sure fire Negro problem stuff."

"But that's ancient history, Brother," protested Bunny. "These ducks won't fall for that any more."

"Bunny, I've learned something on this job, and that is that hatred and prejudice always go over big. These people have been raised on the Negro problem, they're used to it, they're trained to react to it. Why should I rack my brain to hunt up something else when I can use a dodge that's always delivered the goods?"

"It may go over at that."

"I know it will. Just leave it to me," said Matthew confidently. "That's not worrying me at all. What's got my goat is my wife being in the family way." Matthew stopped bantering a moment, a sincere look of pain erasing his usual ironic expression.

"Congratulations!" burbled Bunny.

"Don't rub it in," Matthew replied. "You know how the kid will look."

"That's right," agreed his pal. "You know, sometimes I forget who we are."

"Well, I don't. I know I'm a darky and I'm always on the alert."

"What do you intend to do?"

"I don't know, Big Boy, I don't know. I would ordinarily send her to one of those Lying-in Hospitals but she'd be suspicious. Yet, if the kid is born it'll sure be black."

"It won't be white," Bunny agreed. "Why not tell her the whole thing and since she's so crazy about you, I don't think she'd hesitate to go."

"Man, you must be losing your mind, or else you've lost it!" Matthew exploded. "She's a worse nigger-hater than her father. She'd holler for a divorce before you could say Jack Robinson."

"You've got too much money for that."

"You're assuming that she has plenty of intelligence."

"Hasn't she?"

"Let's not discuss a painful subject," pleaded Matthew. "Suggest a remedy."

"She don't have to know that she's going to one of Crookman's places, does she?"

"No, but I can't get her to leave home to have the baby."

"Why?"

"Oh, a lot of damn sentiment about having her baby in the old home, and her damned old mother supports her. So what can I do?"

"Then, the dear old homestead is the only thing that's holding up the play?"

"You're a smart boy, Bunny."

"Don't stress the obvious. Seriously, though, I think everything can be fixed okeh."

"How?" cried Matthew, eagerly.

"Is it worth five grand?" countered Bunny.

"Money's no object, you know, but explain your proposition."

"I will not. You get me fifty century notes and I'll explain later."

"It's a deal, old friend."

Bunny Brown was a man of action. That evening he entered the popular Niggerhead Café, rendezvous of the questionable classes, and sat down at a table. The place was crowded with drinkers downing their "white mule" and contorting to the strains issuing from a radio loud speaker. A current popular dance piece, "The Black Man Blues," was filling the room. The songwriters had been making a fortune recently writing sentimental songs about the passing of the Negro. The plaintive voice of a blues singer rushed out of the loudspeaker:

> "I wonder where my big, black man has gone;
> Oh, I wonder where my big, black man has gone.
> Has he done got faded an' left me all alone?"

When the music ceased and the dancers returned to their tables, Bunny began to look around. In a far corner he saw a waiter whose face seemed familiar. He waited until the fellow came close when he hailed him. As the waiter bent over to get his order, he studied him closely. He had seen this fellow somewhere before. Who could he be? Suddenly with a start he remembered. It was Dr. Joseph Bonds, former head of the Negro Data League in New York. What had brought him here and to this condition? The last time he had seen Bonds, the fellow was a power in the Negro world, with a country place in Westchester County and a swell apartment in town. It saddened Bunny to think that catastrophe had overtaken such a man. Even getting white, it seemed, hadn't helped him much. He recalled that Bonds in his heyday had collected from the white philanthropists with the slogan: "Work, Not Charity," and he smiled as he thought that Bonds would be mighty glad now to get a little charity and not so much work.

"Would a century note look good to you right now?" he asked the former Negro leader when he returned with his drink.

"Just show it to me, Mister," said the waiter, licking his lips. "What you want me to do?"

"What will you do for a hundred berries?" pursued Bunny.

"I'd hate to tell you," replied Bonds, grinning and revealing his familiar tobacco-stained teeth.

"Have you got a friend you can trust?"

"Sure, a fellow named Licorice that washes pots in back."

"You don't mean Santop Licorice, do you?"

"Ssh! They don't know who he is here. He's white now, you know."

"Do they know who you are?"

"What do you mean?" gasped the surprised waiter.

"Oh, I won't say anything but I know you're Bonds of New York."

"Who told you?"

"Oh, a little fairy."

"How could that be? I never associate with them."

"It wasn't that kind of a fairy," Bunny reassured him, laughing. "Well, you get Licorice and come to my hotel when this place closes up."

"Where is that?" asked Bonds. Bunny wrote his name and room number down on a piece of paper and handed it to him.

Three hours later Bunny was awakened by a knocking at his door. He admitted Bonds and Licorice, the latter smelling strongly of steam and food.

"Here," said Bunny, holding up a hundred dollar bill, "is a century note. If you boys can lay aside your scruples for a few hours you can have five of them apiece."

"Well," said Bonds, "neither Santop nor I have been over-burdened with them."

"That's what I thought," Bunny murmured. He proceeded to outline the work he wanted them to do.

"But that would be a criminal offense," objected Licorice.

"You too, Brutus?" sneered Bonds.

"Well, we can't afford to take chances unless we're pro-tected," the former President of Africa argued rather weakly. He was money-hungry and was longing for a stake to get back to Demerara where, since there was a large Negro population, a white man, by virtue of his complexion, amounted to some-thing. Yet, he had had enough experience behind the bars to make him wary.

"We run this town and this state, too," Bunny assured him. "We could get a couple of our men to pull this stunt but it wouldn't be good policy."

"How about a thousand bucks apiece?" asked Bonds, his eyes glittering as he viewed the crisp banknotes in Bunny's hand.

"Here," said Bunny. "Take this century note between you, get your material and pull the job. When you've finished I'll give you nineteen more like it between you."

The two cronies looked at each other and nodded.

"It's a go," said Bonds.

They departed and Bunny went back to sleep.

The next night about eleven-thirty the bells began to toll and the mournful sirens of the fire engines awakened the entire neighborhood in the vicinity of Rev. Givens's home. That stately edifice, built by Ku Klux Klan dollars was in flames. Firemen played a score of streams onto the blaze but the house appeared to be doomed.

On a lawn across the street, in the midst of a consoling crowd, stood Rev. and Mrs. Givens, Helen and Matthew. The old couple were taking the catastrophe fatalistically, Matthew was puzzled and suspicious, but Helen was in hysterics. She presented a bedraggled and woebegone appearance with a blanket around her night dress. She wept afresh every time she looked across at the blazing building where she had spent her happy childhood.

"Matthew," she sobbed, "will you build me another one just like it?"

"Why certainly, Honey," he agreed, "but it will take quite a while."

"Oh, I know; I know, but I want it."

"Well, you'll get it, darling," he soothed, "but I think it would be a good idea for you to go away for a while to rest your nerves. We've got to think of the little one that's coming, you know."

"I don't wanna go nowhere," she screamed.

"But you've got to go somewhere," he reasoned. "Don't you think so, Mother?" Old Mrs. Givens agreed it would be a good idea but suggested that she go along. To this Rev. Givens would not listen at first but he finally yielded.

"Guess it's a good idea after all," he remarked. "Women folks is always in th' way when buildin's goin' on."

Matthew was tickled at the turn of affairs. On the way down to the hotel, he sat beside Helen, alternately comforting her and wondering as to the origin of the fire.

Next morning, bright and early, Bunny, grinning broadly walked into the office, threw his hat on a hook and sat down before his desk after the customary salutation.

"Bunny," called Matthew, looking at him hard. "Get me told!"

"What do you mean?" asked Bunny innocently.

"Just as I thought," chuckled Matthew. "You're a nervy guy."

"Why, I don't get you," said Bunny, continuing the pose.

"Come clean, Big Boy. How much did that fire cost?"

"You gave me five grand, didn't you?"

"Just like a nigger: a person can never get a direct answer from you."

"Are you satisfied?"

"I'm not crying my eyes out."

"Is Helen going North for her confinement?"

"Nothing different."

"Well, then, why do you want to know the why and wherefore of that blaze?"

"Just curiosity, Nero, old chap," grinned Matthew.

"Remember," warned Bunny, mischievously, "curiosity killed the cat."

The ringing of the telephone bell interrupted their conversation.

"What's that?" yelled Matthew into the mouthpiece. "The hell you say! All right, I'll be right up." He hung up the receiver, jumped up excitedly and grabbed his hat.

"What's the matter?" shouted Bunny. "Somebody dead?"

"No," answered the agitated Matthew, "Helen's had a miscarriage," and he dashed out of the room.

"Somebody dead right on," murmured Bunny, half aloud.

Joseph Bonds and Santop Licorice, clean shaven and immaculate, followed the Irish red cap into their drawing room on the New York Express.

"It sure feels good to get out of the barrel once more," sighed Bonds, dropping down on the soft cushion and pulling out a huge cigar.

"Ain't it the truth?" agreed the former Admiral of the Royal African Navy.

# Chapter Nine

"BUNNY, I've got it all worked out," announced Matthew, several mornings later, as he breezed into the office.

"Got what worked out?"

"The political proposition."

"Spill it."

"Well, here it is: First, we get Givens on the radio; national hookup, you know, once a week for about two months."

"What'll he talk about? Are you going to write it for him?"

"Oh, he knows how to charm the yokels. He'll appeal to the American people to call upon the Republican administration to close up the sanitariums of Dr. Crookman and deport everybody connected with Black-No-More."

"You can't deport citizens, silly," Bunny remonstrated.

"That don't stop you from advocating it. This is politics, Big Boy."

"Well, what else is on the program?"

"Next: We start a campaign of denunciation against the Republicans in *The Warning*, connecting them with the Pope, Black-No-More and anything else we can think of."

"But they were practically anti-Catholic in 1928, weren't they?"

"Seven years ago, Bunny, seven years ago. How often must I tell you that the people never remember anything? Next we pull the old Write-to-your-Congressman- Write-to-your-Senator stuff. We carry the form letter in *The Warning*, the readers do the rest."

"You can't win a campaign on that stuff, alone," said Bunny disdainfully. "Bring me something better than that, Brother."

"Well, the other step is a surprise, old chap. I'm going to keep it under my hat until later on. But when I spring it, old timer, it'll knock everybody for a row of toadstools." Matthew smiled mysteriously and smoothed back his pale blond hair.

"When do we start this radio racket?" yawned Bunny.

"Wait'll I talk it over with the Chief," said Matthew, rising, "and see how he's dated up."

*

The following Thursday evening at 8:15 p.m. millions of people sat before their loud speakers, expectantly awaiting the heralded address to the nation by the Imperial Grand Wizard of the Knights of Nordica. The program started promptly:

"Good evening, ladies and gentlemen of the radio audience. This is Station W H A T, Atlanta, Ga., Mortimer K. Shanker announcing. This evening we are offering a program of tremendous interest to every American citizen. The countrywide hookup over the chain of the Moronia Broadcasting Company is enabling one hundred million citizens to hear one of the most significant messages ever delivered to the American public.

"Before introducing the distinguished speaker of the evening, however, I have a little treat in store for you. Mr. Jack Albert, the well-known Broadway singer and comedian, has kindly consented to render his favorite among the popular songs of the day, 'Vanishing Mammy.' Mr. Albert will be accompanied by that incomparable aggregation of musical talent, Sammy Snort's Bogalusa Babies. . . . Come on, Al, say a word or two to the ladies and gentlemen of the radio audience before you begin."

"Oh, hello folks. Awfully glad to see so many of you out there tonight. Well, that is to say, I suppose there are many of you out there. You know I like to flatter myself, besides I haven't my glasses so I can't see very well. However, that's not the pint, as the bootleggers say. I'm terribly pleased to have the opportunity of starting off a program like this with one of the songs I have come to love best. You know, I think a whole lot of this song. I like it because it has feeling and sentiment. It means something. It carries you back to the good old days that are dead and gone forever. It was written by Johnny Gulp with music by the eminent Japanese-American composer, Forkrise Sake. And, as Mr. Shanker told you, I am being accompanied by Sammy Snort's Bogalusa Babies through the courtesy of the Artillery Café, Chicago, Illinois. All right, Sammy, smack it!"

In two seconds the blare of the jazz orchestra smote the ears of the unseen audience with the weird medley and clash of sound that had passed for music since the days of the Panama-Pacific Exposition. Then the sound died to a whisper

and the plaintive voice of America's premier black-faced trou-
badour came over the air:

> *Vanishing Mammy, Mammy! Mammy! of Mi—ne,*
> *You've been away, dear, such an awfully long time*
> *You went away, Sweet Mammy! Mammy! one summer night*
> *I can't help thinkin', Mammy, that you went white.*
> *Of course I can't blame you, Mammy! Mammy! dear*
> *Because you had so many troubles, Mammy, to bear.*
> *But the old homestead hasn't been the same*
> *Since I last heard you, Mammy, call my name.*
> *And so I wait, loving Mammy, it seems in vain,*
> *For you to come waddling back home again*
> *Vanishing Mammy! Mammy! Mammy!*
> *I'm waiting for you to come back home again.*

"Now, radio audience, this is Mr. Mortimer Shanker speaking again. I know you all loved Mr. Albert's soulful rendition
of 'Vanishing Mammy.' We're going to try to get him back
again in the very near future.

"It now gives me great pleasure to introduce to you a man
who hardly needs any introduction. A man who is known
throughout the civilized world. A man of great scholarship,
executive ability and organizing genius. A man who has, practically unassisted, brought five million Americans under the
banner of one of the greatest societies in this country. It affords
me great pleasure, ladies and gentlemen of the radio audience,
to introduce Rev. Henry Givens, Imperial Grand Wizard of
the Knights of Nordica, who will address you on the very
timely topic of 'The Menace of Negro Blood.'"

Rev. Givens, fortified with a slug of corn, advanced nervously
to the microphone, fingering his prepared address. He cleared
his throat and talked for upwards of an hour during which
time he successfully avoided saying anything that was true, the
result being that thousands of telegrams and long distance
telephone calls of congratulation came in to the studio. In his
long address he discussed the foundations of the Republic, anthropology, psychology, miscegenation, coöperation with Christ,
getting right with God, curbing Bolshevism, the bane of birth
control, the menace of the Modernists, science versus religion,
and many other subjects of which he was totally ignorant. The

greater part of his time was taken up in a denunciation of Black-No-More, Incorporated, and calling upon the Republican administration of President Harold Goosie to deport the vicious Negroes at the head of it or imprison them in the federal penitentiary. When he had concluded "In the name of our Saviour and Redeemer, Jesus Christ, Amen," he retired hastily to the washroom to finish his half-pint of corn.

The announcer took Rev. Givens's place at the microphone: "Now friends, this is Mortimer K. Shanker again, announcing from Station W H A T, Atlanta, Ga., with a nationwide hookup over the chain of the Moronia Broadcasting Company. You have just heard a scholarly and inspiring address by Rev. Henry Givens, Imperial Grand Wizard of the Knights of Nordica on 'The Menace of Negro Blood.' Rev. Givens will deliver another address at this station a week from tonight. . . . Now, to end our program for the evening, friends, we are going to have a popular song by the well-known Goyter Sisters, lately of the State Street Follies, entitled 'Why Did the Old Salt Shaker'. . . ."

The agitation of the Knights of Nordica soon brought action from the administration at Washington. About ten days after Rev. Givens had ceased his talks over the radio, President Harold Goosie announced to the assembled newspaper men that he was giving a great deal of study to the questions raised by the Imperial Grand Wizard concerning Black-No-More, Incorporated; that several truckloads of letters condemning the corporation had been received at the White House and were now being answered by a special corps of clerks; that several Senators had talked over the matter with him, and that the country could expect him to take some action within the next fortnight.

At the end of a fortnight, the President announced that he had decided to appoint a commission of leading citizens to study the whole question thoroughly and to make recommendations. He asked Congress for an appropriation of $100,000 to cover the expenses of the commission.

The House of Representatives approved a resolution to that effect a week later. The Senate, which was then engaged in a spirited debate on the World Court and the League of Nations, postponed consideration of the resolution for three weeks. When it came to vote before that august body, it was passed, after long argument, with amendments and returned to the House.

Six weeks after President Goosie had made his request of Congress, the resolution was passed in its final form. He then announced that inside of a week he would name the members of the commission.

The President kept his word. He named the commission, consisting of seven members, five Republicans and two Democrats. They were mostly politicians temporarily out of a job.

In a private car the commission toured the entire country, visiting all of the Black-No-More sanitariums, the Crookman Lying-in Hospitals and the former Black Belts. They took hundreds of depositions, examined hundreds of witnesses and drank large quantities of liquor.

Two months later they issued a preliminary report in which they pointed out that the Black-No-More sanitariums and Lying-in Hospitals were being operated within the law; that only one million Negroes remained in the country; that it was illegal in most of the states for pure whites and persons of Negro ancestry to intermarry but that it was difficult to detect fraud because of collusion. As a remedy the Commission recommended stricter observance of the law, minor changes in the marriage laws, the organization of special matrimonial courts with trained genealogists attached to each, better equipped judges, more competent district attorneys, the strengthening of the Mann Act, the abolition of the road house, the closer supervision of dance halls, a stricter censorship on books and moving pictures and government control of cabarets. The commission promised to publish the complete report of its activities in about six weeks.

Two months later, when practically everyone had forgotten that there had ever been such an investigation, the complete report of the commission, comprising 1789 pages in fine print came off the press. Copies were sent broadcast to prominent citizens and organizations. Exactly nine people in the United States read it: the warden of a county jail, the proofreader at the Government Printing Office, the janitor of the City Hall in Ashtabula, Ohio, the city editor of the Helena (Ark.) *Bugle*, a stenographer in the Department of Health of Spokane, Wash., a dishwasher in a Bowery restaurant, a flunky in the office of the Research Director of Black-No-More, Incorporated, a life termer in Clinton Prison at Dannemora, N. Y., and a gag writer on the staff of a humorous weekly in Chicago.

Matthew received fulsome praise from the members of his organization and the higher-ups in the Southern Democracy. He had, they said, forced the government to take action, and they began to talk of him for public office.

The Grand Exalted Giraw was jubilant. Everything, he told Bunny, had gone as he had planned. Now he was ready to turn the next trick.

"What's that?" asked his assistant, looking up from the morning comic section.

"Ever hear of the Anglo-Saxon Association of America?" Matthew queried.

"No, what's their graft?"

"It isn't a graft, you crook. The Anglo-Saxon Association of America is an organization located in Virginia. The headquarters are in Richmond. It's a group of rich highbrows who can trace their ancestry back almost two hundred years. You see they believe in white supremacy the same as our outfit but they claim that the Anglo-Saxons are the cream of the white race and should maintain the leadership in American social, economic and political life."

"You sound like a college professor," sneered Bunny.

"Don't insult me, you tripe. Listen now: This crowd thinks they're too highbrow to come in with the Knights of Nordica. They say our bunch are morons."

"That about makes it unanimous," commented Bunny, biting off the end of a cigar.

"Well, what I'm trying to do now is to bring these two organizations together. We've got numbers but not enough money to win an election; they have the jack. If I can get them to see the light we'll win the next Presidential election hands down."

"What'll I be: Secretary of the Treasury?" laughed Bunny.

"Over my dead body!" Matthew replied, reaching for his flask. "But seriously, Old Top, if I can succeed in putting this deal over we'll have the White House in a bag. No fooling!"

"When do we get busy?"

"Next week this Anglo-Saxon Association has its annual meeting in Richmond. You and I'll go up there and give them a spiel. We may take Givens along to add weight."

"You don't mean intellectual weight, do you?"

"Will you never stop kidding?"

Mr. Arthur Snobbcraft, President of the Anglo-Saxon Association, an F.F.V. and a man suspiciously swarthy for an Anglo-Saxon, had devoted his entire life to fighting for two things: white racial integrity and Anglo-Saxon supremacy. It had been very largely a losing fight. The farther he got from his goal, the more desperate he became. He had been the genius that thought up the numerous racial integrity laws adopted in Virginia and many of the other Southern states. He was strong for sterilization of the unfit: meaning Negroes, aliens, Jews and other riff raff, and he had an abiding hatred of democracy.

Snobbcraft's pet scheme now was to get a genealogical law passed disfranchising all people of Negro or unknown ancestry. He argued that good citizens could not be made out of such material. His organization had money but it needed popularity—numbers.

His joy then knew no bounds when he received Matthew's communication. While he had no love for the Knights of Nordica which, he held, contained just the sort of people he wanted to legislate into impotency, social, economic and physical, he believed he could use them to gain his point. He wired Matthew at once, saying the Association would be delighted to have him address them, as well as the Imperial Grand Wizard.

The Grand Exalted Giraw had long known of Snobbcraft's obsession, the genealogical law. He also knew that there was no chance of ever getting such a law adopted but in order to even try to pass such a law it would be necessary to win the whole country in a national election. Together, his organization and Snobbcraft's could turn the trick; singly neither one could do it.

In an old pre-Civil War mansion on a broad, tree-shaded boulevard, the directors of the Anglo-Saxon Association gathered in their annual meeting. They listened first to Rev. Givens and next to Matthew. The matter was referred to a committee which in an hour or two reported favorably. Most of these men had dreamed from youth of holding high political office at the national capital as had so many eminent Virginians but none of them was Republican, of course, and the Democrats never won anything nationally. By swallowing their pride for a season and joining with the riff raff of the Knights of Nordica, they saw an opportunity, for the first time in years to get into power; and they took it. They would furnish plenty of money, they said, if the other group would furnish the numbers.

Givens and Matthew returned to Atlanta in high spirits.

"I tell you, Brother Fisher," croaked Givens, "our star is ascending. I can see no way for us to fail, with God's help. We'll surely defeat our enemy. Victory is in the air."

"It sure looks that way," the Grand Giraw agreed. With their money and ours, we can certainly get together a larger campaign fund than the Republicans."

Back in Richmond Mr. Snobbcraft and his friends were in conference with the statistician of a great New York insurance company. This man, Dr. Samuel Buggerie, was highly respected among members of his profession and well known by the reading public. He was the author of several books and wrote frequently for the heavier periodicals. His well-known work, *The Fluctuation of the Sizes of Left Feet among the Assyrians during the Ninth Century before Christ* had been favorably commented upon by several reviewers, one of whom had actually read it. An even more learned work of his was entitled *Putting Wasted Energy to Work*, in which he called attention, by elaborate charts and graphs, to the possibilities of harnessing the power generated by the leaves of trees rubbing together on windy days. In several brilliant monographs he had proved that rich people have smaller families than the poor; that imprisonment does not stop crime; that laborers usually migrate in the wake of high wages. His most recent article in a very intellectual magazine read largely by those who loafed for a living, had proved statistically that unemployment and poverty are principally a state of mind. This contribution was enthusiastically hailed by scholars and especially by business men as an outstanding contribution to contemporary thought.

Dr. Buggerie was a ponderous, nervous, entirely bald, specimen of humanity, with thick moist hands, a receding double chin and very prominent eyes that were constantly shifting about and bearing an expression of seemingly perpetual wonderment behind their big horn-rimmed spectacles. He seemed about to burst out of his clothes and his pockets were always bulging with papers and notes.

Dr. Buggerie, like Mr. Snobbcraft, was a professional Anglo-Saxon as well as a descendant of one of the First Families of Virginia. He held that the only way to tell the pure whites from the imitation whites, was to study their family trees. He claimed that such a nationwide investigation would disclose the various non-Nordic strains in the population. Laws, said he, should then be passed forbidding these strains from mixing or marrying with the pure strains that had produced such fine specimens of mankind as Mr. Snobbcraft and himself.

In high falsetto voice he eagerly related to the directors of the Anglo-Saxon Association the results of some of his preliminary researches. These tended to show, he claimed, that there must be as many as twenty million people in the United States who possessed some slight non-Nordic strain and were thus unfit for both citizenship and procreation. If the organization would put up the money for the research on a national scale, he declared that he could produce statistics before election that would be so shocking that the Republicans would lose the country unless they adopted the Democratic plank on genealogical examinations. After a long and eloquent talk by Mr. Snobbcraft in support of Dr. Buggerie's proposition, the directors voted to appropriate the money, on condition that the work be kept as secret as possible. The statistician agreed although it hurt him to the heart to forego any publicity. The very next morning he began quietly to assemble his staff.

# Chapter Ten

$H$ ANK JOHNSON, Chuck Foster, Dr. Crookman and Gorman Gay, National Chairman of the Republican National Committee, sat in the physician's hotel suite conversing in low tones.

"We're having a tough time getting ready for the Fall campaign," said Gay. "Unfortunately our friends are not contributing with their accustomed liberality."

"Can't complain about us, can you?" asked Foster.

"No, no," the politician denied quickly. "You have been most liberal in the past two years, but then we have done many favors for you, too."

"Yuh sho right, Gay," Hank remarked. "Dem crackahs mighta put us outa business efen it hadn' bin fo' th' admin'strations suppo't."

"I'm quite sure we deeply appreciate the many favors we've received from the present administration," added Dr. Crookman.

"We won't need it much longer, though," said Chuck Foster.

"How's that?" asked Gay, opening his half-closed eyes.

"Well, we've done about all the business we can do in this country. Practically all of the Negroes are white except a couple of thousand diehards and those in institutions," Chuck informed him.

"Dat's right," said Hank. "An' it sho makes dis heah country lonesome. Ah ain't seen a brown-skin ooman in so long Ah doan know whut Ah'd do if Ah seen one."

"That's right, Gay," added Dr. Crookman. "We've about cleaned up the Negro problem in this country. Next week we're closing all except five of our sanitariums."

"Well, what about your Lying-In hospitals?" asked Gay.

"Of course we'll have to continue operating them," Crookman replied. "The women would be in an awful fix if we didn't."

"Now look here," proposed Gay, drawing closer to them and lowering his voice. "This coming campaign is going to be one

of the bitterest in the history of this country. I fear there will
be rioting, shooting and killing. Those hospitals cannot be
closed without tremendous mental suffering to the womanhood of the country. We want to avoid that and you want to
avoid it, too. Yet, these hospitals will constantly be in danger.
It ought to be worth something to you to have them especially
protected by the forces of the government."

"You would do that anyway, wouldn't you Gay?" asked
Crookman.

"Well, it's going to cost us millions of votes to do it, and the
members of the National Executive Committee seem to feel
that you ought to make a very liberal donation to the campaign
fund to make up for the votes we'll lose."

"What would you call a liberal donation?" Crookman inquired.

"A successful campaign cannot be fought this year," Gay replied, "under twenty millions."

"Man," shouted Hank, "yuh ain't talkin' 'bout dollahs, is
yuh?"

"You got it right, Hank," answered the National Chairman.
"It'll cost that much and maybe more."

"Where do you expect to get all of that money?" queried
Foster.

"That's just what's worrying us," Gay replied, "and that's
why I'm here. You fellows are rolling in wealth and we need
your help. In the past two years you've collected around ninety
million dollars from the Negro public. Why not give us a good
break? You won't miss five million, and it ought to be worth it
to you fellows to defeat the Democrats."

"Five millions! Great Day," Hank exploded. "Man, is you
los' yo' min'?"

"Not at all," Gay denied. "Might as well own up that if we
don't get a contribution of about that size from you we're liable
to lose this election. . . . Come on, fellows, don't be so tight.
Of course, you're setting pretty and all you've got to do is
change your residence to Europe or some other place if things
don't run smoothly in America, but you want to think of those
poor women with their black babies. What will they do if you
fellows leave the country or if the Democrats win and you have
to close all of your places?"

"That's right, Chief," Foster observed. "You can't let the women down."

"Yeah," said Johnson. "Give 'im th' jack."

"Well, suppose we do?" concluded Crookman, smiling.

The National Chairman was delighted. "When can we collect?" he asked, "and how?"

"Tomorrow, if yuh really wants it then," Johnson observed.

"Now remember," warned Gay. We cannot afford to let it be known that we are getting such a large sum from any one person or corporation."

"That's your lookout," said the physician, indifferently. "You know *we* won't say anything."

Mr. Gay, shortly afterward, departed to carry the happy news to the National Executive Committee, then in session right there in New York City.

The Republicans certainly needed plenty of money to re-elect President Goosie. The frequent radio addresses of Rev. Givens, the growing numbers of the Knights of Nordica, the inexplicable affluence of the Democratic Party and the vitriolic articles in *The Warning*, had not failed to rouse much Democratic sentiment. People were not exactly for the Democrats but they were against the Republicans. As early as May it did not seem possible for the Republicans to carry a single Southern state and many of the Northern and Eastern strongholds were in doubt. The Democrats seemed to have everything their way. Indeed, they were so confident of success that they were already counting the spoils.

When the Democratic Convention met in Jackson, Mississippi, on July 1, 1936, political wiseacres claimed that for the first time in history the whole program was cut and dried and would be run off smoothly and swiftly. Such, however, was not the case. The unusually hot sun, coupled with the enormous quantities of liquor vended, besides the many conflicting interests present, soon brought dissension.

Shortly after the keynote speech had been delivered by Senator Kretin, the Anglo-Saxon crowd let it be known that they wanted some distinguished Southerner like Arthur Snobbcraft nominated for the Presidency. The Knights of Nordica were intent on nominating Imperial Grand Wizard Givens. The

Northern faction of the party, now reduced to a small minority in party councils, was holding out for former Governor Grogan of Massachusetts who as head of the League of Catholic voters had a great following.

Through twenty ballots the voting proceeded, and it remained deadlocked. No faction would yield. Leaders saw that there had to be a compromise. They retired to a suite on the top floor of the Judge Lynch Hotel. There, in their shirt sleeves, with collars open, mint juleps on the table and electric fans stirring up the hot air, they got down to business. Twelve hours later they were still there.

Matthew, wilted, worn but determined, fought for his chief. Simeon Dump of the Anglo-Saxon Association swore he would not withdraw the name of Arthur Snobbcraft. Rev. John Whiffle, a power in the party, gulped drink after drink, kept dabbing a damp handkerchief at the shining surface of his skull, and held out for one Bishop Belch. Moses Lejewski of New York argued obstinately for the nomination of Governor Grogan.

In the meantime the delegates, having left the oven-like convention hall, either lay panting and drinking in their rooms, sat in the hotel lobbies discussing the deadlock or cruised the streets in automobiles confidently seeking the dens of iniquity which they had been told were eager to lure them into sin.

When the clock struck three, Matthew rose and suggested that since the Knights of Nordica and the Anglo-Saxon Association were the two most powerful organizations in the party, Givens should get the presidential nomination, Snobbcraft the vice-presidential and the other candidates be assured of cabinet positions. This suggested compromise appealed to no one except Matthew.

"You people forget," said Simeon Dump, "that the Anglo-Saxon Association is putting up half the money to finance this campaign."

"And you forget," declared Moses Lejewski, "that we're supporting your crazy scheme to disfranchise anybody possessing Negro ancestry when we get into office. That's going to cost us millions of votes in the North. You fellows can't expect to hog everything."

"Why not?" challenged Dump. "How could you win without money?"

"And how," added Matthew, "can you get anywhere without the Knights of Nordica behind you?"

"And how," Rev. Whiffle chimed in, "can you get anywhere without the Fundamentalists and the Drys?"

At four o'clock they had got no farther than they had been at three. They tried to pick some one not before mentioned, and went over and over the list of eligibles. None was satisfactory. One was too radical, another was too conservative, a third was an atheist, a fourth had once rifled a city treasury, the fifth was of immigrant extraction once removed, a sixth had married a Jewess, a seventh was an intellectual, an eighth had spent too long at Hot Springs trying to cure the syphilis, a ninth was rumored to be part Mexican and a tenth had at one time in his early youth been a Socialist.

At five o'clock they were desperate, drunk and disgusted. The stuffy room was a litter of discarded collars, cigarette and cigar butts, match stems, heaped ash trays and empty bottles. Matthew drank little and kept insisting on the selection of Rev. Givens. To the sodden and nodding men he painted marvelous pictures of the spoils of office and their excellent chance of getting there, and then suddenly declared that the Knights of Nordica would withdraw unless Givens was nominated. The threat aroused them. They cursed and called it a holdup, but Matthew was adamant. As a last stroke, he rose and pretended to be ready to bolt the caucus. They remonstrated with him and finally gave in to him.

Orders went out to the delegates. They assembled in the convention hall. The shepherds of the various state flocks cracked the whip and the delegates voted accordingly. Late that afternoon the news went out to a waiting world that the Democrats had nominated Henry Givens for President and Arthur Snobbcraft for Vice-President. Mr. Snobbcraft didn't like that at all, but it was better than nothing.

A few days later the Republican convention opened in Chicago. Better disciplined, as usual, than the Democrats, its business proceeded like clockwork. President Goosie was nominated for reëlection on the first ballot and Vice-President Gump was again selected as his running mate. A platform was adopted whose chief characteristic was vagueness. As was customary, it

stressed the party's record in office, except that which was criminal; it denounced fanaticism without being specific, and it em-
phasized the rights of the individual and the trusts in the same
paragraph. As the Democratic slogan was White Supremacy
and its platform dwelt largely on the necessity of genealogical
investigation, the Republicans adopted the slogan: Personal
Liberty and Ancestral Sanctity.

Dr. Crookman and his associates, listening in on the radio in
his suite in the Robin Hood Hotel in New York City, laughed
softly as they heard the President deliver his speech of acceptance which ended in the following original manner:

"And finally, my friends, I can only say that we shall continue
in the path of rugged individualism, free from the influence of
sinister interests, upholding the finest ideals of honesty, independence and integrity, so that, to quote Abraham Lincoln,
'This nation of the people, for the people and by the people
shall not perish from the earth.'"

"That," said Foster, as the President ceased barking, "sounds
almost like the speech of acceptance of Brother Givens that we
heard the other day."

Dr. Crookman smiled and brushed the ashes off his cigar. "It
may even be the same speech," he suggested.

Through the hot days of July and August the campaign slowly
got under way. Innumerable photographs appeared in the newspapers depicting the rival candidates among the simple folk of
some village, helping youngsters to pick cherries, assisting an
old woman up a stairway, bathing in the old swimming hole,
eating at a barbecue and posing on the rear platforms of special
trains.

Long articles appeared in the Sunday newspapers extolling
the simple virtues of the two great men. Both, it seemed, had
come from poor but honest families; both were hailed as tried
and true friends of the great, common people; both were declared to be ready to give their strength and intellect to America
for the next four years. One writer suggested that Givens resembled Lincoln, while another declared that President Goosie's
character was not unlike that of Roosevelt, believing he was
paying the former a compliment.

Rev. Givens told the reporters: "It is my intention, if elected, to carry out the traditional tariff policy of the Democratic Party" (neither he or anyone else knew what that was).

President Goosie averred again and again, "I intend to make my second term as honest and efficient as my first." Though a dire threat, this statement was supposed to be a fine promise.

Meanwhile, Dr. Samuel Buggerie and his operatives were making great headway examining birth and marriage records throughout the United States. Around the middle of September the Board of Directors held a conference at which the learned man presented a partial report.

"I am now prepared to prove," gloated the obese statistician, "that fully one-quarter of the people of one Virginia county possess non-white ancestry, Indian or Negro; and we can further prove that all of the Indians on the Atlantic Coast are part Negro. In several counties in widely separated parts of the country, we have found that the ancestry of a considerable percentage of the people is in doubt. There is reason to believe that there are countless numbers of people who ought not to be classed with whites and should not mix with Anglo-Saxons."

It was decided that the statistician should get his data in simple form that anyone could read and understand, and have it ready to release just a few days before election. When the people saw how great was the danger from black blood, it was reasoned, they would flock to the Democratic standard and it would be too late for the Republicans to halt the stampede.

No political campaign in the history of the country had ever been so bitter. On one side were those who were fanatically positive of their pure Caucasian ancestry; on the other side were those who knew themselves to be "impure" white or had reason to suspect it. The former were principally Democratic, the latter Republican. There was another group which was Republican because it felt that a victory for the Democrats might cause another Civil War. The campaign roused acrimonious dispute even within families. Often behind these family rifts lurked the knowledge or suspicion of a dark past.

As the campaign grew more bitter, denunciations of Dr. Crookman and his activities grew more violent. A move was started to close all of his hospitals. Some wanted them to be closed for all time; others advised their closing for the duration of the campaign. The majority of thinking people (which wasn't so many) strenuously objected to the proposal.

"No good purpose will be served by closing these hospitals," declared the New York *Morning Earth*. "On the contrary such a step might have tragic results. The Negroes have disappeared into the body of our citizenry, large numbers have intermarried with the whites and the offspring of these marriages are appearing in increasing numbers. Without these hospitals, think how many couples would be estranged; how many homes wrecked! Instead of taking precipitate action, we should be patient and move slowly."

Other Northern newspapers assumed an even more friendly attitude, but the press generally followed the crowd, or led it, and in slightly veiled language urged the opponents of Black-No-More to take the law into their hands.

Finally, emboldened and inflamed by fiery editorials, radio addresses, pamphlets, posters and platform speeches, a mob seeking to protect white womanhood in Cincinnati attacked a Crookman hospital, drove several women into the streets and set fire to the building. A dozen babies were burned to death and others, hastily removed by their mothers, were recognized as mulattoes. The newspapers published names and addresses. Many of the women were very prominent socially either in their own right or because of their husbands.

The nation was shocked as never before. Republican sentiment began to dwindle. The Republican Executive Committee met and discussed ways and means of combating the trend. Gorman Gay was at his wits' end. Nothing, he thought, could save them except a miracle.

Two flights below in a spacious office sat two of the Republican campaigners, Walter Williams and Joseph Bonds, busily engaged in leading the other workers (who knew better) to believe that they were earning the ten dollars a day they were receiving. The former had passed for a Negro for years on the strength of a part-Negro grandparent and then gone back to the white race when the National Social Equality League was forced to cease operations at the insistence of both the sheriff and the landlord. Joseph Bonds, former head of the Negro Data League who had once been a Negro but thanks to Dr. Crookman was now Caucasian and proud of it, had but recently returned to the North from Atlanta, accompanied by Santop Licorice. Both Mr. Williams and Mr. Bonds had been unable to stomach the Democratic crowd and so had fallen in with the Republicans, who were as different from them as one billiard ball from another. The two gentlemen were in low tones discussing the dilemma of the Republicans, while rustling papers to appear busy.

"Jo, if we could figure out something to turn the tables on these Democrats, we wouldn't have to work for the rest of our lives," Williams observed, blowing a cloud of cigarette smoke out of the other corner of his mouth.

"Yes, that's right, Walt, but there ain't a chance in the world. Old Gay is almost crazy, you know. Came in here slamming doors and snapping at everybody this morning," Bonds remarked.

Williams leaned closer to him, lowered his flame-thatched head and then looking to the right and left whispered, "Listen here, do you know where Beard is?"

"No," answered Bonds, starting and looking around to see if anyone was listening. "Where is he?"

"Well, I got a letter from him the other day. He's down there in Richmond doing research work for the Anglo-Saxon Association under that Dr. Buggerie."

"Do they know who he is?"

"Of course they don't. He's been white quite a while now, you know, and of course they'd never connect him with the Dr. Shakespeare A. Beard who used to be one of their most outspoken enemies."

"Well, what about it?" persisted Bonds, eagerly. "Do you think he might know something on the Democrats that might help?"

"He might. We could try him out anyway. If he knows anything he'll spill it because he hates that crowd."

"How will you get in touch with him quickly? Write to him?"

"Certainly not," growled Williams, "I'll get expenses from Gay for the trip. He'll fall for anything now."

He rose and made for the elevator. Five minutes later he was standing before his boss, the National Chairman, a worried, gray little man with an aldermanic paunch and a convict's mouth.

"What is it, Williams?" snapped the Chairman.

"I'd like to get expenses to Richmond," said Williams. "I have a friend down there in Snobbcraft's office and he might have some dope we can use to our advantage."

"Scandal?" asked Mr. Gay, brightening.

"Well, I don't know right now, of course, but this fellow is a very shrewd observer and in six months' time he ought to have grabbed something that'll help us out of this jam."

"Is he a Republican or a Democrat?"

"Neither. He's a highly trained and competent social student. You couldn't expect him to be either," Williams observed. "But I happen to know that he hasn't got any money to speak of, so for a consideration I'm sure he'll spill everything he knows, if anything."

"Well, it's a gamble," said Gay, doubtfully, "but any port in a storm."

Williams left Washington immediately for Richmond. That night he sat in a cramped little room of the former champion of the darker races.

"What are you doing down there, Beard?" asked Williams, referring to the headquarters of the Anglo-Saxon Association.

"Oh, I'm getting, or helping to get, that data of Buggerie's into shape."

"What data? You told me you were doing research work. Now you say you're arranging data. Have they finished collecting it?"

"Yes, we finished that job some time ago. Now we're trying to get the material in shape for easy digestion."

"What do you mean: easy digestion?" queried Williams. "What are you fellows trying to find out and why must it be so easily digested. You fellows usually try to make your stuff unintelligible to the herd."

"This is different," said Beard, lowering his voice to almost a whisper. "We're under a pledge of secrecy. We have been investigating the family trees of the nation and so far, believe me, we certainly have uncovered astounding facts. When I'm finally discharged, which will probably be after election, I'm going to peddle some of that information. Snobbcraft and even Buggerie are not aware of the inflammatory character of the facts we've assembled." He narrowed his foxy eyes greedily.

"Is it because they've been planning to release some of it that they want it in easily digestible form, as you say?" pressed Williams.

"That's it exactly," declared Beard, stroking his now clean-shaven face. "I overheard Buggerie and Snobbcraft chuckling about it only a day or two ago."

"Well, there must be a whole lot of it," insinuated Williams, "if they've had all of you fellows working for six months. Where all did you work?"

"Oh, all over. North as well as South. We've got a whole basement vault full of index cards."

"I guess they're keeping close watch over it, aren't they?" asked Williams.

"Sure. It would take an army to get in that vault."

"Well, I guess they don't want anything to happen to the stuff before they spring it," observed the man from Republican headquarters.

Soon afterward Williams left Dr. Beard, took a stroll around the Anglo-Saxon Association's stately headquarters building, noted the half-dozen tough looking guards about it and then caught the last train for the capital city. The next morning he had a long talk with Gorman Gay.

"It's okeh, Jo," he whispered to Bonds, later, as he passed his desk.

# Chapter Eleven

"WHAT'S the matter with you, Matt?" asked Bunny one morning about a month before election. "Ain't everything going okeh? You look as if we'd lost the election and failed to elect that brilliant intellectual, Henry Givens, President of the United States."

"Well, we might just as well lose it as far as I'm concerned," said Matthew, "if I don't find a way out of this jam I'm in."

"What jam?"

"Well, Helen got in the family way last winter again. I sent her to Palm Beach and the other resorts, thinking the travel and exercise might bring on another miscarriage."

"Did it?"

"Not a chance in the world. Then, to make matters worse, she miscalculates. At first she thought she would be confined in December; now she tells me she's only got about three weeks to go."

"Say not so!"

"I'm preaching gospel."

"Well, hush my mouth! Waddya gonna do? You can't send her to one o' Crookman's hospitals, it would be too dangerous right now."

"That's just it. You see, I figured she wouldn't be ready until about a month after election when everything had calmed down, and I could send her then."

"Would she have gone?"

"She couldn't afford not to with her old man the President of the United States."

"Well, whaddya gonna do, Big Boy? Think fast! Think fast! Them three weeks will get away from here in no time."

"Don't I know it?"

"What about an abortion?" suggested Bunny, hopefully.

"Nothing doing. First place, she's too frail, and second place she's got some fool idea about that being a sin."

"About the only thing for you to do, then," said Bunny, "is to get ready to pull out when that kid is born."

"Oh, Bunny, I'd hate to leave Helen. She's really the only

woman I ever loved, you know. Course she's got her prejudices and queer notions like everybody else but she's really a little queen. She's been an inspiration to me, too, Bunny. Every time I talk about pulling out of this game when things don't go just right, she makes me stick it out. I guess I'd have been gone after I cleaned up that first million if it hadn't been for her."

"You'd have been better off if you had," Bunny commented.

"Oh, I don't know. She's hot for me to become Secretary of State or Ambassador to England or something like that; and the way things are going it looks like I will be. That is, if I can get out of this fix."

"If you can get out o' this jam, Matt, I'll sure take my hat off to you. An' I know how you feel about scuttling out and leaving her. I had a broad like that once in Harlem. 'Twas through her I got that job in th' bank. She was crazy about me, Boy, until she caught me two-timin'. Then she tried to shoot me.

"Squaws are funny that way," Bunny continued, philosophically. "Since I've been white I've found out they're all the same, white or black. Kipling was right. They'll fight to get you, fight to keep you and fight you when they catch you playin' around. But th' kinda woman that won't fight for a man ain't worth havin'."

"So you think I ought to pull out, eh Bunny?" asked the worried Matthew, returning to the subject.

"Well, what I'd suggest is this:" his plump friend advised, "about time you think Helen's gonna be confined, get together as much cash as you can and keep your plane ready. Then, when the baby's born, go to her, tell her everything an' offer to take her away with you. If she won't go, you beat it; if she will, why everything's hotsy totsy." Bunny extended his soft pink hands expressively.

"Well, that sounds pretty good, Bunny."

"It's your best bet, Big Boy," said his friend and secretary.

Two days before election the situation was unchanged. There was joy in the Democratic camp, gloom among the Republicans. For the first time in American history it seemed that money was not going to decide an election. The propagandists and publicity men of the Democrats had so played upon the fears and prejudices of the public that even the bulk of Jews and Catholics were wavering and many had been won over to the support of a candidate who had denounced them but a few months before. In this they were but running true to form, however, as they had usually been on the side of white supremacy in the old days when there was a Negro population observable to the eye. The Republicans sought to dig up some scandal against Givens and Snobbcraft but were dissuaded by their Committee on Strategy which feared to set so dangerous a precedent. There were also politicians in their ranks who were guilty of adulteries, drunkenness and grafting.

The Republicans, Goosie and Gump, and the Democrats, Givens and Snobbcraft had ended their swings around the country and were resting from their labors. There were parades in every city and country town. Minor orators beat the lectern from the Atlantic to the Pacific extolling the imaginary virtues of the candidates of the party that hired them. Dr. Crookman was burned a hundred times in effigy. Several Lying-In hospitals were attacked. Two hundred citizens who knew nothing about either candidate were arrested for fighting over which was the better man.

The air was electric with expectancy. People stood around in knots. Small boys scattered leaflets on ten million doorsteps. Police were on the alert to suppress disorder, except what they created.

Arthur Snobbcraft, jovial and confident that he would soon assume a position befitting a member of one of the First Families of Virginia, was holding a brilliant pre-election party in his palatial residence. Strolling in and out amongst his guests, the master of the house accepted their premature congratulations in good humor. It was fine to hear oneself already addressed as Mr. Vice-President.

The tall English butler hastily edged his way through the throng surrounding the President of the Anglo-Saxon Association and whispered, "Dr. Buggerie is in the study upstairs. He says he must see you at once; that it is very, very important."

Puzzled, Snobbcraft went up to find out what in the world could be the trouble. As he entered, the massive statistician was striding back and forth, mopping his brow, his eyes starting from his head, a sheaf of typewritten sheets trembling in his hand.

"What's wrong, Buggerie?" asked Snobbcraft, perturbed.

"Everything! Everything!" shrilled the statistician.

"Be specific, please."

"Well," shaking the sheaf of papers in Snobbcraft's face, "we can't release any of this stuff! It's too damaging! It's too inclusive! We'll have to suppress it, Snobbcraft. You hear me? We musn't let anyone get hold of it." The big man's flabby jowls worked excitedly.

"What do you mean?" snarled the F. F. V. "Do you mean to tell me that all of that money and work is wasted?"

"That's exactly what I mean," squeaked Buggerie. "It would be suicidal to publish it."

"Why? Get down to brass tacks, man, for God's sake. You get my goat."

"Now listen here, Snobbcraft," replied the statistician soberly, dropping heavily into a chair. "Sit down and listen to me. I started this investigation on the theory that the data gathered would prove that around twenty million people, mostly of the lower classes were of Negro ancestry, recent and remote, while about half that number would be of uncertain or unknown ancestry."

"Well, what have you found?" insisted Snobbcraft, impatiently.

"I have found," continued Buggerie, "that over half the population has no record of its ancestry beyond five generations!"

"That's fine!" chortled Snobbcraft. "I've always maintained that there were only a few people of good blood in this country."

"But those figures include all classes," protested the larger man. "Your class as well as the lower classes."

"Don't insult me, Buggerie!" shouted the head of the Anglo-Saxons, half rising from his seat on the sofa.

"Be calm! Be calm!" cried Buggerie excitedly, "You haven't heard anything yet."

"What else, in the name of God, could be a worse libel on the aristocracy of this state?" Snobbcraft mopped his dark and haughty countenance.

"Well, these statistics we've gathered prove that most of our social leaders, especially of Anglo-Saxon lineage, are descendants of colonial stock that came here in bondage. They associated with slaves, in many cases worked and slept with them. They intermixed with the blacks and the women were sexually exploited by their masters. Then, even more than today, the illegitimate birth rate was very high in America."

Snobbcraft's face was working with suppressed rage. He started to rise but reconsidered. "Go on," he commanded.

"There was so much of this mixing between whites and blacks of the various classes that very early the colonies took steps to put a halt to it. They managed to prevent intermarriage but they couldn't stop intermixture. You know the old records don't lie. They're right there for everybody to see. . . .

"A certain percentage of these Negroes," continued Buggerie, quite at ease now and seemingly enjoying his dissertation, "in time lightened sufficiently to be able to pass for white. They then merged with the general population. Assuming that there were one thousand such cases fifteen generations ago— and we have proof that there were more—their descendants now number close to fifty million souls. Now I maintain that we dare not risk publishing this information. Too many of our very first families are touched right here in Richmond!"

"Buggerie!" gasped the F. F. V., "Are you mad?"

"Quite sane, sir," squeaked the ponderous man, somewhat proudly, "and I know what I know." He winked a watery eye.

"Well, go on. Is there any more?"

"Plenty," proceeded the statistician, amiably. "Take your own family, for instance. (Now don't get mad, Snobbcraft.) Take your own family. It is true that your people descended from King Alfred, but he has scores, perhaps hundreds of thousands of descendants. Some are, of course, honored and respected citizens, cultured aristocrats who are a credit to the country; but most of them, my dear, dear Snobbcraft, are in what you call the lower orders: that is to say, laboring people, convicts, prostitutes, and that sort. One of your maternal ancestors in the late seventeenth century was the offspring of an English serving maid and a black slave. This woman in turn had a daughter by the plantation owner. This daughter was married to a former indentured slave. Their children were all white and you are one of their direct descendants!" Buggerie beamed.

"Stop!" shouted Snobbcraft, the veins standing out on his narrow forehead and his voice trembling with rage. "You can't sit there and insult my family that way, suh."

"Now that outburst just goes to prove my earlier assertion," the large man continued, blandly. "If you get so excited about the truth, what do you think will be the reaction of other people? There's no use getting angry at me. I'm not responsible for your ancestry! Nor, for that matter, are you. You're no worse off than I am, Snobbcraft. My great, great grandfather had his ears cropped for non-payment of debts and was later jailed for thievery. His illegitimate daughter married a free Negro who fought in the Revolutionary War." Buggerie wagged his head almost gleefully.

"How can you admit it?" asked the scandalized Snobbcraft.

"Why not?" demanded Buggerie. "I have plenty of company. There's Givens, who is quite a fanatic on the race question and white supremacy, and yet he's only four generations removed from a mulatto ancestor."

"Givens too?"

"Yes, and also the proud Senator Kretin. He boasts, you know of being descended from Pocahontas and Captain John Smith, but so are thousands of Negroes. Incidentally, there hasn't been an Indian unmixed with Negro on the Atlantic coastal plain for over a century and a half."

"What about Matthew Fisher?"

"We can find no record whatever of Fisher, which is true of about twenty million others, and so," he lowered his voice dramatically, "I have reason to suspect that he is one of those Negroes who have been whitened."

"And to think that I entertained him in my home!" Snobbcraft muttered to himself. And then aloud: "Well, what are we to do about it?"

"We must destroy the whole shooting match," the big man announced as emphatically as possible for one with a soprano voice, "and we'd better do it at once. The sooner we get through with it the better."

"But I can't leave my guests," protested Snobbcraft. Then

turning angrily upon his friend, he growled, "Why in the devil didn't you find all of this out before?"

"Well," said Buggerie, meekly, "I found out as soon as I could. We had to arrange and correlate the data, you know."

"How do you imagine we're going to get rid of that mountain of paper at this hour?" asked Snobbcraft, as they started down stairs.

"We'll get the guards to help us," said Buggerie, hopefully. "And we'll have the cards burned in the furnace."

"All right, then," snapped the F. F. V., "let's go and get it over with."

In five minutes they were speeding down the broad avenue to the headquarters of the Anglo-Saxon Association of America. They parked the car in front of the gate and walked up the cinder road to the front door. It was a balmy, moonlight night, almost as bright as day. They looked around but saw no one.

"I don't see any of the guards around," Snobbcraft remarked, craning his neck. "I wonder where they are?"

"Probably they're inside," Buggerie suggested, "although I remember telling them to patrol the outside of the building."

"Well, we'll go in, anyhow," remarked Snobbcraft. "Maybe they're down stairs."

He unlocked the door, swung it open and they entered. The hall was pitch dark. Both men felt along the wall for the button for the light. Suddenly there was a thud and Snobbcraft cursed.

"What's the matter?" wailed the frightened Buggerie, frantically feeling for a match.

"Turn on that God damned light!" roared Snobbcraft. "I just stumbled over a man. . . Hurry up, will you?"

Dr. Buggerie finally found a match, struck it, located the wall button and pressed it. The hall was flooded with light. There arranged in a row on the floor and neatly trussed up and gagged were the six special guards.

"What the hell does this mean?" yelled Snobbcraft at the mute men prone before them. Buggerie quickly removed the gags.

They had been suddenly set upon, the head watchman explained, about an hour before, just after Dr. Buggerie left, by a crowd of gunmen who had blackjacked them into unconsciousness and carried them into the building. The watchman displayed the lumps on their heads as evidence and looked quite aggrieved. Not one of them could remember what transpired after the sleep-producing buffet.

"The vault!" shrilled Buggerie. "Let's have a look at the vault."

Down the stairs they rushed, Buggerie wheezing in the lead, Snobbcraft following and the six tousled watchmen bringing up the rear. The lights in the basement were still burning brightly. The doors of the vault were open, sagging on their hinges. There was a litter of trash in front of the vault. They all clustered around the opening and peered inside. The vault was absolutely empty.

"My God!" exclaimed Snobbcraft and Buggerie in unison, turning two shades paler.

For a second or two they just gazed at each other. Then suddenly Buggerie smiled.

"That stuff won't do them any good," he remarked triumphantly.

"Why not?" demanded Snobbcraft, in his tone a mixture of eagerness, hope and doubt.

"Well, it will take them as long to get anything out of that mass of cards as it took our staff, and by that time you and Givens will be elected and no one will dare publish anything like that," the statistician explained. "I have in my possession the only summary—those papers I showed you at your house. As long as I've got that document and they haven't, we're all right!" he grinned in obese joy.

"That sounds good," sighed Snobbcraft, contentedly. "By the way, where is that summary?"

Buggerie jumped as if stuck by a pin and looked first into his empty hands, then into his coat pockets and finally his trousers pockets. He turned and dashed out to the car, followed by the grim-looking Snobbcraft and the six uniformed watchmen with their tousled hair and sore bumps. They searched the car in vain, Snobbcraft loudly cursing Buggerie's stupidity.

"I—I must have left it in your study," wept Buggerie, meekly and hopefully. "In fact I think I remember leaving it right there on the table."

The enraged Snobbcraft ordered him into the car and they

drove off leaving the six uniformed watchmen gaping at the entrance to the grounds, the moonbeams playing through their tousled hair.

The two men hit the ground almost as soon as the car crunched to a stop, dashed up the steps, into the house, through the crowd of bewildered guests, up the winding colonial stairs, down the hallway and into the study.

Buggerie switched on the light and looked wildly, hopefully around. Simultaneously the two men made a grab for a sheaf of white paper lying on the sofa. The statistician reached it first and gazed hungrily, gratefully at it. Then his eyes started from his head and his hand trembled.

"Look!" he shrieked dolefully, thrusting the sheaf of paper under Snobbcraft's eyes.

All of the sheets were blank except the one on top. On that was scribbled:

> Thanks very much for leaving that report where I could get hold of it. Am leaving this paper so you'll have something on which to write another summary.
> Happy dreams, Little One.
>
> G. O. P.

"Great God!" gasped Snobbcraft, sinking into a chair.

# Chapter Twelve

THE afternoon before election Matthew and Bunny sat in the latter's hotel suite sipping cocktails, smoking and awaiting the inevitable. They had been waiting ever since the day before. Matthew, tall and tense; Bunny, rotund and apprehensive, trying ever so often to cheer up his chief with poor attempts at jocosity. Every time they heard a bell ring both jumped for the telephone, thinking it might be an announcement from Helen's bedside that an heir, and a dark one, had been born. When they could no longer stay around the office, they had come down to the hotel. In just a few moments they were planning to go back to the office again.

The hard campaign and the worry over the outcome of Helen's confinement had left traces on Matthew's face. The satanic lines were accentuated, the eyes seemed sunken farther back in the head, his well-manicured hand trembled a little as he reached for his glass again and again.

He wondered how it would all come out. He hated to leave. He had had such a good time since he'd been white: plenty of money, almost unlimited power, a beautiful wife, good liquor and the pick of damsels within reach. Must he leave all that? Must he cut and run just at the time when he was about to score his greatest victory. Just think: from an underpaid insurance agent to a millionaire commanding millions of people—and then oblivion. He shuddered slightly and reached again for his glass.

"I got everything fixed," Bunny remarked, shifting around in the overstuffed chair. "The plane's all ready with tanks full and I've got Ruggles right there in the hangar. The money's in that little steel box: all in thousand dollar bills."

"You're going with me, aren't you, Bunny?" asked Matthew in almost pleading tones.

"I'm not stayin' here!" his secretary replied.

"Gee, Bunny, you're a brick!" said Matthew leaning over and placing his hand on his plump little friend's knee. "You sure have been a good pal."

"Aw, cut th' comedy," exclaimed Bunny, reddening and turning his head swiftly away.

Suddenly the telephone rang, loud, clear, staccato. Both men sprang for it, eagerly, open-eyed, apprehensive. Matthew was first.

"Hello!" he shouted. "What's that! Yes, I'll be right up."

"Well, it's happened," he announced resignedly, hanging up the receiver. And then, brightening a bit, he boasted, "It's a boy!"

In the midst of her pain Helen was jubilant. What a present to give her Matthew on the eve of his greatest triumph! How good the Lord was to her; to doubly bless her in this way. The nurse wiped the tears of joy away from the young mother's eyes.

"You must stay quiet, Ma'am," she warned.

Outside in the hall, squirming uneasily on the window seat, was Matthew, his fists clenched, his teeth biting into his thin lower lip. At another window stood Bunny looking vacantly out into the street, feeling useless and out of place in such a situation, and yet convinced that it was his duty to stay here by his best friend during this great crisis.

Matthew felt like a young soldier about to leave his trench to face a baptism of machine gun fire or a gambler risking his last dollar on a roll of the dice. It seemed to him that he would go mad if something didn't happen quickly. He rose and paced the hall, hands in pockets, his tall shadow following him on the opposite wall. Why didn't the doctor come out and tell him something? What was the cause of the delay? What would Helen say? What would the baby look like? Maybe it might be miraculously light! Stranger things had happened in this world. But no, nothing like that could happen. Well, he'd had his lucky break; now the vacation was over.

A nurse, immaculate in white uniform, came out of Helen's bedroom, passed them hurriedly, smiling, and entered the bath-room. She returned with a basin of warm water in her hands, smiled again reassuringly and reëntered the natal chamber. Bunny and Matthew, in unison, sighed heavily.

"Boy!" exclaimed Bunny, wiping the perspiration from his brow. "If somethin' don't happen pretty soon, here, I'm gonna do a Brodie out o' that window."

"The both of us," said Matthew. "I never knew it took these doctors so damn long to get through."

Helen's door opened and the physician came out looking quite grave and concerned. Matthew pounced upon him. The man held his finger to his lips and motioned to the room across the hall. Matthew entered.

"Well," said Matthew, guiltily, "what's the news?"

"I'm very sorry to have to tell you, Mr. Fisher, that something terrible has happened. Your son is very, very dark. Either you or Mrs. Fisher must possess some Negro blood. It might be called reversion to type if any such thing had ever been proved. Now I want to know what you want done. If you say so I can get rid of this child and it will save everybody concerned a lot of trouble and disgrace. Nobody except the nurse knows anything about this and she'll keep her mouth shut for a consideration. Of course, it's all in the day's work for me, you know. I've had plenty of cases like this in Atlanta, even before the disappearance of the Negroes. Come now, what shall I do?" he wailed.

"Yes," thought Matthew to himself, "what should he do?" The doctor had suggested an excellent way out of the dilemma. They could just say that the child had died. But what of the future? Must he go on forever in this way? Helen was young and fecund. Surely one couldn't go on murdering one's children, especially when one loved and wanted children. Wouldn't it be better to settle the matter once and for all? Or should he let the doctor murder the boy and then hope for a better situation the next time? An angel of frankness beckoned him to be done with this life of pretense; to take his wife and son and flee far away from everything, but a devil of ambition whispered seductively about wealth, power and prestige.

In almost as many seconds the pageant of the past three years passed in review on the screen of his tortured memory: the New Year's Eve at the Honky Tonk Club, the first glimpse of the marvelously beautiful Helen, the ordeal of getting white, the first, sweet days of freedom from the petty insults and cheap discriminations to which as a black man he had always been subjected, then the search for Helen around Atlanta, the organization of the Knights of Nordica, the stream of successes, the coming of Bunny, the campaign planned and executed by him: and now, the end. Must it be the end?

"Well?" came the insistent voice of the physician.

Matthew opened his mouth to reply when the butler burst into the room waving a newspaper.

"Excuse me, sir," he blurted, excitedly, "but Mister Brown said to bring this right to you."

The lurid headlines seemed to leap from the paper and strike Matthew between the eyes:

### DEMOCRATIC LEADERS PROVED OF NEGRO DESCENT

Givens, Snobbcraft, Buggerie, Kretin and Others
of Negro Ancestry, According to Old
Records Unearthed by Them.

Matthew and the physician, standing side by side, read the long account in awed silence. Bunny entered the door.

"Can I speak to you a minute, Matt?" he asked casually. Almost reluctant to move, Matthew followed him into the hall.

"Keep your shirt on, Big Boy," Bunny advised, almost jovially. "They ain't got nothin' on you yet. That changing your name threw them off. You're not even mentioned."

Matthew braced up, threw back his shoulders and drew a long, deep breath. It seemed as if a mountain had been taken off his shoulders. He actually grinned as his confidence returned. He reached for Bunny's hand and they shook, silently jubilant.

"Well, doctor," said Matthew, arching his left eyebrow in his familiar Mephistophelian manner, "it sort of looks as if there is something to that reversion to type business. I used to think it was all boloney myself. Well, it's as I always say: you never can tell."

"Yes, it seems as if this is a very authentic case," agreed the physician, glancing sharply at the bland and blond countenance of Matthew. "Well, what now?"

"I'll have to see Givens," said Matthew as they turned to leave the room.

"Here he comes now," Bunny announced.

Sure enough, the little gray-faced, bald-headed man, came

leaping up the stairs like a goat, his face haggard, his eyes bulging in mingled rage and terror, his necktie askew. He was waving a newspaper in his hand and opened his mouth without speaking as he shot past them and dashed into Helen's room. The old fellow was evidently out of his head.

They followed him into the room in time to see him with his face buried in the covers of Helen's bed and she, horrified, glancing at the six-inch-tall headline. Matthew rushed to her side as she slumped back on the pillow in a dead faint. The physician and nurse dashed to revive her. The old man on his knees sobbed hoarsely. Mrs. Givens looking fifteen years older appeared in the doorway. Bunny glanced at Matthew who slightly lowered his left eyelid and with difficulty suppressed a smile.

"We've got to get out o' this!" shouted the Imperial Grand Wizard. "We've got to get out o' this, Oh, it's terrible. . . . I never knew it myself, for sure. . . Oh, Matthew, get us out of this, I tell you. They almost mobbed me at the office. . . Came in just as I went out the back way. . . Almost ten thousand of them. . . We can't lose a minute. Quick, I tell you! They'll murder us all."

"I'll look out for everything," Matthew soothed condescendingly. "I'll stick by you." Then turning swiftly to his partner he commanded, "Bunny order both cars out at once. We'll beat it for the airport. . . Doctor Brocker, will you go with us to look out for Helen and the baby? We've got to get out right now. I'll pay you your price."

"Sure I'll go, Mr. Fisher," said the physician, quietly. "I wouldn't leave Mrs. Fisher now."

The nurse had succeeded in bringing Helen to consciousness. She was weeping bitterly, denouncing fate and her father. With that logicality that frequently causes people to accept as truth circumstantial evidence that is not necessarily conclusive, she was assuming that the suspiciously brown color of her new-born son was due to some hidden Negro drop of blood in her veins. She looked up at her husband beseechingly.

"Oh, Matthew, darling," she cried, her long red-gold hair framing her face, "I'm so sorry about all this. If I'd only known, I'd never have let you in for it. I would have spared you this disgrace and humiliation. Oh, Matthew, Honey, please forgive me. I love you, my husband. Please don't leave me, please don't leave me!" She reached out and grasped the tail of his coat as if he were going to leave that very minute.

"Now, now, little girl," said Matthew soothingly, touched by her words, "You haven't disgraced me; you've honored me by presenting me with a beautiful son."

He looked down worshipfully at the chubby ball of brownness in the nurse's arms.

"You needn't worry about me, Helen. I'll stick by you as long as you'll have me and without you life wouldn't be worth a dime. You're not responsible for the color of our baby, my dear. I'm the guilty one."

Dr. Brocker smiled knowingly, Givens rose up indignantly, Bunny opened his mouth in surprise, Mrs. Givens folded her arms and her mouth changed to a slit and the nurse said "Oh!"

"You?" cried Helen in astonishment.

"Yes, me," Matthew repeated, a great load lifting from his soul. Then for a few minutes he poured out his secret to the astonished little audience.

Helen felt a wave of relief go over her. There was no feeling of revulsion at the thought that her husband was a Negro. There once would have been but that was seemingly centuries ago when she had been unaware of her remoter Negro ancestry. She felt proud of her Matthew. She loved him more than ever. They had money and a beautiful, brown baby. What more did they need? To hell with the world! To hell with society! Compared to what she possessed, thought Helen, all talk of race and color was damned foolishness. She would probably have been surprised to learn that countless Americans at that moment were thinking the same thing.

"Well," said Bunny, grinning, "it sure is good to be able to admit that you're a jigwalk once more."

"Yes, Bunny," said old man Givens, "I guess we're all niggers now."

"Negroes, Mr. Givens, Negroes," corrected Dr. Brocker, entering the room. "I'm in the same boat with the rest of you, only my dark ancestors are not so far back. I sure hope the Republicans win."

"Don't worry, Doc," said Bunny. "They'll win all right. And how! Gee whiz! I bet Sherlock Holmes, Nick Carter and all the Pinkertons couldn't find old Senator Kretin and Arthur Snobbcraft now."

"Come on," shouted the apprehensive Givens, "let's get out o' here before that mob comes."

"Whut mob, Daddy?" asked Mrs. Givens.

"You'll find out damn quick if you don't shake it up," replied her husband.

Through the crisp, autumn night air sped Fisher's big tri-motored plane, headed southwest to the safety of Mexico. Reclining in a large, comfortable deck chair was Helen Fisher, calm and at peace with the world. In a hammock near her was her little brown son, Matthew, Junior. Beside her, holding her hand, was Matthew. Up front near the pilot, Bunny and Givens were playing Conquian. Behind them sat the nurse and Dr. Brocker, silently gazing out of the window at the twinkling lights of the Gulf Coast. Old lady Givens snored in the rear of the ship.

"Damn!" muttered Givens, as Bunny threw down his last spread and won the third consecutive game. "I sure wish I'd had time to grab some jack before we pulled out o' Atlanta. Ain't got but five dollars and fifty-three cents to my name."

"Don't worry about that, Old Timer," Bunny laughed. "I don't think we left over a thousand bucks in the treasury. See that steel box over there? Well, that ain't got nothin' in it but bucks and more bucks. Not a bill smaller than a grand."

"Well, I'm a son-of-a-gun," blurted the Imperial Grand Wizard. "That boy thinks o' everything."

But Givens was greatly depressed, much more so than the others. He had really believed all that he had preached about white supremacy, race purity and the menace of the alien, the Catholic, the Modernist and the Jew. He had always been sincere in his prejudices.

When they arrived at the Valbuena Air Field outside Mexico City, a messenger brought Bunny a telegram.

"You better thank your stars you got away from there, Matt," he grinned, handing his friend the telegram. "See what my gal says?"

Matthew glanced over the message and handed it to Givens without comment. It read:

*Hope you arrive safely Senator Kretin lynched in Union Station Stop Snobbcraft and Buggerie reported in flight Stop Goosie and Gump almost unanimously reëlected Stop Government has declared martial law until disturbances stop Stop When can I come?*

MADELINE SCRANTON.

"Who's this Scranton broad?" queried Matthew in a whisper, cutting a precautionary glance at his wife.

"A sweet Georgia brown," exclaimed Bunny enthusiastically.

"No!" gasped Matthew, incredulous.

"She ain't no Caucasian!" Bunny replied.

"She must be the last black gal in the country," Matthew remarked, glancing enviously at his friend. "How come she didn't get white, too?"

"Well," Bunny replied, a slight hint of pride in his voice. "She's a race patriot. She's funny that way."

"Well, for cryin' out loud!" exclaimed Matthew, scratching his head and sort of half grinning in a bewildered way. "*What* kind o' *sheba* is that?"

Old man Givens came over to where they were standing, the telegram in his hand and an expression of serenity now on his face.

"Boys," he announced, "it looks like it's healthier down here right now than it is back there in Georgia."

"*Looks* like it's healthier?" mocked Bunny. "Brother, you know damn *well* it's healthier!"

# Chapter Thirteen

TOWARD eleven o'clock on the evening before election day, a long, low roadster swept up to the door of a stately country home near Richmond, Va., crunched to a stop, the lights were extinguished and two men, one tall and angular, the other huge and stout, catapulted from the car. Without wasting words, they raced around the house and down a small driveway to a rambling shed in a level field about three hundred yards to the rear. Breathless, they halted before the door and beat upon it excitedly.

"Open up there, Frazier!" ordered Snobbcraft, for it was he. "Open that door." There was no answer. The only reply was the chirping of crickets and the rustle of branches.

"He must not be here," said Dr. Buggerie, glancing fearfully over his shoulder and wiping a perspiring brow with a damp handkerchief.

"The damned rascal had better be here," thundered the Democratic candidate for Vice-President, beating again on the door. "I telephoned him two hours ago to be ready."

As he spoke someone unlocked the door and rolled it aside an inch or two.

"Is that you, Mr. Snobbcraft?" asked a sleepy voice from the darkness within.

"Open that damned door, you fool," barked Snobbcraft. "Didn't I tell you to have that plane ready when we got here? Why don't you do as you're told?" He and Dr. Buggerie helped slide the great doors back. The man Frazier snapped on the lights, revealing within a big, three-motored plane with an automobile nestling under each of its wings.

"I-I kinda fell asleep waitin' for you, Mr. Snobbcraft," Frazier apologized, "but everything's ready."

"All right, man," shouted the president of the Anglo-Saxon Association, "let's get away from here then. This is a matter of life and death. You ought to have had the plane outside and all warmed up to go."

"Yes sir," the man mumbled meekly, busying himself.

"These damned, stupid, poor white trash!" growled Snobb-craft, glaring balefully at the departing aviator.

"D-D-Don't antagonize him," muttered Buggerie. "He's our only chance to get away."

"Shut up, fool! If it hadn't been for you and your damned fool statistics we wouldn't be in this fix."

"You wanted them, didn't you?" whined the statistician in defense.

"Well, I didn't tell you to leave that damned summary where anybody could get hold of it." Snobbcraft replied, reproach-fully. "That was the most stupid thing I ever heard of."

Buggerie opened his mouth to reply but said nothing. He just glared at Snobbcraft who glared back at him. The two men presented a disheveled appearance. The Vice-Presidential candidate was haggard, hatless, collarless and still wore his smoking jacket. The eminent statistician and author of *The Incidence of Psittacosis among the Hiphopa Indians of the Amazon Valley and Its Relation to Life Insurance Rates in the United States*, looked far from dignified with no necktie, canvas breeches, no socks and wearing a shooting jacket he had snatched from a closet on his way out of the house. He had forgotten his thick spectacles and his bulging eyes were red and watery. They paced impatiently back and forth, glancing first at the swiftly working Frazier and then down the long driveway toward the glowing city.

Ten minutes they waited while Frazier went over the plane to see that all was well. Then they helped him roll the huge metal bird out of the hangar and on to the field. Gratefully they climbed inside and fell exhausted on the soft-cushioned seats.

"Well, that sure is a relief," gasped the ponderous Buggerie, mopping his brow.

"Wait until we get in the air," growled Snobbcraft. "Anything's liable to happen after that mob tonight. I was never so humiliated in my life. The idea of that gang of poor white trash crowding up my steps and yelling nigger. It was disgraceful."

"Yes, it was terrible," agreed Buggerie. "It's a good thing they didn't go in the rear where your car was. We wouldn't have been able to get away."

"I thought there would be a demonstration," said Snobbcraft, some of his old sureness returning, "that's why I 'phoned Frazier to get ready. . . . Oh, it's a damned shame to be run out of your own home in this way!"

He glared balefully at the statistician who averted his gaze.

"All ready, sir," announced Frazier, "where are we headed?"

"To my ranch in Chihuahua, and hurry up," snapped Snobb-craft.

"But—But we ain't got enough gas to go that far," said Frazier. "I-I-You didn't say you wanted to go to Mexico, Boss."

Snobbcraft stared incredulously at the man. His rage was so great that he could not speak for a moment or two. Then he launched into a stream of curses that would have delighted a pirate captain, while the unfortunate aviator gaped indecisively.

In the midst of this diatribe, the sound of automobile horns and klaxons rent the air, punctuated by shouts and pistol shots. The three men in the plane saw coming down the road from the city a bobbing stream of headlights. Already the cavalcade was almost to the gate of the Snobbcraft country estate.

"Come on, get out of here," gasped Snobbcraft. "We'll get some gas farther down the line. Hurry up!"

Dr. Buggerie, speechless and purple with fear, pushed the aviator out of the plane. The fellow gave the propeller a whirl, jumped back into the cabin, took the controls and the great machine rolled out across the field.

They had started none too soon. The automobile cavalcade was already coming up the driveway. The drone of the motor drowned out the sound of the approaching mob but the two fearful men saw several flashes that betokened pistol shots. Several of the automobiles took out across the field in the wake of the plane. They seemed to gain on it. Snobbcraft and Bug-gerie gazed nervously ahead. They were almost at the end of the field and the plane had not yet taken to the air. The pursu-ing automobiles drew closer. There were several more flashes from firearms. A bullet tore through the side of the cabin. Simultaneously Snobbcraft and Buggerie fell to the floor.

At last the ship rose, cleared the trees at the end of the field and began to attain altitude. The two men took deep breaths of relief, rose and flung themselves on the richly upholstered seats.

A terrible stench suddenly became noticeable to the two passengers and the aviator. The latter looked inquiringly over his shoulder; Snobbcraft and Buggerie, their noses wrinkled and their foreheads corrugated, glanced suspiciously at each other. Both moved uneasily in their seats and looks of guilt succeeded those of accusation. Snobbcraft retreated precipitously to the rear cabin while the statistician flung open several windows and then followed the Vice-Presidential candidate.

Fifteen minutes later two bundles were tossed out of the window of the rear cabin and the two passengers, looking sheepish but much relieved, resumed their seats. Snobbcraft was wearing a suit of brown dungarees belonging to Frazier while his scientific friend had wedged himself into a pair of white trousers usually worn by Snobbcraft's valet. Frazier turned, saw them, and grinned.

Hour after hour the plane winged its way through the night. Going a hundred miles an hour it passed town after town. About dawn, as they were passing over Meridian, Mississippi, the motor began to miss.

"What's the matter there?" Snobbcraft inquired nervously into the pilot's ear.

"The gas is runnin' low," Frazier replied grimly. "We'll have to land pretty soon."

"No, no, not in Mississippi!" gasped Buggerie, growing purple with apprehension. "They'll lynch us if they find out who we are."

"Well, we can't stay up here much longer," the pilot warned.

Snobbcraft bit his lip and thought furiously. It was true they would be taking a chance by landing anywhere in the South, let alone in Mississippi, but what could they do? The motor was missing more frequently and Frazier had cut down their speed to save gasoline. They were just idling along. The pilot looked back at Snobbcraft inquiringly.

"By God, we're in a fix now," said the president of the Anglo-Saxon Association. Then he brightened with a sudden idea. "We could hide in the rear cabin while Frazier gets gasoline," he suggested.

"Suppose somebody looks in the rear cabin?" queried Buggerie, dolefully, thrusting his hands into the pockets of his white trousers. "There's bound to be a lot of curious people about when a big plane like this lands in a farming district."

As he spoke his left hand encountered something hard in the pocket. It felt like a box of salve. He withdrew it curiously. It was a box of shoe polish which the valet doubtless used on Snobbcraft's footgear. He looked at it aimlessly and was about to thrust it back into the pocket when he had a brilliant idea.

"Look here, Snobbcraft," he cried excitedly, his rheumy eyes popping out of his head farther than usual. "This is just the thing."

"What do you mean?" asked his friend, eyeing the little tin box.

"Well," explained the scientist, "you know real niggers are scarce now and nobody would think of bothering a couple of them, even in Mississippi. They'd probably be a curiosity."

"What are you getting at, man?"

"This: we can put this blacking on our head, face, neck and hands, and no one will take us for Snobbcraft and Buggerie. Frazier can tell anybody that inquires that we're two darkies he's taking out of the country, or something like that. Then, after we get our gas and start off again, we can wash the stuff off with gasoline. It's our only chance, Arthur. If we go down like we are, they'll kill us sure."

Snobbcraft pursed his lips and pondered the proposition for a moment. It was indeed, he saw, their only chance to effectively escape detection.

"All right," he agreed, "let's hurry up. This ship won't stay up much longer."

Industriously they daubed each other's head, neck, face, chest, hands and arms with the shoe polish. In five minutes they closely resembled a brace of mammy singers. Snobbcraft hurriedly instructed Frazier.

The plane slowly circled to the ground. The region was slightly rolling and there was no good landing place. There could be no delay, however, so Frazier did his best. The big ship bumped over logs and through weeds, heading straight for a clump of trees. Quickly the pilot steered it to the left only to send it head first into a ditch. The plane turned completely over, one wing was entirely smashed and Frazier, caught in the wreckage under the engine, cried feebly for help for a few moments and then lay still.

Shaken up and bruised, the two passengers managed to crawl out of the cabin window to safety. Dolefully they stood in the Mississippi sunlight, surveying the wreckage and looking questioningly at each other.

"Well," whined Dr. Buggerie, rubbing one large sore buttock, "what now?"

"Shut up," growled Snobbcraft. "If it hadn't been for you, we wouldn't be here."

Happy Hill, Mississippi, was all aflutter. For some days it had been preparing for the great, open-air revival of the True Faith Christ Lovers' Church. The faithful for miles around were expected to attend the services scheduled for the afternoon of Election Day and which all hoped would last well into the night.

This section of the state had been untouched by the troubles through which the rest of the South had gone as a result of the activities of Black-No-More, Incorporated. The people for miles around were with very few exceptions old residents and thence known to be genuine blue-blooded Caucasians for as far back as any resident could remember which was at least fifty years. The people were proud of this fact. They were more proud, however, of the fact that Happy Hill was the home and birthplace of the True Faith Christ Lovers' Church, which made the prodigious boast of being the most truly Fundamentalist of all the Christian sects in the United States. Other things of which the community might have boasted were its inordinately high illiteracy rate and its lynching record—but these things were seldom mentioned, although no one was ashamed of them. Certain things are taken for granted everywhere.

Long before the United States had rid themselves of their Negroes through the good but unsolicited offices of Dr. Junius Crookman, Happy Hill had not only rid itself of what few Negroes had resided in its vicinity but of all itinerant blackamoors who lucklessly came through the place. Ever since the Civil War when the proud and courageous forefathers of the Caucasian inhabitants had vigorously resisted all efforts to draft them into the Confederate Army, there had been a sign nailed over the general store and post office reading, "NIGER REDE & RUN. IF U CAN'T REDE, RUN ENEYHOWE." The literate denizens of Happy Hill would sometimes stand off and spell out the words with the pride that usually accompanies erudition.

The method by which Happy Hill discouraged blackamoors who sought the hospitality of the place, was simple: the offending Ethiopian was either hung or shot and then broiled. Across from the general store and post office was a large iron post about five feet high. On it all blacks were burned. Down one side of it was a long line of nicks made with hammer and chisel. Each nick stood for a Negro dispatched. This post was one of the landmarks of the community and was pointed out to visitors with pardonable civic pride by local boosters. Sage old fellows frequently remarked between expectorations of tobacco juice that the only Negro problem in Happy Hill was the difficulty of getting hold of a sufficient number of the Sons or Daughters of Ham to lighten the dullness of the place.

Quite naturally the news that all Negroes had disappeared, not only from their state but from the entire country, had been received with sincere regret by the inhabitants of Happy Hill. They envisioned the passing of an old, established custom. Now there was nothing left to stimulate them but the old time religion and the clandestine sex orgies that invariably and immediately followed the great revival meetings.

So the simple country folk had turned to religion with renewed ardor. There were several churches in the county, Methodist, Baptist, Campbellite and, of course, Holy Roller. The latter, indeed, had the largest membership. But the people, eager for something new, found all of the old churches too tame. They wanted a faith with more punch to it; a faith that would fittingly accompany the fierce corn liquor which all consumed, albeit they were all confirmed Prohibitionists.

Whenever and wherever there is a social need, some agency arises to supply it. The needs of Happy Hill were no exception. One day, several weeks previously, there had come to the community one Rev. Alex McPhule who claimed to be the founder of a new faith, a true faith, that would save all from the machinations of the Evil One. The other churches, he averred, had failed. The other churches had grown soft and were flirting with atheism and Modernism which, according to Rev. McPhule, were the same thing. An angel of God had visited him one summer evening in Meridian, he told them, when he was down sick in bed as the result of his sinning ways, and had told him to reform and go forth into the world and preach the true faith of Christ's love. He had promised to do so, of course, and then the angel had placed the palm of his right hand on Rev. McPhule's forehead and all of the sickness and misery had departed.

The residents of Happy Hill and vicinity listened with rapt attention and respect. The man was sincere, eloquent and obviously a Nordic. He was tall, thin, slightly knock-kneed, with a shock of unkempt red hair, wild blue eyes, hollow cheeks, lantern jaw and long ape-like arms that looked very impressive when he waved them up and down during a harangue. His story sounded logical to the country people and they flocked in droves to his first revival held in a picturesque natural amphitheater about a mile from town.

No one had any difficulty in understanding the new faith. No music was allowed besides singing and thumping the bottom of a wooden tub. There were no chairs. Everybody sat on the ground in a circle with Rev. McPhule in the center. The holy man would begin an extemporaneous song and would soon have the faithful singing it after him and swinging from side to side in unison. Then he would break off abruptly and launch into an old fashion hellfire-and-damnation sermon in which demons, brimstone, adultery, rum, and other evils prominently figured. At the height of his remarks, he would roll his eyes heavenward, froth at the mouth, run around on all fours and embrace in turn each member of the congregation, especially the buxom ladies. This would be the signal for others to follow his example. The sisters and brothers osculated, embraced and rolled, shouting meanwhile: "Christ is Love! . . . Love Christ! . . . Oh, be happy in the arms of Jesus! . . . Oh, Jesus, my Sweetheart! . . . Heavenly Father!" Frequently these revivals took place on the darkest nights with the place of worship dimly illuminated by pine torches. As these torches always seemed to conveniently burn out about the time the embracing and rolling started, the new faith rapidly became popular.

In a very short time nothing in Happy Hill was too good for Rev. Alex McPhule. Every latchstring hung out for him. As usual with gentlemen of the cloth, he was especially popular with the ladies. When the men were at work in the fields, the Man of God would visit house after house and comfort the womenfolk with his Christian message. Being a bachelor, he made these professional calls with great frequency.

The Rev. Alex McPhule also held private audiences with the sick, sinful and neurotic in his little cabin. There he had erected an altar covered with the white marble top from an old bureau. Around this altar were painted some grotesque figures, evidently the handiwork of the evangelist, while on the wall in back of the altar hung a large square of white oilcloth upon which was painted a huge eye. The sinner seeking surcease was commanded to gaze upon the eye while making confessions and requests. On the altar reposed a crudely-bound manuscript about three inches thick. This was the "Bible" of the Christ Lovers which the Rev. McPhule declared he had written at the command of Jesus Christ Himself. The majority of his visitors were middle-aged wives and adenoidal and neurotic young girls. None departed unsatisfied.

With all the good fortune that had come to the Rev. McPhule as a result of engaging in the Lord's work, he was still dissatisfied. He never passed a Baptist, Methodist or Holy Roller church without jealousy and ambition surging up within him. He wanted everybody in the county in his flock. He wanted to do God's work so effectually that the other churches would be put out of business. He could only do this, he knew, with the aid of a message straight from Heaven. That alone would impress them.

He began to talk in his meetings about a sign coming down from Heaven to convince all doubters and infidels like Methodists and Baptists. His flock was soon on the nervous edge of expectancy but the Lord failed, for some reason, to answer the prayer of his right-hand man.

Rev. McPhule began to wonder what he had done to offend the Almighty. He prayed long and fervently in the quiet of his bedchamber, except when he didn't have company, but no sign appeared. Possibly, thought the evangelist, some big demonstration might attract the attention of Jesus; something bigger than the revivals he had been staging. Then one day somebody brought him a copy of *The Warning* and upon reading it he got an idea. If the Lord would only send a nigger for his congregation to lynch! That would, indeed, be marked evidence of the power of Rev. Alex McPhule.

He prayed with increased fervency but no African put in an appearance. Two nights later as he sat before his altar, his "Bible" clutched in his hands, a bat flew in the window. It rapidly circled the room and flew out again. Rev. McPhule could feel the wind from its wings. He stood erect with a wild look in his watery blue eyes and screamed, "A sign! A sign! Oh, Glory be! The Lord has answered my prayer! Oh, thank you, God! A sign! A sign!" Then he grew dizzy, his eyes dimmed and he fell twitching across the altar, unconscious.

Next day he went around Happy Hill telling of his experience of the night before. An angel of the Lord, he told the gaping villagers, had flown through the window, alighted on his "Bible" and, kissing him on his forehead, had declared that the Lord would answer his prayer and send a sign. As proof of his tale, Rev. McPhule exhibited a red spot on his forehead which he had received when his head struck the marble altar top but which he claimed marked the place where the messenger of the Lord had kissed

The simple folk of Happy Hill were, with few exceptions, convinced that the Rev. McPhule stood in well with the celestial authorities. Nervous and expectant they talked of nothing but The Sign. They were on edge for the great revival scheduled for Election Day at which time they fervently hoped the Lord would make good.

At last the great day had arrived. From far and near came the good people of the countryside on horseback, in farm wagons and battered mud-caked flivvers. Many paused to cast their ballots for Givens and Snobbcraft, not having heard of the developments of the past twenty-four hours, but the bulk of the folk repaired immediately to the sacred grove where the preaching would take place.

Rev. Alex McPhule gloated inwardly at the many concentric circles of upturned faces. They were eager, he saw, to drink in his words of wisdom and be elevated. He noted with satisfaction that there were many strange people in the congregation. It showed that his power was growing. He glanced up apprehensively at the blue heavens. Would The Sign come? Would the Lord answer his prayers? He muttered another prayer and then proceeded to business.

He was an impressive figure today. He had draped himself in a long, white robe with a great red cross on the left breast and he looked not unlike one of the Prophets of old. He walked back and forth in the little circle surrounded by close-packed humanity, bending backward and forward, swinging his arms, shaking his head and rolling his eyes while he retold for the fiftieth time the story of the angel's visit. The man was a natural actor and his voice had that sepulchral tone universally associated with Men of God, court criers and Independence Day orators. In the first row squatted the Happy Hill True Faith Choir of eight young women with grizzled old man Yawbrew, the tub-thumper, among them. They groaned, amened and Yes-Lorded at irregular intervals.

Then, having concluded his story, the evangelist launched into song in a harsh, nasal voice:

> *I done come to Happy Hill to save you from Sin,*
> *Salvation's door is open and you'd better come in,*
> *Oh, Glory Hallelujah! you'd better come in.*
> *Jesus Christ has called me to save this white race,*
> *And with His Help I'll save you from awful disgrace.*
> *Oh, Glory Hallelujah! We must save this race.*

Old man Yawbrew beat on his tub while the sisters swayed and accompanied their pastor. The congregation joined in.

Suddenly Rev. McPhule stopped, glared at the rows of strained, upturned faces and extending his long arms to the sun, he shouted:

"It'll come I tell yuh. Yes Lord, the sign will come—ugh. I know that my Lord liveth and the sign will come—ugh. If—ugh —you just have faith—ugh. Oh, Jesus—ugh. Brothers and Sisters—ugh. Just have faith—ugh—and the Lord—ugh—will answer your prayers . . . Oh, Christ—ugh. Oh, Little Jesus —ugh . . . Oh, God—ugh—answer our prayers . . . Save us—ugh. Send us the Sign . . ."

The congregation shouted after him "Send us the Sign!" Then he again launched into a hymn composed on the spot:

> *He will send the Sign,*
> *Oh, He will send the Sign*
> *Loving Little Jesus Christ*
> *He will send the Sign.*

Over and over he sang the verse. The people joined him until the volume of sound was tremendous. Then with a piercing scream, Rev. McPhule fell on all fours and running among the people hugged one after the other, crying "Christ is Love! . . . He'll send the Sign! . . . Oh Jesus! send us The Sign!" The cries of the others mingled with his and there was a general kissing, embracing and rolling there in the green-walled grove under the midday sun.

As the sun approached its zenith, Mr. Arthur Snobbcraft and Dr. Samuel Buggerie, grotesque in their nondescript clothing and their blackened skins, trudged along the dusty road in what they hoped was the direction of a town. For three hours, now, they had been on the way, skirting isolated farmhouses and cabins, hoping to get to a place where they could catch a train. They had fiddled aimlessly around the wrecked plane for two or three hours before getting up courage enough to take to the highroad. Suddenly they both thrilled with pleasure somewhat dampened by apprehension as they espied from a rise in the road, a considerable collection of houses.

"There's a town," exclaimed Snobbcraft. "Now let's get this damned stuff off our faces. There's probably a telegraph office there."

"Oh, don't be crazy," Buggerie pleaded. "If we take off this blacking we're lost. The whole country has heard the news about us by this time, even in Mississippi. Let's go right in as we are, pretending we're niggers, and I'll bet we'll be treated all right. We won't have to stay long. With our pictures all over the country, it would be suicidal to turn up here in one of these hotbeds of bigotry and ignorance."

"Well, maybe you're right," Snobbcraft grudgingly admitted. He was eager to get the shoe polish off his skin. Both men had perspired freely during their hike and the sweat had mixed with the blacking much to their discomfort.

As they started toward the little settlement, they heard shouts and singing on their left.

"What's that?" cried Dr. Buggerie, stopping to listen.

"Sounds like a camp meeting," Snobbcraft replied. "Hope it is. We can be sure those folks will treat us right. One thing about these people down here they are real, sincere Christians."

"I don't think it will be wise to go where there's any crowds," warned the statistician. "You never can tell what a crowd will do."

"Oh, shut up, and come on!" Snobbcraft snapped. "I've listened to you long enough. If it hadn't been for you we would never have had all of this trouble. Statistics! Bah!"

They struck off over the fields toward the sound of the singing. Soon they reached the edge of the ravine and looked down on the assemblage. At about the same time, some of the people facing in that direction saw them and started yelling "The Sign! Look! Niggers! Praise God! The Sign! Lynch 'em!" Others joined in the cry. Rev. McPhule turned loose a buxom sister and stood wide-eyed and erect. His prayers had come true! "Lynch 'em!" he roared.

"We'd better get out of here," said Buggerie, quaking.

"Yes," agreed Snobbcraft, as the assemblage started to move toward them.

Over fences, through bushes, across ditches sped the two men, puffing and wheezing at the unaccustomed exertion, while in hot pursuit came Rev. McPhule followed by his enthusiastic flock.

Slowly the mob gained on the two Virginia aristocrats. Dr. Buggerie stumbled and sprawled on the ground. A dozen men and women fell upon him while he yelled to the speeding Snobbcraft for help. The angular Snobbcraft kept on but Rev. McPhule and several others soon overtook him.

The two men were marched protesting to Happy Hill. The enthused villagers pinched them, pulled them, playfully punched and kicked them during their triumphant march. No one paid the slightest attention to their pleas. Too long had Happy Hill waited for a Negro to lynch. Could the good people hesitate now that the Lord had answered their prayers?

Buggerie wept and Snobbcraft offered large sums of money for their freedom. The money was taken and distributed but the two men were not liberated. They insisted that they were not Negroes but they were only cudgeled for their pains.

At last the gay procession arrived at the long-unused iron post in front of the general store and post office in Happy Hill. As soon as Mr. Snobbcraft saw the post he guessed its significance. Something must be done quickly.

"We're not niggers," he yelled to the mob. "Take off our clothes and look at us. See for yourself. My God! don't lynch white men. We're white the same as you are."

"Yes, gentlemen," bleated Dr. Buggerie, "we're really white men. We just came from a masquerade ball over at Meridian and our plane wrecked. You can't do a thing like this. We're white men, I tell you."

The crowd paused. Even Rev. McPhule seemed convinced. Eager hands tore off the men's garments and revealed their pale white skins underneath. Immediately apology took the place of hatred. The two men were taken over to the general store and permitted to wash off the shoe polish while the crowd, a little disappointed, stood around wondering what to do. They felt cheated. Somebody must be to blame for depriving them of their fun. They began to eye Rev. McPhule. He glanced around nervously.

Suddenly, in the midst of this growing tenseness, an ancient Ford drove up to the outskirts of the crowd and a young man jumped out waving a newspaper.

"Looky here!" he yelled. "They've found out th' damned Demmycratic candidates is niggers. See here: Givens and Snobbcraft. Them's their pictures. They pulled out in airplanes last night or th' mobs wouldda lynched 'em." Men, women and children crowded around the newcomer while he read the account of the flight of the Democratic standard bearers. They gazed at each other bewildered and hurled imprecations upon the heads of the vanished candidates.

Washed and refreshed, Mr. Arthur Snobbcraft and Dr. Samuel Buggerie, each puffing a five-cent cigar (the most expensive sold in the store) appeared again on the porch of the general store. They felt greatly relieved after their narrow escape.

"I told you they wouldn't know who we were," said Snobbcraft disdainfully but softly.

"Who are you folks, anyway?" asked Rev. McPhule, suddenly at their elbow. He was holding the newspaper in his hand. The crowd was watching breathlessly.

"Why-why-y I'm-a-er-a that is . . ." spluttered Snobbcraft.

"Ain't that your pichure?" thundered the evangelist, pointing to the likeness on the front page of the newspaper.

"Why no," Snobbcraft lied, "but—but it looks like me, doesn't it?"

"You're mighty right it does!" said Rev. McPhule, sternly, "and it *is* you, too!"

"No, no, no, that's not me," cried the president of the Anglo-Saxon Association.

"Yes it is," roared McPhule, as the crowd closed in on the two hapless men. "It's you and you're a nigger, accordin' to this here paper, an' a newspaper wouldn't lie." Turning to his followers he commanded, "Take 'em. They're niggers just as I thought. The Lord's will be done. Idea of niggers runnin' on th' Demmycratic ticket!"

The crowd came closer. Buggerie protested that he was really white but it was of no avail. The crowd had sufficient excuse for doing what they had wanted to do at first. They shook their fists in the two men's faces, kicked them, tore off their nondescript garments, searched their pockets and found cards and papers proving their identity, and but for the calmness and presence of mind of the Rev. McPhule, the True Faith Christ Lovers would have torn the unfortunate men limb from limb. The evangelist restrained the more hot-headed individuals and insisted that the ceremonies proceed according to time-honored custom.

So the impetuous yielded to wiser counsel. The two men, vociferously protesting, were stripped naked, held down by husky and willing farm hands and their ears and genitals cut off with jack knives amid the fiendish cries of men and women. When this crude surgery was completed, some wag sewed their ears to their backs and they were released and told to run. Eagerly, in spite of their pain, both men tried to avail themselves of the opportunity. Anything was better than this. Staggering forward through an opening made in the crowd, they attempted to run down the dusty road, blood streaming down their bodies. They had only gone a few feet when, at a signal from the militant evangelist, a half-dozen revolvers cracked and the two Virginians pitched forward into the dust amid the uproarious laughter of the congregation.

The preliminaries ended, the two victims, not yet dead, were picked up, dragged to the stake and bound to it, back to back. Little boys and girls gaily gathered excelsior, scrap paper, twigs and small branches while their proud parents fetched logs, boxes, kerosene and the staves from a cider barrel. The fuel was piled up around the groaning men until only their heads were visible.

When all was in readiness, the people fell back and the Rev. McPhule, as master of ceremonies, ignited the pyre. As the flames shot upward, the dazed men, roused by the flames, strained vainly at the chains that held them. Buggerie found his voice and let out yelp after yelp as the flames licked at his fat flesh. The crowd whooped with glee and Rev. McPhule beamed with satisfaction. The flames rose higher and completely hid the victims from view. The fire crackled merrily and the intense heat drove the spectators back. The odor of cooking meat permeated the clear, country air and many a nostril was guiltily distended. The flames subsided to reveal a red-hot stake supporting two charred hulks.

There were in the assemblage two or three whitened Negroes, who, remembering what their race had suffered in the past, would fain have gone to the assistance of the two men but fear for their own lives restrained them. Even so they were looked at rather sharply by some of the Christ Lovers because they did not appear to be enjoying the spectacle as thoroughly as the rest. Noticing these questioning glances, the whitened Negroes began to yell and prod the burning bodies with sticks and cast stones at them. This exhibition restored them to favor and banished any suspicion that they might not be one-hundred-per-cent Americans.

When the roasting was over and the embers had cooled, the more adventurous members of Rev. McPhule's flock rushed to the stake and groped in the two bodies for skeletal souvenirs such as forefingers, toes and teeth. Proudly their pastor looked on. This was the crowning of a life's ambition. Tomorrow his name would be in every newspaper in the United States. God had indeed answered his prayers. He breathed again his thanks as he thrust his hand into his pocket and felt the soothing touch of the hundred-dollar bill he had extracted from Snobbcraft's pocket. He was supremely happy.

## AND SO ON AND SO ON

In the last days of the Goosie administration, the Surgeon-General of the United States, Dr. Junius Crookman, published a monograph on the differences in skin pigmentation of the real whites and those he had made white by the Black-No-More process. In it he declared, to the consternation of many Americans, that in practically every instance the new Caucasians were from two to three shades lighter than the old Caucasians, and that approximately one-sixth of the population were in the first group. The old Caucasians had never been really white but rather were a pale pink shading down to a sand color and a red. Even when an old Caucasian contracted vitiligo, he pointed out, the skin became much lighter.

To a society that had been taught to venerate whiteness for over three hundred years, this announcement was rather staggering. What was the world coming to, if the blacks were whiter than the whites? Many people in the upper class began to look askance at their very pale complexions. If it were true that extreme whiteness was evidence of the possession of Negro blood, of having once been a member of a pariah class, then surely it were well not to be so white!

Dr. Crookman's amazing brochure started the entire country to examining shades of skin color again. Sunday magazine supplements carried long articles on the subject from the pens of hack writers who knew nothing whatever of pigmentation. Pale people who did not have blue eyes began to be whispered about. The comic weeklies devoted special numbers to the question that was on everyone's lips. Senator Bosh of Mississippi, about to run again for office, referred several times to it in the Congressional Record, his remarks interspersed with "Applauses." A popular song, "Whiter Than White" was being whistled by the entire nation. Among the working classes, in the next few months, there grew up a certain prejudice against all fellow workers who were exceedingly pale.

The new Caucasians began to grow self-conscious and resent the curious gazes bestowed upon their lily-white countenances in all public places. They wrote indignant letters to the newspapers about the insults and discriminations to which they were increasingly becoming subjected. They protested vehemently against the effort on the part of employers to pay them less and on the part of the management of public institutions to segregate them. A delegation that waited upon President Goosie firmly denounced the social trend and called upon the government to do something about it. The Down-With-White-Prejudice-League was founded by one Karl von Beerde, whom some accused of being the same Doctor Beard who had, as a Negro, once headed the National Social Equality League. Offices were established in the Times Square district of New York and the mails were soon laden with releases attempting to prove that those of exceedingly pale skin were just as good as anybody else and should not, therefore, be oppressed. A Dr. Cutten Prodd wrote a book proving that all enduring gifts to society came from those races whose skin color was not exceedingly pale, pointing out that the Norwegians and other Nordic peoples had been in savagery when Egypt and Crete were at the height of their development. Prof. Handen Moutthe, the eminent anthropologist (who was well known for his popular work on *The Sex Life of Left-Handed Morons among the Ainus*) announced that as a result of his long research among the palest citizens, he was convinced they were mentally inferior and that their children should be segregated from the others in school. Professor Moutthe's findings were considered authoritative because he had spent three entire weeks of hard work assembling his data. Four state legislatures immediately began to consider bills calling for separate schools for pale children.

Those of the upper class began to look around for ways to get darker. It became the fashion for them to spend hours at the seashore basking naked in the sunshine and then to dash back, heavily bronzed, to their homes, and, preening themselves in their dusky skins, lord it over their paler, and thus less fortunate, associates. Beauty shops began to sell face powders named *Poudre Nègre, Poudre le Egyptienne* and *L'Afrique*.

Mrs. Sari Blandine (formerly Mme. Sisseretta Blandish of Harlem), who had been working on a steam table in a Broadway Automat, saw her opportunity and began to study skin stains. She stayed away from work one week to read up on the subject at the Public Library and came back to find a recent arrival from Czecho-Slovakia holding down her job.

Mrs. Blandine, however, was not downhearted. She had the information and in three or four weeks time she had a skin stain that would impart a long-wearing light-brown tinge to the pigment. It worked successfully on her young daughter; so successfully, in fact, that the damsel received a proposal of marriage from a young millionaire within a month after applying it.

Free applications were given to all of the young women of the neighborhood. Mrs. Blandine's stain became most popular and her fame grew in her locality. She opened a shop in her front room and soon had it crowded from morning till night. The concoction was patented as Blandine's Egyptienne Stain.

By the time President-Elect Hornbill was inaugurated, her Egyptienne Stain Shoppes dotted the country and she had won three suits for infringement of patent. Everybody that was anybody had a stained skin. A girl without one was avoided by the young men; a young man without one was at a decided disadvantage, economically and socially. A white face became startlingly rare. America was definitely, enthusiastically mulatto-minded.

Imitations of Mrs. Blandine's invention sprang up like weeds in a cemetery. In two years there were fifteen companies manufacturing different kinds of stains and artificial tans. At last, even the Zulu Tan became the vogue among the smart set and it was a common thing to see a sweet young miss stop before a show window and dab her face with charcoal. Enterprising resort keepers in Florida and California, intent on attracting the *haute monde*, hired naturally black bathing girls from Africa until the white women protested against the practice on the ground that it was a menace to family life.

One Sunday morning Surgeon-General Crookman, in looking

over the rotogravure section of his favorite newspaper, saw a photograph of a happy crowd of Americans arrayed in the latest abbreviated bathing suits on the sands at Cannes. In the group he recognized Hank Johnson, Chuck Foster, Bunny Brown and his real Negro wife, former Imperial Grand Wizard and Mrs. Givens and Matthew and Helen Fisher. All of them, he noticed, were quite as dusky as little Matthew Crookman Fisher who played in a sandpile at their feet.

Dr. Crookman smiled wearily and passed the section to his wife.

# THE CONJURE-MAN DIES

## A MYSTERY TALE OF DARK HARLEM

*Rudolph Fisher*

# Chapter One

I

ENCOUNTERING the bright-lighted gaiety of Harlem's Seventh Avenue, the frigid midwinter night seemed to relent a little. She had given Battery Park a chill stare and she would undoubtedly freeze the Bronx. But here in this midrealm of rhythm and laughter she seemed to grow warmer and friendlier, observing, perhaps, that those who dwelt here were mysteriously dark like herself.

Of this favor the Avenue promptly took advantage. Sidewalks barren throughout the cold white day now sprouted life like fields in spring. Along swung boys in camels' hair beside girls in bunny and muskrat; broad, flat heels clacked, high narrow ones clicked, reluctantly leaving the disgorging theaters or eagerly seeking the voracious dance halls. There was loud jest and louder laughter and the frequent uplifting of merry voices in the moment's most popular song:

> "*I'll be glad when you're dead, you rascal you,*
> *I'll be glad when you're dead, you rascal you.*
> *What is it that you've got*
> *Makes my wife think you so hot?*
> *Oh you dog—I'll be glad when you're gone!*"

But all of black Harlem was not thus gay and bright. Any number of dark, chill, silent side streets declined the relenting night's favor. 130th Street, for example, east of Lenox Avenue, was at this moment cold, still, and narrowly forbidding; one glanced down this block and was glad one's destination lay elsewhere. Its concentrated gloom was only intensified by an occasional spangle of electric light, splashed ineffectually against the blackness, or by the unearthly pallor of the sky, into which a wall of dwellings rose to hide the moon.

Among the houses in this looming row, one reared a little taller and gaunter than its fellows, so that the others appeared to shrink from it and huddle together in the shadow on either side. The basement of this house was quite black; its first floor, high above the sidewalk and approached by a long graystone stoop, was only dimly lighted; its second floor was lighted more dimly still, while the third, which was the top, was vacantly dark again like the basement. About the place hovered an oppressive silence, as if those who entered here were warned beforehand not to speak above a whisper. There was, like a footnote, in one of the two first-floor windows to the left of the entrance a black-on-white sign reading:

"Samuel Crouch, Undertaker."

On the narrow panel to the right of the doorway the silver letters of another sign obscurely glittered on an onyx background:

"N. Frimbo, Psychist."

Between the two signs receded the high, narrow vestibule, terminating in a pair of tall glass-paneled doors. Glass curtains, tightly stretched in vertical folds, dimmed the already too-subdued illumination beyond.

2

It was about an hour before midnight that one of the doors rattled and flew open, revealing the bareheaded, short, round figure of a young man who manifestly was profoundly agitated and in a great hurry. Without closing the door behind him, he rushed down the stairs, sped straight across the street, and in a moment was frantically pushing the bell of the dwelling directly opposite. A tall, slender, light-skinned man of obviously habitual composure answered the excited summons.

"Is—is you him?" stammered the agitated one, pointing to a shingle labeled "John Archer, M.D."

"Yes—I'm Dr. Archer."

"Well, arch on over here, will you, doc?" urged the caller. "Sump'm done happened to Frimbo."

"Frimbo? The fortune teller?"

"Step on it, will you, doc?"

Shortly, the physician, bag in hand, was hurrying up the graystone stoop behind his guide. They passed through the still open door into a hallway and mounted a flight of thickly car-peted stairs.

At the head of the staircase a tall, lank, angular figure awaited them. To this person the short, round, black, and by now quite breathless guide panted, "I got one, boy! This here's the doc from 'cross the street. Come on, doc. Right in here."

Dr. Archer, in passing, had an impression of a young man as long and lean as himself, of a similarly light complexion except for a profusion of dark brown freckles, and of a curiously scowl-ing countenance that glowered from either ill humor or appre-hension. The doctor rounded the banister head and strode behind his pilot toward the front of the house along the upper hallway, midway of which, still following the excited short one, he turned and swung into a room that opened into the hall at that point. The tall fellow brought up the rear.

Within the room the physician stopped, looking about in surprise. The chamber was almost entirely in darkness. The walls appeared to be hung from ceiling to floor with black vel-vet drapes. Even the ceiling was covered, the heavy folds of cloth converging from the four corners to gather at a central point above, from which dropped a chain suspending the single strange source of light, a device which hung low over a chair behind a large desk-like table, yet left these things and indeed most of the room unlighted. This was because, instead of shedding its radiance downward and outward as would an or-dinary shaded droplight, this mechanism focused a horizontal beam upon a second chair on the opposite side of the table. Clearly the person who used the chair beneath the odd spot-light could remain in relative darkness while the occupant of the other chair was brightly illuminated.

"There he is—jes' like Jinx found him."

And now in the dark chair beneath the odd lamp the doctor made out a huddled, shadowy form. Quickly he stepped for-ward.

"Is this the only light?"

"Only one I've seen."

Dr. Archer procured a flashlight from his bag and swept its faint beam over the walls and ceiling. Finding no sign of an-other lighting fixture, he directed the instrument in his hand toward the figure in the chair and saw a bare black head inclined limply sidewise, a flaccid countenance with open mouth and fixed eyes staring from under drooping lids.

"Can't do much in here. Anybody up front?"

"Yes, suh. Two ladies."

"Have to get him outside. Let's see. I know. Downstairs. Down in Crouch's. There's a sofa. You men take hold and get him down there. This way."

There was some hesitancy. "Mean us, doc?"

"Of course. Hurry. He doesn't look so hot now."

"I ain't none too warm, myself," murmured the short one. But he and his friend obeyed, carrying out their task with a dispatch born of distaste. Down the stairs they followed Dr. Archer, and into the undertaker's dimly lighted front room.

"Oh, Crouch!" called the doctor. "Mr. Crouch!"

"That 'mister' ought to get him."

But there was no answer. "Guess he's out. That's right—put him on the sofa. Push that other switch by the door. Good."

Dr. Archer inspected the supine figure as he reached into his bag. "Not so good," he commented. Beneath his black satin robe the patient wore ordinary clothing—trousers, vest, shirt, collar and tie. Deftly the physician bared the chest; with one hand he palpated the heart area while with the other he adjusted the ear-pieces of his stethoscope. He bent over, placed the bell of his instrument on the motionless dark chest, and listened a long time. He removed the instrument, disconnected first one, then the other, rubber tube at their junction with the bell, blew vigorously through them in turn, replaced them, and repeated the operation of listening. At last he stood erect.

"Not a twitch," he said.

"Long gone, huh?"

"Not so long. Still warm. But gone."

The short young man looked at his scowling freckled companion.

"What'd I tell you?" he whispered. "Was I right or wasn't I?"

The tall one did not answer but watched the doctor. The doctor put aside his stethoscope and inspected the patient's head more closely, the parted lips and half-open eyes. He extended a hand and with his extremely long fingers gently palpated the scalp. "Hello," he said. He turned the far side of the head toward him and looked first at that side, then at his fingers.

"Wh-what?"

"Blood in his hair," announced the physician. He procured a gauze dressing from his bag, wiped his moist fingers, thoroughly sponged and reinspected the wound. Abruptly he turned to the two men, whom until now he had treated quite impersonally. Still imperturbably, but incisively, in the manner of lancing an abscess, he asked, "Who are you two gentlemen?"

"Why—uh—this here's Jinx Jenkins, doc. He's my buddy, see? Him and me——"

"And you—if I don't presume?"

"Me? I'm Bubber Brown——"

"Well, how did this happen, Mr. Brown?"

"'Deed I don' know, doc. What you mean—is somebody killed him?"

"You don't know?" Dr. Archer regarded the pair curiously a moment, then turned back to examine further. From an instrument case he took a probe and proceeded to explore the wound in the dead man's scalp. "Well—what do you know about it, then?" he asked, still probing. "Who found him?"

"Jinx," answered the one who called himself Bubber. "We jes' come here to get this Frimbo's advice 'bout a little business project we thought up. Jinx went in to see him. I waited in the waitin' room. Presently Jinx come bustin' out pop-eyed and beckoned to me. I went back with him—and there was Frimbo, jes' like you found him. We didn't even know he was over the river."

"Did he fall against anything and strike his head?"

"No, suh, doc." Jinx became articulate. "He didn't do nothin' the whole time I was in there. Nothin' but talk. He tol' me who I was and what I wanted befo' I could open my mouth. Well, I said that I knowed that much already and that I come to find out sump'm I didn't know. Then he went on talkin', tellin' me plenty. He knowed his stuff all right. But all of a sudden he stopped talkin' and mumbled sump'm 'bout not bein' able to see. Seem like he got scared, and he say, 'Frimbo, why don't you see?' Then he didn't say no more. He sound' so funny I got scared myself and jumped up and grabbed that light and turned it on him—and there he was."

"M-m."

Dr. Archer, pursuing his examination, now indulged in what appeared to be a characteristic habit: he began to talk as he worked, to talk rather absently and wordily on a matter which at first seemed inapropos.

"I," said he, "am an exceedingly curious fellow." Deftly, delicately, with half-closed eyes, he was manipulating his probe. "Questions are forever popping into my head. For example, which of you two gentlemen, if either, stands responsible for the expenses of medical attention in this unfortunate instance?"

"Mean who go'n' pay you?"

"That," smiled the doctor, "makes it rather a bald question."

Bubber grinned understandingly.

"Well here's one with hair on it, doc," he said. "Who got the medical attention?"

"M-m," murmured the doctor. "I was afraid of that. Not," he added, "that I am moved by mercenary motives. Oh, not at all. But if I am not to be paid in the usual way, in coin of the realm, then of course I must derive my compensation in some other form of satisfaction. Which, after all, is the end of all our getting and spending, is it not?"

"Oh, sho'," agreed Bubber.

"Now this case"—the doctor dropped the gauze dressing into his bag—"even robbed of its material promise, still bids well to feed my native curiosity—if not my cellular protoplasm. You follow me, of course?"

"With my tongue hangin' out," said Bubber.

But that part of his mind which was directing this discourse did not give rise to the puzzled expression on the physician's lean, light-skinned countenance as he absently moistened another dressing with alcohol, wiped off his fingers and his probe, and stood up again.

"We'd better notify the police," he said. "You men"—he looked at them again—"you men call up the precinct."

They promptly started for the door.

"No—you don't have to go out. The cops, you see"—he was almost confidential—"the cops will want to question all of us. Mr. Crouch has a phone back there. Use that."

They exchanged glances but obeyed.

"I'll be thinking over my findings."

Through the next room they scuffled and into the back of the long first-floor suite. There they abruptly came to a halt and again looked at each other, but now for an entirely different reason. Along one side of this room, hidden from view until their entrance, stretched a long narrow table draped with a white sheet that covered an unmistakably human form. There was not much light. The two young men stood quite still.

"Seem like it's—occupied," murmured Bubber.

"Another one," mumbled Jinx.

"Where's the phone?"

"Don't ask me. I got both eyes full."

"There 'tis—on that desk. Go on—use it."

"Use it yo' own black self," suggested Jinx. "I'm goin' back."

"No you ain't. Come on. We use it together."

"All right. But if that whosis says 'Howdy' tell it I said 'Goo'by.'"

"And where the hell you think I'll be if it says 'Howdy'?"

"What a place to have a telephone!"

"Step on it, slow motion."

"Hello!—Hello!" Bubber rattled the hook. "Hey operator! Operator!"

"My Gawd," said Jinx, "is the phone dead too?"

"Operator—gimme the station—quick. . . . Pennsylvania? No ma'am—New York—Harlem—listen, lady, not railroad. Police. *Please*, ma'am. . . . Hello—hey—send a flock o' cops around here—Frimbo's—the fortune teller's—yea—Thirteen West 130th—yea—somebody done put that thing on him! . . . Yea—O.K."

Hurriedly they returned to the front room where Dr. Archer was pacing back and forth, his hands thrust into his pockets, his brow pleated into troubled furrows.

"They say hold everything, doc. Be right over."

"Good." The doctor went on pacing.

Jinx and Bubber surveyed the recumbent form. Said Bubber, "If he could keep folks from dyin', how come he didn't keep hisself from it?"

"Reckon he didn't have time to put no spell on hisself," Jinx surmised.

"No," returned Bubber grimly. "But somebody else had time to put one on him. I knowed sump'm was comin'. I told you. First time I seen death on the moon since I been grown. And they's two mo' yet."

"How you reckon it happened?"

"You askin' me?" Bubber said. "You was closer to him than I was."

"It was plumb dark all around. Somebody could'a' snook up behind him and crowned him while he was talkin' to me. But I didn't hear a sound. Say—I better catch air. This thing's puttin' me on the well-known spot, ain't it?"

"All right, dumbo. Run away and prove you done it. Wouldn't that be a bright move?"

Dr. Archer said, "The wisest thing for you men to do is stay here and help solve this puzzle. You'd be called in anyway—you found the body, you see. Running away looks as if you were— well—running away."

"What'd I tell you?" said Bubber.

"All right," growled Jinx. "But I can't see how they could blame anybody for runnin' away from this place. Graveyard's a playground side o' this."

# Chapter Two

O F THE ten Negro members of Harlem's police force to be promoted from the rank of patrolman to that of detective, Perry Dart was one of the first. As if the city administration had wished to leave no doubt in the public mind as to its intention in the matter, they had chosen, in him, a man who could not have been under any circumstances mistaken for aught but a Negro; or perhaps, as Dart's intimates insisted, they had chosen him because his generously pigmented skin rendered him invisible in the dark, a conceivably great advantage to a detective who did most of his work at night. In any case, the somber hue of his integument in no wise reflected the complexion of his brain, which was bright, alert, and practical within such territory as it embraced. He was a Manhattanite by birth, had come up through the public schools, distinguished himself in athletics at the high school he attended, and, having himself grown up with the black colony, knew Harlem from lowest dive to loftiest temple. He was rather small of stature, with unusually thin, fine features, which falsely accentuated the slightness of his slender but wiry body.

It was Perry Dart's turn for a case when Bubber Brown's call came in to the station, and to it Dart, with four uniformed men, was assigned.

Five minutes later he was in the entrance of Thirteen West 130th Street, greeting Dr. Archer, whom he knew. His men, one black, two brown, and one yellow, loomed in the hallway about him large and ominous, but there was no doubt as to who was in command.

"Hello, Dart," the physician responded to his greeting. "I'm glad you're on this one. It'll take a little active cerebration."

"Come on down, doc," the little detective grinned with a flash of white teeth. "You're talking to a cop now, not a college professor. What've you got?"

"A man that'll tell no tales." The physician motioned to the undertaker's front room. "He's in there."

Dart turned to his men. "Day, you cover the front of the place. Green, take the roof and cover the back yard. Johnson, search the house and get everybody you find into one room. Leave a light everywhere you go if possible—I'll want to check up. Brady, you stay with me." Then he turned back and followed the doctor into the undertaker's parlor. They stepped over to the sofa, which was in a shallow alcove formed by the front bay windows of the room.

"How'd he get it, doc?" he asked.

"To tell you the truth, I haven't the slightest idea."

"Somebody crowned him," Bubber helpfully volunteered.

"Has anybody ast you anything?" Jinx inquired gruffly.

Dart bent over the victim.

The physician said:

"There is a scalp wound all right. See it?"

"Yea—now that you mentioned it."

"But that didn't kill him."

"No? How do you know it didn't, doc?"

"That wound is too slight. It's not in a spot that would upset any vital center. And there isn't any fracture under it."

"Couldn't a man be killed by a blow on the head that didn't fracture his skull?"

"Well—yes. If it fell just so that its force was concentrated on certain parts of the brain. I've never heard of such a case, but it's conceivable. But this blow didn't land in the right place for that. A blow at this point would cause death only by producing intracranial hemorrhage——"

"Couldn't you manage to say it in English, doc?"

"Sure. He'd have to bleed inside his head."

"That's more like it."

"The resulting accumulation of blood would raise the intra —the pressure inside his head to such a point that vital centers would be paralyzed. The power would be shut down. His heart and lungs would quit cold. See? Just like turning off a light."

"O.K. if you say so. But how do you know he didn't bleed inside his head?"

"Well, there aren't but two things that would cause him to."

"I'm learning, doc. Go on."

"Brittle arteries with no give in them—no elasticity. If he had them, he wouldn't even have to be hit—just excitement might shoot up the blood pressure and pop an artery. See what I mean?"

"That's apoplexy, isn't it?"

"Right. And the other thing would be a blow heavy enough to fracture the skull and so rupture the blood vessels beneath. Now this man is about your age or mine—somewhere in his middle thirties. His arteries are soft—feel his wrists. For a blow to kill this man outright, it would have had to fracture his skull."

"Hot damn!" whispered Bubber admiringly. "Listen to the doc do his stuff!"

"And his skull isn't fractured?" said Dart.

"Not if probing means anything."

"Don't tell me you've X-rayed him too?" grinned the detective.

"Any fracture that would kill this man outright wouldn't have to be X-rayed."

"Then you're sure the blow didn't kill him?"

"Not by itself, it didn't."

"Do you mean that maybe he was killed first and hit afterwards?"

"Why would anybody do that?" Dr. Archer asked.

"To make it seem like violence when it was really something else."

"I see. But no. If this man had been dead when the blow was struck, he wouldn't have bled at all. Circulation would already have stopped."

"That's right."

"But of one thing I'm sure: that wound is evidence of too slight a blow to kill."

"Specially," interpolated Bubber, "a hard-headed cullud man——"

"There you go ag'in," growled his lanky companion.

"He's right," the doctor said. "It takes a pretty hefty impact to bash in a skull. With a padded weapon," he went on, "a fatal blow would have had to be crushing to make even so slight a scalp wound as this. That's out. And a hard, unpadded weapon that would break the scalp just slightly like this, with only a little bleeding and without even cracking the skull, could at most have delivered only a stunning blow, not a fatal one. Do you see what I mean?"

"Sure. You mean this man was just stunned by the blow and actually died from something else."

"That's the way it looks to me."

"Well—anyhow he's dead and the circumstances indicate at least a possibility of death by violence. That justifies notifying us, all right. And it makes it a case for the medical examiner. But we really don't know that he's been killed, do we?"

"No. Not yet."

"All the more a case for the medical examiner, then. Is there a phone here, doc? Good. Brady, go back there and call the precinct. Tell 'em to get the medical examiner here double time and to send me four more men—doesn't matter who. Now tell me, doc. What time did this man go out of the picture?"

The physician smiled

"Call Meridian 7–1212."

"O.K., doc. But approximately?"

"Well, he was certainly alive an hour ago. Perhaps even half an hour ago. Hardly less."

"How long have you been here?"

"About fifteen minutes."

"Then he must have been killed—if he was killed—say anywhere from five to thirty-five minutes before you got here?"

"Yes."

Bubber, the insuppressible, commented to Jinx, "Damn! That's trimming it down to a gnat's heel, ain't it?" But Jinx only responded, "Fool, will you hush?"

"Who discovered him—do you know?"

"These two men."

"Both of you?" Dart asked the pair.

"No, suh," Bubber answered. "Jinx here discovered the man. I discovered the doctor."

Dart started to question them further, but just then Johnson, the officer who had been directed to search the house, reappeared.

"Been all over," he reported. "Only two people in the place. Women—both scared green."

"All right," the detective said. "Take these two men up to the same room. I'll be up presently."

Officer Brady returned. "Medical examiner's comin' right up."

The detective said, "Was he on this sofa when you got here, doc?"

"No. He was upstairs in his—his consultation room, I guess

you'd call it. Queer place. Dark as sin. Sitting slumped down in a chair. The light was impossible. You see, I thought I'd been called to a patient, not a corpse. So I had him brought where I knew I could examine him. Of course, if I had thought of murder——"

"Never mind. There's no law against your moving him or examining him, even if you had suspected murder—as long as you weren't trying to hide anything. People think there's some such law, but there isn't."

"The medical examiner'll probably be sore, though."

"Let him. We've got more than the medical examiner to worry about."

"Yes. You've got a few questions to ask."

"And answer. How, when, where, why, and who? Oh, I'm great at questions. But the answers——"

"Well, we've the 'when' narrowed down to a half-hour period." Dr. Archer glanced at his watch. "That would be between ten-thirty and eleven. And 'where' shouldn't be hard to verify—right here in his own chair, if those two fellows are telling it straight. 'Why' and 'who'—those'll be your little red wagon. 'How' right now is mine. I can't imagine——"

Again he turned to the supine figure, staring. Suddenly his lean countenance grew blanker than usual. Still staring, he took the detective by the arm. "Dart," he said reflectively, "we smart people are often amazingly—dumb."

"You're telling me?"

"We waste precious moments in useless speculation. We indulge ourselves in the extravagance of reason when a frugal bit of observation would suffice."

"Does prescription liquor affect you like that, doc?"

"Look at that face."

"Well—if you insist——"

"Just the general appearance of that face—the eyes—the open mouth. What does it look like?"

"Looks like he's gasping for breath."

"Exactly. Dart, this man might—might, you understand—have been choked."

"Ch——"

"Stunned by a blow over the ear——"

"To prevent a struggle!"

"—and choked to death. As simple as that."

"Choked! But just how?"

Eagerly, Dr. Archer once more bent over the lifeless countenance. "There are two ways," he dissertated in his roundabout fashion, "of interrupting respiration." He was peering into the mouth. "What we shall call, for simplicity, the external and the internal. In this case the external would be rather indeterminate, since we could hardly make out the usual bluish discolorations on a neck of this complexion." He procured two tongue depressors and, one in each hand, examined as far back into the throat as he could. He stopped talking as some discovery further elevated his already high interest. He discarded one depressor, reached for his flashlight with the hand thus freed, and, still holding the first depressor in place, directed his light into the mouth as if he were examining tonsils. With a little grunt of discovery, he now discarded the flashlight also, took a pair of long steel thumb-forceps from a flap in the side of his bag, and inserted the instrument into the victim's mouth alongside the guiding tongue-depressor. Dart and the uniformed officer watched silently as the doctor apparently tried to remove something from the throat of the corpse. Once, twice, the prongs snapped together, and he withdrew the instrument empty. But the next time the forceps caught hold of the physician's discovery and drew it forth.

It was a large, blue-bordered, white handkerchief.

# Chapter Three

## I

"DOC," said Dart, "you don't mind hanging around with us a while?"

"Try and shake me loose," grinned Dr. Archer. "This promises to be worth seeing."

"If you'd said no," Dart grinned back, "I'd have held you anyhow as a suspect. I'm going to need some of your brains. I'm not one of these bright ones that can do all the answers in my head. I'm just a poor boy trying to make a living, and this kind of a riddle hasn't been popped often enough in my life to be easy yet. I've seen some funny ones, but this is funnier. One thing I can see—that this guy wasn't put out by any beginner."

"The man that did this," agreed the physician, "thought about it first. I've seen autopsies that could have missed that handkerchief. It was pushed back almost out of sight."

"That makes you a smart boy."

"I admit it. Wonder whose handkerchief?"

"Stick it in your bag and hang on to it. And let's get going."

"Whither?"

"To get acquainted with this layout first. Whoever's here will keep a while. The bird that pulled the job is probably in Egypt by now."

"That wouldn't be my guess."

"You think he'd hang around?"

"He wouldn't do the expected thing—not if he was bright enough to think up a gag like this."

"Gag is good. Let's start with the roof. Brady, you come with me and the doc—and be ready for surprises. Where's Day?"

The doctor closed and picked up his bag. They passed into the hallway. Officer Day was on guard in the front vestibule according to his orders.

"There are four more men and the medical examiner coming,"

the detective told him. "The four will be right over. Put one on the rear of the house and send the others upstairs. Come on, doc."

The three men ascended two flights of stairs to the top floor. The slim Dart led, the tall doctor followed, the stalwart Brady brought up the rear. Along the uppermost hallway they made their way to the front of the third story of the house, moving with purposeful resoluteness, yet with a sharp-eyed caution that anticipated almost any eventuality. The physician and the detective carried their flashlights, the policeman his revolver.

At the front end of the hallway they found a closed door. It was unlocked. Dart flung it open, to find the ceiling light on, probably left by Officer Johnson in obedience to instructions.

This room was a large bedchamber, reaching, except for the width of the hallway, across the breadth of the house. It was luxuriously appointed. The bed was a massive four-poster of mahogany, intricately carved and set off by a counterpane of gold satin. It occupied the mid-portion of a large black-and-yellow Chinese rug which covered almost the entire floor. Two upholstered chairs, done also in gold satin, flanked the bed, and a settee of similar design guarded its foot. An elaborate smoking stand sat beside the head of the bed. A mahogany chest and bureau, each as substantial as the four-poster, completed the furniture.

"No question as to whose room this is," said Dart.

"A man's," diagnosed Archer. "A man of means and definite ideas, good or bad—but definite. Too bare to be a woman's room—look—the walls are stark naked. There aren't any frills" —he sniffed—"and there isn't any perfume."

"I guess you've been in enough women's rooms to know."

"Men's too. But this is odd. Notice anything conspicuous by its absence?"

"I'll bite."

"Photographs of women."

The detective's eyes swept the room in verification.

"Woman hater?"

"Maybe," said the doctor, "but——"

"Wait a minute," said the detective. There was a clothes closet to the left of the entrance. He turned, opened its door, and played his flashlight upon its contents. An array of masculine attire extended in orderly suspension—several suits of various patterns hanging from individual racks. On the back of the open door hung a suit of black pajamas. On the floor a half-dozen pairs of shoes were set in an orderly row. There was no suggestion of any feminine contact or influence; there was simply the atmosphere of an exceptionally well ordered, decided masculinity.

"What do you think?" asked Dr. Archer.

"Woman hater," repeated Dart conclusively.

"Or a Lothario of the deepest dye."

The detective looked at the doctor. "I get the deep dye—he was blacker'n me. But the Lothario——"

"Isn't it barely possible that this so very complete—er—repudiation of woman is too complete to be accidental? May it not be deliberate—a wary suppression of evidence—the recourse of a lover of great experience and wisdom, who lets not his right hand know whom his left embraceth?"

"Not good—just careful?"

"He couldn't be married—actively. His wife's influence would be—smelt. And if he isn't married, this over-absence of the feminine—well—it means something."

"I still think it could mean woman-hating. This other guesswork of yours sounds all bass-ackwards to me."

"Heaven forfend, good friend, that you should lose faith in my judgment. Woman-hater you call him and woman-hater he is. Carry on."

2

A narrow little room the width of the hallway occupied that extent of the front not taken up by the master bedroom. In this they found a single bed, a small table, and a chair, but nothing of apparent significance.

Along the hallway they now retraced their steps, trying each of three successive doors that led off from this passage. The first was an empty store-room, the second a white tiled bathroom, and the third a bare closet. These yielded no suggestion of the sort of character or circumstances with which they might be dealing. Nor did the smaller of the two rooms terminating the hallway at its back end, for this was merely a narrow kitchen, with a tiny range, a table, icebox, and cabinet. In these they found no inspiration.

But the larger of the two rear rooms was arresting enough. This was a study, fitted out in a fashion that would have warmed the heart and stirred the ambition of any student. There were two large brown-leather club chairs, each with its end table and reading lamp; a similarly upholstered divan in front of a fireplace that occupied the far wall, and over toward the windows at the rear, a flat-topped desk, upon which sat a bronze desk-lamp, and behind which sat a large swivel armchair. Those parts of the walls not taken up by the fireplace and windows were solid masses of books, being fitted from the floor to the level of a tall man's head with crowded shelves.

Dr. Archer was at once absorbed. "This man was no ordinary fakir," he observed. "Look." He pointed out several framed documents on the upper parts of the walls. "Here——" He approached the largest and peered long upon it. Dart came near, looked at it once, and grinned:

"Does it make sense, doc?"

"Bachelor's degree from Harvard. N'Gana Frimbo. N'Gana——"

"Not West Indian?"

"No. This sounds definitely African to me. Lots of them have that N'. The 'Frimbo' suggests it, too—mumbo—jumbo—sambo——"

"Limbo——"

"Wonder why he chose an American college? Most of the chiefs' sons'll go to Oxford or bust. I know—this fellow is probably from Liberia or thereabouts. American influence—see?"

"How'd he get into a racket like fortune telling?"

"Ask me another. Probably a better racket than medicine in this community. A really clever chap could do wonders."

The doctor was glancing along the rows of books. He noted such titles as Tankard's *Determinism and Fatalism, a Critical Contrast*, Bostwick's *The Concept of Inevitability*, Preem's *Cause and Effect*, Dessault's *The Science of History*, and Fairclough's *The Philosophical Basis of Destiny*. He took this last from its place, opened to a flyleaf, and read in script, "N'Gana

Frimbo" and a date. Riffling the pages, he saw in the same script penciled marginal notes at frequent intervals. At the end of the chapter entitled "Unit Stimulus and Reaction," the penciled notation read: "Fairclough too has missed the great secret."

"This is queer."

"What?"

"A native African, a Harvard graduate, a student of philosophy—and a sorcerer. There's something wrong with that picture."

"Does it throw any light on who killed him?"

"Anything that throws light on the man's character might help."

"Well, let's get going. I want to go through the rest of the house and get down to the real job. You worry about his character. I'll worry about the character of the suspects."

"Right-o. Your move, professor."

# Chapter Four

MEANWHILE Jinx and Bubber, in Frimbo's waiting-room on the second floor, were indulging in one of their characteristic arguments. This one had started with Bubber's chivalrous endeavors to ease the disturbing situation for the two women, both of whom were bewildered and distraught and one of whom was young and pretty. Bubber had not only announced and described in detail just what he had seen, but, heedless of the fact that the younger woman had almost fainted, had proceeded to explain how he had known, long before it occurred, that he had been about to "see death." To dispel any remaining vestiges of tranquillity, he had added that the death of Frimbo was but one of three. Two more were at hand.

"Soon as Jinx here called me," he said, "I knowed somebody's time had come. I busted on in that room yonder with him—y'all seen me go—and sho' 'nough, there was the man, limp as a rag and stiff as a board. Y' see, the moon don't lie. 'Cose most signs ain't no 'count. As for me, you won't find nobody black as me that's less suprastitious."

"Jes' say we won't find nobody black as you and stop. That'll be the truth," growled Jinx.

"But a moonsign is different. Moonsign is the one sign you can take for sho'. Moonsign——"

"Moonshine is what you took for sho' tonight," Jinx said.

"Red moon mean bloodshed, new moon over your right shoulder mean good luck, new moon over your left shoulder mean bad luck, and so on. Well, they's one moonsign my grandmammy taught me befo' I was knee high and that's the worst sign of 'em all. And that's the sign I seen tonight. I was walkin' down the Avenue feelin' fine and breathin' the air——"

"What do you breathe when you don't feel so good?"

"—smokin' the gals over, watchin' the cars roll by—feelin' good, you know what I mean. And then all of a sudden I stopped. I store."

"You whiched?"

"Store. I stopped and I store."

"What language you talkin'?"

"I store at the sky. And as I stood there starin', sump'm didn't seem right. Then I seen what it was. Y' see, they was a full moon in the sky——"

"Funny place for a full moon, wasn't it?"

"—and as I store at it, they come up a cloud—wasn't but one cloud in the whole sky—and that cloud come up and crossed over the face o' the moon and blotted it out—jes' like that."

"You sho' 'twasn't yo' shadow?"

"Well there was the black cloud in front o' the moon and the white moonlight all around it and behind it. All of a sudden I seen what was wrong. That cloud had done took the shape of a human skull!"

"Sweet Jesus!" The older woman's whisper betokened the proper awe. She was an elongated, incredibly thin creature, illfavored in countenance and apparel; her loose, limp, angular figure was grotesquely disposed over a stiff-backed arm-chair, and dark, nondescript clothing draped her too long limbs. Her squarish, fashionless hat was a little awry, her scrawny visage, already disquieted, was now inordinately startled, the eyes almost comically wide above the high cheek bones, the mouth closed tight over her teeth whose forward slant made the lips protrude as if they were puckering to whistle.

The younger woman, however, seemed not to hear. Those dark eyes surely could sparkle brightly, those small lips smile, that clear honey skin glow with animation; but just now the eyes stared unseeingly, the lips were a short, hard, straight line, the skin of her round pretty face almost colorless. She was obviously dazed by the suddenness of this unexpected tragedy. Unlike the other woman, however, she had not lost her poise, though it was costing her something to retain it. The trim, black, high-heeled shoes, the light sheer stockings, the black seal coat which fell open to reveal a white-bordered pimiento dress, even the small close-fitting black hat, all were quite as they should be. Only her isolating detachment betrayed the effect upon her of the presence of death and the law.

"A human skull!" repeated Bubber. "Yes, ma'am. Blottin' out the moon. You know what that is?"

"What?" said the older woman.

"That's death on the moon. It's a moonsign and it's never been known to fail."

"And it means death?"

"Worse 'n that, ma'am. It means three deaths. Whoever see death on the moon"—he paused, drew breath, and went on in an impressive lower tone—"gonna see death three times!"

"My soul and body!" said the lady.

But Jinx saw fit to summon logic. "Mean you go'n' see two more folks dead?"

"Gonna stare 'em in the face."

"Then somebody ought to poke yo' eyes out in self-defense."

Having with characteristic singleness of purpose discharged his duty as a gentleman and done all within his power to set the ladies' minds at rest, Bubber could now turn his attention to the due and proper quashing of his unappreciative commentator.

"Whyn't you try it?" he suggested.

"Try what?"

"Pokin' my eyes out."

"Huh. If I thought that was the onliest way to keep from dyin', you could get yo'self a tin cup and a cane tonight."

"Try it then."

" 'Tain't necessary. That moonshine you had'll take care o' everything. Jes' give it another hour to work and you'll be blind as a Baltimo' alley."

"Trouble with you," said Bubber, "is, you' ignorant. You' dumb. The inside o' yo' head is all black."

"Like the outside o' yourn."

"Is you by any chance alludin' to me?"

"I ain't alludin' to that policeman over yonder."

"Lucky for you he is over yonder, else you wouldn't be alludin' at all."

"Now you gettin' bad, ain't you? Jus' 'cause you know you got the advantage over me."

"What advantage?"

"How could I hit you when I can't even see you?"

"Well if I was ugly as you is, I wouldn't want nobody to see me."

"Don't worry, son. Nobody'll ever know how ugly you is. Yo' ugliness is shrouded in mystery."

"Well yo' dumbness ain't. It's right there for all the world to see. You ought to be back in Africa with the other dumb boogies."

"African boogies ain't dumb," explained Jinx. "They' jes' dark. You ain't been away from there long, is you?"

"My folks," returned Bubber crushingly, "left Africa ten generations ago."

"Yo' folks? Shuh. Ten generations ago, you-all wasn't folks. You-all hadn't qualified as apes."

Thus as always, their exchange of compliments flowed toward the level of family history, among other Harlemites a dangerous explosive which a single word might strike into instantaneous violence. It was only because the hostility of these two was actually an elaborate masquerade, whereunder they concealed the most genuine affection for each other, that they could come so close to blows that were never offered.

Yet to the observer this mock antagonism would have appeared alarmingly real. Bubber's squat figure sidled belligerently up to the long and lanky Jinx; solid as a fire-plug he stood, set to grapple; and he said with unusual distinctness:

"Yea? Well—yo' granddaddy was a hair on a baboon's tail. What does that make you?"

The policeman's grin of amusement faded. The older woman stifled a cry of apprehension.

The younger woman still sat motionless and staring, wholly unaware of what was going on.

# Chapter Five

I

DETECTIVE DART, Dr. Archer, and Officer Brady made a rapid survey of the basement and cellar. The basement, a few feet below sidewalk level, proved to be one long, low-ceilinged room, fitted out, evidently by the undertaker, as a simple meeting-room for those clients who required the use of a chapel. There were many rows of folding wooden chairs facing a low platform at the far end of the room. In the middle of this platform rose a pulpit stand, and on one side against the wall stood a small reed organ. A heavy dark curtain across the rear of the platform separated it and the meeting-place from a brief unimproved space behind that led through a back door into the back yard. The basement hallway, in the same relative position as those above, ran alongside the meeting-room and ended in this little hinder space. In one corner of this, which must originally have been the kitchen, was the small door of a dumbwaiter shaft which led to the floor above. The shaft contained no sign of a dumbwaiter now, as Dart's flashlight disclosed: above were the dangling gears and broken ropes of a mechanism long since discarded, and below, an empty pit.

They discovered nearby the doorway to the cellar stairs, which proved to be the usual precipitate series of narrow planks. In the cellar, which was poorly lighted by a single central droplight, they found a large furnace, a coal bin, and, up forward, a nondescript heap of shadowy junk such as cellars everywhere seem to breed.

All this appeared for the time being unimportant, and so they returned to the second floor, where the victim had originally been found. Dart had purposely left this floor till the last. It was divided into three rooms, front, middle and back, and these they methodically visited in order.

They entered the front room, Frimbo's reception room, just as Bubber sidled belligerently up to Jinx. Apparently their entrance discouraged further hostilities, for with one or two

398

upward, sidelong glares from Bubber, neutralized by an inarticulate growl or two from Jinx, the imminent combat faded mysteriously away and the atmosphere cleared.

But now the younger woman's eyes lifted to recognize Dr. John Archer. She jumped up and went to him.

"Hello, Martha," he said.

"What does it mean, John?"

"Don't let it upset you. Looks like the conjure-man had an enemy, that's all."

"It's true—he really is——?"

"I'm afraid so. This is Detective Dart. Mrs. Crouch, Mr. Dart."

"Good-evening," Mrs. Crouch said mechanically and turned back to her chair.

"Dart's a friend of mine, Martha," said the physician. "He'll take my word for your innocence, never fear."

The older woman, refusing to be ignored, said impatiently, "How long you 'spect us to sit here? What we waitin' for? We didn' kill him."

"Of course not," Dart smiled. "But you may be able to help us find out who did. As soon as I've finished looking around I'll want to ask you a few questions. That's all."

"Well," she grumbled, "you don't have to stand a seven-foot cop over us to ask a few questions, do you?"

Ignoring this inquiry, the investigators continued with their observations. This was a spacious room whose soft light came altogether from three or four floor lamps; odd heavy silken shades bore curious designs in profile, and the effect of the obliquely downcast light was to reveal legs and bodies, while countenances above were bedimmed by comparative shadow. Beside the narrow hall door was a wide doorway hung with portières of black velvet, occupying most of that wall. The lateral walls, which seemed to withdraw into the surrounding dusk, were adorned with innumerable strange and awful shapes: gruesome black masks with hollow orbits, some smooth and bald, some horned and bearded; small misshapen statuettes of near-human creatures, resembling embryos dried and blackened in the sun, with closed bulbous eyes and great protruding lips; broad-bladed swords, slim arrows and jagged spear-heads of forbidding designs. On the farther of the lateral walls was a

mantelpiece upon which lay additional African emblems. Dr.
Archer pointed out a murderous-looking club, resting diagonally across one end of the mantel; it consisted of the lower
half of a human femur, one extremity bulging into wicked-
looking condyles, the other, where the original bone had been
severed, covered with a silver knob representing a human skull.

"That would deliver a nasty crack."

"Wonder if it did?" said the detective.

## 2

They passed now through the velvet portières and a little isthmus-
like antechamber into the middle room where the doctor had
first seen the victim. Dr. Archer pointed out those peculiarities
of this chamber which he had already noted: the odd droplight
with its horizontally focused beam, which was the only means
of illumination; the surrounding black velvet draping, its long
folds extending vertically from the bottom of the walls to the
top, then converging to the center of the ceiling above, giving
the room somewhat the shape of an Arab tent; the one apparent opening in this drapery, at the side door leading to the
hallway; the desk-like table in the middle of the room, the visitors' chair on one side of it, Frimbo's on the other, directly beneath the curious droplight.

"Let's examine the walls," said Dart. He and the doctor
brought their flashlights into play. Like two offshoots of the
parent beam, the smaller shafts of light traveled inquisitively
over the long vertical folds of black velvet, which swayed this
way and that as the two men pulled and palpated, seeking
openings. The projected spots of illumination moved like two
strange, twisting, luminous moths, constantly changing in size
and shape, fluttering here and there from point to point, pausing, inquiring, abandoning. The detective and the physician
began at the entrance from the reception room and circuited
the black chamber in opposite directions. Presently they met at
the far back wall, in whose midline the doctor located an opening. Pulling the hangings aside at this point, they discovered
another door but found it locked.

"Leads into the back room, I guess. We'll get in from the hallway. What's this?"

"This" proved to be a switch-box on the wall beside the closed door. The physician read the lettering on its front. "Sixty amperes—two hundred and twenty volts. That's enough for an X-ray machine. What does he need special current for?"

"Search me. Come on. Brady, run downstairs and get that extension-light out of the back of my car. Then come back here and search the floor for whatever you can find. Specially around the table and chairs. We'll be right back."

3

They left the death chamber by its side door and approached the rearmost room from the hallway. Its hall door was unlocked, but blackness greeted them as they flung it open, a strangely sinister blackness in which eyes seemed to gleam. When they cast their flashlights into that blackness they saw whence the gleaming emanated, and Dart, stepping in, found a switch and produced a light.

"Damn!" said he as his eyes took in a wholly unexpected scene. Along the rear wall under the windows stretched a long flat chemical work-bench, topped with black slate. On its dull dark surface gleamed bright laboratory devices of glass or metal, flasks, beakers, retorts, graduates, pipettes, a copper water-bath, a shining instrument-sterilizer, and at one end, a gleaming black electric motor. The space beneath this bench was occupied by a long floor cabinet with a number of small oaken doors. On the wall at the nearer end was a glass-doored steel cabinet containing a few small surgical instruments, while the far wall, at the other end of the bench, supported a series of shelves, the lower ones bearing specimen-jars of various sizes, and the upper, bottles of different colors and shapes. Dart stooped and opened one of the cabinet doors and discovered more glassware, while Dr. Archer went over and investigated the shelves, removed one of the specimen-jars, and with a puzzled expression, peered at its contents, floating in some preserving fluid.

"What's that?" the detective asked, approaching.

"Can't be," muttered the physician.

"Can't be what?"

"What they look like."

"Namely?"

Ordinarily Dr. Archer would probably have indulged in a leisurely circumlocution and reached his decision by a flank attack. In the present instance he was too suddenly and wholly absorbed in what he saw to entertain even the slightest or most innocent pretense.

"Sex glands," he said.

"What?"

"Male sex glands, apparently."

"Are you serious?"

The physician inspected the rows of jars, none of which was labeled. There were other preserved biological specimens, but none of the same appearance as those in the jar which he still held in his hand.

"I'm serious enough," he said. "Does it stimulate your imagination?"

"Plenty," said Dart, his thin lips tightening. "Come on—let's ask some questions."

# Chapter Six

## I

THEY returned to the middle chamber. Officer Brady had plugged the extension into a hall socket and twisted its cord about the chain which suspended Frimbo's light. The strong white lamp's sharp radiance did not dispel the far shadows, but at least it brightened the room centrally.

Brady said, "There's three things I found—all on the floor by the chair."

"This chair?" Dart indicated the one in which the victim had been first seen by Dr. Archer.

"Yes."

The three objects were on the table, as dissimilar as three objects could be.

"What do you think of this, doc?" Dart picked up a small irregular shining metallic article and turned to show it to the physician. But the physician was already reaching for one of the other two discoveries.

"Hey—wait a minute!" protested the detective. "That's big enough to have finger prints on it."

"My error. What's that you have?"

"Teeth. Somebody's removable bridge."

He handed over the small shining object. The physician examined it. "First and second left upper bicuspids," he announced.

"You don't say?" grinned Dart.

"What do you mean, somebody's?"

"Well, if you know whose just by looking at it, speak up. Don't hold out on me."

"Frimbo's."

"Or the guy's that put him out."

"Hm—no. My money says Frimbo's. These things slip on and off easily enough."

"I see what you mean. In manipulating that handkerchief the murderer dislodged this thing."

"Yes. Too bad. If it was the murderer's it might help identify him."

"Why? There must be plenty of folks with those same teeth missing."

"True. But this bridge wouldn't fit—really fit—anybody but the person it was made for. The models have to be cast in plaster. Not two in ten thousand would be identical in every respect. This thing's practically as individual as a finger print."

"Yea? Well, we may be able to use it anyhow. I'll hang on to it. But wait. You looked down Frimbo's throat. Didn't you notice his teeth?"

"Not especially. I didn't care anything about his teeth then. I was looking for the cause of death. But we can easily check this when the medical examiner comes."

"O.K. Now—what's this?" He picked up what seemed to be a wad of black silk ribbon.

"That was his head cloth, I suppose. Very impressive with that flowing robe and all."

"Who could see it in the dark?"

"Oh, he might have occasion to come out into the light sometime."

The detective's attention was already on the third object.

"Say——!"

"I'm way ahead of you."

"That's the mate to the club on the mantel in the front room!"

"Right. That's made from a left femur, this from a right."

"That must be what crowned him. Boy, if that's got finger prints on it——"

"Ought to have. Look—it's not fully bleached out like the specimens ordinarily sold to students. Notice the surface—greasy-looking. It would take an excellent print."

"Did you touch it, Brady?"

"I picked it up by the big end. I didn't touch the rest of it."

"Good. Have the other guys shown up yet? All right. Wrap it—here"—he took a newspaper from his pocket, surrounded the thigh bone with it, stepped to the door and summoned one of the officers who had arrived meanwhile. "Take this over to the precinct, tell Mac to get it examined for finger prints pronto—anybody he can get hold of—wait for the result and bring it back here—wet. And bring back a set—if Tynie's around, let him bring it. Double time—it's a rush order."

"What's the use?" smiled the doctor. "You yourself said the offender's probably in Egypt by now."

"And you said different. Hey—look!"

He had been playing his flashlight over the carpet. Its rays passed obliquely under the table, revealing a grayish discoloration of the carpet. Closer inspection proved this to be due to a deposit of ash-colored powder. The doctor took a prescription blank and one of his professional cards and scraped up some of the powder onto the blank.

"Know what it is?" asked Dart.

"No."

"Save it. We'll have it examined."

"Meanwhile?"

"Meanwhile let's indulge in a few personalities. Let's see—I've got an idea."

"Shouldn't be at all surprised. What now?"

"This guy Frimbo was smart. He put his people in that spotlight and he stayed in the dark. All right—I'm going to do the same thing."

"You might win the same reward."

"I'll take precautions against that. Brady!"

Brady brought in the two officers who had not yet been assigned to a post. They were stationed now, one on either side of the black room toward its rear wall.

"Now," said Dart briskly. "Let's get started. Brady, call in that little short fat guy. You in the hall there—turn off this extension at that socket and be ready to turn it on again when I holler. I intend to sit pat as long as possible."

Thereupon he snapped off his flashlight and seated himself in Frimbo's chair behind the table, becoming now merely a deeper shadow in the surrounding dimness. The doctor put out his flashlight also and stood beside the chair. The bright shaft of light from the device overhead, directed away from them, shone full upon the back of the empty visitors' chair opposite, and on beyond toward the passageway traversed by those who entered from the reception room. They waited for Bubber Brown to come in.

2

Whatever he might have expected, Bubber Brown certainly was unprepared for this. With a hesitancy that was not in the least feigned, his figure came into view; first his extremely bowed legs, about which flapped the bottom of his imitation camels' hair overcoat, then the middle of his broad person, with his hat nervously fingered by both hands, then his chest and neck, jointly adorned by a bright green tie, and finally his round black face, blank as a door knob, loose-lipped, wide-eyed. Brady was prodding him from behind.

"Sit down, Mr. Brown," said a voice out of the dark.

The unaccustomed "Mr." did not dispel the unreality of the situation for Bubber, who had not been so addressed six times in his twenty-six years. Nor was he reassured to find that he could not make out the one who had spoken, so blinding was the beam of light in his eyes. What he did realize was that the voice issued from the place where he had a short while ago looked with a wild surmise upon a corpse. For a moment his eyes grew whiter; then, with decision, he spun about and started away from the sound of that voice.

He bumped full into Brady. "Sit down!" growled Brady.

Said Dart, "It's me, Brown—the detective. Take that chair and answer what I ask you."

"Yes, suh," said Bubber weakly, and turned back and slowly edged into the space between the table and the visitors' chair. Perspiration glistened on his too illuminated brow. By the least possible bending of his body he managed to achieve the mere rim of the seat, where, with both hands gripping the chair arms, he crouched as if poised on some gigantic spring which any sudden sound might release to send him soaring into the shadows above.

"Brady, you're in the light. Take notes. All right, Mr. Brown. What's your full name?"

"Bubber Brown," stuttered that young man uncomfortably.

"Address?"

"2100 Fifth Avenue."

"Age?"

"Twenty-six."

"Occupation?"

"Suh?"

"Occupation?"

"Oh. Detective."

"De—what!"

"Detective. Yes, suh."

"Let's see your shield."

"My which?"

"Your badge."

"Oh. Well—y'see I ain't the kind o' detective what has to have a badge. No, suh."

"What kind are you?"

"I'm a family detective."

Somewhat more composed by the questioning, Bubber quickly reached into his pocket and produced a business card. Dart took it and snapped his light on it, to read:

> BUBBER BROWN, INC., *Detective*
> (formerly with the City of
> New York)
> 2100 Fifth Avenue
> Evidence obtained in affairs of
> the heart, etc. Special attention
> to cheaters and backbiters.

Dart considered this a moment, then said:

"How long have you been breaking the law like this?"

"Breaking the law? Who, me? What old law, mistuh?"

"What about this 'Incorporated'? You're not incorporated."

"Oh, that? Oh, that's 'ink'—that means black."

"Don't play dumb. You know what it means, you know that you're not incorporated, and you know that you've never been a detective with the City. Now what's the idea? Who are you?"

Bubber had, as a matter of fact, proffered the card thoughtlessly in the strain of his discomfiture. Now he chose, wisely, to throw himself on Dart's good graces.

"Well, y'see times is been awful hard, everybody knows that. And I did have a job with the City—I was in the Distinguished Service Company——"

"The what?"

"The D. S. C.—Department of Street Cleaning—but we

never called it that, no, suh. Coupla weeks ago I lost that job and couldn't find me nothin' else. Then I said to myself, 'They's only one chance, boy—you got to use your head instead o' your hands.' Well, I figured out the situation like this: The only business what was flourishin' was monkey-business——"

"What are you talking about?"

"Monkey-business. Cheatin'—backbitin', and all like that. Don't matter how bad business gets, lovin' still goes on; and long as lovin' is goin' on, cheatin' is goin' on too. Now folks'll pay to catch cheaters when they won't pay for other things, see? So I figure I can hire myself out to catch cheaters as well as anybody—all I got to do is bust in on 'em and tell the judge what I see. See? So I had me them cards printed and I'm r'arin' to go. But I didn't know 'twas against the law sho' 'nough."

"Well it is and I may have to arrest you for it."

Bubber's dismay was great.

"Couldn't you jes'—jes' tear up the card and let it go at that?"

"What was your business here tonight?"

"Me and Jinx come together. We was figurin' on askin' the man's advice about this detective business."

"You and who?"

"Jinx Jenkins—you know—the long boy look like a giraffe you seen downstairs."

"What time did you get here?"

" 'Bout half-past ten I guess."

"How do you know it was half-past ten?"

"I didn't say I knowed it, mistuh. I said I guess. But I know it wasn't no later'n that."

"How do you know?"

Thereupon, Bubber told how he knew.

3

At eight o'clock sharp, as indicated by his new dollar watch, purchased as a necessary tool of his new profession, he had been walking up and down in front of the Lafayette Theatre, apparently idling away his time, but actually taking this oppor-tunity to hand out his new business cards to numerous theater-goers. It was his first attempt to get a case and he was not surprised to find that it promptly bore fruit in that happy-go-lucky, care-free, irresponsible atmosphere. A woman to whom he had handed one of his announcements returned to him for further information.

"I should 'a' known better," he admitted, "than to bother with her, because she was bad luck jes' to look at. She was cross-eyed. But I figure a cross-eyed dollar'll buy as much as a straight-eyed one and she talked like she meant business. She told me if I would get some good first-class low-down on her big boy, I wouldn't have no trouble collectin' my ten dollars. I say 'O.K., sister. Show me two bucks in front and his Cleo from behind, and I'll track 'em down like a bloodhound.' She reached down in her stockin', I held out my hand and the deal was on. I took her name an' address an' she showed me the Cleo and left. That is, I thought she left.

"The Cleo was the gal in the ticket-box. Oh, mistuh, what a Sheba! Keepin' my eyes on her was the easiest work I ever did in my life. I asked the flunky out front what this honey's name was and he tole me Jessie James. That was all I wanted to know. When I looked at her I felt like givin' the cross-eyed woman back her two bucks.

"A little before ten o'clock Miss Jessie James turned the ticket-box over to the flunky and disappeared inside. It was too late for me to spend money to go in then, and knowin' I prob'ly couldn't follow her everywhere she was goin' anyhow, I figured I might as well wait for her outside one door as another. So I waited out front, and in three or four minutes out she come. I followed her up the Avenue a piece and round a corner to a private house on 134th Street. After she'd been in a couple o' minutes I rung the bell. A fat lady come to the door and I asked for Miss Jessie James.

"'Oh,' she say. 'Is you the gentleman she was expectin'?' I say, 'Yes ma'am. I'm one of 'em. They's another one comin'.' She say, 'Come right in. You can go up—her room is the top floor back. She jes' got here herself.' Boy, what a break. I didn' know for a minute whether this was business or pleasure.

"When I got to the head o' the stairs I walked easy. I snook up to the front-room door and found it cracked open 'bout half an inch. Naturally I looked in—that was business. But, friend, what I saw was nobody's business. Miss Jessie wasn't

gettin' ready for no ordinary caller. She look like she was gettin' ready to try on a bathin' suit and meant to have a perfect
fit. Nearly had a fit myself tryin' to get my breath back. Then I
had to grab a armful o' hall closet, 'cause she reached for a kimono and started for the door. She passed by and I see I've
got another break. So I seized opportunity by the horns and
slipped into her room. Over across one corner was———"

"Wait a minute," interrupted Dart. "I didn't ask for your life
history. I only asked———"

"You ast how I knowed it wasn't after half-past ten o'clock."

"Exactly."

"I'm tellin' you, mistuh. Listen. Over across one corner was
a trunk—a wardrobe trunk, standin' up on end and wide open.
I got behind it and squatted down. I looked at my watch. It
was ten minutes past ten. No sooner'n I got the trunk straight
'cross the corner again I heard her laughin' out in the hall and
I heard a man laughin', too. I say to myself, 'here 'tis. The
bathin'-suit salesman done arrived.'

"And from behind that trunk, y'see, I couldn't use nothin'
but my ears—couldn't see a thing. That corner had me pretty
crowded. Well, instead o' goin' on and talkin', they suddenly
got very quiet, and natchelly I got very curious. It was my
business to know what was goin' on.

"So instead o' scronchin' down behind the trunk like I'd
been doin', I begun to inch up little at a time till I could see
over the top. Lord—what did I do that for? Don' know jes'
how it happened, but next thing I do know is 'wham!'—the
trunk had left me. There it was flat on the floor, face down,
like a Hindu sayin' his prayers, and there was me in the corner,
lookin' dumb and sayin' mine, with the biggest boogy in
Harlem 'tween me and the door.

"Fact is, I forgot I was a detective. Only thing I wanted to
detect was the quickest way out. Was that guy evil-lookin'?
One thing saved me—the man didn't know whether to blame
me or her. Before he could make up his mind, I shot out o'
that corner past him like a cannon-ball. The gal yelled, 'Stop
thief!' And the guy started after me. But, shuh!—he never had
a chance—even in them runnin'-pants o' his. I flowed down
the stairs and popped out the front door, and who was waitin'
on the sidewalk but the cross-eyed lady. She'd done followed

me same as I followed the Sheba. Musta hid when her man went by on the way in. But when he come by chasin' me on the way out, she jumped in between us and ast him where was his pants.

"Me, I didn't stop to hear the answer. I knew it. I made Lenox Avenue in nothin' and no fifths. That wasn't no more than quarter past ten. I slowed up and turned down Lenox Avenue. Hadn' gone a block before I met Jinx Jenkins. I told him 'bout it and ast him what he thought I better do next. Well, somebody'd jes' been tellin' him 'bout what a wonderful guy this Frimbo was for folks in need o' advice. We agreed to come see him and walked on round here. Now, I know it didn't take me no fifteen minutes to get from that gal's house here. So I must 'a' been here before half-past ten, y'see?"

4

Further questioning elicited that when Jinx and Bubber arrived they had made their way, none too eagerly, up the stairs in obedience to a sign in the lower hallway and had encountered no one until they reached the reception-room in front. Here there had been three men, waiting to see Frimbo. One, Bubber had recognized as Spider Webb, a number-runner who worked for Harlem's well-known policy-king, Si Brandon. Another, who had pestered Jinx with unwelcome conversation, was a notorious little drug-addict called Doty Hicks. The third was a genial stranger who had talked pleasantly to everybody, revealing himself to be one Easley Jones, a railroad man.

After a short wait, Frimbo's flunky appeared from the hallway and ushered the railroad man, who had been the first to arrive, out of the room through the wide velvet-curtained passage. While Jones was, presumably, with Frimbo, the two ladies had come in—the young one first. Then Doty Hicks had gone in to Frimbo, then Spider Webb, and finally Jinx. The usher had not himself gone through the wide doorway at any time—he had only bowed the visitors through, turned aside, and disappeared down the hallway.

"This usher—what was he like?"

"Tall, skinny, black, stoop-shouldered, and cockeyed. Wore

a long black silk robe like Frimbo's, but he had a bright yellow sash and a bright yellow thing on his head—you know—what d'y' call 'em? Look like bandages——"

"Turban?"

"That's it. Turban."

"Where is he now?"

"Don't ask me, mistuh. I ain't seen him since he showed Jinx in."

"Hm."

"Say!" Bubber had an idea.

"What?"

"I bet he done it!"

"Did what?"

"Scrambled the man's eggs!"

"You mean you think the assistant killed Frimbo?"

"Sho'!"

"How do you know Frimbo was killed?"

"Didn't—didn't you and the doc say he was when I was downstairs lookin' at you?"

"On the contrary, we said quite definitely that we didn't know that he was killed, and that even if he was, that blow didn't kill him."

"But—in the front room jes' now, didn't the doc tell that lady——"

"All the doctor said was that it looked like Frimbo had an enemy. Now you say Frimbo was killed and you accuse somebody of doing it."

"All I meant——"

"You were in this house when he died, weren't you? By your own time."

"I was here when the doc says he died, but——"

"Why would you accuse anybody of a crime if you didn't know that a crime had been committed?"

"Listen, mistuh, please. All I meant was, *if* the man *was* killed, the flunky *might* 'a' done it and hauled hips. He could be in Egypt by now."

Dart's identical remark came back to him. He said less sharply:

"Yes. But on the other hand you might be calling attention to that fact to avert suspicion from yourself."

"Who—me?" Bubber's eyes went incredibly large. "Good Lord, man, I didn't leave that room yonder—that waitin'-room —till Jinx called me in to see the man—and he was dead then. 'Deed that's the truth—I come straight up the stairs with Jinx —we went straight in the front room—and I didn't come out till Jinx called me—ask the others—ask them two women."

"I will. But they can only testify for your presence in that room. Who says you came up the stairs and went straight into that room? How can you prove you did that? How do I know you didn't stop in here by way of that side hall-door there, and attack Frimbo as he sat here in this chair?"

The utter unexpectedness of his own incrimination, and the detective's startling insistence upon it, almost robbed Bubber of speech, a function which he rarely relinquished. For a moment he could only gape. But he managed to sputter: "Judas Priest, mistuh, can't you take a man's word for nothin'?"

"I certainly can't," said the detective.

"Well, then," said Bubber, inspired, "ask Jinx. He seen me. He come in with me."

"I see. You alibi him and he alibis you. Is that it?"

"Damn!" exploded Bubber. "You is the most suspicious man I ever met!"

"You're not exactly free of suspicion yourself," Dart returned dryly.

"Listen, mistuh. If you bumped a man off, would you run get a doctor and hang around to get pinched? Would you?"

"If I thought that would make me look innocent I might —yes."

"Then you're dumber'n I am. If I'd done it, I'd been long gone by now."

"Still," Dart said, "you have only the word of your friend Jinx to prove you went straight into the waiting-room. That's insufficient testimony. Got a handkerchief on you?"

"Sho'." Bubber reached into his breast pocket and produced a large and flagrant affair apparently designed for appearance rather than for service; a veritable flag, crossed in one direction by a bright orange band and in another, at right angles to the first, by a virulent green one. "My special kind," he said; "always buy these. Man has to have a little color in his clothes, y'see?"

"Yes, I see. Got any others?"

"'Nother one like this—but it's dirty." He produced the mate, crumpled and matted, out of another pocket.

"O.K. Put 'em away. See anybody here tonight with a colored handkerchief of any kind?"

"No suh—not that I remember."

"All right. Now tell me this. Did you notice the decorations on the walls in the front room when you first arrived?"

"Couldn't help noticin' them things—'nough to scare anybody dizzy."

"What did you see?"

"You mean them false-faces and knives and swords and things?"

"Yes. Did you notice anything in particular on the mantelpiece?"

"Yea. I went over and looked at it soon as I come in. What I remember most was a pair o' clubs. One was on one end o' the mantelpiece, and the other was on the other. Look like they was made out o' bones."

"You are sure there were two of them?"

"Sho' they was two. One on——"

"Did you touch them?"

"No *suh*—couldn't pay me to touch none o' them things— might 'a' been conjured."

"Did you see anyone touch them?"

"No, suh."

"You saw no one remove one of them?"

"No, suh."

"So far as you know they are still there?"

"Yes, suh."

"Who was in that room, besides yourself, when you first saw the two clubs?"

"Everybody. That was befo' the flunky'd come in to get the railroad man."

"I see. Now these two women—how soon after you got there did they come in?"

"'Bout ten minutes or so."

"Did either of them leave the room while you were there?"

"No, suh."

"And the first man—Easley Jones, the railroad porter—he had come into this room before the women arrived?"

"Yes, suh. He was the first one here, I guess."

"After he went in to Frimbo, did he come back into the waiting-room?"

"No, suh. Reckon he left by this side door here into the hall."

"Did either of the other two return to the waiting-room?"

"No, suh. Guess they all left the same way. Only one that came back was Jinx, when he called me."

"And at that time, you and the women were the only people left in the waiting-room?"

"Yes, suh."

"Very good. Could you identify those three men?"

" 'Deed I could. I could even find 'em if you said so."

"Perhaps I will. For the present you go back to the front room. Don't try anything funny—the house is lousy with police-men."

"Lousy is right," muttered Bubber.

"What's that?"

"I ain't opened my mouth, mistuh. But listen, you don't think I done it sho' 'nough do you?"

"That will depend entirely on whether the women corroborate your statement."

"Well, whatever that is, I sho' hope they do it."

## Chapter Seven

"**B**RADY, ask the lady who arrived first to come in," said Dart, adding in a low aside to the physician, "if her story checks with Brown's on the point of his staying in that room, I think I can use him for something. He couldn't have taken that club out without leaving the room."

"He tells a straight story," agreed Dr. Archer. "Too scared to lie. But isn't it too soon to let anybody out?"

"I don't mean to let him go. But I can send him with a couple o' cops to identify the other men who were here and bring them back, without being afraid he'll start anything."

"Why not go with him and question them where you find 'em?"

"It's easier to have 'em all in one place if possible—saves everybody's time. Can't always do it of course. Here comes the lady—your friend."

"Be nice to her—she's the real thing. I've known her for years."

"O. K."

Uncertainly, the young woman entered, the beam of light revealing clearly her unusually attractive appearance. With un-disguised bewilderment on her pretty face, but with no sign of fear, she took the visitors' chair.

"Don't be afraid, Mrs. Crouch. I want you to answer, as accurately as you can, a few questions which may help determine who killed Frimbo."

"I'll be glad to," she said in a low, matter-of-fact tone.

"What time did you arrive here tonight?"

"Shortly after ten-thirty."

"You're sure of the time?"

"I was at the Lenox. The feature picture goes on for the last time at ten-thirty. I had seen it already, and when it came on again I left. It is no more than four or five minutes' walk from there here."

"Good. You came directly to Frimbo's waiting-room?"

"No. I stopped downstairs to see if my husband was there."

"Your husband? Oh—Mr. Crouch, the undertaker, is your husband?"

"Yes. But he was out."

"Does he usually go out and leave his place open?"

"Late in the evening, yes. Up until then there is a clerk. Afterwards if he is called out he just leaves a sign saying when he will return. He never," she smiled faintly, "has to fear robbers, you see."

"But might not calls come in while he is out?"

"Yes. But they are handled by a telephone exchange. If he doesn't answer, the exchange takes the call and gives it to him later."

"I see. How long did stopping downstairs delay you?"

"Only a minute. Then I came right up to the waiting-room."

"Who was there when you got there?"

"Four men."

"Did you know any of them?"

"No, but I'd know them if I saw them again."

"Describe them."

"Well there was a little thin nervous man who looked like he was sick—in fact he was sick, because when he got up to follow the assistant he had a dizzy spell and fell, and all the men jumped to him and had to help him up."

"He was the first to go in to Frimbo after you arrived?"

"Yes. Then there was a heavy-set, rather flashily-dressed man in gray. He went in next. And there were two others who seemed to be together—the two who were in there a few minutes ago when you and Dr. Archer came in."

"A tall fellow and a short one?"

"Yes."

"About those two—did either of them leave the room while you were there?"

"The tall one did, when his turn came to see Frimbo."

"And the short one?"

"Well—when the tall one had been out for about five or six minutes, he came back—through the same way that he had gone. It was rather startling because nobody else had come back at all except Frimbo's man, and he always appeared in the hall doorway, not the other, and always left by the hall doorway also. And, too, this tall fellow looked terribly excited. He beckoned to the short one and they went back together through the passage—into this room."

"That was the first and only time the short man left that room while you were there?"

"Yes."

"And you yourself did not leave the room meanwhile?"

"No. Not until now."

"Did anyone else come in?"

"The other woman, who is in there now."

"Very good. Now, pardon me if I seem personal, but it's my business not to mind my business—to meddle with other people's. You understand?"

"Perfectly. Don't apologize—just ask."

"Thank you. Did you know anything about this man Frimbo —his habits, friends, enemies?"

"No. He had many followers, I know, and a great reputation for being able to cast spells and that sort of thing. His only companion, so far as I know, was his servant. Otherwise he seemed to lead a very secluded life. I imagine he must have been pretty well off financially. He'd been here almost two years. He was always our best tenant."

"Tell me why you came to see Frimbo tonight, please."

"Certainly. Mr. Crouch owns this house, among others, and Frimbo is our tenant. My job is collecting rents, and tonight I came to collect Frimbo's."

"I see. But do you find it more convenient to see tenants at night?"

"Not so much for me as for them. Most of them are working during the day. And Frimbo simply can't be seen in the daytime—he won't see anyone either professionally or on business until after dark. It's one of his peculiarities, I suppose."

"So that by coming during his office hours you are sure of finding him available?"

"Exactly."

"All right, Mrs. Crouch. That's all for the present. Will you return to the front room? I'd let you go at once, but you may be able to help me further if you will."

"I'll be glad to."

"Thank you. Brady, call in Bubber Brown and one of those extra men."

When Bubber reappeared, Dart said:

"You told me you could locate and identify the three men who preceded Jenkins?"

"Yes, suh. I sho' can."

"How?"

"Well, I been seein' that little Doty Hicks plenty. He hangs out 'round his brother's night club. 'Cose ev'ybody knows Spider Webb's a runner and I can find him from now till mornin' at Patmore's Pool Room. And that other one, the railroad man, he and I had quite a conversation before he come in to see Frimbo, and I found out where he rooms when he's in town. Jes' a half a block up the street here, in a private house."

"Good." The detective turned to the officer whom Brady had summoned:

"Hello, Hanks. Listen Hanks, you take Mr. Brown there around by the precinct, pick up another man, and then go with Mr. Brown and bring the men he identifies here. There'll be three of 'em. Take my car and make it snappy."

2

Jinx, behind a mask of scowling ill-humor, which was always his readiest defense under strain, sat now in the uncomfortably illuminated chair and growled his answers into the darkness whence issued Dart's voice. This apparently crusty attitude, which long use had made habitual, served only to antagonize his questioner, so that even the simplest of his answers were taken as unsatisfactory. Even in the perfectly routine but obviously important item of establishing his identity, he made a bad beginning.

"Have you anything with you to prove your identity?"

"Nothin' but my tongue."

"What do you mean?"

"I mean I say I'm who I is. Who'd know better?"

"No one, of course. But it's possible that you might say who you were not."

"Who I ain't? Sho' I can say who I ain't. I ain't Marcus Garvey,

I ain't Al Capone, I ain't Cal Coolidge—I ain't nobody but
me—Jinx Jenkins, myself."

"Very well, Mr. Jenkins. Where do you live? What sort of
work do you do?"

"Any sort I can get. Ain't doin' nothin' right now."

"M-m. What time did you get here tonight?"

On this and other similar points, Jinx's answers, for all their
gruffness, checked with those of Bubber and Martha Crouch.
He had come with Bubber a little before ten-thirty. They had
gone straight to the waiting-room and found three men. The
women had come in later. Then the detective asked him to describe in detail what had transpired when he left the others and
went in to see Frimbo. And though Jinx's vocabulary was
wholly inadequate, so deeply had that period registered itself
upon his mind that he omitted not a single essential item. His
imperfections of speech became negligible and were quite ignored; indeed, the more tutored minds of his listeners filled in
or substituted automatically, and both the detective and the
physician, the latter perhaps more completely, were able to observe the reconstructed scene as if it were even now being
played before their eyes.

3

The black servitor with the yellow headdress and the cast in
one eye ushered Jinx to the broad black curtains, saying in a
low voice as he bowed him through, "Please go in, sit down,
say nothing till Frimbo speaks." Thereupon the curtains fell to
behind him and he was in a small dark passage, whose purpose
was obviously to separate the waiting-room from the mystic
chamber beyond and thus prevent Frimbo's voice from reaching the circle of waiting callers. Jinx shuffled forward toward
the single bright light that at once attracted and blinded. He
sidled in between the chair and table and sat down facing the
figure beneath the hanging light. He was unable, because of
the blinding glare, to descry any characteristic feature of the
man he had come to see; he could only make out a dark shadow
with a head that seemed to be enormous, cocked somewhat
sidewise as if in a steady contemplation of the visitor.

For a time the shadow made no sound or movement, and Jinx squirmed about impatiently in his seat, trying to obey directions and restrain the impulse to say something. At one moment the figure seemed to fade away altogether and blend with the enveloping blackness beyond. This was the very limit of Jinx's endurance—but at this moment Frimbo spoke.

"Please do not shield your eyes. I must study your face."

The voice changed the atmosphere from one of discomfiture to one of assurance. It was a deep, rich, calm voice, so matter of fact and real, even in that atmosphere, as to dispel doubt and inspire confidence.

"You see, I must analyze your mind by observing your countenance. Only thus can I learn how to help you."

Here was a man that knew something. Didn't talk like an African native certainly. Didn't talk like any black man Jinx had ever heard. Not a trace of Negro accent, not a suggestion of dialect. He spoke like a white-haired judge on the bench, easily, smoothly, quietly.

"There are those who claim the power to read men's lives in crystal spheres. That is utter nonsense. I claim the power to read men's lives in their faces. That is completely reasonable. Every experience, every thought, leaves its mark. Past and present are written there clearly. He who knows completely the past and the present can deduce the inevitable future, which past and present determine. My crystal sphere, therefore, is your face. By reading correctly what is there I know what is scheduled to follow, and so can predict and guard you against your future."

"Yes, suh," said Jinx.

"I notice that you are at present out of work. It is this you wish to consult me about."

Jinx's eyes dilated. "Yes, suh, that's right."

"You have been without a job several weeks."

"Month come Tuesday."

"Yes. And now you have reached the point where you must seek the financial aid of your friends. Being of a proud and independent nature, you find this difficult. Yet even the fee which you will pay for the advice I give you is borrowed money."

There was no tone of question, no implied request for confirmation. The words were a simple statement of fact, presented as a comprehensive résumé of a situation, expressed merely as a basis for more important deductions to follow.

"So far, you see, my friend, I have done nothing at all mysterious. All this is the process of reason, based on observation. And now, though you may think it a strange power, let me add that there is nothing mysterious either in my being able to tell you that your name is Jenkins, that your friends call you Jinx, that you are twenty-seven years old, and that you are unmarried. All these matters have passed through your mind as you sat there listening to me. This is merely an acuteness of mental receptivity which anyone can learn; it is usually called telepathy. At this point, Mr. Jenkins, others whom you might have consulted stop. But at this point—Frimbo begins."

There was a moment's silence. The voice resumed with added depth and solemnity:

"For, in addition to the things that can be learned by anyone, Frimbo inherits the bequest of a hundred centuries, handed from son to son through four hundred unbroken generations of Buwongo kings. It is a profound and dangerous secret, my friend, a secret my fathers knew when the kings of the Nile still thought human flesh a delicacy."

The voice sank to a lower pitch still, inescapably impressive.

"Frimbo can change the future." He paused, then continued, "In the midst of a world of determined, inevitable events, of results rigidly fashioned by the past, Frimbo alone is free. Frimbo not only sees. Frimbo and Frimbo alone can step in at will and change the course of a life. Listen!"

The voice now became intimate, confidential, shading off from low vibrant tones into softly sibilant whispers:

"Your immediate needs will be taken care of but you will not be content. It is a strange thing that I see. For though food and shelter in abundance are to be your lot sooner than you think, still you will be more unhappy than you are now; and you will rejoice only when this physical security has been withdrawn. You will be overjoyed to return to the uncertain fortunes over which you now despair. I do not see the circumstances, at the moment, that will bring on these situations, because they are outside the present content of your mind which I am contemplating. But these things even now impatiently await you—adequate physical necessaries, but great mental distress.

"Now then, when you have passed through that paradoxical period, what will you do? Let me see. It is but a short way—a few days ahead—but——" Into that until now completely self-assured tone crept a quality of puzzlement. It was so unexpected and incongruous a change that Jinx, up to this point completely fascinated, was startled like one rudely awakened from deep sleep. "It is very dark——" There was a long pause. The same voice resumed, "What is this, Frimbo?" Again a pause; then: "Strange how suddenly it grows dark. Frimbo——" Bewilderment dilated into dismay. "Frimbo! Frimbo! *Why do you not see?*"

The voice of a man struck suddenly blind could not have been imbued with greater horror. So swift and definite was the transition that the alarmed Jinx could only grip the arms of his chair and stare hard. And despite the glaring beam, he saw a change in the figure beyond the table. That part of the shadow that had corresponded to the head seemed now to be but half its original size.

In a sudden frenzy of terror, Jinx jumped up and reached for the hanging light. Quickly he swung it around and tilted it so that the luminous shaft fell on the seated figure. What he saw was a bare black head, inclined limply sidewise, the mouth open, the eyes fixed, staring from under drooping lids.

He released the light, wheeled, and fled back to summon Bubber.

4

All this Jinx rehearsed in detail, making clear by implication or paraphrase those ideas whose original wording he was otherwise unable to describe or pronounce. The doctor emitted a low whistle of amazement; the detective, incredulous, said:

"Wait a minute. Let me get this straight. You mean to say that Frimbo actually talked to you, as you have related?"

" 'Deed he did."

"You're sure that it was Frimbo talking to you?"

"Jest as sure as I am that you're talkin' to me now. He was right where you is."

"And when he tried to prophesy what would happen to you a few days hence, he couldn't?"

"Look like sump'm come over him all of a sudden—claim he couldn't see. And when he seen he couldn't see, he got scared-like and hollered out jes' like I said: 'Frimbo—why don't you see?'"

"Then you say *you* tried to see *him*, and it looked as though his head had shrunken?"

"Yes, suh."

"Evidently his head-piece had fallen off."

"His which?"

"Did you hear any sound just before this—like a blow?"

"Nope. Didn't hear nothin' but his voice. And it didn't stop like it would if he'd been hit. It jes' stopped like it would if he'd been tellin' 'bout sump'm he'd been lookin' at and then couldn't see no more. Only it scared him sump'm terrible not to be able to see it. Maybe he scared himself to death."

"Hm. Yea, maybe he even scared up that wound on his head."

"Well, maybe me and Bubber did that."

"How?"

"Carryin' him downstairs. We was in an awful hurry. His head might 'a' hit sump'm on the way down."

"But," said Dart, and Jinx couldn't know this was baiting, "if he was dead, that wound wouldn't have bled, even as little as it did."

"Maybe," Jinx insisted, "it stopped because he died jes' about that time—on the way down."

"You seem very anxious to account for his death, Jenkins."

"Humph," Jinx grunted. "You act kind o' anxious yourself, seems like to me."

"Yes. But there is this difference. By your own word, you were present and the only person present when Frimbo died. I was half a mile away."

"So what?"

"So that, while I'm as anxious as you are to account for this man's death, I am anxious for perhaps quite a different reason. For instance, I could not possibly be trying to prove my own innocence by insisting he died a natural death."

Jinx's memory was better than Bubber's.

"I ain't heard nobody say for sho' he was killed yet," said he.

"No? Well then, listen. We know that this man was murdered. We know that he was killed deliberately by somebody who meant to do a good job—and succeeded."

"And you reckon I done it?" There was no surprise in Jinx's voice, for he had long had the possibility in mind.

"I reckon nothing. I simply try to get the facts. When enough facts are gathered, they'll do all the reckoning necessary. One way of getting the facts is from the testimony of people who know the facts. The trouble with that is that anybody who knows the facts might have reasons for lying. I have to weed out the lies. I'm telling you this to show you that if you are innocent, you can best defend yourself by telling the truth, no matter how bad it looks."

"What you think I *been* doin'?"

"You've been telling a queer story, part of which we know to be absolutely impossible—unless——" The detective entertained a new consideration. "Listen. What time did you come into this room—as nearly as you can judge?"

"Musta been 'bout—'bout five minutes to eleven."

"How long did Frimbo talk to you?"

"'Bout five or six minutes I guess."

"That would be eleven o'clock. Then you got Bubber. Dr. Archer, what time were you called?"

"Three minutes past eleven—according to the clock on my radio."

"Not a lot of time—three minutes—Bubber took three minutes to get you and get back. During those three minutes Jenkins was alone with the dead man."

"Not me," denied Jinx. "I was out there in the hall right at the head o' the stairs where the doc found me—wonderin' what the hell was keepin' 'em so long." This was so convincingly ingenuous that the physician agreed with a smile. "He was certainly there when I got here."

"During those few minutes, Jenkins, when you were here alone, did you see or hear anything peculiar?"

"No, 'ndeed. The silence liked to drown me."

"And when you came back in this room with the doctor, was everything just as you left it?"

"Far as I could see."

"M-m. Listen, doc. Did you leave the body at all from the time you first saw it until I got here?"

"No. Not even to phone the precinct—I had the two men do it."

"Funny," Dart muttered. "Damn funny." For a moment he meditated the irreconcilable points in Jinx's story—the immobility of Frimbo's figure, from which nevertheless the turban had fallen, the absence of any sound of an attack, yet a sudden change in Frimbo's speech and manner just before he was discovered dead; the remoteness of any opportunity—except for Jinx himself—to reach the prostrate victim, cram that handkerchief in place, and depart during the three minutes when Jinx claimed to be in the hall, without noticeably disturbing the body; and the utter impossibility of any man's talking, dead or alive, when his throat was plugged with that rag which the detective's own eyes had seen removed. Clearly Jenkins was either mistaken in some of the statements he made so positively or else he was lying. If he was lying he was doing so to protect himself, directly or indirectly. In other words, if he was lying, either he knew who committed the crime or he had committed it himself. Only further evidence could indicate the true and the false in this curious chronicle.

And so Dart said, rather casually, as if he were asking a favor, "Have you a handkerchief about you, Mr. Jenkins?"

" 'Tain't what you'd call strictly clean," Jinx obligingly reached into his right-hand coat pocket, "but——" He stopped. His left hand went into his left coat pocket. Both hands came out and delved into their respective trousers pockets. "Guess I must 'a' dropped it," he said. "I had one."

"You're sure you had one?"

"M'hm. Had it when I come here."

"When you came into this room?"

"No. When I first went in the front room. I was a little nervous-like. I wiped my face with it. I think I put it——"

"Is that the last time you recall having it—when you first went into the front room?"

"Uh-huh."

"Can you describe it?"

Perhaps this odd insistence on anything so unimportant as a handkerchief put Jinx on his guard. At any rate he dodged.

"What difference it make?"

"Can you describe it?"

"No."

"No? Why can't you?"

"Nothin' to describe. Jes' a plain big white handkerchief with a——" He stopped.

"With a what?"

"With a hem," said Jinx.

"Hm."

"Yea—hem."

"A white hem?"

"It wasn' no black one," said Jinx, in typical Harlemese.

The detective fell silent a moment, then said:

"All right, Jenkins. That's all for the present. You go back to the front room."

Officer Brady escorted Jinx out, and returned.

"Brady, tell Green, who is up front, to take note of everything he overhears those people in there say. You come back here."

Obediently, Officer Brady turned away.

"Light!" called Dart, and the bluecoat in the hall pressed the switch that turned on the extension light.

# Chapter Eight

"WHAT do you think of Jenkins' story?" Dr. Archer asked.

"Well, even before he balked on the handkerchief," answered Dart, "I couldn't believe him. Then when he balked on describing the blue border, it messed up the whole thing."

"He certainly was convincing about that interview, though. He couldn't have just conjured up that story—it's too definite."

"Yes. But I'm giving him a little time to cool off. Maybe the details won't be so exact next time."

"As I figure it, he could be right—at least concerning the time the fatal attack occurred. It would be right at the end of the one-half hour period in which I first estimated death to have taken place. And in the state of mind he was in when Frimbo seemed to be performing miracles of clairvoyance, he might easily have failed to hear the attack. Certainly he could have failed to see it—he didn't see me standing here beside you."

"You're thinking of the crack on the head. You surely don't suppose Jenkins could have failed to see anyone trying to push that handkerchief in place?"

"No. But that could have been done in the minute when he ran up front to get Bubber. It would have to be fast work, of course."

"Damn right it would. I really don't believe in considering the remote possibilities first. In this game you've got to be practical. Fit conclusions to the facts, not facts to conclusions. Personally I don't feel one way or the other about Jenkins— except that he is unnecessarily antagonistic. That won't help him at all. But I'm certainly satisfied, from testimony, that he is not the guilty party. His attitude, his impossible story, his balking on the blue-bordered handkerchief——"

"You think it's his handkerchief?"

"I think he could have described it—from the way he balked.

If he could have described it, why didn't he? Because it belonged either to him or to somebody he wanted to cover."

"He was balking all right."

"Of course, that wouldn't make him guilty. But it wouldn't exactly clear him either."

"Not exactly. On the other hand, the Frimbo part of his story—what Frimbo said to him—is stuff that a man like Jenkins couldn't possibly have thought up. It was Frimbo talking—that I'm sure of."

"Through a neckful of cotton cloth?"

"No. When he was talking to Jenkins, his throat was unobstructed."

"Well—that means that, the way it looks now, there are two possibilities: somebody did it either when Jenkins went up front to get Bubber or when Bubber went to get you. Let's get the other woman in. All right, Brady, bring in the other lady. Douse the glim, outside there."

Out went the extension light; the original bright horizontal shaft shot forth like an accusing finger pointing toward the front room, while the rest of the death chamber went black.

2

Awkwardly, not unlike an eccentric dancer, the tall thin woman took the spotlight, stood glaring a wide-eyed hostile moment, then disposed herself in a bristlingly erect attitude on the edge of the visitor's chair. Every angle of her meagre, poorly clad form, every feature of her bony countenance, exhibited resentment.

"What is your name, madam?"

"Who's that?" The voice was high, harsh, and querulous.

"Detective Dart. I'm sitting in a chair opposite you."

"Is you the one was in yonder a while ago?"

"Yes. Now——"

"What kind o' detective is you?"

"A police detective, madam, of the City of New York. And please let me ask the questions, while you confine yourself to the answers."

"Police detective? 'Tain't so. They don't have no black detectives."

"Your informant was either ignorant or color-blind, madam. —Now would you care to give your answers here or around at the police station?"

The woman fell silent. Accepting this as a change of heart, the detective repeated:

"What is your name?"

"Aramintha Snead."

"Mrs. or Miss?"

"Mrs." The tone indicated that a detective should be able to tell.

"Your address?"

"19 West 134th Street."

"You're an American, of course?"

"I is now. But I originally come from Savannah, Georgia."

"Occupation?"

"Occupation? You mean what kind o' work I do?"

"Yes, madam."

"I don't do no work at all—not for wages. I'm a church-worker though."

"A church-worker? You spend a good deal of time in church then?"

"Can't nobody spend too much time in church. Though I declare I been wonderin' lately if there ain't some things the devil can 'tend to better'n the Lord."

"What brought you here tonight?"

"My two feet."

Dart sighed patiently and pursued:

"How does it happen that a devoted church-worker like you, Mrs. Snead, comes to seek the advice of a man like Frimbo, a master of the powers of darkness? I should think you would have sought the help of your pastor instead."

"I did, but it never done no good. Every time I go to the Rev'n the Rev'n say, 'Daughter take it to the Lord in prayer.' Well, I done like he said. I took it and took it. Tonight I got tired takin' it."

"Tonight? Why tonight?"

"Tonight was prayer-meetin' night. I ain' missed a prayer-meetin' in two years. And for two years, week after week—every night for that matter, but specially at Friday night prayer-meetin'—I been prayin' to the Lord to stop my husband from drinkin'. Not that I object to the drinkin' itself, y'understand. The Lord made water into wine. But when Jake come home night after night jes' drunk enough to take pleasure in beatin' the breath out o' me—that's another thing altogether."

"I quite agree with you," encouraged Dart.

In the contemplation of her troubles, Mrs. Snead relinquished some of her indignation, or, more exactly, transferred it from the present to the past.

"Well, lo and behold, tonight I ain't no sooner got through prayin' for him at the meetin' and took myself on home than he greets me at the door with a cuff side o' the head. Jes' by way of interduction, he say, so next time I'd be there when he come in. And why in who-who ain't his supper ready? So I jes' turn around and walk off. And I thought to myself as I walked, 'If one medicine don' help, maybe another will.' So I made up my mind. Everybody know 'bout this man Frimbo—say he can conjure on down. And I figger I been takin' it to the Lord in prayer long enough. Now I'm goin' take it to the devil."

"So you came here?"

"Yes."

"How did you happen to choose Frimbo out of all the conjure-men in Harlem?"

"He was the only one I knowed anything about."

"What did you know about him?"

"Knowed what he done for Sister Susan Gassoway's boy, Lem. She was tellin' me 'bout it jes' a couple o' weeks ago— two weeks ago tonight. We was at prayer-meetin'. Old man Hezekiah Mosby was prayin' and when he gets to prayin' they ain't no stoppin' him. So Sister Gassoway and me, we was talkin' and she told me what this man Frimbo'd done for her boy, Lem. Lem got in a little trouble—wild boy he is, anyhow—and put the blame on somebody else. This other boy swore he'd kill Lem, and Lem believed him. So he come to this Frimbo and Frimbo put a charm on him—told him he'd come through it all right. Well you 'member that case what was in the *Amsterdam News* 'bout a boy havin' a knife stuck clean through his head and broke off and the hole closed over and he thought he was jes' cut and didn't know the knife was in there?"

"Yes. Went to Harlem Hospital, was X-rayed, and had the knife removed."

"And lived! That was Lem Gassoway. Nothin' like it ever heard of before. Anybody else'd 'a' been killed on the spot. But not Lem. Lem was under Frimbo's spell. That's what saved him."

"And that's why you chose Frimbo?"

"'Deed so. Wouldn't you?"

"No doubt. At just what time did you get here, Mrs. Snead?"

"Little after half-past ten."

"Did anyone let you in?"

"No. I did like the sign say—open and walk in."

"You came straight upstairs and into the waiting-room?"

"Yes."

"Did you see anybody?"

"Nobody but that other girl and them two fellers that was 'bout to fight jes' now and a couple o' other men in the room. Oh, yes—the—the butler or whatever he was. Evilest-lookin' somebody y'ever see—liked to scared me to death."

"Did you notice anything of interest while you were waiting your turn?"

"Huh? Oh—yes. When one o' them other two men got up to go see the conjure-man, he couldn't hold his feet—must 'a' been drunker'n my Jake. 'Deed so, 'cause down he fell right in the middle o' the floor, and I guess he'd been there yet if them other men hadn't helped him up."

"Who helped him?"

"All of 'em."

"Did you notice the mantelpiece?"

"With all them conjures on it? I didn't miss."

"Did you see those two clubs with the silver tips?"

"Two? Uh–uh—I don't remember no two. I 'member one though. But I wasn't payin' much attention—might 'a' been a dozen of 'em for all I know. There was so many devilish-lookin' things 'round."

"Did you see anyone with a blue-bordered white handkerchief—a man's handkerchief?"

"No, suh."

"You are sure you did not see any such handkerchief—in one of the men's pockets, perhaps?"

"What men is got in they pockets ain't none my business."

3

There were, at this point, sounds of a new arrival in the hall. The officer at the hall door was speaking to a man who had just appeared. This man was saying:

"My name is Crouch. Yes, I have the funeral parlor downstairs. I'd like to see the officer in charge."

"Ask Mr. Crouch in, Brady," called Dart. "Mrs. Snead, you may return to the front room, if you will."

"To the front room!" expostulated the woman. "How long do you expect me to stay in this place?"

"Not very long, I hope. Brady, take the young lady up front. Come right in, Mr. Crouch. Take that chair, will you please? I'm glad you came by."

"Whew! It's dark as midnight in here," said the newcomer, vainly trying to make out who was present. He went promptly, however, to the illuminated chair, and sat down. His manner was pleasantly bewildered, and it was clear that he was as anxious to learn what had occurred as were the police. He grasped at once the value of the lighting arrangement of which Dart had taken advantage and grinned. "Judas, what a bright light! Clever though. Can't see a thing. Who are you, if I may ask?"

Dart told him.

"Glad to know you—though so far you're just a voice. Understand I've lost a tenant. Came back expecting to put the finishing touches on a little job down stairs, and found the place full of officers. Fellow in the door took my breath away—says Frimbo's been killed. How'd it happen?"

Dart's sharp black eyes were studying the undertaker closely. He observed a youngish man of medium build with skin the color of an English walnut, smooth, unblemished, and well cared for. The round face was clean shaven, the features blunt but not coarse, the eyes an indeterminate brown like most Negroes'. His hair was his most noteworthy possession, for it was as black and as straight as an Indian's and it shone with a bright gloss in the light that fell full upon it. His attire was quiet and his air was that of a matter-of-fact, yet genial business man on whom it would be difficult to play tricks. His manner, more than his inquiry, indicated that while there was no need of getting excited over something that couldn't be restored, still it was his right, as neighbor and landlord, to know just what had come about and how.

"Perhaps, Mr. Crouch," replied Dart, "you can answer your own question for us."

If the detective anticipated catching any twitch of feature that might have betrayed masquerading on the undertaker's part he was disappointed. Crouch's expression manifested only a curiosity which now became meditative.

"Well," he said reflectively, "let me see now. You know that he was killed, of course?"

"More than that. We know how he was killed. We know when. We even have evidence of the assailant's identity."

"Assailant? Oh, he was assaulted then? One of his customers, probably. Why, say, if you know that much, you shouldn't have much trouble. It would be narrowed down to whoever was here at the time who wanted to kill him. But that's just your difficulty. Who'd want to kill him?"

"Exactly. That's where you may be able to help us. You knew Frimbo, of course?"

"Only as a landlord knows a tenant." Crouch smiled. "Even that isn't quite true," he amended. "Landlords and tenants are usually enemies. Frimbo, on the contrary, was the best tenant I've ever had. Paid a good rent, always paid it on time, and never asked for a thing. A rare bird in that respect. I'll hardly get another one like him."

"How long was he your tenant here?"

"Nearly two years now. Built himself up quite a following here in Harlem—at least he always had plenty of people in here at night."

"You've had your place of business here how long?"

"Five years this winter."

"And in spite of the fact that you and he have been neighbors for two years, you knew nothing about him personally?"

"Well," again Crouch smiled, "we weren't exactly what you'd call associated. The proximity was purely—geographical, would you call it? You know, of course, that this isn't my residence."

"Yes."

"To be frank, Frimbo always seemed—and I don't mean this geographically—a little above me. Pretty distant, unapproachable

sort of chap. Part of his professional pose, I guess. Solemn as
an undertaker—I honestly envied him his manner. Could have
used it myself. Occasionally we'd meet and pass the time of
day. But otherwise I never knew he was here."

"Your relations were purely of a business nature, then?"

"Quite."

"In that case you really had to see him only once a month—
to collect his rent."

"At first, yes. But during the last few months I didn't even
have to do that. My wife collects all the rents now."

"Isn't that rather a dangerous occupation for a woman? Carrying money about?"

"I suppose so. We hadn't thought about that angle of it. You
know how women are—if they haven't anything much to do
they get restless and dissatisfied. We haven't any kids and she
has a girl to do the housework. When she asked me to let her
collect the rents it struck me as quite sensible—something to
occupy her time and give me a little more freedom. I'm on call
at all hours, you see, so I appreciated a little relief."

"I see. That is probably why she was here tonight."

"Was she? That's good."

"Good? Why?"

"Why—I guess it sounds a little hard—but—of course I'm
sorry for Frimbo and all—but death is such a common experience to me that I suppose I take it as a matter of course. What
I meant was that at least he didn't die in our debt."

So bald a statement rendered even the illusionless Dart silent
a moment, while Dr. Archer audibly gasped. Then the detective said:

"Well—evidently you didn't know Frimbo as well as I had
hoped. You knew no one who would want him out of the
way?"

"No. And whoever it was certainly didn't do me any favor."

"You were here earlier this evening, weren't you, Mr.
Crouch?"

"Yes. I left about nine o'clock. From then until a few minutes ago I was at the Forty Club around the corner playing
cards." He smiled. "You can easily verify that by one of the
attendants—or by my friend, Si Brandon, whom I plucked
quite clean."

"Tell me—could any one get into this room and out without being seen by people in the hall or in the waiting-room?"

"Indeed I don't know. This is the first time since Frimbo came that I've been in here."

"Is that so?"

"Yes."

"Even when you collected rents yourself, you never had to come in here?"

"No. I used to wait in the hall there. Frimbo's man would tell him I was here for the rent and he would send it out. I'd hand the receipt over to the man and that was all."

"I see."

"And there are no concealed passages in this house by which some one could get about undetected?"

"Not unless Frimbo put 'em in himself. I never bothered him or nosed around to see what he was up to. His lease required him to leave things at the end as he found them at the beginning and I let it go at that. But in a room like this I should think a lot of undetected movement would be easy for anyone who put his mind to it. The darkness and those wall drapes and all——"

"Of course. How long did the lease still have to run?"

"Three more years—and at a rate considerably higher than I'll be able to get from anyone now in this depression."

"Was there anything peculiar about your lease agreement—special features and such?"

"No. Nothing. Except perhaps the agreement about heating. I paid for the coal and he paid for the labor. That is, he had his man keep the fires. There's only one boiler, of course."

"His man would have to pass through your part of the house quite often then to tend the fire, put out ashes, and so on?"

"Yes—he did."

"Well, Mr. Crouch, I suppose that's all then for the present. Except that an apology is due you for making use of your parlor downstairs without permission. Dr. Archer here moved the victim down there to examine him better—before he knew he was dead."

"Oh, is that you there, doc? Look like anybody else in the dark, don't you? Don't mention it—glad to have been able to help out. Perhaps if you'd tell me the circumstances, officer, I might run across something of value. Unless, of course, you have reasons for not disclosing what is known so far."

"Don't mind telling you at all," decided Dart. "The victim was stunned by a blow with a hard object—a sort of club—then stifled by a handkerchief pushed down his throat."

"Judas Priest!"

"We have the handkerchief. The club is being examined for finger prints. It was last seen—prior to Frimbo's death I mean—shortly after ten-thirty, resting in its apparently usual place on the mantelpiece in the front room. No one admits seeing it after that time until we found it here on the floor beside this chair, in which Frimbo's body was discovered. Testimony indicates that Frimbo was alive and talking as late as five minutes to eleven. The club was removed therefore by someone who was in the front room after ten-thirty and used by someone who was out of the front room by five minutes to eleven. Presumably the person who removed it was the person who used it. This person, of course, could have hidden until five minutes to eleven in the darkness or behind the drapes of the walls. But certainly he was one of the people who passed from that room into this room during that twenty-five-minute period."

"Say—that's a swell method. Beats a maxim silencer, doesn't it?"

"Well—I don't know. Leaves more evidence, apparently."

"Yes, but the more the evidence the more the possibility of confusion."

"True. But if the two clues we are studying—the ownership of the handkerchief and the identification of the finger prints—coincide, somebody'll be due for a toasting. On a specially designed toaster."

"I don't think you'll find any finger prints on your club though."

"Why not?"

"I'll bet the chap handled the club with the handkerchief."

"Hm—that's a good suggestion. But we'll have to wait for the results of the examination of the club to check that."

"Well," Crouch rose, "if I can think of anything or find anything that might help, I'll be glad to do so. I'm easy to get hold of if you need me again."

"Thank you, Mr. Crouch. I won't detain you." Dart called to the bluecoat at the hall door: "Pass Mr. Crouch out. Or did you say you had something to do downstairs, Mr. Crouch?"

"Well, I did, but it can wait till morning. I might be in your way now—searching around and all. Tomorrow'll be time enough—last few touches you know. Easier to handle a dead face than a live one—I've found that out."

"Interesting," commented Dart. "I never thought of an undertaker as a beautician."

"You'd be surprised. We can make the dark ones bright and the bright ones lighter—that seems to be the ambition in this community. We can fatten thin ones and reduce fat ones. I venture to say that, by the simplest imaginable changes, I could make Doc Archer there quite unrecognizable."

"The need," murmured the doctor, "may be present, but I trust the occasion does not soon arise."

"Well, good luck, officer. Good-night, doc. See you again sometime when things are brighter."

"Good-night."

"Good-night, Crouch."

4

"Why," asked Dr. Archer, "didn't you let him know his wife was still here?"

"She was here when the thing happened. I may need her. If I'd told him she was still here he'd have wanted to see her and she'd have wanted to leave with him."

"You could keep him too, then."

"Had no reason to keep him. His story checked perfectly with his wife's in spite of my efforts to trick him. And I can easily check his previous whereabouts, just as he said—he wouldn't have been so definite about 'em if they couldn't have been verified."

"He could pay liars."

"But he actually wasn't here. Brown, Jenkins, Mrs. Snead, or his wife—surely one of them would have mentioned him."

"That's so."

"And Frimbo was a goose that laid golden eggs for him."

"If it was anybody else besides Martha, I might be suspicious of——"

"Of what?"

"What she might have laid for Frimbo."

"Doctor—spare my blushes!" Then seriously, "But you're sure that she's an irreproachable character. And I'm just as sure Frimbo was not interested in women. That all argues against any outraged husband theory. There's absolutely no basis for it and even if there was, there's nothing that could possibly incriminate Crouch."

"You're right. But don't forget to check up." The doctor fell to ruminating in his wordy and roundabout way. "And keep your pupils dilated for more evidence. I have an impression—just an impression—that bright plumage oft adorns a bird of prey. Curious fellow, Crouch. Bright exterior, genial, cheerful even, despite his doleful occupation; but underneath, hard as a pawnbroker, with an extraordinarily keen awareness of his own possessions. Imagine a man congratulating himself on acquiring an extra month's rent before his tenant came to grief."

"Well, I don't know. Suppose a patient of yours died during an operation for which you had already collected the fee. Would you give back the fee—or would you be glad you had got it first?"

"I would desire with all my heart," murmured the doctor, "to reimburse the bereaved relatives. But since that would resemble an admission that my operation was at fault and would hence endanger my professional reputation, no course would remain except to rush speedily to the bank and deposit the amount to my credit."

"Self-preservation," grinned Dart. "Well, we can't blame Crouch for the same thing. He spoke bluntly, but maybe the man's just honest."

"Maybe everybody is," said Dr. Archer with a sigh.

# Chapter Nine

I

MEANWHILE Bubber Brown, riding beside Officer Hanks in Detective Dart's touring car was evincing a decided appreciation of his new importance. Over his countenance spread a broad grin of satisfaction, and as the machine swung up the Avenue, he reared back in his seat and surveyed his less favored fellow men with a superior air. The car swung into 135th Street, pulled up at the curb in front of the station-house, and acquired presently a new passenger in the person of an enormous black giant named Small, who managed to crowd himself into the tonneau. As it drew away, Bubber could contain himself no longer.

"Hot damn!" he exclaimed. "In power at last!" As the little five-passenger car started off again— "Y'all s'posed to follow my directions now, ain't you?"

"Yep," said Hanks. "Where to now?"

"Henry Patmore's Pool Room—Fifth Avenue and 131st Street. And do me jes' one kind favor, will you Mr. Hanks?"

"What?"

"See that red traffic light yonder?"

"Yep."

"Run on past it, will you please?"

Shortly they reached their objective, got out, and, with Bubber expansively leading the way, entered Patmore's well-known meeting-place.

Patmore's boasted two separate entrances, one leading into the poolroom proper, the other into the barroom by its side. These two long, low rooms communicated within by means of a wide doorway in the middle of the intervening wall, and also by means of a small back gaming-room into which one might pass from either the speakeasy or the billiard parlor. It was into the poolroom that Bubber led the way. He and his uniformed escort paused just within the entrance to survey the scene.

Two long rows of green-topped tables extended the length of the bare wooden floor. Players in shirt sleeves moved about, hats on the backs of their heads, cigarettes drooping from their lips; leaned far over the felt to make impossible shots, whooped at their successes, cursed their failures, thrust cue-points aloft to mark off scores, or thumped cue-butts upon the floor to signal an attendant.

One of these gentlemen, seeing the entrance of Bubber's familiar rotund figure flanked by two officers of the law, called sympathetically:

"Tough titty, short-order. What they got you for this time?"

"They ain't got me," responded Mr. Brown glowing with his new importance. "I got them. And you get fly, I'll get you, too. Now what you think o' that?"

"I think you jes' a pop-eyed liar," said the other, dismissing the matter to sight on a new shot.

Bubber asked the manager, standing nearby, "Say, boy, you seen Spider Webb?"

The one addressed looked at him and looked at the policemen. Then he inquired blandly, "Who'n hell is Spider Webb?"

"Damn!" Bubber murmured, pushing back his hat and scratching his head. "You boogies sho' get dumb in the presence of the law. Listen, this ain' nothin' on him—jes' want to get some dope from him, that's all. Y'see, I'm doin' a little detective work now"—he produced one of the cards he had shown Detective Perry Dart—"and I want Spider's slant on a little case."

"So I *got* to know him?" bridled the other.

"You did know him."

"Well, I done forgot him, then."

"Thanks, liar."

"You welcome—stool."

Ordinarily Bubber would have resented the epithet, which was much worse than the one he himself had used; but he was now in such lofty spirits that the opinion of a mere poolroom manager could not touch him.

"You all wait here," he suggested to the officers. "The Spider might try a fast one if he feels guilty."

But before this expedition had started, Hanks had caught a

sign from Detective Dart that Mr. Bubber Brown must be brought back as well as those whom Mr. Brown identified; and so now Hanks offered an amendment:

"We'll leave Small at the door," he said, "and I'll come along with you."

So it was agreed, and Bubber with Hanks at his heels made his way to the back room of the establishment. As they approached it, Bubber saw the door open and Spider Webb start out. Looking up, Webb recognized Bubber at a distance, stopped, noted the policeman, stepped back and quickly shut the door. Bubber reached the door and flung it open a few seconds later, but his rapid survey revealed a total and astonishing absence of Spider Webb.

"Where'd that boogy go?" inquired Bubber blankly.

"Who?" said the house-man, sitting on a stool at the mid-point of one side of the table, running the game.

"Spider Webb."

The house-man looked about. "Any o' you all seen Spider Webb?" he asked the surrounding atmosphere. The players were so intent on the game that they did not even seem to hear. Upon receiving no response, the house-man appeared to dismiss the matter and also became absorbed again in the fall of cards. Bubber and his policeman were decidedly outside the world of their consideration.

But the newly appointed champion of the law now caught sight of the door at the other end of the room leading into the bar which paralleled the poolroom. With more speed than consideration for those he swept past, he bustled along to the far end of the chamber, opened that door and burst forth into the long narrow barroom. Hanks was but a moment behind him, for Hanks was as concerned with keeping close to Bubber as Bubber was with overtaking Webb. The barroom, however, was as innocent of Spider Webb as had been the blackjack chamber, and Bubber was still expressing his bewilderment in a vigorous scratching of the back of his head when the gentleman pursued appeared. He came through the wide doorway by which the barroom communicated directly with the poolroom. He came, in other words, out of the poolroom. The mystery of how he managed to appear from a place where he certainly had not been—for had not Bubber and Hanks just traversed the poolroom?—was submerged in the more important fact that he was proceeding now very rapidly toward the street door.

"Spider! Hey, Spider!" called Bubber.

Mr. Webb halted and turned in apparent surprise. Bubber and the policeman overtook him.

"What's on your mind?" inquired the Spider quite calmly and casually, quite, indeed, as though he had not been in any hurry whatever and had no other interest in the world than the answer to his question.

"How did you get in yonder?" Bubber wanted to know.

"How," inquired Webb, "did you and your boy friend get in here?"

Bubber abandoned the lesser mystery to pursue his interest in the original one. "Listen. Somebody put that thing on Frimbo tonight. We all got to get together over there and find out who done it. Everybody what was there."

"Put what thing on him?"

"Cut him loose, man. Put him on the well-known spot."

"Frimbo——"

"Hisself."

"Killed him?"

"If you want to put it that way."

"Good-night!" Spider Webb's astonishment yielded to a sense of his own implication. "So what?" he inquired rather harshly.

"So you, bein' among those present, you got to return to the scene of the tragedy. That's all."

"Yea? And who knew I was on the scene of the tragedy?"

"Everybody knew it."

"Reckon the police knew it, huh? All they had to do was walk in, and they knew I'd been there, huh? The peculiar perfume I use or somethin'?" There was somber menace in Spider's tone.

"Well," admitted Bubber, "you know I been doin' a little private detective work o' my own, see? So I'm helpin' the police out on this case. Naturally, knowin' you was there, I knew you'd want to give all the information you could, see? Anything else would look like runnin' away, y'understand?"

"I see. You're the one I got to thank for this little consideration."

"I'm givin' you a chance to protect yo'self," said Bubber.

"Thanks," Webb responded darkly. "I'll do the same by you sometime. Be watchin' out for it."

"Let's go," suggested Officer Hanks.

They went into the poolroom and with Small, returned to the car at the curb.

2

"Know how to drive?" Hanks asked Bubber.

"Who me? Sho'. I can drive anything but a bargain."

"Take the wheel—and plenty o' time."

Bubber obeyed. Shortly the expedition arrived at its next port of call, the Hip-Toe Club on Lenox Avenue. Leaving Small and the ominously silent Spider Webb in the car, Officer Hanks and Bubber left to seek Doty Hicks.

"How you know he's here?" Hanks said.

"His brother runs the place. Spats Oliver, they call him. Real name's Oliver Hicks. Everybody knows him, and everybody knows Doty. Doty's been up for dope-peddlin' coupla times—finally the dope got him—now it's all he can do to get enough for himself. This is his hang-out."

"It would be," observed Hanks. They had passed under a dingy canopy and into a narrow entrance, had negotiated a precipitate and angular staircase, and so with windings and twistings had descended eventually into a reclaimed cellar. The ceiling was oppressively low, the walls splotched with black silhouetted grotesqueries, and the atmosphere thick with smoke. Two rows of little round white-topped tables hugged the two lateral walls, leaving between them a long narrow strip of bare wooden floor for dancing or entertainment. This strip terminated at a low platform at the far end of the room, whereon were mounted a pianist, a drummer, a banjo-player and a trumpeter, all properly equipped with their respective instruments and at the moment all performing their respective rites without restraint.

In the narrow strip of interspace, a tall brown girl was doing a song and dance to the absorbed delight of the patrons seated nearest her. Her flame chiffon dress, normally long and flowing, had been caught up bit by bit in her palms, which rested nonchalantly on her hips, until now it was not so much a dress as a sash, gathered about her waist. The long shapely smooth brown limbs below were bare from trim slippers to sash, and only a bit of silken underthing stood between her modesty and surrounding admiration.

With extraordinary ease and grace, this young lady was proving beyond question the error of reserving legs for mere locomotion, and no one who believed that the chief function of the hips was to support the torso could long have maintained so ridiculous a notion against the argument of her eloquent gestures.

Bubber caught sight of this vision and halted in his tracks. His abetting of justice, his stern immediate duty as a deputy of the law, faded.

"Boy!" he said softly. "What a pair of eyes!"

Sang the girl, with an irrelevance which no one seemed to mind:

> *I'll be standin' on the corner high*
> *When they drag your body by—*
> *I'll be glad when you're dead, you rascal you.*

"Where," said the unimpressionable Hanks, "is this bozo named Doty Hicks?"

"If he ain't here," returned Bubber, still captivated by the vision, "we'll jes' have to sit down and wait for him."

"I'll stand here. You look."

"I'm lookin'."

"For Hicks, if it ain't askin' too much."

Reluctantly obedient, Bubber moved slowly along the aisle, scanning the patrons at this table and that, acutely aware that his march was bringing him momentarily nearer the dancing girl. No one had he yet seen who faintly resembled Doty Hicks. The girl's number ended just as Bubber was on the point of passing her. As she terminated her dance with a flourish, she swung merrily about and chucked the newcomer under his plump chin.

"You're short and broad, but sweet, oh Gawd!"

Bubber, who was as much a child of the city as she, was by no means embarrassed. He grinned, did a little buck and wing step of his own, ended with a slap of his foot, and responded:

"You're long and tall and you've got it all!"

"O.K., big boy," laughed the girl and would have turned away, but he stopped her. Offering her one of his detective-cards, he said:

"Sis, if you ever need a friend, look me up."

She took the card, glanced at it, laughed again.

"Here on business, mister?"

"Business, no lie," he said ruefully. "Seen my friend Doty Hicks?"

"Oh—that kind o' business. Well who's that over in the corner by the orchestra?"

He looked, and there indeed was Doty Hicks, a little wizened black fellow, bent despondently over the table at which he sat alone, his elbows resting on the white porcelain surface, which he contemplated in deep meditation, his chin in his hands.

"Thanks, sister. I'll do better when I can see more of you. Right now at present, duty calls." And lamenting the hardships of working for law and order, Bubber approached the disconsolate figure at the corner table.

Remembering how he had been received by Spider Webb, Bubber approached the present responsibility differently:

"Hello, Doty," he said pleasantly and familiarly.

Doty Hicks looked up, the protrusiveness of his eyes accentuated by the thinness of his face. He stared somewhat like a man coming out of anesthesia.

"Don't know you," he said in a voice that was tremulous but none the less positive. And he resumed his contemplation of the table top.

"Sure you know me. You and me was at Frimbo's tonight —remember?"

"Couldn't see Frimbo," said Doty. "Too dark." Whether he referred to the darkness of Frimbo's room or of Frimbo's complexion was not clear. Bubber went on:

"Frimbo's got somethin' for you."

"Yea—talk. Thass all. Lot o' talk."

"He ain't expected to live—and he wants to see you befo' he dies."

For a moment the little man made no sound, his great round eyes staring blankly at Bubber Brown. Then, in a hoarse, unsteady whisper he repeated:

"Ain't expected to live?"

"Not long." Bubber was pursuing the vague notion that by hiding the actuality of the death he would achieve easier coöperation and less enmity. "It took him sort o' sudden."

"Mean—mean Frimbo's dyin'?"

"Don't mean maybe."

Doty Hicks, unsteadily, jerkily, more like a mechanism than like a man, got to his feet, pushed back his chair, stood teetering a dizzy moment, then rubbed the back of his hand across his nose, shook his head, became steadier, and fixed Bubber with an unwavering stare, a look in which there was a hint of triumph and more than a hint of madness.

"It worked!" he said softly. "It worked!" A grin, vacant, distant, unpleasant to see, came over his wasted features. "It worked! What you know 'bout that?" said he.

Bubber did not care for this at all. "I don't know nothin' 'bout it, but if you comin', come on, let's go."

"If I'm comin'? You couldn't keep me 'way. Where is he?"

Bubber had to hold him by the arm on the way out, partly to support him, partly to restrain the trembling eagerness with which he sought to reach Frimbo ere the latter should die.

3

"Where," inquired Bubber of Officer Hanks as they wedged the diminutive Doty Hicks into the already well-occupied rear seat and resumed their journey, "are we go'n' put Brother Easley Jones—if any?"

"We'll have to drop these men off and come back for him."

"Won't need no car for him—told me he lived right there in the same block, a few houses from Frimbo."

"You know everybody, don't you?"

"Well, I recognized these two in the waitin'-room there

tonight. Anybody that travels the sidewalks o' Harlem much as I do knows them by sight anyhow. This Easley Jones I struck up a conversation with on purpose. He was a jolly sort of a feller, easy to talk to, y' see, and when I found out he was a railroad man, I knew right off I might have a customer. Railroad men is the most back-bitten bozos in the world. They what you might call legitimate prey. That's, of co'se, if they married. Y' see, they come by it natural—they so crooked themselves. Any guy what lays over forty-eight hours one time in New York, where his wife is, and forty-eight hours another in Chicago, where she ain't, is gonna curve around a little in Chicago jes' to keep in practice for New York. Y' see what I mean?"

"Is that what this Easley Jones was doin'?"

"He didn't say. But he give me the number o' the house he rooms at in New York—*his* wife is in Chicago—and asked me to drop in and advise him some time."

"Some time'll be tonight."

"Right."

The two material witnesses were escorted back to Frimbo's and were left on the way upstairs in Officer Small's care. Hanks and Bubber walked the short distance back along the block to the address Easley Jones had given. Bubber mounted the stoop and rang the bell of a dwelling much like that in which the African mystic had lived and died.

After a moment the dark hall lighted up, the door opened, and a large, yellow woman wearing horn-rimmed spectacles gazed inquisitively upon them.

"Mr. Jones in?" asked Bubber.

"Mr. who?"

"Mr. Jones. Mr. Easley Jones."

The lady glanced at the uniformed officer and said resolutely, "Don' nobody stay here by that name. You-all must have the wrong address."

"We don't want to arrest him, lady. We want him to help us find somebody, that's all. He's a friend o' mine—else how'd I know he lived here?"

The woman considered this. "What'd you say his name was?"

"Jones. Easley Jones. Light brown-skin feller with freckles all over his face and kinks all over his head. He's a railroad man

—runs from here to Chicago—him and me used to work together. Yes ma'am. Sho' did."

The horn-rimmed lenses were like the windows of a fortress.
"Sorry—y'all done made a mistake somewhere. No sech person lives in this house. Know a Sam Jones," she added helpfully,
"that lives in Jamaica, Long Island. He's a butler—don' run on
no road, but he commutes to New York mos' ev'y night."

"Too bad, lady, but we can't take no substitutes. If it ain't
genuwine Easley, we can't use it. Thanks jes' the same. But if
you do run across a Easley Jones, tell him Frimbo wants to see
him again tonight—right away—please."

"Hmph!" responded the gracious lady and shut the door
abruptly.

"That's funny, ain't it?" reflected Bubber as the two turned
back toward the house of tragedy.

"It's all funny to me," confessed Officer Hanks. "It's all jes'
a mess, what I mean. Everybody I've seen acts guilty."

"You ain't been lookin' at me, is you, brother?"

"You? You're mighty anxious to put it on somebody else—I
see that."

Bubber sighed at the hopelessness of ever weaning a cop
from indiscriminate suspicion.

# Chapter Ten

I

THE officer who had taken the club to be examined for finger prints returned and reported that the examination was under way, that photographic reproductions would be sent over as soon as they were ready, and that a finger-print man would come with them to take additional data, make comparisons, and establish or eliminate such possible identities as Detective Dart might be seeking.

This officer was returned to his post as Doty Hicks and Spider Webb were ushered up the stairs by the gigantic Officer Small. Sensing their arrival, Dart had the extension light again turned off.

"If those are the men we're waiting for send them up front."

Accordingly, Small came in alone to report. "We got two of 'em. Little dopey guy and Spider Webb, the number-runner."

"Where are the others—Brown and Jones?"

"Brown's gone with Hanks to get Jones—right down the street here."

"Good. You wait outside, Small. Brady, bring Hicks—the little one—in first."

Doty Hicks, though of none too steady a gait, was by no means reluctant to come in. With his protruding eyes popping and mouth half open, he entered the shaft of light and stood peering into the well-nigh impenetrable blackness that obscured the seated detective and the doctor standing beside him.

Dart waited. After a long moment of fruitless staring, Doty Hicks whispered, "Is you dead yet?"

"No," said the detective softly.

"But you dyin', ain't you?" The little fellow was trembling. "They tol' me you was dyin'."

Dart followed the obvious lead, though he could only guess its origin.

"So you tried to kill me?"

450

A puzzled look came over Doty Hick's thin black face.
"You don't sound right. Yo' voice don't sound——"
"Sit down," said Dart.
Still bewildered, Hicks mechanically obeyed.
"Why did you try to kill me?"
Hicks stared dumbly, groping for something. Suddenly his
features changed to an aspect of unwilling comprehension,
then of furious disappointment. He leaned forward in his chair,
catching hold of the edge of the table. "You ain't him!" he
cried. "You ain't him! You tryin' to fool me! Where's he at—I
got to see him die. I got to——"
"Why?"
"Else it ain't no use—I got to see him! Where's he at?"
"Take it easy, Hicks. Maybe we'll let you see him. But you'll
have to tell us all about it. Now, what's the idea?"
A plaintive almost sobbing tone came into Doty's high, quavering voice.
"Who is you, mister? What you want to fool me for?"
"I don't want to fool you, Hicks. I want to help you. You
can tell me all about it—you can trust me. Tell me the whole
thing, and if it's straight, I'll let you see Frimbo."
"Lemme see him first, will you, mistuh? He may die before
I get to him."
"If he isn't dead yet he won't die till you get to him. You'll
have to tell your story first, so you better tell it quickly. Why
did you come here tonight at ten-thirty? Why did you try to
kill Frimbo, and why must you see him before he dies?"
Doty sank back in his chair. "All right," he said, dully. Then,
quickened by the realization of the urgency, he leaned forward
again. "All right—I'll tell you, I'll tell you. Listen." He paused.
"I'm listening."
Drawing a deep breath, Doty Hicks proceeded:
"Frimbo's a conjure-man. You know that."
"Yes."
"I come here tonight because Frimbo was killin' my brother."
He hesitated. "Killin' my brother," he repeated. Then, "You
know my brother—everybody knows my brother—Spats Oliver
Hicks—runs the Hip-Toe Club on Lenox Avenue. Good guy,
my brother. Always looked out for me. Even when I went
dopey and got down and out like I is now, he never turned me

down. Always looked out for me. Good guy. If it'd been me Frimbo was killin', 'twouldn' matter. I'm jes' a dope—nobody'd miss me. But he was killin' my brother, see? Y'see, Frimbo's a conjure-man. He can put spells on folks. One kind o' spell to keep 'em from dyin' like that boy what got the knife stuck in his head. Another kind to set 'em to dyin'—like he was doin' my brother. Slow dyin'—misery all in through here, coughin' spells, night sweats, chills and fever, and wastin' away. That's what he was doin' to Spats."

"But why?" Dart couldn't help asking.

" 'Count o' my brother's wife. He's doin' it 'count o' my brother's wife. Spats married a show-gal, see? And hadn't been married a month befo' she met up with some guy with more sugar. So she quit my brother for the sugar-papa, see? And natchelly, bein' a regular man and not no good-for-nothin' dope like me, my brother went after her, see? He grabbed this sugar-daddy and pulled him inside out, like a glove. And one day he met the gal and asked her to come back and she called him somethin' and he smacked her cross-eyed. Well, 'cose, that give her a fever, and she come straight here to Frimbo. She could get plenty o' what it took from the new daddy, and she brought it with her. Frimbo told her what to do. She made be-lieve she was goin' back to live with my brother, and he like a fool took her in. She stayed jes' long enough to do what Frimbo'd told her to do, whatever it was. Day she left, my brother had a fit—jes' like a cat in a alley—a fit. And ever since, he's been goin' from bad to worse. Doctor don' help, nothin' don' help. Y'see, it's Frimbo's spell."

"And that's why you tried to kill him?"

"Yea—that's why."

"How did you go about it?"

Doty Hicks looked around him into the enshrouding dark-ness. He shook his head. "Can't tell you that. Can't tell nobody how—that'd break the spell. All I can tell you is that they's only one way to kill a conjure-man—you got to out-conjure him. You got to put a back-conjure on him, and it's got to be stronger 'n the one he put on the other feller. 'Cose you can't do it alone. Got to have help."

"Help? What kind of help?"

"Somebody has to help you."

"Who helped you with this?"

"Can't tell you that neither—that'd break the spell. Can I see him now?"

"Why do you have to see him before he dies?"

"That's part of it. I have to see him and tell him how come he's dyin', else it don't do no good. But if I see him and tell him how come he's dyin', then, soon as he die, my brother gets well. See? Jes' like that—gets well soon as Frimbo die."

"Did you pay the person to help you?"

"Pay him? Sho'—had to pay him."

"And do you realize that you are making a confession of deliberate murder—for which you may be sentenced to die?"

"Hmph! What I care 'bout that? I been tired livin' a long time, mistuh. But you couldn't prove nothin' on me. I did a stretch once and I know. You got to have evidence. I got it fixed so they ain't no evidence—not against me."

"Against somebody else, maybe?" Doty Hicks did not answer.

"Frimbo was a pretty wise bird. He must have known you wanted to conjure him—the way he could read people's minds. What did he say when you came in?"

"Didn't say nothin' for a while. I asked him to lay off my brother—begged him, if he had to conjure somebody, to conjure me—but he jes' set there in the dark like he was thinkin' it over, and then he begins talkin'. Say: 'So you want to die in place of your brother? It is impossible. Your brother is incurably ill.' Then he kep' quiet a minute and he say, 'You have been misinformed, my friend. You are under the impression that I have put an evil spell upon your brother. That is superstitious nonsense. I am no caster of spells. I am a psychist—a kind of psychologist. I have done nothing to your brother. He simply has pulmonary tuberculosis—in the third stage. He had had it for at least three months when your sister-in-law came to me for advice. I could not possibly be responsible for that, since until then I did not know of his existence.' 'Course I didn' believe that, 'cause my brother hadn' been sick a day till after his wife came here, so I kep' on askin' him to take off the spell, so he finally says that everything'll be all right in a few days and don' worry. Well, I figure he's jes' gettin' rid o' me, and I gets up like I'm on my way out and come through that side door there, but 'stead o' goin' on downstairs, I slips back in again and—and——"

"Put your counter-spell on him?"

"I ain' sayin'," said Doty Hicks, "I'm jes' tellin' you enough so I can see him. I ain' sayin' enough to break the spell."

"And you refuse to say who helped you?"

"Not till I see Frimbo die; then I'll tell maybe. 'Twon' make no difference, then—the spell'll be broke. Now lemme see him, like you said."

"There's no hurry. You can wait up front a few minutes."

"You said if I tol' you——" Doty Hicks was changing from abjection and pleading to suspicion and anger. "What you want to say so for if you wasn't go'n'——"

"I said you must tell your story first. You've only told part of it. I also said that if Frimbo wasn't dead when you came in, he wouldn't be when you finished. That was true. He was already dead when you came in."

The face of the tremulous little man in the illumined chair was ordinarily ugly in a pitiful, dissolute, and rather harmless way. But as the meaning of Dart's statement now slowly sank into his consciousness that usual ugliness became an exceptionally evil and murderous ugliness. Doty Hicks leaned forward still further where he sat, his white eyes more protruding than ever, his breath coming in sharp gasps. And suddenly, as if a high tension current shot through him, he lurched to his feet and lunged forward toward Dart's voice.

"Gimme sump'm!" he screamed, his hands groping the table top in the dark. "Gimme sump'm in my hand! I'll bust yo' head open—you cheat! I'll——"

By that time Brady had him.

"Take him up front," instructed Detective Dart. "Have somebody keep a special eye on him. He's worth holding on to."

Struggling, cursing, and sobbing, Doty Hicks was dragged from the room.

2

"He wanted something with which to 'bust your head open,'" reflected Dr. Archer.

"So I noticed," said Detective Dart.

"Frimbo's head was—ever so slightly—'busted' open."

"Yes."

"Memory-suggestion?"

"Or coincidence? Anybody in a rage might want to get his hands on a weapon."

"With which to 'bust open' an offending cranium. No doubt. Rather over-effective way to 'put a spell' on a fellow though."

"Exactly. Wouldn't have to put a spell on him if you were going to brain him with a club."

"No. Yet—if you weren't going to brain him—if you just wanted him to keep still while the spell was being put on——"

"Yes—but a handkerchief is a pretty substantial thing, also, to use as a spell. And it wasn't put on. It was put in."

"In other words, whoever helped Doty Hicks, wasn't taking any chances."

"Something like that."

"Turn on the light a minute. I want to look at that—spell."

Dart gave the order. The extension lamp went on, throwing its sharp radiance into the darkness and giving an unnatural effect which disclosed well enough the men, the two chairs, the table, the black-hung walls, but somehow did not in any way relieve the oppressive somberness of the place—a light that cut through the shadow without actually dispelling it.

The physician stooped and, using his forceps, took the blue-bordered handkerchief out of his bag. He dropped it on the table, and with the instrument poked it about till it lay flat.

"What sort of a person," he meditated in a low tone, "would even think of using a device like that?"

## 3

Whatever Dart might have answered was cut off by the uncere-monious and rather breathless entrance of Bubber Brown. Hanks, like a faithful guardian, was at his heels.

"We got two of 'em—see 'em?" Bubber breathed. "Doty Hicks was no trouble—too anxious to get here. But that Spider Webb—we had to chase that nigger all over Pat's."

"Yes, thanks. But where's Easley Jones?"

"We went to where he said he lived, couple o' doors up the street. But the landlady claim she didn' know him. I think she got leery when she saw my boy's brass buttons here and jes' shut up on general principles. But we left word for him to come by."

"That's not so good. Guess we'll have to put out feelers for him."

"How come 'tain' so good?"

"Nobody's anxious to get mixed up in a murder case."

"How he know it's a murder case?" Bubber said, using the same logic Dart had used on him earlier. "All I said was Frimbo wanted to see him right away. If he don't know it's a murder case, he'll figure Frimbo's got some more advice for him or sump'm and come a-runnin'. If he do know it's a murder case, he's long gone anyhow, so leavin' the message can't do no more harm than's done already."

Dart looked at Bubber with new interest.

"That's good reasoning—as far as it goes," he remarked. "But the woman—the landlady—may have been telling the truth. Maybe Easley Jones doesn't live there."

"Well then," Bubber concluded promptly, "if he lied 'bout his address in the first place, he was up to sump'm crooked all along. He didn't *have* to invite me to come advise him 'bout his trouble, jes' 'cause he saw my card. I can see why his land-lady would lie—to protect him—but there wasn't no reason for him to lie to me."

"Then what is your opinion, Brown?"

"My 'pinion's like this: I believe he gimme the right address. She'll tell him—if he's still there to tell. If he had anything to do with this he'll stay 'way. If he didn't have nothin' to do with it, and don't know it's happened, curiosity to see what else Frimbo wants will bring him back."

"In other words, if Easley Jones does come back, he isn't the man we're after. Is that it?"

"Yes, suh. That's it. And if he don't come back, whether it's 'cause he lied 'bout the address or 'cause he got the message and is scared to come—y'all better find him. He knows sump'm. Any man that runs away, well, all I say is, is been up to sump'm."

"The attendant seems to have run away," Dart reminded him.

"It's between the two of 'em then—less'n they show up."

"What about Doty Hicks? He's confessed."

"No!"

"Sure—while you were out."

"He did? Well, I don't pay that no mind. That nigger's crazy. Smokes too many reefers."

"There may be a good deal in what you say, Brown. Anyhow, thanks for your help. Just go up front and keep your eyes and ears open, will you?"

"Sho' will," Bubber promised, proud of his commendation. But as he was on the point of turning away, his eye fell on the table where the blue-bordered handkerchief lay.

"Jinx been in here, ain't he?" said he.

"Jenkins? Yes, why?"

"I see he left his handkerchief. Want me to give it to him?"

Dart and the physician exchanged glances.

"Is that his?" the detective asked, feigning mild surprise.

"Sho' 'tis. I was kiddin' him 'bout it tonight. Great big old ugly boogy like Jinx havin' a handkerchief with a baby blue border on it. Can y' imagine? A baby blue border!"

"But," Dart said softly, "I asked you before if you'd seen anybody here with a colored handkerchief, and you said no."

"Yea—but I thought you meant really colored—like mine. That's white, all 'cep'n' the hem. And anyhow, when you ast me if I'd seen any o' these people here with a colored handkerchief, I wasn't thinkin' 'bout Jinx. He ain't people. He never even crossed my mind. I was thinkin' 'bout them three men."

"Brady, ask Jenkins to come in again."

When Jinx returned, the unsuspecting Bubber, whose importance had by now grown large in his own eyes, did not wait for Dart to act. He picked up the handkerchief and thrust it toward Jinx saying:

"Here, boy, take your belongin's with you—don't leave 'em layin' 'round all over the place. You ain't home."

The tall, freckled, scowling Jinx was caught off guard. He looked doubtfully from the handkerchief to Bubber and from Bubber to the detective.

The detective was smiling quite guilelessly at him. "Take it if it's yours, Jenkins. We found it." Not even in his tone was there the slightest implication of any earlier mention of a handkerchief.

"Ole baby blue," mocked Bubber. "Take it boy, take it. You know it's yours—though it's no wonder you 'shamed to own it. Baby blue!"

But the redoubtable Jinx had by now grown normally wary.

" 'Tain' none o' mine," he growled. "Never seen it before. This here's the boy that goes in for colors."

"Well," grinned Bubber, unaware that he was driving nails in his friend's coffin, "it may not be yours, but you sho' was wipin' yo' face with it when you come in here tonight."

Dart was still smiling. "Never mind," he remarked casually, "if it isn't Jenkins' he doesn't have to take it. That's all for the present. Just step up front again, will you please?"

A moment later, the doctor was saying, "Looks bad for Jenkins. If he'd accepted it right off, it would've been better for him."

"Right."

"But refusing to acknowledge it when it's now so clearly his—that's like being caught with the goods and saying 'I didn't take it.' "

"Jenkins is lying to cover up. That's a cinch."

"He may, of course—in ignorance—be just denying everything on general principles, without knowing specifically why himself."

"Yea," said Dart ironically. "He may. Brady, did you get that last down exactly?"

"Sho' did," said Brady.

"It wouldn't take much more," mused Dart, "to justify arresting our lanky friend, Jenkins."

"He hasn't admitted ownership of it."

"No. But knowing it's his, we can probably—er—persuade him to admit it, if necessary."

"But you've already got to hold that Hicks—on his own confession."

"His confession—if that's what it was—mentioned a sort of accomplice, as I remember it."

"So it did," reflected Dr. Archer.

"Jenkins might be that accomplice."

"Well—there's one strong argument against that."

"Name it."

"Jenkins' character. He just isn't the coöperating kind."

Detective Dart grinned.

"Doc, did you ever hear," he said, "of the so-called filthy lucre?"

Dr. Archer's serious face relaxed a little.

"I even saw some once," he murmured reminiscently.

# Chapter Eleven

## I

FROM the hall came the sound of an unsubdued and frankly astonished masculine voice, high-pitched in tone, firm, smooth in timbre, decidedly southern in accent, exclaiming:

"Great day in the mornin'! What all you polices doin' in this place? Policeman outside d' front door, policeman in d' hall, policeman on d' stairs, and hyer's another one. 'Deed I mus' be in d' wrong house! Is this Frimbo the conjure-man's house, or is it the jail?"

"Who you want to see?"

"There 'tis again. Policeman downstairs tole me come up hyer. Now you ask me same thing he did. Frimbo jes' sent for me, and I come to find out what he want."

"Wait a minute."

The officer thus addressed came in to Dart.

"Let him in," Dart said. But the order was unnecessary for the newcomer was already in.

"Bless mah soul!" he ejaculated. "I never see so many polices in all my life. Look like a lost parade." He came up to the physician and the detective. "Which a one o' y'all is Mr. Frimbo?" he inquired. "When I was hyer befo' it was so dark I couldn' see, though 'cose I heard every word what was said. Fact, if one o' y'all is him, jes' speak and I'll know it. Never fergit that voice as long as I got holes in my ears."

"You're Easley Jones?"

"At yo' service, brother."

"Mr. Frimbo is gone, Jones. Gone on a long journey."

"Is that a fact? Well, I'm a travelin' man myself. I run on the road—y' know—New York to Chicago. But say—how could he send me word to come back here if he's done gone away?"

"You received the message?"

"Sho' I did. Ha! That landlady o' mine's all right. Y' know, she figured I been up to sump'm, so she made out like she didn' know me when that cop come by jes' now. But I knowed

460

I ain' done nothin' wrong, and I figured best thing to do was breeze on back and see what's up. Where's he gone, mistuh?"

"Frimbo's dead. He was killed while you were here to-night."

For the first time, the appearance of Easley Jones became definite, as if this statement had suddenly turned a floodlight full upon him. He was of medium height, dressed in dark clothing, and he carried a soft gray felt hat in his hand. The hat dropped to the floor, the man stood motionless, his brown eyes went widely incredulous and his light brown face, which was spattered with black freckles, grew pale so that the freckles stood out even blacker still. Loose-mouthed, he gazed upon the detective a long moment. Then he drew a deep breath, slowly bent his kinky head and recovered his hat, stood erect again, and sighed:

"Well I be dog-goned!"

"I'm a police officer. It was I who sent for you, not Frimbo. It speaks in your favor that you have come. If you will be kind enough to sit down there in that chair, I'd like to ask you a few questions."

"Ask *me* questions? 'Deed, brother, I don' know what good askin' me anythin's go'n' do you. Look like to me I ought to be askin' you the questions. How long he been daid?"

"Sit down, please."

There was no evading the quiet voice, the steadfast bright black eyes of the little detective. Easley Jones sat down. At a word from Dart, the extension light went out. Thereupon, Easley Jones promptly got up. He made no effort to conceal the fact that the absence of surrounding illumination rendered the situation decidedly uncomfortable for him.

"Why—this is jes' like it was befo'—befo'. Listen, brother, if you 'specks to get a straight tale out o' me, you better gimme plenty o' light. Dark as 'tis in hyer now, I can't make out what I'm sayin'."

"Nothing's going to hurt you. Just sit down and answer truthfully what I ask you."

"Aw right, mistuh. But tellin' a man somebody been killed, and then turnin' out all the lights and talkin' right from wha' he was—dat ain't no way to get the truth. I ain' 'sponsible for nothin' I say, I tell you that much, now. And jes' lemme hear one funny little noise and you'll find yo'self starin' at a empty chair."

"You won't get far, my friend."

"Who? I tol' you I was a travelin' man. If anything funny happen, I'm go'n' prove it."

"You run on the railroad?"

"Yas, suh. Dat is, I rides on it."

"Company?"

"Never has no company. No suh. Always go alone."

"What railroad company?"

"Oh. Pullman—natchelly."

"Porter, of course?"

"Now what else do the Pullman Company put niggers on trains for?"

"How long've you been with them?"

"Ten years and five months yestiddy. Yestiddy was the first o' February, wasn't it?"

"What run?"

"You mean now?"

"Yes."

"New York to Chicago over the Central."

"Twentieth Century?"

"Yas indeedy—bes' train in the East."

"What's its schedule?"

"Two forty-five out o' New York, nine forty-five nex' morning in Chicago."

"Same hours on the return trip?"

"Yas, suh. 'Cep'n' week-ends. I lay over Saturday night and all day Sunday—one week in Chicago, nex' week in New York. Tonight's my Saturday in New York, y'see?"

"That's how you happened to choose tonight to see Frimbo?"

"Uh-huh. Yea."

"What time did you get here tonight?"

"Ten-twenty on the minute."

"How can you say that so positively?"

"Well, I tole you I'm a railroad man. I does ev'ything by the clock. When I arrive someplace I jes' natchelly look at my watch —fo'ce o' habit, y'see."

"You went straight into the waiting-room?"

"Yea—they was a flunky standin' in the hall; he showed me in."

"Describe him."

"Tall, black, and cock-eyed."

"Which eye had the cast in it?"

"Right eye—no—lemme see—left—tell you the truth I don' know. I never could tell, when it come to folks like that, which eye is lookin' at me and which ain't. But it was one of 'em—I knows that."

"Who was present when you arrived?"

"Nobody. I was first."

"What did you do?"

"I sat down and waited. Nothin' else for me to, was they?"

"What happened?"

"Nothin'. Too much nothin'. I sat there waitin' a while, 'bout eight or ten minutes I guess, and then a little feller come in that looked—well, he looked kind o' dopey to me. Nex', right behind him, come a sporty lookin' gent in gray—kind o' heavy-set he was, and tight-lookin', like he don' want no foolishness. Then two other men come in together, a long thin one and a short thick one. We all set around a minute or so, and then this short one begin to walk around and look at them decorations and charms in yonder, and the tall one with him. He started talkin' to the tall one 'bout them little freakish-lookin' figures on the wall, and them knives and spears. He say, 'Boy, you know what them is?' His boy say, 'No, what?' He say, 'Them's the folks this Frimbo's done chopped loose, and these implements hyer is what he chopped 'em loose with.' So the other say, 'What of it?' And the little one say, 'Know how come he kilt 'em?' 'No,' the long boy says. So the little one say, ''Cause they was so ugly. That make it look bad for you, son.' Long boy say, 'Why?' Shorty say, ''Cause they was all better lookin' than you is!' I figgered he might know sump'm 'bout them things sho' 'nough, so I went over where he was and struck up a conversation with him. Turned out he was a sort o' home detective, and I figgered he might be of some use to me, so I invited him to come by and see me some time when I was in town. Said he would. Say—I guess that's how y'all knowed where to find me at, huh? He must 'a' tol' you."

"What particular decorations or charms did you and he discuss?"

"None of 'em. Started—but right off he handed me his card and we got to talkin' 'bout other matters and fust thing I know, there was the flunky ready to show me in to Frimbo. So I went back to my chair, picked up my hat, and follered the flunky. Thought I might see this li'l detective ag'in, but 'stead o' goin' out the way I come in, Frimbo tole me to go out by this side hall-door hyer."

"Did you see two clubs on opposite ends of the mantel-piece?"

"Clubs? Uh-uh. Not far as I 'member now. Them funny-faces and things on the wall—I 'member them. Wait a min-ute—you mean two bones?"

"Yes."

"B'lieve I did. One 'cross one end of the mantelpiece, and one 'cross the other. Yea—sho' I did."

"What did you wish to see Frimbo about, Mr. Jones?"

"Now right there, brother, is where you gettin' personal. But I reckon I kin tell you—though I don' want to see it in no papers."

"There are no reporters here."

"Well, then, y'see it's like this. I got a wife in Chicago. I fig-ger she gets kind o' lonesome seein' me only every other week-end—that is, for any length o' time. Three four hours in the middle o' the day is jes' enough to say howdy and goo'by. So with all them evenin's full o' nothin' special to do, I got kind o' worried—y' understand? And one o' the New York boys on the train was tellin' me this Frimbo could tell the low-down on doings like that, so I figgered I'd come up and see him. So up I come."

"Did he give you the information you were looking for?"

" 'Deed he did, brother. He set my mind at rest."

"Just what was said when you came in to see him?"

"Well, I say I was hyer to ask 'bout my wife—was she true *to* me or f'ru *with* me. But he didn' say nothin' till he got good and ready, and then he didn' say much. Tole me I didn' have nothin' to worry 'bout—that he seen I had murder in my heart for somebody, but there wasn' no other mule in my stall sho' 'nough and to go on forgit it. 'Course them wasn' his 'zack words, but dass what he meant. So I went on—'cep'n' as I was 'bout to go down the stairs, the flunky 'peared in the hall there and collected my two bucks. Then I lef'."

Detective Dart turned his flashlight on the table where the blue-bordered handkerchief still lay.

"Ever see that before?"

The railroad porter leaned forward to inspect the object. "Seen one jes' like it," he admitted.

"When and where?"

"Tonight. In the front room yonder. That tall feller was wipin' his face with it when he fust come in. Couldn't miss it. 'Cose I can't say it's the self-same one——"

"That's all for the present, Jones. Thank you. Wait up front a few minutes, please."

"Yas, *suh*. And if they's anything I kin do, jes' lemme know. Who you reckon done it, chief?"

"When do you count up your tips, Jones?"

"Suh?"

"In the middle of the trip—or at the end?"

"Oh." Jones grinned widely, his round freckled face brightening. "I see what you mean. Yas, suh. I count 'em after the train's pulled in."

"Right. This train isn't in yet. But we know where it's headed and we know who's on board."

"O.K., brother engineer. But bring her in on time, please suh. I got me a little serious wringin' and twistin' to do later on tonight."

2

"I'm getting interested in the servant with the evil eye," murmured Dr. Archer. "Terribly careless of him to disappear like this."

"We'll find him, if it boils down that far."

"Are you by any manner of chance beginning to draw conclusions?"

"Not by chance, no. Getting tired?"

"The neurons of my pallium are confused but extraordinarily active. The soles of my feet, however, being, so to speak, at the other extreme as to both structure and function——"

"Brady, bring in Spider Webb and bring along a chair for Dr. Archer."

"Thoughtful of you," said Dr. Archer.

"Excuse me, doc. I forgot you were standing all this time."

"I only remember it in the intervals myself. And this is possibly the last. However, better tardy than when parallel lines meet—what's this?"

"Wait a minute, Brady. Lights, Joe," the detective called. "Who's there now? Oh, hello there, Tynes. This is our local finger-print hound, doc. What'd you find, Tynie?"

"They had some trouble," the Spaniard-like newcomer in civilian dress said, "gettin' a man up from downtown, and long as I was hangin' around——"

"Glad you were. Maybe we'll make a killing for our own office. Be nice to carry this through by ourselves. So what've you got?"

"I've got one isolated print. Smudgy, but definite. Didn't even have to bring it out—just photographed it like it was."

He reached into a small black Boston bag he was carrying. "Got the other stuff here, too." He brought forth a flat rectangular slab with a smooth metal surface a foot long and three inches wide, and placed it on the table, then a small roller with a handle, which he laid beside the slab. Next he withdrew a bundle wrapped in a silk cloth and handed it to Dart. "There's your bone or club or whatever it is. Next time wrap it in something soft like a silk handkerchief."

"Had a handkerchief all right," Dart said, "but it wasn't silk."

"Anything beats a newspaper—damn near scratched the thing useless."

"Don't hold us up for an argument, Tynie. Bring on your print."

"Well, there's probably lots of old finger marks on that bone—it's gooey as hell. But this one is new. It's a little spread, but there'd be no mistaking it."

He withdrew now a metal cigarette-case. "Best thing in the world to carry a moist print in—see?" He opened it, revealing, beneath either transverse guard, a single photograph of a thumb print. "The slight bulge accommodates the curl of the wet paper and the guards hold it in place without touching anything but the edges."

"Smart boy," said Dart.

"Smarter than that," said the physician, "if you can read those smudges."

"Now listen, young expert," said Dart, "hold that here a minute. After I see this next bird, I want you to print everybody here and see if you find a print identical with that one. If you do, there's a few free nights in jail for somebody."

"O.K., Perry."

"I hope so anyway—it'll save sending out an alarm for the tall dark gentleman with the cock-eye."

"External strabismus is the term," said the doctor gravely.

"The hell it is," said Dart. "Douse that light. All right Brady, let's have the Spider."

# Chapter Twelve

SPIDER WEBB, an alert mouse-faced gentleman, perhaps thirty-five years old, was of dusky yellow complexion, rather sharp yet negroid features, and self-assured bearing. He was decidedly annoyed at the circumstances which had thus involved him, and his deep-set green-gray eyes glowed with a malicious impatience as he sat facing the well-nigh invisible detective.

His curt answers to Dart's incisive questioning revealed nothing to contradict the essential points already established. But the eliciting of his reasons for coming tonight to see Frimbo opened an entirely new realm of possibility.

At first he surlily refused to discuss the interview between himself and the African. It had been strictly personal he said.

"No more personal," the detective suggested, "than being held for murder on suspicion, was it?"

Spider was silent.

"Or being arrested for number-running? You know we can get you there on several counts, don't you?"

"Can't help that. Whatever you know, you also know I can't talk. That's suicide."

"So's silence. Telling the truth, Spider, will get you out of this—if you're not guilty—out of this and several other counts I could hold you on. You've enjoyed a lot of freedom, but this is a matter of life and death. A man has been killed. You're suspected. You can't keep quiet but so long. You know that?"

Webb said nothing.

"Now if it really was a personal matter you came here on tonight, telling me about it won't affect your—er—professional standing. If it wasn't, it had something to do with your number game. I know about that already—you won't be telling me anything new. The only thing talking now will do is clear you if you're innocent. Silence is equal to a confession."

Spider's receding chin quivered a bit; he started to speak, but didn't.

"You can get plenty, you know, for withholding evidence, too."

468

"I'd rather go to jail," Spider growled, "than take lead."

"Oh. So you're afraid of getting shot? Then you do know something. You'd better spill it, Spider, now that you've gone that far. Who sent you here to get Frimbo?"

A little of Webb's assurance dropped away.

"Nobody. On the level. Nobody."

"The man behind you is Brandon. Did he send you?"

"I said nobody."

"Let's see now. Brandon has only one real competitor as a policy-king here in Harlem. That's Spencer. Spider, your silence means one of two things. Either Brandon or Spencer had it in for Frimbo. If it was Spencer, you won't talk because you did it. If it was Brandon, you're afraid to squeal because he might find out."

In the bright illumination of the horizontal beam of light, Spider's face twitched and changed just enough to convince Dart that he was on the right track. He took a long chance:

"Spencer has been hit hard several times in the past month, hasn't he?"

"How—how'd you know?" came from the startled Spider.

"We watch such things, Spider. It helps us solve lots of crimes. Your chief, Brandon, however, has shown no signs of loss. He's going strong."

Again Spider Webb's expression betrayed a touch for the detective.

"Of course, if you let me do all the talking, Spider, I won't be able to give you any of the credit. I'll have to put you in jail just the same—on all the outstanding counts. Understand, the only reason you're not in jail now is that you might be of value in just such a case as this."

Uneasily, Spider stirred in his chair.

"You tried to escape coming here tonight, too, didn't you, Spider? In Pat's—when you saw a policeman with a man you had seen here earlier tonight. You tried to duck. I guess you're our man all right. Brady, put the bracelets on——"

"Wait a minute," said Spider. "Is this going to be on the level—no leaks?"

"Give you my word. Wait, Brady. Go ahead, Spider."

"O. K."

"Good. You're only protecting yourself," said Dart.

"This Frimbo was a smart guy—much too smart," Spider Webb began.

"Yes?"

"Yea. He had a system of playing the game that couldn't lose. I don't know how he did it—whether he worked out somethin' mathematical or was just a good guesser or what. But he could hit regular once a week without fail. And he played ten dollars a day, and I collected it."

"Go on."

"When he hit the third week in succession, the boss set up a howl. You know the percentage—six hundred to one. Hit for a dollar, you get six hundred minus the ten percent that goes to the runner. Hit for ten bucks, you're due six thousand minus the six hundred—five thousand four hundred dollars. Well, even a big banker like Brandon can't stand that—he only collects four grand a week."

"Only," murmured Dart.

"And when it happened the third week, it looked bad for me—I was gettin' six hundred out of each time this guy hit. I been with Brandon a long time, but he began to look at me awful doubtful. But he paid off—he always does—that's why he's successful at it. Also he told me, no more bets from this Frimbo. But then he begun to figure, and what he figured was this—that maybe he could use some o' this Frimbo's smartness for himself. Smart guy, Brandon. Here's what he did.

"First he accused me of playin' crooked. Runners try that once in a while, y' know. We have a list o' names on a slip, with the number and amount of money being played by each person beside the name. Well, the slips are s'posed to be turned in at nine forty-five every A.M., but it takes some time to get 'em in. Ten o'clock, the clearing-house number on which the winner is based is announced downtown. There's ways of holdin' the slip just a few seconds after ten, having a buddy telephone the winning number up, say, to the house next door, or downstairs someplace, where another buddy signals what it is by tapping on the wall or a radiator or something. Then the runner adds the winning number to his list beside a fake name, collects the money later, and splits with his buddies. Brandon, of course, knows all them tricks, and accused me of 'em. I showed him I wasn't dumb enough to try it three weeks in succession. So he had to admit this Frimbo must be just smart.

"So he figured he could trust me and he told me what to do. I was to keep on takin' Frimbo's ten bucks a day, and the numbers he played. Brandon had some of his boys play the same numbers with Spencer—but for twenty bucks. Result—when the numbers hit, Brandon lost six grand to Frimbo and won twelve from Spencer. The rest of his income stood like it was before. Spencer couldn't stand more than two or three twelve-grand hits—he'd have to quit. That would clear the field for Brandon. Then he could just stop taking Frimbo's bets and be sitting pretty."

"So what?" inquired Detective Dart.

"So that's why I was here tonight, that's all. To get Frimbo's number."

"Did he give you the number?"

"Sure he did—right from where you're sitting now."

"And the ten bucks?"

"Nope. He never handles money himself. The flunky collects all the people's fees as they go out of that door there. So I always got the ten bucks from the flunky. He'd either be waiting there or he'd come out in a moment."

"Come out? Out of where?"

"Out of the back room there."

"The back room? Oh. Could Spencer have learned of this and put Frimbo out of the way?"

"If he was smart enough. He'd be bound to get suspicious, no matter how Brandon played his twenty—it wouldn't look right. And he'd investigate. He'd check the bets each night before, find twenty bucks of the same number, and trace those players. But he'd have to pay 'em, once he'd taken the money. And he couldn't tell who not to take beforehand, either, because they could change their names, or if he did find a leak and got the lowdown, there'd be only one way out for him. He'd have to paralyze Frimbo or be ruined himself. Pure self-defense."

Perry Dart sat silent a moment, then said, "You know, doc, there's one thing that keeps worrying me. All these people agree up to now that Frimbo talked to them—talked to them personally about personal matters. How could a murdered man conduct an intelligent conversation *after* his death? That's why I haven't taken Jenkins already. The victim couldn't have been sitting here dead in the chair all the time, talking—through a stuffed neck."

"True," said the physician, "but the visitors preceding Jenkins might have found the man dead just as Jenkins did and slipped out without saying anything, to avoid incriminating themselves. Or the assistant might have been doing the talking through some trick or device, without knowing his master was dead. Everyone agrees the servant didn't come in here. So don't bank on the end of the conversation as the moment of death. Death could have occurred a half an hour or more earlier, without changing the testimony at all."

Another silence, then Dart said:

"Put on that light."

As the sharp radiance cut the shadow, Spider Webb exclaimed:

"Judas Priest! If I'd known you had all them listeners——"

"Don't worry—we'll see it doesn't cost you anything. Brady, bring everybody in here. All ready, Tynie?"

"All ready, Perry," said Tynes.

# Chapter Thirteen

## I

IN THE crystalline underlighting from the glaring extension, a thin brightness through which shot the horizontal beam from Frimbo's curious illumination, a semicircle of people stood facing the table. Behind it now stood the detective and the physician. The latter was busy with his handkerchief, wiping from his fingers a dark film which had stuck to them while he had been sitting in the chair which Brady had brought. It was a small, erect wooden chair with short arms on one of which he had rested a hand during Spider Webb's testimony. At the moment he paid the stuff no further attention, considering it merely a sort of furniture polish which had been too heavily applied, and had become gummy on standing.

The detective was addressing the people facing him. "I'm going to ask the coöperation of all of you folks. Before doing so, I want you to know just what I have in view." He paused a moment, considered, decided. "Among the facts brought out by what we have found and by your testimony are these: Frimbo, a man of close habits and no definitely known special friends or enemies, was killed here in this chair tonight between ten-thirty and eleven o'clock. He was stunned by a blow, presumably from this club, and then choked to death by this handkerchief, which was removed from his throat in my presence by Dr. Archer."

He paused again to observe the effect of this announcement. Outstanding were two reactions, quite opposite: Mrs. Crouch's horrified expression, and Bubber Brown's astonished comment:

"Doggone! They's some excuse for chokin' on a fish-bone—but a handkerchief!"

"There are several possible motives that have come to light. But before following these motives any further, we must establish or complete such evidence as we already have in hand. We have reliable testimony on the ownership of this handkerchief.

We must now determine who handled this club. You all know the meaning of finger prints. On this club, we have found a fresh print which will have to be compared with certain of your finger prints. But first I want to give you a chance now to admit having hold of this weapon tonight—if you did. Is anyone here ready to admit that he—even accidentally—touched this club tonight?"

Everyone looked at everyone else. No one spoke but the irrepressible Bubber. "Not tonight," murmured he, "nor las' night, either."

"Very well, then. I shall have to ask you all to submit to what you may consider an indignity, but it's quite necessary. And any who objects will have to be arrested on suspicion and for withholding of evidence, and will then have to submit anyhow. You will please come forward to this table in turn, one by one, beginning with Mrs. Crouch on that end, and allow Officer Tynes to take your prints. These prints will not be held as police records unless you are arrested in connection with this case."

"Wait a minute." It was Dr. Archer who spoke. "Better take mine first, hadn't you? I'm a suspect, too."

Dart agreed. "Right you are, doc. Go ahead."

Tynes had prepared his flat slab meanwhile by touching to it a dab of thick special ink from a flexible tube, then rolling this to a thin smooth even film which covered the rectangular surface. Dr. Archer submitted his hand. Tynes grasped the physician's right thumb, laid its outer edge upon the inky surface, rolled it skillfully over with a light even pressure till its inner edge rested as had its outer, lifted it, and repeated the maneuver within a labeled space on a prepared paper blank. The result was a perfectly rolled thumb print.

"I'm pretty sure it's a thumb on the club," Tynes said, "but I'll take the others, too, for safety."

"By all means," said the tall physician gravely. And in a few minutes Tynes had filled all ten of the spaces on the blank. Then he produced a small bottle of gasoline and a bit of cheese cloth. "That'll take it off," he said. He looked at the prints. "Your left thumb's blurred. Must have been dirty."

"Yes. It was, now that you mention it. Gummy furniture polish or something on the arm of that chair I was sitting in."

"Never mind, it'll do. Next."

"Mrs. Crouch—if you don't mind," said Dart.

Martha Crouch stepped forward without hesitation. The others followed in turn. The dexterous Tynes required only a minute for each person: Mrs. Snead, highly disgruntled, but silent save for an occasional disgusted grunt, Spider Webb, sullen, Easley Jones, grinning, Doty Hicks, trembling, and Jinx Jenkins scowling. Bubber's turn came last. Jinx's paper with his name across the head lay in plain view among those scattered out to dry on the table. Bubber cocked his head sidewise and peered at it as he submitted his digits to Tynes.

"Listen, brother—ain't you made a mistake?" he asked.

"How?" said Tynes, working on.

"Honest now, them ain't Jinx's *finger* prints, is they?"

"Sure, they are."

"Go on, man. You done took the boy's foot prints. Ain' no fingers made look like that."

"They're his, though."

"Tell me, mistuh, does apes have finger prints?"

"I suppose so."

"Well, listen. When you get time, see if them there don't belong to a gorilla or sump'm. I've had my doubts about Jinx Jenkins for quite a long time."


2


Tynes gathered the papers indiscriminately, so that they were not in any known order, faced them up in a neat pile, and procured a large hand-glass from his bag. He was the center of attention—even the officers in the corners of the room drew unconsciously a bit nearer. The doctor insisted on his sitting in one of the two chairs, he and the detective both being now on their feet. Tynes complied, sitting at the end of the table toward the hall with his back to the door. The physician stood so that he could direct his flashlight from the side upon the objects of Tynes' observations.

The latter now removed from the cigarette case one of the two photographs of the print which he had found on the club. This he kept in his left hand, the hand-glass in his right, and holding the original so that it was beside each labeled space in turn, methodically began to compare under the glass, the freshly made prints with the photograph.

Intently, silently, almost breathlessly, the onlookers stood watching the bent shoulders, the sleek black head, the expressionless tan face of Tynes. The whole room seemed to shift a little each time he passed from one comparison to the next, to hang suspended a moment, then shift with him again. So complete was the silence that the sound of a fire-siren on the Avenue a quarter-mile away came clearly into the room, and so absorbed was everyone in this important procedure that occasional odd sounds below were completely ignored.

It appeared that Tynes was making two separate piles, one of which, presumably, contained cases dismissed as out of the question, the other of which contained cases to be further studied and narrowed down. The long moments hung unrelaxed; the observers stared with the same fascinated expectancy that might have characterized their watching of a burning fuse, whose spark too slowly, too surely, approached some fatal explosive.

Yet Tynes' work was proceeding very rapidly, facilitated by the fortunate accident that the original print belonged to one of the simpler categories. In an apparent eternity which was actually but a few minutes, he had reduced the final number to two papers. One of these he laid decisively aside after a short reinspection. The other he examined at one point long and carefully. He nodded his head affirmatively once or twice, drew a deep breath, put down his hand-glass, and straightened up. He handed the paper to Detective Perry Dart, standing behind the table.

"This is it, Perry. Right thumb. Exactly like the photograph."

Dart took the paper, held it up, looked at it, lowered it again. His bright black eyes swept the waiting circle, halted.

"Jenkins," he said quietly, "you're under arrest."

# Chapter Fourteen

## I

"YOU, Hicks," Dart continued, "will be held also on your own testimony, as a possible accessory. The rest of you be ready to be called at any time as witnesses. For the present, however——"

At this moment a newcomer pressed into the room, a large, bluff, red-faced man carrying a physician's bag, and puffing with the exertion of having climbed the stairs.

"Hello, Dart. Got you working, hey?"

"Hello, Dr. Winkler. How long've you been here?"

"Long enough to examine your case."

"Really? I heard some noises downstairs, but I didn't realize it was you. Shake hands with Dr. Archer here. He was called in, pronounced the case, and notified us. And he's a better detective than I am—missed his calling, I think."

"Howdy, doctor," said the florid medical examiner pleasantly. "This case puzzles me somewhat."

"I should think it would," said Dr. Archer. "We have the advantage over you."

"Can't figure out," went on Dr. Winkler, "just what evidence of violence there was to make you call in the police. Couldn't find any myself—looked pretty carefully, too."

"You mean you didn't see a scalp wound over the right ear?"

"Scalp wound? I should say I couldn't. There isn't any."

"No?" Dr. Archer turned to Dart. "Did you see that, Dart, or was it an optical illusion?"

"I saw it," admitted Dart.

"And unless I'm having hallucinations," the local physician went on, "it contained a fresh blood clot which I removed with a gauze dressing that now rests in my bag." He stooped deliberately, procured and displayed the soiled dressing, while the medical examiner looked first at him, then at Dart, as if he was not sure whether to doubt their sanity or his own. Dr.

477

Archer dropped the dressing back into his bag. "Then I probed it for a fracture," he concluded.

"Well," said Winkler, "I don't see how I could've missed anything like that. I went over her from head to foot, and if she wasn't a cardiorenal I never saw one——"

"You went—where?"

"I went over her from head to foot—every inch——"

*"Her?"* burst from Dart.

"Yes—her. She's been dead for hours——"

"Wait a minute. Doctor Winkler," said Dr. Archer, "we aren't discussing the same subject. I'm talking about the victim of this crime, a man known as Frimbo."

"A man! Well, if that corpse downstairs is a man, somebody played an awful dirty trick on him."

"Stand fast, everybody!" ordered Dart. "Tynes, take charge here till I get back. Come on, you medicos. Let's get this thing straight."

Out of the room and down the stairs they hurried, Archer, Dart, and Winkler. The door of Crouch's front room was open, but the couch on which the dead man had been placed was in a position that could not be seen from the hall. So far did Dr. Archer out-distance the others that by the time they got inside the room, he was already standing in the middle of the floor, staring dumbfoundedly at an unquestionably unoccupied couch.

"The elusive corpse," he murmured, as the other two came up. "First a man, then a woman, then—a memory."

"He was on that couch!" Dart said. "Where's Day? The cop covering the front? Day! Come here!"

Officer Day, large, cheese-colored, and bovine, loomed in the doorway. "Yas, suh."

"Day, where's the body that was on this couch?"

"Body? On that couch?" Day's face was blank as an egg.

"Are you on duty down here—or are you in a trance?"

"'Deed, I ain' seen no body on that couch, chief. The only body down here is back yonder in the room where the telephone is. On a table under a sheet."

"He's right there," said Winkler.

"Day, don't repeat this question, please: When did you first come into this room?"

"When the medical examiner come. I took him in and showed him back yonder, but I didn' stay to look—I come right back here to my post."

"When you first came here tonight, didn't you see the corpse on this couch?"

"No 'ndeed. I was the last one in. You and the doc went in there and left the rest of us here in the hall. I couldn't see 'round the door. And when you come out, yo' orders to me was 'cover the front.' And I been coverin' it." Officer Day was a little resentful of Detective Dart's implied censure. "When the medical examiner got here I took him in. And they sho' wasn't no corpse on no couch then. Only corpse in here was back yonder, under the sheet. Natchelly I figured that was it."

"You would. Doc——"

But Dr. Archer was already returning from a quick trip to the rear room. "It's a woman all right," he said. "Frimbo is apparently A.W.O.L. Inconsiderate of him, isn't it?"

"Listen, Day," Dart said, refraining with difficulty from explosive language. "Has anyone come through this door since you came down here?"

"No 'ndeed. Nobody but him." He pointed to Dr. Winkler. "The undertaker started in, but when I told him what had happened he asked where y'all was, and I told him upstairs yonder, so he went straight up. Then, when he come down again, he went on out. Asked me to turn out the lights and slam this door when we was through, that's all."

"All right, Day. That's all. You keep on covering the front. Don't let it get away from you. Doc, you and the M. E. wait here and keep your eyes open. I'll tear this shack loose if necessary—nobody's going to get away with a stunt like that."

"Wait a second," said Dr. Archer. "How long has it been since we were down here?"

"Damn!" exploded Dart, looking at his watch. "Over an hour."

"Well," the local physician said, "whoever removed that stiff has had plenty of time to get it off the premises long before now. Just a hasty harum-scarum search won't dig up a thing, do you think?"

"I can't help it," Dart replied impatiently. "I've got to look, haven't I?" And out of the door he sped and bounded up the stairs.

2

The tall, pale, bespectacled Dr. Archer summarized the situation for the medical examiner's benefit while they waited. He described how they had found the strange instrument of death and later the club, devised of a human femur, which must have delivered the blow. He gave the evidence in support of his estimate of the period during which death had occurred, the medical examiner readily approving its probability.

"Testimony indicated," the local physician went on, "and Dart checked each witness against the others, that the two women and one of the six men present were very unlikely as suspects. Any one of the other five men, four of them visitors and one the assistant or servant, could have committed the crime. One of them, an obvious drug addict, even admitted having a hand in it—rather convincingly, too; although the person who voluntarily comes forward with an admission is usually ignored——"

"Some day," the medical examiner grinned, "that sort of suspect is going to be ignored once too often—he'll turn out guilty in spite of his admission."

"Well, there's more to this chap's admission than just an admission. He had a good motive—believed that Frimbo was slowly killing his brother by some mystic spell, which only Frimbo's own death could break. And he indicated, too, that he had a paid accomplice. That, plus his obvious belief in the superstition, was what really lent a little credibility to his admission. But there was another motive brought out by Dart: One of the other men was a policy-runner. He said Frimbo had a winning system that was being used to break his boss's rival, and that the rival might have found it out and eliminated Frimbo in self-defense. Even so, of course, the actual murderer would have to be one of those five men present. Because one of them had to take that club from the front room back to the middle room where we found it—it couldn't move by itself, even if it was a thigh-bone once. Of course, the same thing applies to the handkerchief. There was the servant too, who managed to disappear completely just before the murder was discovered. He'd hardly kill the goose that laid his golden eggs, though."

"But he did disappear?"

"To the naked eye."

"What about the undertaker who came in and went out?"

"He didn't enter the front room at any time. You see, both the handkerchief and the club were unquestionably in the front room before Frimbo was killed with them. The undertaker, or anybody else, would have had to be in that room at some time—and so be seen by the others—to have got possession of those two objects.— And the undertaker had every apparent reason to want Frimbo to stay alive. Frimbo paid him outrageously high rent—and always on time."

"So who did it?"

"Well, I'll give you a list—if I don't forget somebody—in the order of their probable guilt. First is Jenkins, against whom both the clues point. It's his handkerchief, as two others testify. What makes it look worse for him is that he denies it's his. It may be just apprehension or perversity that makes him deny it—he's a hard-boiled, grouchy sort of person; but it looks on the face of it, more like he's covering up. But worse still, his right thumb print was identified on the club—which, again, he'd denied touching."

"Dart's holding him then?"

"Has to. And that's evidence that even a smart lawyer—which Jenkins probably can't afford—couldn't easily explain away. Then next, I should say, is Doty Hicks, the drug-addict, about whom I just told you. Possibly the accomplice he admits paying is Jenkins. Then—let's see—then would come Spencer—the number-king mentioned by the runner, Spider Webb. Not Spencer himself, of course, but some one of those present, paid by Spencer. That again suggests Jenkins, who might be in Spencer's employ. Or the railroad porter, Jones—Easley Jones. He might be Spencer's agent, though he tells a simple, straightforward story which can easily be checked; and there isn't a scrap of evidence against him. In fact he went in to see Frimbo first and Frimbo talked to him, as well as to three others following him. Obviously even an African mystic couldn't tell fortunes through a throat plugged up as tightly as Frimbo's was."

"Not unless he used sign language," commented the medical examiner.

"Which he couldn't in the dark," answered Dr. Archer. "Well next—the servant, against whom the only charge is his disappearance. He could figure as somebody's agent too, I suppose. But it wasn't his thumb print on the club, nor his handkerchief. Then there was Brown, a likable sort of Harlem roustabout, who, however, did not leave the front room till after the attack on Frimbo. And finally the two women, who didn't even know the man had been killed till we told them, some time after examining him."

"Well, you know how the books tell it. It's always the least likely person."

"In that case, evidence or no evidence, the guilty party is Mrs. Aramintha Snead, devout church-member and long-suffering housewife."

"Oh, no. You've very adroitly neglected to mention the really most unlikely person. I'm thinking of the physician on the case. Dr. Archer is the name, I believe?"

"Quite possible," Dr. Archer returned gravely. "Motive—professional jealousy."

"If that theory applied here," the medical examiner laughed, "I'd have to clear out myself. I'm obviously the murderer: I was ten miles away when it happened."

"Of course. You put Jenkins' thumb print on that club by telephoto, and the handkerchief——"

"I blew the handkerchief out of Jenkins' pocket and down Frimbo's throat by means of a special electric fan!"

"Some day I'm going to write a murder mystery," mused Dr. Archer, "that will baffle and astound the world. The murderer will turn out to be the most likely suspect."

"You'd never write another," said the medical examiner.

3

For half an hour, Perry Dart and three of the more experienced bluecoats searched the house. They prowled from roof to cellar in vain. At one moment, Dart thought he had discovered an adequate hiding-place beneath the laboratory bench, which stretched across the posterior wall of the rear on the second floor; for the doors to the cabinets under the bench were locked. But he soon saw that this was an impossible lead: the two doors were not adjacent; an easily opened compartment was between them filled with mechanical bric-a-brac; and the size of this and all the other unlocked compartments indicated that the locked ones were far too small to accommodate a full sized cadaver.

Again a possibility appeared in the old dumbwaiter shaft, which extended from the basement to the first floor. But inspection of this, both from above and below, disclosed that it did not contain even the dumbwaiter which must originally have occupied it. A few old ropes and a set of pulleys dangled from its roof, at the level of the first floor ceiling; between these, flashlights revealed nothing but musty space.

Eventually, the detective returned alone to the two physicians. He was still grim and angry, but thoroughly composed again. "Somebody," he said, "is going to get in trouble."

The medical examiner grinned.

"What do you make of it?"

"Only one thing to make of it—you can't prove a murder without a corpse. It's an old trick, but it's the last thing I'd expect up here."

"Somebody's smart," commented Dr. Archer.

"Exactly. And the somebody isn't working alone. Everybody who could possibly have done the job is upstairs in that room now; not a single suspect has been down here since we left the body. Every one of them has been under some policeman's eye."

"The undertaker was down here."

"In the hall, but not in this room. Day might not be as bright as his name would indicate, but surely he could see whether Crouch came in here. Day says positively that he didn't; he went straight up, and came down and went straight out. He couldn't get back in here any other way without being seen, either. The back yard and back door are covered. The roof is covered. Every possible entrance and exit have been covered from almost the moment we left this room with Frimbo on that couch."

"Then," Dr. Archer said, "the fact of the matter must be that the gentleman is still in our midst. Maybe you're dealing with secret passages and mysterious compartments."

"Wouldn't be surprised," said the medical examiner amusedly. "He was a man of mystery, wasn't he? He ought to have a few hidden chambers and such."

"We can take care of them," Dart said. "I'll have a departmental expert here early tomorrow morning—even if it is Sunday. This morning, as a matter of fact. We'll go over the house with a pair of micrometer calipers. There never was a secret chamber that didn't take up space. And one thing is sure: Jenkins knows who did this. Whoever paid him, paid for the removal of the corpse also. It's the final stroke—protects everybody, you see. No corpse, no killing. Damn!"

"Somehow," Dr. Archer reflected, "I've a very uncomfortable feeling that something is wrong."

"Not really?"

"I mean something in the way we've been reasoning. It's so easy to ignore the obvious. What obvious circumstance can we have been ignoring?" He deliberated without benefit of the others' aid. Rather suddenly he drew a breath. "No," he contradicted his own inspiration, "that's a little too obvious. And yet——"

"What the dickens are you mumbling about?" Dart asked, with pardonable impatience.

"Let's divide all the suspects," said Dr. Archer, "whom we have considered here tonight into two groups. The first will be a group about whom we can definitely say they couldn't have made off with this body. The second will be a group about whom we can't say that."

"Go ahead."

"All right. Everybody that's been here will fall into the first group—except one."

"Who?"

"The servant."

"Mmm."

"Nobody knows that servant's whereabouts since he bowed Jenkins into Frimbo's room. And if it's a matter of knowing the layout, he ought to be more qualified than anybody else to bring off this last bit of sleight-of-hand."

"How'll we prove it?"

"Find him. He has all the additional information you need. He's your key."

"If he didn't leave before we got here."

"In that case he couldn't have got back to recover the remains—not if all avenues were covered. So that he may still be—with his gruesome companion. Keep your avenues guarded until you can go over the place with—calipers, did you say? And even if he isn't here, he's got to be found. I suspect his remarks on this whole matter would save us considerable energy, even if he didn't remove the body."

"All right, doc, I accept your suggestion. But Jenkins is a bird in the hand, and I think we can persuade him to talk. Hicks, too, may have something more to say under the right circumstances. And I've a mind to hold the other two also until the body is found. A few pertinent suggestions might improve their knowledge of the case. But it may be better to let 'em go, and have 'em trailed. Find out more that way. Yep—I'm going to have everybody I let out of here tonight trailed. I won't even tell 'em about this. That's the idea——"

"Well," the medical examiner sighed, gathering himself for departure, "I can't examine what isn't here. When you guys get a body let me know. But don't find it till I've had a few hours' sleep. And no more false alarms, please."

"O.K., Dr. Winkler. It won't be a false alarm next time."

"Good-night, doctor."

Before the outside door slammed behind the departing medical examiner, Dart had reached the telephone in the rear room. He got headquarters, made a brief preliminary report of the case, and instituted a sharp lookout, through police radio broadcast and all the other devices under headquarters' control, for a Negro of the servant's description, and any clues leading to possible recovery of the dead body.

Then he and the doctor returned to the death chamber above.

# Chapter Fifteen

I

"GREAT day in the mornin'!" exclaimed Mrs. Aramintha Snead. "What under the sun is it now?"

"Sit tight, everybody," advised Tynes. "They'll be right back."

"'Twouldn' be so bad," commented Easley Jones good-humoredly, "if we was sittin'—tight or loose. But my dawgs is 'bout to let me down."

As for the customary volubility of Bubber, that had for the moment fled. The actuality of his friend's arrest had shocked him even more than it had Jinx, for Jinx had half-anticipated it, while Bubber hadn't given the possibility a thought. He stood near his long, lanky, uncomely friend, looking rather helplessly into his face. Jinx was scowling glumly into the distance. Finally Bubber spoke:

"Did you hear what the man said?"

"Hmph!" grunted Jinx.

"Is you got any idea what it means?"

"Hmph!" Jinx grunted again.

"Hmph hell-ie!" returned Bubber, sufficiently absorbed in his ally's predicament to be oblivious of the heretofore hampering presence of ladies. "Here you is headed straight for the fryin'-pan, and all you can do is grunt. What in the world is you tol' the man to make him think you done it?"

"Tol' him little as I could," muttered Jinx.

"Well, brother, you better get to talkin'. This here's serious."

"You tellin' me?"

"Somebody got to tell you. You don' seem to have sense enough to see it for yo'self. Look here—did you have a hand in this thing sho' 'nough?"

"Hmph!" said Jinx.

"Well, you could 'a. Man might 'a' said sump'm 'bout yo' ancestors, and you might 'a' forgot yo'self and busted him one. It's possible."

486

"I tol' 'em what the man said—word for word—near as I could. This is what I get for that."

"Guess you jes' born for evil, boy. Good luck come yo' way, take one look at you, and turn 'round and run. You sho' you ain't done it?"

"Hmph," issued a fourth time from the tall boy's nose.

"Listen, Jinx. 'Hmph' don' mean nothin' in no language. You better learn to say 'no' and say it loud and frequent. You didn't fall asleep while the man was talkin' to you? Did y'?"

"How'm I go'n' sleep with all that light in my eyes?"

"Shuh, man, I've seen you sleep with the sun in yo' eyes."

"Hadn' been for you," Jinx grumbled, "I wouldn' be in this mess."

"Hadn' been for me? Listen to the fool! What'd I have to do with it?"

"You tol' the man that was my han'kerchief, didn' y'?"

"'Cose I did. It was yo' han'kerchief. But I sho' didn' tell 'im that was yo' finger print on that club yonder."

"'Tain' no finger print o' mine. I ain' touched no club."

"Now wait a minute, big boy. Don' give the man no argument 'bout no finger print. You in trouble enough now. This ain't the first time yo' fingers got away from you."

"And 'tain't the first time yo' tongue's got away from you. You talk too doggone much."

"Maybe. But everything I've said tonight is a whisper side o' what that finger print says. That thing shouts out loud."

2

Mrs. Aramintha Snead came up to them. "Young man," she addressed Jinx, "your time has come. I'm gonna pray for you."

At this, everyone exchanged uncomfortable, apprehensive glances, and Bubber, gathering the full significance of the church lady's intention, looked at Jinx as if the latter's time had indeed come.

"Stand one side, son," ordered the lady, elbowing Bubber well out of the way.

"Yas'm," said Bubber helplessly, his face a picture of distress.

"Young man, does you know the Ten Commandments?"

Jinx could only look at her.

"Does you know the *six'* commandment? Don't know even a single one of the commandments, does y'? Well, you's a hopeless sinner. You know that, don't y'? Hopeless—doomed—on yo' way," her voice trembled and rose, "to burn in hell, where the fire is not quenched and the worm dieth not."

"Lady, he ain't no worm," protested Bubber.

"Hush yo' mouf!" she rebuked; then resumed her more holy tone. "If you'd 'a' obeyed the commandments, you wouldn't 'a' been a sinner and you wouldn't 'a' sinned. But how could you obey 'em when you didn' even know 'em?"

The silence accompanying her pause proved that this was an unanswerable point.

"If you'd obeyed the six' commandment," her voice was low and impressive, "you wouldn't 'a' killed this conjure-man here tonight. 'Cause the six' commandment say, *'Thou shalt not kill!'* And now you done broke it. Done broke it—done kilt one o' yo' fellow men. Don' matter whether he was good or bad—you done kilt him—laid 'im out cold in the flesh. The Good Book say 'A eye for a eye and a toof for a toof.' And inasmuch as you did it unto him, it shall likewise be done unto you. And you got to go befo' that great tribunal on high and 'splain why—'splain why you done it. They's only one thing, you can do now—repent. Repent, sinner, befo' it is too late!"

"Can I do it for 'im, lady?" Bubber offered helpfully.

"Let us pray," said Mrs. Snead serenely. "Let us pray."

She stood erect, she folded her arms, she closed her prominent eyes. That helped. But the benefit to Jinx of what followed was extremely doubtful.

"Lawd, here he is. His earthly form returns to the dust frum whence it came, and befo' his undyin' soul goes to eternal judgment, we want to pray for 'im. We know he's got to go. We know that soon his mortal shell will be molderin' in the ground. It ain't for that we prayin'—it ain't for that——"

"The hell it ain't," devoutly mumbled Bubber.

"Hit's for his soul we prayin'—his soul so deep-dyed, so steeped, so black in sin. Wash him, Lawd. Wash him and he shall be whiter than snow. Take from him every stain of transgression, and bleach him out like a clean garment in the sunlight of righteousness."

For an unconscionable length of time she went on lamenting the hopeless sinner's iniquitous past, that had culminated in so shameful a present, and picturing the special torments reserved in hell for the impenitent dead.

"We know he's a hopeless sinner. But, oh, make him to see his sins—make him know it was wrong to steal, wrong to gamble, wrong to drink, wrong to swear, wrong to lie, and wrong to kill—and make him fall on his knees and confess unto salvation befo' it is too late. Make him realize that though he can't save his body, they's still time to save his soul. So that when that las' day comes, and he reaches Jordan's chilly shore, and Death puts forth his cold icy hand and lays it on his shoulder and whispers, 'Come,' he can rise up with a smile and say, 'I'm ready—done made my peace callin', and election sho', done cast off this old no'count flesh and took on the spirit.'"

Then she opened her eyes and looked at the young man for whose soul she had so long pleaded. "There now," she said, "Don't you feel better?"

"No, ma'am," said Jinx.

"Lawd have mercy!" breathed the lady, and shaking her head sadly from side to side, she abandoned him to the fate of the unrepentant, returning to her place with the air of one who at least has done his duty.

3

When the second search was over and the detective and the physician returned to the room where the others waited, they found a restless and bewildered company.

"What was it, doc?" Bubber promptly wanted to know, "a boy or a girl?"

"Neither," said the physician.

"Mph!" grunted Bubber. "Was Frimbo like that too? It's gettin' so you don' know who to trust, ain't it?"

"Brown," said Detective Dart, "you heard what I told Jenkins before I went out?"

"Sho' did."

"He's a good friend of yours, isn't he?"

"Who—Jenkins? Friend o' mine? No 'ndeed."

"What do you mean?"

"I mean I barely know the nigger. Up till night befo' las' we was perfect strangers."

"You were pretty chummy with him tonight. You and he came here together."

"Purely accidental, mistuh. Jes' happen' to meet him on the street; he was on his way here; I come along too, thinkin' the man might gimme some high lowdown. Chummy? Shuh! Didn' you and the doc burst in on us in the front room there where we was almost 'bout to fight? Friend o' mine! 'Deed you wrong there, brother. I don' have nothin' to do with gangsters, gunmen, killers, or no folks like that. I lives above reproach. Ask anybody."

Jinx's jaw sagged, his scowl faded into a stare of amazement. It was perhaps the first time in his life when he had failed to greet the unexpected obdurately. Not even the announcement of his arrest for murder had jolted him as did this. He had never been excessively articulate, but his silence now was the silence of one struck dumb.

"All right, Brown," Dart said. "I'm glad to hear that."

"Yes, *suh*," vowed Bubber, but he did not look at Jinx.

"Now listen, you people," went on Dart. "I'm letting you go, with the exception of Jenkins and Hicks, but you're not to leave town until further word from me. Jones, that means you too. I'm sorry to have you lose any time from your job, but you may have to. Can you manage it?"

"Yas, indeed," smiled Easley Jones. "I'm layin' over till Monday anyhow, y'see, and another day or two won' matter. I can fix it up with the boss-man—no trouble 'tall."

"Good. Then you and the others are free to go."

The word "go" was scarcely out of his mouth before the whole place went suddenly black.

"Hey—what the hell!"

Even the hall lights were gone. In the sudden dark, Mrs. Snead screamed aloud, "Sweet Jesus have mercy!" There was a quick soft rustle and bustle. Dart remembered that Jinx was

nearest to the hall-door. "Look out for Jenkins!" he yelled.
"Block that door—he's pullin' a fast one!"

He reached into his pocket for the flashlight he had dropped
there, and at the same time Dr. Archer remembered his. The
two fine beams of white light shot forth together, toward the
spot where Jinx had been standing; he was not there. The lights
swept toward the door, to reveal Officer Green, who had automatically obstructed the exit, earnestly embracing Jinx's long
form, and experiencing no small difficulty in holding the young
man back. At the same time Jinx looked back over his shoulder
and saw the two spots of light. To him they must have appeared
to be the malevolent eyes of some gigantic monster; for with a
supreme effort he wriggled out of Green's uncertain hold, and
might have fled down the stairs and out into the night, had he
not tripped and fallen in the hall. Green, following him blindly,
tripped over him, landed upon him, and so remained until Dart's
pursuing flashlight revealed the tableau.

"Smart boy," muttered the detective grimly, for it did not
seem to him that Jinx's behavior might have been occasioned
by momentary panic. "Who's workin' with you? Who switched
off those lights? Where's the switch?"

Under Green's weight, it was all Jinx could do to answer,
"Dam' 'f I know!"

"Oh, no? Got bracelets, Green? Use 'em. Where the——"

A deep strong voice in the middle of the death room struck
silence to all the rising babel.

"Wait!"

Profound, abrupt quiet.

"You will find a switch in this room beside the rear door."

Somebody drew a single sharp startled breath. Dr. Archer,
who had not moved from where he had been standing, swung
his light around toward the sound. It fell on the head and
shoulders of a stranger, seated in Frimbo's chair.

Through the subsequent silence came Martha Crouch's
voice, uttering one lone, incredulous word:

*"Frimbo!"*

From the hall Dart called: "Find that switch!" One of the
patrolmen stationed inside the room obeyed. The horizontal
beam, and the bright sharp extension light came on together

as suddenly as they had gone out. Dart came rushing back into the room. He halted, staring like everyone else with utterly unbelieving eyes at the figure that sat in the chair from which the dead body had been removed: a black man wearing a black robe and a black silk head-band; a man with fine, almost delicate features, gleaming, deep-set black eyes, and an expression of supreme intelligence and tranquillity.

Quickly, ere Dart could speak, Martha Crouch stepped forward in wide-eyed wonder.

"Frimbo—you're—alive . . . ?"

"Yes, I am alive," said the deep clear voice of the man in the chair. Something just less than a smile touched the handsome dark face.

"But they said—they said you were dead——"

"They were correct," affirmed Frimbo, without emotion.

# Chapter Sixteen

## I

EVERYONE in the room perceptibly shrank. So terrible a thing, so calmly said, at once impelled them to flight and held them captive.

"My Gawd!" breathed Aramintha Snead. "The man done come back!" And she with the others drew away staring and terrified. For a moment it seemed they would have fled, had the air not been turned to jelly, holding them fast. "He done done a Lazarus!" Bubber Brown whispered.

But Perry Dart's amazement gave way to exasperation. He stepped forward. "Say, what is all this, anyway? Who the devil are you?"

There was something extraordinarily disconcerting in the unwavering deep-set black eyes of the man in the chair. Even the redoubtable Dart must have felt the penetrating, yet impenetrable calmness and vitality of that undisturbed gaze as it switched to meet his own.

"I am Frimbo. You heard this lady?"

"Oh, yea? Then who was killed?"

"I was."

"You were, were you? I suppose you've risen from the dead?"

"It is not the first time I have outwitted death, my friend."

"Do you mean to sit there and tell me that you are the man I saw lying dead on that couch downstairs?"

"I am the man. And if you will be patient, I will try to explain the matter to your satisfaction."

"But how did you—what did you do? Where did you go? What's the idea dousing the lights? What do you think we are, anyway?"

"I think you are a man of intelligence, who will appreciate that coöperation achieves more than antagonism. I trust I am correct?"

"Go ahead—talk," said Dart gruffly.

"Thank you. I hope you will understand. The facts are these:

493

At the time I was attacked—I am uncertain myself of the precise moment, for time is of little importance to me personally
—I was in a state of what you would probably call suspended
animation. More exactly, I was wholly immune to activities of
the immediate present, for I had projected my mind into the
future—that gentleman's future—Mr. Jenkins'. During that
period I was assaulted—murderously. Physically, I *was* murdered.
Mentally I could not be, because mentally I was elsewhere. Do
you see?"

"I never heard of such thing," said Dart, but he spoke uncertainly, for nothing could have been more impressive than
this cool, deliberate deep voice, stating a mystic paradox in
terms of level reason.

"Your profession, Mr. Dart," returned Frimbo, "should
embrace an understanding of such matters. They do occur, I
assure you, but at the moment I must not take the time to
convince you personally. I can, if necessary. Now, since my apparently lifeless body, which you and Dr. Archer abandoned
downstairs, was not seriously damaged in any vital particular,
the return of consciousness, which is to say, the return of present mental activity, was naturally accompanied by a return of
physical activity also. In short, I came to. I realized what must
have happened. Naturally, I decided to assist your further
efforts.

"But I have certain aversions, Mr. Dart. One is to be im-
peded physically, particularly by such worthy but annoying
persons as gigantic minions of the law. I therefore desired to
return to this room, where you were, without being obstructed
by your deputies. It was not difficult to reach my laboratory
without being detected, but the hallway there could not be so
easily negotiated. And so I adopted the simple, if theatrical,
device of completing my journey under cover of darkness. It
was much simpler and pleasanter for me, you see."

For the first time tonight Dart was uncertain of procedure.
Nothing in his training, thorough as it had been, covered this
situation where, with a murder on the verge of solution and
the definitely incriminated assailant in handcuffs, the victim
walked in, sat down, and pronounced himself thoroughly alive.
It swept the very foundation out from under the structure
which his careful reasoning had erected and rendered it all

utterly and absurdly useless. So, for the present at least, it seemed.

But Frimbo continued with a statement altogether startling in its implications:

"The fact remains, of course, that a murder was committed. I live, but someone killed me. Someone is guilty." The voice took on a new hardness. "Someone must pay the penalty."

Something in that suggestion brought method back into Dart's mind. "Where were you when we were searching the house just now?" said he.

"Obviously, we simply were not in the same place at the same time. That is nothing extraordinary."

"How do I know it was you who was killed?"

"You saw me, did you not? My identity is easy to establish. Mrs. Crouch knows me, as she has indicated, by sight. The other visitors may not have been able to see me well, but they will perhaps recognize my voice."

"Sho' is the same voice," vowed Jinx, unaware that he was testifying against himself.

"Are you sure of that?" Dart asked.

"Sho' is," repeated Jinx, and the others murmured assent.

"Well," Dart turned to the doctor, "at least it wasn't the servant doing the talking."

But Dr. Archer now spoke. "I beg your pardon, Dart, but may I point out that it is of no consequence whether this gentleman is Frimbo or not. The only question of importance is whether he is the man whom we saw downstairs."

Thereupon Frimbo said, "Dr. Archer, who pronounced me dead, will naturally be most reluctant to identify me with the corpse, since the implication would be that he had been mistaken in his original pronouncement. Thereupon I must insist that he examine me now."

The physician was slightly surprised. "I should think you would prefer someone less prejudiced," he said.

"On the contrary. If you identify me with the man you yourself pronounced dead, there can be no further question. You are the only person who would be reluctant to do so. You will allow only the most reliable evidence to overcome that reluctance."

Dr. Archer stared for a moment from behind his spectacles

into the serene dark face of this astonishing fellow, sensing for the first time perhaps how his own irrepressible curiosity was to lead him shortly into an investigation of the most extraordinary personality he had ever confronted.

Then he went over to the seated figure. "Will you please remove your head-band? The wound would hardy be healed so soon."

"You will find the wound unhealed," said Frimbo, complying. The silken headdress removed, there appeared a small white dressing affixed by adhesive, over the right temple. "Look beneath the dressing," suggested the African.

Dr. Archer appreciated the ever so faintly malicious little irony, for he answered gravely:

"I shall look even further than that."

He detached the dressing, removed it, and examined a short scalp wound thus disclosed, a wound apparently identical with the one he had probed over an hour ago.

"I delayed a moment to dress it, of course," said Frimbo.

The physician inspected carefully every peculiarity of feature that might answer the question. To the lay eye, certainly there was nothing in this strikingly vivid countenance to recall that other death-distorted visage. But violent death—or even near death—often performs strange transfigurations. Dr. Archer eventually stood erect.

"As nearly as I can determine," he said, "this is the same man. I should request him to submit to a further test, however, before I commit myself finally—a test which will require some little time."

"Whatever the doctor wishes," agreed Frimbo.

"I have in my bag a small amount of blood on a dressing with which I swabbed the wound before probing it. There are one or two tests which can be used as convincing evidence, provided I may have a sample of your blood now for comparison."

"An excellent idea, doctor. Here"—Frimbo drew back the wide sleeve of his black satin robe, baring a well-formed forearm—"help yourself."

The physician promptly secured a tourniquet just above the elbow, moistened a sponge with alcohol, swabbed a small area, where large superficial veins stood out prominently, carefully removed a needle from its sterile tube container, deftly inserted it into a vein, caught a few drops of blood in the tube, loosed the tourniquet, withdrew the needle, and pressed firmly a moment with his swab on the point of puncture.

"Thank you," he said, the operation over.

"How long will this take you, doc?" Dart asked.

"At least an hour. Perhaps two. I'll have to go back to my office to do it."

"You will do the usual agglutination tests, of course?" Frimbo inquired.

"Yes," said Dr. Archer, unable to veil his astonishment that this apparent charlatan should even know there were such tests. "You are familiar with them?"

"Perfectly. I am somewhat of a biologist, you see. Psychology is really a branch of biology."

"You subscribe to the Spencerian classification?" Dr. Archer said.

It was Frimbo's turn to express surprise, which appeared in the slight lift of his lids.

"In that particular, yes."

"I should like to discuss the subject with you."

"I should be very glad indeed. I have met no one competent to do so for years. Today is Sunday. Why not later today?"

"At what hour?"

"Seven this evening?"

"Splendid."

"I shall look forward to seeing you."

2

At this point, a surreptitious remark from Bubber, who had been unwontedly silent, drew attention back to the matter in hand.

"He sho' can talk—for a dead man, can't he?"

"Listen, Frimbo," said Dart. "You say you were killed. All right. Who killed you?"

"I don't know, I'm sure."

"Why don't you?"

"I have tried to explain, Mr. Dart, that I was in a mental state equivalent to being absent. My entire mind was elsewhere— contemplating that gentleman's future. I can no more answer your question than if I had been sound asleep."

"Oh, I see. Would it be asking too much of this strange power of yours if I suggested that you use it to determine the identity of your assailant?"

"I'm glad you suggested it, even ironically. I was reluctant to interfere with your methods. You already have what you be- lieve to be damning evidence against Jenkins. You may be right. But you still have to make sure of the items of motive and possible complicity. Is that not true?"

"Yes."

"Since I am the victim and thus the most personally inter- ested party, I suggest that you allow me to solve this matter for you."

"How?"

"By the use of what you sarcastically call my strange power. If you will have all the suspects here on Monday night at eleven, I will provide you with the complete story of what took place here tonight and why."

"What are you going to do—reconstruct the crime?"

"In a sense, yes."

"Why can't you do that now? All the suspects are here. Here's Jenkins. His finger print on the club that inflicted that wound can't mean but one thing—he handled that club. Why don't you just read his mind and find out what made him do it?"

"It's not so simple as that, my friend. Such a thing requires preparation. Tonight there is not time. And I am tired. But see, I am not suggesting that you neglect doing any single thing that you would have done anyway. Proceed as if I had not returned—I insist that my being alive does not alter the fundamental criminal aspect of this case—proceed, hold whom you will, determine such facts as you can by every means at your disposal, establish your case—then accept my suggestion, if you care to, simply as a corroboration of what you have con- cluded. Consider what I shall show you on Monday night as just a check on what you already know."

Dart was impressed by the turn of the suggestion. "I

suppose," he mused, "I could change the charge to felonious assault——"

Frimbo said, "You are working on a common fallacy, my friend. You are making the common assumption that any creature who is alive cannot have been dead. This is pure assumption. If a body which has presented all the aspects of death, resumes the functions of life, we explain the whole thing away merely by saying, 'He was not dead.' We thus repudiate all our own criteria of death, you see. I cannot think in this self-contradictory fashion. Physically, I was dead by all the standards accepted throughout the years as evidence of death. I was so pronounced by this physician, who has already shown himself to be unusually competent. Had I been anyone else on earth, I should still be dead. But because I have developed special abilities and can separate my mental from my physical activities, the circumstances were such that I could resume the aspects of life. Why must you, on that account, assume that the death was any less actual than the life? Why must you change the charge from murder, which it unquestionably was, to assault, which is only part of the story? Must I pay a premium for special abilities? Must I continually reexpose myself to a criminal who has already carried out his purpose? He has killed—let him die also. If he is able, as I was, to resume life afterwards, I am sure I shall have no objection."

Dart shook his head. "No living person could convince a judge or a jury, that he'd been really murdered. Even if I believed your argument, which I don't, I couldn't arrest this man for murder. A conviction of murder requires the production of a corpse—or tangible evidence of a corpse. I can't present you as a corpse. I'd be the joke of the force."

"Perhaps you are right," Frimbo conceded. "I had not considered the—force."

"Still," Dr. Archer injected, "Mr. Frimbo's suggestion can do no harm. All he says is proceed as if he had not returned. That's what you'd have done anyway. Then, if you like, he will produce additional evidence—Monday night. Personally, I'd like to see it."

"So would I," Dart admitted. "Don't misunderstand me. My only point is that if this is the same man, it's no longer murder."

"There's still plenty to be answered, though," the doctor reminded him. "Jenkins' stout denial in the face of the strongest evidence, the probability of complicity, the motive——"

"And," popped unexpectedly from Bubber, "where that flunky disappeared to, all of a sudden."

Frimbo apparently rarely smiled, but now his awesome dark face relaxed a little. "That need not worry you. My assistant has been with me a long time. He is like a brother. He lives here. He could not possibly be guilty of this crime."

"Then," inquired Bubber, "how come he hauled hips so fast?"

"He is free to leave at eleven every night. It is our understanding and our custom. At that hour tonight, he no doubt took his departure as usual."

"Departure for where—if he lives here?" asked Dart.

"Even servants are entitled to their hour or two of relaxation. He takes his at that time. You need have no doubts about him. Even if I found him guilty, I should not press charges. And I assure you he will be present Monday night."

Later, Detective Dart conveyed to Dr. Archer the considerations which had influenced his decision. First, it had been his experience that in Harlem the most effective method of crime detection was to give your man enough rope with which to hang himself. If Jenkins' denial was true, in whole or part, careful observation of the behavior of the other suspects would reveal something incriminating. Believing himself free and unwatched, the actual criminal—or accomplice—would soon betray himself. The forty-eight hour interval would reveal much about all the suspects. Secondly, if any suspect demurred on the matter of returning or actually failed to return on Monday night, that fact, together with whatever was discovered meanwhile by trailers, would carry its own weight. In short, it was Dart's persuasion that in Harlem one learned most by seeking least—to force an issue was to seal it in silence forever.

And therefore, he now complied with the suggestion that the company be reassembled here on Monday night.

"Very well. I agree. Jenkins and Hicks will be returned under guard. Do any of you other ladies and gentlemen feel that you will be unable to be present?"

No one demurred.

"It is understood, then, that you will be present here at eleven P.M. on Monday. That is all. You are free to go."

The visitors departed, each in his own manner: Jinx, shackled to Officer Green, glowered unforgivingly at Bubber, who for once did not indulge in an opportunity to mock. Doty Hicks glared helplessly at the superbly calm figure of the man whose death he had admittedly sought and failed to effect. Martha Crouch seemed about to stop and speak to Frimbo, but simply smiled and said, "Good-night." Easley Jones and Aramintha Snead made their way out almost stumblingly, so unable were they to remove their fascinated stares from the man who had died and now lived.

### 3

The detective and the doctor took leave of each other in the street below.

"I will start this test tonight and finish it in the morning," promised the latter. "You'll get the result as soon as I am reasonably certain of it."

"Could he really be the same guy, doc? Is that suspended animation stuff on the level?"

"Cases have been reported. This is the first in my experience."

"You sound skeptical."

"I am more than skeptical in this case, my suspicious friend. I am positively repudiative. Somehow, I stubbornly cling to the belief that the man I examined was dead, completely and permanently."

"What? Well, why didn't——"

"And I too am of the common persuasion which Mr. Frimbo so logically exposed, that one who comes to life was never dead. Logic to the contrary notwithstanding, I still believe the dead stay dead. And, while the corpse may be hard to produce, I still believe you have a murder on your hands."

"But you practically admitted he was the same man. Why?"

"I found no evidence to the contrary—nothing decisive. He looked enough like the dead man, and he had an identically similar wound."

"Explainable how?"

"Self-inflicted, perhaps."

"Not unless he had seen the original."

"If he removed the corpse, he did see the original."

"Then why didn't you spring that removable bridge on him? I saw you look at his teeth."

"Because his teeth were perfect."

"What! Why, that would have shown he wasn't the same man right there!"

"Wait a minute now. When the bridge was first found, we considered the possibilities: It might be the corpse's, it might be his assailant's——"

"And decided it must be his—the corpse's."

"But we didn't check that up by going back to the corpse at once. We said we'd do so when the medical examiner arrived. But when the medical examiner arrived the corpse was gone."

"But you just said Frimbo's teeth were perfect. So the bridge can't possibly be his."

"That doesn't prove it belonged to the corpse. It might or might not—we never did establish the point."

"That's right—we didn't," Dart admitted.

"Which allows for a third possibility which we haven't even considered—that the bridge may belong to neither the victim nor the assailant. It could conceivably belong to anybody."

"You've got me there. Anybody who'd ever been in that room could have dropped it."

"Yes—out of a pocket with a hole in it—after having found the thing on the street."

"All Frimbo would have to do would be know nothing about it."

"Exactly. The identification of the ownership of that bridge is to find the person it was made for. And it must fit that person. So you see I had only a conviction—no tangible support whatever. It would have been worse than useless to show our cards then and there. But now, if these two blood specimens reposing in my bag present certain differences which I anticipate, I shall advise you to proceed with the total demolition of yonder dwelling—a vandalism which you have already contemplated, I believe?"

"Gosh, doc, it would be so much easier in French. Say it in French."

"And if you shouldn't find the elusive corpse there—a possibility with which I have already annoyed you tonight—you may proceed to demolish the house next to the right, then the next to the left, and so on until all Harlem lies in ruins. An excellent suggestion, I must say. You, after all, would only be doing your duty, while ever so many people would be infinitely better off if all Harlem did lie in ruins."

"And if we do find a corpse, Frimbo becomes a suspect himself!"

"With things to explain."

Dart whistled. "What a mess that would be!"

"Testicles," mused the other.

"All right, doc. It's irregular, of course, but I believe it's the best way. And I'd rather work with you than—some others. I'm dependin' on you."

"You have the house covered?"

"Sewed up back and front. And we'll keep it sewed up from now till we're satisfied."

"Satisfied—hm—have you reflected on the futility of satisfaction, Dart?"

"Never at one o'clock in the morning, doc. So long. Thanks a lot. See you in Macy's window."

"Shouldn't be at all surprised," murmured Dr. John Archer.

# Chapter Seventeen

WITH an unquestionable sense of humor, the sun grinned down upon the proud pageantry of Seventh Avenue's Sunday noontime, beaming just a little more brightly and warmly than was strictly necessary for a day in February. Accordingly, the brisk air was tempered a little, and the flocks that flowed out from the innumerable churches could amble along at a more leisurely pace than winter usually permitted. This gave his celestial majesty time to observe with greater relish the colorful variety of this weekly promenade: the women with complexions from cream to black coffee and with costumes, individually and collectively, running the range of the rainbow; the men with derbies, canes, high collars, spats, and a dignity peculiar to doormen, chauffeurs, and headwaiters.

Bubber Brown had his place in the sun, too, and he swaggered proudly along with the others, for although Bubber was molded on the general plan of a sphere, his imitation camel's hair overcoat was designed to produce an illusion of slenderness and height, with broad shoulders, a narrowly belted waist and skirts long enough to conceal the extraordinary bowing of his legs. Although he boasted no derby, no cane, and no spats, still with his collar turned swankily up, the brim of his felt hat snapped nattily down, and his hands thrust nonchalantly into his coat pockets, even the rotund Bubber achieved fair semblance of a swagger.

This he maintained as he moved in the stream of church people by humming low yet lustily the anything but Christian song of the moment:

*"I'll be glad when you're dead, you rascal you. . . ."*

On he strolled past churches, drugstores, ice-cream parlors, cigar stores, restaurants, and speakeasies. Acquaintances standing in entrances or passing him by offered the genial insults which were characteristic Harlem greetings:

"What you say, blacker'n me?"

"How you doin', short-order?"

"Ole Eight-Ball! Where you rollin', boy?"

In each instance, Bubber returned some equivalent reply, grinned, waved, and passed on. He breathed deeply of the keen sweet air, appraised casually the trim, dark-eyed girls, admired the swift humming motors that flashed down the Avenue.

But at frequent intervals a frown ruffled his customarily bland countenance, and now and then he foreswore his humming and bowed his head in meditation, shaking it vainly from side to side.

When he reached the corner of 135th Street, he stopped. The stream flowed on past him. He looked westward toward the precinct station-house. Heaving a tremendous sigh, he turned and headed in that direction.

But when he reached the station-house, instead of stopping, he strode on past it as rapidly as if no destination had been further from his mind. At Eighth Avenue he turned south and walked three blocks, then east toward Seventh again. A moment later he halted, aware of a commotion just across the street.

This was a quiet side street, but people were stopping to look. Others, appearing from nowhere, began to run toward the point of agitation, and soon dozens were converging upon the scene like refuse toward a drain. Bubber approached the rim of the clutter of onlookers and craned his neck with normal curiosity.

The scene was the front stoop of an apartment house. Two men and a girl were engaged in loud and earnest disagreement.

"He did!" the girl accused hotly. "He come up to me on that corner——"

"If you was jes' man enough to admit it," menaced her champion.

"Aw, boogy, go diddle," the accused said contemptuously. "I never even seen your——"

Clearly, whatever his epithet might have signified at other times, at this moment it meant action; for hardly had Bubber time to comment, "Uh-oh—that's trouble——" before the girl's protector had smacked the offender quite off the stoop and into the crowd.

The latter, somewhat like a ball on an elastic, came instantaneously and miraculously back at the other. As he flew forward, the girl was heard to yell, "Look out, Jim! He's got a knife!" Jim somehow flung off the attack for the moment and reached for his hip. Apparently every onlooker saw that sinister gesture at the same instant, for the crowd, with one accord, dispersed as quickly and positively as a moment ago it had converged upon this spot—as though indeed, some sudden obstruction had caused the drain to belch back. Two quick loud pistol reports punctuated that divergent scattering. Inquisitive dark heads thrust out of surrounding windows vanished. The victim lay huddled with wide staring eyes at the foot of the stoop, and the man with the gun and his girl sped back into the foyer, appropriated the empty elevator, banged the gate shut, and vanished upward.

2

Bubber did not slacken his rapid pace till he was back at the corner of Eighth Avenue and 135th Street, a few feet from the precinct station. Then he removed his hat and with his bright-colored handkerchief mopped his beaded brow and swore.

"Damn! What a place! What is this—a epidemic?" The thought recalled his superstition. He opened his mouth and gazed awestruck into space. "Jordan River! That's number two! One las' night and another one today. Wonder whose turn it'll be nex'?"

Inadvertently, pondering the horror of the mysterious, he allowed his feet to wander whither they listed. They conveyed him slowly back toward the station-house, the abrupt presence of which struck so suddenly upon his consciousness as almost to startle him into further flight. But his feet were in no mood for further flight; they clung there to the pavement while Bubber's original purpose returned and made itself felt.

For a moment he stood hesitant before the imposing new structure, peering uncertainly in. There was no visible activity. He moved closer to the entrance, gazed into the spacious, not uninviting foyer, looked up and down the street and into the foyer again.

"They's an excuse," he mumbled, "for gettin' dragged into jail, but jes' walkin' in of yo' own free will—ain' no sense in that. . . ."

Nevertheless, with an air of final resolution, he mounted the steps, tried and opened the door. "Hope it works jes' as easy from the other side," he said, and entered.

He approached the desk sergeant.

"Y'all got a boy in here name Jinx Jenkins?"

"When was he brought in?"

"Las' night."

"Charge?"

"Suh?"

"What charge?"

"Couldn' been no charge, broke as he was."

"What was he brought in for—drunk, fightin', or what?"

"Oh. He didn' do nothin'. He jes' got in the wrong house."

"Whose house?"

"Frimbo's. You know—the conjure-man."

"Oh—that case. Sure he's here. Why?"

"Can I see him?"

"What for?"

"Well, y'see, he figgers sump'm I said put him in a bad light. I jes' wanted to let him know how come I said it, that's all."

"Oh, that's all, huh? Well that ain't enough."

But the lieutenant on duty happened to be crossing the foyer at the time and heard part of the conversation. He knew the circumstances of the case, and had planned to be present at the questioning for which, in part, Jinx was being held. With the quick grasp of every opportunity for information that marks the team-work of a well-trained investigative organization, he nodded significantly to the sergeant and promptly departed to arrange a complete recording of all that should transpire between Jinx and his visitor.

"You a friend o' his?" the sergeant asked.

"No—we ain' no special friends," said Bubber. "But I don't aim we should be no special enemies neither."

"I see. Well, in that case, I guess I could let you see him a few minutes. But no monkey-business, y'understand?"

"Monkey-business in a jail-house, mistuh? Do I look dumb, sho' 'nough?"

"O.K."

### 3

In due time and through proper channels, it came to pass that Bubber confronted his tall lean friend, who stood gloomily behind a fine steel grille.

"Hello, Judas," was Jinx's dark greeting.

"Boy," Bubber said, "it's everybody's privilege to be dumb, but they ain' no sense in abusin' it the way you do."

"Is that what you come here to say?"

"I done nearly had what I come here to say scared out o' me. I done seen number two."

"Number two?"

"Yea, man."

"Number two—that's what the little boy said to his mammy. You big and black enough to——"

"Death on the moon, boy. First one las' night, second one today—not ten minutes ago—'round on 132nd Street. Two boogies got in a li'l argument over a gal, and first thing you know—bong—bong! There was one of 'em stretched out dead on the ground and me lookin' at him."

"No."

"Yea, man. This Harlem is jes' too bad. But I tol' you I'm go'n' stare three corpses in the face. They's one mo' yet."

"Hmph. And you call me dumb."

"What you mean?"

"That wasn' no corpse you stared in the face las' night. Las' I remember, he was sittin' up in that chair talkin' pretty lively, like a natchel man."

"Yea, but he ain' no natchel man—he's a conjure-man. He was sho' 'nough dead, jes' like he said. He 'jes knows sump'm, that's all."

"He knows sump'm, I don't doubt that. Tol' me plenty. But any time a man knows enough to come to life after he's dead, he knows too much."

"Reckon that's how come he got kilt, 'cause he knows too much. Sho' was the same man though, wasn't he?"

"Far as I could see. But 'course that don' mean much—all coons look alike to me."

There was a moment's silence, whereupon Jinx added, with meaning, "And no matter how well you know 'em, you can't trust 'em."

"Listen, boy, you all wrong. 'Course I know you can't help it, 'cause what few brains you had is done dried up and been sneezed out long ago. But even you ought to be able to see my point."

" 'Cose I see yo' point. Yo' point was, you was savin' yo' own black hide. If you admit you a friend o' mine, maybe you inhale some jail-air too. Jes' like all boogies—jes' let the man say 'Boo!' and yo' shirt tail roll up yo' back like a window shade."

"All right—all right. But see if this can penetrate yo' hard, kinky head. What good am I——"

"None whatsoever."

"Wait a minute, will you please? What good am I to you if I'm right here in jail alongside o' you?"

"What good is you to me anywhere?"

"Well, if I'm out, at least I got a chance to find out who done it, ain't I?"

Jinx relented a little, reluctantly comprehending.

"Yea, you got a chance," he muttered. "But you go'n' need mo'n a chance to find out who done that. Right under my nose, too, with me sittin' there—and if I seen anybody, you did."

"Well cheer up, long boy. You ain' got nothin' to worry 'bout. The man's alive and you heard what the detective said— all they can hold you for is assault."

"No," reflected Jinx sardonically. "I ain' got nothin' to worry 'bout. They tell me the most I can get for assault is twenty years."

"Twenty—whiches?"

"Years. Them things growin' out the side o' yo' head. And all twenty of 'em jes' that color. It sho' is a dark outlook."

"Mph!"

"Who's gruntin' now?"

"Both of us. But shuh, man, they can't do that to you."

"I know they can't. You know they can't. But do they know they can't?"

"Don't worry, boy. Leave everything to me. I'll find out who done this if it takes me the whole twenty years."

"Hmph! Well, it's time you done sump'm right. When you could 'a' kep' yo' mouth shut, you was talkin'. 'Sho' that's Jinx's handkerchief.' And when you could 'a' talked, you kep' yo' mouth shut. 'Friend o' mine? No 'ndeed!'—All right. Whatever you go'n' do, get to doin' it, 'cause these accommodations don't suit me. Twenty years! Twenty years from now Harlem'll be full o' Chinamen."

"Don't blame me for all of it. I never would 'a' been in the conjure-man's place if you hadn't said 'come on let's go.'"

"What you go'n' do?"

"I'm go'n' do some detectin', that's what. What's use o' bein' a private detective if I can't help out a friend? I'm workin' on a theory already, boy."

"First work you done since you quit haulin' ashes for the city."

"That was good trainin' for a detective. I used to figure out jes' what happened the night befo' by what I found in the ash can nex' mornin'. If I see a torn nightgown and a empty whiskey bottle——"

"I've heard all 'bout that. What's yo' theory?"

"The flunky, boy. He done it, sho's you born. I'm go'n' find him and trick him into a confession."

"What makes you think he done it?"

" 'Cause he run away, first thing."

"But didn't you hear the man say he was s'posed to leave by eleven o'clock?"

"That would make it all the easier for him, wouldn't it? If he s'posed to be gone th'ain't nothin' suspicious 'bout him *bein'* gone, don't you see?"

"M-m."

"He figured on that."

"How'n hell'd he get my handkerchief?"

"He took it out yo' pocket. 'Member when Doty Hicks fell down in a faint and we all scrambled 'round and helped him up?"

"Yea——"

"That's when he took it."

"He could 'a'. But what would he want to kill his boss for?"

"Boy, ain't you ever had a boss? They's times when you feel like killin' the best boss in the world, if you could get away with it."

"Well, whoever you hang it on, it's all right with me."

"If worse comes to worse," Bubber's voice sank to a whisper, "I can swear I seen him take yo' handkerchief out yo' pocket."

"No," Jinx demurred, "ain' no need o' you goin' to hell jes' 'cause I go to jail."

"I'm go'n' get you out o' this."

"When you startin'?"

"Tonight."

"Don' hurry. Nex' week'll be plenty o' time."

"Tonight. By tomorrer I'll have the dope on that flunky. You watch."

"I'm watchin'," said Jinx. "And all I got to say is, Sherlock, do yo' stuff."

# Chapter Eighteen

BY ELEVEN-THIRTY the same Sunday morning, Dr. Archer had completed his morning calls—both of them. He returned to his office, where he found three gentlemen awaiting him. Two were patients, the third was Detective Perry Dart.

"Urgent?" he asked Dart.

"Nope. Take the others."

The others were soon disposed of; the first pleaded a bad cold and got his liquor prescription, the second pleaded hard times and borrowed three dollars.

"Come in here," the physician then summoned Dart, and led the way through his treatment room with its adjustable table, porcelain stands, glass-doored steel cabinets shining with bright—and mostly virgin—instruments, into a smaller side room which had done duty as a butler's pantry in the days before Harlem changed color.

"Something like Frimbo's," commented the detective, looking admiringly around.

"In part, yes. That is, Frimbo has some clinical stuff, but that's only a fraction of his, while it's all of mine. He has chemistry apparatus that a physician's lab would never need except for research, and few practicing physicians have time for that kind of research. More than that, he has some electrical stuff there that only a physicist or mechanic would have, and I'm sure I saw something like a television receptor on one end of the bench—remember that affair like a big lens set in a square box? Those specimens sort of stole the show and we didn't take time to examine around carefully. But all I've got is what's necessary for routine clinical tests—some glassware, a few standard reagents, a centrifuge, a microscope, and that's about all."

"I guess all labs look alike to me."

"Well, there's enough here to investigate certain properties of our friend's blood, any day. If the two specimens present no differences that we can determine, we're stumped—so far as murder goes. But if they do——"

"Is this something new, doc?"

"New? No, why?"

"Well, of course I knew they could tell whether it was human blood. I know of plenty of cases where blood was found on a weapon, and the suspect claimed it was chicken's blood or sheep's blood, but the doctors came along and showed it was human. I should think that would be hard enough."

"Not so hard. A chap—Gay, I believe—sensitized some lab animals—guinea pigs or rabbits or whatever happened to be around—to various serums. You see, if you do it right, you can inject a little serum into an animal and he'll develop what they call antibodies for that serum. Antibody's a substance which the blood manufactures to combat certain things that get into it but haven't any business there. But the point is that each antibody is specific—hostile to just one certain thing. From the viewpoint of the health of the human family, that's too bad. Be swell if you could just inject a little of anything and get a general immunity to everything. But from the viewpoint of criminology it's useful, because if you're smart enough, you can tell whether your suspect is lying or not about the blood on his weapon. You just dissolve your blood off the weapon, and test it against the sensitized blood from each of your known animals. When you get a reaction you know, your unknown is the same as the one which reacted to it. See?"

Dart shook his head.

"I'll take you guys' word for that stuff. But if it's that hard to tell human blood from other kinds, I should think it would be still harder to tell one human's blood from another human's blood." Dart looked around. "And I don't see the first guinea pig."

"So it would seem. But there are many ways in which one man's blood differs from another's. Take the Wasserman reaction. Mine may be negative and yours positive——"

"Hold on, doc, don't get personal."

"Or we may both be positive, but different in degree."

"That's better."

"And there are plenty of other germs, which, like the germ of syphilis, bring about definite changes in the blood. In many cases these changes can be determined, so that you can say that this blood came from a fellow who had so-and-so, while that blood came from a fellow who didn't have so-and-so."

"Go ahead. How about Frimbo's?"

"Or take blood transfusions. You know everybody can't give his blood to everybody—in many cases it would be fatal—was fatal before blood types were known about. Now it's known a man might be eager to give his blood to save his sweetheart, and yet that might be the quickest way of killing her."

Dart's black eyes were alive with interest.

"That's right. I remember——"

"That's because one blood may contain something that doesn't harmonize with something in another blood."

"Like what, doc?"

"It's mainly a matter of serum and red corpuscles. Some serum will destroy some corpuscles——"

"Oh, I see," said Dart.

"So to make sure this doesn't happen, every transfusion now has to be preceded by a certain blood examination known as typing. Couple of bright gentlemen named Janski and Moss looked into the matter not so many years ago and found that all human blood falls into four general types. Since then a flock of sub-types have been established, but the four basic ones still suffice for ordinary procedures. Everybody falls into one of the four groups—and stays there."

Dart was eagerly curious.

"And Frimbo's blood isn't in the same group with the other?"

"I don't know. Haven't tested it out yet—just got ready and had to go deliver twins. That allowed you to get here just in time for the performance. But for intrahuman differences, you'd hardly find any two people with every degree of every blood reaction precisely identical."

"Do your stuff, doc. I'm getting nervous."

"All right. Now look. See this?" He held up a test tube in the bottom of which was a small amount of pinkish fluid. "This is the unknown serum, extracted from the dressing with which I sponged the wound in the dead man's scalp. It's diluted, of course, and discolored because of haemolysis of the red cells——"

"Don't mind me, doc. Go right ahead."

"—but that doesn't matter much. And this tube is Frimbo's serum, and this is a suspension of Frimbo's red cells, which I made last night. By the way, Dart, would you give up some of your blood to find this thing out?"

"How much, doc?"

"He hesitates in the pursuit of his duty," murmured the doctor. "Well, never mind—I may not need it. I may not even need my own."

"You mean you were figuring on bleeding yourself, too?"

"I happen to know I'm under Type II. You remember I mentioned that all tests are checks against a known specimen."

"And you've got to have a known specimen?"

"Unless we're very lucky. We may be able to prove these two specimens different without actually having to type them. Well, now look. We'll take this capillary pipette and remove a drop of this unknown serum and place it thus on a microscopic slide. Then we'll take a nichrome loop so, and remove a loopful of Professor Frimbo's best red cells, and stir them gently into the drop of serum, thus, spreading same smoothly into a small circular area in this manner. Watch carefully. The hand is quicker than the eye. Now then, a cover glass, and under the microscope it goes. We adjust the low power with a few deft turns and gaze into the mysteries of the beyond. Dart, we seldom reflect upon what goes on at the other end of the barrel of a microscope: challenge, conquest, combat, victory, defeat, life, death, reproduction—every possible relationship of living beings—the very birth of the world there in a droplet of moisture." With both eyes open he was manipulating the fine adjustment. "Do you know what a fellow said to me once? I came up behind him and asked him what he was staring down his mike so steadily for—what did he hope to find? He said one word without looking up. He said, 'God.'" He focused the instrument satisfactorily, peered a moment, then stood aside, "You and I are more practical, aren't we? All we hope to find is a murderer. Come on—try your luck."

"Me?"

"Of course. Look, look, and keep looking. If you see anything happen, don't keep it a secret."

Dart, squinting one eye shut, gazed with the other down the barrel. "A lot of little reddish dots," he announced.

"What are they doing?"

"Nothing." Dart grinned. "Must be Negro blood."

"Jest not, my friend. It is Sunday. All blood reposes. But keep looking."

"Well, maybe they are moving a little. Hey—sure! They *are* moving—so slow you can hardly see it, though."

"In what direction?"

"Every direction. Boy, this is good. They can't make up their minds."

"That sounds as though——"

"Hey—Judas Priest—what's this? Look, doc!"

"You look and tell me about it. I might let my imagination run away with me."

"These things are going into a huddle. No—into a flock of huddles. No kidding—they're slowly collecting in little bunches."

"Are you sure?"

"Am I sure? What does it mean, doc? Here, take a look."

Dr. Archer complied. "Hm—I think I can safely say your observations are correct—though 'agglutination' is a far more elegant term than 'huddle.'"

"But what's the answer?"

"The answer is that nobody's red cells could conceivably behave like that in their own serum. Not even a magician's."

"You mean that's the destruction you were talking about?"

"Yes, sir. The first step in it. That's as far as we need to go in vitro. In vivo, the process goes on to dissolution, disintegration, haemolysis—oh, there's lots of nice words you can call it. But whatever you call it, this serum gives those corpuscles —hell."

Dart's eyes glowed.

"Then Frimbo and the corpse were two different people?"

"And still are. And you and I are two lucky people, because we don't have to play school any longer—not with these, anyway."

"The son of a bedbug! I'm going to put him *under* the jail—trying to kid somebody like that. Where's my hat?"

"What's your hurry, mister? He isn't going anywhere."

"How do I know he isn't?"

"Can he get out without being seen by your men?"

"That's right. But why wait?"

"If you grab him now—if you even let him suspect what we know, he'll close up like a vault. My humble opinion is that he's got a lot of information you need—if he gets lockjaw, you'll never convict him."

"Then what's your idea?"

"Indulge me, my friend. I'm smart. I want to keep that appointment with him this evening——"

"He may be back in Bunghola, or wherever he hails from, by then."

"Not the slightest chance. Frimbo is staging a party tomorrow night for just one reason—he's going to fasten the blame for that murder, as he still calls it, and rightly, on somebody—somebody else. Your best bet is to have all the counter-evidence ready to confront him with at the same time. Don't worry, he'll be there."

"Well this certainly is enough to make him a suspect."

"You've got suspects enough already. What you want now is a murderer. It's true that Frimbo was not the corpse. This proves that. It is also true that he must have managed to make away with the corpse; then, to cover that, masqueraded as the corpse—even inflicted a wound on his head resembling that of the corpse." Dr. Archer could talk very plainly and directly on occasion. "But there are lots of things between that conclusion and proof of his being the murderer. All that we know is that Frimbo lied. We do not know why he lied. And he isn't the only liar in this case—Jenkins lied, probably Hicks lied, for all I know Webb lied——"

"Say that reminds me! That Webb was on the right track. He was telling the truth, at least in part. I meant to tell you, but I got so interested in this other thing. There was a knock-down and drag-out shooting this morning on 132nd Street. Apparently an argument over a girl, but who do you suppose the victim was? One of Brandon's best-known runners. Yes, sir. Well, it took the boys exactly forty-five minutes to nab the guy that did it. And who do you s'pose *he* was? Spencer's first lieutenant, boy named Eagle Watson. Of course he'll get out of it—good lawyers and all—girl'll swear the victim attacked her and turned on him when he came to her rescue—plenty o' bona fide witnesses—self-defense—easy. But we know what's behind it—and Webb told the truth about it. There actually is a Spencer-Brandon policy feud on; Spencer's getting the worst of it, and he's declared war on the whole Brandon outfit. The reason why he's getting the worst of it can only be because he's losing a lot of money and losing it fast, and the reason he declares war on the rival outfit is because he figures they are responsible. If he figures that, he may have got wind of this Frimbo's having a hand in it and tried to pull a fast one last night. Only that doesn't hitch up with this blood business at all, does it?"

"There was once a man—nice fellow, too, even though he was a policeman—who delivered some remarks on premature conclusions. His idea was to fit conclusions to facts, as I recall, not facts to conclusions. And he admitted—nay, insisted—that, by such a system, it would only be necessary to accumulate enough facts and they'd sort of draw their own conclusions. You will observe that this fellow was a lineal descendant of Francis Bacon—despite their difference of complexion—in that he inherited the tendency to reason inductively rather than deductively. But such is the frailty of human-kind that even this fortunate chap occasionally fell into the error of letting his imagination, instead of his observation, draw the conclusions; whereupon he would suddenly look about in bewilderment and say that something didn't hitch up with something."

"O.K., doc. The point of all that being it's still too soon to speculate?"

"The point being that where more facts can be gathered, it is always too soon to speculate."

"Well—I guess he'll keep. But if you let him get away from me——"

"My dear fellow, permit me to remind you that in that case the situation would be no different from what it was before I suggested the blood comparison."

"Beg your pardon, doc. But what about the corpse? We've got to have a corpse—you know that. If it's still somewhere in that house, Frimbo's going to have plenty of time to destroy it."

"Have you—if I'm not too personal—ever tried to destroy a corpse, Dart?"

"Almost impossible to destroy it completely by ordinary

methods. But there are acids. As much stuff as he's got there——"

"You searched the house pretty well."

"Yes, but we've got experts that do nothing else, doc. They could find places that I wouldn't dream of looking for. They measure and calculate and reconstruct to scale, and when they get through, there isn't a place left big enough to hide a bedbug in."

"They take time, though, and their presence would arouse Frimbo's suspicions and hostility. Believe me, Dart—Frimbo himself is the only answer to this riddle. Jump him too soon and you'll destroy the only chance. I'm sure of that. I'm as curious about this thing as you are. I'm funny that way. And I'd like to see you and the local boys get the credit for this whole thing—not a lot of Philistines from downtown. You said you were depending on me. All right. Do that. And let me depend on you."

"Gee, doc, I didn't realize you were as interested as all that. It sure would mean a lot to me personally to get credit for this. We don't grab off a funny one like this often. If that's really how you feel about it——"

"Fine. Now all you've got to do is make no report of this last finding and hold off Frimbo till I'm through with him. Before tomorrow night I hope to have a pretty good idea of what makes him go 'round. After all, a gentleman who turns out to be one of the suspects in his own murder case deserves a little personal consideration."

"A suspect in his own murder—say, that's right! That's a brand-new one on me! But he's smart all right. Wonder why he didn't object to the blood test? He must have known it might prove incriminating."

"Of course he knew it. But what could he do? To refuse would have put him in a bad light too. All he could gracefully do was acquiesce and take a chance on the two bloods being so much alike that the small amount of the unknown would be exhausted before we could distinguish it from his own. That failing, he would simply have to depend on his wits. Did you hear him ask me whether I would use the ordinary agglutination tests? He's ready with an alibi for this lie right now, I'll bet you. That's another reason for not rushing in yet. We've got to get something he can't anticipate."

Dart looked at the physician with genuine admiration. "Doc, you're all right, no lie. You ought to've been a detective."

"I am a detective," the other returned. "All my training and all my activities are those of a detective. The criminal I chase is as prime a rascal as you'll ever find—assailant, thief, murderer —disease. In each case I get, it's my job to track disease down, identify it, and arrest it. What else is diagnosis and treatment?"

"I never thought of it that way."

"In this Frimbo case, I'm your consultant—by your personal invitation. I'm going to make as extensive an examination as I can before I draw my conclusions. Your allowing me to do so is proper professional courtesy—a rare thing for which I thank you deeply." He bowed solemnly to the grinning Dart. "And meanwhile you will be finding out every move of every visitor to that place last night?"

"Right. They're all being tailed this minute. And I've already checked everybody's story, even the undertaker's. They're all O.K. Brown came around to the precinct this morning to see Jenkins—they eavesdropped on him but didn't get anything except that Jenkins is still denying guilt. And his friend is willing to perjure himself to save him."

"I still find it hard to believe that Jenkins, even for the dirty lucre you so cogently brought forward, actually did this. Jenkins is a hard one all right, but it's all external. He's probably got the heart of a baby, and has to masquerade as a tough customer to protect himself."

"As you like. But that very masquerade could lead him into something from which he couldn't turn back."

"But not murder."

"Well, explain how he masqueraded his finger print onto that club and you'll do him a great favor."

"He may be lying about not touching the club the same as he is about the handkerchief."

"He's lying all right if he says he didn't touch that club. There's no other way the print could have got there."

"Isn't there?" the physician said, but the detective missed the skepticism in the tone and went on with his enumeration.

"Doty Hick's brother really is sick with T.B. and refuses to go to a hospital. I told you this morning about the killing that harmonizes with Webb's story. And Easley Jones has been employed by the Pullman Company for ten years—the man spoke very highly of him. I went by the Forty Club last night after leaving you. Three different members told me Crouch the undertaker had been there as he said."

"What about the women?"

"Well, you yourself vouched for Mrs. Crouch. And I'm almost willing to vouch for that other one. If she's got anything to do with this, I have."

"I was wondering about that. Have you?"

"Sure, doc," Dart's bright smile flashed. "I'm the detective on the case, didn't you know?"

"Do you know who committed the crime?"

"Not for certain."

"I see. Then you couldn't have done it yourself. Because if you had, you'd know who did it and it would be a simple matter for you to track yourself down and arrest yourself. Of course you might have done it in your sleep."

"So might you."

"I have a perfect alibi, my friend. Doctors never sleep. If it isn't poker it's childbirth—a pair of aces or a pair of pickaninnies."

"Seriously, doc, there's one objection to your trying to get something on Frimbo tonight."

"What?"

"Why do you suppose that guy was so quick to invite you back alone? Because you're his chief worry. You may be the cause of putting him on the frying-pan. He's evil. He must know your purpose. And if you get too warm, he'll try to rub you out."

"He'll find me quite indelible, I'm sure," Dr. Archer said.

# Chapter Nineteen

JOHN ARCHER opened a desk drawer and picked up a revolver which lay there. He gazed thoughtfully upon it a moment, then gently replaced it. He shut the drawer, turned and made his way out of the house. His front door closed behind him, and he stood contemplating the high narrow edifice across the dark street. It was two minutes to seven; the air was sharp and ill-disposed and snapped at him in passing. Absently he hunched his ulster higher about his shoulders, thrust his hands, free of the customary bag, deep into his pockets and studied Frimbo's shadowy dwelling. Rearing a little above its fellows, it was like a tall man peering over the heads of a crowd. "Wonder if I'm expected?" the physician mused. As if in answer, two second-story windows suddenly lighted up, like eyes abruptly opened.

"I am expected." Slowly he crossed the dim street, halted again at the foot of the stoop to resume his meditative stare, then resolutely mounted to the door and, finding it unlocked, entered.

His host was awaiting him at the head of the stairs. Frimbo's tall figure was clad tonight in a dressing-gown of figured maroon silk; this, with a soft shirt open at the throat, and the absence of any native headdress, gave him a matter-of-fact appearance quite different from that of the night before. Tonight he might have been any well-favored Harlemite taking his ease on a Sunday evening in leisure which he could afford and intended to enjoy.

But the deep-set eyes still held their peculiar glow, and the low resonant voice was the same.

"Let us go up to the library," he said. "It will be more comfortable."

He reached into the front room as they passed and snapped a wall switch, leaving the room dark. "I turned those on for your benefit, doctor. We must not be disturbed by other visitors. I have been looking forward to seeing you."

He led the way to that rear third-floor chamber which the physician had visited the night before.

"Choose your own chair—you will find most of them comfortable." The man's attitude was entirely disarming, but Dr. Archer took a chair that was disposed diagonally in a corner with bookshelves to either side.

Frimbo smiled.

"I have some fair sherry and some execrable Scotch," he offered.

"Thank you. You evidently prefer the sherry—I'll follow your example."

Shortly the wine had been procured from the adjacent kitchen; glasses were filled—from the same container, the physician noted; cigarettes were lighted; Frimbo seated himself on the divan before the fireplace, in which artificial logs glowed realistically.

"You were speaking," he said, as if almost a whole day had not intervened, "of Herbert Spencer's classification of the sciences."

"Yes," the physician said. "Psychology considered as the physiology of the nervous system."

Easily and quickly they began to talk with that quick intellectual recognition which characterizes similarly reflective minds. Dr. Archer's apprehensions faded away and shortly he and his host were eagerly embarked on discussions that at once made them old friends: the hopelessness of applying physico-chemical methods to psychological problems; the nature of matter and mind and the possible relations between them; the current researches of physics, in which matter apparently vanished into energy, and Frimbo's own hypothesis that probably mind did likewise. Time sped. At the end of an hour Frimbo was saying:

"But as long as this mental energy remains mental, it cannot be demonstrated. It is like potential energy—to be appreciated it must be transformed into heat, light, motion—some form that can be grasped and measured. Still, by assuming its existence, just as we do that of potential energy, we harmonize psychology with mechanistic science."

"You astonish me," said the doctor. "I thought you were a mystic, not a mechanist."

"This," returned Frimbo, "*is* mysticism—an undemonstrable

belief. Pure faith in anything is mysticism. Our very faith in reason is a kind of mysticism."

"You certainly have the gift of harmonizing apparently opposite concepts. You should be a king—there'd be no conflicting parties under your régime."

"I am a king."

For a moment the physician looked at the serene dark countenance much as if he were seeing his first case of some unusual but clear-cut disease. Frimbo, however, tranquilly took a sip of sherry, gently replaced the fragile glass on a low table at his elbow, and allowed the phantom of a smile to soften his countenance.

"You forget," he said, lighting a fresh cigarette, "that I am an African native." There was a pride in the statement that was almost an affront. "I am of Buwongo, an independent territory to the northeast of Liberia, with a population of approximately a million people. My younger brother rules there in my stead." A reminiscent air descended momentarily upon him. "Often I long to go back, but it would be dull. I am too fond of adventure."

"Dull!" Archer exclaimed. "Why—most people would consider that an extraordinarily exciting life."

"Most people who know nothing of it. Excitement lies in the challenge of strange surroundings. To encounter life in the African brush would exhilarate you, certainly. But for the same reasons, life in a metropolis exhilarates me. The bush would be a challenge to all your resources. The city is a similar challenge to mine."

"But you can't be so unaccustomed to this now. You have finished an American college, you have mastered the ways of our thinking enough to have original contributions of your own to make—surely all that is behind you once and for all."

"No," said Frimbo softly. "There are things one never forgets."

"You make me very curious."

The kindled black eyes regarded him intently a long moment. Then Frimbo said, "Perhaps I should satisfy that curiosity somewhat . . . if you care to listen. . . ."

And the dark philosopher who called himself king, with a faraway look in his eyes and a rise and fall in his deep low voice, painted a picture twenty years past and five thousand miles away.

2

"In some countries night settles gently like a bird fluttering down into foliage; in Buwongo it drops precipitately like a bird that has been shot. It is as if the descending sun backed unaware upon the rim of a distant mountain, tripped on the peak, and tumbled headlong out of sight into the valley beyond. The bright day has been mysterious enough—the blank, blue sky, the level rice fields, the arrogant palms, the steaming jungle. But it is obvious, bold mystery—it must reveal itself before it can strike. Night clothes it in invisibility, renders it subtle, indeterminate, ominous. Brings it close.

"All day we have traveled southward—my father, a hundred fighting men, and I. I am only twelve, but that is enough. I must now begin to take part in the feasts of our tributary villages. We are on the way to Kimalu, a town of a thousand people. I am very tired—but I am the eldest son of a chief. I stride proudly beside my tireless father. Some day I shall be like him, tall, straight, strong; I shall wear the scarlet loin cloth and the white headdress of superior rank. I must not falter. We have not stopped for food or drink—for shall we not feast lavishly tonight? We have ignored the beckoning paths that lead off our main trail—paths to other villages, to cool green tributaries of the Niger, to who knows what animal's hideout. And in the flattening rays of the sinking sun we at last see the rice fields outside our destination and presently the far off thatched roofs of Kimalu's dwellings. We are on a slight rise of ground. Yet before we can reach Kimalu, night overtakes us and devours us.

"But already there is the glow of village fires, a hundred spots of wavering yellow light; and shortly we enter Kimalu, my father leading, with me by his side, the men in double file behind us. All fatigue drops away as the shouts of greeting and welcome deluge our company like a refreshing shower.

"The ceremonies are scheduled to begin three hours hence, at the height of the moon. Meanwhile preparations go on. Our company is welcomed respectfully by the elderly headman, who receives with effusive thanks our two bullocks, each suspended by its feet on a horizontal pole and carried on the shoulders of eight of our carriers. These will augment the feast that follows the ceremony and help provide for our party on the morrow. We are conducted to the central square before the dwelling of the headman, a large house, thatch-roofed, walled with palm and bamboo, and surrounded by a high rampart of tall interlaced *timwe* trunks, the sharpened top of each one treated with a poison that is death to touch. Even the most venomous snake could not crawl over that rampart and live. The square is large enough to accommodate all the people of the village, for here they must assemble at regular intervals to hear the issuing of edicts relative to their governing laws and their local and national taxes. Here too, the headman sits in judgment every other day and pronounces upon both moral and civil offenders sentences ranging from temporary banishment to castration—the latter a more dreaded penalty than beheading.

"Around the enormous square, as we enter it, we see many fires, over which stews are simmering in kettles, and barbecues of boar, bullock, or antelope are roasting on poles. Savory odors quicken our nostrils, cause our mouths to water. But we may not yet satisfy our appetites. First we must wash and rest. And so we go down to the edge of the river beside which the village lies; there is a broad clearing and a shallow bit of beach upon which more fires burn for illumination and protection. Here we wash. Then we return to the rim of the square and stretch out to doze and rest till the feast begins.

"It is the Malindo—the feast of procreation—and of all the rites of all our forty-eight tribes, none is more completely symbolic. An extremely wide circle—one hundred and fifty feet in diameter—of firewood has been laid in the center of the square. Outside this at intervals are piles of more firewood, short dry branches of fragrant trees.

"At the height of the moon, the headman gives the signal for the ceremony to begin. The band of drummers, stationed to one side of the rampart gate, is ready. The drums are hollow logs; one end is open; over the other is stretched a tympanum of boarskin; they lie horizontally side by side; vary in length from two to twenty feet, but are so placed that the closed ends are in alignment facing the circle of firewood; they vary in diameter also, but even the smallest is a foot high. Each drummer sits astride his instrument above its closed end, upon which he plays with his bare hands and fingers.

"At the chief's signal, the player of the largest drum stretches his arms high over his head and brings the heels of both hands down hard on the face of his instrument. There is a deep, resounding boom, a sound such as no other instrument has ever produced; as low and resonant as the deepest organ note, as startlingly sudden as an explosion. A prowling cat five miles away will halt and cringe at that sound. The stillness that follows trembles in the memory of it; as that tremor dwindles the drummer strikes again—the cadence is established. Again, again. Slowly, steadily the great drum booms, a measure so large, so stately, so majestic, that all that follows is subordinated to it and partakes of its dignity.

"The people of the village have already gathered around the margin of the square; some sit on the ground, some stand, all are raptly intent. My father is seated on a platform directly in front of the rampart gate; I am on his left, the headman on his right, our hundred men seated on the ground further along. There is no movement anywhere save the flicker of low fires, and no sound save the steady tremendous boom of the great drum.

"But now something is happening, for a new note creeps subtly into the slow period of the drumbeat—another smaller drum, then another, then another, sounding a submeasure of lesser beats, quicker pulsations that originate in the parent sound and lift away from it like dwindling echoes. From the far side of the clearing a procession of shadowy figures emerges, and in their midst appear six men bearing on their shoulders a large square chest. The figures move slowly, in time with the fundamental measure, till they are on this side of the circle of firewood; then the six bearers turn toward the circle, and the others, in front of them and behind them, turn toward us. The bearers, still in time, move forward toward the circle, step over the wood with their burden, and deposit it in the center of the ring, while the others, also keeping to the measure, approach our position, about face, and seat themselves on the ground to either side of our platform.

"Still another motif now enters the rhythmic cadence—all the remaining drums, at first softly, almost imperceptibly, then more definitely, take up this new, lighter, quicker variation, which weaves itself into the major pattern like brocaded figures into damask—the whole a rich fabric of strength, delicacy, and incredible complexity of design. And now a file of torches appears far across the clearing, comes closer—they seem numberless, but are forty-eight, I know—one for each of our tribes. And we see that they are borne aloft, each in the hand of a slim naked girl whose dancing movements are in accord with the new lighter measure of the drums. The file passes before us, each member gracefully maintaining the rhythmic motif, till, equally spaced, they face the circle, each the stem of a bright flower in a swaying garland of flame.

"For a few minutes they dance thus, keeping their relative positions around the circle, but advancing periodically a few feet toward the center then withdrawing; and they do this so perfectly in unison that, while their feet and bodily gestures obey the lighter, quicker rhythm, their advances and retreats are tuned to the original, fundamental pulse, and the flares in their hands become jewels of flame, set in a magic ring which contracts . . . dilates . . . contracts . . . dilates . . . like a living heart, pumping blood. Then, with a sudden swell and dwindling of the lesser drums, there is a terminal, maximal contracture—the girls have advanced quite to the circle of firewood, dropped their torches upon it each at her respective point; have then, without seeming to lose a rhythmic movement, executed a final retreat—faded back from the circle like so many shadows, and fallen on the ground perfectly straight, each in a radial line, each as motionless as if she were bound to a spoke of some gigantic wheel.

"The great circle of wood soon kindles into an unbroken ring of fire, symbol of eternal passion; and as the flames mount, the drumming grows louder and more turbulent, as if the fire were bringing it to a boil. A warrior, whose oiled skin gleams in the light, leaps through the flames into the inside of the circle, reaches the large square chest in the center, unfastens and turns back the lid, and vanishes through the far rim of the fire.

"Every eye is focused on the chest beyond the flames. There is a slight shift of the rhythm—so slight as entirely to escape an unaccustomed ear. But the dancing girls catch it, and instantly are on their feet again in another figure of their ceremonial gesture—a languorous, lithe, sinuous twist with which they again advance toward the fiery circle. They incorporate into this figure of their dance movements whereby they take branches from the extra piles and toss them into the fire. The blaze mounts steadily. No one is noticing the girls now, however; no one is aware of the pervasive incense from the fragrant burning wood. For something is rising from the chest—the head of a gigantic black python, that rears four—five—six feet above the rim and swings about bewildered by the encircling fire.

"Now the warrior reappears, holding aloft in his two hands an infant of the tribe. Swiftly, with the infant so held as to be out of reach of the licking flames, again he bounds through the fire into the circle. At the same time the most beautiful maiden of the tribe, her bare body oiled like the warrior's, appears within the ring from the opposite side. The python, still bewildered, swings back and forth. The warrior and the maiden dance three times in opposite directions around the serpent. And now, though none has seen it happen, the girl has the infant in her arms; the python, sensing danger in the entrapping flames and the tumult of the drums, withdraws into his chest. The warrior closes and fastens the lid and vanishes through the far wall of fire. The drums have gone mad. The girl, holding the baby aloft in both hands, faces us, dashes forward with a cry that transcends the crescendo of drumming, a shriek like that of a woman in the last spasm of labor, leaps high through the blaze, runs toward our platform, and gently lays the unharmed infant at our feet. . . ."

3

There was a long silence. Frimbo sat looking into the flickering mock-embers on his artificial hearth, seeing those faraway genuine ones of woods that burned with a fragrance like incense. John Archer was silent and still, absorbed in the other man's fine dark face. Perhaps he was wondering, "Could this man have committed a murder? Whom would he want to kill? Why?

What is he—charlatan or prophet? What is his part in this puzzle—what indeed is not possible to this mind that in a moment steps out of cold abstract reason into the warm symbolic beauty of a barbaric rite?"

But what the physician actually said was, "Rather a dangerous ceremony, isn't it?"

Frimbo gathered himself back into the present, smiled, and answered, "Are conception and birth without danger?"

After a moment the doctor said, "My own youth was so utterly different."

"Yet perhaps as interesting to me as mine would have been to you."

"The age of twelve," laughed the other, "recalls nothing more exciting than a strawberry festival in the vestry of my father's church."

"Your father was a minister?"

"Yes. He died shortly after I finished college. I wanted to study medicine. One of my profs had a wealthy friend. He saw me through. I've been practicing nearly ten years—and haven't finished paying him back yet. That's my biography. Hardly dramatic, is it?"

"You have omitted the drama, my friend. Your father's struggle to educate you, his clinging on to life just to see you complete a college training—which had been denied him; your desperate helplessness, facing the probability of not being able to go on into medicine; the impending alternative of teaching school in some Negro academy; the thrill of discovering help; the rigid economy, to keep the final amount of your debt as low as possible—the summers of menial work as a bell boy or waiter or porter somewhere, constantly taking orders from your inferiors, both white and black; the license to practice—and nothing to start on; more menial work—months of it—to accumulate enough for a down payment on your equipment; the first case that paid you and the next dozen that didn't; the prolonged struggle against your initial material handicaps—the resentment you feel at this moment against your inability to do what you are mentally equipped to do. If drama is struggle, my friend, your life is a perfect play."

Dr. Archer stared.

"I swear! You actually are something of a seer, aren't you?"

"Not at all. You told me all that in the few words you spoke. I filled in the gaps, that is all. I have done more with less. It is my livelihood."

"But—how? The accuracy of detail——"

"Even if it were as curious as you suggest, it should occasion no great wonder. It would be a simple matter of transforming energy, nothing more. So-called mental telepathy, even, is no mystery, so considered. Surely the human organism cannot create anything more than itself; but it has created the radio-broadcasting set and receiving set. Must there not be within the organism, then, some counterpart of these? I assure you, doctor, that this complex mechanism which we call the living body contains its broadcasting set and its receiving set, and signals sent out in the form of invisible, inaudible, radiant energy may be picked up and converted into sight and sound by a human receiving set properly tuned in."

He paused while the doctor sat speechless. Then he continued:

"But this is much simpler than that. Is it at all mystifying that you should walk into a sick room, make certain examinations, and say, 'This patient has so-and-so. He got it in such-and-such a way approximately so long ago; he has these-and-these changes in such-and-such organs; he will die in such-and-such a fashion in approximately so long'? No. I have merely practiced observation to the degree of great proficiency; that, together with complete faith in a certain philosophy enables me to do what seems mystifying. I can study a person's face and tell his past, present, and future."

The physician smiled. "Even his name?"

"That is never necessary," smiled Frimbo in the same spirit. "He always manages to tell me that without knowing it. There are tricks in all trades, of course. But fundamentally I deceive no one."

"I can understand your ability to tell the present—even the past, in a general way. But the future——"

"The future is as inevitably the outcome of the present as the present is of the past. That is the philosophy I mentioned."

"Determinism?"

"If you like. But a determinism so complete as to include everything—physical and mental. An applied determinism."

"I don't see how there can be any such thing as an applied determinism."

"Because——?"

"Because to apply it is to deny it. Assuming the ability to 'apply' anything is free will, pure and simple."

"You are correct," agreed Frimbo, "as far as you go."

"Why," the doctor continued warmly, "anyone who achieved a true freedom of will—a will that had no reference to its past —was not molded in every decision by its own history—a power that could step out of things and act as a cause without being itself an effect—good heavens!—such a creature would be a god!"

"Not quite a god, perhaps," said the other softly.

"What do you mean?"

"I mean that such a creature would be a god only to those bound by a deterministic order like ours. But you forget that ours is not—cannot be—the only order in the universe. There must be others—orders more complex perhaps than our simple cause-and-effect. Imagine, for instance, an order in which a cause followed its effect instead of preceding it—someone has already brought forward evidence of such a possibility. A creature of such an order could act upon our order in ways that would be utterly inconceivable to us. So far as our system is concerned, he would have complete freedom of will, for he would be subject only to his order, not to ours."

"That's too much metaphysics for me," confessed the physician. "Come on back to this little earth."

"Even on this little earth," said Frimbo, "minds occasionally arise that belong to another order. We call them prophets."

"And have you ever known a prophet?"

"I know," said the other in an almost inaudible voice, "that it is possible to escape this order and assume another."

"How do you know?"

"Because I can do it."

Had he shouted instead of whispering, John Archer could not have exhibited greater amazement.

"You can—what?"

"Do not ask me how. That is my secret. But we have talked together enough now for you to know I do not say anything lightly. And I tell you in all seriousness that here, in a world of

rigidly determined causes and effects, Frimbo is free—as free as
a being of another order."

The doctor simply could not speak.

"It is thus I am able to be of service to those who come to
me. I act upon their lives. I do not have to upset their order. I
simply change the velocity of what is going on. I am a catalyst.
I accelerate or retard a reaction without entering into it. This
changes the cross currents, so that the coincidences are different from what they would otherwise be. A husband reaches
home twenty minutes too soon. A traveler misses his train—and
escapes death in a wreck. Simple, is it not?"

"You've certainly retarded my reactions," said Dr. Archer.
"You've paralyzed me."

4

It was ten o'clock when finally the physician rose to go. They
had talked on diverse and curious topics, but no topic had
been so diverse and curious as the extraordinary mind of
Frimbo himself. He seemed to grasp the essentials of every discussion and whatever arose brought forth from him some peculiar and startling view that the physician had never hitherto
considered. Dr. Archer had come to observe and found himself
the object of the observation. To be sure, Frimbo had told
how, as an adventurous lad, he had been sent to a mission
school in Liberia; how at twenty he had assumed the leadership
of his nation, his father having been fatally injured in a hunting
expedition; but after a year, had turned it over to his brother,
who was ten months younger than he, and had departed for
America to acquire knowledge of western civilization—America
because of his American mission school beginning. He had
studied under private tutors for three years in preparation for
college; had been irregularly allowed to take entrance examinations and had passed brilliantly; but had acquired a bitter
prejudice against the dominant race that had seemed to be
opposing his purpose. Many episodes had fostered this bitter-
ness, making it the more acute in one accustomed to absolute
authority and domination. But all this, even as it was being
told, had somehow increased the physician's sense of failure in

this first meeting. It was too much under Frimbo's direction. And so he suggested another call on the morrow, to which Frimbo agreed promptly.

"I have a little experiment in which you would be interested," he said.

"I had really intended to discuss the mystery of this assault," the doctor declared. "Perhaps we can do that tomorrow?"

Frimbo smiled.

"Mystery? That is no mystery. It is a problem in logic, and perfectly calculable. I have one or two short-cuts which I shall apply tomorrow night, of course, merely to save time. But genuine mystery is incalculable. It is all around us—we look upon it every day and do not wonder at it at all. We are fools, my friend. We grow excited over a ripple, but exhibit no curiosity over the depth of the stream. The profoundest mysteries are those things which we blandly accept without question. See. You are almost white. I am almost black. Find out why, and you will have solved a mystery."

"You don't think the causes of a mere death a worthy problem?"

"The causes of *a* death? No. The causes of death, yes. The causes of life and death and variation, yes. But what on earth does it really matter who killed Frimbo—except to Frimbo?"

They stood a moment in silence. Presently Frimbo added in an almost bitter murmur:

"The rest of the world would do better to concern itself with why Frimbo was black."

Dr. Archer shook hands and departed. He went out into the night in somewhat the state of mind of one waking from odd dreams in a dark room. A little later he was mounting his own stoop. Before opening his door he stopped for a moment, looking back at the house across the street. With a hand on the knob, he shook his head and, contrary to his custom, indulged in a popular phrase:

"What a man!" he said softly.

# Chapter Twenty

I

EVENING had fallen and still Bubber Brown, Inc., had not been able to decide on a proper course of action. He had wandered about Harlem's streets unaware of its Sunday-best liveliness and color. Sly, come-hither eyes that fell upon him had kindled no sheikish response, trim silken calves had not even momentarily captured his dull, drifting stare, bright laughter of strolling dark crowds had not warmed his weary heart. Even his swagger had forsaken him. He had rolled along, a frankly bow-legged man, and the mind behind his blank features had rolled likewise, a rudderless bark on a troubled sea of indecision.

A mystery movie in which the villainous murderer turned out to be a sweet young girl of eighteen had not at all quickened Bubber's imagination. Leaving the theater, he had stopped in Nappy Shank's Café for supper; but the pigtails and hoppin'-john, which he meditatively consumed there from a platter on a white porcelain counter, likewise yielded no inspiration.

Eventually, in the early evening, his wandering brought him to Henry Patmore's Pool Room, and after standing about for a few minutes watching the ivory balls click, he made his way to the rear room where blackjack was the attraction.

An impish fate so contrived matters that the first player he saw was Spider Webb, whose detention he had brought about the night before. Spider at first glared at him, then grinned a trifle too pleasantly.

"Detective Brown, as I live!" he greeted. "Do you guys know the detective? Who you squealin' on tonight, detective?"

Bubber had forgotten until now Spider's threat last night. The abrupt reminder further upset his already unsteady poise. It was clear now that Spider really meant to square the account. To conceal his discomfiture, Bubber calmly seated himself at the table and bought two dollars' worth of chips.

"Deal me in," said he casually, ignoring Spider Webb.

"Sure—deal him in. He's a good guy."

Had the situation been normal it is likely that Bubber would promptly have lost his two dollars, got up, and departed. But inasmuch as his mind was now on anything but the cards, his customarily disastrous judgment was quite eliminated, and the laws of chance had an opportunity to operate to his advantage. In the course of an hour he had acquired twenty dollars' worth of his fellow players' chips and had become too fascinated at the miraculous, steady growth of his pile to leave the game. And of course, no one, not even an ordinarily poor gambler like Bubber, could run away from luck, not only because of what he might miss thereby but also because the losers expected a sporting chance to win back their money and could become remarkably disagreeable if it should be denied them.

But Bubber continued to win, the only disturbing part of this being that most of his gain was Spider Webb's loss. He did not know that Spider was gambling with money collected from policy-players, money that must be turned in early tomorrow morning; but he knew that Spider was taking risks that one rarely took with one's own hard-earned cash. And he soon saw whither this was directed. For whenever Bubber won a deal by holding a blackjack, Spider grimly undertook to break him by "stopping the bank"—that is by wagering at every opportunity an amount equal to whatever Bubber possessed, hoping thus to pluck him clean on the turn of a single hand.

With luck running in Bubber's direction, however, this plunging soon proved disastrous to Spider. By the time Bubber's twenty dollars had swelled to forty, Spider, certain that the moment was at hand when the tide must turn, "stopped" the forty dollars with all he had. Chance chose that moment to give Bubber another blackjack. Spider's curses were gems.

The heavy loser had now no recourse save to leave the game, and he did so with ill grace. A few minutes later, one Red Williams, a hanger-on at Pat's who was everybody's friend or enemy as profitable opportunity might direct, came into the card room from the pool parlor and called Bubber aside.

"Is you won money from Spider Webb?" he inquired in a

low tone that clearly indicated the importance of what hung on the answer.

"Sho'," admitted Bubber. "Does it pain you too?"

"Listen. I heard Spider talkin' to Tiger Shade jes' now. Seem like Spider had it in for you anyhow. I don't know what you done to him befo', but whatever 'twas he could 'a' scrambled you with pleasure. But when you ups and wins his money too, that jes' 'bout set 'im on fire. Fu'thermo', that wasn't his money he los'—that was players' money. If he don' turn in nothin' in the mornin', his boss Spencer knows he's been stealin' and that's his hips. If any o' his players git lucky and hit and don't git paid, that's his hips too. Either way it's his hips. So from what I heard him whisperin' to his boy, Tiger, he's plannin' to substitute yo' hips fo' his'n."

"Talk sense, man. What you mean?"

"Mean Tiger is done agreed to lay for you and remove both yo' winnin's and yo' school gal complexion. Tonight."

"You sho'?"

"I heard 'em. You better slip on out befo' they git wise you onto 'em."

"O. K. Thanks."

"Thanks? Is that all it's worth to you—much as you done won?"

"Wait a minute." Bubber made extravagant excuses to the house and cashed his chips. He returned to the waiting informer and handed him a dollar. "Here—git yo'self a pint o' gut-bucket. See y' later."

Sourly, Red Williams gazed upon the bill in his hand. "Hmph!" grumbled he. "Is this all that nigger thinks his life is worth?" Then he grinned. "But it won't be worth this much when Tiger Shade git hold of 'im. No, *suh!*"

2

Bubber sought to elude those who conspired against him by making a hasty exit through the barroom instead of through the poolroom, where apparently the plot had been hatched. This would have been wholly successful had not Tiger Shade already taken his stand on the sidewalk outside, between the poolroom and barroom entrances.

"Hello, there, Bubber, ol' boy," he greeted as Bubber came out and started to walk rapidly away.

It was perhaps the most unwelcome greeting Bubber had ever heard. He returned it hurriedly and would have kept going, but the Tiger called pleasantly, "Hey, wait a minute—I'm goin' your way. What's y' hurry?"

"Got a heavy date and I'm way late," came over Bubber's shoulder.

But in what seemed like three strides, the Tiger had overtaken and was beside him. For Tiger Shade was by a fair margin the tallest, widest, and thickest man in Harlem. He was bigger than the gigantic Officer Small, one of Bubber's companions of last night—and one for whose presence Bubber would have been most grateful now. And the Tiger was as bad as he was big. His was no simulated malice like Jinx's, no feigned ill-humor arising as a sort of defense mechanism; no, the Tiger simply enjoyed a congenital absence of sympathy. This had been too extreme even for those occupations where it might have been considered an advantage. He might have been a great boxer, but he simply could not remember to take the rules seriously. When he got interested in putting an opponent out, he saw no sound objection to doing so by hitting him below the belt or by snapping his head back with one hand and smiting him on the Adam's apple with the other. And when the opponent thus disposed of lay writhing or gasping as the case might be, Tiger always thought the hisses of the crowd were meant for the fallen weakling.

Hence he didn't rise high in the pugilistic firmament; but nobody crossed his path in that lowly part of Harlem where he moved. His reputation was known, and his history of destruction was the more terrible because it was so impersonal. He proceeded in combat as methodically as a machine; was quite as effective when acting for someone else as when acting for himself, and in neither case did he ever exhibit any profound emotion. True, he had a light sense of humor. For example, he had once held an adversary's head in the crook of his elbow and with his free hand torn one of the unfortunate fellow's ears off. He was given to such little drolleries; they amused him much as it amuses a small boy to pull off the wings of a fly; but it was quite as impersonally innocent.

It is hardly accurate to say that Tiger walked along beside Bubber. He walked along above Bubber, looming ominously like a prodigious shadow, and fully as tenacious. He did so without effort, smoothly, taking approximately one step to Bubber's three; he glided. Bubber bounced along hurriedly, explaining how he had allowed the time to get away from him and must rush but did not want to inconvenience his unexpected companion by so swift a pace. Tiger assured him that the pace was anything but exhausting.

It was about the hour at which his moonsign had appeared to him on the night before. "Wonder do you see yo'self when you dead?" he asked himself. "Maybe the third one is me!"

"Huh?" inquired Tiger.

"Nothin'. Jes' thinkin' out loud."

It was a mistake that he did not make again. But what he thought further, as the two progressed southward along Harlem's Fifth Avenue, was evident from what he presently did.

"I ain't got but one chance to shake this boogy loose. That's 'cause he don't know that I know what he's aimin' to do. He didn't see Red come in the card-room and tell me the bad news. So the thing to do is surprise him; got to stay here on the Avenue till I get a chance to duck around a corner and run like hell up a side street. By the time he realize' what I've done, not expectin' me to know nothin', I'll have a start on him. When he look he won't see nothin' but the soles o' my feet. I'll be runnin' so fas' he'll think I'm layin' down.—But what's the use runnin' if I ain' got no place to run to? Lemme see. Hot damn—I got it! The doctor—right in the next street. I was goin' to see him anyhow, see if he could tell me how to help Jinx. Now I *got* to see him. Feet, get ready. And fo' Gawd's sake keep out o' each other's way!"

They crossed 130th Street. As they mounted the far curb and would have passed the building line, suddenly Bubber pointed in astonishment. "Good-night! Look a yonder! Done been a accident!" And as Tiger Shade innocently peered ahead, the trickster did a right turn, snatched off his hat, and flew.

He had estimated Tiger's reaction correctly. Tiger even walked on past the building line before he realized that he was alone, and Bubber was at the physician's stoop before Tiger's pursuit got under way.

The front door was at that moment opening to let out a patient who had come to see the doctor and found him out. The patient was in a bad humor. He needed treatment for certain scratches, abrasions, and bruises which his physiognomy had sustained before he had been able to subdue a violent wife. The wife had taken it upon herself to follow a certain private detective to a certain private residence the night before, and had come thus to discover her husband in an unexplainably trouserless state. The misunderstanding which had arisen then had waxed into an energetic physical encounter this morning; and though the lady had been duly subdued, she had, so to speak, made her mark first. Further the patient's present ill humor had been increased by the difficulty of getting a physician on a Sunday evening. Dr. Archer had been his fifth unsuccessful attempt, and he emerged from the hallway, where a housekeeper had told him the doctor was out for the evening, in a state of repressed, scowling rage which was the more rancorous because it was facially painful to scowl. Indeed he was at the moment praying to high heaven that the blippety-blipped so-and-so that got him in the jam in the first place be delivered into his hands just for sixty seconds.

It was therefore not coincidence but the efficacy of honest prayer which brought Bubber bounding up the stoop just as the large, disappointed gentleman turned to descend. There was just enough light before the door closed for each to recognize the other. And it might have inspired a new philosophy of the organism had some competent observer been there to see how so utterly different emotions in so utterly dissimilar men produced so completely identical reactions: malicious glee on the gentleman's part, consternation on Bubber's, but abrupt and total immobility in both cases. Before action could relieve that mutual paralysis, Tiger Shade was at hand.

At such moments, imbecility becomes genius. Bubber, accordingly, became a superman. "Come on, boy!" he shouted to the leaping Tiger. "Here he is—this the guy I was chasin'! He grabbed my money at the corner and run! Come on, let's get 'im!" Whereupon he lunged upward and tackled the dumbfounded husband about the knees. Tiger, whose real interest lay in recovering the money, of which he was to receive part, hesitated now but a moment; swept up the stairs and lay hold of the accused, whom Bubber promptly released below. When Doctor Archer's housekeeper opened the door again to see what the sudden rumpus was about, her astonished eyes beheld two heavyweights engaged in a wrestling match. It ended as she watched.

"Hand it over," she heard the victor, sitting astride the other, advise.

"I ain't been near no corner!" panted the uncomfortable underling. "I'm after that tubby runt, too! Where'd he go? Lemme up! Which a way'd he go?"

"Get off my stoop, you hoodlums," cried the outraged house-keeper, "else I'll call the police. Go on now! Get off o' my stoop!"

Her admonitions were unnecessary. Bubber's absence was sufficient evidence of his stratagem. Tiger desisted, whipping about just in time to see the elusive Bubber enter the house directly opposite across the street and carefully close the door behind him.

"There he goes!" exclaimed he. "Come on—let's get him!"

3

Across the street they sped, scuffled up the brownstone stoop and burst through the door. Tiger, who was first, glanced up the stairs, which the fugitive could not possibly yet have traversed.

"He's down here some place—on this floor. Let's look. Come on."

His new ally hesitated.

"Say—you know what this is?"

"What?"

"This place is a undertaker's parlor!"

"I don't care if it's a undertaker's bathroom, I'm goin' in here and look for that boogy. He can't pull no fast one on me like that."

They found Undertaker Crouch's rooms invitingly accessible and apparently quite empty. They went into the parlor and stopped. There was a faint funeral fragrance in the air, and a strange, unnatural quiet over all that immediately subdued their movements to cautious tiptoeing and their voices to low muttering.

"I ain' crazy 'bout lookin' for nobody in here," announced the husband.

"Aw, what you scared o'?" the Tiger reassured him. "Dead folks ain' no trouble."

"They ain' no trouble to me—I don't get that close to 'em."

"Well—you don't see none do you?"

"I ain' looked. First one I see, I bids you both good-evenin'."

"I thought you wanted some o' this guy?"

"Some of him? In a place like this, I couldn't use two of him. My mind wouldn't be on what I was doin'."

"Well, I'm go'n' get 'im tonight. He's got eighty bucks o' my buddy's dough. If he gives me the slip tonight, them bucks is long gone."

"And if I hear any funny noises, I'm long gone."

"Come on. Let's look back yonder."

"Go ahead—I'll wait for you."

"He's tricky—it'll take both of us to find 'im."

"O.K. I'm behind you. But I ain't lettin' nothin' get 'tween me and the door."

"Did you leave it open?"

"I sho' did."

But the words were no sooner out of his mouth than the door was heard to swing gently shut.

"The wind," explained Tiger Shade.

"Oh, yea?"

"What else could it be?"

"The Spirit of St. Louis for all I know."

"Come on."

"What you waitin' for?"

"Come on."

"O.K. Start out. If you turn round and don't see me you'll know I jes' lost my enthusiasm."

None too eagerly, Tiger started out, followed by his reluctant ally. Several tubbed palms stood supercilious and motionless along the walls, and these the two searchers eyed distrustfully as they passed. They reached the wide doorway of the rear room without noting any evidence of their quarry. The rear room was dark save for what shadowy illumination reached it from the dim light of the parlor. Close together, the husband peering around the more venturesome Tiger, their wide eyes trying vainly to discern the contents of the room, they halted on the threshold.

It occurred to both of them to feel for a switch-button on the wall beside the door, and still eyeing the shadows they simultaneously felt. Contact with an open live wire could have given either no greater shock than he got at this unexpected contact with a hand. For one palsied moment their fingers stuck together as if to an electrified object which, once grasped, could not be released. Then the husband snatched his hand away, wheeled and took the first stride in flight. Only the first. The Tiger, having wheeled also, was so close behind him as to be able to grab him from behind, and his comrade, not knowing what held him, gave a hoarse moan, slipped on the polished hardwood floor, and sprawled.

"Hey you dumbbell," muttered Tiger, recovered and master of himself again, but still noticeably dyspnœic. "That was only me. Come on—snap out of this monkey-business."

"I felt a human hand!" the other whispered getting up sheepishly.

"Well, don't I look human?"

"Was it you? Huh—well—yea, you look human all right. But if you grab hold o' me the next time I start to run, you won't look human no mo'. You'll look like you been ridin' a wild steer."

"Come on. That guy is hidin' in there."

"Somehow I done los' interest in that guy."

At this moment a curious sound rose to their ears.

"What's *that?*"

It was startlingly close—a distinct chorus of voices singing. Even the words of the song were easily distinguishable:

> "*Am I born to die?*
> *Oh, am I born to die?*
> *Lord, am I born to die—*
> *To lay this body down?*"

"What kind o' house is this?"

Tiger's wealth of reassurance was rapidly being exhausted. "Can't you think o' none o' the answers? That's somebody's radio."

> "*One of these mornings bright and fair,*
>    *Lay this body down—*
> *Going to take my wings and try the air,*
>    *Lay this body down—*
> *Lord am I born to die?*"

"No radio never sounded like that. Them's sho' 'nough voices and they's in this house."

> "*Oh, am I born to die*
>    *To lay this body down?*"

"Not me!"

"Listen," said Tiger. "That's only a radio. Let's give this place one mo' look. He got to be in there. If he can go in there, so can we."

"All right. But no holdin' in the clinches."

Again, in the closest possible formation and in utter silence, they advanced to the rear room door.

"Whyn't you feel for the light ag'in?"

"Wait. I'll strike a match." The Tiger did so with none too steady fingers. By its fluttering, feeble, yellow flare two pairs of dilated eyes surveyed what could be seen of the room—a large desk on the right in the far corner, two windows in the back wall, a chair or two, and—

"Lawd have mercy—look a yonder!"

But the Tiger had needed no such admonition—he was looking with one hundred percent of his eyesight. Along the left wall stretched a long table, upon which, covered with a sheet, lay an unmistakably human form.

The match went out.

The pair stood momentarily cataleptic, their eyes fixed on the body which, once seen, remained now vaguely but positively visible even in the shadows. Before their shock passed a mysterious thing, an awful thing, began to happen, holding them fast in a horrified moment of fascination: slowly the white form moved in the shadow, seemed to change shape, to lift and widen like vapor. At the moment when their very eyeballs seemed about to burst, singing voices came again with that disturbing query:

*"Am I born to die?"*

Their spastic paralysis broke into convulsions of activity.

"Not here!" gasped the husband. And this time Tiger Shade did not overtake him till they both hit the sidewalk at the base of the front stoop and headed in opposite directions for more light.

Bubber, sitting fully erect now on the side of the table, cast the sheet aside and stood up with a sigh of relief. "Frimbo ain't got a thing on me," said he. "If that ain't risin' from the dead, what is it?"

But the chorus of the singing was disturbing him as much as it had his pursuers. While allowing the latter time to retreat to a safe distance he decided to investigate the former. "Might as well find out all I can 'bout this morgue. Which a way——?"

He listened. He moved toward the door which led from the room directly into the back of the first-floor balcony. At the head of the stairs leading down to the basement he saw light below, and realized that the sound was coming from that direction. The singing had stopped. Just over his head, in the flight above, soft footsteps were distinctly audible. He waited, listening. Presently the front door clicked shut.

"Wonder if that was that flunky goin' out?"

It was too late to attempt to follow, however, and so he pursued his present investigation. The singing had stopped. Bubber went on down the stairs as noiselessly as he could. In the hall below, which corresponded to its fellows above, he paused and listened again. The light he had seen came from a door which was only partly open; the prowler could not see around it without going too close. But he heard significant sounds:

"Is they anybody heah," a deep evangelic voice was saying, "what don't expect to shake my hand up in glory?"

"No!" shouted a number of voices.

"The spirit of the Lord has been in this place tonight!"

"Yes!" avowed the chorus.

"Did you feel it?"

"Yes!"

"Did it stir yo' soul?"

"Yes, Jesus!"

"Move you to do good deeds?"

"Yes, indeed. Amen, brother!"

"Aw right then. Now let's take up the collection."

Silence, abrupt and unanimous.

Bubber grinned in the hall outside. "Church meetin'—and 'bout to break up."

He was right. Some of the members of the little group that evidently used Crouch's meeting-room Sundays were already shamelessly heading for the hall door, en route to the freer manifestations of divine presence out of doors. Bubber retreated to the rear of the hall so as to attract no attention, and found himself at the head of the cellar stairs. It occurred to him that his tour of inspection might as well include the cellar, especially since that would allow the occupants of the meeting-room time to take up their collection and depart. Then he could return and investigate the basement floor.

4

He had procured at a drugstore during his wanderings today, an inexpensive pocket flashlight in imitation of the physician and detective who had found such devices so useful last night. This he now produced and by its light started down the cellar stairs. He had to proceed cautiously for this staircase was not so firmly constructed as those above; but he was soon in the furnace-room below the sidewalk level, and his small pencil of light traced the objects which his predecessors had observed the night before: the furnace, the coal bin, the nondescript junk about the floor, the pile of trunks, boxes, and barrels up front. He saw the central droplight but could not turn it on, since its switch was at the head of the stairs he had already passed.

And so he moved inquisitively forward toward the pile of objects up front. A few minutes of nosing about revealed nothing exciting, and he became conscious that the sounds of shuffling feet overhead had stopped.

He was about to abandon the cellar, whose chilly dampness was beginning to penetrate, when, without sound or warning, the center droplight went on. Feeble as it was, its effect was startling in the extreme, and Bubber felt for the moment trapped and helpless. He recovered his wits enough to crouch down among the shadows of the objects around him, and slowly came to realize that no one else was in the place. He awaited a footfall on the staircase. None came. At the moment when curiosity would have overcome better judgment, he heard a sound which came from beyond the stairs, toward the distant back wall. Cautiously looking around the corner of a packing case, he saw a figure emerge from the dimness. The figure approached the foot of the stairs, and Bubber saw that it was Frimbo, bareheaded, clad in a black dressing-gown. Frimbo carefully and silently went up the stairs; there was the sound of a bolt sliding; then Frimbo came down again.

Fortunately Bubber's protection was now nothing so unstable as an outspread wardrobe trunk, for he was quite unmindful of anything but the strange man's movements. And curious enough they were. Frimbo grew dim again in the shadow, then reëmerged with a paper bundle in his arms. He laid this down several feet from, and in front of the furnace, which was against the left wall and facing toward the center. The bundle thus rested almost directly beneath the droplight, and Bubber could see that its paper wrapping had a greasy appearance, as if its contents had been dripping with oil. Frimbo went to the furnace door and flung it wide. The red of the bright coals touched his awesome face to a glow, contrasting oddly with the yellow light behind him. He seized a long-handled shovel standing beside the furnace and returning, lifted the bundle upon it, reapproached the open door and thrust the thing in. The ignition of the package was instantaneous, the flames from it belching out of the aperture before Frimbo closed it. Now he replaced the shovel, went up the stairs again, unbolted the door at the top, came down, and disappeared in the darkness at the rear. There was a soft sound like the one that had heralded Frimbo's appearance, and a moment later the center light went out.

Among all the bewildering questions which must have presented themselves to Bubber now, the greatest was surely, "What's he burnin'?" For a long time, perhaps half an hour, the spy remained where he was, afraid to move. Eventually, the compelling impulse to look into the furnace and trust to providence for escape, if necessary, moved him out of his refuge and toward the fire.

Every foot or two he stopped to make sure there was no sound. It was clear that Frimbo had some means of traveling about the house other than the stairs, and it was probable that he would not return to the cellar without switching on the light from whatever distant connection he had contrived. But Bubber had to reassure himself somewhat as to the mysterious avenue of approach before satisfying his major curiosity. He invaded the territory through which Frimbo had departed, and could discover no ordinary exit. There was no cellar door leading up to the back yard; the walls were solid cement. All that he could find was the base of the dumbwaiter shaft, and his little beam of light, directed up the channel, was sufficient to disclose, some feet above, the dangling gears and broken ropes which attested the uselessness of the device.

In a state of mind which the shifting shadows about him did nothing to relieve, he quickly returned to the furnace and flung open the door. Whatever Frimbo had used to accelerate combustion had already reduced his bundle to a fragile-looking char; its more susceptible parts had already stopped blazing, and the remainder lay crumbling like the embers of a frame house that has burned down. Pocketing his light and working by the illumination from the coals, Bubber took the shovel and, with as little noise as possible, gently retrieved a part of what had been consigned to the flames. He laid it, shovel and all, on the floor, shut the furnace, and examined it with his flash. So intent was he now that it would have been easy to approach and catch him unawares. But the contents of the shovel, from which the glow had already faded, presented nothing susceptible to Bubber's knowledge; his puzzled stare disclosed to him only that he must get the find out of this place and subject it to more expert inspection.

It did not take him long to find a wooden box into which he could deposit what he had retrieved. Having done so, he replaced the shovel beside the furnace, and with the box under one arm, quietly mounted the stairs. The basement floor was dark. He did not stop to investigate that now, however, but, succeeding in making his exit by way of the basement front door, without a moment's delay he ran across the street to Dr.

Archer's house and, no less excitedly than twenty-four hours before, rang the front-door bell.

Again the doctor himself answered the summons.

"Hello, Brown! What's up?"

"I done 'scovered sump'm!"

"In that box? What?"

"You'll have to answer that, doc. Damn 'f I know."

"Come in."

5

In the warmth and brightness of the physician's consulting-room, Bubber related what he had seen and done. Meanwhile the doctor was examining the contents of the box on his desk, poking about in it with a long paper knife. He stopped poking suddenly, then, very gently resumed. Much of what he touched crumbled dryly apart. At last he looked up.

"I should say you have discovered something."

"What is it, doc?"

"How long did you say this burned?"

" 'Bout half an hour. Took me that long to make up my mind to get it out."

"Are you sure it didn't burn longer?"

"With me snoopin' 'round 'spectin' to be bumped off any second? No, s*uh!* If it was half an hour that was half an hour too long."

"Did it blaze when he first put it in the furnace?"

" 'Deed it did. Looked like it was 'bout to explode."

"Let me see now. How could he have treated human flesh so as to make it so quickly destructible by fire?" The doctor mused, apparently forgetting Bubber's presence. "Alcohol would dehydrate it, if he could infiltrate the tissues pretty well. He could do that by injecting through the jugulars and carotids. But the alcohol would evaporate—that would explain the rapid oxidation. Greasy? Oh, I have it! He's simply reinjected with an inflammable oil—kerosene, probably. Of course. Hm—what a man!"

"Doc, would you mind tellin' me what you talkin' 'bout?"

"Have you any idea what this stuff is?"

"No, suh."

"It's what's left of a human head, neck and shoulder, a trifle over-cooked."

"Great day in the mornin'!"

"Quite so. The extent of destruction has been sped up by treating the dead tissues with substances which quickly reduced the water content and heightened the inflammability. Maybe alcohol and kerosene—maybe chemicals even more efficient—it doesn't matter."

He stopped his poking and gently lifted from the box an irregular, stiff, fragile cinder. He placed it very carefully on a piece of white paper on his desk.

"This is exhibit A. Notice anything? No, don't handle it—it's too crumbly and we can't afford to lose it. What do you——"

"Ain't them teeth?" Bubber pointed to three little lumps in the char.

"Yes. And apparently the only ones that haven't fallen loose. I believe we may be able to use them. Further, this cinder represents parts of two bones, the maxillary, in which the upper teeth are set, and the sphenoid which joins it at about this point."

"You don't mean to tell me?" gaped Bubber.

"I do. I do indeed. And I mean to tell you this also: that the presence of the sphenoid, or most of it, in a relatively free state like this is proof that its owner has left this world. On this bone, in life, rests a considerable part of the brain."

"S'posin' a guy's brainless, like Jinx?"

"Even Jinx couldn't make it without his sphenoid. So you see that in that fragile bit of the fruit of the crematory, we have an extraordinary bit of evidence. We have proof of a death. You see that?"

"Oh, sho' I see that."

"And we may have a means of identifying the corpse. You see that?"

"Well, that ain't quite so clear."

"Never mind. It will be. And finally we have your testimony to the effect that Frimbo was destroying this material."

"Huh. Don't look so good for Mr. Frimbo, do it?"

"Thanks to your discovery, it doesn't."

"Will that help Jinx out?"

"Possibly. Even probably. But the case against Frimbo is not quite complete, you see, even with this."

" 'Tain't? What mo' you need?"

"It might be important to know who was killed, don't you think?"

"Tha's right. Who?"

"I'm sure I don't know. Maybe nobody. These may be the remains of an old stiff he was dissecting—who knows? That we must find out. And there is one more thing to learn—Frimbo's motive. Not only whom did he kill—if anybody—but why?"

"Why you reckon?"

"That may be a hard point to convey to you, Mr. Brown, so late in the evening. But this much I will tell you. You see, while you have been ruminating in the depths of Frimbo's cellar, I have been ruminating in the depths of my mind."

"I hope 'tain't as full of trash as that cellar was."

"It has its share of rubbish, I'm not ashamed to say. But what it holds just now is the growing conviction that Frimbo is a paranoiac."

"A—which?"

"A paranoiac."

"The dirty son of a gun. Ought to be ashamed o' hisself, huh?"

"And so, my worthy collaborator, if you don't mind leaving this precious clue in my hands, I'll spend a little time and energy now freshening my mind on homicidal tendencies in paranoia —a most frequent symptom, if I recall correctly."

"Jes' what I was thinkin'," agreed Bubber. "Well, I'll come 'round again tomorrow, doc. I was on my way here tonight, but I got sorta side-tracked. I thought you might be able to tell me how to help Jinx out."

"If this is any indication," smiled the doctor, pointing to the evidence, "the best thing you can do for Jinx is to get side-tracked again."

Bubber thought over the day's episodes, grinned and shook his head.

"Uh—uh," he demurred resolutely. "He ain't wuth it, doc."

# Chapter Twenty-one

I

"IN THIS respect," Dr. Archer confessed to Detective Dart, who sat facing him across his desk the next morning, "Frimbo would call me a mystic. I have implicit faith in something I really can't prove."

"Is it a secret?"

"Yes, but I'll share it with you. I believe that the body, of which these humble remnants are ample evidence, is the same as the one I pronounced dead on Saturday night."

"Shouldn't think there'd be any doubt about that."

"There isn't. That's the mysticism of it. There isn't any doubt about it in my mind. But I haven't proved it. I have only yielded to a strong suspicion: somebody is killed, the body disappears. Frimbo steps up claiming to be the body. He is lying as our little blood test proved, and later he is seen destroying vital parts of a body. This might be another body, but I am too confirmed a mystic to believe so. I am satisfied to assume it is the same."

"You know damn well it's the same," said the practical Dart.

"We won't argue the point," smiled Dr. Archer. "Assuming it is the same—there will be reasons why Frimbo destroys a murdered man."

"Protecting himself."

"An omnipresent possibility. The victim was sped into the beyond either by Frimbo himself or by someone in league with Frimbo, whom Frimbo is trying to protect. Yes. But do you recall that we drew the same conclusions about Jinx Jenkins?"

"Well—bad as this looks for the conjure-man, it doesn't remove the evidence against Jenkins. That handkerchief could be explained, but that club—and the way he tried to scram when the lights went out——"

"Very well. Nor does it eliminate the actuality of a feud between the two policy kings, Spencer and Brandon, in which that runner was an unfortunate sacrifice yesterday. Personally, I pay no more attention to that than I do to the ravings of Doty Hicks."

"Me, personally," responded Dart, "I pay attention to both of 'em. I suspect 'em all till facts let 'em out. And I still think that the simplest thing may be so. Why make it hard? Hicks or Brandon, the one out of superstition, the other out of greed, either one may have hired Jenkins to do the job. Jenkins somehow didn't get Frimbo but got—say! I know—he got Frimbo's flunky! That's your dead body! The flunky!"

The physician demurred.

"Inspiration has its defects. Remember. The flunky ushered Jenkins to the entrance of the room. Jenkins went in. The victim was already in the chair waiting. Would the flunky have obligingly hurried around through the hall and got in place just so that Mr. Jenkins could dispose of him? That would be simple indeed—too simple."

"Well, maybe I'm prejudiced. But——"

"You are. Because that isn't all you ignore. Why would Frimbo claim to be the victim if what you suggest were true? Why would he destroy the body of his servant? One would rather expect him to want to find and punish the murderer."

"All right, doc. You can out-talk me. You give us the answer."

"I'm only part way through the problem. But I had an interesting interview with the gentleman last night. And I'm reasonably sure he's a full-fledged paranoiac."

"Too bad. If he was a Mason, now, or an Odd Fellow——"

"A paranoiac is a very special kind of a nut."

"Well, now, that's more like it. What's so special about this kind of a nut?"

"First, he has an extremely bright mind. Even flashes of brilliance."

"This bird is bright, all right."

"You don't know the half of it. You should hear him tie you up in mental knots the way he did me. Next thing, he has some trouble—some unfortunate experience, some maladjustment, or something—that starts him to believing the world is against him. He develops a delusion of persecution. Frimbo concealed his pretty well, but it cropped out once or twice. He came to America to study and had some trouble getting into college. He took it personally, and attributed it to his color."

"Where's the delusion in that?"

"The delusion in that is that plenty of students the same color, but with more satisfactory formal preparation, have no such difficulty. Also that plenty the same color with unsatisfactory preparation don't draw the same conclusion. And also that plenty *without* his generous inheritance of pigment and with unsatisfactory preparation have the same difficulty and don't draw the same conclusion."

"Call it a delusion if you want to——"

"Thanks. Now your paranoiac couldn't live if something didn't offset that plaguing conviction. So he develops another delusion to balance it. He says, 'Well, since I'm so persecuted, I must be a great guy.' He gets a delusion of grandeur."

"I know flocks of paranoiacs."

"Me too. But you don't know any with the kind of delusion of grandeur that Frimbo has. It's the most curious thing—and yet perfectly in case. You see, his first reaction to the persecution idea was flight into study. He got steeped in deterministic philosophy."

"What the hell is that?"

"The doctrine that everything, physical and mental, is inevitably a result of some previous cause. Well, Frimbo evidently accepted the logic of that philosophy, and that molded his particular delusion of grandeur. He said, 'Yes, everything is determined—nature, the will of man, his decisions, his choices—all are the products of their antecedents. This is the order of our existence. *But I—Frimbo—I am a creature of another order.* I can step out of the order of this existence and become, with respect to it, a free agent, independent of it, yet able to act upon it, reading past and present and modifying the future. Persecution cannot touch me—I am above it.' Do you see, Dart? Does it mean anything to you?"

"Not a damn thing. But it doesn't have to. Go on from there."

"Well, there you are—still paranoia. But when it gets as bad as in Frimbo's case, they get dangerous. They get homicidal. Either the first delusion moves them to eliminate their supposed persecutors, or the second generates such a contempt for their inferiors that they will remove them for any reason they choose."

"Gee! Nice people to ride in the subway with. Are you sure about this guy?"

"Reasonably. I'm going back for more evidence today."

"So he can remove you?"

"Not likely. I think he's taken a fancy to me. That's another symptom—they make quick decisions—accept certain people into their confidence as promptly as they repudiate others. I seem to be such a confidant. Something I said or did Saturday night appealed to him. That's why he accepted me so quickly—invited me back—took me in—exchanged confidences with me. No normal mind under similar circumstances would have done so."

"Well—be careful. I don't mind nuts when they're nuts. But when they're as fancy as that they may be poison."

"Don't worry. I know antidotes."

After a pause, Dart said:

"But who the hell did he kill?"

"You mean who's dead? We only surmise that Frimbo——"

"I mean who was the bird on the couch?"

"Have you that removable bridge in your pocket?"

"Sure. Here it is. What of it?"

"I don't dare hope anything. But let's see." He took the small device. Its two teeth were set in a dental compound tinted to resemble gums and its tiny gold clamps reached out from either end to grasp the teeth nearest the gap it bridged.

"Look." The doctor pointed to the three teeth in the bony char which still lay on the piece of white paper. "Upper left bicuspid, a two-space gap, and two molars. That means first bicuspid and second and third molars. Now this bridge. Second bicuspid and first molar. See?"

"Don't you ever talk English?"

"The gap, Dart, old swoop, corresponds to the bridge."

"Yea—but you yourself said that doesn't prove anything. It's got to fit. Fit perfect."

"Oh, thou of little faith. Well, here goes. Pray we don't break up the evidence trying to get a perfect fit." With deft and gentle fingers, the physician brought the bridge clamps in contact with the abutments of the cinder and ever so cautiously edged them in place, a millimeter at a time. He heaved a sigh.

"There you are, skeptic. The gums are gone of course. But

the distance between the teeth has been maintained, thanks to the high fusion point of calcium salts. Am I plain?"

"You are—but appearances are deceiving."

"Here's one you can depend on. Find out who belongs to this bridge and you'll know who, to put it quite literally, got it in the neck on Saturday night."

Dart reached for the bridge.

"Gently, kind friend," warned the doctor. "That's your case—maybe. And leave it in place."

"There's probably," observed the detective, "three thousand and three of these things made every day in this hamlet. All you want me to find out is whose this was."

"That's all. It'll be easy. See your dentist——"

"I know—twice a year. What time'll you be back here?"

"Four o'clock. And bring that club with you."

"Right. I'll see you—if Frimbo lets you out whole."

2

With the clue resting like a jewel upon soft cotton in a small wooden box, Detective Dart sought out one Dr. Chisholm Dell, known to his friends, including Perry Dart, as Chizzy. Chizzy was a young man of swarthy complexion, stocky build, and unfailing good humor, whose Seventh Avenue office had become a meeting-place for most of the time-killing youth of Harlem—ex-students, confidence boys, insurance agents, promoters, and other self-confessed "hustlers." The occasional presence of a pretty dancing girl from Connie's or the Cotton Club, presumably as a patient awaiting her turn, kept the boys lingering hopefully about Chizzy's reception room.

Detective Dart was not deceived, however, and rose promptly when Chizzy, in white tunic, came out of his operating-room.

"Can you give the law a hot minute?"

"I couldn't give anybody anything right now," grinned Chizzy. "But I'll lend you one. Come on in."

Dart obeyed. He produced his exhibit.

"Take a look."

"What the devil's that?" Chizzy exclaimed after glancing at it.

Dart explained, adding, "As I get it, this bridge is a pretty accurate means of identification. Is that right?"

"I've been practicing ten years," said Chizzy, "and I haven't seen two exactly alike yet."

"Good. Now is there any way to tell who this belonged to?"

"Sure. Whose bone is it?"

"Don't be funny. Would I ask for help if I knew that?"

Chizzy considered. "Well—it can be narrowed down, certainly. I can tell you one thing."

"No?"

"Sure. That bridge is less than two months old."

"Yea?"

"See this part here that looks like gums?"

"Is that what it's supposed to look like?"

"Yea. That's a new dental compound called deckalite. Deckalite has been on the market only two months. I haven't made a case yet."

"Know anybody in Harlem that might have?"

"When you limit it to Harlem, that makes it easy. Do you know it was made in Harlem?"

"No. But it was made for a Harlemite. The likelihood is that he went to a local dentist."

"I doubt it. I haven't seen a patient for so long I believe all the Harlemites must be going to Brooklyn for their teeth. But if he did go to a Harlem dentist, it's easy."

"Hurry up."

"Well, you see there are only two dental mechanics up here that can handle deckalite. As it's a recent product it requires a special technique. Not one of the regular dentists knows it, I'm sure. Whoever your unknown friend went to would just take the impression and send it to one of those two men to be made up. All you've got to do is to go to each of the two mechanics, find out what dentist he's made deckalite uppers for, go back to the referring dentist and trace down your particular bridge."

"Beautiful," said Dart. "Two names and addresses, please."

Chizzy complied. "You'll find 'em in now, sitting down with their chins in their hands, wishing for something to do."

"Thanks, Chizzy. If you weren't so damned funny-lookin', I'd kiss you."

"Is that all that prevents you?" Chizzy called—but Dart was already banging the outside door behind him.

3

"Come into my laboratory, doctor," Frimbo invited Dr. Archer. "I'm glad you could return, because, if you remember, I promised to demonstrate to you a little experiment. Let's see, this time you have your bag, haven't you? Good. Have you a gauze dressing?"

Dr. Archer produced the requested article and handed it over. Frimbo removed it from the small, sealed tissue paper envelope which kept it dry and sterile, and dropped it into a sealed glass beaker. Then he rolled up the left sleeve of his robe, the one he had worn the night before.

"Please, doctor, remove a few cubic centimeters of blood. Put a little in that test tube there, which contains a crystal of sodium citrate to prevent clotting, and the rest in the empty tube beside it. You will be interested in this, I'm sure."

The physician applied a tourniquet, procured a syringe, touched a distended vein of Frimbo's forearm with alcohol, and obeyed the latter's directions. Frimbo, the tourniquet removed, pressed the swabbing sponge on the point of puncture a moment, then discarded it and dropped his sleeve.

"Now, doctor, there are my red cells, are they not?" He indicated the first tube. "And in a moment we shall have a little of my serum in this other tube, as soon as the blood clots and squeezes the serum out." They awaited this process in silence.

"Good. Now I take your sterile dressing and pour onto it some of my serum. In a general way, now, this dressing might have wiped a bloody wound on some part of my body—except that it has upon it only serum instead of whole blood. A mere short cut to my little demonstration. I return the dressing to the beaker and add a few cubic centimeters of distilled water from this bottle. Then I remove the dressing, thus, leaving, you see, a dilute sample of my serum in the beaker."

"Yes," Dr. Archer said thoughtfully.

"Now on this slide, with this loop, I place a drop of my diluted serum"—he stressed "my" whenever he used it—"and mix with it a loopful of my red cells, so. Now. Will you observe with the microscope there, what takes place?"

The doctor put the slide on the stage of the microscope, adjusted the low power, and looked long and intently. Eventually he looked up. He was obviously astonished.

"Apparently your serum agglutinates its own cells. But that's impossible. One part of your blood couldn't destroy another—and you remain alive."

"Perhaps I am dead," murmured Frimbo. "But there is a much simpler explanation: Your dressings are evidently treated with some material which is hostile to red cells. In such a procedure as this, where the serum has to be soaked out of the dressing, this hostile material is soaked out also. It is this material that is responsible for the phenomenon which we usually attribute to hostile serum. Let us prove this."

Thereupon he repeated the experiment, discarding the dressing, and using a dilution of his serum made directly in another test tube. This time the microscope disclosed no clumping of red cells.

"You see?" the African said.

The doctor looked at him. "Why did you show me this?" he asked.

"Because I did not wish you to interpret falsely any observations you might have made in your investigation of night before last."

"Thank you," Dr. Archer said. "And may I say that you are the most remarkable person I have ever met in my life."

"Being remarkable also in my lack of modesty," smiled the other, "I quite agree with you. Tell me. How do you like my little laboratory?"

"It certainly reveals an unusual combination of interests. Biology, chemistry, electricity——"

"The electricity is, with me, but a convenience. The biochemistry is vital to my existence."

"Isn't that a television receiver over there?"

"Yes. I made it."

"Small, isn't it?"

"Therein lies its only originality."

"I hope you'll pardon my curiosity; you have taken me somewhat into your confidence, and if I presume you must pardon me. But you seem so absorbed in more or less serious pursuits—have you no lighter moments? I should think you would have to relax—at least occasionally—to offset your habitual concentration."

"I assure you I have—lighter moments," smiled the other.

"You are a bachelor?"

"Yes."

"And bachelors—you may look upon this as a confession if you like—are notoriously prone to seek relaxation in feminine company."

"I assure you," Frimbo returned easily, "that I am not abnormal in that respect. I admit I have denied myself little. I have even been, on occasion, indiscreet in my affairs of the heart—perhaps still am. But," he promptly grew serious, "this," he waved his hand at the surrounding apparatus, "this is my real pleasure. The other is necessary to comfort, like blowing one's nose. This I choose—I seek—because I like it. Or," he added after a pause, "because a part of it lifts me out of the common order of things."

"What do you mean?" The voice of Dr. Archer was not too eager.

"I mean that here in this room I perform the rite, which has been a secret of my family for many generations, whereby I am able to escape the set pattern of cause and effect. I wish I might share that secret with you, because you are the only person I have ever met who has the intelligence to comprehend it and the balance not to abuse it. And also because"—his voice dropped—"I am aware of the possibility that I may never use it again."

The doctor drew breath sharply. But he said quietly:

"It is always the greatest tragedy that a profound discovery should remain unshared."

"Yes. Yet it must be so. It is the oath of my dynasty. I can only name it for you." He paused. Then, "We call it the rite of the gonad."

"The rite of the gonad." With the greatest difficulty the physician withheld his glance from the direction of the shelf whereon he had observed a specimen jar containing sex glands.

"Yes," Frimbo said, a distant look creeping into his deep-set eyes. "The germplasm, of which the gonad is the only existing sample, is the unbroken heritage of the past. It is protoplasm which has been continuously maintained throughout thousands of generations. It's the only vital matter which goes back in a continuous line to the remotest origins of the organism. It is therefore the only matter which brings into the present every influence which the past has imprinted upon life. It is the epitome of the past. He who can learn its use can be master of his past. And he who can master his past—that man is free."

For a time there was complete silence. Presently Dr. Archer said, "You have been very kind. I must go now. I shall see you tonight."

"Yes. Tonight." A trace of irony entered the low voice. "Tonight we shall solve a mystery. An important mystery."

"Your death," said the doctor.

"My death—or my life. I am not sure."

"You—are not sure?"

"The life of this flesh, my friend."

"I do not follow you."

"Do not be surprised. Released of this flesh, I should be freer than ever."

"You mean—you think you may be—released?"

"I do not know. It is not important now. But Saturday night, an odd thing happened to me. I was talking to the man, Jenkins. I had projected my mind into his life. I could foresee his immediate future—up till tonight. Then everything went blank. There was nothing. I was as if struck blind. I could see no further. You see what that means?"

"A sort of premonition?"

"So it would be called. To me it is more than that. It meant the end. Whether of Jenkins' body or mine, I can not say at the moment. I was with him, of him, so to speak. But you see—the abrupt termination which cut off my vision could be either his—or—mine."

The doctor could say nothing. He turned, went out, and slowly descended the stairs.

# Chapter Twenty-two

I

AGAIN Bubber Brown called on his friend Jinx Jenkins and
again was permitted to see him. Jinx had never been of
cheerful mien; but today he had sunk below the nadir of de-
spondency as his glum countenance attested. But Bubber wore
a halo of hope and his face was a garland of grins.

"Boy, I told you I'd get you out o' this!"

"Where," asked the sardonic prisoner, "is the key to the
jail?"

"Far as you concerned, it's on Doc Archer's desk."

"That's a long way from this here lock."

"I been goin' after mo' evidence, boy. And I got it. I give it
to the doc and, what I mean, yo' release is jes' a matter of time."

"So is twenty years."

"You' good as out, stringbean."

"Not so long as I'm in. Look." He laid hold of the grille between them and shook it. "That's real, man; that's sump'm I
can believe, even the holes. But what you're sayin' don't widen
nothin' but yo' mouth."

"Listen. You know what I found?"

And he related, how, at great personal risk, which he ignored
because of his friend's predicament, he had voluntarily entered
the stronghold of mystery and death, ignored the undertaker's
several corpses—four or five of them lying around like chickens
on a counter—descended past the company of voodoo wor-
shipers who would have killed him on sight for spying on their
secrets, and so into the pit of horror, where the furnace was
merely a blind for the crematory habits of the conjure-man.

"He come straight out o' the wall," he related, "and me
there hidin' lookin' at him. Come through the wall like a ghost."

"Ghos'es," Jinx demurred, "is white. Everybody know that."

"And so was I," avowed Bubber.

"Well," Jinx conceded, "you might 'a' turned white at that
—when you seen Frimbo come out o' that wall."

Bubber went on with his story. "And," he eventually concluded, "when Doc Archer seen what I'd found, he said that settled it."

"Settled what?"

"That proved somebody's been killed sho' 'nough. See?"

Jinx gazed a long time upon his short, round friend. Finally he said, "Wait a minute. I know I didn't hear this thing straight. You say that what you found proves it was murder?"

"Sho' it do."

"Boy, I don't know how to thank you."

"Oh that's all right. You'd 'a' done the same for me."

"First you get me pulled in on a charge of assault. But you ain' satisfied with that. Tha's only twenty years. You got to go snoopin' around till you get the charge changed to murder. My pal."

"But—but——"

"But my ash can. You talkin' 'bout dumbness and ignorance. Well, you sho' ought to know—you invented 'em. All right; now what you go'n' do? You got me sittin' right in the electric fryin'-pan. Somebody got to throw the switch. You done arranged that too?"

"Listen, boy. All I'm doin' is tryin' to find enough facts to clear you. You ain't guilty sho' 'nough, is you?"

"I didn't think so. But you got me b'lievin' I must be. If you keep on bein' helpful, I reckon I'll jes' have to break down and confess."

"Well, what would you 'a' done?"

"What would I 'a' done? First place, I wouldn' 'a' been there. Second place, if the man wanted to burn up sump'm in his own furnace, he could 'a' burned it. He could 'a' got in the furnace and burned hisself up for all I'd 'a' cared. But you—you got to run up and stop the thing from burnin'—you rather see me burn."

"Aw man, quit talkin' lamb-yap. If Frimbo's tryin' to get rid o' remains, who's responsible for 'em bein' remains? Frimbo, of course. Frimbo put his flunky up to killin' somebody; then he got the flunky away and tried to get rid o' the remains."

"Yea? Well, I don' see Frimbo in this jail house. I'm here. I'm holdin' the well-known bag. And all you doin' is fillin' it."

"I wish I could fill yo' head with some sense. Maybe when

you get yo' big flat feet out on the street again you'll appreciate what I'm doin' for you."

"Oh, I appreciate it now. But I never expect to get a chance to show you how much. That'll be my only dyin' regret."

Bubber gave up. "All right. But you needn' never fear dyin' in nobody's electric chair."

"No?"

"No. Not if they have to put that electric cap on yo' head to kill you. Yo' head is a perfect non-conductor."

With this crushing remark Bubber terminated his call and gloomily departed.

2

"You're ahead of time," said Dr. Archer.

"This won't wait," returned Perry Dart. "It took me less than an hour to get the dope. Here's your club." He laid a package on the desk. "And here," he put the box containing Bubber's discovery down beside the other package, "is your removable deckalite bridge. And I'll bet a week's wages you can't guess who that bridge belonged to."

"I can't risk wages. Who?"

"A tall, slender, dark gentleman by the name of N. Frimbo."

The physician sat forward in his chair behind the desk. The gray eyes behind his spectacles searched Dart's countenance for some symptom of jest. Finding none, they fell to the box, where they rested intently.

"And his address," the detective added, "is the house across the street."

"Unless I've been seeing things," said Dr. Archer, "Frimbo's teeth are very nearly perfect. Those two teeth are certainly present."

"This patient differed from our friend in only one respect."

"How?"

"The dentist who treated him insists that he was cock-eyed."

"I'm beginning to wonder aren't we all?"

"Frimbo's servant was cock-eyed."

"And otherwise much like his master—tall, dark, slender."

"With the same name?"

The physician regarded the detective a solemn moment. "What's in a name?" he said.

3

Before the detective could answer, Dr. Archer's door bell rang again. The caller proved to be Bubber Brown; and a more disconsolate Bubber Brown had never appeared before these two observers.

"Sit down," said the doctor. "Found anything else?"

"Gee, doc," Bubber said, "my boy Jinx is got me worried. He brought up a point I hadn't thought about before."

"What point?"

"Well, if that clue I brought you last night changes the charge to murder, Jinx'll have to do life at least. 'Cose life in jail with nothin' to worry 'bout, like meals and room rent, has its advantages. But the accommodations is terrible they tell me, and I don't like the idea that I messed my boy up."

"Is that what he thinks?" asked Dart.

" 'Deed he do, mistuh, and it don't sweeten his temper. He's eviler than he would be if he really had killed the man."

"There is evidence that he did kill the man," Dart reminded him.

"Must be sump'm wrong with that evidence. Jinx wouldn't kill nobody."

"I thought you didn't know him so well?"

Bubber was too much concerned for his friend to attempt further subterfuge. "I know that much about him," he said. "That Negro ain't bad sho' 'nough. He's jes' bad-lookin'."

"You yourself identified his handkerchief. It had been stuffed down the victim's throat, you'll remember."

"Well—I knowed he didn't do it befo'. But, far as I see, that proved he didn't do it."

"How?"

"Listen, mistuh. Jinx might 'a' hit somebody with that club jes' sorter thoughtless like. But stuffin' a handkerchief down his throat—that wouldn't even occur to him. He's too dumb to think up a smart trick like that."

"An opinion," Dr. Archer said, "in which I wholly concur.

Nothing in Jenkins' character connects him with this offense, either as author or agent. Someone in that room simply made him the dupe."

"Possibly you can explain, then, how his thumb print got on that club," Dart said.

"Possibly I can. In fact I had just that in mind when I asked you to bring it along."

He reached for the first package which Dart had put on the desk, and unwrapped it carefully.

"Remember, we don't know," he observed meanwhile, "that this club or bone actually delivered the blow. There was no blood on it for the simple reason that it had bounced back from the point of impact before hemorrhage, which was moderate, got under way. But it is permissible to assume that it was used."

He lifted the club by its two ends, using the tips of his fingers, and slowly rotated it about its own axis. His glance shuttled back and forth over the ivory-colored surface. "This is the incriminating print?" he asked, indicating a dark smudge.

"Yes. That's what Tynie photographed."

"He didn't dust the bone with powder first, did he?"

"No. How'd you know?"

"Because there's no powder on it elsewhere. This surface has a thick viscous film over it as though it had been oiled or waxed. It isn't oil or wax. It's a film which oozes from the pores of the incompletely prepared specimens, due to the presence of undestroyed marrow inside. If Tynie had dusted this bone there'd be particles of powder stuck all over it. Fortunately, he looked first and found preparation unnecessary—his print had been prepared for him. Now let's have a look.

"I've a magnifying glass hereabouts somewhere—here it is." He studied the smudge a moment. Then he put the bone down, looked up at Dart and smiled. "Easiest thing in the world," he said.

"What is?"

"Transferring a finger print."

"Are you kidding me, doc?"

"Not at all. Simple statement of fact. The discovery of a finger print is not necessarily any better evidence of its owner's presence than the discovery of any other object belonging to him. Don't misunderstand me. I know that as a means of identification, its value is established. But as proof that the owner's fingers put it where it was found—that's another matter. That is a belief based on an assumption. And the fact that the assumption is usually correct does not make it any the less an assumption."

"But just what is the assumption?"

"That there is but one way to put finger prints on an object, namely, direct contact between the fingers and the object. That is the unconscious assumption that is always made the moment a finger print is discovered. We say 'A-ha, finger print.' We identify it as John Doe's finger print. Then we say, 'A-ha, John Doe was here.'"

"Of course," said Dart. "What else would anyone think?"

"Apparently nothing else. But I assure you that as a matter of demonstrable fact, John Doe may never have been near the place. He may have been ten miles away when his finger print was put on the object."

"You'll have to produce plenty evidence to convince me of that, doc."

"Look. You were perfectly willing to believe that Jinx Jenkins' handkerchief might have been taken by somebody else and put where we found it, weren't you? So willing that you did not arrest him on that evidence alone. But when his thumb print was found on the club—that settled it: Jinx must have had a hand in it. Now, I believe I can show you that, aside from a lot of minor assumptions there, your major assumption could have been wrong. Jinx Jenkins didn't have to be anywhere near this club. His finger print could have been deliberately put on it to incriminate him, just as his handkerchief could have been used as it was for the same purpose."

"I'm looking, doc. Go ahead."

"All right. Let us suppose that I want to rob that safe in the corner. I'd be an awful ass, because I wouldn't get a dime's worth of anything. But I don't know that. I want to rob it and I want the circumstances to incriminate you. I decide that since people think as they do, it would incriminate you if right after the robbery your finger prints—even a lone thumb print—could be demonstrated on that safe door.

"Here is a box of fine grade talcum powder. It's a professional sample, otherwise it wouldn't be so fine. I'll put a little on the arm of your chair—smooth, polished wooden surface. Now grasp the arms of your chair with your hands, as you might if you didn't think I was putting something over on you. Good. Incidentally, look at your thumb—has a fair film of powder, hasn't it? All right. Change seats with me. . . . Now again grasp the arms of your chair naturally. Take your hands away. Look at the right arm of your chair. See anything?"

"Sure. A perfect thumb print in white powder! But——"

"Too early for buts. Get up now and stand behind the chair. You are now ten miles away. All right. Here is a rubber glove, such as I rarely nowadays have the opportunity to use. I put it on my hand thus. The rubber is of course perfectly smooth, and if I wish I can increase the coefficient of adhesion——"

"Wait a minute, doc."

"My error. I can make it just a very little bit sticky by rubbing into the palm of it thus, a bit of vaseline, cold cream or what have you. This is not strictly necessary, but tends to improve the clearness of the transfer. Now, with proper stealth, I approach the talcum-powder thumb print which you have so obligingly left on the arm of your chair. I lean over the chair thus and carefully, as if it were a curved blotter, I roll the heel of my hand once, only once, over our powder print. And you see, I have the powder tracing on my glove.

"Of course this is not your thumb print. It is the negative of your thumb print, or rather, the mirror-image of it. If now I go to the safe and smear a tiny bit of vaseline on the safe door thus, it is a simple matter to roll your thumb print off my glove onto the black surface of the door. And there it is. Doesn't even have to be dusted. Photograph it, bring it up on the high contrast paper, and you, my friend, are under arrest for robbing my safe. Yet you have never been near my safe and you were ten miles away when the crime was committed."

Perry Dart silently went over to the safe and gazed upon the smudge of powder. He came back to the desk, picked up the doctor's hand glass, returned to the safe door and studied the transferred print. It was not the crisp image of the original, but the fine granules of powder, primarily arranged in a definite pattern by the tiny grooves of his own skin, had not been sufficiently disarranged by the transposition to obliterate that pattern.

"If you wish," said Dr. Archer, "I can improve on that beautifully by using the same technique with printer's ink. It comes up astonishingly when dusted with finger-print powder afterwards. But this is sufficient to indicate the possibilities."

"You're going to get yourself in trouble thinking up things like that," muttered the detective.

"I didn't think it up," was the answer. "Our unknown murderer —if any—thought it up and used it. Only, since he had a light-colored and fairly gummy object to work toward, he used a black substance instead of a white. I remember getting some of it on my hand from that chair Brady brought me; possibly the same chair Jenkins used—or maybe several chair-arms had been so treated. Lamp-black would do nicely, plain or in a paste like shoe polish. If you examine that print on the bone as you did the one on the safe, you will note a general similarity. Both look as though they might have been put on by a somewhat dirty finger, that's all. Both, however, were actually put on by a smooth-surfaced applicator, which spread the lines just a little, but not too much."

"You know, I thought it was funny Tynes' saying he didn't even have to prepare the thing."

"Still," the physician said, "this only indicates that Jenkins didn't have to touch the club or deliver the blow. It doesn't indicate that he did not actually do so. But something else does."

"What?"

"The position of the print. Even if the transferability of a finger print couldn't be demonstrated, still this print would not prove that Jenkins delivered a blow with this club. On the contrary, it proves that he could not have delivered an effective blow with his thumb in that spot. Look. To deliver an effective blow he would grasp the club in his hand like this—no danger, I'm using my gloved hand and I've wiped off the remains of your thumb print—like this, near the smaller end, so that the condyles—those big bumps which help form the knee part of the bone—would land on the victim's head. Grasping it so, his fingers would surround the shaft thus, completely, and his thumb, you see, would rest on the outside of his fingers; it couldn't possibly produce a print on the surface of the bone because it wouldn't even touch the surface of the bone. But beyond that, the position of the print is near the big end—the clubbing-end here. Notice that the print is close to this condyle and directed obliquely toward it. If your hand grasped this bone so that your thumb fell in that position, your fingers would have to be around the club end like this, and the shaft of the bone, you see, would then fall along your forearm, so that you could not possibly deliver a blow. Any attempt to do so would only endanger your own fingers."

"Gee, doc, you ought to be a lawyer."

"I am. I'm Jenkins' lawyer right now. And I contend, your honor, that if the handkerchief was insufficient basis for indictment, so is the thumb print. Only more so."

"Hot damn!" came an unexpected cry from the admiring Bubber. "Go to it, doc! You're the best!"

4

Bubber's ensuing expressions of appreciation literally carried him away. He backed and sidled out through the doctor's several doors on a transporting flood of gratitude, much like a large rubber ball twisting this way and that on the surface of a flowing stream.

The physician turned again to the detective and smiled. "What does your honor say about Jenkins?"

"Sort of lost my enthusiasm for Jenkins," grinned Dart.

"Well, then, since we're beginning to eliminate, let's attempt a diagnosis."

"O.K. doc. Take 'em one by one. That'll bring up some things I've found out that I haven't told you. I was too interested in Frimbo's servant when I came in."

"Jinx Jenkins."

"Hardly, after your defense."

"Thanks. Doty Hicks."

"Oh, yes. Well, here's the dope on Hicks. Remember, he said that to break Frimbo's spell on his brother it was necessary to put a counter-spell equally fatal on Frimbo. But he had to have somebody's help. The immediate possibility was, of course, that Jenkins was that somebody. But your argument practically eliminates Jenkins on the one hand; and on the other we've found out by further questioning just who he meant. He was talking about a hoodoo artist named Bolus in 132nd Street, who gave him some kind of goofer dust to sprinkle on Frimbo's floor. That's the gray powder we found under the table."

"You found this Bolus?"

"Had no trouble getting a check-up out of him. I told him he was under suspicion for murder, having deliberately conjured and killed a professional competitor. Well, sir, he nearly died himself trying to convince me that his goofer dust was just ordinary coal ashes. Of course, I knew that already. Got the report last night. So then I promised to come back and take him for fraud."

"Doty Hicks, then, is no longer a suspect?"

"Hardly."

"Ironic business all around, Dart. Hicks, in all good faith, put his goofer dust at the feet of a man who may even then have been dead. And he and Jenkins, the only two you could reasonably have held, are probably the least likely suspects of the lot. Well—the two women."

"They're out. We know from checked testimony that they didn't enter the death room till after the thing was done."

"All right by me. Nice girl, Martha Crouch. Easley Jones, the railroad man?"

"Excellent record on his job. Long, faithful service. Hasn't been out of his rooming-house but twice since Saturday night, both times for food."

"Also decidedly untutored—same sort of man that Aramintha Snead is of woman. By no means the character of mind who would think up this particular scheme to incriminate someone else."

"Who's next?"

"Spider Webb."

"Yes, Webb. Well, Webb told a straight story. And Frimbo tried to dispose of the servant's remains. The only way to connect Webb with the crime now is to assume that he and Frimbo were conspiring. But why they'd be conspiring to kill Frimbo's servant—that's beyond me."

"You're sure Webb told a straight story?"

"About the feud, yes. We've gone into it thoroughly. That killing yesterday morning means all I told you it meant. Further, Brandon, Spencer's rival policy king, has disappeared. He always does when somebody has to take the rap."

"That leaves us Frimbo himself."

"Nobody else but."

"Hm—the house is open for suggestions."

"You know, I'm beginning to see daylight in this thing." An idea was growing on Dart. "By Judas! I do see daylight!"

"Show me, O master."

"Look. Suppose Brandon did find out that Frimbo was the cause of his downfall. It's not hard to believe you know. Dumber people than Frimbo are remarkably clever at this number-playing game. They hit on some system and it works. They get so good that bankers actually turn down their bets. Well, Frimbo could have doped out such a system. Suppose he did, and suppose that through it, Spencer was playing heavily with Brandon and winning. Brandon couldn't wipe out Spencer —that would be open confession. But nothing in the world would stop him from trying to wipe out Frimbo. Nothing except that Frimbo isn't easy to get at alone, except at night in a private interview. To take Frimbo, therefore, Brandon's got to finesse. You see?"

"So far."

"So what does he do? He finds somebody who is close to Frimbo, who has access to him, and who is not likely to be suspected. In short, he finds the servant. The servant, who no doubt is already envious of his master's success—the way black servants are with black masters—is offered a big handful of change to put his boss out—any way he can. All right. He agrees. But he's not going to jam himself by doing it during the day when he is known to be in the place alone with Frimbo! He's going to wait till night when the office is full. And he's going to bring the whole thing off in a way that will incriminate somebody else who happens to be present. Wouldn't you? Wait a minute—I know what you're going to say. The answer is that the servant was on the point of carrying the scheme through. He had snatched Jenkins' handkerchief in the scramble there when Doty Hicks fainted. He had already by some scheme such as you just demonstrated got Jenkins' finger print on the club. But Frimbo's smart. Frimbo reads his mind or gets a hunch or anything you want to call it. Frimbo discovers what's up just in time to turn the tables—frustrates the attack and gives the servant his own medicine, club, handkerchief, and all!"

Dart paused to emphasize this twist of interpretation; then went on:

"But Frimbo hasn't got time to dispose of the body then and there. So he exchanges the servant's yellow turban and sash for his own, props the body up in his own chair, hides in the dark and goes on telling visitors their fates, intending to get them all out without arousing any suspicions. But our crusty friend Jenkins discovers the fact that the man talking to him is a corpse—and that changes his plans. See?"

The physician meditated upon this. "You have lapsed into brilliance, Dart," he commented finally. "Brilliance is likely to be blinding. . . . Wasn't it the servant who ushered each visitor to Frimbo's door?"

"Hell, no. That was Frimbo, himself. He took each one to the door, then, while they were going in, blinded by that light, he'd run around, enter the hall door, hide behind the corpse, and talk to 'em."

"All coons look alike, to be sure. But I've seen no sign of external strabismus in either of Frimbo's eyes."

"What?"

"The servant in general resembled Frimbo. But he was cock-eyed. Frimbo isn't. The people who testified all saw the servant and all agreed that he was cock-eyed. Somehow, Dart, I dislike that term—extremely misleading isn't it? But strabismus, now —there's a word! External strabismus—internal strabismus— see how they roll off your tongue."

"I'm particular what rolls off my tongue."

"Nevertheless, external strabismus is not an easily assumed disguise. I have never heard of anyone who could render himself cock-eyed at will."

"You haven't?" grinned Dart. "Ever try cooked whiskey?"

"The phenomenon you have in mind is an illusion—an optical illusion, if you like. The victim enjoys diplopia—the impression of seeing the world double, an impression which he believes cock-eyed people must have at all times. Thus the illusion is twofold: cock-eyed people really don't see double; and the happy inebriate actually has no external strabismus, he has only a transitory internal strabismus. I insist therefore, that, remarkable as Frimbo is, voluntary external strabismus is an accomplishment which we must not grant him lightly. But all this is not the prime objection to your startling vision. The prime objection is that Frimbo would surely not leave thwarted his own plan. Would he?"

"He didn't. Jenkins——"

"He did. Jenkins would have gone on being mystified by Frimbo's revelations, had it not been for Frimbo's own startled words. The thing that made Jenkins jump up and turn the light on the corpse was Frimbo's sudden exclamation, 'Frimbo, why don't you see?' Frimbo would not have said that if he had been planning to get Jenkins and the others out as quickly and unsuspectingly as possible. Something happened to Frimbo about that moment."

"But Jenkins' word is all we have for that remark."

"Jenkins' word, now that he is pretty well exonerated, should be worth something. But even if by itself it isn't, I have Frimbo's word in support."

"You what?"

"Frimbo himself said to me today that he went blind, so to speak, while talking to Jenkins. He saw so far ahead—then everything went blank."

"Hooey."

"All right. Maybe this is hooey too: You say that Frimbo hid behind the corpse near enough to make his voice seem to come from the corpse."

"Yes."

"Then, when Jenkins suddenly jumped up and without warning swung the light around why didn't he see Frimbo hiding?"

"I don't know—maybe Frimbo ducked under the table or some place."

"Hooey. Hooey. An eloquent word, isn't it?"

"Well, the details may not be exact, but that isn't far from what happened. It's the only thing I can think of that even nearly fits the facts."

"Nearly won't do."

"All right, professor. You guess."

"There's something malicious in the way you say that. However, innocent and unsuspecting as I am, I will guess. And I guess, first off, I'll leave out the number racket. That'll make it easier for me, you see."

"But the number racket can't be ignored——"

"Who's doing this guessing?"

"O.K. doc. Guess away."

"I guess the same thing that you guess, that Frimbo killed his servant. But not because of the number racket, or any attack upon him growing out of the number racket."

"But because he's a nut."

"Please—not so bluntly. It sounds crude—robbed of its nuances and subtleties. You transform a portrait into a cartoon. Say, rather, that under the influence of certain compulsions, associated with a rather intricate psychosis, he was impelled to dispose of his servant for definite reasons."

"All right. Say it anyhow you like. But to me it's still because he was a nut."

" 'Nut' in no wise suggests the complexity of our friend's psychology. You recall my description of his condition; its origin in his type of mind, its actual onset in an experience, its primary and secondary delusions."

"Yes. I recall all that."

"Well, here's an item you don't recall because it hasn't been mentioned; Frimbo like other paranoiacs, has a specific act as a part of his compensatory mechanism. This act becomes a necessary routine which must be performed, and naturally takes its form from some earlier aspect of his life. In his case it derives from his native days in Buwongo, his African principality. He calls it the rite of the gonad. And though he declines to describe it, I can imagine what it amounts to. It is nothing more or less than his extracting, in that laboratory of his, a kind of testicular extract with which he periodically treats himself. By so doing, he believes that he partakes of matter actually carrying the impress of all the ages past, and so becomes master of that past."

"Deep stuff. Anything in it?"

"Well, I don't know anything about endocrines. But I should think such a practice would produce some kind of hyper-sexuality. Sex gland deficiency can be helped by such treatment, so perhaps a normal person would become, in some respects, oversexed."

"But sex has played no part in this picture."

"I was only answering your question. To return to my guess. Frimbo has to have sex glands—not those of lower animals such as biological houses use to make their commercial extracts, but human sex glands, carrying, to his mind, the effects of human experience from time immemorial. With the compulsion strong upon him to secure human tissues for his rite, he could easily become as ruthless as a drug addict deprived of his drug. But he would be far more cunning. He would choose a victim who would not be missed, and he would arrange circumstances to incriminate someone else. And the insanely brilliant feature is that he would arrange to have himself appear to be the victim. I do not believe that the unusual devices used to commit this crime and divert suspicion indicate the workings of an ordinary mind or knowledge such as a servant would have. They indicate a sort of crazy ingenuity which would not be conceived and carried out by a normal person. Frimbo is the only one in the crowd whose mind fits the details of this crime."

"Well, you're disagreeing with me only on motive. I say self-defense. You say insanity. But both of us say Frimbo did it. From that point on I should think our difficulties would be alike: the cock-eyed business, the blind spot or whatever it was, and the—what was the other thing?"

"His sudden invisibility if he hid behind the dead servant."

"Yea—that."

"The cock-eyed business, yes. But the other business, no. I did not say that he hid behind the servant. I think he had some device or instrument—I'm not sure just what, but we'll find it —that placed his voice so that it seemed to come from the servant. And I do not say that he acted under the urgency of a sudden encounter. I say that he planned the whole thing ahead, deliberately. Even foresaw the possibility of discovery and arranged to rise from the dead, just for effect, as he did. That would be wholly in character. He even had an alibi ready for my blood test. He showed me this afternoon how I might easily have made an error in the little experiment I showed you. He did not know, of course, that Bubber Brown's discovery was on hand as a perfect check.

"He demonstrated how something in my gauze dressing might throw the test off—it would have been very disturbing indeed if I had not known what he was up to. What he did was to substitute for my gauze a piece which he had previously treated with the dead man's serum. He foresaw every possibility. Far from thwarting his own plans, even that sudden loss of prophetic vision, that premonition, did not change his main course of action. That exclamation, 'Frimbo, why don't you see?' startled Jenkins into action, to be sure, and resulted in our rushing on the scene. But even then he would have removed the body anyway from under our very noses—he could have done so simply by shutting off the lights.

"And there's another difference in our theories: If, as you say, it was just self-defense, he is not shown to be dangerous. He can be held for disposing of the remains, but not for murder; self-defense is manslaughter and is likely to go unpunished. But if, as I say, it is insanity, then he's liable to do the same thing again to some other unfortunate fellow; he must be put away in a cool dry place where he's no longer a menace. Don't you see?"

"That's so. You know, doc, just out of sportsmanship you might let me win an argument once in a while."

"We're not arguing. We're guessing. And I have a curious feeling that smart as we think we are, we're both guessing wrong."

"You're good, doc. Anyway it goes now, you're right."

"At least I know one thing."

"What?"

"I know I saw a new specimen jar on one of Frimbo's shelves today. It was next to the one that we noted before. And it contained two more sex glands."

"Judas H. Priest!" said Perry Dart softly.

# Chapter Twenty-three

I

For the first time since the incarceration of his friend Jinx, Bubber Brown enjoyed a meal. The probability of Jinx's release later tonight, a happy eventuality which Bubber himself had helped bring about, more than restored Bubber's appetite to normal and he indulged in gleeful anticipation of what he would say to his grouchy comrade upon the latter's return to freedom. Mumbled mockery pushed its way through prodigious mouthfuls of food.

"Uh—huh," emerged stifled but determined through roast beef and mashed potatoes. "Here you is. Yo' flat feet is now out in the free air they probably need plenty of. Now get to thankin' me." A succulent forkful of kale crowded its way in with the roast and potatoes, and all this was stuffed securely back with a large folded layer of soft white bread. Even through this there somehow escaped sounds.

"Boy, you was due to go. Go where? Where do folks go what murder folks? I mean it was upon you. If it hadn' been for me and the doc, you'd be on your way to Swing Swing now. Your can was scheduled to rest on a 'lectric lounging chair—they even had the date set. I ain' kiddin' you, boy. You was jes' like that coffee they advertise on the radio—your can was dated."

The next few phrases were overwhelmed with hot coffee. Bubber grinned and substituted a dish of juicy apple cobbler for his denuded dinner plate. "From now on," he told it, "you listen and I talk, 'cause your head is a total loss to you—jes' extra weight you carryin' around for no purpose." The apple cobbler began miraculously to vanish. "You see, you don't appreciate my brains. I got brains enough for both of us. I don't even have to use all my brains—I got brains in the back o' my head I ain't never used. Some time when you admit how dumb you is, I'll lend you some for a few days, jes' to show you how it feels to have a thought once in a while."

The dessert became a sweet memory, vestiges of which were dislodged with a handy toothpick.

"Now, let's see. Got to be at the place at 'leven o'clock. Guess I'll drop in and see that picture at the Roosevelt Theatre —*Murder Between Drinks*. Wonder 'f I'm go'n' see that third one tonight? Maybe the one in the picture'll be number three. Now there's brains again. Jes' by goin' to see this picture I may save somebody's life. Doggone!—ain't I smart?"

## 2

Promptly at eleven, Bubber Brown mounted the stoop and entered the house. He started up the stairs toward Frimbo's floor, looking above. He stopped, his eyes popping. He brushed his hand across his lids, and stared again toward the head of the stairs. What he saw persisted. It might have been Saturday night again; for there motionless above him stood the tall, black-robed figure of Frimbo's servant, bright yellow turban and sash gleaming in the dim light, exactly as he had been before, even—yes, there it was—even to the definite cast in one solemn eye.

Bubber blinked twice, wheeled about, and would have vanished through the front door as magically as this corpse had reappeared. But at that particular moment the door opened and Perry Dart with half a dozen policemen obstructed the avenue of escape. Bubber came to in Jinx Jenkins' arms, pointed, and gasped:

"Look! is I dreamin'—or is I dreamin'?"

"What's the matter, Brown?" Dart asked.

"Didn't you say the flunky was the one got cooked?"

"Yes."

"Well, look up yonder! He's there—I seen him!"

"Yeah?" Dart stepped forward, looked up the stairs. He smiled. "So he is, Brown. We must have made a mistake. Come on, let's go—can't let a little error like that worry us."

"So," muttered Jinx, "you is wrong again. What a brain!"

"You can go if you want to, brother," demurred Bubber. "Me—I've never felt the need of fresh air the way I do now. People in this house don't suit me. They jes' don't pay death no mind."

"Come on, Brown," insisted Dart. "I'll need your help. Don't let me down now."

"All right. I'll follow. But don't count on me for no help. I'm go'n' stay 'live long as I can. I ain't learnt this Lazarus trick yet."

In the hallway above, Dart gave due orders in stationing his men, so that all natural exits were covered. The servant ushered them then to the reception room, where every one was present but Dr. Archer. The detective noted each person in turn: Mrs. Aramintha Snead, Mrs. Martha Crouch, Easley Jones, Doty Hicks, Spider Webb, and Jinx Jenkins, whom he had brought with him.

The physician arrived a moment later. "I summon Frimbo," said the servant who had escorted him in also. The servant bowed. The doctor looked after his retreating form quizzically, then turned to Detective Dart and smiled. Dart grinned back. Bubber observed the exchange and murmured, "You all could see jokes in tombstones, couldn't you?"

Perry Dart said to the physician, "Now what?"

"Wait," answered Dr. Archer. "It's his show."

They waited. Shortly the gold turban and sash returned. "This way, please," said the servitor, and gestured toward the wide entrance to the consulting-room.

"Everybody?"

"Please."

Again the servant retreated by way of the hall. The others, directed by the detective and led by the physician, entered the black chamber from the front room and stood in an expectant semicircle facing the table in the center. Over the far chair, which still sat behind the table just as it had when the body had been found in it, hung the device which projected a horizontal beam of light toward the entrance. Most of the visitors fell to the one or the other side of this beam, but at the distance of the semicircle, its rays diverged enough to include two figures directly in its path, those of Martha Crouch and Spider Webb. Mrs. Crouch's dark eyes were level and clear, her lips slightly compressed, her expression anticipative but not apprehensive. Spider Webb also betrayed interest without profound concern, his countenance manifesting only a sort of furtive malignancy. The rest were mere densities in the penumbra.

3

As they stood watching, the darkness beyond the table condensed into a black figure, much as mist might condense into a cloud. This figure silently came to occupy the chair beneath the light. Then from it issued the low rich voice of Frimbo.

"A return into the past," it said, "observes events in their reverse order. May I therefore ask Mr. Jenkins, who was the last to occupy that chair on Saturday evening, to be the first to do so tonight?"

Nobody moved.

Bubber's sharp whisper came forth.

"Go on, fool. Get yo'self freed."

With obvious and profound reluctance, Jinx's figure moved forward into the light. Those toward one side could see tiny beads of sweat glistening on his freckled countenance. He sidled into the chair on this side of the table, facing the voice and the shadow. His face was brightly illuminated and starkly troubled.

"Mr. Jenkins," Frimbo's voice went on smoothly, "it is again Saturday night. You have come to consult me. All that reached your consciousness is again before you. You will conceal nothing from the eyes of Frimbo. The light shall lay open your mind to me, book-wise. I shall read you. Be silent, please."

There was scant danger of Jinx's being anything else. Even his usual murderous scowl had been erased, and Frimbo's intent contemplation of his face could be sensed by every onlooker. They too were steadily staring upon him from behind or from the side, according to their position, much as if they expected him at any moment to leap to his feet and confess the crime.

Then a change of color came over Jinx's face. Those who were in position to see observed that the light freckled skin over the eminences of his bony countenance was growing darker. Alarmingly the change progressed, like an attack of some grave cyanotic disease. Jinx was actually turning blue. But it at once became apparent that his color was due to a change in the light which illumined him. Slowly that light changed again.

"Each hue," said Frimbo's voice, "makes its particular disclosure."

Jinx became yellow.

"Got to do mo'n that to make a Chinaman out o' him," came Bubber's whisper.

Diabolically red flushed the subject's lean visage, and finally a ghastly green. Throughout it all Frimbo's intense inspection created an atmosphere of vibrant expectancy. One felt that the lines of vision between his eyes and Jinx's face were almost tangible—could be plucked and made to sing like the strings of an instrument.

Eventually Frimbo said, "No," and the spell was broken. "This is not the man." The light came white again. "That is all, Mr. Jenkins."

There was a general sigh of relief. Jinx returned to the circle, where Bubber greeted him with an inevitable comment:

"The red light turned you red, boy, and that green light turned you green. But that white light couldn't do a thing for you. It was jes' wasted."

Frimbo said, "Now, Mr. Webb, please."

But Perry Dart interrupted. "Just a minute, Frimbo." He stepped forward to the side of the table. "Before we go any further, don't you think it fair to have your servant present?"

Frimbo's voice became grave. "I regret that I have already permitted my servant to leave."

"Why did you do that?"

"It is his custom to leave at eleven, may I remind you?"

"And may I remind you that we are investigating a serious crime; also that you promised to have him present."

"I kept my promise. He was here. You all saw him. I did not promise that he would remain after his hours."

"Very well. You say he is gone?"

"Yes."

"He has left the house?"

"Yes."

"Then perhaps you will tell me just how he got out. Every exit is covered by an officer, with orders to bring to me anyone who tries to leave this house."

There was a pause; but Frimbo said easily, "That I cannot tell you. I can tell you, however, that by interrupting this procedure you are defeating your own investigation, with which I am endeavoring to help you."

Dart achieved a trace of Frimbo's own irony. "Your consideration for my interest touches me, Frimbo. I am overwhelmed with gratitude. But your servant is a necessary witness. I must insist on his being here—with you."

"That is impossible."

"Well, now you are at least telling the truth. Or perhaps you can do for him what you did for yourself?"

"You are obscure."

"Look harder, Frimbo. It's the bad lighting. I mean that perhaps you can make him rise from the dead, as you did."

Bubber could not suppress a mumbled, "Come on, Lazarus. Do yo' stuff."

"You believe then," Frimbo said, "that my servant is dead?"

"I know that your servant is dead. I have in my hand positive evidence of his death."

"Of what nature?"

"Evidence that was retrieved from your furnace downstairs by one of my men——"

"Hot damn!" breathed Bubber. "Tell 'em 'bout me!"

"—when you were trying to destroy it. I have a piece of the bone upon which his brain rested during life. I have a removable bridge which is known to be his, and which fits that bone—or rather the teeth in the bone joined to it. Frimbo, this is a farce. You killed your servant, who also went by the name of Frimbo. You slipped around through this house somehow on Saturday night while I was investigating this case, and moved his body to some hiding-place on these premises. You treated that body to make it burn quickly and to make what bone was left crumble easily. You dismembered it and tried to dispose of it by way of your furnace. You were seen doing this by Bubber Brown, who was in your cellar last night and who recovered a part of the bone before it crumbled. To avert suspicion, you masqueraded as your servant by a trick of your eyes. I see no point in continuing this nonsense. You're the guilty party and you're under arrest. Am I still obscure?"

4

For a long moment no other word was spoken. At last Frimbo said quietly:

"Since I am already under arrest, it would be useless, perhaps, to point out certain errors in your charges. . . . However, if you would care to know the truth——"

"You are at liberty to make any statement you please. But don't try anything funny. We've anticipated some of your tricks."

"Tricks," Frimbo said softly, "is an unkind word. The fact is, however, that I have killed no one. It is true that I have disposed of my servant's remains. If that box contains what you say it does, and if Brown was in the cellar when you say he was, he undoubtedly saw me in the course of performing what was nothing more or less than a tribal duty."

"Tribal duty?"

"The servant was a fellow tribesman of mine whom I took in and protected when his venture into this civilization proved to be less fortunate than mine. He was of my clan and entitled to use the name, Frimbo. His distinguishing name, however—what you would call his Christian name, had he not been a heathen and a savage—was N'Ogo. It is our tradition that the spirit of one of our number who meets death at the hands of an—an outsider, can be purged of that disgrace and freed from its flesh only by fire. The body must be burned before sunset of the third day. Since the circumstances made this impossible, I assumed the risk of removing and properly destroying my tribesman's flesh. For that and for whatever penalty attaches to it, I have no regret. My only regret, Mr. Dart, is that you have interrupted, and perhaps for the time defeated, my effort to complete the duty which this death has imposed upon me."

Dart was impressed. The man's total lack of embarrassment, his dignity, his utter composure, could not fail to produce effect.

"Complete the duty——?"

"It is a part of my duty, as the king of my people, to find the killer and bring him to the just punishment which he has earned. In my own land I should take that part of the matter into my own hands. Here in yours it was my intention to find the killer and turn him over to you. But as for killing N'Ogo myself—you would have to be one of us, my friend, to appreciate how horribly absurd that is. I would sooner kill myself than one of my clan. And he—he could not under the most extraordinary circumstances imaginable bring himself to do a thing against his king. He simply could not have committed an offense against me that would have caused me to decree or execute his death. Against one of his own or lower rank, perhaps, but not against me."

The detective, ordinarily prompt in decision, was for the moment bewildered. But habit was strong. "Look here," he said, "how can you prove that what you say is true—that you didn't kill this man?"

"It is not of the slightest importance to me, Mr. Dart, whether you or the authorities you represent believe me or not. My concern is not for my own protection but for the discharge of my obligation as king. If I can not complete my duty to this member of my clan, I do not deserve to have been his king. The greatest humiliation I could suffer would be death at the hands of a strange people. That is no more than he has suffered."

This was an attitude which Dart had never encountered. The complete and convincing unimportance to Frimbo of what was paramount to the detective left the latter for the moment without resource. He was silent, considering. Finally he asked:

"But why did you have to do so much play-acting? Accepting what you say as true, why did you have to pull all that hokum about rising from the dead?"

"Do you not see that it was necessary to my plans? I had to have time in which to dispose of N'Ogo's body. I had to account for its disappearance. It is easy for me to pass undiscovered from almost any part of this house to any other part. I have a lift, electrically operated and practically undiscoverable, in the old dumbwaiter shaft. It travels from this floor to the cellar. What appears on examination to be the roof of the old shaft, with rusty gears and frazzled rope hanging down, is really not the roof but the bottom of the floor of the lift. N'Ogo's remains reposed on that lift, securely hidden, during the latter part of your search. So did I until the proper moment for my entrance. What better way can you think of to account for the disappearance of a body than to claim to be that body? I even wounded myself as N'Ogo had been wounded, in anticipation of the good doctor's examination. I took every possible precaution—even inviting the doctor alone here to determine the extent of his investigations and divert him from the truth if possible."

"What about those sex glands?"

"They too are a part of the tradition. They alone, of all his flesh, must be preserved as a necessary item in the performance of one of our tribal rites, one which I went so far as to mention to Dr. Archer today. That I can not speak further of, but I think the doctor's excellent mind will comprehend what it can not fully know."

"But this is unheard of. You haven't told the whole story yet. You say you don't know who killed this servant or tribesman of yours. Do you know when he was killed?"

"Not even that. I know only that one of the people who came here to see me killed him, thinking he was I."

"How could anybody make that mistake?"

"Easily. You see, it has always been our custom, as is true of many peoples, that the chief, in whom resides the most important secrets of the nation, should not be unnecessarily exposed to physical danger. Just as a lesser warrior in medieval days donned the white plume of his commander to deceive the enemy and prevent the possibility of their concentrating upon the leader, killing him early, and demoralizing the troops by eliminating competent direction, so with us for many hundreds of years a similar practice has been in effect. The king is prohibited by tribal law from unnecessarily endangering the tribal secrets residing in his person. My servant knew of certain dangers to which I was exposed here. I had devised a mathematical formula whereby I was able to predict a certain probability in the popular policy game of this community. My part in the dwindling fortunes of one of the so-called bankers was discovered through the disloyalty of a disgruntled underling in the rival camp which my information was aiding. The loser intended to eliminate me. Whether this actual killing was his doing or not I am not sure—that was one possibility. There was another.

"At any rate, N'Ogo and I exchanged rôles. It had been so

for several days. I am able through a divertissement learned in youth to diverge my eyes as easily as most people converge theirs, and so, to the casual observer, could easily pass for my own servant.

"My servant had only to sit here in this chair in the darkness. I myself, dressed in his costume, would usher the visitor to the entrance there, turn aside, and come down the hall to my laboratory at the rear. There a device of mine enabled me to convince the visitor, now seated in that chair opposite, that it was really I who sat there. This light over my head is far more than a light. It is also a mechanism whereby I can see the illuminated face of whoever occupies that chair, and whereby also I can transmit my voice to this point. It comprises nothing mechanically original or unusual, except, perhaps, its compactness. By means of it, I was able to carry on my observation of a visitor and talk to him quite as if I were really in this chair, except that I could see only his face. Thus, you see, by the use of two rather simple mechanisms, my lift and my light, I enjoyed remarkable freedom of movement and considerable personal security in case of necessity.

"But on Saturday night, I had no need, any more than on any other night, for entering this room. Visitors were always accustomed to paying their fees to the assistant in the hall as they departed. So negative was my assistant's part in this masquerade that I did not—and do not—know just when he was attacked. But the strange experience—what you will call a premonition—that momentarily startled me during Mr. Jenkins' interview made me exclaim in a way that startled him also, so that he jumped up to investigate. The crime had been done before that moment. It was done between the time when some prior visitor rose to go—disappearing from view in my mechanism—and the time when I collected the same visitor's fee in the hall. Or perhaps between the time when I bowed him into this room and reached my laboratory.

"From that point on you know what happened. I could do only what I did do. Tonight I had every reason to believe, before your interruption, that I should determine the identity of the murderer. Perhaps I may do so yet—I have arranged certain traps. In case of the unexpected, Mr. Dart, be careful what you touch——"

A wholly strange voice suddenly shot out from the deep shadow behind Frimbo.

"So it's really you this time, Frimbo? Why weren't you careful what you touched?"

At the last word a pistol banged twice.

In that frozen instant, before any of the dumbfounded bystanders could move, Frimbo's light was abruptly blotted out and the room went utterly black. At the same moment a shriek of unmistakable pain and terror broke through the dark from the direction of the two shots.

"Brady—that light—quick!" came Dart's sharp voice. The powerful extension light flashed brilliantly on.

There was no need for haste, however. Against the wall at the rear of the black-draped chamber, whence the distressed cry had come, everyone saw a figure slumped limply down, as if it would fall but could not. It moaned and twitched as if in a convulsion, and one arm was extended upward as if held by something on the wall.

Dr. Archer reached the figure before the detective, started to lift it, looked up at the point where the hand was clinging, and changed his intention.

"Wait—be careful!" he warned the detective. The man's hand was grasping the handle of the switch-box which occupied that point on the wall. "That handle's live in that position. Here— push it up by lifting him by his clothing—that's it—a little more—I'll push up his elbow—there!" The hand fell free.

Supporting his limp figure between them, they got the man to his feet. They swung him, more unnerved than hurt, around into the light and drew him forward.

It was the railroad porter, Easley Jones.

5

Dr. Archer first did what he could for Frimbo, who, still sitting in the chair, had fallen face-down on the table; lifted his shoulders so that he resumed an erect posture, and began to loosen his clothing in order to examine his wounds. Frimbo, rapidly weakening, yet was able to lift one hand in protest. He smiled ever so faintly and managed a low whisper:

"Thank you, my friend, but it is of no use. This is what I foresaw."

Martha Crouch had come forward like one walking in a daze. Now she was beside Frimbo. Her face was a portrait of bewilderment and dread. Frimbo's head sank forward on his chest.

"The Buwongo secret," he murmured, "dies. . . ."

The young woman put her arm about his sagging shoulders. Her horror-struck face turned to Dr. Archer, mutely questioning. He shook his head a little sadly.

"How about the car downstairs, doc?" Dart was asking. "Shoot right over to Harlem Hospital if you say so."

Dr. Archer stood beside Frimbo a moment longer without answering. Then he sighed and turned away. "It's too late," he said. "Have him taken up to his room."

He approached Easley Jones, who stood between two policemen, looking down at the palm of his left hand, where the live switch handle had burned him. The doctor picked up the railroad porter's hand, inspected it, dropped it.

"Just what under the sun," he said, looking the man up and down, "could you have had against Frimbo?"

Easley Jones said nothing. His head remained sullenly lowered, the bushy kinks standing out like a black wool wig, the dark freckles sharply defined against pale brown skin.

"Have you anything to say?" Dart asked him.

Still he was silent.

"You sneaked around in the dark until you were near that switch Frimbo mentioned Saturday night. Then you shot Frimbo from behind, intending to throw off the switch and get back to your place during the excitement. We were looking for something like that, otherwise this extension would have been useless. We plugged it in downstairs on another circuit."

"But it was Frimbo," Dr. Archer said, "who caught him. Frimbo had wired that switch box so that the handle would go live when it was pulled down. Frimbo anticipated all this—he said so. Deliberately exposed himself to another attack in order to catch the killer. He even knew he was going to die."

"What this guy's grudge was I can't imagine. But he's saved us a lot of trouble by trying again. I suppose he would have tried it before if he hadn't known he was being trailed. How'd you know we were trailing you, Jones?"

No answer.

"Incredible," Dr. Archer was muttering. "Nothing about him to suggest the ingenuity——"

"Frimbo!"

The physician swung around, stepped back to Martha Crouch, who had uttered the name as one might cry out in torture. Never on any face had he seen such intense grief.

"Why, Martha—what in the world? Does this mean all that to you?"

Her eyes, wide and dry, stared impotently about in a suppressed frenzy of despair. Clearly, she would have screamed, but could not.

"You mean"—the physician could not bring himself to accept the obvious—"that you and Frimbo——?"

It was as if that name coupled with her own was more than she could endure. She wheeled away from him, and from the sudden tense immobility of her figure he knew that in a moment all that she was now curbing by long self-discipline would explode in one relieving outburst.

Suddenly she about-faced again. This time her eyes, fixed on a point behind John Archer, had in them the madness of hysteria. The doctor manifested an impulse to restrain her as she passed him. He hesitated a trifle too long. Before anyone knew her intention, she had swept like a Fury upon the man whose arms were in the grasp of the two officers. Low words came from between her clenched teeth as her hands tore at his face.

"You—killed—the only man——"

They managed after a moment to pull her away. What shocked her, however, out of that moment of mania into a sudden stupor of immobility was not the firm grasp of friendly hands but the realization that in her tightly closed fingers was a wig of kinky black hair, and that the sleek, black scalp of the man before her, despite the freckles which so well disguised his complexion, was that of her husband, the undertaker, Samuel Crouch.

## Chapter Twenty-four

JINX JENKINS, released, and his ally, Bubber Brown, walked together down Seventh Avenue. It was shortly after midnight and the Avenue at this point was alive. The Lafayette Theatre was letting out somewhat later than usual, flooding the sidewalk with noisy crowds. Cabs were jostling one another to reach the curb. Brightly dressed downtowners were streaming into Connie's Inn next door. Habitués of the curb stood about in commenting groups, swapping jibes. The two friends ambled through the animated turbulence, unaware of the gaiety swirling around them, still awed by the experience through which they had passed.

"Death on the moon, boy," Bubber said. "What'd I tell you?"

"You tol' me," Jinx unkindly reminded him, "it was the flunky done it."

"The flunky done plenty," returned Bubber. "Got hisself killed, didn't he?"

"Yea—he done that, all right."

"His name was N'Ogo," Bubber said, "but he went."

They emerged from the bedlam of that carnival block.

"Smart guy that Frimbo," observed Bubber. "Y' know, I wouldn't mind bein' kind o' crazy if it made me that smart."

"That Crouch wasn't no dumbbell."

"Dart say Crouch must 'a' known all about a railroad porter named Easley Jones, and made out he was him."

"Hmph. Guess now he wishes he was him sho' 'nough."

"Sho' was different from his own self—act different, talk different."

"He wasn't so different. He was still actin' and talkin' cullud, only more so."

Bubber's hand was on the roll of bills in his pocket which he had won at blackjack, but his mind was still in Frimbo's death chamber.

"Them artificial freckles—that man must 'a' been kind o' crazy too—jealous crazy—to sit down and think up a thing like that. Freckles sump'm like yourn, only his comes off."

"Mine liked to come off too when I seen who he was. How you reckon he got my finger print on that thing?"

Bubber described with enthusiasm the physician's demonstration.

"Say, that's right," Jinx recalled. "My chair arm was kind o' messy on one side, but I thought it was jes' furniture polish and sorter blotted it off on a clean place."

"Then we got up and went over to the mantelpiece and was talkin' 'bout all them false-faces and things."

"Yea."

"That's when this guy come up and joined the conversation. But he had dropped his hat in your chair. While he was standin' there talkin' so much, he got your han'kerchief and that club. Then it come his turn to go in to Frimbo. On the way he leaned over your chair to pick up his hat. That's when he got your thumb print—off the clean place. Didn't take him a second."

"The grave-digger," Jinx muttered. "He sho' meant to dig me in, didn't he?"

"If it hadn't been you, 'twould 'a' been somebody else. He jes' didn't mean to lose his wife and his life both. Couldn't blame him for that. Jes' ordinary common sense."

A gay young man on the edge of the pavement burst into song for the benefit of some acquaintance passing by with a girl:

> "*I'll be glad when you're dead, you rascal you—*
> *I'll be glad when you're dead, you rascal you—*
> *Since you won't stop messin' 'round,*
> *I'm go'n' turn yo' damper down—*
> *Oh, you dog—I'll be glad when you're gone!*"

"Boy," murmured Bubber, if he only knew what he was singin'."

And deep in meditation the two wandered on side by side down Seventh Avenue.

# BLACK THUNDER

*Arna Bontemps*

TO
ALBERTA

# CONTENTS

# BOOK ONE

# JACOBINS

# *One*

VIRGINIA COURT records for September 15, 1800, mention a certain Mr. Moseley Sheppard who came quietly to the witness stand in Richmond and produced testimony that caused half the States to shudder. The disclosures, disturbing as they were, preceded rumors that would positively let no Virginian sleep. A troop of United States cavalry was urgently dispatched, and Governor James Monroe, himself an old soldier, paced the halls of Ash Lawn with quaking knees and appointed for his estate three special aides-de-camp.

It is safe to say, however, that on the night this history begins, early in June of the same year, Mr. Moseley Sheppard slept well. That night the planter's great house was as dark as death. The rooms, cavernous and deep, were without sound, except when a gray squirrel scampered over the roof or when Ben, the old slave, rattled a plate in the pantry. A tall clock, ticking hoarsely on a landing, changed its tone occasionally and suggested the croaking of a bullfrog. Mr. Moseley Sheppard breathed heavily behind his mosquito netting, turned now and again on his high-piled mattresses, but slept well.

Old Ben twisted a scrap of paper, got a fragment of flame over the pantry lamp and went into the kitchen. There were candles on a table in the corner. He lit one and threw the punk that was burning his fingers into a kettle of ashes.

Following the taper, the old servant's face glowed like a drunken moon behind a star. He was smiling. There was gray wool on the sides of his face as well as on his head. Ben wore satin breeches and shoes with white paste buckles; his savage hair was long and tied with a black string at the back of his neck.

On the landing he opened the clock and began winding it with a brass key. He had placed the candle above his head, and it threw on his shoulders a dull blue radiance weaker than the light a ghost carries. Ben's thin hands kept turning the key, winding the tall clock. He was still turning, still winding, when young Robin Sheppard let himself in by a side door and came quietly through the unlighted great room. He reached the staircase and paused. Ben closed the clock, took his candle and came down. The boy's embroidered cuffs covered his pale hands. There was glossy braid on his knee-length coat.

"Listen, Ben," he said. "You're not supposed to see things, and you're not supposed to hear."

"No, suh, young Marse Robin. I don't hear and I don't see."

"You don't know what time I came in—understand?"

"I don't know nothing," Ben said, "nothing."

"That's it. Have you got anything handy in the pantry, Ben?"

The boy followed him out to the larder, took a stool beneath the pantry lamp and waited while Ben trimmed the breast of a cold roasted duck, opened an earthen jar of preserves and poured wine from a reed-covered jug. Home from the College of William and Mary, Robin seemed strangely unfamiliar to Ben, not at all like the youngster he had seen grow up in that same house; but he was showing his Sheppard blood all right, keeping such hours before he was twenty-one and drinking like a congressman. Ben knew what to expect of the quality.

"You know where I've been, Ben?"

"I don't know nothing, young Marse Robin. Not a thing."

"You know, but you're not supposed to say. I want you to know, Ben. I might need you some time. You see, she's yellow."

"Yes, suh. I know and *don't* know."

"The horse is tied to a tree on the drive."

"I'll put him up myself," Ben said. "No need to call Pharoah."

"Thanks, Ben. You're a good boy."

The old gray-haired Negro smiled. He went through the kitchen and out on the gravel way. His heart fluttered with pleasure; he was a good boy.

Mr. Moseley Sheppard was still asleep behind his mosquito netting, his toes peeping out of the cover, but cocks were crowing. The handsome great house was dark as death inside, but in the fields thousands of gleaming birds were crowing up the sun. Old Ben, a shadow among shadows, wavered on the path that led beneath the walnut trees. He was smoking a corncob pipe, and in his hand there was an empty bowl covered with a napkin. He let himself into the kitchen.

Later, when Drucilla came with her grown daughter and started cooking breakfast, Ben returned to the back steps, bringing the silverware in a plush bag, and commenced polishing the pieces one by one on a bench. It was a big job, one that would take most of the morning, and he was glad to get an early start.

He worked steadily. By and by the sky flushed. There was a blue mist on the world. Ben always felt mellow at that hour. Somewhere, in some hedge or thicket a thrasher called; a thrasher called him somewhere. A few moments passed. The mist stretched and broke like a cobweb, and through it crept Bundy, an extremely thin Negro carrying a fat earthen jug.

" 'Mawnin', Ben."

They were near the same age, but Bundy was not gray, had no hair to be gray, in fact, and had no frizzly whiskers on his face.

"What's on yo' mind?" Ben said.

Bundy turned his jug bottom up.

"Look: dry's a bone," he said. "Can't you give me another little taste of that old pizen rum, Ben?"

"You drinks worser'n a gentaman, Bundy. But I reckon maybe Marse Sheppard can spare you one mo' jugful. I'll just fill it anyhow and ask him about it some other time. He sleep now."

"That's the ticket, Ben. You oughta be a mason."

"A mason?"

"Sure. I'm one. You oughta come j'ine."

Ben came out of the cellar a few moments later hammering with his palm on the cork of Bundy's jug.

"There you be."

"Much obliged, Ben. But sure 'nough, you oughta come on j'ine the masons."

"I ain't got time for no such chillun's foolishness as that, Bundy."

"If you come find out what it is, you might change that song."

"Nah, not me, boy."

"Listen. I'm going to come get you next week just the same."

"Don't bother, Bundy. I'm too busy."

"I just want you to talk to Gabriel; I ain't asking you to j'ine no mo'."

"I'm too busy," Ben said. "That's all chillun's foolishness."

"You just wait'll Gabriel 'splains it. I'm going to come get you next week."

"Aw, Bundy——"

"Don't say a word. Just you wait'll you talks to Gabriel. Much obliged, Ben."

"Don't mention it, Bundy. It wa'n't nothing."

Bundy left with his jug. The mist had broken into scraps. Ben could feel the softness of the young day. It amused him to see Bundy making his way across the fields on such unsteady legs with such a fat jug. Join the masons! Lordy, what a notion! Where was it the thrasher called him, to what green clump? Mr. Moseley Sheppard was probably still sleeping, his toes looking out from under the sheet, but bacon was frying in the kitchen and Ben thought he had better go up and wake him now.

# *Two*

MR. THOMAS PROSSER was waiting beside a water oak in the low field when the sky flushed that morning. His lips were soiled with snuff; his pippin cheeks were bright. He had on a wig, a three-cornered hat and a pair of riding breeches, but he had neglected his shirt, and he stood expanding a hairy chest in the dewy air and smiting his boot with the firm head of a riding whip. His horse whinnied and pawed the earth.

Some Negroes were already in the field hoeing. Old Bundy came over a knoll, crossed a meadow and climbed a fence. Still toiling with the fat jug, he got in a corn row and followed it. His legs seemed less and less secure.

Mr. Thomas Prosser flung himself into the saddle, drove his horse up to the end of the corn. The lines around his mouth and eyes tightened. A worthless old scavenger, that Bundy. Too old for hard work, too trifling and unreliable for lighter responsibilities. Not worth his keep. No better'n a lame mule. And here coming home from God knows where with a jug of rum as big as himself.

Old Bundy saw something coming and veered away, his arm thrown up to protect his head. He saw it again and started side-stepping. He dropped the jug, threw the other hand up and felt the butt end of a riding whip on his elbow. His arms became suddenly paralyzed. Again he veered anxiously. This time he went down on his knees in a clump of rank polk and began crying like a child.

The jug rolled into the corn row without loosing its cork. The Negroes, hoeing in another field, raised their heads, their faces wrenched with agony. Somewhere the thrashers called. The Negroes cupped their hands, whispered through the tall corn.

Something struck Bundy's head. Was it the horse or the man? Both were above him now; both showed him clinched teeth. Bundy regained his feet and made a leap for the bridle. He grasped something, something. . . . But there was darkness now.

Old Bundy's eyes were open, but he didn't see. His mouth was open, and his face had a tortured look, but he said nothing.

Mr. Thomas Prosser was obliged to use his foot to break the critter's grip on the stirrup. Was Bundy trying to resist? The old sway-backed mule. The lick-spittle scavenger. Well, take that. And here is some more. This. And this.

Yes, suh, Marse Prosser, I'm taking it all. I can't prance and gallop no mo'; I'm 'bliged to take it. Yo' old sway-backed mule —that's me. Can't nobody lay it on like you, Marse Prosser, and don't nobody know it better'n me. Me and my jug has a hard time with you, a hard time. That jug done got to be bad luck for a fact. Every time I puts it under my arm I meets trouble. Lordy, me. Ain't that 'nough, Marse Prosser? Ain't you done laid on 'nough for this one time? You see me crumpled up here in the bushes. Howcome you keeps on hitting? Howcome you keeps on hitting me around the head, Marse Prosser? I won't be no mo' good to you directly. Lordy, what was that? Felt like a horse's foot. Lordy. . . .

# *Three*

THE colt called Araby kicked up his heels in the deep clover. He swept his lowered head over the sweet green surf that broke and foamed about his knees and struck across the field in a joyous race with his shadow. He was as glossy and black as anthracite; his legs, still a trifle long for his body, twinkled in the sunlight. After the fetid stable, the stale straw for a bed and the damp planks underfoot, after the dark indoor prison and the days and weeks of longing at a tiny window, the meadow seemed too good to be true. He bounded again, inscribed a huge circle in the fine gritty turf and came back to the whitewashed gate, the water trough and the cake of salt under the chestnut tree.

The young coachman in varnished hat, high boots and tailed coat turned toward the barn, the halter in his hand. Then he paused, put his foot on the gate again. That jet colt was happiness itself, pure joy let loose. The coachman shook his head. His own eyes were wretched; old Bundy was dying.

"That's all right for you, Araby," Gabriel said. "You ain't a horse yet, and you ain't a nigger neither. That's mighty fine for you, feeling yo' oats and trying to out-run the wind. You don't know nothing yet. Was you a white colt, I reckon I'd have to call you *mister* Araby."

He took a lump of sugar from a pocket in his coat tail and held it between the crosspieces of the gate. Araby's lips touched the immense boyish hand. Gabriel could have cried with melancholy pleasure at the sudden feeling of this confidence, but instead he smiled.

"Nothing like that," he said. "Get on back there in the clover, you and them monstrous flies. I'm got to drive Marse Prosser to town directly."

The horses were hitched, waiting in the door of the carriage room. Taking Araby to the meadow had been an afterthought. Gabriel was fond of the colt. Criddle, the stable boy, would never have thought of it; he was too busy pitching manure out the back window. His little stupid head was a bullet; his eyes were no more than the white spots on a domino.

All about the place Negroes were whispering. They stood in pairs behind the stable, under the low trees, in the tobacco rows, bowed till their corncob pipes nearly touched, cupped their hands and whispered.

High on the driver's seat Gabriel gave the lines a twitch. He was almost a giant for size, but his head was bowed. The tall shiny hat seemed ready to fall on his knees at any minute. One leg hanging loosely beside the footboard gave a suggestion of his extraordinary length. His features were as straight as a Roman's, but he was not a mulatto. He was just under twenty-four and the expression of hurt pride that he wore was in keeping with his years and station. He was too old for joy, as a slave's life went in Henrico County, Virginia, too young for despair as black men despaired in 1800. The gleaming golden horses were out from under the shed with a leap. The newly painted carriage flashed on the gravel path.

The tallest of three uncommonly tall brothers, Gabriel was also what they considered a man of destiny. His reputation was about a year old. It dated from an encounter with Ditcher, Negro "driver" on a near-by plantation.

Long before, Solomon and Ditcher had fought. Gabriel was fifteen then, but he remembered well the fierce struggle his oldest brother put up against the powerful barrel-chested black that ruled the Bowler slaves in the place of the usual white overseer. He remembered the shiver of powerful muscles and the blowing of powerful nostrils near the ground, and he remembered the thuds of blows in the darkness after night fell on the contest. Finally, too, he remembered how they brought Solomon home unconscious.

Three years later Martin, the second brother, met Ditcher in the clump of trees behind the barn. He and Ditcher were nearer the same age, but Martin didn't last as long as did Solomon against the roaring beast. Two or three years passed, and it was Gabriel's turn, the third of the Prosser giants.

Ditcher, naked to the waist, came to the little grove in the twilight. He carried a whip that had been in his hand all day; and when Gabriel approached him in the clearing, straight and unflinching, he tossed it on the ground and slapped his great chest with a proud air. They locked mighty grips. Again there was that wanton display of strength. Again the muscles tightening till they shivered and the two giants tumbling on the ground.

A score of round-eyed blacks encircled the two. For them the earth rocked. The stars shook like lamps swinging in a storm. They thought: Them three big Prosser boys is *some* pun'kins, and this here Gabriel is just too fine to talk about, but that there Ditcher ain't no man: he's a demon. Yet and still, Gabriel ain't scairt of devils or nothing else, he ain't. Look a-yonder. God bless me, he's giving Ditcher the time of his life.

Suddenly Gabriel shook himself free and sprang to his feet. Ditcher rose slowly. The tide had turned. Gabriel leaped to the attack with a bitter grin on his boyish face. He showered blows on the demon that had whipped his two older brothers. It couldn't last. Ditcher curled up on the ground, and the Bowler crowd carried him home, snickering and giggling as they crossed the fields. One of the youngsters took the whip for a plaything.

"That there Gabriel can whup anything on two feet," an old man said. "He ain't biggity neither."

Gabriel didn't like to think about it any more, because he and Ditcher were friends now. Ditcher wasn't really mean; he simply had a loud ugly way of talking and doing things. He had been somewhat spoiled by the feeling of authority. But Ditcher could be depended on to stand by a friend. Of course Ditcher knew right well who was the biggest and the baddest nigger in Henrico County, but Gabriel didn't see any reason to talk about it or rub it in.

The horses stopped in the drive near the front steps. Gabriel's varnished hat inclined a little forward as he waited. His eyes were sad. Being massive and strong didn't make one happy. Being a great slave made Marse Prosser richer, perhaps, but it didn't put any pennies in Gabriel's pocket. Of course there was some compensation in the fine clothes of a coachman, and it was a pleasure to drive to town occasionally and to sport around in a tall hat instead of working in the fields or the shop. These were compensations, but they were brief, very brief.

Beyond the tall columns the door swung open. A lackey

with white stockings stepped out first and stood bowing till the master followed. The pippin-cheeked man with three-cornered hat, knee breeches, a white wig and a cane under his arm came down the path fingering a small sheaf of papers.

"I'm going to the notary first, Gabriel."

"Yes, suh."

"Walk the horses. I have some things to read over."

"H'm."

Having only recently inherited the plantation on the outskirts of Richmond, Mr. Thomas Prosser seemed endlessly occupied with legal papers and long conversations at the notary's office. And it may have been, Gabriel imagined, that these concerns were responsible for his curt manners and quick flashes of indignation. At any rate, he was a hard man to serve.

The morning sun mounted. There were grouse dusting in the road and bluejays annoying squirrels in the low branches of trees. A swarm of sparrows covered a green coppice like flies on a carcass. The horses were eager to be gone; at first Gabriel had to hold them in check. Marse Prosser was still fingering his papers, still belching periodically and periodically snapping the top of his snuffbox.

The road went over a hill and down along the edge of a creek. Later it found another rise and beyond that some green slopes and low fields. At best it gave a jolting ride; but it did not stop the flutter of Mr. Thomas Prosser's papers; it failed even to topple the coachman's varnished hat. In time Gabriel was so deeply absorbed by his daydream that his chin fell against his shirt front, the reins fell slack in his hands and he awakened to hear Marse Prosser shouting in his ears.

"Are you asleep there, billy goat? Or are you trying to turn the carriage over?"

"Nah, suh," Gabriel murmured in a deep voice. "I ain't going to turn you over, Marse Prosser."

"Well, if you can't keep those horses in the road, I have a cane here that I can bloody well teach you with."

"Yes, suh."

Gabriel got his wheels out of the ditch promptly. He drew himself more erect in the seat.

"You can let them take a trot from here in."

"H'm."

*

The streets had a quiet air in the forenoon. Richmond's six or seven thousand people were so scattered the town seemed even smaller than it was for population. Shops were doing a slow business here and there; carriages and saddle horses were tied at hitching bars, and little groups of free blacks and poor whites lolled at the public watering troughs and under the oak trees. There were slaves too, trusted family servants going through the town on errands, the males trotting in the dusty streets, carrying little mashed-up hats in their hands, the women balancing huge baskets on their heads, slapping their bare feet in the footpaths.

There was always the hum of fiddles at the dancing school and the flutter of clean, crisp-looking children in crinolins with pompous black attendants. The dancing master was a Frenchman, as was also his friend the printer, whose shop attracted Gabriel while he waited for Marse Prosser to complete his conversations with the notary.

M. Creuzot had a visitor, and the two were talking very rapidly and in deep earnestness. The rather young visitor wore thick-lensed glasses; he was short and dark and his hair was thick. M. Creuzot was tall and fair and his hair was thin. The printer had also a hoarseness in his throat and a perpetual cough on his chest. He shook a long nervous finger before his face as he talked.

Gabriel walked over to the window where M. Creuzot's red-haired shop boy was setting type so fast it was scarcely possible to follow his fingers. The boy had moved a case and his copy near the window in order to enjoy the better light and the suggestion of a breeze outside. He did not seem interested in the conversation of M. Creuzot and his Philadelphia visitor. But Gabriel, his eyes on the plump red-haired fellow, was innocent of letters and interested only in the words of the other men.

Presently M. Creuzot grew tired, his voice weak.

"Here in Richmond," he said with an accent, "I am an outsider. I am not trusted too far."

"I know," the younger man said. "I know."

"They have catalogued me with the radicals for some reason. I don't know why. I never talk."

"They have heard of Sonthonaz and the *Amis des Noirs*."

"It is an inconvenience," M. Creuzot said.

They paused. There were blue shadows outside the back window. Through the front, yellow sunlight slanted in shafts. After a while Alexander Biddenhurst said vigorously, "The equality of man—there's the pill. You had the filthy nobles in France. Here we have the planter aristocrats. We have the merchants, the poor whites, the free blacks, the slaves—classes, classes, classes. . . . I tell you, M. Creuzot, the whole world must know that these are not natural distinctions but artificial ones. Liberty, equality and fraternity will have to be won for the poor and the weak everywhere if your own revolution is to be permanent. It is for us to awaken the masses."

"Perhaps," said M. Creuzot weakly. "Perhaps. I do not say. It baffles me. I have read Mr. Jefferson's *Notes on Virginia*, and I understand that Judge Tucker, here at William and Mary College, makes a strong proposal for gradual abolution in his *Dissertation on Slavery*, but it all seems hopeless in this country."

"Never say hopeless, M. Creuzot. Even now the blacks are whispering."

"Perhaps not hopeless entirely. But the blacks are *always* whispering. It baffles me."

"The trouble is that those statesmen you named do not go far enough in the direction they indicate."

They were all just words, but they put gooseflesh on Gabriel's arms and shoulders. He felt curiously tremulous. Standing at the window he felt one chill after another run along his spine. He knew that he was delaying longer than he should, but his feet were planted. He was as helpless as a man of wood. He stood facing the funny little typesetter but seeing nothing; he was bewitched. Here were words for things that had been in his mind, things that he didn't know had names. Liberty, equality, frater—it was a strange music, a strange music. And was it true that in another country white men fought for these things, died for them? Gabriel reeled a trifle, but his feet were hopelessly fastened. So they had noticed the blacks whispering, had they?

The men talked on. After a while the young man from Philadelphia came out, slapped the immense Negro on the shoulder and pointed to the typesetter.

"Would you like to learn things like that?"

Gabriel came out of his trance. He managed to get turned around so that he faced the carelessly dressed visitor.

"I reckon I would, suh. I reckon so."

"Are you a free man?"

Gabriel's shoulders rounded, his arms hung a bit in front of his body, the tall hat tilted forward on his head.

"No." His head went lower. "I ain't free."

Young Mr. Biddenhurst looked at him a long time in silence, looked up at the great stature, the powerful shoulders, looked at the sober melancholy face.

"That's a pity. Listen. Peep in the wine shop by the river bridge some time. I do my reading there. I'll buy you a drink, maybe."

When he had turned away, Gabriel felt the hand on his shoulder again. He was so embarrassed by the white man's attention he could not speak. He was now thinking about Marse Prosser and the danger of keeping him waiting, but that was a small thing as compared to Mr. Biddenhurst's astonishing words.

M. Creuzot went back to the form he was making up on the flat stone in the corner. The red-haired boy threw a glance or two out of the window, but he had not interrupted his work. Across the street and down a few paces the fiddles were still humming. They were upstairs over a tailoring establishment, and there were young girls, dancing pupils, at the windows with fans. Downstairs two black crones sat on a stone smoking corncob pipes. Others, like them, were leaning against carriage wheels, giggling with the glossy males who held the horses. Alexander Biddenhurst carried a book under his arm, but he wore no hat. His long natural hair looked odd and wild, and he walked with a sharp step. Gabriel went the other way, staggering.

Marse Prosser was walking back and forth beside his carriage, the sheaf of papers in one hand, his cane in the other. Gabriel came up like a drunken man.

"You left the horses, fool."

"They wa'n't fidgety. I just walked a little piece."

"But you kept me *waiting*. I'll teach you to gad around when I'm on business. There. Let that be a lesson to you. And that."

Twice the cane whistled. Once it fell on Gabriel's arm, the

second time across the side of his face. He raised his head slowly. Something tightened in his shoulders.

"Yes, suh. Yes, suh, Marse Prosser."

Mr. Thomas Prosser took a pinch of snuff and climbed to his seat. His pippin cheeks were no redder than they had been, but his three-cornered hat and the wig under it were sitting a bit off kilter. Gabriel took his place and gave the driving lines a jerk. For some reason he felt less wretched than he had felt earlier. Marse Prosser's licks didn't actually hurt him much; even though they left a long welt on his arm and another on his face, they were really nothing.

# *Four*

M. CREUZOT's shop apron suggested a huge penwiper. It was inked so thoroughly he must have long ago despaired of making a new smear on a fresh spot. Had the cloth been black from the beginning, the effect might have been less like a stipple job now, but the garment could hardly have been more completely darkened. He stood at the window rubbing his fingers on it sadly and looking out at the shaded street— stood and rubbed as if his sadness were occasioned by his failure to make another impression on the hopeless apron.

Once, apparently, he had chosen to wipe his hands on his cheek, and there he had been more successful. A vivid three-fingered smudge ran downward, reached his chin. But this did not reassure M. Creuzot's despondent eyes. They were as melancholy as if the whole world were blackened and all smears made.

Not that M. Creuzot pined to besmear the earth actually— possibly the picture suggests too much. M. Creuzot longed to see justice prevail. He had come to the new world before the storm broke in his former home, but he had been deeply stirred by the triumph of the third estate, and he often cried in his heart for another sight of the little singing village he had left too soon. In this city where he was not trusted, where the poor man was as wretched as a feudal serf, he stood at his window, hearing violins that seemed to be playing in the branches of the trees across the street, seeing poverty-stricken youngsters flee before the approach of proud horses on the cobblestones, and felt sick for another breath of Norman air, for another night in a little stone house he remembered and another stroll in a field of tiny haycocks.

Yet he did not think, as did the young man with the bushy hair, the thick-lensed spectacles and the copy of the *Dictionnaire Philosophique* under his arm, that there was hope for the masses in Virginia, that white and black workers, given a torch, could be united in a quest. He could not feel hopeful or buoyant as did Alexander Biddenhurst. His own head was usually low. Perhaps, he thought, it was because of his lungs, that confounded barking cough, that persistent rattle in his chest. There were many who said that a man's thoughts could make him ill; perhaps it was also true that a man's illness could corrupt his thoughts. M. Creuzot turned to the pudgy red-haired boy who was no longer standing before the case of type.

"Have you finished that galley, Laurent?"

"Yes, sir. This is the last."

Even as he spoke he was removing the type from his stick, balancing the orderly pile between his fingers.

"Good. Perhaps I can read the proof before the children bring my lunch."

"I'll take it directly."

The boy inked the type with a small hand roller, took an impression and brought it to the pale man. M. Creuzot moved a stool to the window.

"This is very clear. You might make another one, though, so that we can compare our corrections."

"Yes, sir."

They read a few moments in silence, M. Creuzot on his stool, Laurent standing with his elbows on the sill. Suddenly the older man looked up astonished.

"Something's wrong. This doesn't make sense."

"Where's that?"

"Between the third and forth paragraphs. He is giving here instances in which great fish have been known to swallow men, in support of the Jonah legend, and then in the next sentence he is speaking of the various ranks of angels."

"I followed copy."

"Yes? Where is that copy?"

The fat, round-faced boy gathered all the scattered pages, assembled them and handed them to M. Creuzot.

"It was all hard to follow."

"Yes, these pamphlet-writing preachers are generally as incoherent as they are dull. They write like schoolboys."

"I thought perhaps the fault was mine."

"Just partly, Laurent. Your wits are normal, but it may be true that some spiritual things elude you for *other* reasons."

The boy became intensely red. He dropped his eyes as he tried to smile.

"I hadn't thought I was so wicked as all that."

M. Creuzot looked up with a twinkle.

"Perhaps not. Perhaps I misjudged you. But, seriously, if pamphlet-writing clergymen are no credit to letters, they *are* a boon to printers. Here—just what I thought—there *is* a page missing."

"I didn't discover it."

"The pages were unnumbered when we got them. I suppose you had better run over there and ask the Rev. Youngblood if he can supply the other sheet."

Laurent looked out at the sun. It stood almost directly above the street.

"Shall I eat my lunch first?"

"I'd rather not. I can work while you eat if you go now."

The boy put an absurd little round cap on his head and went out, walking reluctantly. The stockings he wore with his knee breeches had been white. They were dust-colored now, and there were holes in them, and they had a tendency to wrinkle on his legs.

On his stool at the window M. Creuzot smiled without mirth and gave his thought once more to the pages in his hand.

The youngsters André and Jean were as dark and rugged as Tartars and nothing at all like M. Creuzot; nothing, that is, except that André was inclined to be a trifle tall for his years and that Jean's eyes were bluish. The little heavy fellow carried the lunch in a basket, and André brought a warm dish with a cover and the bottle of wine, and each had a hoop that he was not able to roll because his hands were too full.

"Papa, there's something here that will surprise you. May I have a little taste of it?"

"Now, what is that? What have you brought that you want to eat from me, little pig?"

"He had one already," André said. "They're tarts."

"Mine was awfully small," Jean protested. "May I have just a taste of yours? You have two big ones."

M. Creuzot uncovered the small basket and divided one of his tarts between his sons. Then he spread the lunch on the stone make-up table in the corner and sat down and blessed himself. The boys went past the window slapping their hoops with one hand, clasping the fragments of their dainty in the other. M. Creuzot coughed behind his napkin, munched his bread sullenly and at intervals drank from the bottle.

For some reason Laurent delayed. He was gone longer than it would ordinarily require for a boy to go and return twice. And when M. Creuzot's bottle was nearly empty, he began throwing anxious glances at the door. He finished the mutton stew and raked the crumbs of bread from the table into the bowl. The table cleared, he folded his napkin, put the bowl in the basket and went back to the stool at the window with his bottle and tart.

A fastidious young man with fancy riding gloves and frills on his shirt-front went by on a white horse. A poor farmer walked beside his ox cart, and a barefoot boy was sleeping on a sack of meal thrown across a scrawny mare's back. There were people walking too, more of them than there had been an hour or two earlier, but Laurent was not among them. His round, moth-eaten cap was nowhere in sight; his round, pock-marked face was nowhere. M. Creauzot took another bite of his tart, another swallow from his bottle.

When the boy did finally return, his cap was in his hand; he had been running, and he was breathless. His red hair had fallen on his forehead in a shaggy bang.

"You had to run?"

"Yes, sir. Here's the other page of copy."

"But you could have gone and returned three times at the gait of an ox."

"I was detained," Laurent said with embarrassment.

"Not by the Rev. Youngblood?"

"Some town boys."

"The same ones as usual?"

"Some were the same, but there were others. They were hiding behind a fence. When I passed, they leaped over and gave me a broadside of green apples."

"Were you hurt?"

"Just a little. I ran for it. I was at the Rev. Youngblood's in a wink, but I couldn't stop. They stayed at my heels till I reached the edge of town, and I had to wait there till they went away."

"You should have led them into our own neighborhood and there returned their fire."

"There wasn't time to think."

"Did they call you a Jacobin?"

"Yes, that's always the first thing. Then something about my red hair. Some of the big fellows were really men."

"They are dogs, not men. That's their amusement as mine is my fiddle and a game of chess."

"It's a mean sport," Laurent said.

"Perhaps when they learn that we do not wish to impose our views on them, they may be more willing to tolerate us, Laurent. Even now *some* conditions are improving a trifle."

"You wouldn't have thought so had you been in my shoes a few minutes ago."

M. Creuzot smiled, took a few steps toward the back of the shop.

"I suppose that *was* a hypothetical remark. You'd better eat your lunch now. I'll set that."

# Five

T‌HE impartial sun kept its course. The first pearl-gray flush gave the great Prosser house a silver glow, and the same flush filled the chink holes in Gabriel's cabin with a duller silver. There was still the reek of fried greens, ham hocks and coffee grounds in the hut. Gabriel turned fretfully on his bed of rags. Something like a powerful cobweb constricted his arms, bore down upon his chest. He was neither asleep nor awake; he felt paralyzed, yet he continued to struggle. The same thoughts ran through his mind over and over again and he couldn't stop them. They were like snakes crawling. Suddenly the cobweb tightened, tightened till he thought the breath would go out of him, and he wakened in the arms of Juba, the tempestuous brown wench.

"Go on back to sleep, big sugar," she said. "You ain't slept enough to do a scarecrow."

"I know, gal. I know I ain't slept much."

"Put yo' head on my breast, boy. Sleep some mo'. There, like that. Go on back to sleep now."

"H'm."

A pause.

"Soft?" she asked.

"Soft as goose feathers."

"Well, howcome you can't sleep no mo'? Howcome that?"

"I can't sleep, and I don't know howcome, gal."

Her arms half-around him, she patted his shoulders and looked frightened. Her eyes were bright in the dark corner, her mouth round. She raised her head and saw the dull silver in the chink holes. There was a bitter sweetness in her voice.

"Big sugar?"

"Little bit."

"Maybe it's a yellow woman on yo' mind?"

"No womens but you, gal, no womens."

"That yellow white man's woman that they calls Melody, maybe?"

618

"No woman they calls Melody; just you."

"Ain't the place where you's laying sweet no mo'? Ain't it sweet and soft no mo', boy?"

"Too sweet, gal, too sweet. Yo' breast, soft. Yo' lips, sweet, sweet as ripe persimmons."

"Sweet, hunh?"

She patted his shoulders with both her hands, rocking a little as she patted.

"Too sweet. Yet and still—I can't sleep no mo'."

He yawned and stretched the length of a giant. The muscles quavered and ran under his skin. He saw the silver welding in the chink holes and wondered why the bell hadn't rung. There was a pig outside, rooting against the bottom log.

"Is you—" She stopped short.

"What you go to say, gal?"

"Ne' mind."

"Go on, say it."

"Is you thinking, boy?" she whispered. "Is that howcome you can't sleep no mo'?"

He looked ashamed.

"I reckon so. I reckon that's it, gal."

"That's bad."

"I know. I can't help it, though."

"What you thinking about, big sugar?"

"Thinking about I don't know my mind and I ain't satisfied no mo'."

"Ain't satisfied?"

"No mo'n a wriggletail."

She clasped him tighter, rocking, patting his shoulders again.

"Stop it, boy; stop thinking like that. It ain't good."

"You say stop, but you don't say how."

"Yo' head on my breast; there. . . . Yo' arms; there. . . . Stop thinking."

"Soft. Sweet too, but I can't stop thinking."

"Thinking about *what*?"

"Thinking about how I'd like to be free—how I'd feel."

Juba cried. Real tears came in her eyes.

"You thinking it too, hunh? You fixing to leave me soon."

"No, I ain't fixing to run away, and I ain't going to leave you soon. But I wants to be free. I wonder how it'd feel."

"The police'll get you for just thinking like that, boy. It's bad, bad."

"I reckon so, but I can't help it."

The bell rang. Criddle, the short black stable boy with the bullet head and the eyes like white spots on a domino, was already in the barn. The mules were geared. Presently there were little puffs of smoke above each cabin. The sleepy slave folks, as crochety as things scissored from black paper, crept out half-naked. Each had his corncob pipe, his tuft of rebellious wool. Here and there one cupped his hand, threw a glance over his shoulder and whispered to a round-eyed neighbor.

Gabriel and Juba came up from the creek dripping. They lit their pipes at an outdoor fire, and the girl, who wasn't yet eighteen, ran back to the hut. Gabriel walked down toward the shops.

# Six

OLD BUNDY was dying when Ben got the word. It was night again, and the old great house was still and dark, but Ben was not alone. While Mr. Moseley Sheppard and his son slept in the large bedrooms at the top of the stairs, the frizzly whiskered major-domo and the female house servants buzzed quietly in the kitchen.

Drucilla was preparing her next day's vegetables by the flicker of a candle, and Mousie, the grown daughter that did the scrubbing, had stayed to help her. Mousie was picking and cleaning greens while her old black mother shelled peas. Ben stood at the lamp table blowing his breath on a smoked chimney and polishing it with a soft cloth. There was an octagonal ring on his finger. It was about the thickness of a woman's wedding band, and it kept clicking against the glass as Ben turned his hand inside the chimney.

Presently there was a little scraping noise at the back door, a sound like the pawing of a dog. Ben opened it and looked out. Criddle was there, terrified and panting, the two little domino spots showing plain on his bullet head.

"Bundy——"

"Hush that loud talk, boy. The white folks is sleep," Ben said.

"Well, I help you to say hush," Drucilla whispered.

"What about Bundy?"

"He's dying, I reckon."

"Dying!"

"H'm."

"Dying from what?"

"From day before yestiddy; from what happened in the field."

They all became silent and looked one at the other. The candle on the table gasped as if catching its breath. Ben put the lamp chimney down, knotted his brow and looked at the boy.

"I ain't heard nothing about day before yestiddy."

"Marse Prosser whupped Bundy about coming here," Criddle said. "He whupped him all up about the head and stepped on him with his horse."

Mousie turned her head petulantly.

"That's one mo' mean white man, that Marse Prosser."

"H'm," Criddle murmured. "That's what Gabriel and the rest of them is saying now. They say it ain't no cause to beat a nigger up about the head and step on him in the bushes with a horse."

"Po' old Bundy," Ben said. "He was worried about making me a mason."

"That's howcome he sent me," Criddle said. "He say don't you stay away on account of him. He want you to talk to Gabriel about j'ining up."

"I wasn't aiming to go," Ben said. "I ain't strong on that chillun's foolishness, but you needn't mention it to Bundy if he's all that bad off."

"I reckon he dying all right."

"Bundy used to talk a heap about freedom," Drucilla said. "Used to swear he's going to die free."

"He ain't apt to do that now."

"Nah," Criddle said; "leastwise, not less'n the good Lord sets him free."

"Po' old Bundy," Ben said. "He kept drinking up all that rum because he couldn't get up enough nerve to make his get-away."

"Must I tell him you said yes, Uncle Ben?"

"Tell him I said I reckon. That mason business is chillun's foolishness."

Criddle slipped away, dissolved in the shadows. Ben took a candle and went through the dark house trying the doors, adjusting the windows and hangings. His hand trembled on the brass knobs. Old Bundy was dying. A squirrel sprang from a bough, ran across the roof. Poor old Bundy. It seemed like just the other day since he was a young buck standing cross-legged against a tree and telling the world he was going to die free. He had grown old and given up the notion, it seemed, but Ben could well imagine his feelings. A slave's life was bad enough when he belonged to quality white folks; it must have been torment on that Prosser plantation.

They were praying for old Bundy's life when Criddle returned. Moonlight made shadows of uplifted arms on the wall above his heap of rags. There was a chorus of moaning voices. There were faces bowing to the earth and bodies swaying like barley.

Oh, Lord, Lord-Lord. . . . Knee-bent and body-bound, thy unworthy chilluns is crying in Egypt land. . . . Laaawd, Lord. . . . Wilt thou please, Oh, Massa Jesus, to look upon him what's lowly bowed and raise him up if it is thy holy and righteous will. Oh, La-aawd. La-aaaawd-Lord! . . .

"Amen," old Bundy said feebly. *"Amen!"*

They were praying for old Bundy's life, but there was one who didn't pray. He stood naked to the waist in the hot cabin, stood above the others with hands on his hips and head bowed sorrowfully. His shadow, among the waving hands on the wall, was like a giant in a field of grain.

Old Bundy's eyes opened; he looked at the big fellow.

"That there head of yo's is mighty low, long boy, mighty low."

"Yeah, old Bundy, I reckon it is. I reckon it is," Gabriel said.

"And it don't pleasure me a bit to see it like that neither."

"I'm sorry, old man; I'm sorry as all-out-doors. I'd lift it up for a penny, and I'd pleasure you if I could."

"It's that yellow woman, I 'spect, that white men's Melody waving her hand out the window."

"No woman, old Bundy, no woman."

"That brown gal Juba then—her with her petticoats on fire?"

"She belongs to me, that Juba, but she ain't got my head hung down."

"Not her? Well, you's thinking again, boy."

"Thinking again. It's all like we been talking. You know."

"H'm. I was aiming to die free, me. I heard tell how in San Domingo——"

"Listen, old man. You ain't gone yet."

"I don't mind dying, but I hates to die not free. I wanted to see y'-all do something like Toussaint done. I always wanted to be free powerful bad."

"That you did, and we going to do something too. You know how we talked it, you and me. And you know right well how I feel when my head's bowed low."

"Feel bad—I know. I feel bad too, plenty times."

One of the moaners on the ground raised a fervent voice, cried in a wretched sing-song.

"When Marse Prosser beat you with a stick, how you feel, old man?"

"Feel like I wants to be free, chile."

Gabriel gave the others his back, strolled to the door, rested one hand on the sill overhead. The chant went on.

"When the jug get low and you can't go to town, how you feel?"

"Bound to be free, chillun, bound to be free."

Gabriel left the others, walked outdoors.

"When the preacher preach about Moses and the chillun, about David and the Philistines, how you feel, old man?"

"Amen, boy. Bound to be free. You hear me? Bound to be free."

Gabriel did not turn. Even when the moaning and chanting stopped, he continued to walk.

# *Seven*

---

THEN the days hastened. M. Creuzot and his friend the dancing master were at a game of chess when sharp heels clicked on the doorstep. Both of them paused, looked up and waited for the knocker. When it sounded, M. Creuzot rose slowly. Hugo Baptiste took the board. The two men had been holding it on their knees, but now M. Baptiste placed it on the edge of a table. The eager, hopeful voice of Alexander Biddenhurst came from the vestibule. Laurent, the red-haired boy, was with him.

"We had a bottle of wine at the *Dirty Spoon*," Biddenhurst said. "All the blacks have the jumps. Something's up."

"It's nothing. The Negroes are always jumpy, always whispering."

"I think they're waking up. I really do."

"More's the pity," M. Creuzot said. "They are far better off asleep."

M. Baptiste stroked his fine chin whiskers with a wan hand.

"Better to sleep," he echoed.

"But I disagree," said Biddenhurst. "Think of the white peasantry, our own poor."

"Yes, do," said M. Creuzot, "but it is better to sit while thinking of them. Laurent, go in the kitchen and ask my wife to put one of her aprons on you. You know your job."

M. Creuzot pushed open the tall shutters of his living room. There was a light flutter of hangings before a frame of stars. M. Baptiste reclined in a straw-stuffed seat; Biddenhurst took a straight-backed chair, tilted it on its hind legs. In the kitchen Angelique and her small sons were laughing boisterously at Laurent.

"This may interest you," Biddenhurst said, taking a handbill from his pocket.

The dancing master read it aloud.

*"Slavery and the Rights of Man."*

"More of that stuff intended to incite the proletariat," the printer said, bowing over the other's shoulder. "Trouble is the proletariat is innocent of letters. They know of only one use for clean sheets of paper like this."

"A boon to the outhouses—that's what they are. Especially at a time when cornshucks are not plentiful."

Biddenhurst laughed with them.

"But there is a striking thing about this one," he said seriously.

"The subject is trite."

"That's true. But the gossips in town have it that this one was written by Callender."

"Callender?"

"Yes, sir, Thomas Callender, Jefferson's friend, right here in the Richmond prison where he's serving time for sedition. They are saying everywhere that he's the anonymous author."

"What a mad thing to distribute at a time like this," M. Baptiste said. "Where did you get this copy?"

"Two French Negroes, boys from Martinique, were distributing them among the free colored folks and the slaves—who probably took them for wedding certificates or something of the sort. The boys were assisted by a United Irishman. All there were strangers. The boys were from the French boat that was docked here yesterday. They have just sailed."

"Do you suppose they knew what they were scattering?"

"Of course not, but they knew to whom they should give them. I had the devil's own time wrangling them out of one."

Laurent came in with bottles and tall greenish glasses. He looked grotesque in the white apron Mme. Creuzot had pinned around him. Beyond the dining room the faces of Jean and André could be seen in the candlelight, giggling in the kitchen door. They felt sure they had made a clown of Laurent, but the men did not notice the apron or the way the boy's red hair had been ruffled. M. Baptiste continued to read, M. Creuzot looking over his shoulder and both holding full glasses.

"I doubt that Callender would be guilty of an attempt to incite the Negroes," M. Creuzot said.

"Possibly not," said Biddenhurst, "but it gives you an idea what they're whispering about. *Some*body published it."

"It mentions the San Domingo uprisings, I see."

"Yes, the Negroes talk about that too. It's one of the things that make me suspect they're awakening."

M. Creuzot emptied his glass and held it out for the boy to refill.

Then something occurred to him. A twinkle came into his eye.

"It would be too bad for poor Laurent should we live to see any real discontent among the masses here. They call him a Jacobin on the streets now, and sometimes they pelt him when he passes."

Laurent blushed a deeper red.

"That's partly because of his red hair," said M. Baptiste laughing. "But it is true that all Virginians have a tendency to associate the slogans of the *States-Général* with every show of discontent among slaves. They blame those principles for the San Domingo uprisings, and they resent the resumption of commercial relations with that country. Such things as that possibly come into their minds when they see poor Laurent with his round face and run-down stockings. He is just the type. He could scarcely suit them better if he had a shaggy beard. A Jacobin, they fancy, is an abandoned, villianous person with a foreign accent and a soiled shirt."

"I hadn't thought of that," Laurent lamented. "I'll have to spruce up."

"Don't grieve, Laurent," Biddenhurst said lightly. "The worm can turn. You may well pelt them some day."

"Let us hope that M. Baptiste and I, poor souls like us with our less combative spirits, have moved on by then. There'll be bitter days ahead when Laurent pelts the town boys in Richmond. It will be an omen."

They all laughed. Laurent went into the kitchen and returned with a tray of cheese, cold meat and bread. The men laughed again. Young Biddenhurst threw out his feet with hearty pleasure.

"Will John Adams be re-elected this fall, Mr. Biddenhurst?"

"No, I think not. Mr. Jefferson's popularity is increasing. This sliced turkey—it *is* good, M. Creuzot. Where do you shoot these days?"

"There's a bottom out of town, a place where the creek broadens and the thicket is dense. The Brook Swamp."

"Well, now, that's a fortune."

"One can't amuse himself with the fiddle *all* the time, and M. Baptiste is occasionally unavailable for chess."

"By the by," M. Baptiste said, "you were in Paris last year?"

"Yes."

"Ah——"

"One gets homesick some time, I daresay?"

"Homesick? *Mon Dieu!* Who is seen at the old Procope nowadays, Mr. Biddenhurst?"

"A very interesting crowd. Poets, musicians, artists, and a great many others who'd like to be poets or musicians or artists. They were mostly young. Perhaps they're a new crowd, a younger generation than you knew."

"Yes, yes. Of course, they are. What memories that café holds! I can remember seeing Voltaire there when I was a student in the Latin Quarter. Murat and Danton and Robespierre came too. Time flies, Mr. Biddenhurst. You do not know yet. Wait till you pass fifty-five."

"I shall not mind passing fifty-five at all if I am as nimble as M. Hugo Baptiste, the dancing master, is at that age."

They all laughed. Laurent stumbled going into the kitchen with his empty tray, but he did not fall. The small boys came to the kitchen door again, laughing hard. Laurent had stepped on his apron.

# Eight

MELODY, the apricot-colored mulattress, swept her rooms with a sage-straw broom, dusted the chairs and table with a spray of turkey feathers. The windows were open, the curtains knotted high and the shutters thrown out as she cleaned, and through the house there went an early morning breeze from the river. Her skirt was folded up and caught at the back, and her leaf-green petticoat kept turning at the bottom, turning up the frill of a yellow one underneath. Melody's headcloth was a faded red, but beneath it there was enameled black hair and barbarous hoops in her ears.

The broom, a handful of straw bound to the stick with a cord, was in her hand when she stood at the window looking down at the quiet street. She nipped a twig with her fingernails and chewed it a moment. Then she dipped the frayed tip into a snuffbox on the table and put it in her mouth against the gums.

A few minutes passed. Melody twirled the broom. She thought: He's a funny one with them thick specks of his'n and that book underneath of his arm all the time. Favors a Jew more'n he does a Englishman. I reckon he reads too much. One thing's mighty sure, though: Him and his equality of mens, his planter aristocrats, as he calls them, and all like of that is going to get his Philadelphia pants hung wrong-side-out on a sour apple tree if he don't mind out. And it's worse'n a shame, too, because he talks like he mean what he say, and I thinks he likes poor folks a heap.

Another thing too: My name'll be mud if folks start saying he come up here to get drunk on peach brandy and to big-talk about how all the money in the country ought to be divided up equal amongst everybody. The rich white folks in this here town, leastwise the menfolks, ain't going to put up with no such running on. Next time he knock on the door, I'm going to have company, full house. If I don't, I'm going to come across myself leaving town one these fine mornings.

629

The old slave called General John Scott was cutting weeds in
the back yard with a scythe. He had no teeth, strictly speaking,
only a half-dozen crooked brown fangs in front, and it was a
miracle how he managed a chew of tobacco. Yet there was always that lump in his cheek, that busy gnawing of his lower
jaw and that periodic dark spout. His whiskers were gray and
frizzled, and his butternut pants, suspended from his shoulder
by a single strap, were perhaps the most thoroughly patched
homespuns in Virginia. His old arched body was as scrawny
and shriveled as a dead oak leaf. He paused once, fished into a
pocket that dropped below his knee and brought out a whetstone with which he touched up his blade. In a moment, the
edge restored, his lower jaw was busy again, his sharp blade
was whispering to the grass roots.

"How you come along, Gen'l John?" Melody called from
the back window.

"Tolerably, Miss Melody," he said. "Just tolerably."

"Well, did you hear all that commotion down by the river
just now?"

He straightened up as best he could, let the blade touch the
ground.

"I ain't heard a thing," he said. "Did it sound like something
to you?"

"Indeed it did, Gen'l. Some of them was hollering loud
enough for it to of been a boat coming up."

"Well, bless me, I ain't heard a thing. There was a Norfolk
boat just the other day."

"I know," she said. "There it is again. Hear them, Gen'l?
Hear that hollering?"

"I'm got both ears pricked."

"Run down to the river road and see what it is."

"I'm gone already, Miss Melody. I'll tell you about it directly."

Melody's rooms were upstairs over an abandoned shop;
weeds were high on either side, and there were no other houses
near. The place had once been a grove, and still many trees
were standing, but people passed on a carriage path now, and
only a stone's throw away was the big road that ran by the
river.

General Scott snatched the tiny crown of a hat off his head

and shambled around to the front. Melody was there looking out of her little plush parlor when he got on the path. A lock of the enameled black hair had fallen down on her neck; one end of the red headcloth was hanging. Her smile, compounded not only of excitement and pure pleasure, was no less comely. She leaned over the row of tiny plants in earthen pots and watched the ragged old slave scuffling the dust on the foot-path.

Partly, General John Scott came to cut weeds in Melody's back yard because he was too old to do a real day's work in the field where the other slaves were cutting tobacco, and partly he came because his tipsy middle-aged master wanted to do something handsome for a rosy buff-colored girl. It made no difference at all to General John. He didn't have to work any harder than he was pleased to work; Melody usually put a shilling in his hand when he finished, and just a short way down the river road was the rum shop beloved of the black folks. Melody had a habit of sending him there before the day's work was done.

The old fellow couldn't run, his time for that sort of kicking up had passed, but he swung his arms gingerly as he went and threw enough dust with his excited heels to well represent a running man. A boat! Children dancing along the river. Black folks opening their eyes in the warm sunlight, rousing from sleep on the stacked boxes at the landing, coming out of the *Dirty Spoon*, whistling, waving their hands. . . . It was mighty fine. The old man's heart fluttered.

Yes, sir, that was it; a boat was coming up the river just as Melody suspected. General John crossed the road and went on to the crest of a slope. There he stood, hat in hand, mouth open and eyes fixed. The patches in his pants were as bright as stars. He had lost his chew of tobacco, perhaps swallowed it, but that didn't matter now. He was busy thinking.

Yonder she come. And a pretty one she is, I thank you. Them white sails and that rigging. They ain't giving her much canvas now, just enough to bring her upstream easy and slow-like. Them flags—well, what kind of flags *is* them? Aw, sail it, Cap'n Bud, sail it.

A finger touched General's elbow, touched it a second time, then a third. He felt it. It was just a little push, nothing to hurt a body. He didn't mind it; he was looking at the boat. There were children scampering around, and the air was full of voices. He didn't mind them either; he was looking at the boat, thinking.

There's some black boys on her too, hauling at them ropes. Well, bust my breeches, what kind of nigger is that one? Red pants fastened at the ankles like a woman's bloomers, bare feet, no shirt and a pair of earrings in his ears. And will you look at that head? Just like a briar patch. He oughta cut some of that mess off if he don't aim to keep it combed and plaited. But he sure looks sassy in that pretty boat. She's fixing to land, too.

That finger on his elbow pushed again, pushed so hard General John dropped his hat and turned to see what touched him. He smiled when he saw the huge young fellow standing beside him in a two-foot hat.

"Quit yo' foolishness, boy," he grinned.

"Was you visioning, Gen'l John?"

"Sure I's visioning. I visions all the time."

Gabriel laughed.

"That's the boat from San Domingo," he said. "Indigo, coffee, cocoa and all like of that."

"Howcome it ain't stopped at Norfolk?"

"I reckon it did stop there. What you doing here?"

"Melody wanted me to find out what all the noise was about. How you come?"

"Taking a walk," Gabriel said. "Just strolling-like."

"Where'bouts yo' Marse Prosser?"

Gabriel shrugged insolently.

"I'm bigger'n him, ain't I?"

"Yes, you's bigger, but you might ain't so loud."

"They're pulling her up at the landing."

"H'm."

"How much money we got in the treasury now, Gen'l?"

"Well, sir, I ain't spent nothing this week, and I laid hands on ten dollar more."

"That's good."

The two started down toward the landing and toward the *Dirty Spoon* that wasn't far away. There was a good crowd in the road, all hurrying. They quickly rushed past old General John and Gabriel. But after them came one who did not rush.

She carried a leaf-green parasol, and she had changed to a plum-colored dress. And when the two men stopped by the lamp post to talk, she went past them, walking with a languid and insolent twitch, and entered the wine shop called the *Dirty Spoon*.

"Money ain't nothing to us," Gabriel said. "We going to have plenty to eat from the crops and cattle and hogs and all. But you and Ben'll need a little for expenses. Pharoah, too."

"Pharoah?"

"Yes. I made up my mind to send Pharoah up to Caroline County with Ben."

"Howcome?"

"I don't trust that pun'kin-colored nigger."

"I thought he was hankering to lead a line."

"He was. I don't trust him, though."

"Well, maybe you did right. Get him far way as you can if his eye ain't right."

The ragged old man looked at Gabriel long and earnestly. His own eyes rounded, then sharpened. Now, take Gabriel here —there was an eye you could bank on. He'd stand up to the last, that Gabriel; he was a nachal-born general, him. General John's mouth dropped open, but he did not speak.

Some noisy sailors came up from the boat, went into the *Dirty Spoon*.

# Nine

MINGO knew how to read. He held the Book on his knee and fluttered the crimped leaves with a damp forefinger. A freedman and a saddle-maker, Mingo was also a friend to the slaves. They came to his house on Sundays because he welcomed them and because they liked to hear him read. The room was hot and small, and Gabriel stood in the midst of the tattered circle that surrounded the reader's chair with his coachman's hat pushed back, his coachman's coat flung open.

"There, there," he said abruptly. "Hold on a minute, Mingo. Read that once mo'."

Mingo looked over his square spectacles. A cataracted left eye blinked. He smiled, turned the page back and repeated.

"He that stealeth a man and selleth him, or if he be found in his hand, he shall surely be put to death. . . ."

"That's the Scripture," Gabriel said. "That's the *good* Book what Mingo's reading out of."

The Negroes murmured audibly, but they made no words. Mingo fluttered a few more pages.

"Thou shalt neither vex a stranger nor oppress him; for ye were strangers in the land of Egypt. . . . Thou shalt not oppress a stranger, for ye know the heart of a stranger. . . .

"Therefore thus saith the Lord: Ye have not harkened unto me, in proclaiming liberty, every one to his brother, and every one to his neighbor: behold, I proclaim a liberty for you, saith the Lord, to the sword——"

"Listen!" Gabriel said.

"——to the pestilence, and to the famine; and I will make you to be removed into all the kingdoms of the earth. And I will give the men that have transgressed my covenant, which have not performed the words of the covenant which they had made before me, when they cut the calf in twain, and passed between the parts thereof, the princes of Judah, and the princes of Jerusalem, the eunuchs, and the priests, and all the people of the land, which passed between the parts of the calf; I will even give them into the hand of their enemies, and into the hand of them that seek their life; and their dead bodies shall be for meat unto the fowls of the heaven, and to the beasts of the earth. . . ."

Mingo thumbed the crimped pages awkwardly.

"Don't stop, Mingo. Read some mo'," Gabriel said. "That's the Scripture, ain't it?"

"Scripture," Mingo said. "Scripture——

"Is not this the fast that I have chosen to loose the bands of wickedness, to undo the heavy burdens, to let the oppressed go free, and that ye break every yoke?"

"Read some mo', Mingo. Keep on reading some mo'."

"He sent a man before them, even Joseph,

"Who was sold for a servant;

"Whose feet they hurt with fetters:

"He was laid in iron——"

"Lord help; Lord help."

"Mm-mm. Do, Jesus. Do help."

"—Until the time that his word came,

"The word of the Lord tried him.

"The king sent and loosed him——

"Even the ruler of the people, and let him go free."

"Yes, Jesus, let him go free. Let him go free."

Mingo cleared his throat. The black folks in chairs, on boxes, kneeling with folded arms, sitting on the floor, rocked reverently as they murmured. Gabriel flipped his coat a little self-consciously and went to the window, giving the others his back.

"One is your master, even Christ; and all ye are brethren . . .

"Rob not the poor because he is poor; neither oppress the afflicted in the gate: for the Lord will plead their cause, and spoil the soul of those that spoil them. . . .

"The people of the land have used oppression, and exercised robbery, and have vexed the poor and needy; yea they have oppressed the stranger wrongfully. And I sought for a man among them that should make up the hedge, and stand in the gap before me in the land, that I should not destroy it: but I found none. Therefore have I poured out mine indignation upon them. . . .

"Woe unto him that buildeth his house by unrighteousness,

and his chambers by wrong; that useth his neighbor's service without wages, and giveth him not for his work. . . .

"Behold the hire of the labourers who have·reaped down your fields, which is of you kept back by fraud, crieth; and the cries of them which have reaped are entered into the ears of the Lord of Saboath. . . .

"And I will come near you to judgment; and I will be a swift witness against the sorcerers, and against the adulterers, and against false swearers and against those that oppress the hireling in his wages. . . ."

Gabriel swung around, one hand at his side, the other still on his hip.

"God's hard on them, Mingo. He don't like ugly, do he?"

Mingo shook his head.

"God's hard on them, and he don't like ugly," he said.

"It say so in the book, and it's plain as day," Gabriel said. "And, let push come to shove, He going to fight them down like a flock of pant'ers, He is. Y'-all heard what he read. God's aiming to give them in the hands of they enemies and all like of that. He say he just need a man to make up the hedge and stand in the gap. He's going to cut them down his own self. See?"

The Negroes stopped rocking and looked up. There was a glint of something bright in Gabriel's eye. Their mouths dropped open; they gazed without speaking.

# Ten

M R. MOSELEY SHEPPARD, slim, silvered, a man with a military air, waited at the foot of the stairs for his candle. Ben brought it to him in a saucer with a handle like a teacup. The old Negro bowed gravely in the shadows.

"All the black folks are terribly nervous, Ben. What's the trouble?"

Ben shook his head slowly.

"I don't get round a heap, Marse Sheppard. I don't hear much talk."

"There must be *some*thing. Why, you see little groups of them whispering under every tree. When you start toward them, they bow their heads and break up."

Ben thought for a long moment. Then he looked up.

"Old Bundy's dead," he said. "You reckon it's that?"

"Who's Bundy?"

"Marse Thomas Prosser's old Bundy. He died from a whupping he got for slipping away, and they's aiming to bury him tomorrow."

"Oh, him."

"Yes, suh, him."

"Well, I suspect that's it. I reckon the niggers are learning that Mr. Prosser doesn't take the foolishness from his slaves that some of us take."

"H'm. They's learning that, Marse Sheppard."

"Good-night, Ben."

"Good-night, suh."

Ben stood at the foot of the stairs till the frail, slim man closed a door overhead. Then he went into the front room and started trying the doors and windows. He remembered that young Marse Robin wasn't in yet, so he left the bolt unfastened on the side door.

Drucilla and Mousie were still slipping about softly in the kitchen and pantry. Ben heard the click of plates they touched, heard the chair legs drag when they moved. He was standing at a tall window, looking out through a lacework of shadows on the lawn.

Marse Sheppard must be the most lonesomest old man in the country, he thought. He must of been that for a fact, what with no mo' womens in the house and him going to bed early like he did because he didn't have nobody to sit around and drink and talk with. And it was just like him to worry hisself about a lot of niggers that didn't even belong to him and that wasn't no ways as lonesome as him.

Ben's heart melted.

And there was young Marse Robin that wasn't a heap of comfort to the old man neither. That college boy had his daddy's quality and manners all right, but he went in stronger for merry times. His heart was a leaf. There he was this very evening out getting hisself drunk with a yellow woman with enameled black hair and hoops in her ears. He wasn't a heap of comfort to his daddy—leastwise, not when the old man felt his lonesomeness coming down.

A small wind fluttered the curtain. Ben closed the window and went through the large dining hall to the kitchen. Mousie was pealing peaches, fishing them out of a bucket of water. Drucilla was getting ready to set her light rolls before leaving for the night. Her hands were full of dough. Ben went into the pantry and came out with a plate of food he had left here half-eaten. He placed it on the kitchen table across from Mousie and went back for his coffee.

"Maybe I can get through eating now," he said.

"I reckon so," Drucilla smiled. "Here, let me set yo' coffee on the back of the stove. I bound you it's stone cold now."

"You's right about that. Thanks."

There was a pone of bread on the plate in a puddle of pot liquor. A small ham hock, partly demolished, stood at the side like a mountain. There had been a half-dozen pots from which to choose, but Ben knew his own mind and he knew his own palate. Let others tear at the tenderloin steaks; let them mop up the gravy and devour the garnishings; let them lick the artichoke's succulent petals if they chose; he would bear them no malice and no envy. He crushed his pone quietly in the puddle of pot liquor and smiled somewhere amid his frizzly whiskers.

"Old Bundy's dead," Mousie muttered over her peaches. "Lord, it don't seem real."

"The last thing I heard him say was something another about rum," Drucilla said.

Ben's mouth was full, but not too full to for him to talk.

"He was worrying me to be one of them colored masons, and I reckon he died with it on his mind."

"H'm," Drucilla answered. "And he'll come back to you with it, if you don't mind out."

"He didn't 'zactly ask me to j'ine up," Ben said. "He ended with asking me to see Gabriel and listen to him talk. He didn't say j'ine, not 'zactly."

"Was I you, Ben, I'd do just about like Gabriel say do about that when you see him. That is, I'd do it if I didn't want to be pestered by no dead mens. It won't cost nothing to oblige him that little bit on account of his last request."

"I reckon it won't cost nothing, but it's a peck of trouble. Yet and still, I ain't after having trouble with no devilish hants and the like of that."

Mousie looked up sharply, her eyes round.

"Lordy, what was that noise I heard?"

"Nothing," Ben said. "Just a squirrel jumped on the roof, I reckon."

They all waited a moment without speaking or moving. Then there was something again.

"Squirrel nothing," Drucilla said. "It's upstairs, Ben."

"Upstairs, hunh?"

"Sound like Marse Sheppard stumbling."

Ben got his feet from under the table as quickly as he could, snatched one of the candles and started through the dining room. When he reached the stairs, he heard the old man opening the bedroom door. Ben rushed up.

Marse Sheppard came into the hall supporting himself by keeping one hand on the door frame. He was pale and his candle trembled in his hand. He looked like an old woman in his nightcap and his long sleeping shirt, but Ben saw only the distressed face.

"My God," he said, "my knees gave away, Ben."

"Yes, suh, Marse Sheppard. Here, lean on me. You oughta

be laying down. There, now, suh. Easy. Lean on me, Marse Sheppard, you be all right."

"Get me the salts, Ben."

"Yes, suh. Lay down there; I'll get them directly. There . . . now."

Ben darted around the room while the old silvered man lay in his nightcap. He held the smelling salts to Marse Sheppard's nose, then poured a peg of whiskey into a small glass. The old man tossed it off and leaned back on his pillow. Ben lit two long rows of candles in the room and picked up a coat his master had dropped on the floor.

"Funny, these confounded spells. I'm not as old as you, am I, Ben?"

"No, suh, Marse Sheppard, but you got so much mo' to think about. That's howcome I don't have no spells like you. I got *you* looking out after me, but who's you got?"

The old man smiled a little.

"You're a good boy, Ben, but you're an awful liar about some things."

"Nah, suh, that ain't no tale."

"You'd make me feel good if you could, Ben."

Ben was glad to hear that; glad, too, that Marse Sheppard had called him a good boy.

Drucilla and her grown daughter were in the door now, gawking foolishly, waiting for a word from Ben. But he didn't need them, and after a few moments they went back downstairs. Ben took a seat near the bed and prepared to sit up with the sick man. Half an hour later young Marse Robin crept upstairs on unsteady legs, went directly to his own room. Ben did not call him. That tipsy boy wouldn't be able to help any, he thought; besides, Robin was too young for troubles like sickness in the family, too young, too merry.

# *Eleven*

THEY were burying old Bundy in the low field by the swamp. They were throwing themselves on the ground and wailing savagely. (The Negroes remembered Africa in 1800.) But there was one that did not wail, and there were some that did not wail for grief. Some were too mean to cry; some were too angry. They had made a box for him, and black men stood with ropes on either side the hole.

Down, down, down: old Bundy's long gone now. Put a jug of rum at his feet. Old Bundy with his legs like knotty canes. Roast a hog and put it on his grave. Down, down. How them victuals suit you, Bundy? How you like what we brung you? Anybody knows that dying ain't nothing. You got one eye shut and one eye open, old man. We going to miss you just the same, though, we going to miss you bad, but we'll meet you on t'other side, Bundy. We'll do that sure's you born. One eye shut and one eye open: down, down, down. Lord, Lord. Mm-mm-mm-mm. Don't let them black boys cover you up in that hole, brother.

They had raised a song without words. They were kneeling with their faces to the sun. Their hands were in the air, the fingers apart, and they bowed and rose together as they sang. Up came the song like a wave, and down went their faces in the dirt.

Easy down, black boys, easy down. I heard tell of niggers dropping a coffin one time. They didn't have no more rest the balance of their borned days. The dead man's spirit never would excuse a carelessness like that. Easy down, black boys. Keep one eye open, Bundy. Don't let them sprinkle none of that dirt on you. Dying ain't nothing. You know how wood burns up to ashes and smoke? Well, it's just the same way when you's dying. The spirit and the skin been together like the smoke and the ashes in the wood; when you dies, they separates. Dying ain't nothing. The smoke goes free. Can't nobody hurt smoke. A smoke man—that's you now, brother. A *real* smoke man. Smoke what gets in yo' eyes and makes you blink. Smoke what gets in yo' throat and chokes you. Don't let them cover you up in that hole, Bundy. Mm-mm-mm-mm.

Ben crossed a field and came to the place. The sun was far in the west; it was slipping behind the hills fast. But there were small suns now in every window on the countryside, numberless small suns. A blue and gold twilight sifted into the low field. The black folks, some of them naked to the waist, kept bowing to the sun, bowing and rising as they sang. Their arms quivered above their heads.

That's all right about you, Bundy, and it's all right about us. Marse Prosser thunk it was cheaper to kill a old wo'-out mule than to feed him. But they's plenty things Marse Prosser don't know. He don't even know a tree got a soul same as a man, and he don't know you ain't in that there hole, Bundy. We know, though. We can see you squatting there beside that pile of dirt, squatting like a old grinning bullfrog on a bank. Marse Prosser act like he done forgot smoke get in his eyes and make him blink. You'll be in his eyes and in his throat too, won't you, Bundy?

Ben knelt down and joined the song, moaning with the others at the place where the two worlds meet. He watched the young black fellows cover the hole, and he kept thinking about the old crochety slave who loved a jug of rum. Bundy wanted Ben to talk with Gabriel, and Ben knew now he would have to do it. There was something about a dead man's wish that commanded respect. The twilight thickened in the low field. Two or three stray whites who had been standing near by walked away.

Dead and gone, old Bundy. Something—something no denser than smoke—squatting by the hole, grinning pleasantly with one eye on the jug of rum.

The Negroes became still; and Martin, the smaller of Gabriel's two brothers, stood up to speak.

"Is there anybody what ain't swore?"

Ben wrinked his forehead, scratched his frizzly salt-and-pepper whiskers.

"Swore about what?" he murmured.

"I reckon you don't know," Martin said. "Here's the Book, and here's the pot of blood, and here's the black-cat bone. Swear."

"Swear what?"

"You won't tell none of what you's apt to hear in this meeting. You'll take a curse and die slow death if you tells. On'erstand?"

Ben felt terrified. All eyes were on him. All the others seemed to know. Something like a swarm of butterflies was suddenly let loose in his mind. After a dreadful pause his thought became clear again. Well, he wouldn't be swearing to do anything he didn't want to do; he would just be swearing that he'd keep his mouth closed. It was no more than he'd have done had he not come to the burying. And by now, anyhow, so great was his curiosity, he couldn't possibly resist the desire to hear. Gossip was sweet at his age.

"I won't tell nobody, Martin," he said. "I swears."

There were a few others to be sworn. This done, Martin knelt quietly, and Gabriel took his place in the center of the circle. Near him on the ground was Ditcher, powerful and beast-like. General John Scott knelt in his rags. Criddle looked up, his mouth hanging open, the domino spots bright in his bullet head. Juba, the thin-waisted brown girl with hair bushed on her head, curled both feet under her body and leaned back insolently, her hands behind her on the ground. Solomon, Gabriel's oldest brother, sat with his chin in his palm like a thinker. His head was bald in front, and his forehead glistened. Something imaginary, perhaps the smoke of old Bundy, squatted beside the hole that the black boys had covered, squatted and grinned humorously, one eye on the jug of rum. Gabriel called for a prayer.

Oh, battle-fighting God, listen to yo' little chilluns; listen to yo' lambs. Remember how you brung deliverance to the Israelites in Egypt land; remember how you fit for Joshua. Remember Jericho. Remember Goliath, Lord. Listen to yo' lambs. Oh, battle-fighting God. . . .

"That's enough," Gabriel said. "Hush moaning and listen to me now. God don't like ugly. Some of y'-all heard Mingo read it."

He gave a quick summary of the Scriptures Mingo had read. Then he paused a long time. His eye flashed in the growing dusk. He looked at those near him in the circle, one by one, and one by one they broke their gaze and dropped their heads.

Another sweeping gaze. Then he spoke abruptly.

"We's got enough to take the town already. This going to be the sign: When you see somebody riding that black colt Araby, galloping him for all he's worth in the big road, wearing a pair of Marse Prosser's shiny riding boots, you can know that the time's come. You going to know yo' captains, and that's going to be the sign to report. You on'erstand me?"

Ben caught his breath with difficulty. Lordy. The young speaker was deeply in earnest, but Ben couldn't make himself believe that Gabriel meant what his words seemed to mean. It sounded like a dream. Two or three phrases, a few words, fluttered in his mind like rags on a clothes wire. Take the town. Captains. . . . Ben shuddered violently. Somebody wearing Marse Prosser's riding boots, galloping Araby in the big road. Where would Marse Prosser be when they took his shiny boots off him? Did they mean that they were going to murder?

And so this was what old Bundy wanted him to hear from Gabriel, was it? Did he think Ben would get mixed up in any such crazy doings? Ben's lips twitched. His thought broke off abruptly. Something squatting beside the covered hole turned a quizzical eye toward the frizzly whiskered house servant. Ben wrung his hands; he bowed his head, and heavy jolting sobs wrenched his body. He wasn't in for no such cutting up as all that. The devil must of got in Bundy before he died. What could he do now with that eye on him? Ben bowed lower.

"Oh, Lord Jesus," he said, crying.

A powerful elbow punched his ribs, and Ben raised his head without opening his eyes.

"What's the matter, nigger, don't you want to be free?"

Ben stopped sobbing, thought a long moment.

"I don't know," he said.

Gabriel was talking again by now.

"This the way how you line up: Ditcher's the head man of all y'-all from across the branch. Gen'l John is going to—" He stopped talking for a moment. A little later he whispered, "Who that coming across that field?"

"Marse Prosser."

"It is, hunh? Well, strike up a song, Martin."

They began moaning softly. The voices rose bit by bit, a full wave. Again there was the same swaying of bodies, the same shouts punctuating the song. Gabriel faced the west, his hands locked behind him, his varnished coachman's hat tilted forward. Ben fell on his face crying. It became quite dark.

# Twelve

MELODY watered the pot plants between the green shutters of her upstairs window. A lock of the enameled black hair fell against her cheek and the large earrings jangled beneath the rose-colored headcloth. General John came around from the back, passed beneath the window and walked toward the river road. There was no bounce in his stride, but he stepped briskly and walked with an air of great importance despite his hopeless rags. He was the busiest man in Richmond.

Three languid blacks lolled in front of the *Dirty Spoon*, one on a chair tilted against the brick wall, one on the doorstep and one standing with legs crossed and hands thrust into the pockets of tattered jeans. There was only the ghost of a breeze in the bright, quiet morning, but the old lamp post swayed in its place a few steps from the door of the wine shop. A tall three-master, its canvas all in, rocked against the river wharf.

General John purchased the wine for which he had been sent and hurried back to Melody's upstairs rooms. She poured him a drink in a tumbler. He stood at the head of the back steps, his mashed-up hat in his hand, and tossed it off.

"Well, if you ain't got nothing else for me to do, I reckon I'll trot along, Miss Melody."

"No need to hurry, Gen'l John. You can sit on the bench under my fig tree and rest yourself some."

He looked at her earnestly.

"Can't rest," he said. "Leastwise, not yet nohow."

She had a slow eye, that yellow woman called Melody. She had finished her sweeping and dusting, and she stood against the door in her billowing furbelows.

"It's mighty funny about you and Gabriel getting so busy all of a sudden."

"It ain't nothing, Miss Melody. Just I'm got to see a friend of mine about something another this morning."

"I ain't seen that Gabriel standing still since I-don't-know-when."

"A brown gal named Juba—that's all."

"His head been mighty low for a nigger what's got the gal he wants. You better tell me right, Gen'l John. You and Gabriel got something up yo' sleeve."

"Just thinking, maybe," he said. "Just thinking how it would feel to be free, I reckon."

"See there. You been talking to that Philadelphia lawyer, ain't you?"

General John shook his head.

"I ain't talked to no white man about nothing," he said. "But you couldn't on'erstand like us. Things ain't the same with you. You's free."

"I got a good mind how you feels," she said. Then after a pause, "That ain't telling me howcome you always keeps so busy, though."

General John just grinned a wide crooked-toothed grin.

"I'm got to trot along."

He hurried down the stairs and around the house to the street.

Suddenly Melody thought of something. She ran through her rooms to the front window and called down to General John.

"Wait a minute," she said.

She went quickly to a table and dipped a quill into an ink pot. Then she began writing hastily on a sheet of notepaper. When she had finished and sealed the brief missive, she returned to the window and tossed it down to General John.

"Mail it?" he asked.

"No, leave it with M. Creuzot at his printing shop. Ask him if he will deliver it, please."

"H'm."

She remained at the window, watching the old black man out of sight.

# *Thirteen*

THE days were not long enough now. Gabriel and a young fellow called Blue went to get Ben at night. They left a group whispering on the floor of a hut, crept silently down a corn row, climbed a fence and went over a low hill. Then, finding a wagon path beneath a line of poplars, they walked another half-mile.

Ben was not in his cabin yet, so they started up toward the big house and met him on the path.

"Did Criddle give you the word?" Gabriel said.

Ben quaked.

"Yes, he been here."

"Well, ain't you coming?"

"I reckon so. But I ain't fit for a lot of cutting up now. I ain't young like y'-all."

"Don't you want to be free, fool," Blue said.

"I reckon I does."

"You *reckon?*"

"Listen," Gabriel said, "you ain't got to fight none. We got something else for you to do. Come along."

Ben walked between the other two.

Solomon, General John and Ditcher lay on their bellies in the hut. They were whispering with their faces near the dirt floor. Gabriel and Blue came in with Ben. No greetings, no useless words passed. The three got down and made a circle. An eery blue light pierced a crack in the wall, separated the dull silhouettes. No preliminary words, no Biblical extenuations preceded the essential plans this time. Ben knelt beside Gabriel and saw the huge young coachman touch the earth with his extended index finger.

"Listen. All the black folks'll j'ine us when we get our power. This here thing'll spread like fire. That's howcome we's sending Gen'l John down to Petersburg. He's aiming to get up a crowd there and start kicking up dust directly after we done made our attack. We want Ben to go to Caroline County. Him and Gen'l John can get off and travel 'thout nobody thinking nothing. They's old and trusted-like. Nothing much they going to have to do: just be there to tell folks what's what when the time come.

"But the main plan is right here. We going to meet at the Brook Swamp where the creek go through the grove. On'er-stand? There ought to be about eleven hundred of us by then. Mingo's got the names. We going to divide in three lines. One'll go on each side the town; one'll take the old penitentiary what they's using for a arsenal (they ain't but a handful of guards there), and the left wing'll hit at the powder house. The third band is the one that carries the guns and the best of the pikes and blades. Them's the ones that's got to hit the town in the middle and mop up. They ain't going to spare nothing what raises its hand—nothing. By daybreak, and maybe befo', every one of us'll have a musket and all the bullets and powder we can shoot. The arsenal is busting open with ammunition.

"The middle column is going to break in two so it can come in town from both ends at the same time. They's been some talk about not hurting the French folks. We'll find out about that later on. But we's aiming to make one of the biggest fires these here white folks is ever seen. Ditcher and Blue is captains of them two lines, and we can let them carry all the guns we got, all the scythe-swords, all the pikes, everything like that. I'm leading the wing what goes after the arsenal. That's a touchy spot. Everything hangs on that. But we can take it with sticks about as well as we could with guns. We got to move on cat feet there and take the guards by surprise. We got to be all around them like shadows, snatching the guns out of they hands and bashing they skulls with sticks. Solomon will take the powder house the same way."

Ben tried hard to keep his lips moist, but they kept drying up like paper. His breath made so much noise he felt ashamed. He imagined the others were listening to it and judging him harshly. Suddenly there were tears in his eyes and a moment later he cried audibly, his face in his hands.

"I can't do it," he said. "Lordy, it's killing and murder and burning down houses. I can't do it."

Gabriel turned sternly, paused and then spoke.

"It's the onliest way. Besides, I reckon that wa'n't murder when Marse Prosser kilt old Bundy."

Ben sniffled and became silent again. The picture of that scrawny old good-humored ghost squatting near his fat jug came into his mind again and his flesh quaked, but he made no other sound. Then there was another man in his thoughts, too, a man whose feet they hurt with fetters, according to the Book, who was laid in irons—*until the time that his word came.*

Curiously, at the same instant Gabriel said, "This here is the time. There ain't no backing up now. Is you going to Caroline County or must we get somebody else?"

"I reckon I'm going," Ben said faintly.

"Well, that's settled. Gen'l John is carrying the money. He'll give you some for expense. We got a peck of bullets and about a dozen scythe-swords now. Solomon's fixing these in the blacksmith shop and I'm making the handles. They'll do the work."

"We need mo' weapons," Blue said.

"We can have them too," Gabriel answered. "But we don't need many's you reckon. They ain't mo'n twenty-three muskets in the town, and we ain't going to give them time to put they hands on them what they's got. What's mo' God's going to fight them because they oppresses the poor. Mingo read it in the Book and you heard it same as me."

"H'm."

They all murmured. Their assent, so near the ground, seemed to rise from the earth itself. H'm. There was something warm and musical in the sound, a deep tremor. It was the earth that spoke, the fallen star.

Ben's eyes burned for sleep. He went from window to window raising blinds and throwing open shutters, but there was no sun and the handsome high-ceilinged rooms remained dull and cheerless. Ben was tortured with a vision of filthy black slaves coming suddenly through those windows with pikes and cutlasses in their hands, their eyes burning with murderous passion and their feet dripping mud from the swamp. He saw the lovely hangings crash, the furniture reel and topple, piece by piece, and he saw the increasing black host storm the stairway.

In another moment there were the quick, choked cries of the dying, followed by wild jungle laughter. Then it occurred to Ben which side he was on, and he covered his eyes with his hand. It was going to be an impossible thing for him to do, a desecrating, sinful thing.

# Fourteen

M. Creuzot stopped in the open door of Mingo's saddle-shop. Outside a horse hitched to a small buck wagon was tied to the crossbar. The printer rested his musket and held a wild turkey up for the free Negro to inspect.

"He one mo' beauty," Mingo said, passing his hand over the enameled feathers. "Where'bouts you shoot him, Mistah Creuzot?"

"Out on the creek. I prefer duck, but you don't see many of them this early."

"I reckon not. They start coming this way about October."

"Yes, or possibly later. I want to hang the bird behind your shop here, Mingo. When Laurent comes, I'll have him carry it home."

"Yes, suh. Help yo'self," Mingo said.

"Thanks."

M. Creuzot went out into the small yard behind. Weeds were tall, and there was a rubbish pile that had grown remarkably. He tied the feet of his turkey to a hook as high as he could reach on the wall. Mingo was busy with an awl when he returned.

"How about leaving that there musket here a few days too?" the Negro suggested.

"Well, I don't mind. You want to try your luck?"

"H'm. I might."

"You'll have to get some small shot."

When he was gone, something that Alexander Biddenhurst had said occurred to M. Creuzot. The blacks are whispering; something's up. Suddenly, and for the first time, the Frenchman seriously wondered if there were reason for the observation. Actually, *could* it be? Could these tamed things imagine liberty, equality? Of course, he knew about San Domingo, many stories had filtered through, but whether or not the blacks themselves were capable of that divine discontent that turns the mill of destiny was not answered. There had been, or so he had been told, strong forces at work in France; there had possibly been paid and experienced agitators supported by groups of people who sometimes had political as well as humanitarian aims. Young mulattos had been to Paris to school and had met certain of the *Amis des Noirs*. . . . M. Creuzot found the long thread tiresome. The blacks were not discontented: they couldn't be. They were without the necessary faculties.

He let himself into his printing shop, picked up two small jobs that had been slipped under the door with written instructions and went to the back windows to let in light and air. The morning was fine, and a shaft of yellow sun fell across the room. M. Creuzot tied on his ink-spattered apron and began clearing the composing stone.

Laurent looked drowsy when he came in a little later. His hair had not been combed and the queer little cap seemed ready to fall at any moment.

"Shame," said M. Creuzot. "You look as if you could hardly drag your feet. And such a fine morning it is. Why, I've been out to the grove and shot a turkey already."

"I didn't sleep well," Laurent said weakly.

"Too much rum?"

"No, I only took a trifle."

"That was too much. Did you see Biddenhurst last night?"

"Yes, it was he that bought the drink."

"Well, I hope you reminded him that we have a note for him here."

"He said he'd be by this morning. Where's the turkey?"

"Hanging behind Mingo's saddle-shop. I want you to carry it home for me when you deliver that job to the greengrocer on our corner."

A little later M. Creuzot looked up from the job he was locking in the form. Laurent had taken his place on a stool in front of his case and his fingers were darting rapidly.

"I keep remembering what Biddenhurst said about the Africans."

"They do whisper a lot," Laurent said. "Has some one else mentioned the same thing?"

"No, I don't know what put it in my mind."

They became silent again, but after a short time M. Creuzot did conclude what suggested the thought to him. It must have been Mingo. He had thought about it first when leaving the saddle-shop. Mingo had mentioned or inferred nothing suspicious, of course; it must have been his asking to use the musket. That *was* it. M. Creuzot rejoiced to trace his thought successfully to its source.

It would surely be a grave thing for Alexander Biddenhurst, following his bold quotations from Voltaire and other makers of the French Revolution, should discontent be manifest among the proletariat and particularly among the blacks. They bore so many insults that might call forth horrible retaliation. It would be miserable for Laurent, whom the town boys already, quite absurdly, called a Jacobin. The ground might even get hot under the feet of M. Creuzot and his friend the dancing master, what with the Presidential election approaching and with the Federalist press accusing the party of Thomas Jefferson of getting its philosophy from the *States-Général* and inclining very radically toward the left. No Federalist paper, wishing to win votes, missed an opportunity to hurl the anathema of that dreaded word *Jacobin* into the air. They didn't bother to analyze or define carefully. They were glad to have the public catch the misleading implications they had succeeded in putting into the term: redistribution of wealth, snatching of private property, elevation of the blacks, equality, immediate and compulsory miscegenation. The masses were pitifully abused and frightened, M. Creuzot thought. But the fact that he had a more temperate burden for their rise than had Alexander Biddenhurst would help him little in a moment of general passion. The same mark was on him. He was sorry that he had let Mingo have his gun; it gave him unpleasant thoughts, made him nervous. He would get it back as soon as possible.

The writing on the envelope was an illiterate scrawl. Alexander Biddenhurst read the misspelled name, smiled and dropped it into his pocket.

"It is just for laughter, M. Creuzot. Nothing important."

The sunlight was so fine in the back of the shop that Biddenhurst removed his coat, took a chair beneath the window and opened his book. A customer came in and engaged M. Creuzot in the front doorway. Biddenhurst read from his book with quiet absorption.

*Man is a stranger to his own research;*
*He knows not whence he comes, nor whither goes.*
*Tormented atoms in a bed of mud,*
*Devoured by death, a mockery of fate;*
*But thinking atoms, whose far-seeing eyes,*
*Guided by thoughts, have measured the faint stars.*
*Our being mingles with the infinite;*
*Ourselves we never see, nor come to know.*
*This world, this theatre of pride and wrong,*
*Swarms with sick fools who talk of happiness . . .*
*Seeking a light amid the deepening gloom. . . .*

# *Fifteen*

The brown girl curled on the floor in front of the circle of men. Mingo sat on a stool; the others had drawn up benches, work tables and boxes. They were meeting in the saddle-shop because Mingo had said, "Never twice in the same place—on'erstand? Here this time and somewheres else the next."

"That's enough reading this time," Gabriel said. "We going to have all the help we needs once we get our hands in. It's most nigh time to strike, and we got to make haste."

Gabriel, silent and dreamy usually, spoke with a quick excitement these days. There was an urgency in his manner that got under the skin at once. He didn't talk in a loud voice; in fact, he didn't talk at all. He simply whispered. Yet Ditcher's mouth dropped open as he listened; he leaned forward and the muscles tightened on his shoulders. His huge hands, dangling at his sides, closed gradually and gradually opened again. He was ready to strike. Blue, hearing every word, pulled the heavy lips over his large protruding teeth, hunched himself somberly on his box. General John Scott, as scrawny and ragged as a scarecrow, rubbed his brown bark-like hands together, blinked nervously. Ben, wearing gloves, stood with a new Sunday hat in his hand, his head bowed. Some of the group trembled. They were all ready.

They had come into the shop through the back way. They had selected this place for their Sunday gathering because the shops on either side were closed and they were able to feel safely secluded.

"What's going to be the day?" Ditcher said.

"The first day in September," Gabriel told him.

"That falls on a Sad-dy," a pumpkin-colored fellow said quietly.

General John showed his brown fangs without malevolence.

"Sad-dy, hunh?"

"Yes, the first day of September come next Sad-dy," Ben said.

"I's just thinking," the yellow Negro muttered. "I's just thinking it might be better to strike on a Sunday."

"Howcome that?" Gabriel asked.

"Well, it's just like today. The country folks can leave home and travel mo' better on a Sunday. Nobody's going to ask where they's going or if they's got a note. That's what I's thinking. Sunday's a mo' better day for the back-country folks to get together."

"We don't need none of them what lives that far in the country—not right now nohow. We done set Sad-dy for the day and Sad-dy it's going to be—hear? We got all the mens we need to hit the first lick right round here close."

"Well, I reckon maybe that's right too. That other was just something what come in my head."

"This what *you* got to remember, Pharoah: You's leaving for Caroline County with Ben next Sad-dy evening. You can send word up by the boys going that a-way so everything'll be in shape. We going to write up something like that what Mingo read from Toussaint, soon's we get our power, and you ain't got to do nothing up there but spread the news. Them's all our brothers. I bound you they'll come when they hears the proclamation."

"H'm. They'll come," General John said. "They'll come soon's they hears what we's done."

Ben turned the new Sunday hat round and round in his hands. He was nervous and tremulous again. He turned General John's words in his mind: They'll come. Anything wants to be free. Well, Ben reckoned so; yet and still, it seemed like some folks was a heap mo' anxious about it than others. It was true that they were brothers—not so much because they were black as because they were the outcasts and the unwanted of the land—and for that reason he followed against his will. Then, too, there was old Bundy buried in the low field and that something else that squatted by the hole where he lay.

"They'll come," Ben echoed weakly. "Anything wants to be free—I reckon."

"You mighty right," Gabriel whispered. "Some of y'-all can commence leaving now. Remember just two by two, and don't go till the ones in front of you is had time to get round the square. That's right, Criddle, you and George. You two go first. Ben and Pharoah—you next. Keep moving and don't make no fuss."

Now they were getting away slowly. They were slipping down the ally by twos and the saddle-shop was emptying gradually. Gabriel stood above the thin-waisted brown girl, his foot on the edge of the bench, one elbow on his knee.

"It's a man's doings, Juba. You ain't obliged to keep following along."

"I hears what you say."

"The time ain't long, and it's apt to get worse and worser."

"H'm."

"And it's going to be fighting and killing till you can't rest, befo' it's done."

"I know," she said.

"And you still wants to follow on?"

"Yes."

"Well, it ain't for me to tell you no, gal."

"I'm in it. Long's you's in it, I'm in it too."

"And it's win all or lose all—on'erstand?"

"I'm in it. Win all or lose all."

Mingo stood by listening. His spectacles had slipped down on his nose. He had a thin face for a black and a high receding forehead. He listened to Gabriel's words and Juba's short answers and tried to tear himself away. Somehow he couldn't move. It was win all or lose all. He became pale with that peculiar lavender paleness that comes to terrified black men. There was death in the offing, death or freedom, but until now Mingo had thought only in terms of the latter. The other was an ugly specter to meet.

He looked at Gabriel's face, noted the powerful resolution

in his expression. Sometimes, he thought, the unlearned lead the learned and teach them courage, teach them to die with a handsome toss of the head. He looked at Juba and saw that she was bewitched. She would indeed follow to the end. He was a free Negro and these were slaves, but somehow he envied them. Suddenly a strange exaltation came to his mind.

"Yes," he said, breaking into their conversation. "It's win all or lose all. It's a game, but it's worth trying and I got a good notion we can win. I'm free now, but it ain't no good being free when all yo' people's slaves, yo' wife and chilluns and all."

"A wild bird what's in a cage will die anyhow, sooner or later," Gabriel said. "He'll pine hisself to death. He just is well to break his neck trying to get out."

# *Sixteen*

---

THE pumpkin-colored mulatto was outside, standing beneath a willow tree near the back doorstep. Ben could see him from the kitchen window, and at first he was puzzled, but in a moment he recognized that it was Pharoah. He was a field-hand, that Pharoah, and his jeans were encrusted with earth. He was obsequious beyond reason, and he had a wide, open-mouth smile and little obscure eyes like the eyes of a swine. He belonged to Marse Sheppard, but Ben saw him rarely.

Standing over the lamp table, cleaning chimneys with a silk cloth, Ben could watch him from the window without even rising on his tiptoes. Pharoah waited patiently in the dusk, his back against the willow, his hands in his pockets. And Ben could have gone out promptly, but he delayed. He felt certain that Pharoah had come on some mission connected with the bloody business just ahead, and for that reason Ben was in no hurry.

Drucilla was at the stove, her head tied in a cloth, bowing over a pot of something she was stirring with a long wooden spoon. Presently she went into the pantry for a pinch of salt, and Ben put down his lamp chimney and slipped out of doors. Pharoah began to grin and bow almost as if he had forgotten that it was not a white person who was approaching him.

"S-sorry, Uncle Ben," he said. "I didn't go to disturb you."

"You ain't disturbing me. What's on yo' mind?"

"Well, I been thinking a heap, Uncle Ben."

"Too late to be thinking now, ain't it?"

"I don't know if it is or if it ain't. I been thinking just the same. Is you going to let them send you up to Caroline County, Uncle Ben?"

Ben averted his face. Pharoah came a step nearer, his shoulders hunched, his mouth open.

"You heard the plan well as me. There ain't nothing else left for me *but* go."

"Gabriel's getting biggity," Pharoah said. "You ain't obliged to do *everything* he says, is you?"

"It'll be better going there than staying here. It'll be murder and killing here. Up there it'll just be——"

"I don't know," Pharoah said. "I can't help thinking sometimes, though. Here. Gabriel sent this here."

"Three shillings, hunh?"

"Yes. It's the money for our expense in Caroline County."

"Kind of skimpy change."

"That's what I been thinking. Gen'l John had a roll of bills in his old raggety pockets fit to choke a crocodile. They could of give us a little mo'n this."

Ben kept looking at Pharoah and trying to make out what he meant by talking that way. But he learned nothing. Pharoah just naturally seemed dissatisfied and peeved and possibly sorry that he was involved in the plot at all.

"I reckon we can make out," Ben said absently. "When do we go?"

"Sad-dy evening, I reckon. That's the last thing Gabriel said at the meeting. We is supposed to get up a good crowd that'll rise up like a flock of sparrows in a wheat field soon's they get the news that Richmond's in Gabriel's hands."

"If we don't get no news, they don't rise up?"

"I reckon they don't." Then after a pause, "I wanted to lead a line into Richmond, me. Gabriel's so biggity he won't listen to nobody. He say I got to go with you."

"You can lead the Caroline County crowd," Ben said.

Suddenly twilight came to the trees behind the great house. The fat, pumpkin-colored Negro crossed the yard and followed the gravel carriage path out to the big road. Ben returned to the kitchen.

Ben placed the candles on the supper table and touched a small brass gong on the sideboard. He had an eye for niceties, that Ben, and he refrained from drawing the blinds against the blue dusk till Marse Sheppard and young Marse Robin were seated at the table. When grace had been said, he served the soup. This done, he hung his cloth neatly across his left wrist and made the rounds of the windows. Ben knew that that was as it should have been. He could even feel the warmth and security that came to Mr. Moseley Sheppard's supper table. Ben stood in a corner of the room, the white cloth on his wrist, his back against an old-rose hanging. There, without warning, the devil spoke to his mind.

What cause you got feeling sorry for a rich old white man that God don't even love? You ought to know them kind by now. They oppress the stranger, and they oppresses the poor. They kills the old horse when he gets wind-broke. Wa'n't it Marse Prosser that said it's cheaper to kill a wo'-out nigger than to feed him? Leastwise, he must of thought it if he didn't say it. He kilt old Bundy with his riding whip, stepped on him with his horse. Old rum-drinking Bundy with his spindle legs and his laughing and his cutting up. Lord, it was a shame; it was a shame befo' Jesus.

Robin waited for his father to finish his soup, and Ben promptly carried the two bowls into the kitchen. The food was ready; Drucilla was waiting, slightly provoked at the lazy tempo of things. Ben took the steaming platters out to the table. It was a routine that called for little thought. Yet in doing it he did reflect upon the trustfulness of masters who eat food prepared by servants they have despitefully used. Of course they had no reason to fear; he had heard of attempts by slaves to poison their masters, but he had never witnessed an instance. Well, it was good that folks couldn't read one another's minds. Yes, suh, and that wa'n't no lie. Ben returned to the kitchen when he had placed the food on the table. Once he came back with warm rolls and again with warm gravy, but he tried to be inconspicuous while the father and son talked across the platters and candles.

In the kitchen Drucilla's glossy round face became increasingly serious. Her forehead wrinkled.

"Marse Sheppard didn't clean his soup dish."

"No, he left some," Ben said.

"That ain't his way. He ain't supposed to turn away from no oyster soup."

"He ain't got the appetite he used to had. He ain't as young, I reckon."

"Maybe he ain't as well, neither. Them spells——"

A little later Ben went in with the sweet dish. Marse Sheppard looked at his and shook his head. Then while young Robin was at his, the old man pushed his chair back and started to rise. But something stopped him, a sudden weakness and a constriction near the base of his ribs on the left side. Robin didn't see it, didn't even raise his eyes, but Ben was by the old planter's side in a wink, saying nothing, but lending his arm and leading Marse Sheppard toward the staircase. They climbed the steps slowly, and Ben blinked with sorrow in his eyes.

He was playing out, Marse Sheppard was, like some old plush-covered music box running down. Yes, suh, his days was few and they was numbered. Ben was getting old too, but somehow he seemed to be lasting a little bit better, thanks the Lord. Nobody couldn't tell, though. He might kick the bucket hisself befo' long. Time didn't stand still. Funny too: it didn't seem long. Yet he had been a full-grown man when Marse Sheppard bought him from old Sol Woodfolk, and that was yonder about fifty year ago. Marse Sheppard had out-lived two young wives since then, but he wouldn't out-live nara another two. No, nor one either.

It was right sad to think about it all. And it was going to be hard to go away to Caroline County and leave him like this. But it would be a heap better'n staying home and seeing the crowd of mad savages coming through the windows with scythe-swords and pikes. Lordy!

They reached the top of the stairs.

"I'm going to be all right," Marse Sheppard said. "Fix the candles."

"Yes, suh."

But Ben knew that when Marse Sheppard became so anxious about light in his room it was because he feared he *wasn't* going to be all right.

# *Seventeen*

ALEXANDER BIDDENHURST hastily took the coach to Fredericksburg. Something was in the air. There was no longer room for doubt. It was leaving time. The Negroes were whispering, and some had whispered a bit too loudly. Nothing was certain, of course, but the prudent act for a stranger who had quoted Rousseau quite freely on the equality of man was to secure passage on the first public conveyance going north.

Laurent was outside, standing on the cobblestones when the horses pulled away. The stagecoach was filled, and there were other people at the junction for saying farewells. They bustled noisily in the street, waving handkerchiefs and, in one case at least, throwing kisses. There were two women with small bright parasols; they wore furbelows and little dainty hats that didn't cover the back of the head. There was a young man with white stockings and a three-cornered hat. And there were others, like Laurent, whose clothes were plain and whose appearance left no remarkable impression.

Laurent followed the footpath beneath the trees along the street. The dust was deep. It had powdered the trees, and Laurent recalled that there had been no drop of rain in more than seven weeks. The earth thirsted. Some small birds rested beneath a shrub, their wings hanging, their tiny throats quavering.

In the shop door he confronted the tall, gentle printer.

"Biddenhurst just took the stage to Fredericksburg."

"So? Is he returning directly?"

"Hardly. He said it was becoming unhealthy for him here."

M. Creuzot looked at his ruddy apprentice with a long puzzled gaze. Then his mouth dropped open. Laurent heard the breath wheezing between the older man's teeth.

"So there *is* something up?"

"He didn't say so to me, not as pointedly as that, anyway."

"He'd have no other reason to flee. He's gotten himself involved in mischief all right. Are you in it too, Laurent?"

"There is nothing that I know, nothing more than I've talked with you."

Again that look on M. Creuzot's face, that serious, intent gaze. But when he spoke finally, his voice was tired and he seemed that he would presently cry.

"Anything may happen, Laurent. They think we're Jacobins and revolutionaries. If the mob spirit is aroused, we'll just have to be ready for the worst."

The two went to the front window and looked out on the parched leaves and the dusty street. Heavy green flies boomed above a puddle of filth beside the nearest hitching bar. There were fiddles overhead, sounding through the trees that shaded M. Baptiste's dancing school.

"We're innocent, though," Laurent murmured. "We've done nothing to injure anyone."

"It's all the same. If they say we're Jacobins, that's quite enough to put them on us."

Alexander Biddenhurst re-read Melody's letter as the stage-coach lumbered over the difficult road. The dust and heat made a vile journey of it, and the large woman and her handsome daughter, who shared the coach with the young lawyer and an older gentleman, kept their handkerchiefs before their faces most of the time. The traveling bags jostled in their carrier overhead. Disregarding the faces around him, Alexander Biddenhurst read:

> I think you're right about what you said the other night. Something *is* up among the slaves. And if you been talking round town like you talked here when you was drinking I think you best to lay low till it quiets down. If anything was to happen somebody might be apt to blame you beingst you're a stranger and all and throw up to you all that book-reading about the natural-born equality of men and all like of that I never did hear no such talking as that amongst the rich white men down here and I reckon as to how they'd hate it a plenty so don't come here again whilst all this whispering is going around and if you are bound and determined to stay in town and see it through it might be healthy to lay mighty low something is up amongst the colored folks and that's a fact as sure's you born. I never before seen them carrying on like now and I'm scared a little myself so don't come here again till it all blows over. Somebody is apt to start looking at me funny too. . . .

Biddenhurst folded his arms tightly when he settled back into his seat. If the town boys pelted Laurent with green apples and called him Jacobin just because he was a Frenchman with red hair, the men were likely to have little mercy on a stranger whom they suspected of inciting slaves to rise against their masters. It was definitely leaving time. Yet the signs were hopeful, in one way of thinking, Biddenhurst thought; there was a definite foment among the masses in this state. The revolution of the American proletariat would soon be something more than an idle dream. Soon the poor, the despised of the earth, would join hands around the globe; there would be no more serfs, no more planters, no more classes, no more slaves, only men.

The stagecoach lurched; dust poured through the open windows.

# Eighteen

NOBODY questioned Criddle's presence in the stable after dark. Even Marse Prosser, slapping his boots with a riding whip, went by without raising his head. But the domino spots in the boy's black face were like silver dollars now. Criddle set the lantern against a stanchion wall and crept into the next room. There he went to a loose floorboard that he knew by sound, removed it and, falling on his belly, ran his arm far back underneath and brought out a monstrous hand-made cutlass with a well-turned handle. Criddle got his hands on a whetstone, and in the dark alone he worked on the edge of his blade.

"Everything what's equal to a groundhog want to be free," he thought.

Ditcher spat on the ground in the door of his cabin. A round orange moon confronted him on a low hill. He was without a shirt, and his jeans were frayed away at the knees. But he carried a driver's whip and wore leather bands on his wrists.

"Pretty night, woman," he said, addressing the moon.

A voice in the black hut said, "Yes, I reckon so."

A pause, the earth whispering, the thrashers speaking in the thickets.

"Tomorrow's our night, woman."

"Yes, I knows. You better be getting yo'self together, too."

"H'm. *You* better be having that there baby, you."

"Soon be daylight, son."

The dreamy mulatto boy was fishing in the creek. A few paces away sat his old black mammy. The moon was gone now.

"Yes, mammy."

"I'm going to cook you a breakfast what'll make yo' mouth water, dreamy boy."

"You always cooks good, mammy."

Silence, the earth whispering, the water lapping the bank with a black tongue. . . .

666

"What you thinking about, son?"

"A heap of things, mammy."

"You ain't fixing to go with Gabriel tomorrow night, is you?"

"I's just thinking, that's all. Didn't you ever want to be free, mammy? Didn't you ever wonder how you'd feel?"

"Hush, boy. Hush that kind of talk."

"Yes, mammy."

Mingo, the freed Negro, locked the door of his shop and said farewell to the stimulating odors of new saddles and leather trimmings. The whole adventure was going to be a plunge into the dark, he reasoned, but at least one thing was certain— nothing would be the same thereafter. The saddle-shop, if he returned to it again, would hold a new experience. His slave wife and children out on Marse Prosser's place—well, they could count on something different. It looked like win all or lose all to Mingo, but he was ready for the throw. Anything would be better than the sight of his own woman stripped and bleeding at a whipping post. Lordy, anything. He raised a hand to cover his eyes from the punishing recollection, but he failed to put by the memory of the woman's cries.

"Pray, massa; pray, massa—I'll do better next time. Oh, pray, massa."

Mingo locked his shop with a three-ounce key, turned away from the familiar door and hurried down the tree-shaded street. Nothing was going to be the same in the future, but anything would be better than Julie stripped and bleeding at a whipping post and the two little girls with white dresses and little wiry braids growing up to the same thing. Lord Jesus, anything would be better than that, anything.

"Well, here's where us parts company, boy," Blue said. He un- hooked the mule's collar and slapped the critter's flank. "Kick up yo' heels if you's a-mind to. Sun's going down directly and it might not rise no mo'. Right here me and you parts company for keeps."

He tossed the harness on the barn floor and hurried down the path to the cabins. Fast moving clouds streaked the mauve sky. The other field Negroes were knocking off too; they fol- lowed the line of mules up the narrow path. Blue tried to imagine how it would feel to be free. He could see himself, in his mind's eye, shooting ducks in the marsh when he should have been following a plow, riding in a public stagecoach with a cigar in his mouth, his clothes well-ordered, his queue neatly tied, drinking rum in a waterfront tavern, his legs crossed, one foot swinging proudly, but he couldn't imagine how it would feel.

"About time to stir now," he said aloud.

Old Catfish Primus was busy all day.

"Here, boy, tie this round yo' neck likea that—on'erstand? It'll do the work. Leastwise, it'll do the work if somebody else ain't already put a bad hand on you."

"Thanks a heap, Old Primus. What I really needs is a black cat bone, but it's too late to get one now."

"Ne'mind, this'll do the work. This a fighting 'hand.' You heard tell about a money hand, a gambling hand, a woman hand and all like of that to help a man out? Well, this fighting hand is just the thing now. I don't reckon nobody else is done put a bad hand on none of y'-all."

"Thanks a heap."

"You other boys—you want the same kind?"

"Same kind, Catfish."

"Well, wait outside then."

"Us ain't got long to wait."

"I knows. Look kinda like rain, don't it?"

"H'm. Mind out what you's doing there, Old Primus. Don't get yo' conjur mixed up, hear?"

"Hush, boy."

"Well, I just don't want no hand to make the womens love me when I needs to be fighting. That's all."

The streaks moved faster and faster across the sky. Then suddenly there were flashes playing on the rushing clouds. Araby whimpered, his lovely head at the open window of his stall. He was bridled and ready. The stables were peopled with shadows slipping from place to place. Outside a few dry leaves were gathered up in a quick swirl. They danced for a moment like tiny wretched ghosts on the barn roof, then fled.

There was a girl's hand on the colt's bridle.

She wore a shiny pair of men's riding boots and a cut-off skirt that failed to reach her knees.

"Not yet," she said, seeking the colt's forelock. "Not yet, boy."

A taller shadow bowed its head and entered the door.

"You, Juba?"

"H'm."

"I's just seeing was everything ready."

"Everything ready," she said.

"Good. I'll be back directly, then."

Gabriel hurried out. The lightning crackled around him like the sound of a young pine fire. The clouds were growing darker.

# Nineteen

"A LITTLE rain won't hurt none," Gabriel kept saying. "Let it rain, if that's what it's up to. A little rain won't hurt and it might can help some."

Presently it was full night, full night with heavy clouds scudding up the sky.

Rain or no rain, wet or dry, it was all the same to Juba. That brown gal wasn't worried. She sat astride Araby's bare back, her fragmentary skirt curled about her waist, her naked thighs flashing above the riding boots, leaned forward till her face was almost touching the wild mane and felt the warm body of the colt straining between her clinched knees.

Out from behind the stable, across a field, down a shaded lane, over a low fence and across another field and she came to the big road. The gangling young horse, warming to the gait, beat a smooth rhythm with his small porcelain feet. Juba heard the footfalls now, heard the sweet, muffled clatter on the hardened earth and her breathing became quick and excited. It occurred to her benumbed mind that she was giving the sign.

Those were not shadows running down to the roadside, pausing briefly and then darting back into the thickets. Those were not shadows, merely. Juba knew better. She understood.

Y'-all sees me, every lasting one of you. And you knows what this here means. Gabriel said it plain. Dust around now, you old big-foot boys. Get a move on. Remember how Gabriel say it: you got to go on cat feet. You got to get around like the wind. Quick. On'erstand? Always big-talking about what booming bed-men you is. Always trying to turn the gals' heads like that. Well, let's see what you is good for sure 'nough. Let's see if you knows how to go free; let's see if you knows how to die, you big-footses, you.

There it was now—thunder. Yes, and rain too. There it was, a sudden spray in her face, a few big broken drops.

Araby tossed his head, nickered, caught his second wind and bounded forward like a creature drunk with pleasure. His heart was a leaf.

# BOOK TWO

## HAND ME DOWN
## MY SILVER TRUMPET

# One

THEY were going against Richmond with eleven hundred men and one woman. They were gathering like shadows at the Brook Swamp. Through the relentless downpour there went the motley rattle of their scythe-swords and the thump of bludgeons hanging from their belts. The ghostly insurrection-naires raked wet leaves overhead with pikes that stood against their shoulders. They splashed water ankle-deep in the honey-locust grove.

"A little rain won't hurt none," Gabriel said, his back against a sapling.

"No, I reckon it won't," Martin whispered. "Yet and still, it might be a sign, mightn't it?"

"Sign of what?"

"I don't know. Bad hand or something like that, maybe."

"Humph! Whoever heard tell about rain being a sign of a bad hand against you?"

Martin's voice faded into the slosh of water, the swish and thrum in the tree-tops and the rattle of home-made side arms. Bare feet churned the mud. One of the Negroes with an extremely heavy voice had a barking cough on his chest. All of them were restless; they kept plop-plopping like cattle in a bog. Now and again a flash brightened their drenched bodies.

Near Gabriel, beneath the next tree, the thin-waisted girl sat like a statue on the black colt. Her wet hair had tightened into a savage bush. She still wore Marse Prosser's high riding boots, but above her knees her thighs were wet and gleaming. She sat rapt, only the things she had fastened to her ears moving.

"How many's here?" Gabriel asked.

"Near about fo'-hundred."

"Some of them's slow coming."

"The rain's holding them back, I reckon."

"They needs to get a move on. Time ain't waiting and the rain ain't fixing to let up. Leastwise, it don't seem like it is."

"It's getting worser. We going to have a time crossing the branches between here and town if we don't start soon."

"You better go on back with the other womens, gal; you's apt to catch yo' death out in all this water."

"Anybody what's studying about freedom is apt to catch his death, one way or another, ain't he?"

"But it's a men-folks' job just the same. It ain't a fitten way for womens to die."

Thunder broke and a fresh shower began before the old one had diminished. Presently another followed and again another, like waves succeeding waves on a tortured reef. The invisible Negroes milled more and more restlessly in the sloppy grove.

"I don't aim to go back, though."

Gabriel knew how to answer that. He decided to forget the matter.

"Ditcher and his crowd ain't here yet," he said.

"It's the rain, I reckon."

"We got to get started just the same. It ain't good to wait. Some of them'll start talking about signs and one thing and another. We got to keep on the move now we's here. Martin. You Martin!"

The older brother wasn't far away. He came near enough to whisper.

"You 'spect it's too much water tonight, Gabriel?"

"Too much water for what?"

"I's just thinking maybe Ditcher and the country crowd's hemmed in. Them creeks out that a-way might be too deep and swift to cross after all this."

"Well *we's* here. There's near about fo'-hundred of us, and we'll go without the others if they don't come soon. You and Solomon and Blue line them up. Find Criddle and send him here. We got to get a move on. There's creeks for us 'tween here and town, and I bound you there's high water in them too. Hush all the talking and make everyone stand still for orders. Hurry. Get Criddle first."

Martin was gone, splashing a lot of water.

"What line you want me in?" Juba said.

"You can take Ditcher's place till he come. Araby'll be something for the line to follow. That you, Criddle?"

"Yes, this here me."

"You know your first job?"

"H'm. That little old house this side of town."

"That's it. Just stay in the yard till the line pass by. There's a old po' white man there that's apt to jump on his horse and start waking up the town folks do he hear us passing. You stay in the yard till the line get by—on'erstand?"

"H'm. I on'erstands."

"Well, light out then. You's going to wait there for us. If anything happen, you's got yo' blade and you oughta know by now what you got it for. Blue——"

"I'm right here."

"Get my crowd in line. We got to lead the way—hear?"

"They's ready."

"Well and good then. That you, Martin?"

"Yes, this me."

"Why in the nation don't you hurry and get yo' crowd in line?"

"Some of them's thinking maybe all this here thunder and lightning and rain's a sure 'nough bad sign."

"Listen. Listen, all y'-all." Gabriel raised his voice, turning around in excitement. "They ain't a lasting man nowheres ever heard tell of rain being a sign of a bad hand or nothing else. If any one of you's getting afeared, he can tuck his tail and go on back. I'm going to give the word directly, and them what's coming can come, and them what ain't can talk about signs. Thunder and lightning ain't nothing neither. If it is, I invites it to try me a barrel." He put out a massive chest, struck it a resounding smack. "Touch me if you's so bad, Big Man." A huge roar filled the sky. The lightning snapped bitterly. Gabriel roared with laughter, slapping his chest again and again. "Sign, hunh! Is y'-all ready to come with me?"

"We's ready," Blue said.

There was a strong murmur of assent. Then a pause, waiting for the orders. The colt whinneyed and the thin rider pulled him around so that his face was away from the force of the rain.

"Remember, we's falling on them like eagles. We's hushing up everything what opens its mouth—all but the French folks. And we ain't aiming to miss, neither, but if anything *do* go wrong, there won't be no turning back. The mountains is the only place for us then." No one spoke. After a pause he turned to the girl. "Juba, I reckon you could hurry back and see for sure is Ditcher and his crowd coming. Tell them we's starting down the creek and they can meet us at the first crossing place."

Araby wheeled, sloshing water noisily, hastened away. Lightning played on the girl's wet garment. Solomon's voice came out of a pocket of darkness.

"We's waiting for the word," he said.

"Stay ready," Gabriel told him. "I'm going to give it directly."

# *Two*

NOTHING like it had happened before in Virginia. The downpour came first in swirls; then followed diagonal blasts that bore down with withering strength. The thirsting earth sucked up as much water as it could but presently spewed little slobbery streams into the wrinkles of the ground. Small gullies took their fill with open mouths and let the rest run out. Rivulets wriggled in the wheel paths, cascaded over small embankments. The creeks grew fat. Water rose in the swamps and in the low fields, and gradually Henrico County became a sea with islands and bays, reefs and currents and atolls.

Cattle, knee-deep in their stalls, set up a vast lamentation. An old sow, nursing her young in a puddle of slime, let out a sudden prolonged wail and scampered into a hay mow with her eleven pigs. Down by a barn fence a lean and sullen mule stood with lowered head, his hinder parts lashed tender by the storm. A flock of speckled chickens went down screaming when the wind whipped off a peach bough.

General John Scott stood in a barn door with a lantern in his hand. He wore a frayed overcoat with sleeves that covered his hands and a wet, fallen-down hat with a brim that covered his eyes. His light hollowed out an orange hole in the blackness, and into it rain poured.

"Here I'm is," the old slave muttered, "'tween the earth and the sea and the sky, and how I'm going to get the rest of the way to Richmond to catch the stagecoach is mo'n a nachal man can tell."

The door flew open and a gust like a bucket of water slopped into his face.

Well, suh, if this here storm ain't the beatingest thing yet. Just when everybody was all fixed and fitten to go, here comes a plague of rain to put the whole countryside under water. Now how in the nation is folks going to get together? Lordy, Lordy. Listen, Lordy. You remember about the chillun of Israel, don't you? Well, this here is the very same thing perzactly. . . .

677

The Lord was on their side, sure as you're born, but some of his ways was mysterious plus.

Another bucket of water splashed in the General's face.

"Confound this tarnation door," he said aloud. "It keep on blowing open. This here rain don't let up directly, I'm going to light out walking again anyhow."

In a thicket on the edge of town wind raked the shingles of a small log house. The undersized cabin, hidden in a tangle of wild plum, columbine and honeysuckle, squatted like a hurt thing under a bush. A light burned inside one of the tiny rooms.

Grisselda stood at the window in an outing night dress that covered her feet. She held a lamp so that it would throw a small beam into the yard. Presently the withered voice of her old father came out of the little dark chamber beyond the kitchen.

"You ain't scairt of the wind, air ye, Grisselda?"

"Oh, no. I don't mind the wind, papa."

"Well, why don't you blow the lamp out then?"

"I was just going to blow it out, papa."

She returned to the high bed. In a moment she was again conscious of the old man's snoring. She lay very still, hearing beams groan after the gusts and squalls. Her face must have been flushed; it felt very warm. Suddenly she heard the thing again and the sound brought her bolt upright in the bed. It was a noise the rain could not make, a tearing of twigs that was unlike wind, and Grisselda knew that if it were not a living creature, it was the very beast of ill weather. She waited and heard it rubbing against the house, something heavier than a cat, something with softer feet than a yearling, a more elastic body than a dog. And the girl would have sprung from the bed and rushed into the kitchen screaming, but at that moment the breath was out of her and she could not move.

For many moments she was sitting there imagining the kind of things that might seek a tangled thicket off the big road on a night like this. A panther? A thug? Was the creature hiding or prowling? What would he seek in the cabin of a widowed old man and his young daughter, destitude white folks who were poorer than black slaves?

Grisselda remembered that she was sixteen now; she knew why a young farmer had noticed the color of her hair and why the middle-aged storekeeper had recently pinched her cheek. A lewd word dropped into her thought like a pebble falling into a well. She curled her feet uneasily, but in the next moment she was cold with fear again. The thing seemed to be setting its weight against the door. Grisselda sprang from the bed and ran into the kitchen.

"Papa!"

"Still prowling, air ye?"

"Didn't you hear nothing at all, papa?"

"God bless me, who could help hearing a storm like this, gal?"

"Not that—something in the yard, something against the door?"

"Against the door, hunh?"

She put a hand on the table and felt her own quaking for the first time. The old man murmured something. They waited.

# *Three*

I T WAS going to be like hog-killing day. Criddle had a picture in his mind; he remembered the feel of warm blood. He knew how it gushed out after the cut. He remembered the stricken eyes. Then more blood, thicker and deeper in color. Criddle knew.

The only difference was that hogs were killed on a wintry day nearer the end of the year. Hog-killing required weather that was cold enough to chill the meat but not cold enough to freeze it. On such a morning three stakes were driven into the earth and bound at the top to form a tripod. From the apex a fat, corn-fed swine was suspended by his hind feet. After a very few moments, exhausted by struggle, the blood forced down into his head, he was ready for the blade.

Criddle knew how to hush their squeals: for a long time that had been his job. It was right funny too, the way Marse Prosser always called on him to use the knife. But it wasn't hard; you just stuck the knife in where that big vein comes down the throat; you gave the blade a turn and it was all over. Hog-killing wasn't a bad preparation for tonight's business.

"I'm going to start in right here, me."

He had lost the path, so it was necessary to tear a way through the undergrowth. Later there appeared a lighted window in the house and that helped. In his bare feet and naked chest Criddle felt as drenched and slick as a frog. When he reached the yellow patch of light, he squatted silently beneath a bush and paused to make up his mind about several small details. It was then that he noticed the face beside the lamp.

He passed a thumb meditatively down the edge of his scythe-sword and derived an unaccountable pleasure from the thought of thrusting it through the pale young female that stood looking into the darkness with such a disturbed face. Yet she looked flower-like and beautiful to him there, and Criddle, though he didn't know his own mind, was sure he meant the girl no harm. She reminded him of a certain indentured white girl in town, a girl who made free with the black slaves of the same master and woke up one morning with a chocolate baby. That wasn't the kind of cutting he was up against tonight, though. Yet and still, there *were* similarities. The domino spots brightened.

Listen here, church, y'-all white folks better stay in yo' seats and look nice. They ain't going to be no wringing and twisting this night. Anything what's equal to a gray squirrel want to be free. That's what kind of business this here is. Us ain't sparing nothing, nothing what raises its hand. The good and the bad goes together this night, the pretty and the ugly. We's going to be as hard as God hisself. That's right, gal; you just as well to blow out that lamp. It'll help you get used to the dark. That's about the very best thing for you now.

The rain was almost taking his breath there under the bush. Could he really hurt that girl? Could he make his hands do it? Well, they had nobody to blame but themselves. Had no business buying and selling humans like hogs and mules. That rain! Criddle darted over to the house, crept along the rough, mud-plastered walls and came around to the door. There was a tiny ledge overhead; it offered a partial shelter. He wondered how long he would have to wait for the columns with Gabriel leading. The road passed near the house. There was a rise just above the clump through which he had wormed his way, and over it the road passed. But there were other ways to town, and the old farmer, detecting the black rabble, could easily beat the lines into town by leaping on a horse. He would be sure to hear them on the road. Somebody would be sure to talk too loud. But the lucky thing about it all was that these possibilities had been provided for. Criddle could visualize a small, ineffectual old man squirming on the end of his sword. He leaned against the door, laughing. Then abruptly he became silent.

What was that sound? Voices inside?

The black stable boy stepped back a stride, faced the door coldly and waited. Don't you come out here, Mistah Man. If you does, you ain't going nowheres. On'erstand? You ain't carrying no news to town this night.

He held his sword arm tense; the scythe blade rose, stiffened, stiffened and remained erect.

"I'm going to start in right here, me."

# Four

M R. MOSELEY SHEPPARD enjoyed a good rainstorm as much as anybody, but his enjoyment of this one was tempered by the thought that possibly it would prove more costly than he could afford. Then there was this cursed wind. Though the windows were closed, he noticed that Ben found it difficult to keep a flame on his wicks.

"Is it still in your head to make that trip you spoke to me about, Ben?"

"Yes, suh—please you, Marse Sheppard."

The old planter moved a window drape aside. Two fingers of the other hand went into the pocket of his satin waistcoat. Ben was laying kindling for a small fire. The night hadn't turned cold, but with such sloppy weather outside the house seemed damp and uncomfortable.

"You shouldn't do it, though. It's not a fit night for ducks, much less people."

"Niggers ain't people, Marse Sheppard."

"I won't argue that with you. They cost a lot of money just the same. If I did right, I wouldn't let you expose yourself like that."

"That's a fact for true," Ben agreed. "Yet and still, them grown gal young-uns of mine ain't seen me in I don't-know-how-long. I done sent the word and they going to be hanging they head out the window, looking. Since you sold them——"

"If they hang their heads out in this rain, they won't have any heads left when you come, not if it's storming there like it is here."

"You know how a nigger feel about his own chillun what he don't see much. Since you sold them gals——"

"I'm not stopping you, remember," Marse Sheppard said quickly.

Ben grinned. Now and again he could hear Drucilla and Mousie moving about in the kitchen. Young Marse Robin was in his room early for once, perhaps writing a careful letter to a pretty cousin who lived in Roanoke. Ben's hand trembled with the splinters and small wood. The fire was catching on and the pink warmth of the great living room reminded him that colossal things were supposed to happen tonight, colossal things in which he was supposed to have a part. Ben knew that by now the Negroes were gathering in the grove by the creek, the place called the Brook Swamp, that when they had gone against Richmond, God willing, they would turn on the planters and their rich harvests, their country homes. Oh, it was hard to love freedom. Of course, it was the self-respecting thing to do. Everything that was equal to a groundhog wanted to be free. But it was so expensive, this love; it was such a disagreeable compulsion, such a bondage.

Ben grieved with his thoughts. Here he was getting fixed to call on his gal young-uns. Bless God, he'd never told Marse Sheppard such a bare-faced lie in all his days. And God might take it on hisself to let a certain lying colored man meet the devil the best way he could, since the fellow was so careless with the truth. Come to think about it, all this big rain just at this time was a caution in itself. How in God's name was all them eleven hundred folks going to cross the streams going into Richmond? There wasn't a sign of a bridge across most of them.

But dying wasn't the only hold-back. Everybody had to die some time. Another thing was leaving this house. Then there was the old frail man standing at the window. It had been so long, their association. They understood each other so well. They were both so well satisfied with their present status. It was a pretty thing to think about and a right sad one too. Ben began to wilt. Then suddenly another thought shouted in his head.

Licking his spit because he done fed you, hunh? Fine nigger you is. Good old Marse Sheppard, hunh? Is he ever said anything about setting you free? He wasn't too good to sell them two gal young-uns down the river soon's they's old enough to know the sight of a cotton-chopping hoe. How'd he treat yo' old woman befo' she died? And you love it, hunh? Anything what's equal——

"Get the toddy bowl, Ben."

"Yes, suh."

Rain poured against the tall windows, rattled the overfilled gutters. Ben went into the kitchen and found Drucilla and Mousie trying to shoo a frightened bird out of the house. Pharoah was standing near the stove, his coat and hat drying on a chair. The bird had evidently come in when he opened the door. It was a bad luck sign and had to be driven out at once. Drucilla and her daughter were shaking towels at it and giving the poor creature no rest. They were still swiping at it when Ben went into the living room with his bowl of toddy.

Marse Sheppard had taken a chair.

"This is good. Did you taste it, Ben?"

Ben, smiling, set the bowl at his master's elbow.

"No, suh," he said.

Then, rather nervously, he busied himself by needlessly touching the window hangings and adjusting chairs. Mr. Moseley Sheppard drank meditatively, his gaze on the small red fire. With the second glass he put out his feet and relaxed.

"What's going on in the kitchen, Ben?"

"They's shooing a bird."

"Shooing what kind of a bird?"

"Just a little old something or other like a field lark or a swift. It come in when Pharoah opened the do', I reckon."

"Pharoah?"

"H'm."

"What's Pharoah doing here?"

"Drying his coat."

"Oh. Well, maybe you'd better tell those gals to keep the door closed from now on."

"I done told them that, Marse Sheppard."

"And tell Pharoah that's a new wrinkle, him coming in the kitchen here to dry his coat by the stove."

"Yes, suh, I'm going to tell him too."

"If you change your mind about that trip, Ben, you can keep the lights burning till the rain lets up."

"Yes, suh."

"If you go, tell Drucilla to keep them."

The two black women stood wilted and panting in the middle of the floor when Ben returned to the kitchen. Fat, pumpkin-colored Pharoah was behind the stove, his back to the fire. The kitchen was in disorder, and a chair had been upset.

"The bird gone yet?" Ben said.

"Yes, thanks the Lord. Us got to start scrubbing now. All that there water slopped in whilst George was holding the door open for us to shoo it out."

Mousie got buckets and rags from a small closet. She tied her skirt above her knees and got down to dry the floor. Drucilla followed.

"If anything give me the all-overs, it's to see a devilish bird get in the house," Mousie said.

"I ain't never seen it to fail," Drucilla said. "It's a sign, sure's you born."

"Sign of what?" Pharoah shot a glance over his right shoulder.

"Sign of death, that's what. Somebody's going to die."

"Peoples is dying all the time," Ben said.

"Well, this just mean one mo' gone," Drucilla told him. "And it's most apt to be somebody close by."

"Hush, gal."

She turned her head languidly, looked up at him from the floor with a strangely quizzical face.

"You don't believe it, hunh?"

"I ain't said I does and I ain't said I doesn't. I said hush up."

"Oh."

"Pharoah, you best throw something round you and get on out somewheres. Marse Sheppard's asking me howcome you in here drying yo' coat like as if you lived here."

"You reckon we can make it in all this rain, Ben?"

Ben went into the pantry without answering. When he returned, he said, "Maybe the rain'll let up soon."

"Better say you *reckon* it'll let up. There ain't no signs of good weather out there now."

"I said maybe."

"But what good it going to do us even do it stop raining after the water get chin-deep over everything?"

Ben put on a hat and a long cape that had been hanging on a nail behind the pantry door. He offered Pharoah a blanket.

"Marse Sheppard say keep the lights burning long's the storm keep up," he told Drucilla.

The two men stood in the doorway a few moments. They looked as solemn as ghosts. A gust of wind flickered the lights as the door opened. The tumult and agony of great trees filled the night. Ben uttered a small, audible groan. Pharoah walked behind him with fearful steps and a wrenched face.

# *Five*

THE crackle of lightning ceased in the fields, but the sky still gave a pulsating blue light. Pharoah stood beneath a live oak holding the jack's bridle while Ben climbed into the buck wagon.

"It's a fool's doing," Ben admitted. "The Lord don't like it."

Pharoah lowered his head, his forehead touching the animal's hard face.

"Gabriel won't listen to sense. It ain't a fit night to break free."

"For a penny I'd stay home."

"Me too."

Pharoah made no move to follow Ben into the wagon. He stroked the jack a few times, and suddenly a palsied frenzy shook him. A moment later, when he heard Ben speaking again, he recovered partially, but his strength was gone so that he needed support to keep him on his feet.

"We can't get to no Caroline County tonight," Ben said. "That's all there is to it."

"H'm. That's what I been——"

"We couldn't make it way up there tonight in all this was we birds with wings. I didn't know it was this bad."

"Reckon we ought to tell Gabriel?"

"I bound you they's left already."

"It ain't late," Pharoah said. "They's most like to be at the Brook Swamp yet."

"We's going to be obliged to get this here jackass and wagon of Mingo's back to town anyhow. They ain't no place to keep it out here. Leastwise, we better get it back if we don't want to answer too many questions."

"That's a fact."

They reached the big road, jogging miserably in the slush. There was still the noisy lamentation of the trees and the downpour slopping against them by the bucketful. Pharoah held the driving lines sullenly.

"Hold on a minute," Ben said abruptly.

"Whop! Hold on for what?"

"Ain't that somebody yonder?"

They waited and presently a half-naked black boy slipped from the roadside shadows. He seemed, in the pitch darkness, as if he gave a strange light from his body, an unearthly luster such as the sky offered. Quickly, without waiting for him to speak, a curious animal-like sense of recognition passed between him and the Negroes on the wagon.

"Daniel?" Pharoah said.

"Yes, this me."

"What done happen—you lost?" Ben said.

"No. Me and Ditcher was going down to the Swamp to meet Gabriel."

"Well, howcome you going back?"

"We met Juba."

"Talk sense, boy. What's the trouble?"

Ben's voice showed excitement now. Daniel fumbled for words.

"The country crowd is hemmed in. They can't make it over here, and they is scairt stiff. Me and Ditcher swimmed and paddled and pulled till we got across, and we went to tell Gabriel. But we met Juba."

"Well, howcome you going back?"

"Juba and Ditcher say tell them to come what's coming and them to stay what's staying. They's going free tonight, them. They's hitting Richmond tonight, do they have to hit it by their lonesomes."

"The others wa'n't fixing to come, hunh?"

"No. They wants to put it off two-three days."

There was a pause. Ben struggled to keep his thoughts in order. He could hear his own heartbeats screaming in his ears.

"Where'bouts you seen Juba?"

"Up the road. She was coming on the colt to see what done happen to us—us taking so long to get there and all."

Ben turned his head. At his side he saw Pharoah faintly, a shadow ready to jump off the seat.

The wagon got started again, the wheels churning mud almost axle-deep, the jack behaving like the wild thing he was. Daniel splashed away very excited. The tiny storm-ridden earth rocked like a great eye in a vast socket. There had been nothing to equal it among all the cloudbursts and tempests in Ben's long memory.

# *Six*

"Romance won't mend the roof of your house," Midwick observed cautiously.

"No, but it's useless to fight against a thing like that when it's in your blood—don't you think so too?"

Fat and red and round of face, Ovid, who had just discovered that the seat of his pants was scorching, wheeled around, rubbing the spot briskly, and gave the other guard his face across the fire.

"Well, if you fail to grow out of it normally at the proper age, perhaps, God willing, it might be a hopeless fight."

There was a plenty of wood, the fire burned well, and the stable was a luxury on such a night. Midwick still relished a dark neglected hole where he could smell earth. That was the thing in his blood; it reminded him of Bunker Hill, Valley Forge and White Plains. The most vivid part of these campaigns, as he remembered them, was the smell of the earth. A thing could get in your blood all right. Midwick was pulling on his shoes. They were not thoroughly dry, but it was about time to go out again and take a stroll around the arsenal. The blasted muskets of the sovereign state might start popping off if a man in uniform failed to go around and try the doors every half-hour. And if an unimportant official should get drunk and run into the place by mistake, he'd end his natural life when he failed to see a guard immediately, even in such weather as this. Ovid looked at the bats clinging overhead, his hands locked behind him.

"You don't really understand me, Midwick. It's a very adult sentiment—the thing I mentioned. I feel sort of like a caged thing that needs the open."

"Open country?"

"No, no. That's figurative. My blood requires adventure—delightful women, that sort of thing."

"Oh, God willing, it's a hankering after harlots. The town's got its share. And Norfolk——"

"Not ill-famed women. Lovely women. You know—young

689

and dimpled. Can't you get the picture? One is standing on a white beach in threatening weather. Her hair is loose, her feet bare; white birds circle above her head."

"Yes, God bless me, I know. I know the kind that goes traipsing around barefoot when rain's coming up and she ought to be to home, but I can't see why a family man like you would worry his head about that kind."

"You don't understand." Ovid looked sorrowful. "Maybe you've wanted to put out with a good ship some time?"

"Not much. It was always soldiering for me when I was a lad, and now it's staying at home."

"I should have soldiered. It might have cured me," Ovid said. "Now, it's my luck to cry over what I've missed. But I'm still a good man. There might be a fling for me yet. Maybe a ship. A year in the Caribbees, taverns, orange trees, Spanish galleons anchored a mile or two out, pirate's daughters left at home."

"You should have soldiered. But here, give me the blanket. I'll make a turn around the place."

He went outside. A short while later Ovid heard him talking to someone in the rain, so he buttoned his own coat, snatched his musket and followed him around to the street side of the old penitentiary building. There were other men there, but he could not see them. They were talking to Midwick.

"Stand there," Ovid said boyishly.

"The night watch of Richmond, Ovid," Midwick answered.

"Oh. A nasty night, I'd say."

"Not even fit for ducks and geese. Good-night."

When they returned to the stable again, Midwick promptly removed his shoes once more.

"They won't turn water," he said.

Ovid sat on a heap of litter within reach of a jug. A little later he threw out his feet, leaned back and tilted the thing above his head.

# *Seven*

T HAT same blue brightness flickered over the line of stumbling shadows. Gabriel could hear a boisterous plop-plopping behind him, and he could see, when he turned his head, a parade of blurred silhouettes in the rain. Juba was back now, moving at his side on the fretful colt.

"We's got a crowd what can do the work. On'erstand?"

"I reckon so. They'll do the work if you's leading. But the country folks was many again as this. We's obliged to get along without them, and that's a care for sure."

"Too many is a trouble some time. A nigger ain't equal to a grasshopper when he scairt, and a scairt crowd is worser'n a scairt one."

The leader's immense shoulders slouched. He tramped in the heavy mud with a melodious swing of loose limbs. He had shed his coachman's frock-tailed coat, but the coachman's tall hat was still on his head; the front of his drenched shirt was open.

"Whoa, suh. Easy now, Araby," the girl said, pulling up the bridle and slapping the colt's face. "Easy, suh."

The rain was whipping him badly, but Araby decided to behave.

"We can do as good 'thout the others. Ditcher's here. It's bad to turn back."

"They's feeling mighty low-down now, I bound you— beingst they's left out."

"I reckon—maybe. The rain's bad and all, but I don't just know."

"You don't know what?"

"I don't know was it the deep water or was it something else that's holding them up."

"You talk funny. What you mean something else?"

Gabriel threw a glance over his shoulder. The line was coming down a rise. Here and there, in the blur and the downpour, a stray glint caught the point of a tall pike. Gabriel led them beneath a clump of willows and discovered an immense bough torn from one of the trees and hurled across the way. He went around it, churning mud up to his knees. Araby had a brief struggle before regaining firm ground.

"You ain't seen nothing, gal? You ain't noticed nothing funny?"

"I don't know what you means, boy."

Again Gabriel refrained from answering promptly. He walked a short way, swinging arms meditatively, then paused to wipe the water from his face with an open hand.

"The line's getting slimmer and slimmer," he said.

Juba took a sudden quick breath through her open mouth. "No!"

"It's the God's truth. I can tell by they feet. They ain't as many back there now."

"Hush, boy. I ain't seen none leave."

"Some's left, though. But that ain't nothing. They'll all come back tomorrow, the country crowd too. There won't be nothing else for them to do after we gets in our lick. Nobody's going to want a black face around they place tomorrow. You mind what I say, it's going to be who shall and who sha'n't, do we get in a good lick tonight. Do we fall down, the niggers what's left'll be looking for us too. They going to find out that the safest place is with yo' own crowd, sticking together."

"What make you so sure they's leaving, though? What you think make them go way like that?"

"Afeared," Gabriel said.

"Afeared to fight?"

"No, not afeared to fight. Scairt of the signs. Scairt of the stars, as you call it. You heard them talking. 'The stars is against us,' they says. They says, 'All this here rain and storm ain't a nachal thing.'"

There was a light in a tiny house beyond the thicket to the left. The line didn't pause, however. Gabriel swung along beside the colt, his elbow now and again touching the naked thigh of the girl astride. He glanced at the light, but he knew that no stone had been left unturned. The thing for the present was to keep going. The rain was no lighter; the wind was not letting up, and somewhere ahead a branch could be heard roaring like a river.

A little later Gabriel whispered, "I'm tired of being a devilish slave."

"Me, too. I'm tired too, boy."

"There ain't nothing but hard times waiting when a man get to studying about freedom."

"H'm. Like a gal what love a no-'count man."

"He just as well to take the air right away. He can't get well."

"No, not lessen he got a pair of wings. They ain't no peace for him lessen he can fly."

"H'm. No peace."

"Didn't you used to loved a yellow woman, boy? A yellow woman hanging her head out the window?"

"Hush, gal. I'm a bird in the air, but it's freedom I been dreaming about. Not no womens."

"You got good wings, I reckon."

"Good wings, gal. Us both two got good wings."

There was still the line of stumbling shadows behind. Suddenly they halted. They were at the crossing of the stream that lay between the plantations and the town. The colt whinnied and shivered, his front feet in the fast water.

"Wide," Juba said. "Deep, too."

Gabriel stood with his feet in it. Rain whipped his back. There was grief in the treetops, a tall wind bearing down. Gabriel could see the flash and sparkle of water through the blackness. He bowed his head, heavy with thoughts, and waited a long moment without speaking.

Meanwhile the storm boomed. The small branch, swollen beyond reason, twisted and curled in its channel, hurled its length like a serpent, spewed water into the air and splashed with its tail.

# *Eight*

MEANWHILE, too, each in his place, the quaint confederates fought the storm, kept their posts or carried on as occasion demanded.

General John, his strength failing, crept into an abandoned pig sty and gave up the journey. He bent above his lantern, muttering aloud and trying to shield it from the wind.

'Twa'n't no use, nohow. Nothing outdoors this night but wind and water, God helping. Lord a-mercy, what I'm going to do with my old raw-boned self? Here I is halfway 'twixt town and home and as near played out as ever I been. They ain't no call to turn back, though. After Gabriel and Ditcher and them gets done mopping up, it ain't going to be no place for we-all but right with the crowd. Gabriel said it and he said right. Do they get whupped, us going to have to hit for the mountains anyhow, so there ain't no cause to study about turning back. Yet and still, Richmond ain't for this here black man tonight, much less Petersburg. No, suh, not this night.

He squatted, his hands locked around his knees, and gave himself to meditation. Now and again a humorless grin altered his face, exposed the sparse brown fangs. The general's mood became first sluggish then mellow.

His head fell on his knees. A little later, his lantern gone out, he tumbled over on a heap of damp litter and slept.

The buck wagon came to a standstill midway the creek. The jack fretted and presently got himself at right angles with the cart.

"It's way yonder too deep for driving across," Ben said.

"Well, what I'm going to do now?" Pharoah asked.

"Turn round or stay here—one thing or t'other."

Pharoah moaned softly, sawing the reins back and forth while the animal danced in the fast current.

"These is bad doings," he said passionately. "I ain't never seen no sense in running a thing in the ground."

"Listen," Ben told him curtly. "Come to think about it, you

694

was the nigger kneeling down side of me at old Bundy's burying."

"Maybe I was. What that got to do with all this here fool-headed mess?"

"Nothing. Only I remembers as to how you jugged yo' elbow in my belly that day and says, 'Don't you want to be free, fool?' Seem to me you was a big one on the rising then."

"Anybody gets mad some time. Freedom's all right, I reckon."

"But if you'd kept yo' elbow out of my belly, I'd of like as not been in my bed this very minute."

"You can't put it on me, Ben."

"No. Not trying to. Just getting you told. You making mo' fuss than me."

The jack whimpered and danced. Suddenly Pharoah rose to his feet in the cart, braced himself and put all his strength on the lines. The terrified, half-wild animal threw up his heels, bounded forward with a violent effort that jerked the shafts from the cart and sent the fat, pumpkin-colored Negro hurtling forward into the creek. The jack leaped again, and Pharoah felt the hot lines tear through his hands, heard the broken thills pounding the ground and the terrified animal galloping against the rain, fury against fury.

Ben climbed over the wheel and waded waist deep to the sloppy bank. He heard Pharoah slushing the mud on his hands and knees, heard him calling God feverishly.

"Lord Jesus, help. Lord a-mercy, do."

Ben felt a quick chill. He noticed that his good clothes were near ruined; and as he stood there trembling, he closed his eyes and tried to imagine himself tucked in a dry feather bed at home. But it was no good. He was wet to the bone, and that was a fact.

It was like hog-killing day to Criddle. He knew the feel of warm blood, and he knew his own mind. He knew, as well, that his scythe-sword was ready to drink. He could feel the thing getting stiffer and stiffer in his hand. Well, anyhow, he hadn't told anyone to snatch that door open and come legging it outside without looking where he was going.

Criddle had heard the columns in the road. They were not noisy, but there was something different in the sound they made. It was something like the rumble of the creek, nothing like the swish and whisper of poplars. He heard them go by, and he felt as if he were free already. He could just as well run and catch up with them now. Why not? But for some reason there wasn't much run left in his legs. They were, for the moment, scarcely strong enough to hold him up.

Cheap old white man, poorer'n a nigger. That's you, and it's just like you, hopping around like a devilish frog. You won't hop no mo' soon. Plague take yo' time, I didn't tell you to be so fidgety. You could of stayed in yonder and woke up in the morning. This here ain't no kind of night to be busting out-doors like something crazy.

And that there gal in the long nightgown and the lamp in her hand. Humph! She don't know nothing. Squeeling and a-hollering round here like something another on fire. She need a big buck nigger to—no, not that. Gabriel done say too many times don't touch no womens. This here is all business this night. What that they calls it? Freedom? Yes, that's the ticket, and I reckon it feel mighty good too.

Where the nation that gal go to? Don't reckon I ought to leave her running round here in that there nightgown like a three-year filly. Where she go?

Criddle knew what blood was like. He remembered hog-killing day.

# Nine

GABRIEL heard the murmur that passed down the line as he stood in the water. He turned slowly, put out his hand and touched the nearest shadow.

"You, Blue?"

"Yes, this me."

"Where'bouts Martin and Solomon?"

"Back in the line, I reckon."

"Call them here."

He was gone with the word, and the confused and frightened Negroes began circling like cattle in the soft mud. Now and again one groaned at the point of hysteria. Gabriel didn't doubt that the groaners presently vanished and that the others lapsed directly into their former animal-like desperation. Juba was on the ground now, twitching her wet skirt lasciviously and clinging to the colt's bridle.

"Tired, boy?"

He shook his head.

"Tired ain't the word," he said. "Low."

"Niggers won't do."

"They's still leaving, slipping away—scairt white. How we's going to get them across this high-water branch is mo'n I know."

"We could of been gone from here, was it just me and you. Biggest part of these others ain't got the first notion about freedom."

"Maybe. That wouldn't do me, though. I reckon it's a birthmark. Running away won't do me no good long's the others stays. The littlest I can think about is a thousand at a time when it come to freedom. I reckon it's a conjure or something like that on me. I'm got to do it the big way, do I do it at all. And something been telling me this the night, the onliest night for us."

"It won't be the night if they keeps slipping away, though."

"I reckon it won't, gal. It won't be the night if we can't get them across this high-water branch."

"H'm. It's wasting time staying here if we can't cross. Just as well to be home pleasuring yo'self in a good sleeping place, dry, warm maybe, two together maybe."

"H'm."

They gathered quickly, Martin, Solomon, Blue and Ditcher with Gabriel and Juba. The others kept mulling in a sloppy low thicket beneath boughs that drooped under the relentless punishment.

"The branch is deep," Gabriel said. "And they's two mo' to cross like it further on. Y'-all reckon we can get this crowd in town tonight?"

Blue lost his breath.

"Quit the game now?"

"The weather's bad," Gabriel said. "It ain't too bad, but the niggers is leaving fast. They's scairt white, and they ain't more'n two hundred left, I reckon. We might could get them together again in two-three days."

"They's leaving for true," Ditcher said. "I heard some talk and I seen some go. They's afeared of the water and they's scairt to fight 'thout the whole eleven hundred. But they's most scairt of the signs. It look like bad luck, all this flood."

"It's bad to turn round and go back," Gabriel said. "Something keep telling me this here's the night, but you can't fight with mens what's scairt. What you say, Solomon?"

"You done said it all, Bubber. They ain't no mo'."

Gabriel turned first to one, then to the other, the question still open.

"You said it all," Blue echoed.

"They ain't no mo'," Juba murmured. "No mo' to say, boy."

"Well, then, it's pass the word along. Pass it fast and tell them all to get home soon's they can. On'erstand? If they don't mind out somebody'll catch up with them going back. Send somebody to tell Criddle ne'mind now and somebody to town to head off Ben and Gen'l John and tell Mingo and them that's with him. Somebody got to wade out to tell the country folks, too. We's got to turn round fast. It's bad to quit and go back. It's more dangerouser than going frontwise. These fools don't know it."

In a few moments the crowd left the low thicket, scurrying across fields by twos and threes. Gabriel walked in the slushy path, his shoulders slouched wistfully, his hand hooked in Araby's bridle. Rain blew in Juba's face. She sat erect, feeling the pure warmth of the colt's fine muscles gnawing back and forth between her naked thighs. There was something sadly pleasant about retreat under these circumstances. Hope was not gone.

"We's got tomorrow," she said.

"Not yet," Gabriel answered. "The sun ain't *obliged* to rise, you know."

"I hope it do."

"H'm."

The storm boomed weakly, flapping the shreds of a torn banner.

# Ten

THE cabins on the Prosser place were running a foot of water. Negroes sleeping in the haymow opened their eyes stupidly and tottered over to the loft window. A village of corn shocks in the low field was completely inundated. A scrawny red rooster, looking very tall and awkward on a small raft, drifted steadily downstream. He had not lost his strut, but his feathers were wet and he seemed, in his predicament, as dismayed as an old beau. The rain was over; there was a vague promise of sunshine in a sky that was lead-colored.

Mingo's frightened jack was still running, an arm of the broken thills dangling from his harness, sliding over the ground with a bump-bump-bump. Something had snapped in his head. He imagined the devil would pounce on him if he lost a single bound. He was running in circles sometimes and sometimes straightening out for a mile at a stretch. Leaping streams, plowing up flower beds, tearing through thickets and underbrush, it did not occur to him that the storm was over.

Ben and Pharoah stood in mud by the roadside, their heads together. They were still dripping wet and their clothes were mud-spattered from heel to crown. The wagon in the creek near by had been thrown on its side by the current; its wheels were lodged on the underside.

"It was a pure fool's doings, Ben."

"No need to stand here saying that all day. We best get gone."

"I reckon."

"That's all what's left to do. Come on."

Pharoah cried shamelessly.

Ben whispered beneath his breath.

Criddle was bewildered when he met the other two on the road.

"What done come of everybody?"

"Gone home. Ain't you heard?"

"I ain't heard nothing. Gone home for what?"

"Tell him, Pharoah."

The pumpkin-faced Negro tried to explain.

"They couldn't make it on account of the water and all. They's telling everybody to lay low two-three days and wait till the weather clear up. They didn't get across the first branch. Somebody was looking for you directly after the lines broke up."

"They broke up, hunh?"

"They *been* broke up. They been gone since before midnight, I reckon."

Criddle's domino spots got smaller and smaller. Finally they disappeared altogether.

"You ain't fixing to cry about it, is you?" Ben said. "It just going to be two-three mo' days."

"I ain't crying, but I don't see how they going to wait no two-three days with that white gal running lose in her nightgown. She'll let it out befo' you can spit."

"How she know?"

"Gabriel told me what to do, and I done it, me. I don't know what come of the gal?"

"I help you to say she going to tell it."

Ben thought of nothing but the broken wagon in the creek and Mingo's half-wild jack running furiously. He began to pray under his breath again, crying in his mind like a child. Pharoah stood like a wooden man, his mouth hanging open, his swine-like eyes extremely bright. Suddenly he quaked violently. Then he covered his face and cried, cried absurdly loud and long for a grown man. When he recovered again and looked up, his eyes were quite empty. Some strange, inarticulate decision of his blood made a new man of him. It was evident on his face.

The three of them started walking. Ben led the dazed Pharoah by the hand a little way. Criddle followed, his shoulders rounded, his long arms hanging a bit in front of his short body as he walked. It was sloppy weather for a Sunday.

# Eleven

Mr. Moseley Sheppard was early to his counting room that Monday. A shaft of fine sunlight stood against the window. The silvered old man sat at a desk profuse with papers. He was carefully dressed; the small pink flower in his buttonhole was responsible for an appearance of almost springtime cheerfulness.

The planter was feeling fit again, and his spirits rose accordingly. His cares seemed small that morning. The fact that young Robin was strong for a yellow wench was nothing. That crops had undoubtedly suffered by the storm (such of them as remained in the fields) was only an incident. That he was growing old and lonesome in a great house, that his friends were few (those he could really count on)—these were no more than moods that good health dispelled.

Leaning far back in his chair, Mr. Moseley Sheppard took an inconsiderable pinch of snuff and looked out on a clean, fresh world tinted with pastel shades. And so pleased was he with the view he did not hear the door open. He was not astonished, however, when he saw a Negro standing timidly before him. The old fellow had been careful to close the door, but now, confronting his master, he was nervous and mute. He was neatly dressed, his face covered with salt-and-pepper whiskers, and he waited with bowed head. Plainly, there was something of moment that he wanted to say, but he was in no hurry whatever to say it.

"Well——"

The Negro's head went lower. His shoulders tightened and the flesh of his arms was suddenly pricked by innumerable needles. His fingernails hurt the palms of his hands.

"Marse Sheppard——"

"Yes." Then after a pause, "Go ahead, Ben."

Suddenly the aged Negro dropped to one knee, his hands resting on the arm of the planter's chair, and began weeping aloud.

# Twelve

"Hush," Gabriel said. "Don't talk. A nigger done kilt a old white trash. That ain't telling nothing about the rising. That ain't so much as telling who done the killing. That ain't a thing to stop us. On'erstand?"

He was polishing the carriage with an oily cloth. Martin and Criddle and Juba were under the shed, Martin keeping watch in the doorway, Criddle leaning on a manure shovel, and Juba, sitting in the carriage like a great lady, twitching her foot and pulling on a corncob pipe.

"The Book said the stars in they courses fit against Sistra," Martin said.

"H'm. I reckon that Sistra must of been a rich old white man then," Gabriel said. "Them's the ones Jesus don't like. You mind my word. God's against them like a gold eagle is against a chipmunk. You heard Mingo read it."

None of them had rested well. Their faces were drawn and tired; Criddle's mouth snapped open with a tremendous yawn. He failed to follow the others in their allusions to Sistra or to the possible effect of the white man's death on the whole scheme.

"I could do with about two-three days' sleep, me."

"Us both two," Martin said. "All I can do to drag."

"Y'-all had yestiddy to sleep," Gabriel said.

"I laid down, Bubber, but sleep ain't been here yet."

"Tonight's another day," Gabriel told them. "The rain done played out. We's got to beat the drum and beat it hard this evening."

Juba got a sensuous pleasure out of the excitement. A little familiar shiver ran over her flesh. She could hardly wait to put on Marse Prosser's stolen riding boots again. She could still feel Araby twitching and fretting between her clinched knees. Lordy, that colt. He was pure joy itself. Almost as much fun as a man, that half-wild Araby.

Then very soon, as the day waxed and the puddles gradually diminished in the road, a half-crazed yellow Negro was streaking toward Richmond, his hat in his hand, his queue in the air. Before sundown he would reach the town if his wind lasted. In half-an-hour they would all know. Drums would beat. Bells would ring. Insurrection. Insurrection. Insurrection. The blacks were rising against their masters. The dogs had gone mad. They were in arms and organized to the number of eleven hundred. Richmond was threatened with fire and butchery. Other near-by cities were not safe. . . . His face wrenched, his eyes empty, the heavy Negro ran as if spurs were digging into his ribs.

Later Ditcher and General John came to the shed, and after them Mingo. Blue and Solomon joined the circle, and they lay on their bellies in a dying coppice as dusk came to the trees behind the stables.

"Ben and Pharoah ought to done been here," Gabriel said. "Us got to be turning round mighty fast two-three hours from now."

"Four-five hour," Martin said.

"Ne' mind. Some's going to be dusting befo' that even —hear?"

"H'm."

"Well, I'm telling you so. Listen. We wants them all to meet like how we planned it befo'. Onliest thing different is we's going down the line this time, and I don't mean I *reckon* so. On'erstand?"

Ditcher felt the flames in Gabriel's angry eyes. Blue ground his teeth.

"Hush a minute. What's that yonder?" General John said, straining his old cataracted eyes.

The others rose on their elbows or knees. A running fury inscribed an arc in the low field half-mile away. The thing was only a trifle more substantial than the twilight itself, but it gave the Negroes a breathless moment.

"Yo' jack, Mingo," Gabriel said. "He still running. Ne' mind that, though. Do we take Richmond, you going to have mo' horses and things than you can shake a stick at. Do we get whupped, us going to have to run so fast a lazy old jack like that couldn't keep up. Let me tell you the whole plan one mo' time."

"Everybody know the plan," Ditcher said. "Tell us what time."

Gabriel waited a moment, apparently irritated.

"Make sure you does then. Midnight is the time. We's meeting in the grove and marching double quick. And do anything go wrong, we ain't coming back here no mo'. Them hills off yonder was made special for niggers what's obliged to use they wings."

"It sound good," General John said. "It sound mighty good, Gabriel, and I like it a heap, I *tell* you. I been had my mind set on freedom a long time."

"H'm, but it ain't no good 'thout all the rest goes free too," Mingo said. "You ain't free for true till all yo' kin peoples is free with you. You ain't sure 'nough free till you gets treated like any other mens."

"That's good to talk about. We's got to start turning around now. Get yo' bellies off of these here leaves and start doing something now. Come on, all y'-all."

Six miles never did seem so long before. But he'd get there if his wind lasted. By night there would be a troop in front of the courthouse. The local guard would be in the streets with long, out-of-date muskets. There would be drums. There would be bells. Pharoah tore through the dry hedges, splashed through muddy water. He had to tell it now. He was sure he would burst if he didn't tell it right away. Bloody insurrection. Bloody, bloody . . .

Little splinters of moonlight showered the dark hut. They fell in gusts as faint and fine as the spray of imaginary sparklers on an imaginary holiday. The tall Negro tossed his limbs boyishly on the floor. Beside him the thin-waisted girl tossed.

"It was right pretty how Toussaint writ that note. I'm going to get Mingo to write me some just like it. We can send them to all the black folks in all the States. Let me see now. How it going to read. 'My name is Gabriel—*Gen'l* Gabriel, I reckon—you's heard tell about me by now.' Ha-ha! How that sound, gal?"

"Right pretty, boy."

"Well, that's how it going to begin."

He couldn't lie still with the hour so near. He twitched his head, flipped an arm and threw one leg out. Juba stretched and drew up to a sitting position, her skirt in a tangle around her waist. Broken splinters of light still came through the chink holes overhead. Presently there were a few Negroes outside, moving on cat feet, whispering.

"Some of them's ready, gal."

"Yes, I hears."

A pause—Gabriel's hands locked under his head, the girl's shoulders gleaming in the darkness.

"That was right pretty how Toussaint writ that note all right."

"What else he say?"

*"Come and unite with us, brothers, and combat with us for the same cause."* He slapped his flank. "Sing it, church! Ain't that pretty?"

"Pretty 'nough, boy."

*"I have undertaken to avenge your wrongs.* You hear it, don't you?"

"H'm."

*"It is my desire that liberty and equality shall reign in*—well, when Mingo write mine, I'll have him say *shall reign in Virginia.—I am striving to this end. Come and unite with us, brothers."*

"It do sound good a-plenty."

"Them folks is getting noisy outdoors."

"Maybe scairt."

"Sound like a big crowd now."

"They's mo' now than they was a few minutes ago."

"And they's scuffling round a *heap* mo'."

Gabriel lay on his elbow a moment, his brow furrowed. Then he sprang to his feet and rushed outside. Presently a thought halted him, the memory of a single word he had dictated into his imaginary letter to the black folks of the States. *Gen'l* Gabriel. He turned abruptly, went back into the hut and put on his shiny boots, his frock-tailed coat and his varnished coachman's hat. It was all very important when you really thought it over.

Scrawny black figures milled up and down the cabin row. They seemed unnecessarily jumpy. At first Gabriel got the impression they were running in circles. There was a great deal of whispering, all very rapid, very breathless. All the crochety old silhouettes had their corncob pipes in their hands. Humorous little tufts stood on their heads or stuck out behind for those who had enough hair to make queues. They were all gesturing with their pipes, throwing out excited arms.

Gabriel started toward a small group by a woodpile. A pale fragmentary moon was pushing up. There was no mistaking the alarm that had spread among the blacks. Their agitation was too plain. Solomon slipped from a shadow and met Gabriel on the path.

"It's something what'll burn yo' ears like fire to hear, Bubber."

"Tell me. Tell me!"

Gabriel forgot to whisper. His voice was a roar.

"The game's up, Bubber."

"What you mean? Tell me, I say!"

Solomon, fluttering like a bird, put his hand on his taller brother and tried to speak. Gradually the thought took shape. Pharoah had betrayed them. Volunteers were already being armed in Richmond to meet the attack. There was another tempest in the offing.

Every bell in the town was ringing. For nearly an hour drums had gone up and down the streets. Men and boys gathered in groups under the trees. They were being assigned to their leaders; they were listening prick-eared to the hasty instructions. Consternation, terror, confusion increased with every bell toll, with every drum beat. All the available horses were being herded into an enclosure behind the courthouse.

And on a near-by street corner, empty-eyed, exhausted, alone, stood Pharoah, the pumpkin-colored mulatto. He was breathing hard. Now he could start home, he thought. Nobody would know who gave the alarm. The white folks would thank him. They wouldn't tell. They would protect him. Now he could start home in the heavy shadows.

"If Gabriel had of listened to me, he'd of fared a heap better. He wasn't fixing to do no good nohow, the way how he was going about it. I wanted to lead a line, me."

BOOK THREE

MAD DOGS

# *One*

GET down, Criddle. Get down underneath of them sassafras switches, down amongst the dead leaves and all. Moon bright as day out yonder—get down low. You knows right well they ain't far away. They done nipped you once already. They nipped you like a man nips a grouse on the wing.

Killing a nachal man ain't nothing like hog-killing, boy. On'erstand?

You's got yo' chance now, maybe. You's free, I reckon. You's got a chance equal to the chance a gray squirrel's got—a gray squirrel what's been nipped. A gray squirrel bleeding with a chunk of lead in his belly. You's got a equal chance, Criddle. Get down; hush.

Marse Jesus, I knows you is a-listening. You's got yo' hand behind yo' ear. You is listening to hear me pray. But I don't know nothing about no praying, me. I's low-down as I-don't-know-what, but I ain't no moaning man, Jesus. I been working for Marse Prosser all the time. I ain't seen nothing but the hind parts of horses, me. I been shoveling up manure in the stable; I ain't had time for no praying. You know yo'self I ain't, Marse Jesus. Howcome you looking at me with yo' hand behind yo' ear? I don't know nothing about no praying. I been pitching manure all the time, me.

Get down, boy. You don't hear them horses yonder? Can't bend, hunh? Look across the hill. Ah, Gabriel is the one to entertain them biggity white mens. They better be studying about him, too—do they know what's good.

Them's them all right: soldiers. Scratch down underneath of the leaves and switches and things. No? Hurt too bad, hunh?

"Well, ne' mind. That there chunk of lead was mo'n a nip maybe. Feel bigger'n a watermellon now. Manure pitching in Marse Prosser's stable wasn't bad, was it? And the smell of the horses and the smell of the harness was right good, come to think about it. What you say, Criddle? What you say now? No mo' hog-killings, I reckon. No mo' Decembers, maybe. No mo' manure. Hush; get down, boy, low.

# *Two*

MEANWHILE the young nation gasped and caught its breath, trembled with excitement. Fanned by newspaper tales and swift rumors, its amazement flared.

"For the week past," wrote the Virginia correspondent to the Philadelphia *United-States Gazette*, "we have been under momentary expectation of a rising among the Negroes, who have assembled to the number of nine hundred or a thousand, and threatened to massacre all the whites. They are armed with desperate weapons and now secrete themselves in the woods. God only knows our fate: we have strong guards every night under arms. . . ."

Another reported: "Their arms consist of muskets, bludgeons, pikes, knives and the frightful scythe-swords. These cutlasses are made of scythes cut in two and fitted with well-turned handles. I have never seen arms so murderous. One shudders with horror at the sight of these instruments of death."

A gentle letter writer remarked to a distant friend that "Last night twenty-five hundred of our citizens were under arms to guard our property and lives. But it is a subject *not to be mentioned*; and unless you hear of it elsewhere, say nothing about it."

A score of Federalist editorials, quick to make a political use of the plot by applying it to the campaign between Thomas Jefferson and John Quincy Adams, hurled Mr. Jefferson's own words disrespectfully into his face with profuse capital letters, "The Spirit of the Master is abating, that of the Slave rising from the dust, his condition mollifying."

Elsewhere the disturbed country sawed at its morning bacon and read the story with bulging eyes—

"It is evident that the French principles of liberty and equality have been infused into the minds of the Negroes and that the incautious and intemperate use of the words by some whites among us have inspired them with confidence. . . .

"While the fiery Hotspurs of the State vociferate their *French babble* of the natural equality of man, the insulted Negro will be constantly stimulated to cast away his cords and to sharpen his pike. . . .

"It is, moreover, believed, though not yet confirmed, that a great many of our profligate and abandoned whites (who are disguised by the burlesque appellation of *Democrats*) are implicated with the blacks. . . . Never was terror more strongly depicted in the countenances of men. . . ."

And as the nation read, it had the assurance that a strong detachment of United States cavalry was moving on to Richmond, the arrogant horses striking a brisk jog, splashing now and again in the little lingering puddles. . . .

A mellow golden morning arched the road. There was a pleasant rattle of side arms, a delicious squeak of new saddle leather, an immoderate splendor of buttons and chevrons. Captain Orian Des Mukes, straight, aristocratic, cavalier, gave his young orderly a profile on which was written a type of languid, moonlight bravery. He was talkative this morning, but for some reason he had insisted on such an immense chew of tobacco that he was obliged, periodically, to suspend a phrase long enough to avert his face and spit with a solemn gurgle.

"Well (splut), this, I bound you, is no exception. Men fight for just three things. The rest (hep) is all (splut) sham. There is no such thing as equality."

At Ash Lawn, Governor James Monroe slumped into a stuffed settee, festooning his arms on the high back. Beyond his window he could see gawdy autumn trees so heavy with color they seemed unreal. The tireless bluejays were still annoying the gray squirrels. On the gravel drive an inexpensive cariole waited at a respectful distance, a small Negro holding the bridle. The nearer bustle of surreys and coaches he could not see from his window, but their presence was disturbingly manifest. There was increasing excitement in the outer rooms. And presently, the Governor knew, the throng would be upon him. His attendants could delay but not withhold them.

A slender man at the writing desk tapped the inkpot with his quill.

"There's a strong impression that it comes of a too hasty resumption of commercial relations with the revolutionary government in San Domingo," he said.

"I don't know. I don't know. But there is no need to deny the obvious. The blacks are in an uprising. Frustrated for the moment by betrayal, they have fled to the swamps and hills. Minimizing their powers will not help us quell the disturbance. By all means, let us have a price offered for the arrest of the chiefs. The cavalry has been dispatched. Let us have added guards here for our own safety and suggest that the night patrols be at least doubled in Petersburg, Norfolk, Roanoke and the other cities."

"But these evidences of serious concern on our part may hearten the blacks. They may imagine that they have a chance if they see us showing them attention."

"By the very nature of things in our state, the very number of blacks and the personal trust that is imposed in so many of them, we are left exceedingly vulnerable to this sort of hostility. I would like to feel that it could be disregarded. There is the political angle that I also regret, but who is going to tell us the extent of our *actual* danger? Who knows exactly how far-reaching this thing is? What Negro can you point to and say definitely he is not involved?"

The younger man curled his feet beneath his chair. The fine yellow sunlight, mocking former tempests, seemed to fairly burst upon them as the morning waxed. Outside on the lawn a uniformed guard strode across the view, a tall musket on his shoulder. The Governor let his arms fall, rose from the settee and paced the room with a far-away smile while the secretary busied himself with his pen.

# *Three*

A BLUE light sifted through the small barred window overhead. In his Richmond cell a man with agitated eyes paced
the floor, folding and unfolding his hands with a transparent,
remote air. He was a Scotsman, his queue tied with a black ribbon, his face furrowed beyond his years. Now and again his
eye caught the flicker of a bright leaf falling past his window
like a flake of gold, his ear caught the tiny golden clang as it
touched the ground.

But the melancholy of Thomas Callender was compounded
of more than autumn leaves and a blue window. Certainly there
were brighter leaves than these in his memory, bluer skies. In
his youth there had been well-heads clothed with growing
vines and singing peasants with pitchers in their arms. But the
shattering came so early, the broken wheel, the neglected
watering place, the leaves falling sorrowfully, one by one—so
early.

Perhaps, he thought, this was the end of his gawdy talents,
the reward of his brilliance. Fate always chose the strangest
turnings in his case. Once he had written poetry, and it had
seemed then that a fire burned in his breast, a fire that would
consume his life if he failed to put verses upon it. But the verses
were second-rate and later the fire demanded prose. So prose it
had been, pages and pages of it, the biting, acid prose of a man
sick with the need of liberty.

It had seemed almost certain, a few years ago, that the bright
fulfillment was at hand; but now, after all the blood, after the
writhing, after the breathless flights, the dream was still a far-
away thing. He had found it necessary to flee England to escape
punishment for political writings. Then came Philadelphia and
the job on the *Gazette*, that lasted till 1796 and again his own
need proved his undoing. Hoping to escape again, perhaps for
good and all this time, he became a teacher. But it was laugh-
able, this notion that he could live without writing, and almost
at once he was publishing the *American Annual Register* with
the support of Thomas Jefferson and others. This brought no

immediate disaster, so presently he was off to Richmond, at Jefferson's suggestion, to become a writer for the *Examiner*. But even then the gods were conspiring. The rest was too disgusting to recall. That foul medievalism, the *Sedition Act*. A sharply barbed pamphlet entitled *The Prospect Before Us*. And then the gaol.

Good men had come to grief before, Callender reflected wistfully, but the thought failed to cure his own melancholy. In fact, it was more agreeable to consider the slow golden rain of autumn leaves outside his high blue window. He was sick to his belly from the offal stench of political wrangling. Far better the red leaves. Far better. But now there were voices at the door. A guard was turning a key in the lock.

A tired young man followed the uniformed attendant into the cell. There was urgency on his face but he seemed almost too worn to speak.

"They are saying you caused it, sir."

"I don't know what you're talking about."

"The insurrection of the blacks. One hears no name so often as Callender."

"Cant. Federalist cant. The nincompoops of John Quincy Adams are braying again. Where is the insurrection?"

The young man told him briefly what had happened.

"Everyone knows that Mr. Jefferson has been your friend. It hasn't taken them a day to make a campaign use of the disturbance."

Callender slumped into a chair, folding and unfolding his hands. His gaze strayed upward to the small indigo window.

"An asinine lie. No Democrat would have been fool enough to encourage a thing that could only help the opposition."

"What do you suggest?"

"I'll write a piece to the *Epitome*."

"Thanks. That may help."

# *Four*

ALL that afternoon they gathered in rum shops and taverns and in the public square. Excited and nervous, the men of the town wanted eagerly to be doing something but couldn't make up their minds where to start. There were so many things to be considered. At dusk somebody lit a flambeau in an apple grove and a crowd of gangling boys began to mill under the small trees.

"They'll thank us for doing it," a thick-chested boy said.

"Sure—Jacobins. That's what they are. They're Jacobins," whispered a boy with a harelip.

"Lots of times I've heard the old man say they're dangerous." The third speaker was lank; his face was small, lorn and doll-like.

The thick-chested boy twitched impatiently.

"Fits, yes. Let's get together. They're next things to—to—why they're almost heathen when it comes to being low."

They were all of a class accustomed to running the streets after dark, when they could elude the watch, and there were among them boys with holes in their stockings and some who were emphatically unwashed. But they were all intoxicated by the bold light of their flambeau and by the delicious whisper of loose leaves underfoot. There was also a holiday feeling of license based on the general bewilderment of their elders and the continuous parade of soldiers and volunteers through the streets.

"They're against religion, too," the whisperer said with an effort. "Infidels. The cursed Africans practice devil-worship and nakedness, but these are next thing to them."

There were bugles in another part of town and occasionally the sound of drums. The streets were far from empty, and it was hard to imagine that night had come. The boys with their little minute-man hats, their loose hair falling on their shoulders, clustered nearer the leaders shouting their readiness to undertake anything, relevant or absurd, so long as it was immediate.

Above all things they wanted to move. Waiting was the one torture they couldn't endure.

The lean, doll-faced boy deposited a slingshot in his pocket. "Why, I've even heard the old man say——"

"Never mind," the heavy fellow said. "Let's start. Everybody'll need two big stones. We can get a crowbar behind the blacksmith shop."

They followed the torch and rallied like any other troopers under its glow, but the light was unnecessary. A moon rose and brightened the footpath so that they could even see the color of the trees. Heaven, perhaps, the lorn, small-faced boy imagined, had spilled its paint pots on the leaves too soon. Autumn was early this year, bright and early.

There were farmers in the streets, delaying their ox carts after dark, still exchanging impressions in high-pitched voices and trembling at the prospect of long journeys into the infested country. Their cheeks were bulged, but the incredible spouts they sent splashing into the road were now invisible. Yet the farmers kept drawing the backs of their hands across their mouths and talking very rapidly.

"I've heard the old man say some pretty hard things about some of them foreign radicals."

"Never mind, we'll show them something."

The crowd delayed noisily while two or three of the larger boys plundered the blacksmith's back yard for irons that would serve as crowbars. They returned promptly and again the crowd moved. Presently they came to a final halt. That portion of town was as dark and tree-shaded as any and as quiet, but overhead across the street there were lights and fiddles sawing on little childish gavots. Apparently there were no pupils in the dancing school.

"Save your stones, boys."

"Stand back a minute. Let Hamlin and Willowby at the door. There; get the bar under the lock. Both together. Now push. Good, she's coming."

A terrified black child went by on a mule. Shadows were darting under the trees now and again, shadows deeply preoccupied with their own errands. Presently a wild beast shout went up from the crowd, a shout at once joyful, fiendish, playful and victorious, and the young animals swept into the print shop. M. Baptiste hastened to his window and tried futilely to see through the leaves.

Then the real storm broke. Cases went over with a clash and boom. Some boys began at once to tug on the presses with their wild, intoxicated strength, having the debauch of their young lives. The composing table was upturned, smashed to splinters. The stools instantly got the same medicine. Then followed a hideous dismemberment of the small pieces; one by one, the last clinging joints were separated.

Meanwhile, by some miracle of happy exuberance, the presses were drawn outside. There, by dint of stones and crowbars, they were wantonly leveled. Then the boys remembered the windows and let their remaining stones fly.

M. Baptiste started across the street but retreated promptly when a stone careered near his feet. Others ran out into the darkness and started turning round and round in a hopeless bewilderment. What, in God's name, was happening?

"Dash the light," the harelipped youngster whispered. "Run for it."

Inside somebody stumbled over the wreckage, scrambled to his feet and came thundering out with the horde.

"Cut across the fields. Over that fence and back to the grove from behind. Scatter when you get out there. You can't tell——"

# Five

M. CREUZOT's first thought ran to his musket; he was now quite certain that his mind had warned him against lending it to Mingo. It was a tall weapon of a French make and easily recognizable. No need to weep now, though, now with the town full of drums, militiamen and men and boys who had volunteered. The situation, where M. Creuzot and his family were concerned, was beyond tears. The wan printer blessed himself at the draped window of his front room and tried to extricate himself, mentally, from the desperate snare. Would he bow down and face the music, or would he attempt flight with a stout wife and two small boys? And Laurent. He would have to be considered one of them now; their problem was the same.

A few moments later, eating supper around a rude kitchen table, M. Creuzot looked at his meat and wine without desire. André and Jean were ravenous as usual. Their mother stood over the stove like one unaccustomed to a table and moistened a morsel of bread in the gravy left in a pot.

"They're everywhere," André said. "Listen, I hear drums over by the river."

"Can't we go out tonight, papa?" Jean said. "We've been in the house all day."

"Maybe. If your mama wants to walk with you."

"You come too," André said.

"Not tonight."

"Are you sick, papa?"

"No, not sick."

"Well, why don't you eat?"

"Why, oh, yes, I'm going to begin now, son."

His wife rattled a kettle self-consciously. Her heavy black hair seemed almost sinister without a direct view of her large smiling face, but when she turned there was reassurance enough.

"Never mind your papa. Eat, Jean. Don't sit staring," she said.

"It's an awful confusion," M. Creuzot said. "Maybe we'll be going away from Richmond soon."

"Why?" Jean said.

"Well, lots of things. All this noise—these soldiers."

"Will they hurt us?"

"No. Business is not so good here, you know. Mr. Biddenhurst says Philadelphia is a finer place."

The boys still looked bewildered. M. Creuzot drank his wine, nibbled at his meat and pretended to disregard their rigid attention. Soon someone was at the front door and M. Creuzot sprang up with a suddenness that frightened the others. Taking one of the candles, he went through the door and into the adjoining room. M. Baptiste materialized from the empty blackness of the doorway. His face, apart from his pointed whiskers, was chalk-white, and there was a ghostly distress on his features.

*"Mon Dieu,"* the printer said, looking at him.

"Have you heard it?"

"We haven't heard anything. But your face——"

"Hell's loose, my friend."

"I know that, but what's happened?"

"Vandals. They've broken in your shop."

"*Broken* in?"

"They've annihilated everything. 'Jacobin' is the word they used. We're all involved somehow in the uprising of the blacks."

"The blacks? What are the blacks doing?"

"Who knows?"

They went into the next room and stood facing each other over a round table. Mme. Creuzot came in, wiping her hands on her apron, and the youngsters followed as far as the door. There they stood, gazing in wonder. The white-paste buckles of the dancing master twinkled nervously. M. Creuzot's face suddenly went haggard.

"Mingo borrowed my musket," he whispered. "Is he among the blacks who have made trouble?"

"A leader of some sort, I daresay."

"The musket *could* be offered as evidence against me, but I am innocent. What can one do?"

"The stages are running. Had you thought of that?"

"I'd like to find Laurent."

"I'll send him. I'll go by his room from here."

"Thanks. Tell him to hurry."

"I've been thinking about Charleston for myself. I have friends there."

There were a few more words, a few more details and M. Baptiste was outside again, facing the candle with that same woe-begone countenance. Then he turned and was gone, and the door closed. Mme. Creuzot was back at the kitchen door, entreating the youngsters to finish their supper, while her husband kept blessing himself in the shadows of the front door.

# *Six*

"AND you acknowledge complicity?"

"Don't know as I does *that*, yo' honor."

"But you were one of them? You plotted with the others to massacre the people of Richmond?"

"No, suh. Befo' God, I ain't done that."

The court of *Oyer and Terminer*, composed of Henrico County justices, had no occasion to nod. Crowded into a clerk's small office, the wigged justices wearing hats and street clothes had taken seats on tables, stools and desks. Three or four newspaper reporters had wormed in with guards and spectators; they had promptly appropriated the writing places. The wheels of customary court justice were too sluggish for a crisis such as this one. The fastidious old slave, the salt-and-pepper whiskers quivering on his face, stood before the circle of men twisting a pair of faun-colored driving gloves in his hands. Presently, for no apparent reason, the tone of inquisition changed. The questioner paused abstractedly. When he opened his mouth again, his voice took a new note.

"You Ben Woodfolk?"

"Yes, suh."

"You the property of Mr. Moseley Sheppard?"

"I is, suh."

"How long?"

"Fifty year, I reckon. Near about that long, leastwise."

"Well, how did you become associated with the plot?"

The Negro's eyes roved. There was a bough sweeping against the blue window at his shoulder. Ben became aware of perspiration on his face and of the new Sunday hat crushed under his arm. He recalled an ugly grinning thing squatted beside a burying hole in Marse Prosser's low field. Suddenly the experiences of the past weeks seemed far away.

Ben moistened his lips and began telling the impromptu court how it had been that old Bundy's invitation to become a "mason" had led to his reluctant interview with Gabriel and

Blue and how the long net, against his will, had seemed to in-
volve him without actually taking him in.

The newspaper men began writing rapidly.

"Who were the leaders?"

"Too many to talk about, suh. Gabriel's the head man. Him
and Ditcher."

"Ditcher?"

"Yes, suh. He is named Jack Bowler. They calls him Ditcher."

"Oh. And who else that you know?"

"Gabriel's two brothers, Solomon and Martin. Marse Prosser's
Blue. Gen'l John Scott——"

"Who is he?"

"Gen'l John belong to Marse Greenhow. He work for Marse
McCrea some time."

"Well, what was his part in the plan?"

"Gen'l John? He carried the biggest end of the money, him.
He was going to lead a rising in Petersburg, too."

"Yes, yes. Possibly he is the one somebody saw take ten dollars from his ragged jeans recently."

"H'm. I reckon so."

"Were there any free Negroes? Any white people?"

"Well, suh, Mingo was one. He kept the names. I don't know
was there any white folks, yo' honor."

"But how were they going about it, Ben? What weapons do
they have, and how did they hope to take the city?"

"They's got plenty scythe-swords and pikes and like of
that."

"Any muskets?"

"About a dozen flintlocks, I reckon."

"Um hunh. How many bullets?"

"A peck," Ben said soberly.

"That's pretty slim ammunition, isn't it?"

"I don't know. They figured how they wasn't many guards at
the arsenal or the powder house. I reckon they figured on
starting in there."

At this disclosure the justices all became sober and ceased to
smile.

Mr. Moseley Sheppard twitched fretfully in his seat. He had
noted the scarlet bough outside the tall window, but his eyes

were now on the perplexed old Negro trembling before the circle of inquisitors. The justices sat with their hats on, and some of them rested gloved hands on the knobs of canes that stood between their feet. Now and again a quick sniffle came from the dour circle, a short catch of the breath attending the intake of snuff. Mr. Moseley Sheppard could almost have wept for Ben's distress. In fact, his eyes were watery when the presiding justice abruptly turned to him with a question.

"Mr. Sheppard——"

"Yes."

"Is that substantially the same confession that the defendant made to you?"

"Yes, sir. Quite the same."

"How long ago was it made?"

"Monday morning last."

"And you'd be disposed to vouch for the credibility of the testimony?"

"Quite."

"Well, now, a few more questions to the defendant——"

The voices continued, purged of emotion, repressed, cold, unmoved, yet quavering faintly with a guarded, hidden excitement that amounted to terror. The sky darkened, and a great shadowy leaf fell from the bough.

Thus it befell that Mr. Moseley Sheppard produced his astonishing testimony in a Richmond court. How could any Virginian sleep? How could he be sure from now on that the black slave who trimmed his lamps was not waiting to put a knife in his heart while he slept? How could he know his cook was not brewing belladonna with his tea? This sickness called the desire for liberty, equality, was plainly among the pack. Where would the madness end?

# *Seven*

A BLANKET had been thrown over the seat to protect the cariole's upholstery from early dew. Ben threw it aside nervously, climbed to his place and twitched the driving lines. The old Negro felt like a child new-born. His heart was a leaf.

He say I's clear, that's what he say. He say, You's a good boy, Ben. Don't you let none of these evil niggers tangle you up in nara another such mess, though. Hear? He sure was scairt a heap, I know that. Him and the rest of them white mens was scairt *plenty*. I reckon they won't feel right good again long's Gabriel and Ditcher and the others is on the wing neither.

Ben's heart quickened at the thought of the big crowd at large on the countryside and perhaps in the hills. For some reason it *did* tickle him to see a mighty powerful black fellow acting right sassy, scampering and cutting up like a devilish pant'er or a lion. It did him more good than a pint of rum. But it was bad doings and dangerous this time. Ben wasn't ready to die. He was past that reckless age. He wasn't even studying about freedom any more. At first, of course, he had been drawn along, but he was glad to be out of it now—now that he was clear and didn't have Gabriel's eyes to face. It was a burden lifted; yes, it was like a new day for Ben.

New-borned, Lordy. New-borned, new-borned, thanks Jesus. I heard tell about a woman come walking up out of the ocean, a brand-new woman come up dripping clean out of that there green water and them white waves and all. I heard tell about such a woman plenty times, but I just now knows how she felt. The man say I's clear's the day I's borned. Marse Sheppard he say——

Suddenly in the midst of his rejoicing a kind of nausea commenced rising from Ben's stomach. Nothing from his head, mind you, nothing in his thought telling him he was a no-'count swine and lower than any dog, just something from his stomach making him so sick he wanted to vomit. He pictured his ruffled shirt-front soiled by his sickness, smeared loathsomely, and with a shiver of revulsion, he found his hand across his breast.

Lordy, Jesus, I ain't being no dog. I ain't being lowdown. I's just being like you made me, Marse Jesus. This here freedom and all ain't nothing to me. There's blood in it, Lordy, and the sight of blood make me sick as I-don't-know-what.

The little mare had a pleasant gait. For a while the cariole rattled over cobblestones, then came the gritty dirt path with tiny lanes for the wheels. There was a flambeau burning in front of the *Dirty Spoon*; the river, with a burnished metallic brightness, gave an indigo flash. There were shadows creeping along the waterfront, and in the light of the rum shop a ragged Negro sleeping face downward on the ground. Ben heard only the whir of wheels, a small legendary whir resounding against the dim wall of sound that was the river.

On it rolled, the night darkening steadily, the feet of the small alert animal showing like upturned teacups on the black road. In less than an hour Ben observed that the mare had turned without his direction and that the little hooves were twinkling on Marse Sheppard's own gravel drive.

"Well, suh, bless me if you don't know the way home, little Miss. Was I blind I wouldn't need no better guiding. You is all eyes and footses once you get yo' head turned this way."

For once there was no lantern hanging in the carriage shed. Ben drew up the reins and stepped to the ground. The broken, fragmentary moon sprang up beyond the stable. The place was frightfully quiet. But Ben knew better than to expect a stable boy now with half the black men on the wing and the other half quaking in their huts. He began unhitching the little mare. Presently a heavy figure tumbled out of the haymow and crept down beside the cariole.

"Listen——"

"That you, Pharoah?"

"Yes, this me. You heard anything?"

"Anything like what?"

"Somebody say Criddle is long gone."

"Long gone, hunh?"

"H'm. He dead out yonder 'neath of a palma Christe tree."

"Bullets?"

"Yes, I reckon. Soldiers. That ain't the beginning neither."

"It ain't?"

"No."

Ben carried an armful of harness into the stable. He was inside several minutes, feeling his way along the wall and putting things on the proper hooks. When he returned he did not speak at once but began passing a dry cloth over the neck and flanks of the horse. Pharoah stood with a petrified stare, hunched at the shoulders and breathing audibly. His arms hung loose.

"Well, what in the nation was you doing in that there devilish haymow?"

"I tell you things is a-popping round here."

"I reckon," Ben said. "They is a-popping in town too. But you—*you* ain't obliged to hide from nobody, is you?"

Pharoah chose to ignore the question. He put his hands together and began twisting an old hat. His queue was untied and his hair had risen on his head like a porcupine's bristles.

"They went by just now with two-three of Marse Bowler's slaves."

"Which ones?"

"Don't know which ones. Mousie say they pulled them out a pigsty. Them pudden-head boys crawled in there in such a big hurry they left they feet sticking out."

"Nobody's hunting *you*, is they?"

"The niggers is saying I'm the one what told——"

Pharoah lost his voice. His eyes kept darting across the yard.

"Saying you's the one what told, hunh?"

"Somebody was hiding in the bushes, and when I passed, they throwed this here out at me."

He held a knife in his hand.

"You should of stayed in town."

"Did somebody tell you it was me that told?"

Ben became uncommonly grave. He walked the little mare around to the barnyard. When he returned, he was shivering. He backed the cariole into the shed by hand and raised the thills.

"Everybody know you told."

"I ain't named no names."

"Naming names ain't nothing. You just as well to named

names. You told plenty. White folks can look and see for they-
selves who's gone. Naming names ain't a thing."

"Where you been? Ain't *you* told nothing?"

"Me told?"

Ben coughed. Then he became silent for a space.

"I been in court. They was trying me."

"Is you clear?"

"H'm."

"Well, ain't you had to tell nothing?"

"Nothing much. Nothing amounting to nothing."

"I wish I's locked up in jail."

Pharoah disappeared beneath some fruit trees, and Ben
started up the path to the great house. There were candles in
the kitchen and in the front a porch lamp flickered in its sconce.
Ben's feet seemed heavy on the gravel path. Somewhere, in
some dying thicket, a brown thrasher called. Shadows of leaves
made a charcoal lacework on the ground. A nervous little
cough escaped Ben and he raised a thin palsied hand to muffle
it. At the same instant something whistled through the shrub-
bery; something as damp and cold as an icicle brushed his coat
sleeve and slipped through his hand. The old slave swayed back
on his heels, tottered a moment and then went down on his
knees.

It was as Ben imagined. There was at once a scuffling and
scampering on the dead leaves beneath the hedge, followed by
running feet on the slope beyond. Ben waited to reassure himself, then rose, his hand sopped by unaccountable mud, and
started toward the house again. In the light before the window
he saw the cut in his palm and was about to go back and look
for the knife when a sudden panic took him. The first thing, he
decided, was to staunch the blood. Furthermore, daylight
would be safer time for prowling in the leaves. He cupped his
wounded hand to hold the blood and let himself into the
kitchen.

# Eight

ALEXANDER BIDDENHURST got the story from newspapers and the accounts he read, like those read by the country at large, were marked by hinted implications more serious than were indicated in the testimony of Ben and the report of Pharoah. It is true that the Salem *Gazette*, with other papers, resented this campaign of reticence and suggestion, but the same veiled reports continued. "The minutiæ of the conspiracy have not been detailed to the public," this journal remarked, "and perhaps, through a mistaken notion of prudence and policy, will not be detailed in the Richmond papers." New York's *Commercial Advertiser* had been informed that a conditional amnesty was to be sought, since the plot, it was felt, involved immense numbers and would demand that nearly all the Africans in that part of the country be apprehended and punished. Later that paper expected the whole procedure to wait on a special secret session of the Virginia legislature, scheduled to meet as soon as the men could be gathered.

Yet reports came through and, straight or warped, the newspapers printed and reprinted them. They told of Gabriel's sober, thoughtful face, his obsession for the same romantic dream that was the lasting creed of the poor, the unwanted, the world over. An immense fellow, amazingly young to exercise such influence, was conjured into the imaginations of thousands; he was a black of vast abilities and life-long preparations. Since the age of twenty-one (he was twenty-four now) he had traveled about, with apparent innocence, recruiting confederates and accumulating stores of arms. He was now at large with hundreds of followers, and his shadowy figure standing on the summit of a twilight hill recalled the savage uprisings in San Domingo that put the slaves in the masters' saddles. The possibility of such a wide conspiracy, when one considered the desperate and fatalistic temper of the serfs, was hard to overestimate.

Mr. Alexander Biddenhurst polished the thick lenses of his spectacles with a silk handkerchief. In his upstairs rooms at the corner of Coats Alley and Budd Street he had drawn away from the writing desk and reclined in a low chair surrounded by frayed Ottomans, shabby cushions and books turned face downward on the floor. His lamp was spitting feebly, and it occurred to him that there was no more oil in the house. He decided to dash the flame and conserve his little remaining fuel for a possible need during the night. One never knew, when he tucked his coverlet over his shoulders, who would knock on his door before morning. That, at least, had been Mr. Biddenhurst's experience in Philadelphia, at the corner of Coats and Budd. He went into the bedroom, feeling the way by hand, and began undressing.

He awakened to a crisp morning and a shaft of golden light against his window. Mr. Chubbs had already let herself into the small apartment and was busy with the coffee pot. Mr. Biddenhurst pulled on his shirt and tied his curly black hair indifferently. A moment later, one arm in his coat, he was flying to the door in answer to urgent raps.

Alexander Biddenhurst felt singularly exuberant this morning, and the noise of his own heels gave him an immense pleasure.

"Hail, goddess," he shouted to the fat housekeeper as he whisked past the door without giving her a chance to reply. But an instant later, his hand on the knob, the sound of voices downstairs gave him pause. They were nervous, covered voices, and Mr. Biddenhurst's speculation ran at once to the fugitive blacks who were stopping at his door more and more frequently these recent days, seeking brief succor and guidance to the next imaginary post on their shadowy flight to the town of St. Catherine, across the Canadian border. Why it would come to be a business soon—these runaways would develop a regular transit line if they continued this system, he reflected. And always it was like this too: just after daybreak, following a night of travel, they would call on him and he would give them directions to one of the addresses on his list. At the homes of freed Negroes or gracious whites they would find pallets in attic or cellar and warm porridge for their bones sometimes. An unimportant young lawyer, a foreign-born citizen of a great city that knew him hardly at all, Mr. Biddenhurst felt that this small contribution to the cause of freedom and equality in the large, cheerfully rendered, justified in some part a life that otherwise meant but little to anyone now. And there was melancholy in the thought, too, though indeed it gave him no hurt at this exuberant hour of the morning. The door swung open.

Gasps and shrieks of astonishment.

The roly-poly red-haired fellow stood with arms dangling, his face rent with an embarrased smile, his ill-fitting hat clinging to his head by a strand, but Mr. Biddenhurst threw his own arms into the air, embraced the boy and began presently to slap him on the back.

"Laurent!"

"It's me. I'm sorry to take you like this, so sudden-like."

"But I don't believe it. That's *not* you."

"Did you ever see a Frenchman you could mistake for me?"

Mr. Biddenhurst laughed heartily and made a motion to close the door behind the excited boy.

"Hardly," he said. "But you could be an apparition. Let me touch the wounds."

"Fortunately I have none, no serious ones at any rate. But you have another surprise in store."

"Let me get near the sofa. Now. You can tell me now."

"There are others downstairs," Laurent said. "Shall I call them?"

"Of course. I heard the voices but seeing you made me forget. Who is it?"

"I'll go down. I had the feeling you were spying me through the keyhole—your hand was on the knob so long."

"The incurable dreamer, you know. Who's down there?"

"I'll get them."

In a moment the little group was on the stair, their hesitant, disciplined steps scarcely audible in the rooms above. Mr. Biddenhurst stood in the door and recognized with a jolt the top of M. Creuzot's hat. The printer was followed by his wife and small sons, and behind them all came Laurent, a heavy traveling bag in each hand this time. There were warm embraces all around.

"But I'm speechless, M. Creuzot."

"It's the season of blowing leaves," the printer said mirthlessly. "You know how leaves behave."

"Sudden, delightful swirls—I know, but still——"

"There's a tempest in Richmond," the other murmured. "A crowd of boys, shouting 'Jacobin' at the top of their lungs, demolished my shop."

"And you suspected they'd demolish you?"

"That's one way of saying it."

Mr. Biddenhurst managed to be silent for a spell. His eyes ran to the small boys peeping into the kitchen, to their mother busy with the folds of her shawl and to the lugubrious red-haired Laurent holding a drape aside as he peered out on the street.

"We cannot escape it," he said at length. "There is a struggle that takes us in. It takes us in against our wills. There is no escape for men of conscience."

"It is unjust."

"Of course, just as poverty is unjust. Just as slavery and class distinctions are unjust. The consequences of these evils fall back on us indirectly. We're marked."

André and Jean had inched their way into the kitchen. They were making friends with Mrs. Chubbs. Suddenly they were laughing. Mr. Biddenhurst, hearing them, threw out his feet and laughed too. M. Creuzot's blue eyes were still downcast.

"We'll want to get settled somewhere today," he said.

"Let's think about coffee now. That other will follow in its time."

Meanwhile the sun went higher. A beam fell across the shelves of inexpensive books, and Laurent turned and began scanning the titles along the wall, his eye obviously running to typographical features rather than subject matter. Mme. Creuzot, wearied of fussing with folds, finally decided to remove her shawl completely. A fresh burst of laughter came from the kitchen, and Mr. Biddenhurst threw out his feet again.

# Nine

STILL the blurred rattle of kettle drums was unbroken, and swarms of uniformed guardsmen gave the streets of Richmond no rest. A hysterical woman wearing a night shift ran out of her house in the early dawn with screams and declarations that she had heard voices in her cellar. A crochety old man leading a cow by a tether carried an immense stone in his right hand. He was followed by a linty old hag who walked with a gnarled corkscrew cane. In the public square a jittery morning crowd was slowly dispersing. Half a dozen obscure blacks had just been hanged following a summary hearing before the wigged justices who composed the *Oyer and Terminer* tribunal for the emergency. This stern show of retribution, as had been expected, was proving itself a useful sedative, but the city was still mad, still frothing at the mouth; and now that the real slave chiefs were known, it was not likely to be long pacified by the blood of a nameless rabble. An immense dog, imprisoned in an outhouse, scratched at the wall and howled bitterly. A fine, silvery mist stretched over the city, over the trees and lawns and finally broke like a cobweb.

A pippin-cheeked man wearing a brown suit and brown shoes with buckles came out of a notary's office and tacked a full-page leaflet on the announcement board. A moment later, leaving a circle of gawking peasants around the bulletin, he spat gingerly into the gutter and walked away. Carriages were on the streets early, rumbling on the cobblestones. And just the night before, the man reflected, there had been such a crowd of them wedged and jammed at the square, it had seemed they would never be disentangled; yet here they were again coming back as eagerly as they had gone. And so much the better, too; why, here was an announcement from Governor Monroe that would raise their hair. The brown-clad man selected a lamp post near the waiting rooms of the stagecoach line and again put up a copy of his bulletin. There was still a small sheaf of the papers in his hand, so he slipped away again as a new crowd began to gawk over his shoulders.

In the courtyard stood the yellow woman with the black enameled hair. She was swinging a scarlet parasol with a vacuous air. There were two horses at the hitching bar and a swarm of pigeons near the water trough and on the ground. Melody's heavy bracelets jangled softly but her furbelows were still. She was watching a troop of guards haul a cowed Negro through the streets. They were flogging him freely and making a scene that drew a medley of spectators.

She began walking again, the lacey parasol twirling, and passed through the crowd with quiet self-conscious hauteur. Suddenly she saw the face of Mingo the freed Negro flickering between the other heads like a drowned moon in a bog. He had lost his hat, and his queue was untied so that he had momentarily the look of a savage. Melody thought: It's ugly doings for true. This here town is going to the dogs, and the peoples is getting meaner'n apes. I wonder how Philadelphia is.

A moment later she turned her face on the sight and began walking once more. Down the empty blue street she passed half a dozen squares. Shops were opening to the soft morning, and there was a string of carts beneath the cottonwoods on a noisy side street. Farmers in filthy homespuns were holding up yams, cabbages, rutabagas and ears of corn and vying noisily for the small indifferent trade. Melody passed them and turned into a neatly arranged shop where she was known.

"He was putting up a fight, that Mingo."

"I wasn't looking. A dozen bananas, please. Some grapes."

"Grapes, bananas—yes. He was the third this morning."

"Third?"

"Yes, the others I didn't know."

"These quinces——"

"A penny for two. We've got the Democrats to thank—plague take them."

"I reckon we has. Four, please."

A little later she stopped before the announcement board outside the notary's office. Two farmers in leather jackets had put their heads together and were reading the small type laboriously. Melody, glancing over their shoulders, between their heads, paused long enough to spell out in part the bold headline of the governor's offer. REWARDS FOR CAPTURE.

. . . SLAVE CHIEFS. . . . PLOT TO MASSACRE. . . .
GABRIEL PROSSER $300.00. . . . Jack Bowler. . . . The
lines were broken up and confused by the two heads that
bobbed and shifted before her line of vision; and presently
such letters as she saw clearly, wrinkled and curled and danced
in her excited eyes. Suddenly she became aware of coarse remarks coming from a crowd of men withdrawn to the edge of
the road. Melody gave them a slow, bitter, sidewise glance and
started walking again. She twirled her parasol lightly, but there
was perspiration in the palm of her hand and she was not gay.

# *Ten*

THOMAS CALLENDER put down his heels hopelessly. Even now, though a prisoner by reason of the Sedition Act, he seemed as actively involved as ever in the political snares of his day. It didn't seem right. He was a sensitive writing man, a poet at heart. Those conscienceless men who were trying to bring about the re-election of John Quincy Adams would halt at no lying inference, no false interpretation to befuddle the voters. Everyone knew, for example, where he (Callender) stood on the question of slavery and on the question of wealth and private property and the equality of men; everyone knew where Thomas Jefferson stood. Yet these Federalist swine now sought to identify both of them with hated atheistic propaganda and with the French *Amis des Noirs* and their encouragement to the slaves to free themselves by armed insurrection. It was fairly obvious guile, Callender thought. He curled his feet beneath the writing table and put another paragraph on his paper.

> . . . An insurrection at this critical moment by the Negroes of the Southern States would have thrown everything into confusion, and consequently it was to have prevented the choice of electors in the whole or the greater part of the states south of the Potomac. Such a disaster must have tended directly to injure the interests of Mr. Jefferson, and to promote the slender possibility of a second election of Mr. Adams.

Such a statement should not be necessary, he told himself, but dishonesty was so rife in the opposing party one had to say something to spare the innocents. Callender leaned back, festooning his writing arm on the back of his chair, and waited for the approach of a guard whose heels were at the moment clicking in the aisle outside.

"A young man wants to know if the letter to the Norfolk *Epitome of the Times* is ready."

"Tell him to wait. He can take it presently."

"Could you say how long?"

"Half an hour, possibly."

Callender dipped his pen in the inkpot and set to work again, more hastily this time.

The sun was pushing up rapidly. An overgrown boy with large feet and a slow wit dashed out of a house and came plop-plopping through the yard carrying an antique matchlock. He shot wild glances in both directions then fled down the street to an open shop at the corner.

"Will this do?" he asked the shoemaker, handing the musket across the counter.

"It's powerfully old."

"Grampa shot turkeys with it, turkeys and Indians."

"I reckon it'll need some tending to."

"There ain't time to fiddle around, is there?" He failed to get an answer from the tiny wizened man with the pipe in his mouth, so he went on talking. "With a lot of wild Africans fixing to scalp us, somebody's got to do something, they're a lot of mad dogs let loose, them niggers. It's true—I heard it from one of the volunteers."

"This won't do. Too much rust. You might scare them with it, though. If somebody seen this looking out of your window, he might change his mind about coming inside."

The boy's eyes rounded; his mouth became a circle. For a moment he could not utter a word. Then his voice returned in a whisper, a whisper that grew with each word.

"Yes, yes. That's topping. I know how: poke it out at them. Like this. Sure, that's it. I know. Thanks. This is it. See? Like this."

He was pointing the thing venomously, driving the unseen savage into a corner. The shoemaker took his pipe in his hand, nodded agreement. The boy bounded out of the store so blindly he ran into a squad of militiamen. But he was up like a cat, hastening to the small inconspicuous house down the road.

The men with Captain Orian Des Mukes were in and out of town at intervals of less than an hour. By turn they followed every road into the country; returning periodically, they offered the townsfolk the pleasant reassurance of squeaky new saddles, burnished sabers and the tock-tock of metal horse-shoes on the cobblestones.

This had continued nearly a week now, but still there had been no clash with insurgents, and the impression was going out that maybe there would be none, that perhaps the blacks were scattered and would have to be ferreted from their holes by searching detachments.

"This parading," Captain Des Mukes said. "It's a cursed tomfoolery, Sergeant."

"I reckon it is for a fact, Cap'n. What's your idea?"

"We'd just as well be hunting rabbits with this outfit. Some-body's got to get out and comb the hills and thickets. Nothing against stationing the cavalry in town, understand. They could be ready for an eventuality."

"That's sense, suh."

"But them ringleaders are like as not out of the state by now. Mark my word, when them black sons hit the bush, they went down on all fours like they been wanting to do for years. They dusted, that's what they did, every blasted one of them. This is nonsense, drilling around here like we were waiting for an attack by an artillery division."

"You're talking sense, Cap'n."

At nightfall Mingo lay face downward on a wooden floor. The room might have been a cave or a den, so far as he could tell; nothing was distinguishable in the blackness. Yet they had taken pains to bind his wrists to the flooring so that he lay on his belly with arms flung out. He wriggled helplessly, his nose pressed against the boards.

No mo' little buck wagon, Mistah Mingo, no mo' saddle shop, no mo' nothing now. Reading's bad for a nigger. You just reads and you reads and pretty soon you sees where it say, Brothers, come and unite with us and let us combat for a com-mon good; then you is plum done for. You ain't no mo' count for bowing and scraping and licking boots. Oh, it's bad when niggers get to holding out they arms, touching hands, saying Brother this and Brother that, they is about to meet the whirl-wind then.

The stars in they courses fought against Sistra, and that's a fact for true. That's howcome all the rain and wind that night. We was fixed to wear them out that night; dog it, we was *ready*. Black folks was as sure to go free here Sad-dy night week ago as God is sure to judge the wicked. We was ready to fall on this here town so fast they wouldn't had time to whistle. The stars was against us, though.

Mingo knew that night had come to the streets and that the night watch had been doubled; he knew too how many times the hangman's trap had been sprung since morning. The sounds came to him distinctly. But he couldn't tell exactly where he was, and he failed at first to understand the strategy that delayed his hanging while others were being rushed to the gallows so breathlessly. Now at last a possible reason was dawning. He had just heard a strange voice talking outside.

"Keep that one," it had said. "There were hands in this plot that haven't been suspected yet. Why, Lord, man, the thing could hardly have failed of success. A surprise blow like this— you mark my word, such audacity and diabolical invention came from a trained mind, possibly a professional revolutionary. Search carefully for papers that might point to Callender, Duane, United Irishmen or to France by way of San Domingo. And by all means hold this Mingo; *he knows how to read*. He was free and in open communication with radical elements. He carried the lists."

Mingo groaned and fretted and twitched till he rubbed the skin off the tip of his nose. His nerves blunted by the torturous anxiety of the past days, he felt that he would sooner take his punishment at once and have it over with than to writhe longer on the floor clutching at a hope too slender for any comfort at all.

Now among the townspeople, however, the first paralyzing consternation was past. The attack, depending entirely upon surprise and audacity for success, had been delayed by the most severe tempest in the memory of any living Virginian. The band of drenched savages, with their chiefs, were scattered. It was not likely that they would reunite, their numbers having dwindled greatly and their design having been betrayed. Many of the rebelling slaves were back at their places, protesting their innocence and laying all blame on the leaders who inveigled them; more than a score had been punished publicly.

Now the town was gathering its wits, but the ringleaders were still at large. That wizened and sinister old sack of rags they called General John Scott—what had become of him and his grinning brown fangs? That giant stud called Ditcher, the one with the immense shock of hair, where was he? And the incredible Gabriel, twenty-four, massive, dour-visaged and un-disputed leader of them all, had he given up the game?

There was a woman too, they said, a thin-waisted brown gal with a penchant for wearing her master's riding boots, twisting her skirt around her hips and galloping a fiery black colt in the big road. There were lots of stories about her. Not much was known definitely.

Richmond was armed to the teeth now, and men could sleep. Ovid, night guard at the arsenal, stood long at his picket gate as night darkened. The sky was too heavy with stars. Leaves were falling like shadows on the gabled roof of his small house, and through the door he could see the numerous faces of his children in the circle of light around a lamp. Ovid filled his pipe leisurely.

"No more cause to fret yourself, Birdie." He stroked a small hand.

The woman's voice came out of the shadows.

"Not fretting, Ovid, thanking God. Think how it might have been with you and Mr. Midwick there alone."

He could toss his head about it now.

"I don't know. There's always something in a brave man that rises to the occasion. My taste for adventure and danger——"

"Oh, it's fine to think about it like that."

"I must trot now, Birdie."

# Eleven

ALEXANDER BIDDENHURST read Governor Monroe's proclamation in the newspapers, and the thing that struck him
was the smallness of the price placed on the rebel heads as
compared with the gravity and earnestness of the governor's
statement and the obvious concern of the state manifest in
their calling of the United States cavalry and the doubling of
patrols and guards in every city of consequence. Possibly, he
concluded, the very gravity of the situation made a larger money
offer unnecessary.

He was standing beneath a tree, his elbows resting on a cob-
blestone fence. Before him and beyond this wall crisp fields
tumbled away into knolls and broken declivities. Small bright
pumpkins were scattered across dun acres of reaped cornstalks.
Mr. Biddenhurst folded his paper, shoved it into a coat pocket
and resumed his morning walk.

Would the frustration of this bold plot delay or hasten the
great emancipation of all serfs and bondmen? Surely it was becoming increasingly plain that liberty and equality for any poor
class could not prevail so long as the system of chattel slavery
continued to mock them. But this thwarted attempt by Gabriel,
this colossal advertisement of wild discontent and desperate
hope, would it not put the planter class on its guard, give them
a chance to fortify their inequitable position?

Certainly no one could be blamed, especially since it was
everywhere conceded that, barring the storm, the blacks could
hardly have failed to duplicate the recent success (within certain bounds) of their brothers in San Domingo. But life was like
that: beauty beats a frail wing and the scales of fate are shaken
by a bubble. Now the hope of freeing the slaves was more remote than ever in the United States and would have to wait for
the slow drip of spring to cut a way through stone. And eventually the stone *would* fail; there could be no doubt of that.
Only now, at this moment, Alexander Biddenhurst felt his own
efforts so futile and unnecessary.

The only thing left for him was to continue his same endeavors. There were many tender old people (with time and money to burn) who longed to see justice triumph, though it reduce their own fortunes. More and more these would be willing to support the small, semi-secret groups working for the deliverance of bondsmen here and there, singly, as the occasion arose. Romantically excited, they would continue to aid those who were trying to establish a secret highway to the Canadian city of St. Catherine. And young men like Alexander Biddenhurst, lawyers, scholars, poets, would receive their support in the discharge of this work while neglecting the saner courses of business. They would keep the spark alive by agitating, agitating, agitating. They would work into the schools, winning the youngsters and the teachers; they would go among the blacks, flaunt the old taboos, slap the hands of the wretches, tell them there was deliverance ahead and to be ready for the revolution at any hour. Comforted by the philosophers and writers, they would carry on their near-hopeless mission; they would be the drip of spring on the determined rock.

An ox cart trudged slovenly in the fine sunlight. A handsome young fellow wearing a red jacket and shiny boots came jauntily out of town with a falcon on his wrist.

On Budd Street, before he reached his own doorstep, Mr. Biddenhurst met the Creuzots coming in from a narrow lane. The tall printer was swinging a cane, but his wife's hands were twisted into the folds of her shawl, her covered head bowed slightly. The boys trotted ahead.

"I think we've found the house we want," Mme Creuzot said with her usual calm cheerfulness. "But Philadelphia's not as pretty as Richmond."

"No, not as pretty. But you'll grow to like it better. There's something about the place that takes hold on you after a time."

"People are straight-laced down there," M. Creuzot said.

"It's something like that—the real difference is. It's a matter of temperament, viewpoint. There's a false, crêpe-paper grandeur down there, a hollowness. How near is the house you're looking at?"

"Only a few squares. Look—I don't know the streets yet— two houses around the second turn there, just beyond the lamp post."

The plump woman, smiling eagerly now, did her best to point.

"People walk faster here," M. Creuzot observed. "We'll have to get adjusted. I don't imagine there'll be time for much chess. Or music."

The younger man laughed.

"You'll manage to squeeze them in."

They were walking again, nearing the doorway where Jean and André waited. Mrs. Chubbs, looking very linty and fluffed in her bonnet and shawl, came down the steps with a basket on her arm. She hurried up the street as if she feared the green grocer would presently close shop; in a moment or two she turned a corner. Mr. Biddenhurst led his guests upstairs and stood against the door while they entered.

"If you're not going to be reading your newspaper right away——"

"Of course not, it's yours, M. Creuzot."

"Thanks."

"Not at all. You know, it offends me just a trifle to see you all so jubilant about leaving my humble——"

"Listen to him," Mme Creuzot laughed. "He's just a boy. As if we could stay here always."

"Why not?"

"He loves to play, that boy. Laurent is still out."

"He's inspecting the town, no doubt."

Jean's eyes were round.

"Are you really a boy, Mr. Biddenhurst?"

"Well, not quite yet, but I soon shall be. You see I used to be an old bent man—like this. I walked with a crooked stick and my back wouldn't straighten up, but now I'm getting younger and younger, and I've just begun getting *smaller*, too. Soon I shall be a little boy, then perhaps a baby."

"Aw, mama, that isn't true, is it?"

"Well—" She threw off her shawl and ran to the window. "Look down there—a man with a monkey."

"But is it true, mama. Is Mr. Biddenhurst——"

She had to face him.

"Well, we'll have to wait and see."

They all laughed, but the smaller boy's eyes were still round.

# Twelve

BEN slept fretfully on chairs behind the great cookstove. Then after daybreak, when he had let Drucilla and Mousie into the kitchen, he went out to the stable and hitched the cariole. There was no hurry, of course; Marse Sheppard was still asleep behind his mosquito nets, and Drucilla's griddle couldn't be heated in a minute. Ben drove the little mare around the gravel path and fastened her reins to a hitching post.

The old Negro had rested poorly, his bones had an aching stiffness, but he was not drowsy. He delayed on the piazza, adjusting a cluster of wooden outdoor chairs around a small table, then walked around to the back and took two wooden water buckets from a stand on the back porch. These were not empty, but Ben poured their remaining contents on the ground and carried them out to the well shed. A moment later he was busy with the sweep, amused by the delightful splash and spatter of water down under the earth.

The two buckets were considerably more than a load for Ben at his age, but there was something about carrying only one at a time that made him unhappy—he had carried two for so many years—and he was more willing to strain his back than to make a second trip. Drucilla opened the door.

"Here you come again, trying to out-do yo'self like some half-grown boy. You ain't fooling nobody but yo'self."

"I ain't old as you might reckon, Miss."

"You done spilt half that water on yo' feet just the same. Now look a-there."

Ben went upstairs and began arranging the old planter's washstand. The great bed on which Marse Sheppard lay looked as feathery and fluffed as a sitting hen. Under one wing and only partly revealed was the white bedroom crock, a shell of a hatched egg. After a while Mousie brought fresh water for the pitcher, and the silvered old man rolled over on the side of the bed so that Ben could untie his nightcap.

Ben sipped a second saucer of coffee behind the stove; and when Marse Sheppard was nearly finished with his meal, he hurried around to the cariole and stood holding the mare's bridle. Marse Sheppard came down the wide white steps, the ruffles of his shirt-front falling like a cascade on his bosom, and took the place beside Ben in the small carriage. A moment later they were in the big road headed for town.

"I reckon they haven't seen hide or hair of them yet? Nothing of Gabriel or of Bowler's big stud either?"

"No, suh, nothing."

"At any rate, nobody that could bring them in has seen them yet."

"I reckon they ain't."

"There was that General John, as they call him, too. How about him?"

"They ain't found him neither."

"Those boys must have meant business."

"H'm. Must of did."

There was a crowd at the courthouse when they reached town. In the midst of them stood Ditcher, surrounded by officers and soldiers. He seemed incredibly large as he stood there. Ben pulled up the little mare. One of the officers had just spoken to the giant Negro. Then a hush fell on the entire group.

"*Nobody* ain't brung me in, suh. I walked down that street yonder on my own two feets. On'erstand?"

"Well, you're under arrest *now*, by——"

"H'm. That's howcome I'm here. I heard tell that the Governor wanted me, and it look like nobody wasn't ever coming to get me."

The swarm of men and boys buzzed around him like hornets. In a moment he walked meekly through a double door, following an officer, followed by dozens of others.

"Well, that accounts for one of them," Marse Sheppard said.

"Gabriel's apt to give them mo' trouble than that," Ben said.

# BOOK FOUR

# A BREATHING OF
# THE COMMON WIND

# One

THEY slipped out of one thicket, ran across a lane and plunged into another. Darkness came down hurriedly like a curtain. Gabriel stroked the girl's long wiry fingers.

"This here's the fork of the road, gal, and yonder's the way back."

"Yonder's the way back, but I ain't a-mind to go, boy. On'erstand?"

The coachman's boots that had suited him so well as a general were far from comfortable now. They squeaked and pinched his toes. The purple coat, the coachman's varnished hat and the ruffles on his shirt bosom were all a care to Gabriel now that the ranks of his crowd were broken, now that every man had his own skin to save.

"Which way Blue go?"

"Through the swamps, I reckon. Trying to catch up with Solomon and Martin."

"He should of gone with them what crossed the river."

"Which way you going, boy?"

His eyes darted, but his face did not alter, and he waited long enough to let her know that some of his thoughts were his own.

"I ain't got a heap of rabbit blood in me," he said. "I ain't got no mind to go scratching through the woods. You better start back now. They ain't studying much about womens in this rising. Maybe Marse Prosser don't know you's in it even."

"Maybe he don't. Maybe he do. I ain't studying Marse Prosser."

"What you studying about, gal?"

"About not leaving you."

He pressed the tenuous fingers again and felt a quick suggestion of their real strength.

"Ne' mind that. No need to hold back. What's going to be is bound to be. On'erstand?"

She shook her head.

"I ain't got no mind for nothing like that. All I knows is I feel bad as all-out-doors and I'd heap sooner take a pure killing 'n go the other way."

"I knows. H'm. Some birds is like that too," he said. "That ain't the thing now, though. You might can help me some time if you go back. See? You might could draw me a drink at the well some morning befo' day. You might could help me out some time when I'm near 'bout give out. You could bring me a jug or a chunk of meat some night, maybe. Down in the low field I might be squatting side of a corn shock some night."

There was nothing she could say to that. Nothing she *would* say, at any rate. They began walking, threading a way through the switches of undergrowth. Presently the carcass of a dead animal was under their feet. Buzzards and possums had already cleaned the bones, but shreds of harness were still on the skeleton and the arm of a broken thill lay under the heap. They looked at it briefly, and Gabriel thought of Mingo and of Pharoah and of Ben. He had a fleeting impression that now Juba would surely speak. But there was nothing she could say.

"See, gal, it's going to be me and them from now till the rope snaps. On'erstand? I ain't fixing to go way and hide in the Dismal Swamp. I ain't got no head to fly across the line or nothing like that. I'm after getting up a crowd of don't-care niggers and punishing them white folks till they hollers calf-rope, me. I'm out to plague them like a hornet. God's against them what oppresses the po'. I ain't fixing to quit now."

"They is all scattered now—Ditcher and Solomon and Mingo and all. You going to be one man by yo' lonesome, boy."

"One man. That's a fact and a caution; but just the same I ain't running away nowheres. I'm laying low but I'm staying here, gal. It ain't the same with me like it is with them. I been the gen'l, I reckon."

"Listen there——"

"Nothing but cottontails."

"You reckon so?"

"You better go back now. Keep one eye on the edge of them trees yonder and the other'n on that little dumpy hill—you know how."

She wasn't paying attention.

"It ain't no trouble to keep the way."

"Well——"

"Well what?"

"Howcome you don't get going?"

"I ain't going now," she said. Then after a pause, "You's right nigh played out, boy. Lay down and rest yo'self."

"Who played out?"

"Stop puffing out yo' chest. You going to pop open one these times. You's tired a plenty."

"Not me, gal. I ain't tired."

"Lay down anyhow. Here, side of me."

"When you going then?"

"Just befo' day, maybe. I want you to sleep some first."

She twisted and turned like an animal on the switches and leaves. Finally, working down to a place of comfort, she stretched tremulously then curled beside the big solemn-faced male. Gabriel threw out his feet but did not lie down at once. He sat with hands behind him on the ground, his face upraised, his varnished hat gleaming bright black in a clump of dull shadows.

# Two

WHOEVER piled light wood against this here fence must of knowed what he was doing, but I'd lay a pretty he didn't know about this here hole he was leaving underneath of the bottom. I bound you he didn't know it was just my size neither. Onliest thing about it is I can't straighten out good and I can't sit up none. Good place to sleep, though. Martin or some of them other lazy niggers is the ones what ought to found this. Yes, suh, sweet as you please for somebody what's studying sleep. I should of put my feet in first. Better crawl out and do that *now*. I'm got to put a knot front of that hole too. Back on out, gen'l; let's go and come again, suh.

Heap better this a-way. I'll be so I can see out some, soon's day come. Whos'n'ever's woodpile this is sure ain't been bothering it much. Weeds about to cover the devilish thing from top to bottom. Don't look like nobody's touched it in a year or mo'. Humph! Just laying out here begging for somebody to crawl under it. . . .

Nothing for a general to crow about, though. Crawling down underneath of a woodpile on his belly. Lordy. I counted on a heap of things, but I sure ain't never counted on this. I heard tell about generals getting kilt and hanged and one thing and another, but I is got my first time to hear tell about one scratching around like a dog under a woodpile. It don't suit a general, this here hole; and it don't suit me a *little* bit. Laying on this sword don't feel good neither. Swords belong to hang down. This here hole ain't going to do me—I see that sticking way out. A general, do he lay down at all, supposes to hang up his sword. Lordy, this ain't me, this sure ain't Gabriel down under here. Gabriel ain't scairt of the living devil; and do he lay down at all for a nachal man, he lay down dead. That's Gen'l Gabriel, Lord, not this here crawling thing.

Yet and still, a good general might would get down low to win; he might would eat some dirt, when his time ain't come, waiting till he can get in his licks good. But that don't look like me. I don't look good to myself eating dirt no kind of way. I'm going to get out of here and hang up my sword, me. Yes, suh, I invites whoever can to come and take the general. 'Member this, though: you takes him standing up, do you take him at all. On'erstand?

The low morning sky was streaked like marble. The peak of a roof here, the silhouette of a grove there, the shape of a hill beyond, each gradually, one by one, took its form from the blackness and assumed its place on the horizon. Cows came to life on a dim slope and a broken-down rail fence suddenly appeared.

The immense Negro, distraught and sleepless, crawled from beneath the light wood and staggered along the fence. The cumbersome sword whipped his left leg. There was a noticeable dent in the top of his two-foot hat. His shirt-front was as smeared and colorless as a gunny sack. He wavered weakly a few steps then leaned against the fence, crossing his legs proudly and festooning his arms on the shoulder-high boards. There, without smiling, he faced the east and soberly invited the sun to rise.

*Humble*—yes—*humble*—I reckon—*humble yo'self, the bell done rung.* Yes, suh, I hears what you say, and I knows what you means. I heard you say see God, too; *see God 'n see God 'n see God.* That's well and good; *see* God then. You say *He'll come riding down the line of time.* Talk about it if you's a-mind to; I reckon He *will* come riding down the line of time; I reckon you's right. You ain't said nothing to the general, though. On'erstand? I know right well you don't mean Gabriel. Humble—humph!

Ring all the bells you please, peoples. The general ain't scratching down underneath of no mo' light-wood pile. This here general is crossing his legs, spitting through his two fingers and calling the turns. Come on up, Mr. Sun. Let's have some daylight. This here is my own neck and I'll keep it if I can, but I ain't wallering in no dirt to keep it. This here country is mo' fulled up with soldiers and mens with guns than it is fulled up with groundhogs. And that's mighty well and good too. I'm going to run them till they tongues hang out, run them till they start going round and round in one place. But I ain't crawling in no hole, peoples. They takes the general standing up, do they take him at all. They takes him with his sword in the air, do he have one then. On'erstand?

# *Three*

THE village of shocks in the field of slain hay was, at that hour, peopled by sparrows. Along the boundary of the acres someone had been building a new stone fence. A drag, neglected in the field, had a dozen egg-shaped boulders still on it, and there was a mortar trough and a sand heap near the spot where work had last ceased. A pair of stolid plow oxen grazed beyond a narrow draw. A lantern blossomed like a yellow flower in the stable door, but already the sky was pale and streaks of light stood ready to show the day.

Gabriel, more the general than ever, followed an obscure lane between hedges of dying spiræa; then, strolling easily with a hand on his steel, he swung into the open, crossed a knoll and came down into a poplar clump.

When they tongues is hanging out and they's running round and round in the same place, that's the time to hit back fast. Me and Ditcher could mash up near about a hundred of them by our lonesomes. But plenty mo' niggers'll come; they'll drop out of the sky when they hears sticks a-cracking together and drums a-beating. They'll came shouting like jackals and hyenas. Something'll happen. Something'll happen for good. Can't say as to how. Maybe all of them get kilt. Good'll come, though. I bound you that, peoples.

It's hitting fast what counts, hitting fast at the right time. Them soldiers and all is feeling mighty spry now, killing off niggers by the dozen—I know about them. Ain't nothing to dying. Humph; you's got to die to find out things, I reckon. You's got to die to find out what you don't know. I ain't moaning about them what dies. Good'll come. I'm worried about getting in hard licks when my time come.

His hand was still on his steel when he came to the stubble field and passed between the tall well-made haycocks. A dewy sweetness rose from the field, and Gabriel was suddenly constrained to loiter. Now and again the muscles tightened on his shoulders, quivered and ran. Then without warning something ripped the air; a musket reported near at hand, and Gabriel, off with the crack, plunged forward with raised hands, his hat tumbling before him. Only one knee touched the ground, however, and his stride was scarcely broken by the business of snatching the jittery headgear from between his feet. Running low, cutting arcs and curlicues between the stacks, dashing, changing pace, the big Negro faded like a mist in the hay field. There was a sort of superiority in his flight, an air not mingled with fear or distress or urgency. It was easy, calculated, catch-me-if-you-can running, and Gabriel pulled up proudly where the haystacks ended. He examined his hat and found that nearly a score of buckshot holes dotted its high crown.

"H'm. Close," he said.

Then, a little self-consciously and with a lordly lassitude, he turned, feet apart, and watched the excitement five hundred yards away. The farmer who had fired the shot was still in the field fiddling with his flintlock. Another armed man had materialized from the blue slope behind the barns and was skirting the field by way of the stone fence. There was a vague commotion around the houses too, doors banging and a blur of voices audible half a mile on the unruffled morning.

Gabriel considered the question of striking out again. Should he wait until they were within musket range and then outdistance them once more, or should he go at once, allowing himself the sweet luxury of walking insolently into the thicket while they tore the dust? A horse and rider left the barn, galloped down toward the big road. Gabriel fancied the spread of alarm on the countryside, perhaps the coming of a squad to comb the woods behind him. He decided to walk nevertheless. So the pursuers, if they saw him at all before he vanished into the thicket, saw him with hat cocked, a hand resting easily on his steel, his shoulders rocking arrogantly.

Safely out of view, he hastened again. Switches whipped his legs. He went through puddles of crisp airy leaves and felt them foam up around his knees and settle down again with a tiny golden splash. Somewhere, incredibly sweet, there was the voice of a brown thrasher. Gabriel recalled a marsh of shallow water, a marsh dense with trees and vines. And now, without his taking thought, something was drawing him toward it.

# *Four*

J UBA moped. She stood outside the circle of savage gossiping hags and settled her weight on one leg. She had given
them her left shoulder and an arm set akimbo on her hip, and
now, running nervous fingers through her wild shock of hair,
she cut her eyes at them spitefully.

At intervals the others leaned forward confidentially, their
heads coming together near the ground, their blunt posteriors
rising and broadening simultaneously. At the center of the circle, beside the outdoor fire, squatted a woman with a baby.
She was moistening a rag in a cup of gruel and offering it to
the infant. Her teeth jutted between sagging lips; lean wrinkled
breasts hung against her belly.

"The way that gal is putting on you'd think he's the last man
in the state what's got a seed to give."

An older woman, wrinkled and witch-like, clasping a clay
pipe in her mouth, picked at the toenails of a scaly foot.

"Gabriel's all right. He a mighty fine boy, even if he is got a
face longer'n a mule's. But all this Jesus talk I hears ain't helping him none."

The sleeves were torn from Juba's garment, and the rag
that remained of the upper half was drawn tight around her
breasts. It had parted from the skirt, too, and there was a
streak of nakedness at her waist. Now that she knew what
they were getting at, she gave her hips a twitch and moved a
few steps.

"You ain't never heard Gabriel moaning and praying. What
you talking about?"

The others looked a little surprised, but they were far from
displeased with their success in piquing her interest and finally
drawing words from her. She had ignored them so long they
had begun to imagine that she failed to hear them, even when
they talked in her presence. The woman with the baby leaned
forward and spat into the fire.

"No sense of you trying to get yo'self hanged, though. You's
a fool; that's what you is."

"Ne' mind about that. If I don't care do I get hanged, that's me. If I's a plum fool, that's me too. On'erstand?"

The shadows gathered quickly, almost hastily, and now, in no time at all, it was night at the cooking place. Juba walked completely around the circle of slave women. Somewhere among the folds of her butternut garment she found a pipe and a moment later she was kneeling at the fire. But she was not one of the crowd on the ground; even when she brushed against them while holding her pipe to the flame, she was as haughty and aloof as a harlot. The old woman scraping at her crusted toenails did not look up.

"A man, do he 'spect to win, is obliged to fight the way he know. That's what's ailing Gabriel and all them. He is obliged to go at it with something he can manage."

Juba looked perplexed, but she did not speak till she was on her feet again.

"What you mean, woman?"

"They talks about Toussaint over yonder in San Domingo. They done forget something."

Her face grew more hideous in the firelight. A frayed stick that she had been chewing hung on her lip.

"Go on. What Gabriel forget?"

"I don't know about all that reading in the Book. All that what say God is going to fight against them what oppresses the po'. That might be well and good—I don't know. Toussaint and them kilt a hog in the woods. Drank the blood."

"He did, hunh?"

"H'm. Gabriel done forget to take something to protect hisself. The stars wasn't right. See? All that rain. Too much listening to Mingo read a white man's book. They ain't paid attention to the signs."

"Gabriel don't know a heap of conjure and signs and charms. He ain't never had no head for nothing like that."

The old female drew up the other foot. Suddenly she seemed far-away and cruelly unconcerned.

"Nah, I reckon he ain't," she said.

"Well, he ain't done for yet. He going to be a peck of trouble to them yet, I bound you."

"Maybe. I tell you there's a heap of them what *is* done for, though. Criddle, Ditcher, Mingo and I don't know how many mo'. Then they's a lot mo' what nobody's seen hide or hair of and what's just as apt to be dead as they is apt to be live."

Juba shrugged.

"Plenty niggers died with Toussaint too, didn't they?"

"It didn't work out the same. You'll see. Toussaint kilt a hog. There's plenty things Gabriel could of done."

"Listen, woman. Maybe some time I might see Gabriel *now* —some night maybe. Has you got a good hand I can give him to put in his pocket?"

The infant, not satisfied with its rag, whimpered and presently set up a faint, croaking lamentation. The four or five women who were not smoking had snuff-smeared mouths; periodically they leaned forward and spat into the fire. Juba squatted down beside the old creature who was still preoccupied with her scaly black feet and waited for an answer.

"Maybe."

"Listen, woman," Juba said. "I don't know nothing about *maybe*. Is you going to make me a hand for Gabriel, one what'll keep him safe whilst he's running?"

"He ought to come hisself. That's the most surest way. I could make you one for him that might help *some*, though."

"Come on." Juba pulled at the other's rags. "Come on now. Some time I might can bring him to you, some night late, but that ain't now. Come on, woman."

"Take yo' hands off'n me, gal. See there, you done pulled it off. I can't be sitting out here buck naked, old as I'm getting."

Juba put the garment under her arm. The old female gave up her toes reluctantly, struggled to her feet.

"Come on now," Juba said. "Here's yo' rag."

"Gabriel should of come hisself. Matter of fact, he should of come long time ago, did he have any sense."

Night had come with emphasis, but bats were still leaving the peaked gable of the barn. They wavered upward, shadowy and fabulous, like legendary birds. When Juba and the old crone reached the door, a foul stench came out of the hut and assailed them like a plague. Juba halted and heard the women they had left cackling around the fire. Then, puffing fast to keep the smoke in her nostrils, she followed the older woman into the hovel.

# Five

THE town of Richmond breathed a bitter murderous resentment, but much of the original excitement had now abated. Militiamen still mulled the streets, however, periodically dragging anonymous Negroes before the justices. For the most part, the first-fruits of this messy harvest were inconspicuous nobodies, but the leaders were marked now and grimly promised to the noose.

Meanwhile the trap was not idle. A crowd swarmed in the open yard. Among them was the dazed, vacuous girl whose parent got himself impaled on Criddle's scythe-sword. All were restless and touchy during the intervals, but the arrival of a fresh victim gave them a moment of pause that permitted the trap to fall during a hush. Then, blinking hard after the jolt, one by one they regained their wits and sought to show a casual air. But the girl, waiting hungrily for each new kill, neither blinked nor recovered. She stared, leaning a little forward, tearing her homespuns absently. There seemed to be an impression among those who had ceased to regard her presence that she was entitled to whatever compensation she could wring from the sights, but she got little attention now.

Somewhere near by, bound face downward to the floor, Mingo caught a change in the voices he heard, discerned the pause and waited for the trap. He could feel gooseflesh rising, and he kicked the floor wildly, imagining that he could not bear the gruesome horror another time. But there it was, a bungling clap-clap, and he wilted again, cold and tremulous and with tears in his eyes. What was it Touissaint said? *Brothers, come and unite with me.* Suddenly Mingo awakened to a meaning he had not previously seen in the words. Toussaint was in jail now, maybe dead. *Brothers, come and unite with me.* Mingo felt momentarily stronger. Do the dead combat for a common cause? Well, he thought, it was possible that they did, quite possible.

Near by old Ben, clean and well-favored, wearing new driving gloves and a hat in neat trim, stood at the curbstone, his

arm hooked in the horse's bridle. His satin breeches were fresh
and glossy, but they were also a bit too loose around his
scrawny old knees. He scarcely filled his coat. A mournful dignity bowed his head, though his shoulders stood back fairly
strong; and as he waited, his lips parted now and again and his
tongue slipped between them, but they were never moistened.
They remained as white as if they had been painted. Hearing
the blurred bustle in the yard and finally the rattle of the
sprung trap, he put a hand over his eyes and groaned aloud.

At the same moment two men came out of a shop door.

"They're at it again."

"H'm. Lot of live stock they're wasting, too."

"Can't be helped. They've gone mad, the black dogs. Some
kind of disease, I reckon. It's got to be stamped out."

Ben opened his eyes and saw their backs against the clear afternoon sky. A barefoot rustic, standing on his horse to see
above the crowd, got down and kicked the animal's ribs.

Gabriel heard nothing that he could distinguish, but he
saw a crowd breaking at the head of the alley and he could
imagine the rest. Presently he threw himself over a back fence
and slipped into an abandoned stable. Frayed and perplexed
and desperate for food, he could at the moment see no special
danger in his position. Matter of fact, the woods had become
unsafe; they were not seeking him in town. Lordy, where was
old Ditcher? What had befell Solomon and Martin? How about
Blue—had he caught up with the others? And General John—
where, where? A good many had swung. Were any of these
among the number? They could swing as many as they were
a-mind to, plague take their time, but the nigger they really
wanted was Gabriel, the general. And it just happened that
there was a plenty fight left in that individual, if they only knew
it. Of course, he couldn't whip a whole squad single-handed,
but he could well-nigh worry them to death if his luck held
out, if he managed to keep his hide free of buckshots.

His hat was battered beyond recognition, and the purple
coat had begun to show its hard use. His shirt was gone. A
strip of bright black nakedness flashed between his buttons.
Gabriel rested his hand on an overhead beam and leaned forward, his long insidious gaze fixed rigidly on nothing. A little
later he sat on a heap of filthy straw, rested his back against the

wall; presently his chin fell against his chest, his eyes closed. His exhaustion was so profound he did not awaken when he finally toppled over on his side.

Then the hours were lost until at length he sprang up fiercely and began hacking at the shadows that crowded the stable. In the midst of this vastly satisfying set-to he awakened, his nerves tingling pleasantly, his feet no heavier than feathers, and replaced his blade. Sleep was gone now. He went out, threw himself over the fence and started up the alleyway. His mind became splendidly active.

Well, now, ain't this a pretty. We-all could of been doing a heap better'n we is doing. Somebody need to be going round and round this town at night; every now and then he need to stop and beat a drum and holler like the devil. Folks would think there was near about a million man-eating Africans in the woods; they wouldn't get no sleep, and that's how we could wear them out. Me and Ditcher and Blue and Solomon and Martin and a few mo' could do that. I'm got to find them. If we can't make no drums, we can sure pop up underneath of a bush every now and then and holler like devils. The others'll hear us, too; they'll come. I'm got to find my crowd, me.

"Stop." The word had been on the surprised man's lips and it leaped out involuntarily and without meaning, for Gabriel was facing him like a beast and in the same instant he sprang at the soldier's face. "Bloody swine—my musket—get your hands off—I'll kill you. Damn black—help, help! No, don't shoot— Oh, God please, no, no. Don't, don't, don'——"

"Here, take yo' musket, suh. Generals don't use 'em. Anyhow a sword'll do the work mo' quiet-like. Got to leave you now. Wa'n't no cause for you to make all that fuss, hollering for help. You wasted yo' breath, Mistah. You could of breathed two-three mo' times, did you keep yo' mouth shut."

There were running feet on the walk. Somebody opened an upstairs window and held a candle out. Presently a horse clattered on the cobblestones. Gabriel charted his directions deliberately. Then, pulling himself together, he slipped between two buildings, leaped a fence, ran a few paces in a lane, scaled another fence and presently faded in a clump of fruit trees.

# *Six*

NORFOLK was unruffled. News filtered through from Richmond, of course, and the papers had much to say about the disclosed plot, but there was less to worry about here. It was true, if one accepted the rumors, that Norfolk had been included by the blacks in their dream of empire, and there had been reports of unexplained slave gatherings outside the town, but nothing had come of these thus far, and, aside from doubling the night patrol, nothing thus far had been done.

The waterfront was the same. Sailing boats tugged at the wharf, rocked sleeplessly as the seas came in. Barefoot deck Negroes shambled along the landing, twisting little useless hats in their hands and kicking up dust along the landing. Without the hats to occupy their hands, they let their arms fly back and forth with an air of important hustle. The fact that it was all mockery and that they were usually bent on a sleeping nook struck them as being apparent, yet their faces disclosed nothing but innocence and industry.

The streets in that part of town were forever cluttered with ox carts, carriages, wains and saddle horses. The air had a flavor. Heaping cargoes of indigo, tobacco and hides waited on the landings. Incoming boats brought sugar, tea, coffee, dates, cinnamon, bananas, cocoanuts, rum and fragrant woods. Some of the argosies were unloaded by black rousters in loin cloths, some by brown men in turbans, emissaries of legendary worlds. A medley of languages was heard.

General John was intoxicated by the aroma of things. He stood behind a crude shed and watched the labor of tiny fishing craft out near the rim of the sky. His long oversized coat was in strings, but he had caught it together at the throat in an effort to cover his naked belly. The coat was a blessing, too. It had pockets, which his jeans had not, and just now pockets were powerfully useful to General John; he had something to put in them.

These here Norfolk people ain't studying me. They ain't paying me no mo' mind than if I wasn't here. Dog take my time, though, they is apt to think something do they see me slipping round here behind this old shed. Yes, suh, bless Jesus, I'm going to walk out yonder big as life, I'm is; I'm going to go over there to the stagecoach station like as if I owned the devilish place. Peoples ain't paying me no mind. This here diving and ducking'll make them think something's rotten. Here go me, peoples.

There now, see? Didn't know me from Adam. Nice down here, all the spice and things, the barrels of rum and the sweet-smelling wood and all, mighty nice. I'd catch me a boat, too, was there one fixing to sail directly. But I can't be waiting around now. Even if they ain't studying me, I can't wait all week. That there stagecoach is the thing. Looka there—see that? This tarnation town is busting wide open with niggers, and every lasting one of them look just alike to the white folks. These peoples don't know me no better'n I knows them, and that suits both two of us mighty fine. Looka there—see?

Go on there, brother, don't *you* start turning round and looking me up and down now. You neither, Mistah Man. Go on about yo' business—on'erstand? H'm. Now, that's a little mo' better. Y'-all don't know me from bullfrog, and if you did, it wouldn't do you a speck of good. The Governor ain't said he's going to pay you for catching anybody except Gabriel and Ditcher. Go catch them if you's big enough. Next town I hits, leastwise the first one across the line, I'm going to buy me some clothes to wear. These rags ain't fitten for a hog. Look a-them shoes: nothing but tops. And my pants, Lord a'mighty, they don't even hide my privates. This old coat is a caution to look at, but it sure do do a heap of good. They wouldn't let a nigger walk through town with pants like this, showing all his— Lordy, no they sure wouldn't.

Well, now, I'm here, ain't I? Soon's that there stage-driving man get his horses out in the yard I'm going to get in and set down too. I sure is tired a plenty; peoples, that ain't no tale, neither. For a fact, I believes I could sleep two-three days 'thout waking up or turning over. Well, suh, what in the name of lands is them folks doing? Oh, buying tickets, hunh? That's something I can do whilst I'm waiting, I reckon.

"Howdy, Mistah Man. Yes, suh, I'm aiming to travel some, I sure am."

The stranger was promptly joined by another, and it occurred to General John that the two looked very little like stagecoach officials. Their eyes were uncommonly stern. And their interest in the wizened old Negro was, to say the least, not a casual curiosity.

"Your papers," General John heard one of them say in the course of a long period, the remainder of which escaped him.

"Papers, hunh? Papers for what, suh?"

Out of a tiny waiting room, curiously, came a uniformed guard. He was armed. Suddenly the three men dropped the veil.

"Where the hell you come from, old nigger? Who you belong to anyhow?"

General John became tense; his old withered lips went white. He shot quick glances at first one man and then another. His head fell forward, but under his rags his shoulders tightened and the quaking old fellow rose on the balls of his feet. His anguished smile revealed the horrid dark fangs that were his teeth, but there was now a shadow of cunning in his eyes that suggested an ancient fox.

"I's a free nigger, suh. I ain't *no*body's, me."

He bowed lower, thinking fast, still poised on his toes, as ready and elastic as a cat. Then his mind fastened on something. One way was hopeless, to be sure, but there were other things he needed to consider. He snatched a paper from his pockets. It was too large; it should have been only half the size. Yet in a flash he crammed more than half of it into his mouth and began swallowing hard as the guards laid hands on him. They snatched a crimped fragment from between his lips, boxed his head severely and bent him double in a frantic attempt to make him cough up what he had swallowed.

"Just what I thought. Search his pockets, rip the insides out of that old coat. Money, too. H'm, I thought so. Calm yourself there, you old dog's vomit, or I'll run you through now. He's one of them. By God, he looked *too* harmless; I thought something was rotten. Here, look——"

General John's courage began to melt. His thought, racing like a squirrel in a cage, slowed down to a walk. The men's hands were on him, clasping viciously. His face smarted from the blows, his head ached. He grinned at them weakly. He was a weird sight.

On the portion of the note that he had saved, the guard read: *Alexander Biddenhurst, corner Coats Alley and Budd Street, Philad—* The writing was a clear, though illiterate, scrawl. The man's eyes danced. Suddenly, harking back to General John's last remark, he added, "You're not going anywhere, old dog." The armed guard had to almost chop a way through the circle of spectators.

# *Seven*

A ND in Richmond, bound to the floor of his cell, Mingo
could still hear the hangman's trap falling periodically.
Obscure Negroes were dragged before the justices in the
morning and hanged the same day. The known leaders, as they
were taken, were not punished immediately, however. There
was still that question of Jacobin hands turning the spoon in
the kettle: Fries, Gallatin, Duane, Callender and certain United
Irishmen had not yet been cleared of suspicion, either. Their
French babble about the natural equality of man had taken
root like dragons' teeth. The black chiefs would have to be
held for questioning. So Mingo, who knew how to read, who
kept the lists, lay with his face to the floor. Ditcher, chained
like a bear, sat on a stool in a dungeon. Rats romped about his
bare feet.

Meanwhile Ben brought the cariole into town alone. The afternoon was fine, and the autumn trees were growing brighter
and brighter. God's upturned paint pots had indeed spattered
them all with red. At the edge of town he saw a familiar young
man standing beneath a balcony, his arm hooked in a horse's
bridle, his hat off, his wig exceedingly white, but Ben had to
look twice before he fully recognized young Marse Robin.
Leaves were falling. The face above had a taunting way of vanishing and reappearing every moment or two. It was wonderful, Ben thought, how oblivious young folks could be to death
and woe. Maybe it was being white that enabled them to be
unconcerned. What did a few niggers more or less mean to
them? God bless them, they weren't studying any evil; they
were just thinking about their own problems. And right now,
seeing that young Robin was just getting himself cured of a
honey-colored woman with hoops in her ears, he must have
had his hands full. Ben twitched his lines, and the little mare's
porcelain-clean feet twinkled again.

You're a good boy, Ben.

Yes, suh, young Marse Robin; thank you, suh. It do pleasure
me a heap to hear you talk that a-way. I's aiming to be good,

befo' God I is. You and yo' pappy is two mo' sure 'nough quality white mens. God bless me, I was about ready to turn my back on y'-alls once, but I bound you I won't do it nara 'nother time. That old dead Bundy—him squatting side of that hole in the low field. Jesus! He the one what was cause of it— him and Gabriel. But God beingst my helper, I'm standing by you from here on, suh. I ain't strong for no such cutting up as Gabriel and them was talking. I been a good nigger, suh, and I's too old to change now.

Pharoah, the pumpkin-colored one, came out of a shop carrying a full basket. Seeing Ben, he threw up his hand pleasantly and stepped down on the street.

"Well, now, what time you make it, old man?"

Ben looked at the sky.

"Two-three hours befo' dark, I reckon. Where you's bound?"

"Home."

"Well, howcome you can't wait and ride piece-ways back with me?"

"I ain't aiming for dark to catch me on the road, Ben."

"Scairt?"

"Nah, just careful-like, I reckon." He shuddered a moment. "The niggers is just nachal-born tired of seeing me live."

Ben didn't answer.

"Listen, Ben, ain't you told it, too?"

"Seem like somebody think I has. Tried to hit me with a knife."

"No?"

"Yes, they did. Leastwise, they throwed it at me. Look at this hand. I ain't saying whether they was trying to kill me or whether they wasn't. It sure look like somebody don't love me much, though."

"Lordy, I can't stand it, Ben. Seem like I'm all the time about half-sleep and half-wake. You reckon they's poisoned me?"

"Conjure poisoning? Well, ain't you carrying nothing?"

"String round my neck. That's all."

"I don't know, Pharoah. Some time I feels mighty funny myself."

"Got to hurry along now. Don't want night to catch me on the road."

"You can just as well ride piece-ways with me."

"Ne' mind, Ben. I can't wait."

Ben clucked to the mare.

An hour later he was back at the same spot, driving out of town. He had tucked the lap rug around his knees and now sat gravely erect in the small carriage. A North African sailor passed him in the road, a turbaned Negro, bright black, barefoot and without a shirt. He looked up, giving his pendants a toss, then promptly averted his face. Suddenly a host of swifts flecked the sky above an old chimney. They kept rising, gushing up like blown-out cinders. Ben set his eyes on the road again. Between the small ears of the small horse he discovered a distant spot near the bend of the road where the bushes were troubled.

Ben took a quick breath, stiffened in his seat and tried to prepare himself for danger. The bushes rustled again, then became still. There was the steady tock-tock of little porcelain feet on the firm road, and the eager animal never slackened pace a moment. In another moment they were at the bend. Ben pulled up the reins and at the same instant the bushes parted. Pharoah sprang out and ran down to the cariole.

"Let me ride some, Ben."

"You ain't home yet?"

"Somebody's after me. Let me ride piece-ways."

"Nobody ain't studying you—not here in the broad daylight, nohow. That's 'magination."

" 'Magination nothing. Let me ride some now. Marse Sheppard won't care none."

"I tried to get you to wait in the first place."

"It's getting dark heap quicker'n I reckoned. Somebody done spied me, too. I heard them amongst the trees. You know I done already had one knife throwed at me."

"Climb on up."

"Much obliged, Ben."

"Maybe you shouldn't of been so burning up to run tell everything you knows. Leastwise, not if you's aiming to live a long time. Get up, Miss."

"It wasn't me what give them the names and all. Ain't you told nothing, Ben?"

"Ne' mind me. It ain't helped *you* none to talk yo'self near about crazy."

"You said they picked you up once, then let you go?"

"Now if you hadn't gone busting to town like you did——"

"Somebody say the white folks let you go cause you told, cause you told them plenty."

"I told them about me. They come and got me. They was aiming to hang me with the rest, I reckon."

The blood left Ben's lips. Pharoah shivered. Again there was a brisk tock-tock on the firm road.

"Some's catching the rope what ain't done nothing, Ben. Howcome they let you go—seeingst you told them about yo'self?"

Ben turned his face.

# Eight

THE small chest-like trunk had been dragged into the middle of the floor, and the young mulattress stood above it in a billowing leaf-green dress. The window hangings were down now, and the room was flooded with yellow light. Melody passed a bright velvet garment through her hands, inspected it lovingly from top to bottom, then knelt to pack the garment away as neatly as possible. There were other articles, too: petticoats hanging on the backs of chairs, capes thrown across the table, pieces of china worth saving, a silver vase, a decanter, a medley of footgear strewn around the gilded box.

Melody felt a certain sadness, but she knew her own mind and she had made her decision. Richmond had suddenly become too small for her. She had a *feeling*. Something told her that she couldn't stay there, enjoying so many conflicting confidences, without becoming entangled. Her imagination was at work, too. Why, for example, was young Marse Robin losing interest? Not that she cared, but might it not have a meaning, coming as it did at this turbulent time? Oh, there were so many angles, so many things involved. Was it suspicion that she saw on his face these last few times?

Well, let it be; she was leaving town. Philadelphia, according to Alexander Biddenhurst, would be a more wholesome place for a young freed woman, particularly an alert and handsome one, despite, in this case, her obvious inclination toward easy virtue. Why, it was a hateful thing, he thought, to sell one's graces to the sons of aristocratic planters. Being the favorite of such men would never help her to serve the cause of liberty and equality. She was selling out her own class, the masses of black folks, the poor, the enslaved. Of course, her sympathies were all right, but of what good was sympathy for the unwanted coming from the darling of their oppressors? No, it was leaving time now. Good-by, peoples. Good-by, church. These zebra-striped stockings—well, toss them into the trunk too. They wouldn't take up much space.

There were, in fact, very definite and substantial things that

771

could bring her trouble if she delayed her departure. There
was the flight of General John with the address she had given
him in his pockets. Lordy, what had come of him? How was he
getting along—him and his raggety self? Do tell, Lordy—po'
old General John. Yes, and there were heaps of people who remembered that Biddenhurst himself had—maybe it was infatu-
ation and maybe it was something very different—at least, he
had known her. And it was funny about him, very funny. Not
very ardent, to be sure, not warm or sensuous, but a curiously
exciting person. All on fire. Liberty, equality, book learning.
. . . He was a case, that Philadelphia man. Looked as if he
might have been part Jew, but he hobnobbed with the
French.

Presently shadows streaked the bright room, and Melody,
rising from her knees, saw clouds in the sky. The storm was less
than a month past, but here was a promise of rain again. No
matter about that, though; old Benbow Bowler understood
that he was to come for her trunk before day in the morning
and deposit it on the schooner *Mary*, scheduled to leave Richmond at dawn. Melody untied her headcloth, went into the
front room and swung the shutters out. She couldn't let folks
see her through the front windows with her hair tied, but by
now she was bored with packing and curious to see who might
be passing.

The street was empty. A mist was gathering down toward
the river. In the other direction two oxen were tied to a tree in
a field where they had been pulled off the road with their cart.
The clouds mounted. Melody leaned across the sill on her elbows, her feet off the floor and swinging childishly. After a
while she closed the shutters and lit a candle. It was time to
prepare supper.

Her mind told her to dash the light. If anyone knocked at
the door, she would lie still and make no sound till the person
was gone. Her house was upset from front to back. She wanted
no visitors, and she wanted no one to carry out the news that
she was leaving town. She wanted to answer no questions.
Melody lay across the bed in a rumpled dress and listened to
the drip of water in the roof drains. The shower itself was so
fine and veil-like it made no sound. Three times she heard the

rattle of broughams on the road. Not one stopped. Melody drew the coverlet above her shoulders and slept.

She awakened to a violent banging downstairs at her back door. And when she snatched on her cape and ran to the window that overlooked the yard, she saw a magical glow over the wet earth. Sheet lightning played like a blue fairy light, seemed to emanate from the very earth. In it she could see a burnished black figure, naked above the waist, wearing a badly battered hat, tottering like a man in a daze: an uncommonly large Negro, sorrowful yet dignified, undismayed, unafraid, turning a slow insidious eye up to her. And suddenly, with a burst of recognition, she put her hand on the sill and felt her own quaking.

"You, Gabriel."

"H'm. Me."

"Lord, boy, howcome you knock at my door this time of night?"

"Ain't nobody here but you," he told her.

"You right sure about that?"

"Right sure, yellow woman."

"Well—" She went to a shelf for the key. He hadn't moved when she returned. "—here then."

It struck the ground at his feet. She went into the next room and waited for him to let himself in. No, better not make a light. She drew the remaining curtains, pushed back the shutters. That was a help. One wouldn't have to stumble over the table with this blue brightness playing on things. Presently Gabriel came through the kitchen, handed her the key.

"Thank you, gal."

"What's that rag in yo' hand?"

"My coat. It's sopping wet."

"Here—let me have it. There's still some coals in the grate."

"I ain't got long."

"I know. Just as well to hang it here, though."

"Thanks a heap." He raised his head. "Mm-mm. Lordy!"

"Lordy what?"

"The perfume and sweetness and all. It's fit to kill and cripple in here."

He was luminous like the earth, giving the same blue light

in the murky darkness. The muscles quivered and ran on his arms and back. When Melody came out of the next room, there was a blanket in her arms.

"Put this round you, boy. Take that old broken-up hat off yo' head, too. Sit down. Rest yo'self some, beingst you's here."

He obeyed. His sword fell against the floor with a clank. If he had only been dry, he would have felt like some*body*. But a general can't feel like somebody as long as he's wearing a pair of sopping wet pants, as long as he can hear water slushing in his shoes. Gabriel's chin fell against his chest. After a long while he looked up slowly.

"Is you seen anybody, gal? Is you heard any talk?"

"Some, I reckon. Why don't you fly, though. Howcome you keep hanging round town, beingst everything's like it is?"

"I don't feel like running. I just feels like fighting, me."

She stared at him for a moment and decided to let that point rest.

"Has you et a plenty?"

"Little bit. Don't feel much like eating here of late."

"No, I reckon you don't. Just the same you need to keep something in yo' stomach if you aims to keep moving."

"Some time I picks up a apple, some time a ear of dry corn, some time nuts or berries or eggs. I ain't plum empty."

"You could do with mo', though; I bound you that."

"Maybe so. What is you heard? Who is you seen?"

"Wait. Let me see what's left in my kettle."

"Tell me now. Has you set eyes on Ditcher or Mingo or Blue? Has you heard tell of Gen'l John or my brothers?"

She reached the door.

"Some of them," she said. "Wait."

# *Nine*

GABRIEL, warmed by the food, relaxing in his chair, threw out one foot majestically, leaned back, his elbows on the arms of the chair, his chin in the palm of his right hand. There, almost lost in shadows, his dark insidious gaze ran from an uncertain point on the floor to the woman on the couch. She had a lazy, indolent air, that Melody, but her presence was so soft and delicate, so charged with fragrant odors, that Gabriel began to feel himself dirtier even than he was, a befouled thing and sorely out of place. His flesh tingled, but there was a drowsiness on his eyes. He could have slept. His head began to rock.

"There, rest yo'self if you's a-mind to, boy. Sleep some. Want to lay down?"

Gabriel remembered his wet pants, his grimy, unclean person. It embarrassed him.

"No," he said, "ne' mind that. Just got to nodding here. What was that about Ditcher?"

"Ditcher give himself up directly after the Governor put up the reward for you and him."

Only Gabriel's eyes showed surprise. His voice came back deep, troubled, but unastonished.

"He in the lock-up, hunh?"

"Been there two-three weeks."

"Not two-three weeks."

"Well, maybe one-two."

"Where'bouts Gen'l John?"

"Philadelphia—if they ain't headed him off."

Gabriel spent several moments with his thoughts. Then suddenly he twitched his feet, stirred in his chair.

"Well, here's one what ain't going to give hisself up. Here's one that ain't aiming to fly away neither."

Melody rose on her elbow, tossing one foot indifferently.

"Was you right *smart*, you'd fly, though."

"I reckon I ain't smart. Not smart 'nough to run."

"Whose house you going to knock at tomorrow night?"

"I don't know. Howcome you say that?"

"See that thing yonder?"

"That there box? Yes."

"That's my trunk. It's all packed up and locked. Benbow be here for it any time now. I'm leaving befo' day on the *Mary*, boy."

"You?"

"Nobody else. It's leaving time, if you ask me."

"Somebody got to stay and fight. It's well and good for you, kicking up yo' heels; you's free. You don't know how it feels."

"'Pears to me, you's free too. Who been telling *you* where to go and what to do these here last two-three weeks?"

"Well, now, I reckon so, me. But a plenty mo' niggers ain't free."

"You can help them mo' better if you's live than if you's dead."

"I might could get up another crowd here."

"You might couldn't, too. Who you think's going to fight now, after seeing all them black mens get kilt—hanged? You can't do a heap by yo'self."

"There ain't nothing else for me, though. I just as well to get kilt. Maybe I can get in two-three mo' good licks befo' my time come. That might would help some others what ain't free."

"It ain't sense. You's big and strong and mighty fine, boy. Was you away somewhere, way away and live, well then, maybe——"

Gabriel pulled himself together in the chair. His hands gripped the arm-rests, and he let the blanket slip down from one shoulder.

"Listen——"

"I hear. A wagon or cart or something."

"It done stop now."

"Benbow, maybe."

She ran to the front window and looked down. The shadowy cart had halted, but no one was apparently getting to the ground. It was a cart, too, a crude two-wheeled affair and not a carriage or brougham or cariole. If it was Benbow, why didn't he come in? He knew where she lived; he knew all the details. Surely he didn't expect to see a light in the window. . . . Come on up, Benbow, stupid nigger; you can't be wasting time. The *Mary* ain't fixing to wait on nobody.

Not getting down, hunh? Moving along. Well, maybe it wasn't Benbow. Funny, though, stopping out yonder like that. Funny as the devil. What's that, now? Sound like something scuffling up leaves across in the field. Something scuffling underneath of them trees all right. Somebody's hogs or something.

"H'm," Gabriel said.

He could not see her across the room, but a shadow was shaking its head.

"Gone now," she said. "Whoever it was. Nobody didn't even get down from the thing."

She waited at the window. Down at the river landing things had begun to stir. There were flares. Now and again a voice identified itself. There was no doubt that they were making ready the *Mary*.

Gabriel rested his chin in his palm again, and his eyes promptly closed. They did not open till Melody returned from the window some time later.

"That's him for sure now. He's coming round to the back," she said, excited.

Gabriel sprang up, confused.

"Coming, hunh?"

"Benbow. Coming to take my trunk."

"Oh. I was about to go to sleep. I couldn't make out who you meant was coming."

"*About* sleep?"

"Maybe I *was* sleep—just that one minute."

"You need to rest, I bound you, but it's near about leaving time now." She ran from window to window, drawing the shutters and pulling together such hangings as were still up. Then she ran into the kitchen and made a small light. "Come on up, Benbow, That's you, ain't it?"

"H'm. This me, Miss Melody."

He came in directly and stood in the door: a short pudgy black with masses of woolly hair pulled together ruthlessly and tied in a queue. Gabriel rose, dropped the blanket, slapped on his hat and stood looking down, his hands on his hips. His air, unintentionally lofty, seemed to disturb the smaller fellow. Benbow's lips went white with surprise.

"Didn't you pass by few minutes ago?" Melody said.

"Mm—yes. Seem like I seed somebody, though; seem like they was police or something—so I kept on moving. Maybe, though, they was looking for Gabriel. Maybe they know he's here."

"No cause for them to stand down there," Gabriel said indifferently. "They got they guns."

Benbow trembled a little.

"You' trunk ready now?"

"That's it there. You better hurry, too, Benbow. Look like they's getting things ready down there at the landing."

"Here," Gabriel said. He raised the small, solidly packed box and waited for Benbow to get under it. "Take it that a-way. See? No trouble to it. Did you see the boys working on the *Mary*, Benbow?"

"Two or three of them was a-stirring."

"That's a good-size schooner, Gabriel. You just as well to be down in it when she pull away. These police and all here waiting to see you come out the front door——"

"Well, maybe I ain't going out the front door."

Benbow was creeping down the steps. Then he was on the path, going around to the front.

"I got to dress in a hurry," Melody said. "Believe I'll ride on the cart with Benbow. It's powerfully dark out yonder."

Gabriel got his coat from the kitchen chair, tossed it across his arm.

"What time you say the *Mary*'s aiming to pull out?"

"Just about day. You better get on it if you can."

"There's a heap of things to think about when you's a general. Right now I don't know my mind. But I'm leaving here, though."

"You better forget some of them things on yo' mind—hot as they is on yo' track. Thing you need to do is see how fast a good general can run when push come to shove." Gabriel was walking away absently, hardly hearing what she said. "Here, wait a minute," she said. She wrote something on a sheet of paper. "Here's somewhere you can go in Philadelphia, do you get away."

Gabriel took it, started down the rear stairs. At the bottom he tore the note up, tossed the pieces on the ground.

# *Ten*

H<small>E SAID</small> he might be squatting side of a corn shock some night. Down in the low field, maybe. That's how I heard him say it, and I sure do wish he'd come right now. He allowed how I might could help him some. A jug of water, maybe, when he's near played out, some meat or bread or like of that. It's all here, boy. Howcome you don't come get it? Everything I can tote, tall boy, everything you talk about I got. It all come out of the big-house kitchen, too, right off of Marse Prosser's table. See here—yams, meat, corn bread, collards, a jug of rum, everything. Me, too; I'm here, boy. What else mo' you want?

Yes, and I got this here charm, too. I know you ain't got no mind for such doings, but it's what you needs. On'erstand? That big rain and all—that was the stars against you, boy. Toussaint and them, they kilt a live hog, drunk the nachal blood underneath of a tree. It made a big difference. You never did hear tell of nobody hunting him like a dog. Martin and all his Jesus; Mingo reading out the Book—nothing to that. Come on back, boy, and get this charm. Come lay down, rest. Nobody's studying you down here this time of night, nobody in the low field but me. Come pleasure yo'self with a blue-gummed gal, boy. Might change yo' luck.

He said he might be squatting side of some corn shock. I heard him say it like that, and I been here time and time again since he said it. But, peoples, it's a heart-sickening thing to keep on waiting when he don't show up.

Nasty night this evening. This little slow misty-like rain. Fit to give a body his death of dampness. Mighty dark, too. Funny how you can see things though. Everything look like it got its own light. Everything got a purple-like shine. Me, too, my hands and legs, this old rag, all shining. I reckon it's the sheet lightning on things.

He'd be shining too, did he come. He'd be something tall, something with a purple shine slipping through the high bushes, wriggling, coming this way. Lordy! He'd slip down side of me.

I know how. I know how. I'll see him easy, do he come. He'll be shining.

Better be stirring now. Freeze yo' round yonder, sitting on this damp ground all night. Need to stir about some.

There were cattle splashing in the bog. Now and again a coon barked in a black clump of trees. The thin-waisted brown girl wriggled out of her rags and stood for a moment rejoicing beside the creek. Lightning played around her. She stood with feet apart, arms thrust overhead. Then, splash! And she was slipping through the water like a moonbeam, a slim, transparent thing that disturbed the stream hardly at all.

Why didn't he come some time? When he was nearly played out, thirsty, hungry, lonesome, why didn't he look for her in the low field? She might be able to help him. It was just like he said. But she couldn't help him if he stayed away. Here was this charm, for one thing. It would be a protection to him. It was a thing he had neglected, an important thing. Was he right safe? Could he possibly be unable to come, or afraid? Had he changed his mind and made a dash for safer ground?

She pulled herself out of the creek, shook the water from her matted hair. The air was cold. Lordy, it was colder than she could endure. She snatched up her rags and ran to the row of huts.

"There's plenty to eat and drink out there, do he come now," she told herself. "But the charm is here in my hand. He wouldn't know what to do with that 'less'n I told him, nohow. Maybe he'll come tomorrow when it ain't so rainy and wet."

# *Eleven*

---

IT WAS a rat, sure as you're born, back behind the rum kegs, down in the hold of the schooner *Mary*. The devilish thing was as big as a cottontail, as full of fight as a porcupine.

Down on his hands and knees, eyes starting from his head and nostrils dilating, Gabriel saw the thing vaguely like a shadow. A moment later, when a scrap of light broke through, he drew his steel and held out a challenge. The rat, desperate in his corner, quickly showed a set of willing teeth. Gabriel came a trifle nearer, put the sword-point practically in the varmint's face.

Bad, hunh? Wants something to set yo' teeth into, do you? Try this here blade one time. See how this taste in yo' mouth, suh. Back on up if you's a-mind to. You can't go nowhere but in that corner. You's got to fight now. Showing me them teeth so big—you got to use them now. There: bite that. There, suh. Just as well to die fighting. I'm got you where I can say what's what now. Oop-oo-oop! No, you don't neither. You ain't getting by me that slick. There now, see what you done? Kilt yo'self. Jumped right straddle across my blade. Well, suh, that's you all right. Look just as nachal as can be. Got on yo' last clean shirt, too.

The schooner was moving along pleasantly. Now and again the kegs jostled. Cries of the men on deck rent the air at intervals. A peculiar lassitude settled on Gabriel. His eyes kept closing involuntarily. None of the usual feelings of sleepiness accompanied it, but periodically his eyes closed and things went black for a few moments.

Just as well be sleep as wake here now. No way to break and run, back behind here with the rats. Just as well to sleep from here to Norfolk. Yes, suh, just as well—ho-hum, just as well to stretch out—just as well—ho-hum.

His body was still asleep when his mind went to work again. He couldn't follow a train of thought, but he was aware of a parched throat. He was thirsty, near perishing for a drink. Water, rum, anything. Lordy——

His eyes opened. He raised himself on an elbow. Were they in Norfolk yet? How long had they been there? Now if he could only get Mott's ear. Lucky for Gabriel, he had seen that young cousin of his as he came on. Otherwise he might not have been so neatly stored. He might not have enjoyed such a long sleep. It was plainly dark outside. Things were quiet aboard. If he could only get Mott's ear about now. He went down on his belly and slept again. Later Mott came and Gabriel put two coins in his hand.

"Norfolk, hunh? Well, I'm staying down here a spell anyhow. I ain't getting off yet a while. That yellow woman——"

"Gone."

"H'm. Well, you can fill me a jug somewheres, if you's a-mind to."

"Stay long is you wants. The *Mary* going to be here a mont', I reckon. Maybe mo'."

"Where it going then?"

"To some them islands."

"Well, I feels like sailing awhile. I ain't getting off just yet."

"I'll bring you the jug directly."

Eleven days had passed. Gabriel had sent Mott to have the jug refilled. Then as he lay on his elbow, he heard stern voices on the deck. He caught a few words. Men were questioning Mott.

"You don't know? We'll take *you* then. Maybe you'll find out before it's too late."

They were fixing to arrest Mott, hunh? Well, suh, nothing like that. They was suspicioning Mott because he kept going and coming with that jug, with bread and meat in a basket, was they? They was aiming to lock him up, hunh? Nothing like that. Mott was powerfully afeard, and that was plain.

"No, suh, I ain't been in no Richmond, me. Leastwise, suh, I ain't been off'n the boat there. No, suh. No, suh, not me."

Gabriel slipped between the stacks of cargo. Then he remembered a bludgeon that had lain beside him and returned for it. Now he was doubly armed. Sunlight was like transparent gold on the deck. He came up, staggered in the intense light and started toward the four policemen who were at the moment haranguing the frightened Mott. The boy clung to his jug, but his knees were smiting.

Gabriel, towering like a giant, reeling noticeably, his clothes in outlandish shape, his eyes vacuous, was upon the group when they first noticed him.

"No, suh," Mott was protesting. "Not me—I ain't seen——"

"I'm the one," Gabriel said in a trance.

They all wheeled in confusion and excitement. For an instant a shadow of fear hung over the entire circle. The men stuttered. He was so obviously the wanted chief, that even Gabriel could see that they were parrying when the first one got a few words out.

"You? You Gabriel?"

They had been too astonished to draw their muskets. Gabriel had been too absorbed in his own daydream to take advantage of their delay. Now they all stepped back, leveled nervously. Gabriel dropped his club.

"I'm Gabriel. You oughta could see that boy ain't——"

"You—you giving up?"

"I ain't running. I wants a drink of water. I'm perishing for something to drink."

They got his blade. Suddenly a thought struck one of the policemen.

"Papers. Letters. Search him."

In a few seconds his clothes were ribbons. He looked at them with calm, detached eyes. His gaze, commonly dark and insidious, became indifferent, far-away.

"Is y'-all through?"

"Funny. Nothing but his money. No letters at all. Mighty funny——"

"You think he could have conceived it all himself?"

"Hard to tell."

"Through now?" Gabriel said.

Mott was slouched against the rain barrel, moaning audibly.

"He does have the look of one that——"

"I ain't got much rabbit in me," Gabriel said. "I ain't much hand at running. I was in for fighting, me."

He was very tired.

# BOOK FIVE

PALE EVENING. . . .
A TALL SLIM TREE

# *One*

---

Now for the second time Virginia was paralyzed with excitement. Benjamin Lundy, living in Richmond, but wisely contemplating a move to Tennessee, wrote letters.

"So well had they matured their plot, and so completely had they organized their system of operation, that nothing but a miraculous intervention of the arm of Providence was supposed to have been capable of saving the city from pillage and flames, and the inhabitants thereof from butchery."

So dreadful was the alarm and so great the consternation, that Congressman John Randolph of Roanoke, speaking with hand on heart, exclaimed, "The night bell is nevermore heard to toll in the city of Richmond, but the anxious mother presses her infant more closely to her bosom."

In Norfolk, meanwhile, crowds surged around the old jail. Bayonets bristled before the gates. In the mulling rabble were dozens of incurably curious blacks. Someone had reported that the dusky chief was about to be moved to Richmond. They had all come to catch a glimpse.

Yes, apparently something was going to happen. Police officers kept going and coming, passing the guards at will, exercising to the limit their prideful prerogative. Each time a lock turned, each time the gate cracked to admit an officer, a ripple of anticipation swept the crowd. Everyone went up on tiptoes, bobbed his head.

Where? Where? Is he coming now?

A sullen black sailor from a San Domingo boat stood with the others. He did not rise on his toes as the rest did; he did not bob his head. He had seen Dessalines ride a horse. He knew the sight of Christophe. He understood now that words like *freedom* and *liberty* drip blood—always, everywhere, there is blood on such words. Still he'd like to see this Gabriel. Was he as tall as Christophe, as broad as Dessalines? Was he as stern-faced as Toussaint, the tiger? They were saying now that the stars were against this Gabriel, that he had neglected the signs.

Yes, something *was* going to happen. They were about ready. Curse those long-necked white people. Couldn't they keep still a single minute? The officers were clearing a way. Evidently they were going to return the prisoner by river boat. There was the coach. Plague take those skinny white people; there they went crowding like swine.

Gabriel stood a moment, seen of all, then walked to the waiting coach. Mounted guards swirled around the conveyance. The crowd broke. The miserable young sailor stood alone, his thick lips hanging wretchedly.

It was an unsatisfactory glimpse. In twenty-four days the legend had become too great; the crowd wanted to know more. They were obliged to get it from the newspapers. In Norfolk they read the *Epitome* story.

"When he was apprehended, he manifested the greatest marks of firmness and confidence, showing not the least disposition to equivocate or screen himself from justice—but making no confession that would implicate any one else. . . . The behavior of Gabriel under his misfortunes was such as might be expected from a mind capable of forming the daring project which he had conceived."

Excitement spread like a fire catching up barn after barn. Wherever there was a black population, slave or free, there was consternation. The Negro became suddenly a dangerous man. In Philadelphia fear was rife. It was proposed there that the use of sky-rockets be forbidden, because in San Domingo they had been employed by the blacks as signals. And Alexander Biddenhurst, hearing the argument, went home and made a note in his journal.

"I can well understand how men's startled consciences make cowards of them. They recognize in the Negro a dangerous man, because they recognize in him an injured one. Injured men like injured beasts are always dangerous. By the same token extremely poor men are dangerous."

Then, pleased with his own words, he went out again, walked beneath the maples and filled his lungs with fresh air.

The *Daily Advertiser* pointed out that "even in Boston fears are expressed and measures of prevention adopted." This reference, of course, was to the advertisement then appearing in Boston newspapers. The police, it seemed, were taking this occasion to enforce an old ordinance for suppressing rogues, vagabonds and the like, an Act which forbade all persons of African descent, with stated exceptions, from remaining more than two months within the Commonwealth. Above a list of about three hundred names the advertisement read:

### NOTICE TO BLACKS

The officers of the police having made returns to the subscriber of the names of the following persons who are Africans or Negroes, not subjects of the Emperor of Morocco nor citizens of any of the United States, the same are hereby warned and directed to depart out of this Commonwealth before the tenth day of October next, as they would avoid the pains and penalties of the law in that case provided, which was passed by the Legislature March 26, 1788.

CHARLES BULFINCH, *Superintendent.*
By order and direction of the Selectmen.

Virginians, for their part, could look forward with hope to the next meeting of the state legislature. With gossips estimating a larger and larger number of Negroes involved, with the reporter for the *Epitome* discovering a meeting of one hundred and fifty blacks near Whitlock's Mills in Suffolk County and getting the assurance that some of these were from Norfolk, with the story of a similar gathering appearing in Petersburg newspapers, with a real insurrection being suppressed near Edinton, N. C., and with all these things being linked more and more closely to the one large design of Gabriel, the opinions of legislators became increasingly necessary. People couldn't sleep as things stood.

# Two

WELL, suh, I done sung my song, I reckon. It wasn't much, though. Nothing like Toussaint. The rain was against us. That Pharoah and his mouth wa'n't no mo'n I looked for. Something told me we was done when we turned back the first time. It was a bad night for such doings as we was counting on. A nachal man can't beat the weather, though. Nothing to do but take the medicine now.

The blacks boys there, working the boat and all—faces longer'n a mule's, every lasting one of them. They'd a-come with us once we got our hand in. They been powerfully polite to me. They know. They know I'm the gen'l. The weather turned out bad, that's all. There's a heap of things what could of been by now. Heap of black mens could of been free in this state, only that big rain come up. Befo' God, it looked to me like the sky was emptying plum bottomside up. Excusing that, niggers would of gone free as rabbits. These black boys know. They know I been a gen'l, me. They been polite, too.

Trees and all, all along the river there, little old houses in the thickets, red leaves a-blowing—mighty pretty. H'm. Didn't see none of this when I was going down two weeks ago. Lordy, me and that old rat was too busy having it out back behind them kegs and things. Yes, suh, worth seeing, too. I shouldn't of come, though. My mind ain't never told me to fly away. There ain't nothing good for Gabriel nowhere but right here where I was borned. Right here with my kinfolks and all. If I can't be free here, I don't want to be free nowheres else, me.

Bless me if I ain't had my time last three-four weeks, though. Ain't seen old Marse Prosser's face since I-don't-know-when. I been free. And, Lordy, I's free from now on, too. Plenty things they might can do to me now, but there ain't but one I'm looking for. Look at them here, lined up round me like the petals round a sunflower. All of them with they guns and everything—they knows what's what. They all know right good and well that they's riding with the gen'l. They know I'm a free man, me.

790

\*

They kept going downstairs. Then, when he could see nothing at all, they opened a door and led him inside.

"Down there—understand?"

He bowed on his knees.

"Flat on yo' belly, nigger. There's points on these muskets if you need a little help."

He put his face on the floor.

"Stretch your arms out. Wide. There now."

They locked the heavy bands around his wrists. Then for the first time he seemed to perceive, without seeing, that there was some one else in the cell, bound to the floor beside him. He couldn't imagine who it was. He wasn't even concerned.

Some of the guards went out. Two remained, and some other men came a moment later. Someone walked over and slapped Gabriel's back with a sword.

"Say, who were some of the foreigners that put it in your head?"

No answer. Then a prick of the pointed blade.

"You—where'd you get the sweet notion to butcher the people of Richmond?"

Gabriel heard the other prisoner squirm. Neither spoke.

"You had money. White men gave it to you, didn't they?"

There was an end of patience. A boot thudded—not against Gabriel's ribs but against the ribs of his companion.

"Talk, dog. You had the lists and the records. Who gave you those pamphlets?"

Then, with a jolt of surprise, Gabriel heard Mingo's voice.

"We didn't read no pamphlets. Them pamphlets didn't have nothing to do with us. We was started long before——"

"How many names did you have listed? Why did you plan to spare the French residents? Why were *you* so active in the thing? You were free."

"We was——"

Gabriel raised his head abruptly.

"Die like a free man, Mingo."

His voice, as he said it, had a savage quaver that suggested a lion. Mingo felt the air suddenly chilled. Trembling, he put his face against the rough boards again. Presently the other men left the two with their guards.

# Three

THE wrinkled black crones made a half-circle before the cabin door. Near by, within easy eyeshot, a host of naked youngsters scampered like little midnight trolls. The old bird-like women sat with scaly bare feet curled beneath them, heads tied in rags, and smoked their pipes in a dreamy haze. Now and again a heavy lip curled, disclosed the want of teeth.

"Ain't that gal young-un of yo's getting heavy, Tisha?"

"Lordy, she *been* getting heavy, chile."

"I thought so all the time. Well, that's good. Two-three days rest from the field'll do her good."

"Yes, she do need a rest. Beulah works so hard. Having a baby'll give her two-three days to kind of catch her breath."

"H'm."

"Hagar, what's that you was saying a little while ago?"

"Oh, about when I was a gal on Marse Bowler's place?"

"Yes, what about it?"

"Well, it look for a long time like I wasn't going to have no chilluns. Marse Bowler, the old one what's dead now, commenced to get worried-like and started talking about selling me down the river whilst I's young. One day I heard him tell some strange white man he didn't believe I could make a baby. That stranger he just turned down the corners of his mouth and say, Bullfrogs! I'm got a stud nigger on my place that'll——"

"Hush that foolishness, Hagar."

"It's truth, gal. And, well-suh, when me and that roaring bull——"

"Hush, gal. You's fixing to say that right away you commenced to spitting out all them ten-twelve babies of yo's. You need to get religion and hush lying. Ain't that Juba coming yonder?"

"She need to be in the field working, do she know what's good for her roundyonder."

"That Juba don't care nothing about her skin."

"She would, did she know what I knows."

"What you doing round here, gal?"

Juba came nearer, her hands on her hips.

"What it look like I'm doing?"

"Snappy, hunh?"

"No, not snappy. Just telling what you ask me."

"You ain't sound to me like you was telling. Sound to me like you was asking me something back."

"Well, I'm doing just what it look like I'm doing. On'er-stand?"

"Oh. Give him that charm yet?"

"I ain't seen him."

"Well, I heard somebody say it's too late now."

Juba put her nose in the air, gave her shoulders a toss.

"I heard that."

"It's true, hunh?"

"I reckon so. Mott say they brung him back this morning."

"Well, now, that's howcome you put down yo' hoe and come back here?"

Juba shrugged. A moment later she slid down beside the others, took a pipe out of her bosom.

It was evening when Marse Prosser called her from her hut.

"You, Juba."

"Yes, suh, Marse Prosser."

She came out into the twilight, her eyes wild, bloodshot. His scowl seized her at once, but she avoided the burning pin-points of his stare. For some reason she had a feeling of being undressed. It was nothing, of course. She waited sullenly.

"How much tobacco you cut this afternoon, gal?"

She rolled her eyes, her gaze rising to meet his attention, then straying off into the darkness. It was an insolent maneuver, but she refrained from speaking.

"I'll teach you, sow."

"You talking to me, Marse Prosser?"

A deep purple red flushed his cheeks.

"You—you varmint. Get on down to the stake. Trot along —trot, I tell you." He prodded her with the butt of his lash. She halted, planted her feet, every time he poked her, and eventually he was obliged to use the lash end on her bare legs.

At the stake she snarled and tossed her hips as she took the place indicated beneath the yard lantern. A crowd of frightened blacks materialized in the dusk, followed at a safe distance, the whites of their eyes, the palms of their hands, their rounded white mouths distinct in the shadows. Later they set up a soft dove-like lamentation.

"Pray, massa, pray. Oh, pray, massa."

"H'ist them clothes."

She understood and obeyed, snatching the old tattered skirt up over her naked buttocks.

The white palms, uplifted, fluttered in the darkness. The mouths, as round as O's, grew large, then small again.

"Lord a-mercy."

"Here's something else to toss up your petticoats for, ma'm. Here's something worth fluttering your hips *about*. Understand?"

She didn't speak, didn't even flinch. Presently her thighs were raw like cut beef and bloody. Once or twice she turned her head and threw a swift, hateful glance at the powerful man pouring the hot melted lead on her flesh, but she didn't cry out or shrink away. The end of the lash became wet and began making words like *sa-lack, sa-lack, sa-lack* as it twined around her thin hips. *Sa-lack, sa-lack, sa-lack.*

"Oh, pray, massa; pray."

Something shook the lantern overhead, and the near shadows began to tremble and bounce back and forth like dervishes. When would Marse Prosser get tired? Maybe he was waiting for that Juba to break down. Maybe he was aiming to take the starch out of her hide. Well, he was certainly a powerful hand at laying it on, anyhow. The voices increased in the thicket, the quaking hands multiplied.

"Another such caper from you, and I'll fix you so you *can't* cut tobacco—then sell you down the river for good measure— sell you down to one of them Georgia cotton raisers—where you'll eat hog slop and sleep in a stable with mules."

She said nothing. She wouldn't even let herself cry. Lordy, she was just so full of meanness, she could almost taste it. Cry? Humph!

*Sa-lack, sa-lack*—

"Pray, massa. Oh, pray, massa."

# *Four*

THE plight of Mrs. Cassandra Rainwater was that she was now too old to accomplish the things she dreamed. In her taffeta and lace she was even too wan and fragile to get around Philadelphia in her own carriage as she wished, and more and more she was obliged to leave with young Biddenhurst errands and contacts that might well have profited by her own attention. This in no wise inferred that the young man's talents were at all short of remarkable or his understanding, his sympathies, less than splendid; but her years, her feminine discernment, her lightness of touch must have offered advantages. Yet her plight was a common one; the sword was outwearing its sheath.

And indeed, over and over again, she had reason to be thankful that she had discovered Alexander Biddenhurst, discovered in him a romantic love of liberty like her own and a rather special burden for abused minority groups. At first there had been their mutual resentment against those who stole the Indians' hunting grounds. And now they were together convinced that liberty, equality and fraternity should prevail in the American States as well as in France. Each had read Rousseau and Voltaire with conviction, and each had been intrigued by the *Amis des Noirs.* Each hoped that somehow slavery would end promptly, even if the end had to come with blood as in San Domingo. The spirit of the master was abating, that of the slave rising from the dust. Jefferson was right; though, of course, he failed to go far enough. They themselves were not afraid to say (to each other, at least) that they approved the Jacobin ideal of utter equality for all men, everywhere. They enjoyed working for it as best they could. But Mrs. Rainwater, widowed and old, could do little of herself now, very little.

Yet she could still contribute her vision—her vision, her insight and, of course, her money. Fortunately she had a plenty of that, and scarcely any dependents. She rested the needlework that had occupied her fingers and adjusted her cushions. The young man rose to go, the afternoon sunlight making grotesque blurs behind his thick-lensed spectacles.

"I don't think you told me you were in a hurry, Alec."

"It's only the stagecoach that I was expecting to meet."

"Oh, yes. You did say—but about your moving. You didn't finish."

"I thought it would be well if they found my lodgings at Coats Alley and Budd Street empty. Of course, it proves nothing that that slave had my name and address when he was captured, but moving will save me the necessity of talking. They may want to make something of my being in Richmond at the beginning of the summer."

"Oh, that. Possibly."

"I couldn't have gone at a more suspicious time, had I actually been inciting the slaves to insurrection."

"You think those with axes to grind would be slow to believe that I sent you merely to look around, to study sentiment and get a cross-section view?"

"They'd never be satisfied with the facts. Being unsuspecting, I *did* say a good many strong things. Mostly I said them to draw out their thoughts, but you see how it's all coming to appear to an outsider."

"Possibly you're right, but they'll find you if they want you badly enough. Be sure to leave your new number anyhow. And come to think about it, why don't you use my carriage to meet the stage?"

"Well, if you say——"

"Of course. Didn't you say she's a young woman?"

"Yes. You and I are becoming a sort of bureau for the aid of fugitives—if nothing more."

"That's something. I hope we're getting at something far deeper, however. Whenever we succor a fleeing creature, I hope we make a soldier for liberty."

"No doubt we do."

"How about the Creuzots and Laurent?"

"Doing well. Their home is simpler than the one they left, but I have no doubt they'll become the kind of influences we want."

"I must have a talk with M. Creuzot. Is he coughing more than usual?"

"Not more."

"That's good. I'm especially eager to get some Negroes, some escaped slaves. They'll bring such an emotional fervor to the work."

"If I may go now——"

"Yes, of course, Alec. Take the carriage."

"Thank you."

Twilight had fallen. There was a cheerful confusion and bustle beneath the elms where the stagecoach unloaded. Mrs. Rainwater's amber coachman held his horses in a soft rain of leaves, while Alexander Biddenhurst ran across the road to meet the veiled woman traveling alone.

A little later, as the horses jogged along indolently, Biddenhurst realized that the carriage was too heavily scented. A dreamy lassitude had settled upon the tired, excited woman. Ah, he thought, it's a strange free-masonry, this love of freedom, a strange free-masonry. Of course, any man might be drawn to a fragrant, faintly tinted creature like this one, but that he should be a partner with her, sharing a secret, working for other ends, was strange. Yet all that did not forestall the joy of living, the pride of the eye.

"Melody—that's the name for you all right."

"You think so, Mist' Alec?"

"Listen. I'm not a rich planter's son, and you're not in Virginia now. *Mist' Alec!*"

She smiled in a drowsy haze. She was very tired.

# Five

"... and are you the one they call the General?"

"I'm name Gabriel."

"I've heard slaves refer to a General something or other."

"Gen'l John, maybe."

"Didn't they call you General?"

"Some time—not so much."

"Then old John there was the leader, not you?"

"No. I been the leader, *me*. I'm the one. Gen'l John is just named that. I'm the one."

"You *are* the General?"

"I reckon so. Leastwise, I'm the leader. I ain't never turned my back to a nachal man. I don't know if I'm a sure 'nough general or if I ain't."

Gabriel, still in the frayed coachman's clothes, sank back into a lordly slouch. Now, suh, curse they ugly hides, they could make up they own minds about the gen'l part. Is I, or ain't I? One hand clasped the arm of the witness chair; the other hung idly across his knee. His eye kept its penetrating gaze, but now there was a vague sadness on his face. It was as if shadows passed before him now and again. It may have been woe or remorse rising in him, but the look was more like the dark, uncertain torment one sees in the countenance of a crushed beast whose spirit remains unbroken.

Only that morning there had been another execution, a small herd of anonymous field Negroes. The townsfolk were hardened to the spectacle now. Even the customary eyewitnesses were missing. The word had gotten about that these were not the ringleaders, and the mere sight of slaughter for its own sake was no longer attractive or stimulating. So many little groups like this had come to the scaffold since mid-September—five, ten, fifteen at a time—so many. It was a routine. These blacks had contracted a malady, a sort of hydrophobia; they were mad. It was necessary to check the spread of the thing. It was a common-sense matter. Only this morning there had been a difference.

At first no one had seen or heard the wiry old man with the turn-down mouth. He had seen the first of the executions, and he had raised his voice then.

"You idiots. You're putting them through too fast, I tell you. No sense in killing off a man's live stock in herds like that unless you know for sure what you're doing."

He scrambled in the crowd and tried to fight his way through. But they thought he was talking about the blacks being idiots. A chorus of approval rose around him. No one saw him as an individual, only as a part of a snarling crowd.

Today, with things much quieter, they had heard, for he succeeded in delaying the hangings half-an-hour.

"See that long yellow boy there. Well, that's John Thomas. That boy's been to Norfolk for me. He just got back last week. And, by God, if you hang him without proof, you'll pay me his worth. Bloody apes, what's wrong with you? Have you gone stone crazy for life?"

John Thomas did not swing. There was a rumor that several other planters had also been to the justices since morning. And already a statement had been issued—some "mistakes" had been made, admittedly. But Gabriel, lying on his face beside Mingo, knew only what the swinging trap indicated. Yet it occurred to him that all this pause, this unhurried questioning, could not possibly have been in keeping with the trials that had preceded his. He concluded at length that the "General" was simply receiving his due recognition, this in spite of the prosecutor's whining, sarcastic voice.

"Here, now, you mean to say you were the one that thought up the whole idea?"

"I was the one. Me."

"Yes, but not all alone, surely——"

"Maybe not all alone."

"Well, then, who were your accomplices? Who helped you think it up?"

Gabriel shrugged.

"You got Ditcher and Mingo and Gen'l John. You done hanged a plenty mo'. I talked to some of them. I told them to come on."

"It's plain that you do not intend to implicate anyone not already in custody. You're not telling all you know."

Gabriel looked at the man long and directly.

"I ain't got cause to talk a heap, suh."

"You haven't?"

"H'm."

Then the prosecutor spun quickly on his heel, barked.

"What do you mean by that, you——"

Gabriel's eyes strayed indolently to the window, to the golden leaves of an oak bough. The court was oppressively rigid, the justices in their wigs and robes, the spectators gaping, straining their necks.

"A man what's booked to hang anyhow——" he mused.

"Oh. So you think——" Then a diplomatic change of tone. "You know, Gabriel, it is not impossible to alter the complexion of things even yet. A—I mean, you have a fine chance to let the court know if you have been made the tool of foreign agitators. If there were white men who talked to you, encouraged——"

That sounded foolish to Gabriel.

"White mens?"

"Yes, men talking about equality, setting the poor against the rich, the blacks against their masters, things like that."

Gabriel was now convinced that the man was resorting to some sort of guile. He fixed his eyes earnestly.

"I tell you. I been studying about freedom a heap, me. I heard a plenty folks talk and I listened a heap. And everything I heard made me feel like I wanted to be free. It was on my mind hard, and it's right there the same way yet. On'erstand? That's all. Something keep telling me that anything what's equal to a gray squirrel wants to be free. That's how it all come about."

"Well, was it necessary to plot such a savage butchery? Couldn't you have contrived an easier way?"

Gabriel shook his head slowly. After a long pause he spoke.

"I ain't got no head for flying away. A man is got a right to have his freedom in the place where he's born. He is got cause to want all his kinfolks free like hisself."

"Oh, why don't you come clean? Don't you realize you're on the verge of hanging? The court wants to know who planted the damnable seeds, what Jacobins worked on you. Were you not treated well by your master?"

Gabriel ignored most of what he said.

"Might just as well to hang."

"That's bravado. You want to live. And the best way for you——"

"A lion what's tasted man's blood is a caution to keep around after that."

"Don't strut, nigger."

"No, suh, no strutting. But I been free this last four-five weeks. On'erstand? I been a gen'l, and I been ready to die since first time I hooked on a sword. The others too—they been ready. We all knowed it was one thing or the other. The stars was against us, though; that's all."

It was astonishing how the thing dragged on, astonishing how they worried and cajoled, threatened and flattered the captive. "Mistakes" *had* been made, due to haste and excitement, but there was no possibility of a mistake here. Gabriel seemed, if anything, anxious to have them get the thing straight, to have them place responsibility where responsibility belonged.

In another room, under heavy guard and awaiting their call, the last of the accused Negroes sulked. Ditcher's massive head was bowed, his wiry queue curled like a pig's tail. It had never been more apparent that he was a giant. His legs suggested tree stumps. The depth of his chest, the spread of his shoulders seemed unreal. His skin was amber. Now, delaying in the guarded room, he was perfectly relaxed. Indeed, he might have nodded had it not been for the jittery, nervous activity of the armed men around him. They annoyed him.

"We could had them on they knees long ago," he was saying in his mind. "Only that devilish big rain. That's what stopped us. We could all been free as squirrels by now. It wasn't the time to hit. We should had a sign."

Mingo's clothes were better, but his hair had been torn from its braid. He had lost his spectacles. His eyes had an uncertain, watery stare. He was not merely downcast; he looked definitely disappointed. Words were going through his mind too, but they made a briefer strain.

"Toussaint's crowd was luckier. Toussaint's crowd was luckier."

There were others, a dozen or more, unimportant fellows. Then near the door the withered old dead-leaf clad in a rag that had once been an overcoat. He kept licking his white, shriveled lips, kept showing the brown fangs. He was trembling now.

"Somebody's obliged to foot the bill," his mind was saying. "Ne' mind, though. Near about everybody dies *one* time. And there ain't many niggers what gets to cross the river free—not many."

Any one of them would have sped the business along had it been his to do it. No cause for a heap of aggravating questions. Them white mens ought to could see that Gabriel didn't care nothing about them; he was going to tell them just what it was good for them to know, and precious little more. But there was nothing they could do, nothing but wait.

". . . and how did you imagine you'd be able to take the city?"

"We was ready to hit fast. We had three lines, and the one in the middle was going to split in two. They was coming in town from both ends at once. They wasn't going to spare nothing what helt up its hand against us."

"How about the other two?"

"Them's the ones what was ready to take the arsenal and the powder house."

"Which line were you to lead?"

"The one what went against the arsenal."

"What arms had you?"

"We didn't need no guns—us what went against the arsenal there. All we needed was to slip by in the dark with good stout sticks. We could manage them few guards."

"Mad dogs—that's what you are. The audacity! It's inconceivable that well-treated servants like——"

"We was tired being slaves. We never heard tell about no other way."

"You'd take the arsenal and powder house by surprise; then with ample arms, with the city in ashes, with the countryside and crops for your food, you thought you'd be able to stand your ground?"

"H'm."

"How many bullets had you to start with?"

"About a peck."

"And powder?"

" 'Nough for that many bullets."

"Any other arms?"

"Pikes, scythe-swords, knives, clubs, all like of that—'nough to do the work."

"How'd you know it would do the work?"

"There wa'n't but twenty-three muskets in town outside the arsenal."

"You knew that!"

Gabriel felt that it was unnecessary to answer.

There was a hush; a shiver passed over the courtroom.

"It was a diabolical thing. Gentlemen——"

He talked for a time with his back to Gabriel. Later he turned to the prisoner again, but this time he spoke like a changed man, an awakened man who had had an evil dream.

"Did you imagine other well-fed, well-kept slaves would join you?"

"Wouldn't you j'ine us, was you a slave, suh?"

"Don't be impudent. You're still a black——"

"I been a free man—and a gen'l, I reckon."

"And stop saying general, too. Ringleader of mad dogs. That's what you've been. I call on this court of justice——"

Gabriel felt the scene withdrawing. It was almost like a dream, almost mystic. Further and further away it receded. Again there was that insulting mockery of words he could not understand, that babble of legal language and political innuendo. It was all moving away from him, leaving him clinging to an arm of his chair, slouched on one elbow. A lordly insolence rose in him. Suddenly he was vaguely aware of that whiney voice again.

"The only question yet raised, sir, was whether or not the wretch was capable of conceiving such a masterpiece of deviltry, such a demon-inspired——"

It was far away. Gabriel's eyes strayed again. The window—blue. The crisp oak leaves—like gold. Demons. Freedom. Deviltry. Justice. Funny words. All of them sounded like conjure now.

"Maybe we should paid attention to the signs. Maybe we should done that," Gabriel thought.

# Six

BEN stood in the kitchen door and watched the fellow sitting on a chopping block beside the woodpile. Early-morning sunlight flooded the yard, and the pumpkin-colored slave sat beneath a bright arch of transparent gold. His elbows rested on his sprawled knees, his brown ham-like hands dangled between. Trouble had dogged old Pharoah since the day he carried the news to Richmond, and now his thoughts were in a whirl.

Lordy, me, I couldn't help telling. I just couldn't live and know all them peoples was fixing to meet they master 'thout knowing it. Seemed like I'd go hog-crazy if I didn't tell it. I *had* to; I didn't mean Gabriel and them no hurt. Just the same, they wants my meat. They wants a piece of my skin, Lord.

Ben watched him and saw the daydream play on his face, saw his lips curl, his eyes flicker. He saw, too, a crisp golden shower of oak leaves on the sorrowful mulatto and on the woodpile. Ben turned to Drucilla who was stirring something in a kettle, her immobile, mask-like face glowing in the heat.

"They's wearing Pharoah down all right, following him around like they do, throwing knives at him every chance they gets."

"What else he 'spect?"

"I don't know."

"H'm. I reckon you don't."

"But it's a powerful bad thing to sit around waiting for yo' medicine when you know you's sure to get it."

"*You* ought to know."

"What you mean, gal?"

"Nothing—just you ought know."

"Howcome *I* ought know mo'n anybody else?"

"I didn't say you ought to know mo'n anybody else."

"It sounded like you meant that."

"Did it?"

He leaned against the doorpost again. She shifted a few pots, stirred a while longer. Ben kept watching Pharoah's bowed head.

A few moments later, when he had decided to say nothing more to Drucilla, he heard her speaking to his back.

"Just like that yellow varmint. Least thing he could do, was he equal to a hound dog, was keep his mouth shut. But, no, he wanted to lead one line; and when they wouldn't let him, nothing would do but he must go tell everything. You and him——"

"Me and him what?"

"Nothing."

"What you keep on hinting at me, gal?"

"Nothing. Call him and see do he want a cup of coffee to ease his mind. You can put a drop of Marse Sheppard's rum in it."

Such fall weather. . . . Lordy! Ben preferred not to raise his voice. He strolled down the gravel walk, went over to the woodpile. He spoke to Pharoah; but the latter, shaking his head woefully, showed no immediate interest in Ben's suggestion. Later, however, he rose reluctantly and followed the other to the kitchen door.

"No need mopping yo'self sick, though."

"I ain't so scairt. That ain't it."

"Howcome you do it, then?"

"I'm sick, Ben. Sure's you borned, I been poisoned."

"Hush. Ain't nothing wrong with you."

"Don't tell me. I been finding frogs' toes and like of that in my pipe. They keeps my bed sprinkled with conjure dust. I been doing everything I know how to fight it, but it don't amount to nothing. I'm got slow poisoning sure's I'm a foot tall."

"Hush. A cup of coffee'll do you good. Then walk around till work time. You can make *yo'self* sick just studying like that."

Drucilla had placed a cup on the stove and poured an inch of rum in it. When they reached the door, she poured the boiling coffee.

"Wait there," she ordered Pharoah.

"H'm."

"Here, now. This'll ease yo' mind."

"You reckon?"

He stood cooling it a few moments, then raised the cup and poured the contents down his throat. His eyes were wide, startled, as if he had seen a spirit. Suddenly he began trembling violently. A moment later he was crying, his hand over his eyes. Ben and Drucilla stood before him paralyzed. Then, abruptly, his shoulders rounded, he gave a little hiccough and the coffee came out of his mouth in an ugly geyser that spouted on the floor of the porch. And when he removed his hand from his eyes and saw it there, he began crying louder.

"Lordy, Ben, look at it. See there. There it is. I told you so. They fixed me. I done puked up a varmint. What is it—a snake or a lizard? Lordy! They done fixed me. Look at it there, Ben."

His crying became louder and louder. Then, without warning, he left Ben and Drucilla in the doorway, bounded across the yard, raising his voice higher and higher, wailing insanely, and raced toward the clump beyond the stables.

Negroes began leaving the outhouses and cabins, coming into the early sun with amazed faces. One by one they started after Pharoah, pursuing him hesitantly, partly curious, partly concerned, but unable to resist following. Ben and Drucilla remained like statues in the doorway.

It was five minutes later when Drucilla went outside and recovered the cup and saucer the crazed fellow had tossed there as he left. She saw some of the black men returning from the tree clump, walking slowly.

"Catch him, George?" Ben called.

"It wasn't no use, Uncle Ben."

"Lord help."

"Done climbed a tree already. Up there barking like a dog."

"Barking, hunh?"

They went on. Drucilla went back into the kitchen. Ben stood wringing his hands. So Drucilla thought it was no more than Pharoah should expect for telling a thing like that? Telling a thing like that! Lordy, what could anybody expect. Anybody.

Ben's hands felt scaly and cold to himself. They were so thin and brittle he imagined they were like the hands of a skeleton. Still he could not restrain the impulse to pass one in and out of the other. He could not move his feet from the place where he stood on the path, either.

# *Seven*

A N AIR of mystery invaded the Virginia State Legislature. Assembled in secret session with drawn blinds and guards at every door, the men sat with bowed heads in a haze of tobacco smoke and flickering lamplight. A warm proud voice engulfed them. Subdued yet distinct in the small chamber, it laid before the group a possible solution for the baffling problem.

"*Resolved*, that the Senators of this state in the Congress of the United States be instructed, and the Representatives be requested, to use their best efforts for the obtaining from the General Government a competent portion of territory in the State of Louisiana, to be appropriated to the residence of such people of color as have been or shall be emancipated, or hereafter may become dangerous to the public safety. . . ."

At length the reading was finished and discussion was allowed. The black-clad men, intensely sober, deeply concerned, shook their heads and murmured. Somewhere in the rear a tired voice was heard saying, "Sir, not yet. The time is not ripe. Our present situation only delays the possibility of such action. There are so many angles. Perhaps slavery itself——"

Yes, the Governor told himself at Oak Lawn, it all led back to the same colossal bugbear. Why such a widespread fret about slavery? Hadn't there always been slaves? But with liberty the fad of the hour, it might well be expected. Some fanatic would always be absent-minded enough to apply his cant to the black man's condition in the American States. Whenever there was a nonsensical thing to be said, nature would provide a fool to say it. So it always went. At any rate, he was still the Governor of Virginia; his personal responsibilities had not ceased. He could at least write the President a letter looking forward to such action by the United States Congress as his own legislature was hesitant to suggest at the moment.

He walked to the window, withdrew the hangings. A frame

of stars. A moment later he returned to his writing table. In the pale orchid light he took a quill and began writing.

"Honorable Sir——"

Now it was different with Gabriel in his cell. He had not been returned to the hole where he had lain chained to the floor beside Mingo. Here there were chains, but now he sat upright on a stool when he wished, rolled on the floor when he felt inclined. There was a barred window, too, a frame of indigo sky with little near stars.

Them white folks is sure a sight. Now they's aiming to make Mingo talk some mo'. They is sure got great heads for figuring out something what ain't. They sure loves to wring and twist about nothing. Nothing going to do them now but to make somebody say white mens was telling us to rise up. Never heard tell of nobody being so set on a thing before.

When the night watch passed, Ovid walked around the corner and whistled for Midwick. Later, plowing his feet through the loose leaves, the older guard came to a pool of light near the main gate.

"Well, doesn't anyone know why she left, Midwick?"

"Don't seem to. Not unless some politician caused it—him or somebody mixed up with this insurrection business."

"Now that's a thing to blind you. I always thought that young Robin Sheppard was great on her."

"Just getting his education, I reckon." He snickered. "They say he's sparking somebody he can marry now."

"The other one was really something to look at, though. Kind of a—I suppose you call it exotic. Apricot-colored, enameled-like hair—most any man could enjoy a little recklessness with——"

"Steady, Ovid. Remember you're a——"

"Dash it all, Midwick. I'm sick of being steady. I want to do incredible things."

"Incredible?"

"Yes, outlandish, glamorous——"

"Well, now, if we go to war again——"

"Oh, you don't understand me, Midwick."

# Eight

A WEEK passed. The gallows-day came, and Gabriel awakened to the clatter of heels and the rattle of side arms outside his cell.

This the day all right. They is sure here early a plenty. Trying to be good as they word, I reckon. Beating the sun up so I won't get to thinking they's gone back on me. Never got up this soon in the morning to feed me, not as I can recollect, nohow.

H'm. Yes, suh, it's still night.

He curled his legs and sat upright, his hands resting on the floor to spare them the weight of the iron wristbands and chains. His naked shoulders gave a faint glow in the darkness. There was a brightness on his cheekbones, on his forehead.

Suddenly there was silence outside. A brief hush blanketed the men with the flambeaus and sabers.

Them is the mens with the milk-white horses, I reckon. I ain't seen nara one of them, but I know right well how they looks. H'm. I got a good mind how they come. I know about *them* all right, all right. . . . Galloping down a heap of clouds piled up like mountains. I know them milk-white horses, me.

His eyes, large, the whites prominent, turned listlessly. He was still sitting on his feet, his hands resting on the floor. Again the sabers rattled, heels clattered and a medley of gross voices rose in confusion.

Put yo' key in the lock, Mistah Man. Give the sign and come in, please you, suh. I heard a nigger say Death is his mammy. His old black mammy is name Death, he say. Well and good, onliest thing about it is Death is a man.

Come on in, suh, if you's a-mind to. I'm ready and waiting, me. I ain't been afeared of a nachal man, and I don't know's I mind the old Massa hisself. I ain't been afeared of thunder and lightning, and I don't reckon I'll mind the hurricane. I don't know's I'll mind when the trees bend down and the tombstones commence to bust. Don't reckon I'll mind, suh. Come on in.

The sky flushed as they put him in the cart, and suddenly Gabriel thought of the others, the ones who were to follow him,
the ones who waited in their cells because of his leadership,
these and others, others, and still others, a world of others who
were to follow.

There was a long over-sized box on the cart, and Gabriel
knew its use. It had to be long, over-sized, for a body of his di-
mensions. He sat on the thing, threw out his feet. A flood of
color burst in the east, rose and orchid and pale gold. The cart
jogged. A clatter of feet went before, and a clatter of feet came
after. Sabers rattled from the belts of shadowy, uniformed men.
Above their heads a score of muskets pointed toward heaven,
pointed like the stiff fingers of black workers rising from their
prayers.

*The trumpet sounds within-a my soul.*

Ditcher, even then was standing at his small window with
bloodshot, sleepless eyes. His face was marked by numerous
small scars. He had been a fighter. Not that he was petulant or
touchy, but the nature of his work frequently got him em-
broiled. The nature of his reputation, before Gabriel deflated
it, obliged him to meet all comers. But fighting had never been
a pleasure to Ditcher; this morning, his massive hands clasping
the window bars, he lamented all wars. Presently, he thought,
so far as he was concerned, the trumpets would blow their last
blast. The sky would flush, redden like a sea of blood, and the
sun would go down on all conflict. . . . Presently. Presently.
Outside the cart lumbered. The pale torches blossomed like
white flowers.

Good-by, Gabriel. Don't nobody need tell *you* how to die, I
reckon. You's the gen'l, you.

Distraught, fluttery, Mingo chewed his lips and dug his
fingernails into the palms of his hands. The Book said some
powerfully hopeful things about the stranger, the servant, the
outcast. The Book was all for abused folks like Negroes. Other
books too, in fact. Mostly them men what writ books was a little
better kind than them what made speeches at the town meetings.

Wagon, hunh? Bright and early, too. Gabriel be the first, I

reckon. Yes, the first, all right. Toussaint was first across yonder; Gabriel's first here. The first robin going north. It was too
soon for Gabriel, though. It wasn't summer. The cold caught
us here, the rain and all. Toussaint drunk blood. Gabriel never
had no head for such doings as that. They was the first, them
two.

Ne' mind, boy.

General John was as scrawny as a hawk now. The days of
waiting had drawn his face so tight and hard it suggested a
bird's face. Inside his torn garment, his shaggy feathers, he
twitched a rattling skeleton-like body.

Was I a singing man, I'd sing me a song now, he thought.
I'd sing me a song about lonesome, about a song-singing man
long gone. No need crying about a nigger what's about to die
free. I'd sing me a song, me.

The horizon was pearl-gray now, but overhead a star or two
lingered. A man gave the word, and Gabriel climbed the steps
to the platform. For an instant he was still, his hands idle.
Across some roof-tops a limp flag rose, ever so lightly, fluttered
a little.

They had chosen to bring him without shirt or coat. He
stood, naked above the waist, excellent in strength, the first for
freedom of the blacks, savage and baffled, perplexed but unafraid, waiting for the dignity of death.

"Have you anything to——"

Then an interruption, another voice.

"Would you ask that of a—of a black?"

"Well, seeing he's getting a hanging like this, I thought
maybe——"

"As you wish."

Then a stuttering followed by bluster.

"You want to talk now, you a—a—scoundrel?"

No answer.

"Want to talk now, I say?"

"Let the rope talk, suh."

"No statement?"

"The rope, please you, suh—let it talk."

The vein grew big in the executioner's forehead. His face
became livid. The narrow scar that was his mouth tightened,

tightened, tightened. Another man, standing beside the one with the ax, stepped forward, stood on tiptoes and placed the cowl on the tall Negro's head.

Somewhere down below feet tramped. The escort jostled, wheeled and withdrew a few paces.

Like night, Gabriel thought, like night with this thing on your head.

A command to the soldiers broke the absolute stillness. A wagon moved. A horse nickered. Then, here and there, the sudden, surprised intake of breath filled the air with a tiny whispering. The sheriff's ax inscribed a vivid arc. The trap banged, and the rope hummed like a violin string. And still there was that arc, inscribed by the ax, lingering there against the sky like a wreath of smoke.

Seated in a cariole a hundred yards away, a blanket tucked about his knees, Ben saw it and gasped. Near him a small crowd of Negroes bowed their heads, covered their faces with their hands. Even when Ben closed his eyes, he could see that arc, hear that violin string.

# Nine

B EN did not wait to see them remove the body. There were errands for him in town. Later he was expected to meet Marse Sheppard and drive him home.

So the morning was spent. Then it occurred to Ben that the sky was no longer clear, clouds were gathering. But now there was no further need for haste. Marse Sheppard was not ready. The old Negro drove his carriage down a street he knew well and remained in the seat, watching something in a corral beyond a low fence. A crowd of white men were mulling in a yard. Saddle horses were strung along all the near hitching bars; and wherever there was space, driving rigs were hitched.

Ben could see the slave block from his seat, could hear the auctioneer's voice, but he had been watching a long while before he realized that the brown girl up for bids was Gabriel's Juba, the tempestuous wench with the slim hips and the savage mop of hair. Her feet were bare. Her clothes were scant. And there was something about her figure, something about the bold rise of her exposed breasts, that put gooseflesh on a man. But her look was downcast, bitter, almost threatening.

Yet the bidding continued lively. Ben decided abruptly that he did not wish to see it through. He pulled on his lines and began threading a way through the thronged carriages of the planters. It was definitely going to rain.

Ben was waiting at a curb for Marse Sheppard when the first flurry came. Then the silvered old man, wrapped to the eyes in his cape, came out, and they started home in the downpour. When they were in the heart of town, lightning flashed, and Ben saw an array of bright red and yellow and green and purple parasols suddenly raised. Men dashed across the wet street, seeking shelter in shops. Carriages jostled. Voices called in the rain and received something better than their own echoes for answer. The clouds bore down. The air had a melancholy sweetness. But Ben could not forget Gabriel's shining naked body or the arc inscribed by the executioner's ax. He could not feel reassured about the knives that waited for him with the sweet brown thrashers in every hedge and clump. For him the rain-swept streets had a carnival sadness.

The little mare's feet played a soothing tune on the cobblestones.

CHRONOLOGY

BIOGRAPHICAL NOTES

NOTE ON THE TEXTS

NOTES

# Chronology

in New York City, attended by some 25,000 delegates. November: James Weldon Johnson becomes executive secretary (and first black officer) of the NAACP. Mamie Smith's "Crazy Blues" is released by Okeh Records. Eugene O'Neill's *The Emperor Jones*, starring Charles Gilpin, opens at the Provincetown Playhouse in Greenwich Village.

**Books**

W.E.B. Du Bois: *Darkwater: Voices from Within the Veil* (Harcourt, Brace & Howe)

Claude McKay: *Spring in New Hampshire and Other Poems* (Grant Richards)

1921    February: Max Eastman invites Claude McKay, just returned from England, to become associate editor of *The Liberator*. March: Harry Pace forms Black Swan Phonograph Company, one of the first black-owned record companies in Harlem; its most successful recording artist is Ethel Waters. May: *Shuffle Along*, a pioneering all–African American production, with book by Flournoy Miller and Aubrey Lyles and music and lyrics by Eubie Blake and Noble Sissle, opens on Broadway and becomes a hit. It showcases such stars as Florence Mills and Josephine Baker. June: Langston Hughes publishes his poem "The Negro Speaks of Rivers" in *The Crisis*. August–September: Exhibit of African American art at the 135th Street branch of the New York Public Library, including work by Henry Ossawa Tanner, Meta Fuller, and Laura Wheeler Waring. December: René Maran, a native of Martinique, becomes the first black recipient of the Prix Goncourt, for his novel *Batouala*; soon translated into English, it will be widely discussed in the African American press.

1922    January: The Dyer Anti-Lynching Bill is passed by the House of Representatives; it is subsequently blocked in the Senate. Spring: *Birthright*, novel of African American life by the white novelist T. S. Stribling, is published by Century Publications. (Oscar Micheaux will make two films based on the book, in 1924 and 1938.) White real estate magnate William E. Harmon establishes the Harmon Foundation to advance African American achievements.

**Books**

Georgia Douglas Johnson: *Bronze* (B. J. Brimmer)

James Weldon Johnson, editor: *The Book of American Negro Poetry* (Harcourt, Brace)

Claude McKay: *Harlem Shadows* (Harcourt, Brace; expanded version of *Spring in New Hampshire*)
T. S. Stribling: *Birthright* (Century)

1923    January: *Opportunity: A Journal of Negro Life*, published by the National Urban League and edited by sociologist Charles S. Johnson, is founded. Claude McKay addresses the Fourth Congress of the Third International in Moscow. February: Bessie Smith's "Downhearted Blues" (written and originally recorded by Alberta Hunter) is released by Columbia Records and sells nearly a million copies within six months. May: Willis Richardson's *The Chip Woman*, produced by the National Ethiopian Art Players, becomes the first serious play by an African American playwright to open on Broadway. June: Marcus Garvey receives a five-year sentence for mail fraud. December: Tenor Roland Hayes, having won acclaim in London as a singer of classical music, gives a concert of lieder and spirituals at Town Hall in New York. *The Messenger*, founded in 1917 by Asa Philip Randolph and Chandler Owen as a black trade unionist magazine with socialist sympathies, begins publishing more literary material under editorial guidance of George S. Schuyler and Theophilus Lewis.

**Books**
Marcus Garvey: *Philosophy and Opinion of Marcus Garvey* (Universal Publishing House)
Jean Toomer: *Cane* (Boni & Liveright)

1924    March: The Civic Club dinner, held in honor of Jessie Redmon Fauset on publishing her first novel *There Is Confusion*, is sponsored by *Opportunity* and Charles S. Johnson. Those in attendance include Alain Locke, W.E.B. Du Bois, Countee Cullen, Eric Walrond, Gwendolyn Bennett, and such representatives of the New York publishing world as Alfred A. Knopf and Horace Liveright. (In retrospect the occasion is often taken to mark the beginning of the Harlem Renaissance.) May: W.E.B. Du Bois attacks Marcus Garvey in *The Crisis* article "A Lunatic or a Traitor." Eugene O'Neill's play *All God's Chillun Got Wings*, starring Paul Robeson and controversial for its theme of miscegenation, opens. Autumn: Countee Cullen is the first recipient of Witter Bynner Poetry Competition. September: René Maran publishes poems by Countee Cullen, Langston Hughes, Claude McKay, and Jean Toomer in his Paris newspaper, *Les Continents.* Louis Armstrong comes to New York from Chicago to join Fletcher Henderson's band at the Roseland Ballroom.

### Books

W.E.B. Du Bois: *The Gift of Black Folk: The Negroes in the Making of America* (Stratford)

Jessie Redmon Fauset: *There Is Confusion* (Boni & Liveright)

Walter White: *The Fire in the Flint* (Knopf)

1925    February: After his appeals are denied, Marcus Garvey begins serving his sentence for mail fraud at Atlanta Federal Penitentiary. March: Howard Philosophy Professor Alain Locke edits a special issue of *The Survey Graphic* titled "Harlem: Mecca of the New Negro"; in November *The New Negro*, an expanded book version, is published by Albert and Charles Boni. The volume features six pages of painter Aaron Douglas's African-inspired illustrations, and includes writing by Jean Toomer, Rudolph Fisher, Zora Neale Hurston, Eric Walrond, Countee Cullen, James Weldon Johnson, Langston Hughes, Georgia Douglas Johnson, Richard Bruce Nugent, Anne Spencer, Claude McKay, Jessie Redmon Fauset, Arthur Schomburg, Charles S. Johnson, W.E.B. Du Bois, and E. Franklin Frazier. May: *Opportunity* holds its first awards dinner, recognizing, among others, Langston Hughes ("The Weary Blues," first prize), Countee Cullen, Zora Neale Hurston, Eric Walrond, and Sterling Brown. Paul Robeson appears at Greenwich Village Theatre in a concert entirely devoted to spirituals, accompanied by Lawrence Brown. August: A. Phillip Randolph organizes the Brotherhood of Sleeping Car Porters. October: The American Negro Labor Congress is founded in Chicago. November: First prize of *The Crisis* awards goes to poet Countee Cullen. Paul Robeson stars in Oscar Micheaux's film *Body and Soul.* December: Marita Bonner publishes essay "On Being Young—A Woman—And Colored" in *The Crisis*, about the predicament and possibilities of the educated black woman.

### Books

Countee Cullen: *Color* (Harper)

James Weldon Johnson and J. Rosamond Johnson, editors: *The Book of American Negro Spirituals* (Viking Press)

Alain Locke, editor: *The New Negro: An Interpretation* (Albert and Charles Boni)

1926    January: The Harmon Foundation announces its first awards for artistic achievement by African Americans. Palmer Hayden, a World War I veteran and menial laborer, wins the gold medal for painting. February: Jessie Redmon Fauset steps down as editor of *The Crisis*. The play *Lulu Belle*, starring Lenore Ulric in blackface as well as the African American actress Edna Thomas, opens to great success on Broadway; it helps create a vogue of whites frequenting Harlem nightspots. March: The Savoy Ballroom opens on Lenox Avenue between 140th and 141st Streets. June: Successive issues of *The Nation* feature Langston Hughes's "The Negro Artist and the Racial Mountain" and George S. Schuyler's "The Negro-Art Hokum." July: W.E.B. Du Bois founds Krigwa Players, Harlem theater group devoted to plays depicting African American life. August: Carl Van Vechten, white novelist and close friend to many Negro Renaissance figures, publishes his roman à clef, *Nigger Heaven*, with Knopf. Although many of his friends—including James Weldon Johnson, Nella Larsen, and Langston Hughes—are supportive, the book is widely disliked by African American readers, and notably condemned by W.E.B. Du Bois. October: Arthur Schomburg's collection of thousands of books, manuscripts, and artworks is purchased for the New York Public Library by the Carnegie Corporation; it will form the basis of what will become the Schomburg Center for Research in Black Culture. November: *Fire!!*, a journal edited by Wallace Thurman, makes its sole appearance. Contributors include Langston Hughes, Zora Neale Hurston, and Gwendolyn Bennett, among others. "Smoke, Lilies and Jade," a short story by Richard Bruce Nugent published in *Fire!!*, shocks many by its delineation of a homosexual liaison as well as by Nugent's suggestive line drawings. Most copies are accidentally destroyed in a fire. December: Countee Cullen begins contributing a column, "The Dark Tower," to *Opportunity*. (It will run until September 1928.)

**Books**
W. C. Handy, editor: *Blues: An Anthology* (Boni & Boni)
Langston Hughes: *The Weary Blues* (Knopf)
Alain Locke, editor: *Four Negro Poets* (Simon & Schuster)

Carl Van Vechten: *Nigger Heaven* (Knopf)
Eric Walrond: *Tropic Death* (Boni & Liveright; story collection)
Walter White: *Flight* (Knopf)

1927    July: Ethel Waters stars on Broadway in the revue *Africana*. August: Rudolph Fisher's essay "The Caucasian Storms Harlem" is published in *The American Mercury*. September: James Weldon Johnson's *The Autobiography of an Ex-Colored Man*, first published anonymously in 1912, is republished by Knopf. October: A'Lelia Walker, cosmetics heiress and Harlem socialite, opens The Dark Tower, a tearoom intended as a cultural gathering place, at her home on West 130th Street: "We dedicate this tower to the aesthetes. That cultural group of young Negro writers, sculptors, painters, music artists, composers, and their friends." The Theatre Guild production of DuBose Heyward's play *Porgy*, with an African American cast, opens to great success. December: Marcus Garvey, pardoned by Calvin Coolidge after serving more than half of five-year sentence for mail fraud, is deported. Duke Ellington and his orchestra begin what will prove a years-long engagement at the Cotton Club of Harlem.

**Books**

Countee Cullen: *Copper Sun* (Harper)
Countee Cullen, editor: *Caroling Dusk: An Anthology of Verse by Negro Poets* (Harper)
Langston Hughes: *Fine Clothes to the Jew* (Knopf)
Charles S. Johnson, editor: *Ebony and Topaz* (Journal of Negro Life/National Urban League)
James Weldon Johnson: *God's Trombones: Seven Negro Sermons in Verse* (Knopf)
Alain Locke and Montgomery Gregory, editors: *Plays of Negro Life* (Harper)

1928    January: The first Harmon Foundation art exhibition opens at New York's International House. April 9: Countee Cullen marries Nina Yolande, daughter of W.E.B. Du Bois; the wedding is a major social event, attended by thousands of people. (The marriage breaks up several months later.) May: Bill "Bojangles" Robinson appears on Broadway in the revue *Blackbirds of 1928*. June: *The Messenger* ceases publication when the Brotherhood of Sleeping Car Porters can no longer financially support the journal. November:

Wallace Thurman publishes the first and only issue of the magazine *Harlem: A Forum of Negro Life*.

**Books**

W.E.B. Du Bois: *Dark Princess: A Romance* (Harcourt, Brace)

Jessie Redmon Fauset: *Plum Bun* (Frederick Stokes)

Rudolph Fisher: *The Walls of Jericho* (Knopf)

Georgia Douglas Johnson: *An Autumn Love Cycle* (Harold Vinal)

Nella Larsen: *Quicksand* (Knopf)

Claude McKay: *Home to Harlem* (Harper)

1929    February: *Harlem*, co-authored by Wallace Thurman and William Rapp, opens on Broadway to mixed reviews. Archibald Motley, Jr. wins gold medal for painting from the Harmon Foundation. October 29: The New York stock market plunges, eliminating much of the funding powering "New Negro" literature and arts.

**Books**

Countee Cullen: *The Black Christ and Other Poems* (Harper)

Nella Larsen: *Passing* (Knopf)

Claude McKay: *Banjo: A Story Without a Plot* (Harper)

Wallace Thurman: *The Blacker the Berry* (Macaulay)

Walter White: *Rope and Faggot: A Biography of Judge Lynch* (Knopf)

1930    February: *The Green Pastures*, a play by Marc Connelly, based on Roark Bradford's *Ol' Man Adam an' His Chillun* (1928), opens on Broadway with an all-black cast; it will be one of the most successful plays of its era. July: The Nation of Islam, colloquially known as the Black Muslims, founded by W. D. Fard in Detroit at the Islam Temple. Dancer and anthropology student Katharine Dunham founds Ballet Nègre in Chicago. James Weldon Johnson publishes a limited edition of "Saint Peter Relates an Incident of the Resurrection Day," a poem protesting the insulting treatment accorded to African American Gold Star Mothers visiting American cemeteries in Europe.

**Books**

Langston Hughes: *Not Without Laughter* (Macmillan)

Charles S. Johnson: *The Negro in American Civilization: A Study of Negro Life and Race Relations* (Henry Holt)

James Weldon Johnson: *Black Manhattan* (Knopf)

James Weldon Johnson: *Saint Peter Relates an Incident of the Resurrection Day* (Viking Press)

1931   April–July: The "Scottsboro Boys," a group of young African American men accused of raping two white women, are tried and convicted; a massive, lengthy, and only partly successful campaign to free them begins. Sculptor Augusta Savage, whose real-life rebuff by the white art establishment becomes part of the back story for *Plum Bun*, establishes the Savage Studio of Arts and Crafts in Harlem.

**Books**
Arna Bontemps: *God Sends Sunday* (Harcourt, Brace)
Sterling Brown: *Outline for the Study of Poetry of American Negroes* (Harcourt, Brace)
Countee Cullen: *One Way to Heaven* (Harper)
Jessie Redmon Fauset: *The Chinaberry Tree* (Frederick Stokes)
Langston Hughes: *Dear Lovely Death* (Troutbeck Press)
George S. Schuyler: *Black No More* (Macaulay)
Jean Toomer: *Essentials: Definitions and Aphorisms* (Lakeside Press)

1932   June: Langston Hughes, Dorothy West, Louise Thompson, and more than a dozen other African Americans travel to the Soviet Union to film *Black and White*, a movie about American racism. (Due to shifting Soviet policies, the movie will never be made.)

**Books**
Sterling Brown: *Southern Road* (Harcourt, Brace)
Rudolph Fisher: *The Conjure-Man Dies* (Covici-Friede)
Langston Hughes: *The Dream Keeper* (Knopf)
Claude McKay: *Gingertown* (Harper; story collection)
George S. Schuyler: *Slaves Today* (Brewer, Warren, and Putnam)
Wallace Thurman: *Infants of the Spring* (Macaulay)
Wallace Thurman and Abraham Furman: *Interne* (Macaulay)

1933   **Books**
Jessie Redmon Fauset: *Comedy: American Style* (Frederick A. Stokes)
James Weldon Johnson: *Along This Way* (Knopf)

Alain Locke: *The Negro in America* (American Library Association)

Claude McKay: *Banana Bottom* (Harper)

1934      January: The Apollo Theater opens. February: *Negro*, an anthology of work by and about African Americans, edited by Nancy Cunard, is published by Wishart in London. March: Dorothy West founds the magazine *Challenge*. May: W.E.B. Du Bois resigns from the NAACP; he is replaced as editor of *The Crisis* by Roy Wilkins. November: Aaron Douglas completes *Aspects of Negro Life*, four murals commissioned by the New York Public Library. December: Wallace Thurman and Rudolph Fisher die within days of one another. Richard Wright writes the initial draft of his first novel, *Lawd Today*, published posthumously in 1963. M. B. Tolson completes sequence of poems *A Gallery of Harlem Portraits*, published posthumously in 1979.

**Books**

Langston Hughes: *The Ways of White Folks* (Knopf; story collection)

Zora Neale Hurston: *Jonah's Gourd Vine* (Lippincott)

James Weldon Johnson: *Negro Americans, What Now?* (Viking Press)

1935      March 19: A riot sparked by rumors of white violence against a Puerto Rican youth results in three African American deaths and millions of dollars in damage to white-owned properties. April: In "Harlem Runs Wild," published in *The Nation*, Claude McKay asserts that the riot is "the gesture of despair of a bewildered, baffled, and disillusioned people." The Works Progress Administration (WPA) established by U.S. President Franklin Delano Roosevelt; writers and artists who will eventually find employment under its aegis include Richard Wright, Ralph Ellison, Dorothy West, Margaret Walker, Augusta Savage, Romare Bearden, and Jacob Lawrence. October: Langston Hughes's play *Mulatto* and George Gershwin's opera *Porgy and Bess* open on Broadway.

**Books**

Countee Cullen: *The Medea and Some Poems* (Harper)

Frank Marshall Davis: *Black Man's Verse* (Black Cat Press)

W.E.B. Du Bois: *Black Reconstruction in America, 1860–1880* (Harcourt, Brace)

Zora Neale Hurston: *Mules and Men* (Lippincott)
James Weldon Johnson: *Saint Peter Relates an Incident: Selected Poems* (Viking Press)

1936    February: The National Negro Congress, representing some 600 organizations, holds its first meeting in Chicago. June: Mary McLeod Bethune is appointed Director of the Division of Negro Affairs of the National Youth Administration, becoming the highest-ranking African American official of the Roosevelt administration.

**Books**
Arna Bontemps: *Black Thunder* (Macmillan)
Alain Locke: *Negro Art—Past and Present* (Associates in Negro Folk Education)
Alain Locke: *The Negro and His Music* (Associates in Negro Folk Education)

# Biographical Notes

**Langston Hughes**     Born James Langston Hughes in Joplin, Missouri, on February 1, 1902, son of James Nathaniel Hughes, a stenographer for a mining company, and Carrie Mercer Langston Hughes, an aspiring writer and actress. (In later years, Hughes used the form James Langston Mercer Hughes as his full name.) Hughes's father left the family shortly after his son's birth, relocating to Mexico. In the absence of his father, and with his mother also frequently away, Hughes was raised mostly by his grandmother, Mary Langston, in Lawrence, Kansas. (Mary Langston's first husband, Lewis Leary, was an associate of John Brown who was killed in the Harpers Ferry raid in 1859; her second husband was also an abolitionist.) After briefly reuniting with his mother in Topeka, Kansas, in 1907, Hughes returned to Lawrence to live with his grandmother until her death in 1915. Subsequently he lived with his mother and her second husband in Lincoln, Illinois, and Cleveland, Ohio. He began to publish poems and stories in school publications. After graduating high school he spent a year with his father in Mexico; relations between the two were stormy, as Hughes's literary ambitions were strongly opposed by his father. He published the poem "The Negro Speaks of Rivers" in *The Crisis* in June 1921, and that autumn began attending Columbia University with support from his father (and majoring in engineering at his father's request); he left Columbia after a year following a break with his father. In Harlem he formed friendships with Jessie Redmon Fauset, Countee Cullen, and other writers. A series of odd jobs was followed in 1923 by a job on a steamship which visited ports in West Africa; the following year he worked his way to Europe but jumped ship and remained in Paris, working at a jazz club in Montmartre. He returned to the United States in 1925, living with his mother in Washington, D.C. for a year before settling in Harlem. He continued to befriend many writers, including Alain Locke, Arna Bontemps, Wallace Thurman, and Carl Van Vechten. In 1926 he published his first collection of poems, *The Weary Blues*, as well as the essay "The Negro Artist and the Racial Mountain"; a second poetry collection, *Fine Clothes to the Jew*, appeared the next year. From 1926 to 1929 he attended Lincoln University in Pennsylvania. A wealthy white woman, Charlotte Mason (whom at her request he referred to as "Godmother"), supported him for three years, underwriting trips to Cuba (1930) and Haiti (1931) and encouraging his first novel, *Not Without*

*Laughter*, published in 1930; the relationship with Mason ended abruptly the same year when she broke with him for reasons not clear to him. Around the same time his friendship with Zora Neale Hurston ended as the result of a quarrel over the authorship of a play, *Mule-bone*, on which they had collaborated. Hughes continued to work prolifically in a range of genres, collaborating with Arna Bontemps on the children's book *Popo and Fifina* (1932), and publishing the poetry collections *Dear Lovely Death* (1931) and *The Negro Mother* (1931) and the story collection *The Ways of White Folks* (1934). With Louise Thompson and a contingent of African American writers and intellectuals he traveled to the Soviet Union in 1932 for the purpose of making a film, never realized, about American race relations. He remained in the Soviet Union, traveling widely in Soviet Asia and going in 1933 to China and Japan; he was expelled from Japan for leftist activities and arrived in San Francisco in August 1933. After residences in Carmel, California, and Mexico (where he lived for a time with the photographer Henri Cartier-Bresson), Hughes returned to New York, where his play *Mulatto* opened in 1935 despite Hughes's protests against changes made by the producers. He traveled to Europe and addressed the Paris Writers' Congress in July 1937, meeting Bertolt Brecht, W. H. Auden, and many others; in Spain, where he reported on the civil war for the Baltimore *Afro-American*, he stayed for three months in Madrid while it was under siege; the following year he returned to Paris with Theodore Dreiser to address a conference of the International Association of Writers. A collection of radical poems, *A New Song*, was published in 1938 by the International Workers Order, and the memoir *The Big Sea*, focusing on his travels in the 1920s, appeared in 1940. In the following year Hughes lived briefly in Los Angeles (where he wrote a film script) and Chicago before settling again in Harlem in 1941. Knopf published the poetry collection *Shakespeare in Harlem* in 1942. His newspaper column "Here to Yonder," which began appearing in the Chicago *Defender* in November 1942, introduced in 1943 the character Jesse B. Semple ("Simple"); these columns were ultimately collected in a popular series of books, beginning with *Simple Speaks His Mind* (1950). Hughes's involvement in many left-wing and anti-fascist organizations came under steady right-wing attack during the 1940s and was denounced repeatedly in testimony before the House Un-American Activities Committee. Beginning in 1944 he organized national reading tours which helped provide him with financial support. In 1953 he was subpoenaed to testify before Senator Joseph McCarthy's anti-subversive subcommittee, and gave testimony disavowing communism but not implicating any individuals. In addition to the Simple books, Hughes in the postwar period published the poetry collections *Fields of Wonder* (1947), *Montage of a Dream Deferred* (1951), *Selected Poems* (1959), and *Ask Your Mama: 12 Moods for Jazz* (1961); the memoir *I Wonder As I Wander* (1954); the story collection *Laughing to Keep From Crying* (1952); the novella *Tambourines to Glory* (1958, based on Hughes's 1956 musical play); and a series of books for children. He continued to be involved in a range of musical and theatrical projects, collaborating with Kurt Weill on *Street Scene* (1947) and William Grant Still on *Troubled Island* (1949). He gave readings of his poetry accompanied by bassist Charles Mingus, published translations of Gabriela Mistral and Federico Garcia Lorca, collaborated with photographer Roy DeCarava on *The Sweet Flypaper of Life* (1955), and with Arna Bontemps edited the anthology *The Poetry of the Negro, 1746–1949* (1949). He was elected in 1961 to membership in the National Institute of Arts and Letters. During the 1960s Hughes traveled widely, making repeated visits to Africa and Europe, and participating in a State Department–sponsored tour of Senegal, Nigeria, Ethiopia, and Tanzania in 1966. A private man, Hughes never married and is not known to have had a longtime companion. He died of complications following prostate surgery on May 22, 1967. The poetry collection *The Panther and the Lash: Poems of Our Times* was published posthumously the same year.

**George S. Schuyler**     Born George Samuel Schuyler on February 25, 1895; his birthplace was Providence, Rhode Island, according to Schuyler's account, although little direct evidence supports this. His parents were George Frances, a chef, and Eliza Jane Fischer Schuyler, a cook; it has been speculated that he may have been adopted. After his father died when he was three, he was raised in Syracuse, New York, by his mother, who remarried in 1900, and his grandmother Helen Fischer. At seventeen he dropped out of high school and enlisted in the Armed Services, joining the 25th Infantry and serving in Seattle and Hawaii; eventually he became a drill instructor and rose to the rank of first lieutenant at Fort Des Moines, Iowa. While based in Hawaii he began to contribute writing to the *Honolulu Commercial Advertiser* and other local publications. With a racist incident in 1918 as catalyst, Schuyler deserted; after turning himself in, he was sentenced to five years on Governor's Island in New York, a term finally reduced to nine months. (Until the end of his life Schuyler never acknowledged this episode.) He worked as an army clerk during and after his imprisonment; discharged at the end of the war, he held a succession of low-paying jobs (porter, factory worker, dishwasher) and returned briefly to live in Syracuse, where he worked in construction. He joined the Socialist Party in 1921 and served as the party's educational director in Syracuse. Returning to New York, he took a room in Harlem and immersed himself in literary and political currents, attending Garveyite meetings at Liberty Hall and taking classes at the Rand School, where his teachers included Thorstein Veblen. Out of work, he lived briefly with a group of hobos in a church basement on the Lower East Side before being hired in 1923 as office messenger and staff writer for *The Messenger*, edited by A. Phillip Randolph and Chandler Owen. He remained at the magazine until it closed in 1928, contributing a column, "Shafts and Darts: A Page of Calumny and Satire," along with much other writing, including stories, essays, and reviews. In 1925 he was invited by the *Pittsburgh Courier* to contribute a weekly column, which after several name changes became "Views and Reviews" and which he continued to write until 1966. Schuyler wrote for many other print outlets as well, including *The Nation*, *The Crisis*, and *The American Mercury*, whose editor H. L. Mencken was an enthusiastic supporter of Schuyler's work. For the *Courier* Schuyler undertook a lengthy investigative tour of the South (1925–26), resulting in the series "Aframerica Today." In January 1928 he married Josephine Codgell, the daughter of a wealthy Texas banker and cattle rancher; their daughter Philippa was born in 1931. The interracial marriage— which Schuyler discussed in "Racial Intermarriage in the United States" (1928)—along with Philippa's recognition as a child prodigy on the piano (as well as her exceptionally high scores on intelligence tests) brought much media attention to the Schuylers. His satirical novel *Black No More* was published by the Macaulay Company in 1931. A second novel, *Slaves Today: A Story of Liberia* (1932), grew out of Schuyler's 1931 trip to Liberia to investigate allegations of domestic slavery as well as the use of forced labor by the Firestone Rubber Company. (In articles and in his novel, Schuyler affirmed the practice of slavery but exonerated Firestone.) Schuyler also published in the *Courier*, under pseudonyms, a series of novellas with African settings, including "Devil Town" (1933), "Golden Gods" (1933–34), "Strange Valley" (1934), "The Ethiopian Murder Mystery" (1935–36), "The Black Internationale" (1936–37), "Black Empire" (1937–38), and "Revolt in Ethiopia" (1938–39). Schuyler vigorously protested the Italian invasion of Ethiopia and the U.S. internment of Japanese Americans during World War II. In other respects, his political views moved steadily to the right. He published *The Communist Conspiracy Against the Negroes* in 1947, and supported the anticommunist campaign of Senator Joseph McCarthy. A virulent attack on Dr. Martin Luther King, Jr. in 1964 attracted much attention, and the *Courier* dismissed him two years later. Subsequently Schuyler published *Black and Conservative: The Autobiography of George S. Schuyler* (1966) and contributed to the conservative New Hampshire newspaper *Manchester Union Leader*, which had published the attack on King; he had joined the

John Birch Society in 1965 and began to write for its publications. Philippa Schuyler became a journalist in the 1960s, and while on a humanitarian mission in Vietnam was killed in a U.S. Army helicopter crash in 1967. Schuyler's wife, who had been in declining health, committed suicide in 1969. Schuyler died on August 31, 1977, at New York Hospital.

**Rudolph Fisher**  Born Rudolph John Chauncey Fisher on May 9, 1897, in Washington, D.C., one of three children of Reverend John Wesley Fisher and Glendora Williamson Fisher. As a small child, Fisher moved with the family to Providence, Rhode Island, where he attended public schools, graduating with honors from Classical High School. In 1919 he graduated from Brown University with a BA in English and biology, and a year later received an MA from Brown. In addition, he won prizes in German and public speaking, and was elected to Phi Beta Kappa. While at Brown he formed a friendship with Paul Robeson (a fellow Phi Beta Kappa attending Rutgers), whom he would sometimes accompany on piano. He received a medical degree from Howard University in 1924. Following graduation he took up a residency at the Freedman's Hospital in Washington, D.C., and a postdoctoral fellowship at Columbia University Hospital, working in bacteriology. His work on viruses and ultraviolet rays led to the publication of two scientific articles, one in the *Journal of Infectious Diseases*. He married Jane Ryder, an elementary school teacher, in 1924; their son Hugh was born two years later. He had begun writing while in college, and his story "The City of Refuge" was published in *The Atlantic Monthly* in 1925, and reprinted the same year in Alain Locke's anthology *The New Negro* (1925) along with "Vestiges: Harlem Sketches." He worked at Bronx and Mount Sinai hospitals in New York before opening a private practice and X-ray laboratory in Harlem in the late 1920s; he was head of the roentgenology department at International Hospital in Manhattan, 1930–32. During the same period he moved to Jamaica, Queens, where he relocated his private practice. Fisher (known to his friends as "Bud") socialized widely in Harlem, and was described by Langston Hughes (in his memoir *The Big Sea*) as "the wittiest of these New Negroes of Harlem . . . who always frightened me a little, because he could think of the most incisively clever things to say—and I could never think of anything to answer." Fisher contributed an article on Harlem nightlife, "The Caucasian Storms Harlem," to H. L. Mencken's *American Mercury* in 1927. In a 1933 radio interview he remarked: "If I should be fortunate enough to become known as Harlem's interpreter, I should be very happy." Other short stories appeared in *The Atlantic Monthly*, *McClure's Magazine*, *The Crisis*, *Opportunity*, and *Story Magazine*, and he published reviews of books by George S. Schuyler, Jessie Redmon Fauset, Wallace Thurman, Countee Cullen, and Claude McKay in the *New York Herald Tribune*. His first novel, *The Walls of Jericho*, was published in 1928 by Knopf. *The Conjure-Man Dies*, often described as the first detective novel written by an African American, was published in 1932 by Covici-Friede. Fisher underwent a series of stomach operations during 1934, and died on December 26, 1934, at Edgecombe Sanitarium in Harlem (Wallace Thurman had died four days earlier). As an officer with the reserve medical corps of the New York National Guard's 369th Infantry, Fisher was buried with an honor guard from his unit in attendance. A dramatization of *The Conjure-Man Dies* was produced in Harlem by the Federal Theater Project in 1936. (Fisher's stories were collected posthumously in 1991 in *The City of Refuge: The Collected Stories of Rudolph Fisher*, edited by John McCluskey, Jr.)

**Arna Bontemps**      Born Arnaud Wendell Bontemps on October 13, 1902, in Alexandria, Louisiana, to Paul Bismark Bontemps, a brick and stone mason also sometimes employed as a jazz trombonist, and his wife Maria Caroline, a public school teacher. In 1906 Bontemps moved with his parents and his mother's parents to California, where they were eventually joined by other members of the extended family, settling in the "Furlough Track," a rural area north of Watts in Los Angeles. During the first year in California, his parents left the Catholic church and converted to Seventh Day Adventism, his father becoming a lay minister. Bontemps's mother died in 1914. He attended predominantly white Adventist schools in Los Angeles, graduating from Pacific Union College in 1923. He spent much time reading independently at the Los Angeles Public Library, and early on developed an interest in African American history. Following graduation he went to work in the post office; after he had a poem accepted by *The Crisis* he decided (apparently on the advice of his friend Wallace Thurman) to move to New York. Of his first year in the city he would write: "In some places the autumn of 1924 may have been an unremarkable season. In Harlem it was like a foretaste of paradise." Supporting himself by teaching at the Adventist high school Harlem Academy, he continued to publish poems, winning several prizes; worked on a novel which remained unfinished; and immersed himself in the social and cultural life of Harlem. Countee Cullen introduced Bontemps to Langston Hughes, with whom he formed a lifelong friendship. In 1926 he married Alberta Johnson; they had six children, born between 1927 and 1945. His novel *God Sends Sunday*, inspired by the wandering life of his great-uncle Joseph Ward ("Uncle Buddy"), was published in 1931 by Harcourt, Brace; the book received some good reviews but was condemned by W.E.B. Du Bois for its "low-life" subject matter.

After Harlem Academy closed, Bontemps relocated to Huntsville, Alabama where he taught at the Adventist-affiliated Oakwood College, 1931–34. He was unhappy at Oakwood and came under criticism from the school's conservative and theologically rigid directors, but continued to keep in touch with Cullen and Hughes; with Cullen he collaborated on a dramatization of *God Sends Sunday*, which was produced in Cleveland in 1934, and with Hughes he wrote a children's book, *Popo and Fifina: Children of Haiti*, published by Macmillan in 1932. After resigning his position at Oakwood he returned to his father's home in Watts, where he completed his second novel, *Black Thunder*, based on the Gabriel Prosser slave revolt of 1800, published by Macmillan in 1936. He moved to Chicago, serving as principal of another Adventist school, Shiloh Academy, 1936–38, until conflicts with the school's administration led to his withdrawal from the Adventist church. He found employment with the Illinois Writers Project while pursuing graduate studies at the University of Chicago. Another historical novel, *Drums at Dusk*, about the Haitian revolution, appeared in 1939. He completed a degree in library science in 1943 and was hired as head librarian at Fisk University, where he remained on staff until 1966 and achieved preeminence as a pioneering archivist and historian in the field of African American studies. In 1946 *St. Louis Woman*, the musical dramatization of *God Sends Sunday* on which he and Countee Cullen had continued to work for years, opened successfully on Broadway. After retiring from Fisk in the 1960s, Bontemps taught at the University of Illinois and Yale University as a visiting professor. In addition to numerous volumes of fiction and nonfiction, much of it aimed at young adult readers, he edited a number of anthologies, including *The Poetry of the Negro, 1746–1949* (with Langston Hughes, 1949), *The Book of Negro Folklore* (also with Hughes, 1958), and *American Negro Poetry* (1963). He died on June 4, 1973 of heart failure.

# Note on the Texts

This volume collects four novels—*Not Without Laughter* (1930), by Langston Hughes; *Black No More* (1931), by George S. Schuyler; *The Conjure-Man Dies* (1932), by Rudolph Fisher; and *Black Thunder* (1936), by Arna Bontemps—associated with what has come to be known as the Harlem Renaissance, a period of great creativity and change in African American cultural life, with its epicenter in New York's Harlem neighborhood. A companion volume in the Library of America series, *Harlem Renaissance: Five Novels of the 1920s*, vol. 1, presents five earlier novels: Jean Toomer's *Cane* (1923), Claude McKay's *Home to Harlem* (1928), Nella Larsen's *Quicksand* (1928), Jessie Redmon Fauset's *Plum Bun* (1928), and Wallace Thurman's *The Blacker the Berry* (1929). The texts of all of these novels have been taken from the first printings of the first editions.

*Not Without Laughter.* Though Langston Hughes had written short stories and two books of poetry—*The Weary Blues* (1926) and *Fine Clothes to the Jew* (1927)—he was reluctant, at first, to tackle the longer form of the novel. He was encouraged to do so by a new patron, Charlotte Mason, who suggested the goal in August 1927 and then in November added a proposal of financial assistance: she would provide Hughes a regular stipend for a year (or longer, if their arrangement proved successful), freeing him of the need to support himself. Hughes would retain the rights to his work, but in return Mason expected to be regularly apprised of his progress. Accepting Mason's terms, Hughes finished his junior year at Lincoln University and then began "The Novel" (as his first draft was called) in June 1928. He finished the draft within about six weeks, in mid-August. "At first I did a chapter or two a day," he later recalled in his autobiography *The Big Sea* (1940), "and revised them the next day. But they seemed bad; in fact, so bad I finally decided to write the whole story straight through to the end before re-reading anything." Hughes made further revisions to the initial draft during the fall (his hand-corrected typescript bears the date December 19, 1928), but he did not return to full-time work on the book until the summer of 1929, after his graduation. In May 1929, Mason sent Hughes a twenty-four-page letter offering detailed comments on his initial draft, enthusiastically praising some sections, recommending "literary welding together" for the whole, and at points registering her objections: "the quality of the writing . . . becomes self-conscious, and has the air of the author's propaganda." (She also dissuaded him from using the titles *So Moves This Swift World* and *Roots of Dawn*; the former, she explained, was "not characteristic enough of you and your writing, which is always original and arresting.")

One scholar has argued that this "literary censorship" on Mason's part "forced Hughes to suppress his increasingly strong left-wing political notions in the novel" (see John P. Shields, "'Never Cross the Divide': Reconstructing Langston Hughes's *Not Without Laughter*," *African American Review* 28.4 [1994]: 601–13). Hughes's manuscripts of successive drafts of the novel (all of which he donated, after publication, to the Negro Collection of the 135th Street Branch Library, now the Schomburg Center for Research in Black Culture) suggest that he did make changes to his work in response to Mason's suggestions, in the midst of his own thoroughgoing process of revision. Mason herself was happy with Hughes's second draft, finished on August 15. Hughes—returning from a trip to Canada—insisted it needed more work. ("I couldn't bear to have the people I had grown to love," he remembered in *The Big Sea*, "locked up in long pages of uncomfortable words, awkward sentences, and drawn-out passages.")

With the help of Louise Thompson, a stenographer Mason had hired to facilitate Hughes's progress on the novel, he finished a third draft during the fall. Alfred A. Knopf—who had been asked by Carl Van Vechten to extend "every tenderness and consideration" to Hughes's work—agreed to publish the book. Alain Locke, enlisted by Knopf as a reader, sought further changes after it was accepted (asking for more detail about the protagonist's "inner emotional conflict" in its later sections), and Mason again noted that "propaganda utterances" had re-emerged in the revised manuscript. Hughes addressed Locke and Mason's suggestions and gave his finished manuscript to Blanche Knopf on February 17, 1930. Hughes read galleys and page proofs with great care, reversing many small changes in spelling and the handling of dialect that had been introduced by Knopf's copy editor and making a few further revisions. *Not Without Laughter* was published in July 1930. Knopf reprinted the novel at least nine times during Hughes's lifetime, without Hughes's involvement. The present volume prints the text of the 1930 Knopf first printing.

*Black No More.* In his 1966 autobiography *Black and Conservative*, George S. Schuyler credits V. F. Calverton—the pen name under which George Goetz edited *Modern Quarterly*—for the suggestion that he begin *Black No More*. Schuyler said that Calverton, who had previously published essays by him, "encouraged me to write my first book . . . a satire on the American race question," and was "instrumental in

getting the Macaulay Company to publish it." Another impetus for
the novel was the widely publicized claim by Japanese biologist Yusaburo Noguchi that he had "developed a technique for changing racial
characteristics, even to the pigment colorings" (*The New York Times*,
October 24, 1929). Writing in the *Pittsburgh Courier* on November
2, Schuyler commented: "I have been prophesying it for some years,
and have even written something built around such a discovery."
Schuyler worked on this initial "something" for "about six or seven
months," he recalled in a 1975 interview with Michael W. Peplow; he
had completed a draft of *Black No More* by July 1930. In late August,
he solicited a preface from H. L. Mencken, in whose *American Mercury* he had been publishing since 1927. Mencken declined in mid-
September, explaining that he did not wish to seem to patronize. ("I
think you are quite right about the requested preface, as you are
about most things," Schuyler replied. "One thing I am very anxious
to avoid is patronizing. There has, I believe, been altogether too
much of it, especially in connection with work done by the dark
brethren.") By September 4, 1930, Schuyler had returned a corrected
set of proofs to his publisher. Later that month, he made a number of
small changes in "expression" and "characterization" after receiving
belated suggestions from the novelist and NAACP national secretary
Walter White, to whom he had written about the novel in July. White
went on to suggest further changes, but on October 3, Schuyler informed him that he had returned his final page proofs "about ten
days ago." The Macaulay Company published *Black No More* in January 1931. It was reprinted, much later in Schuyler's career, by Negro
Universities Press in 1969 and Collier Books in 1971, without any au-
thorial revision. This volume prints the text of the 1931 first edition.

*The Conjure-Man Dies.* Little evidence is known to have appeared
in print about the composition and textual history of *The Conjure-
Man Dies*, Rudolph Fisher's second novel. It was published in New
York by Covici-Friede in late July 1932 and was reprinted once, without revision, before Fisher's death in December 1934. No manuscripts
or other prepublication versions of the novel are known to be extant,
and the main repository of Fisher's papers, Brown University Library,
does not hold any correspondence about it. (Other archival sources,
such as the unpublished correspondence of Carl Van Vechten or Walter
White, may contain further information.) Asked about his recently
published book by a reporter from the *Pittsburgh Courier* at an August 18, 1932, Harlem gala for African American authors, Fisher explained that he chose to write a mystery novel "against the wishes of
his friends," because "there is more money in it, he gets more fun out
of this kind of writing, and it isn't necessary after all, to cater to one's

friends in writing." He returned to *The Conjure-Man*'s main characters, John Archer and Perry Dart, in a novelette, "John Archer's
Nose," published posthumously (*Metropolitan*, January 1935). The
present volume prints the text of the 1932 Covici-Friede first
printing.

*Black Thunder.* Arna Bontemps described the genesis of his second
novel, *Black Thunder*, in an introduction he wrote for a new edition
in 1968. After "three horrifying years of preparation in a throbbing
region of the deep South," he moved with his family into his father's
home in Watts, Los Angeles, in the summer of 1934, where he drafted
the novel "on the top of a folded-down sewing machine." He had had
the book in mind for at least a couple of years. In an undated letter to
Langston Hughes, written around March 1932, he reported "working
a bit on a draft of a new adult novel," probably *Black Thunder*. He
had ultimately been inspired, during an earlier visit to Fisk University
in Nashville, Tennessee, by the Fisk Library's collection of slave narratives, and in particular by accounts of the Gabriel Prosser conspiracy of
1800. *Black Thunder*, which is closely based on these accounts, was
completed by the spring of 1935. Harper & Brothers in New York expressed interest in publishing the book but requested extensive
changes. "Gabriel's Attempt"—an unfinished typescript of 105 pages
now in the Arna Bontemps Papers at Syracuse University Library—
represents Bontemps's effort to revise the novel in response to the
firm's suggestions. He abandoned this effort when he learned that
Macmillan, with whom he and Langston Hughes had published a
children's book, *Popo and Fifina*, in 1932, was willing to accept his
original manuscript without alteration: it was published as *Black
Thunder* on January 28, 1936. The novel was reprinted without Bontemps's involvement in 1964, by Seven Seas Press in Berlin. In 1968,
Beacon Press in Boston published a new edition for which Bontemps
contributed a new introduction (reprinted in the Notes to this volume) but which he did not otherwise alter. The text in the present
volume has been taken from the first edition.

    This volume presents the texts of the editions chosen for inclusion
here but does not attempt to reproduce every feature of their typo-
graphic design. The texts are reprinted without change, except for the
correction of typographical errors. Spelling, punctuation, and capital-
ization are often expressive features, and they are not altered, even
when inconsistent or irregular. The following is a list of typographical
errors corrected, cited by page and line number: 14.5, 'Get; 21.23,
outside!; 22.19, 'Does; 22.20, right!; 77.35, passengers,; 131.25, dear;';
165.36, Old-timy; 185.3, Tempy's; 251.6, frauliens; 266.37–38, Givens

viewed; 301.7, gaunt,; 323.34, he had; 334.18, its a; 340.24, Quite; 340.28, Snobbcraft).; 350.7, chubby, ball; 358.3, passengers, managed; 358.23, fact They; 405.3, doctor." You; 550.7, imflammability; 559.31, as unusual; 566.17, glanced; 651.31, imaagine, liberty; 653.25, Creauzot; 669.1, boats; 673.6–7, insurrectionaires; 761.13, helped:.; 807.14, or small.

# Notes

In the notes below, the reference numbers denote page and line of the present volume; the line count includes titles and headings but not blank lines. Notes are not generally made for material found in standard desk-reference works. For additional information and references to other studies, see: Jeffrey B. Ferguson, *The Sage of Sugar Hill: George S. Schuyler and the Harlem Renaissance* (New Haven: Yale University Press, 2005); Nathan Irvin Huggins, *Harlem Renaissance* (New York: Oxford University Press, 1971); Kirkland C. Jones, *Renaissance Man from Louisiana: A Biography of Arna Wendell Bontemps* (Westport, Connecticut: Greenwood Press, 1992); David Levering Lewis, *When Harlem Was in Vogue* (New York: Alfred A. Knopf, 1980); John McCluskey Jr., ed., *The City of Refuge: The Collected Stories of Rudolph Fisher* (Columbia: University of Missouri Press, 2008); Charles H. Nichols, ed., *Arna Bontemps–Langston Hughes Letters, 1925–1967* (New York: Dodd, Mead, 1980); Michael W. Peplow, *George S. Schuyler* (Boston: Twayne, 1980); Arnold Rampersad, *The Life of Langston Hughes*, 2 vols. (New York: Oxford University Press, 1986–88); Steven Watson, *The Harlem Renaissance: Hub of African-American Culture, 1920–1930* (New York: Pantheon, 1995); Oscar R. Williams, *George S. Schuyler: Portrait of a Black Conservative* (Knoxville: University of Tennessee Press, 2007).

NOT WITHOUT LAUGHTER

2.2    *J. E. and Amy Spingarn.*]   Joel Elias Spingarn (1875–1939) and his wife Amy Einstein Spingarn (1883–1980) were among Hughes's patrons; he had attended Lincoln University with their financial help. Joel, a former Columbia professor of comparative literature, was elected president of the NAACP in 1930. Amy, an heiress and artist, published a limited edition of Hughes poems, *Dear Lovely Death*, at her Troutbeck Press in 1931.

32.21    dicty]   African American slang: snobbish, high-class.

36.3–8    THROW yo' arms . . . done!]   Hughes's adaptation of contemporary blues lyrics. A variant of the opening couplet, credited to Gus Cannon (c. 1883–1979), was recorded by the Memphis Jug Band in 1928 in "Stealin' Stealin'"; see also the "Western Bound Blues" by Tampa Red (1904–1981), first recorded in 1932.

37.29    Ada Walker's]   Ada ("Aïda") Overton Walker (1880–1914), vaudeville dancer and choreographer.

38.10–11    I wonder where . . . watch in pawn.]   See "I Wonder Where My Easy Rider's Gone," a 1913 blues song by Shelton Brooks (1886–1975).

39.6    *parse me la*]   A dance step, also spelled *pasmala*, *possumala*, or *pas ma la*, possibly from the French *pas mêlé*, or mixed step. Ernest Hogan (1859–1909), a minstrel performer, published the song "La Pas Ma La" in 1895 and is credited with popularizing the dance.

40.35    *Casey Jones*]   Folk ballad about railroad engineer Casey Jones (1863–1900), written by Wallace Saunders and first published in 1909.

41.7    W. C. Handy]   Alabama-born musician and composer (1873–1958), sometimes referred to as "father of the blues."

64.28    Sen Sens]   Licorice-flavored candies used as a breath freshener.

68.34–35    *St. Louis Blues*]   1914 twelve-bar blues song by W. C. Handy.

69.21    *Memphis . . . Yellow Dog*]   Blues songs by W. C. Handy, first published in 1912 and 1915, respectively.

72.21    P. I.]   Pimp.

118.24    *Dear Old Southland*]   Popular song (1921) with words by Harry Creamer (1879–1930) and music by Turner Layton (1894–1978).

126.9    "Layovers to catch meddlers."]   A widely varying traditional phrase, persistent especially in the South, used to evade impertinently curious questions.

159.33    balling-the-jack.]   From "Ballin' the Jack," a 1913 dance instruction song with words by James Henry (Jim) Burris (1874–1923) and music by Chris Smith (1879–1949).

167.38–39    Dark was the night . . . ground]   African American spiritual based on a 1792 hymn by Thomas Haweis (1734–1820); a version by Blind Willie Johnson (1897–1945) was recorded in 1927.

174.16–17    Senator Bruce . . . Frederick Douglass.]   Blanche Kelso Bruce (1841–1898), senator from Mississippi, 1875–81; John Mercer Langston (1829–1897), congressman from Virginia, 1890–91 (and Langston Hughes's great uncle); Pinckney Benton Stewart Pinchback (1837–1921), Louisiana governor, 1872–73 (and maternal grandfather of Jean Toomer); and abolitionist Frederick Douglass (c. 1818–1895).

175.16–18    some modern novels . . . Gene Stratton Porter]   Tempy's novels and favored novelists were all bestsellers: *The Rosary* (1909), by English romantic writer Florence L. Barclay (1862–1921); *The Little Shepherd of Kingdom Come* (1903), by Kentucky-born John Fox Jr. (1862–1919); Harold Bell Wright (1872–1944), prolific popular novelist, and Gene Stratton-Porter (1863–1924), Indiana novelist most often remembered for *A Girl of the Limberlost* (1909).

183.12–13    all beat up like Jim Jeffries . . . Jack Johnson]   On July 4, 1910, in what came to be known as the "fight of the century," former heavyweight boxing champion James J. Jeffries (1875–1953) was defeated by the African American current champion Jack Johnson (1878–1946). Jeffries was billed as the "Great White Hope"; widespread rioting followed Johnson's victory.

183.14    sweet-papa Stingaree's]   See "Stingaree Blues" (1920), by Clinton A. Kemp (b. 1895).

187.15–16    *The Doors of Life*]   See *The Doors of Life; or, Little Studies in Self-Healing* (1909), by Walter DeVoe.

192.24–25    Love, O love . . . wine!]   From the traditional song "Careless Love"; a popular blues version was recorded in 1925 by Bessie Smith (1894–1937).

BLACK NO MORE

222.7–8    Mr. V. F. Calverton]   Victor Francis Calverton, pen name of George Goetz (1900–1940), editor of the radical magazine *The Modern Quarterly*; Calverton had encouraged Schuyler to write *Black No More*.

229.31    "Numbers" banker]   Operator of an illegal betting scheme, supplied with customers' bets by a "runner."

234.38    Lafayette Theater]   A celebrated Harlem theater located at 132nd Street and Seventh Avenue, reputed to have been the first in New York City to offer desegregated seating to its audiences.

242.37    "Beale Street"]   A street in Memphis, Tennessee associated with the development of the blues.

243.21    Volstead Law]   The Volstead Act of 1919 regulated the manufacture and sale of alcohol during Prohibition.

248.39    dicty]   See note 32.21.

276.10    Shakespeare Agamemnon Beard]   Commentators on *Black No More* have noted that many characters appear to be thinly veiled satiric portraits of public figures. Beard in some respects resembles W.E.B. Du Bois (1868–1963); Napoleon Wellington Jackson, James Weldon Johnson (1871–1938); Mortimer Roberts, Robert Russa Moton (1867–1940), of the Tuskegee Institute; Walter Williams, Walter White (1893–1955) of the NAACP; Santop Licorice, Marcus Garvey (1887–1940); Mme Blandish, Mme. C. J. Walker (1867–1919) or her daughter A'Lelia (1885–1931).

296.36    Tudor City.]   A large, luxurious residential development on the East Side of Manhattan, begun in 1927.

311.26    "white mule"]   Colorless moonshine or grain alcohol.

320.28    Mann Act]   Officially known as the White-Slave Traffic Act, a 1910 anti-prostitution law; the boxer Jack Johnson was the first to be convicted under the law, in 1912, for transporting a white sex worker across state lines.

330.15–17    to quote Abraham Lincoln . . . earth.'] See Lincoln's Gettysburg Address (1863).

350.40–351.1    Sherlock Holmes . . . Pinkertons] Holmes and Carter were fictional detectives, the former the creation of Sir Arthur Conan Doyle (1859–1930) and the latter a character in dime novels and magazine stories by many authors, beginning with *The Old Detective's Pupil; or, The Mysterious Crime of Madison Square* in 1886. The Pinkertons were agents of the Pinkerton National Detective Agency, founded in 1850.

THE CONJURE-MAN DIES

375.18–22    "*I'll be glad* . . . *you're gone!*"] From "I'll Be Glad When You're Dead, You Rascal You" (1929), written by "Lovin'" Sam Theard (1904–1982) and popularized by Louis Armstrong (1901–1971) and others.

445.20–22    *I'll be standin'* . . . *rascal you.*] See note above.

497.16    the Spencerian classification] See "The Classification of the Sciences," an 1864 essay by English philosopher and sociologist Herbert Spencer (1820–1903).

543.35–38    "*Am I born* . . . *body down?*"] Hymn (1763) by Charles Wesley (1707–1788).

578.20    Swing Swing] Sing Sing, a prison in Ossining, New York ("up the river" from New York City).

BLACK THUNDER

593.1    Bontemps added an introduction to the novel in 1968 when Beacon Press published it in a new edition:

Time is not a river. Time is a pendulum. The thought occurred to me first in Watts in 1934. After three horrifying years of preparation in a throbbing region of the deep south, I had settled there to write my second novel, away from it all.

At the age of thirty, or thereabouts, I had lived long enough to become aware of intricate patterns of recurrence, in my own experience and in the history I had been exploring with almost frightening attention. I suspect I was preoccupied with those patterns when, early in *Black Thunder*, I tried to make something of the old major-domo's mounting the dark steps of the Sheppard mansion near Richmond to wind the clock.

The element of time was crucial to Gabriel's attempt, in historical fact as in *Black Thunder*, and the hero of that action knew well the absolute necessity of a favorable conjunction. When this did not occur, he realized that the outcome was no longer in his own hands. Perhaps it was in the stars, he reasoned.

If time is the pendulum I imagined, the snuffing of Martin Luther King, Jr.'s career may yet appear as a kind of repetition of Gabriel's shattered dream during the election year of 1800. At least the occurrence of the former as this is written serves to recall for me the tumult in my own thoughts when I began to read extensively about slave insurrections and to see in them a possible metaphor of turbulence to come.

Not having space for my typewriter, I wrote the book in longhand on the top of a folded-down sewing machine in the extra bedroom of my parents' house at 10310 Wiegand Avenue where my wife and I and our children (three at that time) were temporarily and uncomfortably quartered. A Japanese truck farmer's asparagus field was just outside our back door. From a window on the front, above the sewing machine, I could look across 103rd Street at the buildings and grounds of Jordan High School, a name I did not hear again until I came across it in some of the news accounts reporting the holocaust that swept Watts a quarter of a century later. In the vacant lot across from us on Wiegand a friendly Mexican neighbor grazed his milk goat. We could smell eucalyptus trees when my writing window was open and when we walked outside, and nearly always the air was like transparent gold in those days. I could have loved the place under different circumstances, but as matters stood there was no way to disguise the fact that our luck had run out.

My father and stepmother were bearing up reasonably well, perhaps, under the strain our presence imposed on them, but only a miracle could have healed one's own hurt pride, one's sense of shame and failure at an early age. Meanwhile, it takes time to write a novel, even one that has been painstakingly researched, and I do not blame my father for his occasional impatience. I had flagellated myself so thoroughly, I was numb to such criticism, when he spoke in my presence, and not very tactfully, about young people with bright prospects who make shipwreck of their lives.

What he had in mind, mainly, I am sure, were events which had brought me home at such an awkward time and with such uncertain plans, but somehow I suspected more. At the age at which I made my commitment to writing, he had been blowing a trombone in a Louisiana marching band under the direction of Claiborne Williams. But he had come to regard such a career as a deadend occupation unworthy of a young family man, married to a schoolteacher, and he renounced it for something more solid: bricklaying. Years later when the building trades themselves began to fade as far as black workers were concerned, under pressure of the new labor unions, he had made another hard decision and ended his working years in the ministry.

He was reproaching me for being less resourceful, by his lights, and I was too involved in my novel to even reply. The work I had undertaken, the new country into which I had ventured when I began to explore Negro history had rendered me immune for the moment, even to implied insults.

Had the frustrations dormant in Watts at that date suddenly exploded in flame and anger, as they were eventually to do, I don't think they would have shaken my concentration; but I have a feeling that more readers might then have been in a mood to hear a tale of volcanic rumblings among angry blacks—and the end of patience. At the time, however, I began to suspect that it was fruitless for a Negro in the United States to address serious writing to my generation, and I began to consider the alternative of trying to reach young readers not yet hardened or grown insensitive to man's inhumanity to man, as it is called.

For this, as for so much else that has by turn intrigued or troubled me in subsequent years, my three-year sojourn in northern Alabama had been a kind of crude conditioning. Within weeks after the publication of my first book, as it happened, I had been caught up in a quaint and poignant disorder that failed to attract wide attention. It was one of the side effects of the crash that bought on the Depression, and it brought instant havoc to the Harlem Renaissance of the twenties. I was one of the hopeful young people displaced, so to speak. The jobs we had counted on to keep us alive and writing in New York vanished, as some observed, quicker than a cat could wink. Not knowing where else to turn, I wandered into northern Alabama, on the promise of employment as a teacher, and hopefully to wait out the bad times, but at least to get my bearings. I did not stay long enough to see any improvement in the times, but a few matters, which now seem important, did tend to become clearer as I waited.

Northern Alabama had a primitive beauty when I saw it first. I remember writing something in which I called the countryside a green Eden, but I awakened to find it dangerously infested. Two stories dominated the news as well as the daydreams of the people I met. One had to do with the demonstrations by Mahatma Gandhi and his followers in India; the other, the trials of the Scottsboro boys then in progress in Decatur, Alabama, about thirty miles from where we were living. Both seemed to foreshadow frightening consequences, and everywhere I turned someone demanded my opinions, since I was recently arrived and expected to be knowledgeable. Eventually their questions upset me as much as the news stories. We had fled here to escape our fears in the city, but the terrors we encountered here were even more upsetting than the ones we had left behind.

I was, frankly, running scared when an opportunity came for me to visit Fisk University in Nashville, Tennessee, about a hundred miles away, get a brief release from tension, perhaps, and call on three old friends from the untroubled years of the Harlem Renaissance: James Weldon Johnson, Charles S. Johnson, and Arthur Schomburg. All, in a sense, could have been considered as refugees living in exile, and the three, privately could have been dreaming of planting an oasis at Fisk where, surrounded by bleak hostility in the area, the region, and the nation, if not indeed the world, they might not only stay alive but, conceivably, keep alive a flicker of the impulse they had detected and helped to encourage in the black awakening in Renaissance Harlem.

Each of them could and did recite by heart Countée Cullen's lines dedicated to Charles S. Johnson in an earlier year:

> We shall not always plant while others reap
> The golden increment of bursting fruit,
> Not always countenance, abject and mute,
> That lesser men should hold their brothers cheap;
> Not everlastingly while others sleep
> Shall we beguile their limbs with mellow flute,
> Not always bend to some more subtle brute;
> We were not made eternally to weep.
>
> The night whose sable breast relieves the stark,
> White stars is no less lovely being dark,
> And there are buds that cannot bloom at all
> In light, but crumple, piteous, and fall;
> So in the dark we hide the heart that bleeds,
> And wait, and tend our agonizing seeds.

Separately and with others we made my visit a time for declaring and reasserting sentiments we had stored in our memories for safekeeping against the blast that had already dispersed their young protégés and my friends and the disasters looming ahead.

Discovering in the Fisk Library a larger collection of slave narratives than I knew existed, I began to read almost frantically. In the gloom of the darkening Depression settling all around us, I began to ponder the stricken slave's will to freedom. Three historic efforts at self-emancipation caught my attention and promptly shattered peace of mind. I knew instantly that one of them would be the subject of my next novel. First, however, I would have to make a choice, and this involved research. Each had elements the others did not have, or at least not to the same degree, and except for the desperate need of freedom they had in common, each was attempted under different conditions and led by unlike personalities.

Denmark Vesey's effort I dismissed first. It was too elaborately planned for its own good. His plot was betrayed, his conspiracy crushed too soon, but it would be a mistake to say nothing came of it in Vesey's own time. The shudder it put into the hearts and minds of slaveholders was never quieted. *Nat Turner's Confession*, which I read in the Fisk Library at a table across from Schomburg's desk, bothered me on two counts. I felt uneasy about the amanuensis to whom his account was related and the conditions under which he confessed. Then there was the business of Nat's "visions" and "dreams."

Gabriel's attempt seemed to reflect more accurately for me what I felt then and feel now might have motivated slaves capable of such boldness and inspired daring. The longer I pondered, the more convinced I became. Gabriel had not opened his mind too fully and hence had not been betrayed as had Vesey. He had by his own dignity and by the esteem in which he was held inspired and maintained loyalty. He had not depended on trance-like mumbo jumbo. Freedom was a less complicated affair in his case. It was, it seemed to me, a more unmistakable equivalent of the yearning I felt and which I imagined to be general. Finally, there was the plan itself, a strategy which some contemporaries, prospective victims, felt could scarcely have failed had not the weather miraculously intervened in their behalf. Gabriel attributed his reversal, ultimately, to the stars in their courses, the only factor that had been omitted in his calculations. He had not been possessed, not even overly optimistic.

Back in Alabama, I began to sense quaint hostilities. Borrowing library books by mail, as I sometimes did, was unusual enough to attract attention. Wasn't there a whole room of books in the school where I worked—perhaps as many as a thousand? How many books could a man read in one lifetime anyway? We laughed together at the questions, but I realized they were not satisfied with my joking answers. How could I tell them about Gabriel's adventure in such an atmosphere?

Friends from Harlem years learned from our mutual friends at Fisk that we were in the vicinity and began dropping in to say howdy en route to Decatur or Montgomery or Birmingham. There was an excitement in the state similar to that which recurred twenty-five years later when black folk began confronting hardened oppression by offering to put their bodies in escrow, if that was required. In 1931, however, the effort was centered around forlorn attempts to save the lives of nine black boys who had been convicted, in a travesty of justice, of ravishing two white girls in the empty boxcars in which all were hoboing.

The boyish poet Langston Hughes was one of those who came to protest, to interview the teen-age victims in their prison cells, and to write prose and poetry aimed at calling the world's attention to the enormity about to be perpetrated. It was natural that he should stop by to visit us. He and I had recently collaborated, mainly by mail, on the writing of a children's story, *Popo and Fifina: Children of Haiti*. He had the story and I had the children, so my publisher thought it might work. Perhaps it would not be too much to say they were justified. The story lasted a long time and was translated into a number of languages. The friendship between the two authors also lasted and yielded other collaborations over the next thirty-five years. But the association was anathema to the institution which had, with some admitted reluctance, given me employment.

As my year ended, I was given an ultimatum. I would have to make a clean break with the unrest in the world as represented by Gandhi's efforts abroad and the Scottsboro protests here at home. Since I had no connection or involvement with either, other than the fact that I had known some of the people who were shouting their outrage, I was not sure how a break could be made. The head of the school had a plan, however. I could do it, he demanded publicly, by burning most of the books in my small library, a number of which were trash in his estimation anyway, the rest, race-conscious and provocative. *Harlem Shadows*, *The Blacker the Berry*, *My Bondage and Freedom*, *Black Majesty*, *The Souls of Black Folk*, and *The Autobiography of an Ex-Coloured Man* were a few of those indicated.

I was too horrified to speak, but I swallowed my indignation. My wife was expecting another child, and the options before us had been reduced to none. At the end of the following term we drove to California, sold our car, and settled down in the small room in Watts in the hope that what we had received for the car would buy food till I could write my book. By the next spring *Black Thunder* was finished, and the advance against royalties was enough to pay our way to Chicago.

*Black Thunder*, when published later that year, earned no more than its advance. As discouraging as this was, I was not permitted to think of it as a total loss. The reviews were more than kind. John T. Frederick, director of the Illinois Writers Project, read the book and decided to add me to his staff. He also commended it warmly in his anthology, *Out of the Midwest*, and in his CBS broadcasts. Robert Morss Lovett mentioned it in his class at the University of Chicago. But the theme of self-assertion by black men whose endurance was strained to the breaking point was not one that readers of fiction were prepared to contemplate at the time. Now that *Black Thunder* is published again, after more than thirty years, I cannot help wondering if its story will be better understood by Americans, both black and white. I am, however, convinced that time is not a river.

Chicago
April 1968

594.2    ALBERTA]    Alberta Bontemps (1906–2004), née Johnson, Bontemps' wife.

599.2    VIRGINIA COURT records]    For information about the historicity of *Black Thunder* and Bontemps's sources, see Mary Kemp Davis, "Arna Bontemps' *Black Thunder*: The Creation of an Authoritative Text of 'Gabriel's Defeat'," *Black American Literature Forum* 23.1 (Spring 1989): 17–36, and Davis, "The Historical Slave Revolt and the Literary Imagination" (PhD diss., University of North Carolina, Chapel Hill, 1984).

610.1    Sonthonaz . . . *des Noirs*."]    Léger-Félicité Sonthonax (1763–1813), a member of the French abolitionist group Société des amis des Noirs (1788–93), served as civil commissioner of Saint-Domingue (now Haiti) from 1792–95, during the Haitian Revolution. Sent to keep the colony under

French control, he upheld the citizenship rights of "free men of color," which had been granted by France in 1792, and emancipated Haitian slaves in 1793, while also seeking their return to plantation life.

610.16–18    Judge Tucker . . . *on Slavery*]    St. George Tucker (1752–1827) published his *Dissertation on Slavery* in 1796.

626.9    Callender]    James Thomson Callender (1758–1803), Scottish-born political writer who emigrated to Philadelphia around 1793, where he attained notoriety as an anti-Federalist pamphleteer. Beginning in June 1800 he served a six-month prison sentence for sedition.

626.19    United Irishman.]    A member of the Society of United Irishmen, an Irish nationalist organization inspired by the American and French revolutions and founded in 1791.

628.7    the old Procope]    Reputedly the world's oldest coffeehouse, founded in 1686 and a center of Parisian literary and political life in the eighteenth and nineteenth centuries.

654.1–11    *Man is a stranger . . . deepening gloom*]    See Voltaire's 1755 "Poem on the Lisbon Disaster," as translated in 1911 by Joseph McCabe.

740.20    Duane]    William John Duane (1780–1865), editor of the anti-Federalist Philadelphia *Aurora*; he later served as Postmaster General (1776–82) and Secretary of the Treasury (1833).

767.8    Fries, Gallatin]    John Fries (1750–1818), convicted of treason for his role in Fries's Rebellion, an armed anti-taxation protest among the Pennsylvania Dutch (1799–1800), and pardoned by John Adams in 1800; Albert Gallatin (1761–1849), an advocate for western Pennsylvanians opposed to new taxes on whiskey during the Whiskey Rebellion of the early 1790s and later Secretary of the Treasury (1801–14).

810.15    *The trumpet . . . my soul.*]    From "Steal Away," an African American spiritual first performed by the Fisk Jubilee Singers in 1871 and attributed to Choctaw freedman Wallace Willis (fl. 1840s–1850s).

# THE LIBRARY OF AMERICA SERIES

The Library of America fosters appreciation and pride in America's literary heritage by publishing, and keeping permanently in print, authoritative editions of America's best and most significant writing. An independent nonprofit organization, it was founded in 1979 with seed funding from the National Endowment for the Humanities and the Ford Foundation.

To subscribe to the series or to order individual copies, please visit www.loa.org or call (800) 964.5778.

This book is set in 10 point Linotron Galliard,
a face designed for photocomposition by Matthew Carter
and based on the sixteenth-century face Granjon. The paper
is acid-free lightweight opaque and meets the requirements
for permanence of the American National Standards Institute.
The binding material is Brillianta, a woven rayon cloth made
by Van Heek-Scholco Textielfabrieken, Holland. Composition by Dedicated Book Services. Printing by
Malloy Incorporated. Binding by Dekker Book-
binding. Designed by Bruce Campbell.